CITIZENS

Citizens

A NOVEL BY
MEYER LEVIN

NEW YORK · THE VIKING PRESS · MCMXL

40-7246

TO

HILDING ANDERSON
ALFRED CAUSEY
LEO FRANCISCO
EARL HANDLEY
OTIS JONES
SAM POPOVICH
KENNETH REED
JOSEPH ROTHMUND
ANTHONY TAGLIORI
LEE TISDALE

IT was a perfect Fourth of July. The sky was speckless blue, smooth as the inside of a machine-turned bowl, the lake a deep green-blue, flat as glass, the sand golden. Mitch Wilner lay on the sand beside Sylvia, his back to the sun. The sun reached into the body as into the earth, and a man could almost feel in himself how it was with things in the earth, growing by the in-reaching of the sun.

The children played industriously in the sand. Jackie built a castle, Judy fetched the sand. She filled her little shovel at her mother's side, balanced it, and wobbled five steps to dump the sand by brother Jackie.

Their grandmother approached and viewed the scene with pleasure. "They are just right for brother and sister," she said. "The boy is older and the girl is cuter."

Sylvia idly heaped a little mound of sand, for Judy to take away, and said: "She's at the stage of carrying things from one spot to another."

"People are just like the animals," the grandmother said contentedly. "A little puppy too, it picks things up and carries them and puts them down. Judy, baby, who do you love?" She knelt in the sand and caught the child, who said: "Gramma" automatically and slipped through her arms like silk, to continue with her task.

"Like the animals," Mitch Wilner dreamed, feeling his thoughts warm-stirred but unformed as the sun-energy gathered in his body. Like little animals, yes; like what about that

[1]

fellow in the psych lab with his quick-learning strain of rats? Now there would be an interesting way to check that Kansas City theory. With animals, you might easily check whether allergics were consistently more intelligent than non-allergics. With humans, there were always too many uncontrolled factors. The allergic children Dr. Harvester had used in Kansas City were after all kids brought to a fancy-priced specialist; probably they were better nourished, better taught than the average group of schoolchildren whose I.Q. they had topped. A better way to make the test would be to use two groups of children of the same economic background.

That intelligence idea couldn't be right. It was too much like a popular assumption—the sensitive mind in the sensitive body. Like an article Turk Fergis had talked about, in one of those psychology journals he kept up with—some tripe about the "hay fever personality" being "a neurotic dreamer, overwhelmingly ambitious." Probably Hitler was an allergic, then. Mitch smiled to himself and relaxed, loose-muscled against the warm sand.

But suppose the Kansas City results were sound: did they prove that people born smart tended to be born allergic or could it be that allergic reaction stimulated the mental processes . . . ?

"Don't the Fergises have a place along the dunes here somewhere?" he asked Sylvia.

"Mitch, you promised to take the day off, and play with the kids," Sylvia reminded him.

"I just thought we might drop in on them."

"Oh, yeah?" She smiled with knowing rue.

"Mitch, you better turn over or you will get sunburned," his mother-in-law admonished.

"Let me put some of this lotion on your back, dear," Sylvia said.

Mitch lifted his face from the sand, eying the bottle. "Sun-safe," he read the label. "I told you that junk is only olive oil

[2]

mixed with a little vinegar." He submitted as she rubbed the oil into his back.

"Dear, you must be losing weight," Sylvia said. "Look at those shoulder-blades! Like knives! You've got to build yourself up! Can't you at least take week-ends off, this summer?"

"You don't have to work so hard, you're a specialist now," his mother-in-law reminded him. "After all, health is the most important thing a person has. You are a doctor, you ought to know that."

Mitch turned on his side. Sylvia's arm, stroking the oil upon him, glowed golden in the sun, contrasting against the dusty lemon tonelessness of his own skin. The kids were nicely tanned, too. Perhaps he could spend more time outdoors, this summer; play a little tennis again, with Sylvia.

Ora came down toward them, in her bandanna-halter costume, which left her mid-section bare. Her toe-nails were bright purple. "Mort is worse than the kids," she complained, pulling a cotton-plug out of each ear. "That's all the Fourth is—an excuse to give the daddies a chance to play with firecrackers."

"It's like Christmas, when they buy the children toys and monopolize them," the grandmother agreed. "I only hope he doesn't start shooting with that pistol. That I can't stand. Shooting always frightens me."

Ora laughed inconsequentially, and gazed down the beach.

If Dr. Feldner would approve, Mitch reflected, maybe he and Turk Fergis could repeat that intelligence investigation, in the allergy clinic. The trouble was, Feldner was always so reluctant about a checking job. New work, new work. You could never get it through his thick head that disproving a mistaken theory was as important as inventing a correct one. If that Kansas City stuff was wrong, it might throw the whole field onto the wrong track for years. And instinctively Mitch felt it was a wrong steer. For one thing, it would indicate that allergic intolerance

[3]

was different altogether from the shock of repeated foreign blood injection—anaphylaxis. But he remembered the day way back in school when a dumb dora injected horse blood serum into the wrong rabbit, and started yelping when it died on her table. Surely it made no difference how intelligent a rabbit was, when it came to blood-shock. If he only had more time for research . . . But he had no right to kick. That Kansas City stuff was done within Harvester's own practice. The thing to do was to find more ways to combine research with his practice, instead of always wanting to crawl off into a lab.

A young fellow, chasing a girl, dodged through their group. The wild-haired, laughing girl, breasts dancing, ran smack upon Jackie's castle, squashing it. Jackie stared uncertainly for that dread moment during which the howl gathers, and just as the boy flung a ball at the girl, hitting her and making her shriek, Jackie sent up his shriek over his ruined castle, and Judy joined, howling.

"Oh, that's too bad, darling," Sylvia hastily consoled Jackie. "Look, Jackie, why don't you build a moat to protect your castle?" He quieted and began to dig.

"You certainly know how to handle him," the grandmother said admiringly.

"You just have to divert their attention," Sylvia explained.

"That gang needs the whole beach!" Ora commented a little enviously on the boisterous youngsters, who were playing a game in which they pitched a ball down a sand groove toward a set of holes.

—That was the trouble with him, pitching the ball down the same groove, in a rut, stymied.

Then one of the kids would snatch the ball and throw it at the fleeing pitcher; if hit, the victim had to crawl the gantlet. The boys and girls lined up with their legs spread; now that shrieking tootsie had to crawl through, while they smacked her behind.

"What is the younger generation coming to!" Ora complained, with a touch of wistfulness.

"It's getting so crowded on this beach," Mrs. Abramson said. "And such a cheap class of people."

"I think a lot of them come from Gary, Polacks from those steel mills," Ora said. "They used to go to Miller's beach, but they've been spreading this way."

"Maybe next season we can sell the house and take a place further up, in the Michigan dunes," her mother-in-law said.

"Gosh, look at that kid, she isn't even wearing a bra," said Ora, as the girl swung her arm to roll the ball, advertising her large silk-molded young breasts.

"Well, wait till they get married and have a couple of kids," Sylvia said. Yet even after two children Syl's breasts weren't bad; they needed a little support but they didn't hang like empty sacks; poor Ora, she had even asked him about surgical lifting.

"The best thing is to have another baby," Mrs. Abramson advised her daughter and daughter-in-law. "Then they will be full, and fine."

"Two is enough," Sylvia said.

"In this world, it's a crime to have children. Lord knows what they'll have to face!" said Ora.

"Do you have to worry for the whole world?" The grandmother sighed philosophically. "Who knows what will be by the time they grow up? Maybe everything will be good. If everybody was afraid like that, the human race would die altogether."

Sylvia gazed at their children. "Well, I suppose people should replace themselves in the world," she said. "We had our two, so we've done our duty, two for two."

[5]

"And what about the people that don't have children?" her mother said, addressing Mitch as well as the girls. "You have to have at least one extra for them. Isn't that right, Doctor? Or the human race will die out."

He had told Syl a couple of times to ask her mother not to address him as Doctor.

"And what about the millions they're going to kill in the next war?" Ora demanded. "I suppose we each have to have twelve kids, to make up for them, so the human race won't die out."

"Anyone that thinks it's such a wonderful world, let them supply the extra children," said Sylvia. He was startled by a profound depression in her voice—as if she were a deeply unhappy person. Why did she wait until they were among others to reveal this of herself?

"Such talk! What a terrible life you lead! How you have suffered!" Sylvia's mother chided her.

Sylvia flushed, and looked quickly to him, as if to reassure him, and he felt her mood was perhaps only a reflection of the bitter temper of the times.

"What do you think, Mitch, is this such a terrible world to live in?" Mrs. Abramson pursued the topic, surveying her gamboling grandchildren, looking upward to the family house on the dune-top.

"I don't know, that's Syl's department." Discussions of world affairs irritated him in a peculiar way; not that he was uninterested, but such talk always reminded him how painfully little he knew; at the same time it made him feel defensively belligerent, in the sense that their knowledge, even Sylvia's glib knowledge of movements and events and foreign affairs, appeared so utterly futile. A man might as well bury himself in his lab, and try to do his own little thing.

"No! Go away!" Jackie was yelling at his sister, who persisted in fetching him sand, even though he was now excavating.

[6]

Judith stood frightened, and you could see her tears forming, like bubbles rising.

"Judy dear, bring sand to Mother." Sylvia adjusted the situation. Like a machine whose lever had been reversed, Judith trotted her sand to Mama. She was an obedient little girl. He wished sometimes he could be more playful with the kids. Even Mort had fun with his kids. There he was now, slushing down the sandhill, his younger son astride his shoulders.

"Mort!" Ora shrieked. For the kid clutched a bunch of firecrackers and, reaching the fuse-end to the cigarette in Mort's mouth, lit it and flung the little chain of explosives toward the family. It made a diminutive machine-gun burst.

"We're dynamitos!" Lester yelled. "Pop and me!"

"*Dinamiteros*," Ora forgivingly corrected her child.

"Like in Spain," Lester explained as Mort halted among the women. "In Spain they light the dynamite on their cigars and they throw it. Right at the tanks. Pow!"

"Mort, are you crazy!" Mrs. Abramson reproved her son.

"Aw, it's the Fourth of July!" Mort swung Lester to the ground, his sweat-glistening belly slopping over his trunks as he bent. The older boy, Raoul, came leaping down the sand and banged into his father, cayoodling: "Come on swim, last one in is a sissy!"

The grandmother got to her feet. "Who's coming?" she called. Mitch noticed a new varicose; he'd have to inject it. The little gang made for the water, leaving Sylvia, Mitch, and their children.

Suddenly Mitch was tired of the scene, of those adolescents with their strenuous ball game, of beach shrieks, and from now on the day would be a continuous thunder of fireworks topped off with a whole arsenal after dark came. Then, the inevitable wienie roast with sand in the pickles, and in the evening listening

[7]

to Mort tell dirty stories about Roosevelt. And finally the inevitable argument, with Syl's folks urging them to stay overnight so they could drive in early and miss the traffic.

"Dear," Syl was saying—sometimes, still, their minds seemed to work in the same groove—"why don't we start home now? it would be so much simpler. We'd miss the traffic, and get the kids home before they're tired and cross. You have to stop in at the hospital, too."

"Suits me," he said, looking at his wristwatch. It was after three. "But you have to break it to them."

"And if we start now," Sylvia said, "we can pass by on the way and see if anything happened at that strike. We can take 18 instead of 20 and go right past the plant. You know they were afraid there might be some trouble there today and Barbara Macey asked me if you could pass by on the way home, just in case."

Mitch shrugged, restraining a slight feeling of annoyance at the way she always saved up her little plans until the moment when it would be more bother to disarrange them than to go through with them. "Why should there be any trouble out there?" he asked.

"Oh, you know those cops. They've already clubbed a lot of the strikers. On Friday about twenty of the fellows had their heads clubbed. Barb was out there and tried to bandage them up. So today they want to be prepared. I told you yesterday, remember, she wants you to fix up a first-aid outfit, at the strike headquarters."

"That girl is always looking for excitement," Mitch said. Some of the new university kids Sylvia had picked up as pals, since going back for those "keep up with the world" courses, were keeping her from being her own age, he thought.

"I don't believe there can really be any trouble today," she

[8]

said, rising and beginning to gather up their stuff. "After all, it's the Fourth of July."

"What's that got to do with it?" He helped her with the junk. Towels and sunglasses, sandpails with Donald Duck stamped on them, and waterwings with Popeye painted on them, and "Judy, honey, what did you do with your bathing cap?" and the sunburn lotion.

The road was almost clear of traffic; he drove at forty-five though he usually stayed around forty. Away from Syl's family, Mitch felt almost good toward them.

Jack sat in the front seat, trying to manipulate the shift lever at every stop. "Mother, I'm helping Daddy drive."

Mitch saw the sign for the turnoff to Route 18, and maneuvered into the right lane to make the turn. "Dear, this is where we turn off on 18," Sylvia reminded him.

"Phew, it stinks," Jackie complained. They were passing through that confusing stretch between Gary and Chicago, where you never knew whether you were in Hammond, Whiting, Indiana Harbor, East Chicago, or what; an area of uninhabited chunks of highgrass swamp, with sometimes a mammoth industrial plant set down scarring the grass, its sudden rows of smokestacks sticking up out of the prairie like clumps of teeth on a broken comb; alternating with a block or two of dwellings, unpainted frame houses with an occasional brick front, or a business block, and a succession of three unnecessary stop-lights, ill-timed, so you had to halt for each one, waiting, while no traffic crossed.

The area was littered with canals, and there would be long flat cargo boats, somehow like dachshunds, bringing coal and stuff to the factories; there was even a Ford plant around here somewhere, and he had seen long boats named Henry Ford

[9]

parked in the canals. "Doesn't the drainage canal go through here?" Sylvia sniffed disgustedly.

"I don't know exactly, I always meant to look it up," he said.

Then they were passing through the area of oil refineries, acres of squat round tanks on both sides of the road, white tanks like huge hatboxes, in glistening rows. And strange constructions: a huge aluminum ball like a stratosphere balloon ready to rise. A stinging sulphurous smell was in the air, yellowish.

"Imagine what they could do to this if there was a war," Sylvia remarked. "I suppose this is one of the first places they would come and bomb."

He too could imagine this entire area erupting in a series of explosions, the earth like a consumptive racked by paroxysms, and the sky red with coughed bloody fire. "I think they have the tanks fixed so they can disconnect them some way," Mitch said, "so that even if one gets hit or catches fire, the rest will be safe."

They crossed a whole series of railroad tracks, came to another bit of town. "It's right off here somewhere," Sylvia said. "I was out here with Barbara yesterday." And just then, at the entrance to a side road, they saw a clot of cops, with motorcycles and a patrol wagon. Blocking the view of the lake, further back, rose a factory mass of brown-rust walls, smokestacks.

"That's the plant," said Sylvia.

"I guess it's in operation all right," Mitch observed, nodding at the smoke coming out of the stacks.

"Barb says that's just tar they're burning to make smoke," Sylvia reported. "Some of the strikers stayed inside the first day, to check up on such things, and when they came out they said it was just tarpaper."

There were houses on both sides of the road now, forming the scattered edges of the Steel Harbor settlement; houses with bits of vegetable garden and poultry yards. At a larger intersection

[1 0]

were more cops, and squad cars. On the left, in vacant lots, hundreds of cars were parked. "It's down here," Syl said, as Mitch turned off to park. "You'd better park."

The crowd was congregated in a log-fence enclosure, entered through a rustic archway, log-lettered "Guzman's Grove." At first glance it looked like just a Fourth of July picnic, the kind politicians used to throw. Popsicle salesmen were doing a rushing business around the gate. On the little stretch of sidewalk in front of Guzman's tavern a group of kids were hurling son-of-a-guns against the concrete. A fellow wearing a white paper armband was trying to make them stop the noise, pointing to a speaker on a truck.

As the Wilners went through the arch, a boy bounced alongside, wanting to sell Mitch a *Daily Worker*. A step further a fattish, blond man stood in their path, holding up the *Daily Worker*.

"They certainly don't miss a chance to be on the spot," Syl said.

The grove swarmed. Several trucks had been driven into the place; they were festooned with red-white-and-blue bunting; some bore signs: Progressive Lodge No. 1551, Win with S.W.O.C., Gary Lodge No. 1342, Unity Lodge. . . .

"What's the S.W.O.C.?" Jackie said, spelling it out. Mitch was stumped.

"It means Steel Workers' Organizing Committee," Syl said.

Fellows in striped polo jerseys, girls in light summer dresses and some in shorts and halters, hundreds of people thronged the grounds, centering at the speaker's truck. The listeners were not pressed together, Mitch noticed. Folks were circulating, meeting, greeting friends in the crowd; and on the fringes little family groups squatted on the grass eating picnic lunches, large women with pink-red faces, wearing dollar cotton-print dresses that had a pressed and somehow dress-up appearance, and the

[11]

men in clean white shirts with collars unbuttoned and sleeves rolled up. Further back, some fellows were pitching a ball.

Mitch caught a few words of the speech. The usual strike stuff: We got them beat already, all we have to do is stick together.

"Oh, Syl, Syl!" Barbara Macey came rushing toward them, her color high with excitement; she was wearing a bright red jersey and blue slacks. "Gosh, Mitch, Dr. Wilner, you're a godsend." She pulled them toward the tavern, chattering all the while—wasn't the turnout terrific! and the spirit! the crowd really had the spirit! and: "Look, you know Carl, don't you, Syl?" she was introducing them to a blond, tall fellow with a smooth almost buttery complexion. "And this is Mitch, Dr. Wilner—Carl Gaul."

The fellow stood against the wall of the building, watching the crowd with the expression of a theater manager surveying the box-office line. "And this is Emil." Barbara introduced another fellow, with Carl.

Emil was the real type you imagined for a steel worker, Mitch reflected; short neck and thick shoulders, a pitted face, huge long arms with big-knuckled hands.

"Carl. Dr. Wilner can set up a first-aid station. Don't you think that's a good idea?" Barbara ran on enthusiastically. "Maybe in that little room, the cloakroom. Did you bring your bag, Doctor?"

"It's in the car," Mitch said; but there was scarcely anything in the bag, a stethoscope, some mercurochrome, lint, cotton, a few applicators, and a few syringes with anti-tetanus shots, which he had chucked in just in case some kid had a Fourth of July accident. Well, he was in for it here, he could see; simplest thing would be to fix them a first-aid outfit; there must be a drugstore somewhere near by; then he could get away.

"But what do you think is going to happen?" he asked.

[1 2]

"They're sure to march," Barbara announced, but with excited misgiving in her voice, and in her eyes as she looked to Carl. Carl nodded glumly. "Probably be some broken heads," he said to Mitch. "A couple of the boys had to have stitches, Friday."

Emil speculated. "They're gonna use gas, on a crowd this big."

Mitch Wilner cast over his knowledge of gas effects. Practically nil. But he didn't suppose they'd use anything lastingly harmful—unless someone happened to get a concentrated dose. Burns were possible, he vaguely knew. "What kind of gas do they use?" he asked.

"Some awful stuff that makes you vomit. And tear gas," Barbara said. "I know. I got some at the Fansteel strike," she added with pride.

Looking at the crowd, Mitch asked: "Why? What are they going to try to do, break into the plant?"

Carl Gaul gave him a quick, curious glance.

"No, they just want to picket," Barbara said. "Captain Wiley won't let them picket."

"But I thought that was legal. It was in the papers." Mitch was puzzled.

"It may be legal, darling, but try and tell it to the cops!" Syl pressed his arm, and smiled to the others as if to ask their indulgence for his simple-mindedness.

"I was just up there," Barbara offered. "I never saw so many cops. Honest, it's simply terrifying. I think maybe the whole thing ought to be called off. Carl, honestly!"

Carl Gaul shrugged almost peevishly. He walked toward someone in the crowd; they saw him take the man aside and bend his head in evidently worried discussion.

"Come on inside," Barbara suggested; "at least we can fix up something so it won't be as bad as Friday. They came in all

[13]

clubbed and bloody and there wasn't even a clean towel in the place. I've been begging the boys all week to make some sort of arrangements. . . ."

At the side door they were stopped by a fellow in a faded blue workshirt and overall-pants. "These are friends of mine, they're all right," Barbara said. He looked at her heavily. "You know me—I'm with Carl Gaul." He stepped aside.

Within was a long, gloomy, windowless tavern room, bare except for the remains of a booth against one wall, a few scattered folding-chairs, and, toward the rear, a bridge table surrounded by chairs and upended boxes. An electric light hung from an extension cord over this table, which was cluttered with newspapers, piles of leaflets, stacks of blue cards, cardboard filing boxes.

There was a huge cracked-plaster area on the wall, where a bar mirror had hung; but the bar itself remained. A bulky foreign-looking woman and a collegiate girl were behind it, serving coffee and sandwiches to strikers.

On the walls were amateurly lettered slogans, newspaper clippings, penciled scrawls: "Win with the C.I.O." The place was dusty and oven-hot.

"There's a kitchen back there," Barbara said. "We can get hot water. But I figured the best place for the first aid would be here, this checkroom." She led Mitch to a shed jutting from the tavern, a lean-to. Its one window was stuck. There was an army cot. "Some of the boys stay here all night," Barbara said. "There's one more cot in back somewhere, I think."

"Well, anyway, this place could stand being cleaned up," Mitch suggested. "And better have some basins handy."

"Okay. I'll find the broom," Barbara agreed. Just then Carl Gaul reappeared, accompanied by the older man whom he had snagged out of the crowd. The man was beefy, and had the look of fellows who hang around bowling alleys. "Jock Kiley,"

Carl introduced him, informing him that Dr. Wilner had volunteered to set up a hospital here, in case anybody got hurt.

"Anything you want, Doc, anything you need, just ask for it," Kiley said.

"Well, it depends on the extent you want to—" Mitch began. Kiley had restless eyes; he seemed not so much to be avoiding a direct glance, as to be unfocused in his mind. "I suppose bruises could be patched up here all right," Mitch said. "But as far as anything serious goes, I haven't even any sutures with me, in case anyone gets cut."

"They had to take some stitches on those fellows Friday," Barbara repeated, worriedly.

Kiley pulled out a small wad of bills, gave Mitch a five, saying: "I guess we need some supplies, you take care of it, Doctor, will you?" and, patting Carl on the shoulder, pounded off toward an excited group at the other end of the room.

Mitch held the five-dollar bill. He felt himself being pushed into something. Sylvia had found a stool at the lunch counter and was parked there with the kids, talking to the collegiate girl. "I don't know," Mitch hesitated, then handed the money to Carl Gaul. "You better handle this."

"Well, what do we need? You're the doctor."

"I suppose what they'll do is use gas today," Barbara said.

"You might get some boric acid." That was all that came to his mind. In case of tear gas. "Yes, get a box of boric."

Carl called Emil over. "Anything else, Doc?" he asked. "Bandages or something?"

All sorts of things might be needed if a real emergency arose— but no use setting up a hospital here. Gauze and stuff, he had in the bag. Sutures—well, anything open should be taken to a hospital and decently cleansed, first. "I guess that'll be enough, for now," he said. "Just the boric acid."

"I haven't got my car," Emil said to Carl. "I'll get Art." He left.

[1 5]

Mitch Wilner went out to fetch his bag. The crowd had changed; it was condensed around the speaker's truck now, and it was laughing. Faces were upturned toward the speaker; like open-beaked birds, they waited for more food for laughter. On the truck platform was a dwarfish man with a wrinkled, screwed-up monkey face, and he hopped around like a monkey as he talked. He would stoop way down, double on his haunches, and then rise up gradually with arms flailing, humor sputtering from him as he rose until at the peak of the jest he was off his feet in the air like a sputtering skyrocket; and then he would come down hard on both feet, nailing his point home.

His comical story was of how he had once been taken to jail, up there in Mohawk County, Wisconsin, for yelling scab at a scab. With good-humored woe he marched himself to jail; the key turned in the lock. Sat in the jail, figuring and figuring how to get hold of that key. No jail breaking, no, sir. Just figuring how, after he got out, he could get hold of that key just for future protection, so if he wanted to call a scab a scab, okay, no jail.

His little eyes blinked brightly from their screwed-up sockets. "Friends, what do you think? Up there in Wisconsin I don't go to jail no more if I call a scab a scab. I don't go to jail if I picket where the law says I can picket. How did we do it?" He slapped his back pocket. "That's how we did it—I've got those keys to that jail, right here in my pocket!"

Expectant grins spread over the upturned faces. Doubling down on his knees, waggling his finger at them, he drove the point home. How did he get the keys to that jail? By getting elected sheriff. Yes, sir, the working men of that county got wise, and elected their own man sheriff, and now, by God, workers on strike could yell scab and they could picket because, by God, they themselves, they had the keys to the jail!

The laughter spread and popped all over the field as some of

[16]

the foreigners slow on English had the strategy explained to them. See, he is Szutak, C.I.O. man, we elected him sheriff up there.

Shaking his finger at them, repeating the point over and over for their uncertain English, Szutak was like a wise old father admonishing big-boned, maturing sons: "That's the way to do the trick, boys. You got the vote. Just vote those keys right inside your own pocket. No more troubles!"

He hopped off the truck as they cheered. A sturdy, black-haired man whom Mitch had seen inside the tavern now stepped forward; he had a striking mouth, the lips wide, flat, and sharply stamped. Just then a voice, near Mitch, was heard above the hub-bub. "Mr. Chairman!"

The fellow on the truck, motioning for silence, pointed almost directly at Mitch, to the man who had his arm raised. Standing beside the man was Emil. "I'm going in a minute, Doc," Emil called apologetically. "Just as soon as Art gets finished here. Got to use his car."

Emil's friend Art was a handsome young man with wavy, carefully combed reddish hair. His shirt was fancy-looking, striped, with a starched collar. He was one of the few men wearing a tie, and Mitch noticed that the tie was held by a trick gilt clasp. Art spoke glibly, as though uttering a rehearsed formula. "I move that we now go and make a picket line, to peacefully picket, according to the way the mayor said we had a right, in front of the plant gate."

"All those in favor?" yelled the chairman from the truck. There was a scattering of loud-voiced ayes. "Opposed?" he asked carelessly, waited a second, and announced: "Unanimous. This meeting will now form into a picket line. Everybody out there on the road."

Emil caught Mitch Wilner's eye, and signaled that he was going right off on that errand. It was sometimes amusing to Mitch,

[17]

how urgently people took a doctor's most trivial request. Part of the trade, to keep them impressed.

The crowd loosened, broke up into little groups, families, couples, knots of serious-faced men talking various languages. Two fellows lifted the flags down from the truck-ends; they went and stood on the road, leaning on the flagstaffs. People trickled over, began to arrange themselves behind the flag-bearers; still in little groups, talking, but thickening on the road until they made the rude form of a column.

Maybe he should have asked for more supplies. Again, as he carried his bag to the tavern, Mitch got that foolish uneasy feeling; perhaps he ought to back out of the whole thing, leave now.

Barbara, with a bandanna tied over her hair, was energetically sweeping out the "hospital." Syl had covered an upended box with a newspaper and set a basin there. The kids squatted, twisting their necks to study the funnies on that paper. Jackie was explaining the pictures to his little sister, inventing the meanings; he couldn't read that well.

Mitch set down his bag and walked to the kitchen with the idea of checking the hot water supply. As the rear door was open, he noticed a group of men in the yard, which was separated from the picnic grounds by a man-high fence. Strikers drifted through the fence-door, where the flat-lipped fellow from the truck—Frank, they called him—stood watching. Stacked against the wall were a large number of freshly lettered signs; these were being passed out.

The placards bore the usual type of strike slogans: Consolidated Steel vs. the People; Don't Scab, Come Out; C.I.O.—Consolidated Is Ours; Come Out and Be a Man; Never Fear, Speer Will Sign on the Dotted Line.

"Okay! Bring on them cops!" One of the boys spat on his hands and hefted his picket sign.

[18]

"Hey, Frank, what kind of wood is this?"

"I just wanna see that sonofabitch that conked me Friday. I know him when I see him!"

"We don't want no soft wood."

"Mike, how's your brother?"

"I dunno. He slept twenty hours but he's still vomiting from that kick in his belly."

"You know who did that? That louse bastard name of Rainey. He's out of the South Chicago station, kind of squint-eyed. I know him."

"Well, you just show him to me, that's all I want is a chance at that sonofabitch."

Kiley, the big fellow who had given him the five dollars, came up behind Mitch. He stood in the kitchen doorway, blinking at the group in the yard, and said: "Take it easy, boys. Don't start anything. We don't want to start anything."

"Nobody's going to start anything," a fellow with inflamed eyes cried almost exultantly. "But if those yellow bastards think they can get away with it this time——"

"Take it easy, Mike," Kiley said with a worried half-smile.

"Sure! I'll take them with one hand!" Mike laughed, as he whittled a grip on the two-by-four to which his sign was tacked. He was the stubby fellow who had been talking about his beaten-up brother.

Mitch drew back into the kitchen. If they had been clubbed last Friday, you couldn't blame the boys for wanting at least a stick in their hands when they went up again to that line of cops. But he felt really uneasy now. The boys were drifting out of the enclosure, carrying the hefty picket sticks bearing the signs.

Carl Gaul was with Kiley, in the kitchen. Mitch tried to remark lightly: "Looks like the cops may need a little first aid, if those boys go out there."

Carl shrugged. "They went out there Friday empty-handed."

[1 9]

Kiley said to Carl: "Maybe we ought to pull Mike Sisto out of there. That screwy punk is liable to lose his head and get hurt."

Carl Gaul shrugged again and said with a trace of bitterness: "Go tell Frank to pull him out. It's his show."

Kiley looked toward the yard, blinking. Gaul toyed with a long pocket-knife, springing the blade. "Mex?" Kiley asked.

"Yah. Little Jesus; you know him." Gaul pulled open the kitchen table drawer and tossed the knife inside. Mitch glimpsed several pistols and knives in the drawer. At the same moment, the collegiate-looking girl who had been serving at the lunch counter walked through the kitchen, and he saw the sudden shock on her milk-fed face as she caught sight of the weapons. She went on out, carrying a coffee pot.

"That's a sonofabitch of a place for that stuff," Kiley said. "They're liable to bust in here any time."

"You better tell him to look his boys over." Carl nodded significantly toward the yard. "They don't want to go out there with any of that stuff on them. I can't even talk to him."

"No; he cleaned them off," Kiley said. "He knows that much anyway. We agreed on that. He had Art go around and clean them off." Laughing, he added: "Mike Sisto had a cannon as big as an elephant's jock. Honest to Christ, that little sonofabitch, you can't stop him!" Kiley went into the yard.

Just then an agitated young fellow—evidently a reporter, with a police card stuck in his hatband—hurried up to Carl. He seemed at first glance to be just a kid, with a freckled, small-featured face and eyes fevered with excitement, like those of a kid playing cops and robbers, or war. He had on an open-collar sport shirt, and tennis shoes.

"Where's Jock Kiley?" the reporter demanded with breath-less urgency. "I've got to talk to him!" Spying Kiley in the doorway, he darted over and seized the big fellow's arm. "Listen, Jock, you better not send those people out there. Call it off, for Christ's sake. I've been over there with those bulls——"

Kiley placed his arm on the little fellow's shoulder, walked him to the further side of the kitchen. Two heavy Polish-looking women went on making sandwiches, undisturbed. "I've been over there drinking with them," the reporter said. Though he was obviously trying to keep his voice down, he was so excited that it carried. "Those saloons have the back doors open. You know they're not supposed to serve the cops."

"Yah, we know they're open; we know all about that."

"Listen, a lot of those coppers are stewed. They been feeding them liquor in that plant, too. I was in there. All the liquor you want. They're wild, I tell you. They're out for blood. One of them got kicked in the crotch, bad, on Friday."

Kiley stared at the kid as if to make sure, then slapped his thigh in delight. "Sonofabitch! Knocked 'em off, huh! Emil was telling me he thought he landed one." He wheezed a tickled laugh.

"It isn't funny, Jock. That bastard is still laid up and they say he may never be able to use them any more. That's what they're saying. I tell you they're out for blood," the youngster repeated. "They've got the flaps of their holsters open, and they're going around patting their guns. It's murder to let those people go out there."

Kiley became thoughtful. "Take it easy," he said soberly.

The reporter talked in the tone of a man who has weighed a situation. "Jock," he said, "you've got to call it off. You can't tell what might happen."

Kiley looked toward the yard. "You told Frank Sobol?"

"No. I just came in. Anyway he wouldn't listen to me."

"Who the hell will he listen to!" Carl Gaul remarked sourly. Just then Frank came in from the yard, glanced at them, and

[21]

passed to the big room, where he discussed something with a tired-looking man who sat at the littered table, going through a card-index. The man had a large burn-patch on one cheek.

Taking a breath almost like a sigh, Kiley lumbered after Frank Sobol. "Frank," he said, "the kid here just come from over there. The cops are nervous on their triggers."

Frank looked at the reporter with mild, not unfriendly attention. "They're all drunk, Mr. Sobol," the reporter said nervously. "I tell you I heard them talking—I don't think it's safe——"

"What do you want us to do, call it off?" Sobol asked softly, his wide lips closing to form an exact plane.

After a moment the reporter answered in a shamed tone: "Under the circumstances, it's just suicide to send——"

"You can go back and tell them we're not calling it off," Sobol stated with the same odd, icily courteous calm.

The reporter colored. "Look, Sobol, you've got me wrong——"

"No, Lindeman, I think I've got you right," Sobol said.

"I only came over to tell you——"

Sobol turned back to the table, and resumed his discussion with the burnt-faced man. Lindeman's mouth contracted bitterly. He rushed out of the place.

Kiley and Carl Gaul walked off a few steps, away from the other group. A Negro who had been standing near by approached the table, and Frank Sobol addressed him, but loud enough for Kiley and his group to hear. "That little sonofabitch stoolie," Frank said. "Who the hell is paying him, that's what I want to know. The *Steel Harbor News* never had any reporters before; they haven't got ten bucks a week to pay a reporter."

"Is Szutak gone?" Carl asked Kiley.

The big fellow nodded. "Just left."

"We could call up Alonzo. He might be in the downtown office."

"Naw, he'll just back up those suckers."

[22]

"Szutak is the only one they'd listen to," Carl concluded dejectedly.

"Well, he's gone. I'm going out there and take a look at those cops," Kiley said.

"Sure they want us to call it off!" Frank Sobol continued. "That's all they need to kill the strike. You call those people back now and the strike is dead." He went aside with the Negro; they talked privately.

Mitch found Sylvia in the yard; she had bought the kids popsicles. "Syl, you'd better wait in the car with the kids," he suggested.

"What's the matter?"

"They might get lost in the crowd, or something."

"Is anything wrong?"

"No. I just don't want to have to hunt all over the place for you, when I want to leave. It's getting late."

"It's awfully hot," she said. "Too hot to sit in the car. We'll stay right near it."

He walked toward the car with Sylvia and the kids. Now he thought he felt an uneasiness in the atmosphere, in the very casual ease of the crowd. Maybe because the air was so still. Ought just to get into the car and drive away. Have to go back for his bag. Besides, now he felt that he might really be needed here, soon. It would be wrong to leave.

"Is this okay, Doc? Is this package big enough?" That fellow Emil was back, with the boric.

"Oh, sure, that'll make a gallon," Mitch said.

He walked to the headquarters, with Emil and his friend, Art Nowis.

Barbara saluted them gaily, waving a lettering brush. She had found a dime-store can of red paint, used in making the picket signs, and now she was drawing a wobbly red cross on the back

[23]

of an old placard. "First Aid," she lettered above the cross. "Emil, find some thumbtacks or something and we'll put this on the hospital door."

"Okay." Emil took the placard; the burnt-faced fellow produced tacks from the littered table.

Art ran a pocket-comb through his hair. "You know what we ought to have, an ambulance car, if those cops start slugging again," he suggested. "It took three guys to carry me off the field there, Friday."

"We can use my car for that," Carl Gaul said.

"How about, hey, kid, fix a couple of those red crosses to put on the cars," Art suggested to Barbara. "We can stick them under the windshield wipers."

Barbara painted crosses on the backs of handbills. Art leaned close to her, kind of on the make.

Outside, the parade was ready to start. The two flag-bearers shuffled off and the column ambled behind them, in twos, in fours, or sometimes sprawling to six and eight abreast. A couple of big girls were standing on the segment of sidewalk in front of the tavern. "Hey, Stan," one of them called to a fellow in the column, and he reached out and grabbed her hand, so that she was drawn into the parade. "Leggo my sister!" the other girl protested, laughing.

"Aw, come on, the two of you. Get some exercise," Stan said.

" 'Stoo hot."

"Will you buy us a beer afters?" the younger sister demanded.

"Sure, kid, only don't tell your old man! I don't want him coming around with a shotgun." He winked to a fellow walking with him. "Watch out for these girls. Everybody knows old man Wyznowieki—catch you buying his girls a coke and you got to marry 'em. Hey, Helen, your old man still got all that wine he made in the basement?"

"Sure, he didn't drink half yet. Come on over afters."

"Look out, Stan, she's gonna hook you when you're stewed!"

"Aw, he could do worse," Helen's sister said.

Mitch Wilner walked along listening to the girls and fellows kidding; then he fell away from the column and stood on the grass, letting the people go by.

1. PORTRAIT OF
A CRANE OPERATOR

LADISLAS WYZNOWIEKI was a scrawny, scratchy, hairy-knuck-led crane operator in the Standard Steel mills. For some reason or other he was a leader among the Poles. He never spent any time in the taverns and he didn't even belong to any of the old coun-try friendship and benefit associations, but if you wanted to get the Poles behind something all you had to do was tell Ladislas. He would go whispering, sniffing, trotting around among his pals, and if you wanted the Poles at a meeting, within four hours his cronies would gather up half the Poles in the Harbor. And Ladislas would be in back somewhere grinning and chattering and quarreling with somebody about the best time to pick cherries for cherry brandy.

He wasn't seen in the taverns because all the time he wasn't working he spent on his farm. This farm was the joke and yet the envy of the Polish population. First, a joke, because it wasn't a farm at all. It was just a few lots, three lots at the edge of East

[25]

Chicago, and the two south of his house didn't even belong to Wyzy. He rented them for five dollars a year, and the great dread of his life was that Mr. Kranow, the real estate man, would manage to sell those lots to someone who would decide to build on them. If that happened, Wyznowieki threatened, he would go someplace and buy a real farm.

On the three lots he had everything complete: a cow, a horse, pigs, chickens, rabbits, a corn patch, vegetables, four cherry trees, two apple trees, and two goats. He had a flock of pigeons on the roof of his "barn"—a Sears-Roebuck garage onto which he had built a loft. He tended beehives between the cherry trees. No one had ever managed to count the cats and dogs around the place.

And the Wyznowieki farm was constantly in production. It was as though that little three-lot ranch was a single, fecund being teeming and swarming with life and new life; litters of kittens were underfoot on the basement steps; hens with new chicks marched beneath Mrs. Wyznowieki's clotheslines; once the cow calved in the tiny garage-barn, and Wyzy carried the gaunt-legged new little beast into the kitchen for comfort.

Every manner of farm tool was there; crowded in the shed and in the basement he had harrows and seeders and reapers enough for a hundred-acre establishment.

Sure, Wyzy used to say, every Polish fellow works in the mills, he says some day I'm gonna have farm. Some day gonna live on farm. Saves up the money and some day he's gonna go home to the old country, have his own farm, that's like in the old country, be a *paritz*, a big lord. Or maybe he's gonna buy farm in Wisconsin, Indiana, big place, good-by mills. Every fellow his whole life he saves and maybe when he is old man, so old he cannot even pull a cow's tit, he's gonna have farm, yah, I tell you: all he's gonna plant is his own dead nuts in a piece of land in the cemetery! Me, enjoy life when I got it!

The way he enjoyed life was to get up at four-thirty every morning to feed his stock. He pulled down fodder for his cows, and pulled up turnips for his rabbits, and stirred a mush for his pigs, and yelled at the old lady and his daughters to hurry up and milk the cows and feed the chickens and take that goat out and tie him to a tree but keep him away from those beehives, and by 6 a.m. the whole farm was a commotion of munching and chewing and creatures breathing the new day, and in the kitchen Ladislas and his wife and their two daughters drank pitchers of warm milk, ate home-baked bread with ham and eggs, Polish ham; he made it here on his own farm.

Wyznowieki's wife was no taller than the man, but monumentally broad; she could make three of her husband. And their daughters were tremendous. In America children grow big, Wyznowieki always said, showing his big American daughters Helen and Theresa. Oversized girls, tall, big-boned, and with big features and voices like for hollering on a ranch. They were now eighteen and nineteen, and sometimes for days they would try to be delicate like little girls, putting napkins on the table and speaking almost in whispers trying to make their voices be soft. Then all of a sudden they would wrestle like boys or strong dogs, laughing so loud the walls shook, rolling on the floor with their legs thrashing and their hair wild, playing.

The old man was always trying to get the boys at the mill to come and see his daughters. Every new fellow coming to work in the scrapyard had to run the risk of getting married to one of Wyznowieki's girls. It was a standing joke, how Wyzy would peer into every department, sniff around the openhearth, investigate the blooming-mill if he heard there was a new man there. It was a gag around the plant. Any new man, Ladislas would walk around him like a sniffing dog. "You come out on my farm Sunday, you get some real Polish ham to eat; I raise him myself, I show you my American daughters. They give you good time."

They give you good time, boy! that was the gag. You try the younger one, Helen, see, take her for a walk down by the barn!

Now in summer it was tough for the girls and they bothered the life out of him. Pa, we never meet anybody here on the farm, we might as well be out in the sticks. All of a sudden they wanted to go to Chicago and take up a nursing course, cost three hundred dollars. But hell damn, he said, he didn't raise two big daughters to learn a trade and be old maids; no, he had girls to get married, have kids, straw-haired little bums running around pulling cats' tails. Hurry up, he wanted to see lots of kids, hear kids yell in the house.

The house was a four-room frame with the kitchen swollen out from several rebuildings; the rooms were crowded with huge, old-fashioned chunks of furniture; the dining-room table was so big that Mrs. Wyznowieki had to squeeze sidewise to get around it. In the front room there were four cages of canaries, and the girls had added a parrot. Everywhere there were rubber plants and geranium pots, on all the window sills, on top of the console radio, and a flower pot had to be moved off the sewing machine before it could be used. On the kitchen window ledge Mama Wyznowieki kept a row of milk bottles filled with water, and potatoes flowering out of the tops of the bottles.

Ladislas ran the magnet crane in the scrapyard. Seven years now he had been on that old crane. Before that, scrap-loader down on the ground. One job he wanted. He wanted to run the big Hulett unloader that grabbed iron ore out of the boats in the slip and deposited it on the ore-dock. That was the best crane job. Four times, in these last years, he figured it had been his turn by rights to get promoted to an ore-dock crane. Nearly four dollars more a day, on the average. But it was not only the money, goddamit. It was to prove to those goddam Swedish and their smart American sons. Here was an old Polack who could clean out a boat as quick and as slick as any of them. He would handle those giant jaws like watchmaker's pincers, picking up the last speck of iron dust from the bottom of the boat. Why wasn't he good enough for the Hulett crane? He had a perfect safety record on his skidding, jerking, cranky old scrap-picker. Besides, he had proved he could handle the ore-unloader because once a couple of years ago, when one of those Swedes took sick, he had worked a week over there on the docks.

That was a clean, quiet job, sitting all enclosed in the fine little control cab, with windows all around, instead of in his open rattly old scrapyard box. That was good, sailing suspended under the long bridge stretched like an arm over the docks with a finger projecting out over the water, and from the tip of that finger sending the gigantic scoop-jaws down into the boats,

[29]

hauling up the rusty dirt, and riding it back along the bridge-arm to unload onto the great hills of ore between the docks and the blast furnaces.

There, as nowhere else in the mill, a man had a sense of making something out of earth: almost like on a farm. There from the height of the ore-dump bridge the entire plant could be seen, stretching for two miles along the lakeshore, as a thing of order and sense instead of the haphazard puzzle it appeared to be when a man had only one small task inside a shed or in an enclosed yard. For there a man dredged the very ore and limestone off the barges; he dumped it to form waiting hills, and from his perch saw those hills eaten away by the transfer cars, rolling the raw dirt to the blast furnaces that stood like a row of earth-eating monsters behind the ore-dumps. Iron ore, limestone, and coke—red, white, and black—he saw the different dusts of earth loaded into the larrycars that crawled up the inclines to the tops of the blast furnaces, dumping the ore, limestone, and coke like fodder into the upturned mouths of the beasts, and streams of molten iron issuing below. From that high bridge, Ladislas could see the iron pouring into ladles on wheels, could see the fuming ladles hauled by train-engines to the next row of buildings, the long high openhearth sheds, seven furnaces, boxcar size, under each roof, and in those furnaces was scrap iron already melting, ready for this boiling pig iron to be added to the soup, to mix and boil and purify and make new steel. From the backs of those boxcar furnaces the steel poured into a great pot, and from the pot ingot-molds were filled, and he could see the long trains of gray-sheathed ingots, like trains of upended iron coffins, pulling toward the stripping-shed where the casings were lifted off the newly poured ingots, leaving the red-glowing blocks of steel bare on the ingot-buggies, and he could see those red-hot naked ingots pulled to the soaking-pits, buried in the heated ground so that the heat might spread evenly through them, all even-baked inside, like a man in a Turkish bath; and he could see glowing ingots emerging from the pits, being carried to the various mills, the blooming-mill where the man-sized blocks of steel would be squeezed into workable chunks, thick slabs or long billets; he could see the chipping-yard behind the bloomer, and the sparks as automatic hammers chipped blemishes from the slabs; and from there, cranes lifting the slabs onto flatcars again, and the slabs hauled to the next row of great barn-shaped sheds where the steel would be rolled down, and down, and passed through shaping-rolls, until it came out girders or sheets, or rods, or as wire; and he could see the boxcars at the far end of the yard, hauling the product away.

And then, in the other direction, beyond the slip into which the oreboats came, he could see the repetition of all these things in the three successive millyards that stretched toward Chicago: the Tri-State, and Midwest, and Consolidated mills, each with its flocks of openhearth smokestacks and its tall, fat blast furnaces reaching above all.

On the Hulett unloader, moving over the hills of raw ore, it was as though he had command over the huge sprawling beast of a mill, by feeding it.

But after that one week on the unloaders, they put Wyznowieki back on his old scrapyard crane, that should itself have been thrown in for scrap. His crane-mount straddled the yard,

[3 1]

fifty feet across, and traveled the length of a block. Wet days, the rails were skiddy; wintry days the wind went through the flimsy crane-box like a bunch of knives. But never mind, he knew his old traveler, knew to the fraction of an inch how much she would skid in rain or snow, and how much play there was in the brakes; he had the feel in his fingers of the very edges of the contact brushes.

That was the busiest crane in the whole damn mill; fifty lifts an hour was nothing. The train of empty charging-boxes for the openhearth furnaces was always waiting below him, like an endless row of empty bread-tins. On the other tracks came carloads of scrap: old busted-down auto bodies, rails, iron barrels, locomotive wheels, farm implements (when he spotted these, Wyzy always spent an hour after work hunting in the scrap pile for parts that might be useful on his farm). And from the mill itself scrap came: shear-ends, and blemished castouts, to be melted down again, poured into steel again.

Wyzy rode over the scrap heaps, lowering his magnet, lifting junk, filling the rows of feed-boxes for the furnaces. And all he wanted was two things: to be an ore-unloader, and to see his big daughters married and making kids around the farm.

There was a good friend of his, Waldemar Vikulik, worked as pitman in the openhearth, who had a son, young Pete, working in the Consolidated mill. Sometimes Waldemar brought young Pete along to the farm, to joke the girls; Pete even took Theresa to the moving pictures a couple of times, but no, you could see they were not a couple, maybe she was not smart enough for him. Smart clean boy, this Pete but, besides, a Communist maybe, a revolutionist, talked always politics. The girls, they listened good, like women, but maybe they wanted to play—give her a push, a chase, throw her on the ground, wrestle! Too solemn, young Pete, but anyway a fine boy!

C.I.O. comes and Pete is the first one with a button, and makes his father wear a button into the Standard mill. "Is going to be union now," Waldemar said. "My eyes are going blind, twenty-five years in this mill. No union, I get nothing. Is going to be union, I get pension for my eyes." Sign up in the union, Ladislas, he said, and they got to give you the job on the big crane.

"Last time we had union," Wyzy reminded him, "your boy he got kick in the pants. Fired quick from Standard Steel."

"Sure. That was different union. Now we got C.I.O."

Next Sunday, Waldemar Vikulik and young Pete came over, bringing with them the C.I.O. man, Frank Sobol.

"Yes, I seen you before someplace," Wyznowieki said. Where were they, his dumb cows, his daughters, why didn't they come sit, bring beer, when two young men were present!

Sure, Frank Sobol said, he had been around the Standard mills a couple of years ago, organizing the United Steel Workers that time. Young Pete was in that union, too.

"Yah, I seen you. The company was terribly down on that union. All Bolsheviks, they said."

"What union ain't they down on?" young Pete asked.

"That's right," Ladislas agreed. The girls came, standing, with foolish eyes.

"But they ain't gonna be down on the C.I.O., the C.I.O. is gonna be on top of them," young Pete said, laughing again. The cow Theresa, why didn't she laugh when Pete made jokes? Then maybe he would go more for her.

[33]

"Well, when you gonna sign up all the Polacks, Wyzy?" Pete wanted to know.

"I ain't sign up myself yet," he said. "I not sure about this C.I.O."

"Oh, sure, we know you're gonna sign up," Pete laughed. "But you got to get some of those old Polacks, they won't listen to Pop but you know how to talk to them, Wyzy!"

"They don't listen to me nothing," Wyznowieki demurred. "Old Polacks is not so foolish. You got good union, they sign it up, that's all. You know I got no sayso, I don't even belong to the Polish-American clubs."

Next day in the mill Ladislas Wyznowieki stopped at No. 4 openhearth to say a word to his friend Waldemar Vikulik, to say come over on the farm Sunday, bring over young Pete, we have some new wine. "Where is Vikulik?" he asked a pitman.

"Old Vikulik? He got bounced. They said he got bad eyes. Can't see good enough any more. That's what he gets wearing that button around here."

So on the following Sunday, Wyznowieki had sixteen of his old cronies sitting under the four cherry trees; Frank Sobol came over with the Vikuliks, and signed them all up in the C.I.O., and all took away extra cards, and pretty soon every goddam Pole in the mill had his name on a card.

Up until that time, two men used to work on the ground helping the crane, guiding the chunks of iron into the boxes. But now the scrapyard foreman took off a man. "Super says one man is enough," he informed Wyznowieki. "Hell, a good crane-man ought to load those boxes without any help at all."

"Always was two men on ground!" Wyznowieki kicked. "Now you gonna have scrap stick out from box tearing up furnace door, maybe scrap falling from boxes, make some accidents too. I will tell super, myself!"

The foreman grinned. "Better take off your button before you talk to him."

"I gonna wear my goddam button. I been here seventeen years this mill; I want to wear C.I.O. button, okay, that's my business."

So all the while he talked, the super, with an easy smile on his face, was looking at that button on his cap. "Okay, Wyzy," the super said, "you claim you can't load those boxes with only one helper. We'll find someone that can do it. You want to come off the crane?"

"Nobody can work that crane so good as me!" Ladislas sputtered. "I am long time in line for Hulett crane. Why you don't give me Hulett crane job on the dock?"

"Why, you say you can't even run your old crane any more."

"I say you got safety rules, you gonna have accident, one man is not enough on ground. You gonna lose time charging furnace, for boxes cannot be loaded good."

"You let me worry about that, Wyzy."

The following week, Ladislas Wyznowieki turned in a report on his crane: she needed new brakes. She was coasting and skidding like some day she would ride clear off the rails. If he hadn't known the feel of her she'd have slammed into the stopper forty times a day.

The foreman came back with his report. "What the hell,

[3 5]

Wyznowieki, here lately you are always bellyaching about something. Pin a button on your cap and nothing is good enough for you any more."

"All I do is, safety rules says report bad crane. I report him."

"We can't afford to lose time on overhaul right now. I'll send the millwright up to check your brakes. You've got to be careful, that's all."

The millwright growled. "They allow me two hours on this job. She needs a complete overhaul, take a week. Your wiring is shot, too."

"I fix them," Wyznowieki muttered.

So one day the crane stalled. She wouldn't budge. Hung out there in mid-ocean over the scrapyard. Wyznowieki calmly blew the whistle for the repair crew.

They labored six hours. Tore the controls apart, and meanwhile found several parts that needed replacement. They saw the wires with frayed, sore-rubbed insulation, and put in a lot of new wiring. By the end of that shift they had the old wreck nearly overhauled. Below, the foreman and super were running in circles, yelling through cupped hands: Hurry up! They even had a labor gang loading scrap by hand. The breakdown had come just when four furnaces were charging, needing scrap.

Finally when he saw they were actually falling behind on loading, Wyzy poked his nose in among the repairmen. "Hey," he remarked, "look this motor brushes. They ain't supposed to be so loose like this, huh?"

The repairmen swore thunderously. Who the hell would dream the brushes could get that loose? Why the hell hadn't he looked at them five hours ago! A few turns with a screwdriver, and she was all set.

Next day, Wyznowieki was grounded, shifted to the labor gang. Unsafe, was the excuse. "Unsafe! Look my record! I been seven years on this crane, no accident. I am next man for dock crane. This crane is unsafe, not me!"

"Take it to the C.I.O. Take it to the Labor Board. Go ahead!" The foreman shrugged.

"Nobody is going to kick me off crane. I go fight this! I not afraid of super or whole Standard Steel company! What they can do to me?" he raged. "Balls they can do to me. I spit on them. Me, I got my farm. I can go home and stay on my farm. I got two big girls they can go to work. Farm is enough for me and my old lady. I fight this case ten years!"

From work he went directly to the union headquarters. "Take it easy," Frank Sobol said. "First, you've got to stay in that mill. We'll bring your case up in a grievance meeting. But no matter what they give you to do, don't quit, see? We'll get you back on that crane."

So Ladislas labored with a pick, with the Mexican gang on the tracks. They sure got it in for old Wyzy, the men said. He's getting too old for pick work, too.

Wait till we get our contract. He's gonna be back up there on that crane, goddamit.

Fat chance. He's lucky he ever got on a crane in the first place; they don't give crane jobs to hunkies. Now you got to be a college graduate engineer!

One day they got caught in No. 4 openhearth with two heats

tapping simultaneously. Only one pit crane was in operation. Ordinarily, if the craneman humped and the heats broke right he could keep up with the seven furnaces, but when two furnaces tapped at the same time, the second crane had to go into action. No. 2 furnace was tapping, the stream of liquid steel already sunrising to the brim of the ladle, and the crane was letting down the big hooks to grab up that bucket and carry it across the pit to teem the waiting ingot-molds, when the head melter came running around No. 5 furnace. "Get that steel out of this pot before it goes through the bottom!"

Wyzy was in the pit with the track gang, cleaning frozen chunks of slop-over slag. He saw Baldy MacIver, the head melter, jumping around No. 5. "What's the matter with Baldy, what's he coming in his pants for?" And the word went down, and across the pit. "No. 5 is burning a hole in the bottom, he's scared she'll go through the bottom."

Baldy yelled to the pit foreman: "Get that other crane going. No. 5 heat has got to be teemed right away!" For the steel soup, being taken out early, underheated, would not remain fluid many minutes. It would make a skull in the ladle, and never pour into the ingot-molds, unless handled with utmost speed. The pit foreman yelled up at Baldy: "I got only one operator here, how the hell do you expect me to teem two heats at the same time!" "You got two cranes, ain't you?" "That bitchn crane don't operate itself!" "Well, put someone on it, dammit, there's five thousand dollars' worth of steel in there!" So the pit foreman ran to the phone and screamed to the front office: "Give me a crane-operator, take off a craneman someplace and send him over here quick!"

In a minute Mr. Crowell, the openhearth super, came running around that furnace, and the whole gang of them, Crowell and MacIver and the first helper, stood there watching the steel fill the ladle as if they were going to haul that big tub across the pit by force of will.

"Get somebody on that crane! Get somebody!" And suddenly the melter spied Ladislas down there calmly picking away at a gob of slag. "Hey, Wyzy, what are you doing here?"

"I work on the labor gang now, Mr. MacIver."

"Thought you was on the crane in the scrapyard."

"They got me on the ground now. Said I be unsafe, I can't handle no crane."

"Well, what did you do? Are you unsafe?"

"Nobody ever got hurt by me, seven year."

"Go on up there and take this heat over and teem it for me," the melter said.

So Ladislas put down his pick and climbed the narrow ladder stairs to the second crane and gently let her out, eased her along over the pit. She bumped and shuddered a little as he testingly brought her to a halt, short of No. 5 furnace; but he was getting the feel of her all right. Sounding the warning-bell, he traveled her over to the furnace, watching the upturned heads of super, melter, foreman—goddam, they could twist their necks off watching before he would make a mistake! He halted her smooth, without so much as a quiver. This two-hundred-ton crane was like a Rolls-Royce compared to that lousy creaking jalopy he had run in the scrapyard. Peering across the pit directly at the furnace spout, he lined the big hooks up with the ladle handles, then let down that pair of hooks. All their eyes followed the hooks now. For an instant he was uncertain of himself, uncertain whether he could bring those hooks down under the handles and swing them forward and up like when you grab somebody under the armpits. But the powerful hooks seemed to be the ends of his own hands—he could feel through the lever how they slotted under the grips, he could feel them come up solid embracing the ladle, and feel the instant when the weight of the ladle was upon those hooks, all set to lift. As easy as if he had been ten years on that job, he touched the lever forward, so smoothly you couldn't tell which instant the 130-ton brimming pot of steel left the ground, balanced in the air. Up she came without a speck of slop-over, no sway, just smooth.

The pit was cluttered, two trains of empty molds backing and switching, and a slagcar parked in the middle of the floor; he lifted the ladle high to ride her over all that junk, and now he had to haul her the length of the pit to the second teeming-shelf. They watched him from the monkeywalk behind the furnace, like people on a pier anxiously watching a departing steamer. Then he saw them clambering down to the pit, to walk across and come up on the shelf and watch him pour.

Wyzy lowered the pot over the first waiting mold. For a moment he was afraid of play in the cable; he might squash her on top of the molds; he lowered carefully, as if the entire weight of that great pot of steel was on his own hands. Nine inches, the perfect clearance from the mold tops, he checked her and she held. He could feel the heat of that steel in his face now; the ladle was almost at arm's reach from his box. The pit foreman hurried over to him, whispering like a manager to a fighter in the ring: "Easy now, Wyzy. Got to get that stopper-hole right over the middle of the mold. You splash the side of the mold and you get a frozen skin on that ingot, never come out of the mold."

He wanted to say: "You don't have to tell me!" Too many times he had watched this done. Leak without spraying the sides of the bowl.

On the shelf, just below him, the steel-pourer shouldered the huge stopper-lever. The pit foreman stepped toward the ladle, poked a rod up the stopper-hole. There was a pop like a paper bag bursting, then the stream of steel hissed out the bottom of the ladle, first as thin as a hose stream, but quickly as thick as a fist. The foreman glanced up to let him know she was set okay, but leaning out of the cab window Ladislas could see for himself that he had the stream feeding directly into the narrow ingot-mold. The heat touched his face like sun turned on, and sparks from the pouring steel died all around his head. Another pit hand, a Pole he knew, stood with a wheelbarrow full of aluminum nuggets, and pitched handfuls of aluminum into the teeming mold. That was to halt the boiling action of the steel.

Nearly full—Wyzy saw the leverman stiffen, shoulder up the lever, inching off the stream, then, straightening, snap the lever full up so that the stopper closed tight. That was his time. Wyzy gave the crane a touch of juice, just enough to start her moving. Not quite far enough. Another touch. She halted directly over the second mold. The pourer bowed under the lever again, releasing the stopper.

Fumes were in Wyznowieki's eyes now, and the steel heat was rotten to breathe. He glanced down the line of waiting molds below him, like a row of open mouths; he would fill them one by one.

And when all the molds were filled, he knew the next thing to do. Riding back to No. 5 furnace, he lifted the ladle over the slag pot, caught his small hook on the ladle-bottom. Like yanking a man up by his pants. He tilted the huge ladle until it hung almost upside down, and the last dregs slid into the pot of hissing slag. She was clean.

He saw Crowell turn and head back for his office.

Wyzy finished up the job, setting the empty ladle back in place below the furnace, then picking up the pot of slag and placing it on a waiting car to be hauled to the dump. Finished; like cooking and washing and hanging up the pots. He ran the crane back to her mooring and came down the ladder. Baldy MacIver, the head melter, stood on the monkeywalk. "Where you going, Wyzy?"

"Back to labor gang. Boss says I am on labor gang, I cannot run no crane."

MacIver rubbed glistening black specks of carbon off his bald dome.

"Teeming job is hardest crane job in the mill, right?" Ladislas said.

"Just about."

"I do her all right."

"Yah. You did her okay." The Scotsman rubbed his head again and chuckled in his throat. "Wyzy, when we got crane work to do we'll give it to you. You don't have to go to any

C.I.O. John L. Lewis ain't going to get you back up there on that crane if we got no crane for you to ride."

Two more hours on his shift, so Wyzy went back and got his pick. But as soon as the shift was over he marched to the C.I.O. office. "Where is Frank, is Frank Sobol here?" The dark curly-headed Sobol came out into the hallway and talked with him. "I got some more dope for my grievance. Today they put me on pit crane, I do everything fine. . . ."

For several more weeks, Ladislas was still down there on the labor gang. And every time he passed MacIver he saw the shine in his eyes, hard as the shine on his bald dome. The Scot would narrow his eyes and gaze at the row of monthly dues-paid buttons that Ladislas wore on his cap, then MacIver would shake his head pityingly and walk away, grinning.

But the big news came, how Standard Steel had signed the C.I.O. contract. And the case came up at a grievance meeting all right: Ladislas Wyznowieki, craneman, why was he grounded? And what do you mean he can't handle a crane? When you're caught short he can handle the toughest crane on the lot—here it is, May 26, called him off of the labor gang to teem a heat in No. 4 openhearth. . . .

The super said: Well, he'd see what he could do.

"I want job on Hulett unloader!" Ladislas put in. "I am next man for unloader crane, but every time they put new man!"

Frank Sobol gave him the wink to take it easy. "This man has lost an average of $3.50 a day for two months now," Frank pointed out. "If we wanted to get tough we could put in a claim for the difference in his pay scale. But the main thing is we want him back on a crane."

[43]

"I'll look into it," the super said. "I'll find out why he was grounded."

And, by golly, next week MacIver called him in. "Think you can handle that teeming-crane? I told you, Wyzy, soon as we have a crane job we'll put you up there. You don't have to go to any union to talk to us."

"Sure, sure," Ladislas grinned, fingering the visor of his cap, where all the buttons were pinned.

One job in hell, he told his wife. You got to sit inside, under the roof, not outside like scrapyard crane. Inside, and all the time smoke, black and yellow smoke, one job in hell. And the machine was not in such fine shape as he had at first thought; the wiring was cheesy. He talked to one of the electricians. "They give me three days to rewire the whole job," the electrician complained. "Used to allow a week. But now you get an order—sixty hours. She's got to be in operation. Got to do it. Hell, all I can do is throw that wire in like a bunch of spaghetti. You see it there, no covered stuff at all, just like quick emergency wiring."

"Yah, everything in a hurry, everything economy now," Wyzy agreed.

That wire was rubbing raw, sparking, shorting all the time. The thinly insulated cable running up the wall got covered with grease and oil drippings from the overhead track of the crane; and one day sparks of fire from a pouring heat of steel ignited that grease, and fire ran up along the wires like a fast fuse burning toward the crane.

Wyznowieki didn't see the fire; but one of the pitmen blew a whistle, and he saw them gesticulating at him, pointing behind him; he shut off the motor and seized the extinguisher. He happened to be midfloor, far from the ladder. Best he could do was climb out on top of the cab and walk the rail. His hands got scorched.

The burn was not really serious, but the company doctor said he had to go to the hospital. "I no go!" Wyzy cried, insisting that the women wouldn't feed the livestock properly, and one of his sows was ready to throw a litter, he had to be home on his farm. But Frank Sobol said better go to the hospital in case there comes any argument about compensation claims, so he went and sat around the hospital three days. The C.I.O. boys sent flowers. One hell of a way to waste five bucks; but it was a great big fine geranium plant, and goddam Wyzy, what does he do coming back to the job? He packs that plant with him and hauls it up and sets it inside that crane-box!

Hey, Wyzy, why don't you bring your cow and chickens and fix up a little farm up there!

And a cage of canary birds!

Every hour he would let down a milk bottle on a string, for water for his plant. Back and forth across the floor of hell he rode, with his pot of blooming geraniums. The other shifts on the crane kidded, but let it alone. The night man on that same crane said he was going to put up lace curtains.

Having the contract, Standard Steel naturally did not go out on strike when the three smaller mills went out. But Wyznowieki stopped in the headquarters in Steel Harbor, the big headquar-

[45]

ters for all three mills, in the ancient, crack-ceilinged Harbor Hall. He saw Frank Sobol there. "You need anything for this strike, you tell me, Frank," he said.

"Oh, everything is okay here in the Harbor," Frank told him. The Midwest plant and Tri-State were closed down tight, not even trying to operate. "But that Consolidated is a sonofabitch. That's right inside the Chicago city limits and those Chicago cops are running the scabs into the plant. They won't even let us have a picket line out there."

Saturday, he met Sobol on the sidewalk. "Hey, Wyzy, I want to see you. I'm going over there to the new headquarters we got near Consolidated, you know that place, Guzman's Grove."

"Yah, I know that place. Beer, picnics."

"Tomorrow we got a big meeting there. We got to have everybody out for that meeting."

"Okay," Wyznowieki nodded, sniffed like when he was getting started on the trail. "Okay, I tell all the Polacks, don't worry. Big Fourth of July picnic, huh?"

"Maybe Pete is going to be there," Helen insisted. "All the boys will be there. Me and Theresa are going too. What do you want us to do, sit around here all day and talk to the chickens? It's the Fourth of July!"

"Bad to leave farm like this," he grumbled. "Nobody on the farm!"

They'd have to get back before sundown, for the feedings, milking, all the jobs with the animals. He piled his wife and big daughters into the '31 Dodge. "Wait, you got those eggs? You

[4 6]

got the ham?" A whole crate of eggs, twenty dozen eggs from his farm for the strikers' free kitchen.

They were on the spot early, before the speeches started. Wyzy shouldered the crate of eggs and delivered it to the kitchen, his broad wife following him like a widening wake after a boat. "I know, we got to make it egg sandwiches," she said, and there she remained in the kitchen, turning the eggs into egg sandwiches. Ladislas wandered outside, around the grove. Friends were beginning to arrive. Soon he was buzzing from one to another, nodding, sniffing, screwing his eyes. All here, every Pole in every mill, by golly, was gonna be here on the spot! He talked to Frank Sobol. "What I tell you, I pass the word, huh? I am better than ten thousand these." He laughed at the handbills. "You want the Polacks to come, you tell Ladislas, that's all!"

"What you been drinking, Wyzy?" Frank laughed.

Pretty soon the speeches began. Wyzy did not listen much, but often cocked back his head in a listening attitude, and smiled approvingly because he knew it was all right, without listening—the crowd, the flags, all the Poles, hear that fine speaker, in American, Mr. Szutak, he is Polish too, a comical speaker, he can tell it to the boss all right, that is how you tell it to the boss! Yes, sir, we got the keys in our pocket now! Wyzy blinked, chuckled, and seeing young Pete Vikulik cried: "Hey, Pete, how you like that! He is Polack too! Szutak! Come on, I buy you one beer. You see my girls here? Both my girls are here!"

Later he glimpsed the girls. They were standing with a fellow.

[47]

Theresa had hold of a fellow. Good! A big one, too, taller than herself! She was eating an ice-cream stick.

"Well, Wyzy, you going to march?"

"Sure! I march in this parade!"

He buzzed through the crowd, gathered some of the older Poles, Jan Byzynski; Waldemar the Goat with his stiff whitening whiskers, a heater in the Standard plant, and he had his two sons with him. They fell in line well up toward the front.

"Got no band, no music, huh?" Ladislas grumbled. "By God, we Polish do this job, we have some music next time, for parade! By God, look all this empty land! Good for farm! Can make gardens here!"

When they came up near the police lines and spread off the road, he spied a patch of garden someone had planted in the prairie. Radish spears and carrots were coming up. "Look this! Hey, don't walk on this! Here is garden!" Wyzy buzzed around the patch like a wing-flapping hen, chasing the marchers away from that tiny seeded area. "Here is garden!"

As Mitch Wilner watched the parade get going, his apprehension lifted. It was just the Fourth of July, just people walking; there was a huge bearish-looking man, Lithuanian or something, riding his kid on his shoulder; there came a cluster of fellows with signs on sticks, some of them he had seen back there in the yard, one was dragging a baseball bat. And not far behind was a group of older men laughing and talking Polish; and walking along in the procession he spotted two little people, a fellow and a girl, walking hand in hand with their faces serious, exactly like drawings of workers in the *New Masses*, you didn't think they actually existed just like that; then came a cluster of housewives in cotton dresses; and, scattered through, more of the fellows carrying signs. As the column lengthened it fanned out until it had no form at all, and reminded him, incongruously, of the field following golfers.

Fellows with white paper armbands walked alongside the column, trying to keep it in shape. Close in, get in line, they repeated, but folks paid no attention, seemingly undecided whether they were a part of the march, or simply spectators; like himself, Wilner noticed, they walked alongside rather than in the parade. As another group of men, obviously strikers, passed him, he saw one fellow stoop and pick up a stone, and heft it. One of the armbanded boys said, half-grinning: "Now, no rough stuff," and the lad with the stone grinned back, but kept the stone.

The buildings petered off; there was one block of open prairie, ending at tracks. Here the column made a right turn, and Mitch saw the factory layout.

Beyond the tracks, on a lip curving into the lake, was the steel plant. The mass of buildings with long high windowless walls and peaked roofs, the batches of smokestacks, stood cut out against lake and sky. There came to him, momentarily, the same sense of inexcusable ignorance he had often felt on driving past such plants, or past oil refineries: how could a man remain so ignorant of these processes that were fundamental to his civilization? He had passed his life within a few miles of all these things, but did not know what the shapes of the buildings held. Why were those smokestacks ranged in series of seven? There

[49]

must be a purpose to that. And what were the tall pipe-entangled structures? And what did the men do in these places? Exactly what were their jobs? What was the work of a steelworker? He had only a vague picture-idea, from the word "puddlers," of giant-muscled men half naked in front of fierce open furnaces, maybe sticking rods into those furnaces and stirring the living molten steel.

The road now ran parallel with the railway tracks, and on these tracks, between the marchers and the steel plant, stood long lines of boxcars. Evidently they were marching toward a track-crossing that led to the plant gate.

They got machine guns in those boxcars, a fellow in the crowd said.

They got machine guns on the roofs.

You know that watertank in the yard? Where they put up the big searchlight? They got guns in there.

Mitch Wilner glanced at the solid double line of boxcars, like a Chinese wall protecting the plant. It was not difficult to imagine men and guns materializing in the gaping black doorways of the cars.

From spots in the crowd, Mitch heard attempts at singing; they were singing "Solidarity," but the song stumbled and faded out; they were not marching to rhythm. A few voices carried the words on awhile, as if singing for themselves rather than in a crowd.

Now they saw the police.

Where tracks and the road took a slight curve, the police line cut the road. It was not yet the entrance to the plant, for the main buildings and a huge sign, "Consolidated Steel Corporation," could be made out, at least two blocks behind the police line.

All had known the police were waiting. All had seen, vaguely, blue forms in the distance, motorcycles and police cars buzzing on the roads. But now the moment of encounter brought a sharp focus. The police were stationed like a company of soldiers in pictures of old-time wars, soldiers lined up to charge. And behind them their wheeled paraphernalia stood like cannon backing the line of soldiers.

The marchers slackened, the pace became sluggish, and then the flag-bearers halted. They were perhaps a hundred yards from the police; the white road between them vibrated in the direct rays of the sun.

The halt did not seem one of confusion. There was an odd sense of intention, of design in all that happened. The straggling column consolidated, as those behind pressed forward, then, further compressed, the column distended and overflowed on both sides of the road. On the left, the police line ended at some scattered houses. On the right were the railroad and the plant. The police moved quickly, paralleling the expanding front of the marchers. Pairs of police ran, leaping across railway tracks, until their line reached the boxcars.

The flag-bearers still waited. A discussion seemed to be going on between leaders. Mitch noticed the burnt-faced man shaking his head, while that excited, stubby fellow, Mike Sisto, gesticulated toward the boxcars. A couple of the men with white armbands took part in the discussion. But none of the people who had seemed to be in charge, in the headquarters, were up in front; neither Kiley, nor Sobol, nor Carl Gaul.

Now a decision seemed to have been reached. The fellows with white armbands scattered over the field calling people back into line.

All waited. Behind the police line, on the porches of houses, photographers scrambled, climbing on railings to take vantage-point pictures. Next to a patrol wagon the newsreel truck stood, and the photographer on the roof of the truck buzzed his camera.

Look, the bitchn finks!

[51]

There, on the low sloping roof of one of the plant buildings, as on sloping bleachers, the scabs were assembled, squatting or standing, perhaps a few hundred men altogether, viewing the scene, just like grandstanders at a Fourth of July parade. Muttering and cursing rose all along the line now; Mitch saw more fellows stoop and pick up rocks. But it was a far throw.

The flag-bearers began to walk again, and the crowd behind them walked, a strange, deliberate, silent walk across the remaining hundred paces of no man's land, a testing walk, as if at each step the ground might give way underneath. The police shifted on their feet, nervously. The white strip of road was eaten, step by step. Then police and strikers stood breathing-close, face to face.

And nothing happened. Like throwing a switch when one is fearful of a fuse blowing; but the connection takes place without explosion. They stood, the crowd, the cops, all motionless. Mitch Wilner wove through the crowd, edged up toward the front. The people in the front lines were talking to the cops. "Let us through, why can't we go through, we got a right. Just to the gate, to picket there." The cops were shaking their heads, some grinning, some bored. There was the burnt-faced fellow, and a woman with him, evidently his wife, quite a good-looking young woman, gesticulating, pointing toward the gate. And in the crowd Mitch saw a fellow whom he had known in the old days, one of the old West Side bunch, Sam Eisen. What was he doing here? Sam was a lawyer now, supposed to be a radical or something. The burnt-faced fellow turned around toward the crowd now, with his arm raised, as though counseling patience.

Whole minutes passed. Nothing would happen. The crowd would turn back. Having demonstrated its will, and its control, it would turn back.

Mitch edged still further toward the houses, and there where the column thinned he came into the very front line. He was within arm's length—clubbing length, he realized—of the facing policemen. At that moment an officer of some sort, captain he guessed, came up behind the police. He was old, with a large seamed face, protruding half-closed eyelids, and an almost catatonic rigidity of expression.

In an automatic voice such as bailiffs use in administering courtroom oaths, he reeled off: ". . . order you in the name of the State of Illinois to disperse and go home . . ." a formula. His voice was low, careless. Directly behind Mitch people were asking: "What did he say?" Others called: "Let us through; come on, give us a break. The mayor said——"

The officer turned and walked back behind his police.

Mitch Wilner was seized with apprehension. Why had the officer recited that rigmarole? Without even raising his voice. Simply as though he were complying to a formula before——

Yes, something would come, now. They had better turn back. He felt an urge to shout: Back, back, better go back before they . . . To jump up on something and shout: Go back.

Then he turned, retreating into the crowd, not only to feel people between himself and the police, but with the thought that those immediately around him might turn as he had turned, and that there might be a turning movement in the crowd.

And at the same time he told himself he was being foolish, panicky; here strikers and police had stood face to face for longer than five minutes; all were controlled. He was well among the people now, in the thick. He heard a firecracker pop; and an instant later, a series of firecrackers, like the string of fireworks Mort had let off on the beach. Mitch looked up into the air and saw a missile, a rock perhaps, flying over the police line. Now it will start, he reflected, with fearing, sinking heart; and only then realized that everyone was running, he too was running back down the road. He halted and looked around.

A cloud of smoke rose lazily like a great cigar-puff, lifting upward in the clear still air. That must be tear gas. There was another rattle of explosions. Maybe shooting blanks into the air.

"They're shooting real bullets!" a woman cried, running; and all around him the same words echoed, uttered with surprise, as if for corroboration. "They're shooting real bullets!" Mitch remained standing, as if his standing still there would prove that the police were not actually firing bullets into the crowd; that could not be. Then he saw a man in a blue workshirt, running toward him, cast himself on the ground, exactly like some soldier in a war movie. Or had the man fallen? Wilner realized he had started to run again, and halted now to go back and look at that man, but the crowd swirled him, and a heavy, bareheaded man with his arm across his eyes blocked his way. This man was staggering. "Don't worry, just tear gas, no permanent effect," Mitch said, turning the blinded man and heading him down the road. "You'll be okay in a couple of hours."

"Shooting," the man mumbled, stumbling on his way.

He ought not to stand here. They'd need him at headquarters. Mitch turned once more for a last look, to convince himself that what was happening was happening. The gas cloud had stretched out sausage-shape and was lifting, thinning like torn gauze; through this, he could see the blue line of police approaching. Again, he was possessed by a sense of unreality. This was all like a scene for a movie, yes, or some act in an arena; all staged like a football game, a mimic war; there sat the bleachers crowd; and there movie cameras turned.

He ran from the advancing police. Alongside him as he ran, Mitch saw that huge Lithuanian, with the kid holding his hand, running; and he reassured himself that Syl and the kids must have stayed in the car, or certainly could not have come out very far toward the police, and must have run back when the trouble started. The Lithuanian's kid halted, lifting one foot as though he had stepped on a thistle. "Pa, I'm shot," the kid said. The

[5 4]

Lithuanian swooped and picked up the child, running on, as the blood from the boy's foot trickled down his shirt.

Now a car came toward them, cutting through the crowd. Mitch noticed the Red Cross sign stuck under the windshield wiper. He jumped on the running-board. Carl Gaul was driving, accompanied by some fellow he didn't know. "Shooting," Mitch cried. "Must be some fallen up there."

Carl nodded. "We heard it."

The gas cloud had practically disintegrated, the air clearing as the mind clears after a wild, confusing deed. They saw the police come to a halt, drawing together in a sort of line, except for a cop here and there chasing a last fleeing striker. One they saw hurl his club after a man who escaped him, and stand laughing as the club conked; the fugitive jerked, stumbled a few steps, then, regaining his balance, ran on, his hand awkwardly feeling for the back of his skull.

But mostly the cops were standing still now, looking around them in half-dazed victory, approaching each other with words. Mitch saw forms flat or huddled on the street and on the prairie. Police bent over the forms, prodded, clubbed. Further back, where the line of encounter had been, there was still a pile-up of people, and cops were pulling at arms and legs, whacking at figures that disentangled themselves and scrambled on all fours, skitterwise, to escape. They seized many. Always two cops working together, never a cop alone, pulling a man to his feet and shoving him to and into the patrol wagon. At last the piled group was dissolved, and only the collapsed wounded lay on that spot, like an evaporation residue.

As Carl brought the car to a stop, four policemen hustled toward it.

"Get the hell—" one of the cops began.

Another scratched his ear. "Sonsabitches. All set with their own ambulance!"

[5 5]

Carl jumped out. "Let us pick up these wounded, officer," he said. "We've got a first-aid station back there. These people need immediate attention. This man is a doctor."

As Mitch wore coat and tie, the cops, momentarily, seemed impressed by his appearance. He hurried to the nearest fallen figure. It was a young, husky fellow, who was just trying to turn himself over as Mitch reached him.

"Get hit?" Mitch asked.

"They shot me," the fellow said, wonderingly. His hand moved toward his middle. Mitch opened the shirt and saw a dark hole, like a cigar burn, directly over the navel. It looked so simple and clean. The full danger formed in his mind: abdominal, probably die. He turned the fellow on his side; there was blood enough where he had lain, on his back. The bullet had entered just above the rump, to the right; probably torn kidney and intestinal punctures. "Help me get this fellow into the car," he called. And as people will when directly ordered, two of the police came over and stooped to lift the wounded man. But seeing police, the striker pushed himself to his feet and, leaning on Mitch and Carl, stumbled toward the car, half falling across the back seat. The police watched, their expressions startlingly contrasted: the one deepening with shame, the other swelling to rage.

Another car had come up, driven by the dude Art. And immediately afterward there came a big maroon sedan, driven by Jock Kiley. Many of the wounded were hoisting themselves, stumbling to the rescue cars. Mitch hurried toward another sprawled figure, but already with the feeling that it was hopeless; what could he possibly do for all these gunshot-wounded, and after them the broken heads, fractures, concussions! Confronted with so much, he could touch nothing, nothing at all. Instead of being here on the field, shouldn't he be back there in headquarters where he had a few bandages? But no; his first job was to sort, to find the worst bleeders, and the abdominals; to check the true emergencies. This one on the ground was unconscious, with blood welling from under his scalp and matting his hair. But no gun wound. Calling to Carl and the others to take the man, Mitch hurried on, examining the fallen. A few yards away he saw Kiley and a white-haired but spry-looking man working over a bleeder. They had a man whose femoral artery was evidently severed, for blood was geysering through a rent in his trouser-leg. The white-haired fellow had pulled off the wounded man's belt and was strapping it around the leg, above the wound, to make a tourniquet. Mitch went to help them. "That's right," he approved the man's nice, quick movements. "But wait a second." He picked up a small flat stone and wedged it under the belt, so as to press against the artery. The bleeding was shut off.

"Cradle," he said, clasping the wrist of the white-haired man; he felt a powerful counter-clasp on his own wrists, and then the heavy drop of the wounded man's arm on his shoulder. They lifted, attempting to cradle-carry him to the car. He was not tall, but hugely thick in the shoulders, and great-chested, a man of about two hundred pounds. Mitch staggered. "Lemme have him, Doc." Kiley slipped his hands under theirs, and the three of them carried the wounded man.

"Know him?" the white-haired helper asked.

Kiley shook his head. The man was muttering his name over for them: "Dombrowsky, Stanley Dombrowsky, me."

They got him into Kiley's car. Dazed, the wounded man felt for the back of his head; he had been clubbed, too. Mitch glanced at the tourniquet. "Ought to hold till you get him there," he surmised, and hurried out onto the field again.

But a pair of cops came charging toward him; the shorter of them, a bull-like man with a blazing red face, cursing in a kind of apoplectic frenzy, and brandishing a long stick, longer than a

[57]

police club. The end of the stick was bloody. "Get the hell off this field before I run you in!"

"These people need emergency care," Mitch said. "I'm a doctor."

"They'll get all the goddam care they need. They're all under arrest. Now you get the hell off this field——"

Mitch backed away, as from a crazed beast. The man seemed out of his senses, possessed by an elation of violence.

Carl Gaul had filled his car with wounded, and turned it around. "Coming, Doc?" he called; and Mitch hopped on the running-board. The maddened policeman stared at the car, rushed it as it drove off. Mitch saw him halt, frustrated, mouth open, exactly like a bull who has run through a cape. "Get those sons of bitches," the cop screamed hoarsely, "they're our prisoners!" Then he wheeled and charged toward Kiley's sedan.

People swarmed around the car as it drove into the yard. All were trying to see the faces of the wounded; all were calling out names. Did anybody see Nick Scallisi? My husband, Jim Carraway, anybody see Jim? You got Hank Russo there? Anybody see Hank? The doorway was jammed with anxious men and women. Carrying the wounded, the rescuers had to push and squeeze through the crowd to get inside the headquarters.

Then, as he stumbled into that dark chamber, Mitch Wilner experienced the ultimate sensation of helplessness; it went all through his being like the dying vibration of a shut-off current. The shock of the scene was like nothing he had ever known before, was far beyond that of the first time he had lost a patient, was altogether different from the prepared-for shock of a first entrance into a dissecting-room. During one long instant he wanted to flee; somehow he would convince himself he had never been here, never been confronted with this task; this scene had never existed.

The wounded were on the floor, lying, sitting, while hundreds of feet scuffed dirt around them. Many leaned huddled against the walls, but some lay in the open room. Relatives, wives, milled around, bending over each figure, seeking their own. And the whole scene was hushed. There was no shrieking; the wounded were not howling their pain; only from a few corners came half-smothered nervous, hysterical weeping. An oppressive terror pervaded the room.

It was difficult to see anyone clearly, for dust from the trampled floors was thick in the air; and there was smoke. The one swath of light, from the doorway, was gray with dust-motes. Mitch glimpsed Barbara Macey standing dazed, holding a basin and a bloody towel, uncertain where to give aid first. And people were still staggering in, being carried into the place.

He had not gone four steps when he nearly walked on a figure lying doubled, in a bloody ooze. It was Emil, lying there on his left side, knees drawn up in fetal position.

Mitch lifted away the soaked shirt and saw the bullet wound. "We'll get you to the hospital," he said. "Hold on for a while. Hold on."

"Yah," Emil muttered. "They got me. Shot in the ass. Shot in the ass." He made a sound in his throat, a miserable attempt at a laugh that ended in a blood-gurgle. "Okay, take it easy," Mitch said. He feared internal hemorrhage.

He arose and stood straddling Emil, to keep others from stumbling over the huddled figure. Looking desperately around for help, Mitch recognized the burnt-faced man. "Listen! Get someone at the doors," he cried. "You've got to get this under control. Get the room cleared, everybody out except the wounded. Then we need a lot of cars to take people to hospitals."

The man nodded. "Okay, Doc"; his eyes beginning to focus.

Just then Sylvia rushed to Mitch. Her body was trembling as she clutched him. "Darling, I couldn't find you, I was afraid——"

He squeezed her hand. "Okay. Okay, Syl."

"You're not hurt . . . ?"

"No, nothing. Syl, get some newspapers, spread them on the floor." At least the new people brought in should be kept off the dirt. "God, I—I don't know what——"

"They're shot," she said, still unbelieving. "With bullets."

"If you see any bad bleeders, call me."

But now things began to come under control. The burnt-faced fellow and Art had collected a squad of men and, beginning at the rear of the room, they were systematically clearing the place of all the unhurt. People obeyed quietly. Only those who had found their relatives were allowed to remain. Again, guards were posted at the door.

As the place cleared, Mitch examined the wounded. He made no attempt to treat them, but sought immediately to segregate the bullet-wounded, get them started to hospitals. About half the injured seemed to have been shot; the rest were clubbed head-wounds, and there was a neat uniformity in these: all toward the back and base of the skull. Well-trained police.

Jock Kiley and Art were lining up the cars now, for ambulances. There was nothing to use as a stretcher. And the wounded could not lie flat in the cars; the best that could be done for a man was to curl him on the back seat.

They moved Emil first. "Jesus, you would go and let them plug you," Art scolded his friend, lamely.

"Right in the ass," Emil mumbled feebly.

Six men carried him, crossing their arms under him as a stretcher, trying to move him gently. They placed him in Kiley's big maroon car. Seeing that car, Mitch suddenly recalled: "Where is that fellow with the cut artery? The tourniquet— I didn't see him outside."

"The sonsabitches got him," Kiley said.

"Who . . . ? But we put him in the car . . . ?"

"They dragged him out. They said he was under arrest . . ." Mitch remembered that wild-faced cop, coat open, running toward Kiley's sedan. "I told them he might bleed to death," Kiley growled. "The sonsabitches dragged him right out of the car."

No use worrying about that one; perhaps the strap tourniquet would hold until he got attention. Right now all these wounded had to be moved to hospitals. The nearest one he could think of was the Jackson Park, miles into town. And the Fourth of July traffic was at its worst. "Know any hospitals near here?" Mitch asked.

Art knew a small hospital on 117th Street, only about a mile away. "Take him there and make sure they get to work on him immediately. And tell them to send their ambulance."

A small woman, girlish small, with two kids tagging onto her, waited until the wounded man had been arranged on the seat. "Please," she said, touching Mitch's arm, "is there anyone named Jim Carraway inside? He's my husband."

The begging, asking, seeking after lost ones had frozen into a condition that must be disregarded, as needle-fright must be disregarded when you are injecting a patient; but sometimes a single factor will pierce and trouble the mind unreasonably, and now this woman's worry became a personal burden to him, and back inside the headquarters Mitch inquired of everybody: "Seen a man named Jim Carraway? His wife's out there worried. Anybody know him?"

The burnt-faced fellow, Al Nees, knew him. "Yah. He's from Gary, I seen him in the march." "Was he hurt? Was he in here?" "I'm pretty sure he wasn't in here," Al said. "Ask Ralph Sims, he might know." "Who?" Mitch looked around. "That *Daily Worker* fellow. He was going around taking names." Nees indicated a lanky lad who didn't look like a striker, or a newspaper man either.

The *Daily Worker* reporter went through his scribbled list of names. "No. No Jim Carraway." "Maybe he was arrested," Al Nees said.

Mitch helped carry out another wounded man. Carraway's wife still stood there, watching the loading automobiles. "He's not inside," Mitch told her. "He's not on the list of wounded. Maybe he was arrested."

"The kids are so tired," she said. "I ought to take them home."

"Maybe you'll find him home," Mitch said, awkwardly.

Several women were helping Syl and Barbara now. Sheets brought from a near-by house had been ripped into bandages. It seemed to Mitch he had been working all day, yet he knew that less than an hour had gone by; and at least the worst cases were all on their way.

"Any more gunshots?" he asked. Barbara Macey brushed fallen hair from her eyes, using the back of her wrist; her fingers were blood-stained. "I saw a fellow in the kitchen . . ." She looked back there, vaguely. "A short fellow."

"You better sit down now, get some rest," Mitch advised.

She pulled up one side of her mouth in a lopsided smile which he already recognized as characteristic. The fancy Eastern girls' college accent returned. "I'm all right," she said, and the simple quality he had felt in her the previous instant, the unpretending quality, vanished. For that one instant she had been like a good nurse when you come together out of a critical room, where fine handling has at last succeeded against a fever crisis. In those moments you sense that no matter what you are, dumb or smart, full of skill or only willing to help, you are together, and together with the sick, too, all are together. But now there returned to him the uneasiness and the faint suspicion he had felt about this girl from the moment of his arrival.

[62]

He went into the kitchen. A stubby fellow sat on the table; one trouser-leg was rolled up, and a woman knelt washing the wounded leg. Mitch recognized the fellow; this was the belligerent kid who had whittled a grip on his stick, while raging about the cops beating up his brother. Mike something.

The woman tending him had been hurt too. A long purplish welt was forming on her jaw. Her right arm was bruised. She looked up, her square, large face solemn in the frame of crinkly black hair. "You get hurt?" Mitch said.

"Copper punch me. You look, here is bullet, Doctor?" She moved aside.

Mike's wound was fairly clean, a flesh wound through the calf. "You got off easy," Mitch said to the lad. "It looks okay. Only you've got to go to the hospital, get an anti-tetanus shot."

"I ain't going to no hospital," Mike refused, spitting.

"You've got to get those shots. You might develop lockjaw."

"Stinking lousy bastards!" Mike raved. "Go up there with a stick! Next time I'm going up there same as they are. Gimme a gun and I'll show them. I ain't afraid of no coppers, gun or no gun. What they did to my brother, I'll fix them sonsabitchn——"

"Take it easy," Mitch said.

"Blow that place to s——, that's what we ought to do! Blow up the yellow s——y cops and the whole goddam—" His shirt was in shreds; sweat-grime was all over his face and body. He had one black eye. "I gave it to one of those lice. Put away your gun, I said, I'll——"

"Take it easy. You'll get a fever." Mitch went for a few men to help carry Mike to a car. He returned with Carl Gaul—but the wounded Mike was gone. The woman was at the sink.

"Where'd that fellow go?"

"He don't want to go to hospital," she said.

[63]

"But he has to. He might get lockjaw."

"In hospital, police come," she said.

"Well, he's no criminal, what's he afraid of?" Then, by the look she gave him, the smile, he understood that others too had vanished with their wounds. Perhaps it was the primitive hiding-instinct of the wounded. Or perhaps—and for the first time he identified the thought that had troubled him, the source of his feeling of unreality as he examined gun wounds and club abrasions: the thought that they all knew, and he knew nothing.

"Best thing is to keep away from police," the woman repeated, and he realized this was not from the criminal's sense of having done wrong. And it wasn't fear. It was some fundamental knowledge he didn't yet possess. A knowledge, perhaps, about the whole way of life, and government.

"Who was it, Mike Sisto?" Carl asked.

She nodded. And Carl nodded knowingly, yet Mitch felt that even this organizer, Carl, did not know, as the woman knew. "These people don't like to get mixed up with the cops," Gaul said as they left the kitchen. "They just figure it's bound to mean trouble sometime."

A car drew up, and Frank Sobol rushed into headquarters. Hadn't he been in the march? Mitch wondered. Sobol stood there immobile, his facial muscles rigid, his lips taut and dry, a man who has come too late.

Barbara Macey confronted him hysterically. "Well, are you satisfied? You've had your revolution, are you satisfied? Sending people out there into that! You knew it was going to happen, you knew! You didn't go out there yourself, I noticed. Oh, no, not you!"

Sobol didn't even turn his head. His eyes moved and half focused on her, on Carl. Carl pulled Barbara aside. "Pipe down," he said. "You know it's no use talking to those guys."

Sobol, having apparently assimilated the shock, walked over

[64]

to Al Nees. "I had to go with Szutak," he explained loudly. "He came back and I had to drive him to the Harbor."

Only now, Mitch went into the little room they had set aside for a hospital. There on the window sill stood the box of boric Emil had brought—his total preparation for these injuries! On the cot lay the child he had seen shot out there. His mother and father were with him. The boy was excited but not in bad shape. Examining the wounded foot, Mitch suspected a fracture just below the ankle. "We'll have to get an X-ray," he said. "We'll take him to a hospital now. You got a car?" The big Lithuanian shook his head.

"He be all right, Doctor? He be able to walk?" the mother asked.

"Oh, sure. In a couple of weeks. I'll get someone to take him to the hospital."

On the one chair in the room sat a Mexican woman, who showed a superficial flesh wound of the shoulder. She was scarcely more than grazed. "I was not there," she repeated, over and over. "I was not there in the march. I was standing right here outside, in the street. I got shot right outside here, in the street!"

But a pistol bullet would not have come this far. It must have been a rifle bullet, then, perhaps fired from the mill. He applied a dressing.

Still there was no ambulance. Nearly an hour, he figured, since Art had gone off. Not much need of it now, the gunshots were practically all cleared out. There wasn't even a phone in this place. He got Carl and Kiley to help him with that kid. The Mexican woman had vanished. Well, she'd probably be all right. He told Carl of the case. "I ought to get her name. Legally I have to report all gunshot wounds."

But Kiley got all excited. Standing way over here, and she

[6 5]

got hit! They must have been firing from those roofs! Sure. He could have sworn a bullet whistled by him where he stood, in the yard. Just when all that shooting began! Snipers, using the cops as a screen. Maybe even starting it off. . . .

Art came in. "Hey, Doc, that hospital I took Emil to, they got no doctors to operate. They said if we got any doctors here, to bring them over. Everybody is out for the Fourth. All they got is a couple of nurses there."

The hospital street was blocked by two patrol wagons. A couple of squad cars were at the curb. Police stood on the stairs and at the doors of the building. Mitch had to show his card to prove he was a doctor before they would allow him to enter.

It was a fairly new, well-equipped place, he could tell at a glance. About fifty beds.

There was no one at the desk. "We took them in back," Art said; and Mitch found the receiving-room. It was crowded almost as badly as Guzman's place had been. Stretcher carts loaded with patients were lined up in a solid bank. The rest of the wounded sat in chairs. A woman he had seen, with a bullet wound through her leg, was slumped against her neighbor. There was no attendant in the room.

On a bench were several men with fresh turban bandages around their heads. "Who's taking care of you?" Mitch asked.

"He just went out. He got called upstairs, the nurse called him."

Wilner glanced quickly over the stretchers. Emil still lay there; and that other abdominal case, the blond young fellow. Fools! Bandaging club wounds while these emergencies lay untended! The door opened; all looked up hopefully, but instead of hospital attendants, three policemen appeared. Their leader pointed his chin toward the row of bandaged men. "Okay, on your feet."

[66]

"These people can't be moved," Mitch objected.

"And who are you?"

"My name is Wilner, Dr. Wilner."

The second cop said, more quietly: "These men are under arrest, Doctor. Every man here is under arrest. We have orders to take them in."

"Take them where?"

"To jail," the first cop said as to an imbecile. "Okay, on your feet."

A few of the men groggily arose. The others eyed Mitch anxiously. For the first time in all that day, he felt direct fury. At the same moment he was aware of the possible complications. Dr. Mitchell Wilner defies police. He'd have to stand for plenty of remarks at Memorial. And he could just see Mort Abramson. . . . He shook off all that. "Officer, I cannot be responsible for the lives of any of these men if they are moved in their present condition," he said. "Every one of them is suffering from shock. There may be internal disorders, concussion, hemorrhage. They haven't even been examined, only had first aid."

"Well we got orders, Doc."

"Better let me talk to your superior."

The policemen looked to each other; the leader shrugged, left his two men there and went off. Meanwhile an interne appeared. He had obviously done his best to maintain a professional calm before the patients, but the moment Mitch introduced himself the interne broke into a relieved sweat. His glasses fogged. "Doctor, I've been all alone here," he gasped. "Just three nurses."

"Let's get at these abdominals," Mitch said.

"I—we've been calling Dr. Whalen. Everybody's away. You know, the Fourth. And we didn't have many patients——"

Probably a second-class interne, in a small joint of this kind. "Any more beds?" Mitch asked.

[6 7]

"They're not made up and we haven't anyone to—" He took his glasses off again, wiped them.

Mitch pulled Emil's cart toward the door. He pointed to the other abdominal, the blond fellow. "We better get these boys upstairs." Emil was unconscious. Need a transfusion. Mitch asked the interne: "Have you got a donor list? Better type this fellow right away." But in a setup like this it would take hours to reach a donor. He noticed Art, still standing there. "Art, we're going to need some blood. Better go back and ask for about a dozen volunteers. Bring them with you."

"Sure. How about myself?" Art offered.

"Maybe. I have to make some tests first. It has to be the same type of blood, so bring a bunch of fellows."

"Okay." Art ducked out.

Mitch pushed Emil's cart toward the elevator. Again he was stopped, this time by plainclothesmen. He shouted angrily: "Can't you see these men need immediate attention! We could use twenty doctors here and we're all alone. Now please stop obstructing us!"

"All right, all right, Doc," one of them said. "We ain't interfering with you and we don't want you interfering with us. These people are under arrest and we're taking them to the station—all those that can go. You pick them out."

"I can't stop what I'm doing to pick out people for you to take to jail! We have emergency cases here."

"There are a lot of reds in that gang and we want them," the plainclothesman insisted.

"I don't give a damn who they are! They're not going to run away," Mitch said. "You've got men at the doors."

"Now listen, Doc——"

Just then a beefy, youngish fellow pounded into the corridor; he wore the angry look of someone interrupted at a fine meal.

[68]

"Who the hell ordered all this shooting!" he exploded. "Somebody is going to get it for this! What a mess!"

"Mr. Corcoran," the plainclothesman hastened to interrupt him, "this is the doctor here, he refuses to let us remove our prisoners, says he ain't got time to examine them."

Corcoran wheeled upon Mitch. "You're obstructing the police in the performance of their duty, Doctor," he rattled off, obviously trying to down the effect of his first indiscreet explosion. And to the police, Corcoran said: "Take your men. I'll be responsible."

They pushed into the receiving-room and herded the bandaged men to the alley door, where a patrol wagon waited.

"The rest haven't even had first aid!" Mitch cried. "They haven't been examined!"

"We'll examine them. We'll fix them up," Corcoran announced heartily. "We want every bastard that can stand on his two feet. Doctor, as you claim, these men may be strangers to you"—he eyed Mitch with insinuating suspicion—"but I know some of these boys. You've got some dangerous reds here."

In his helplessness, Mitch Wilner tried to talk to this state's attorney upon a human basis; after all the fellow was a lawyer, with some education, some intelligence. "Listen, I can't let you do this, I have to consider these people as my patients," he said. "Don't you understand?"

Corcoran eyed him; his toothy smile said he understood, but no soap.

Police scoured the receiving-room, picking among the injured like housewives sampling damaged fruit. "How's this fellow, Doc? Just got nicked in the arm here, that won't kill him, he can go, can't he?" "Hey, Doc, patch this guy up so we can take him out of here." And then they seemed to be swarming all through the hospital; they went through the wards. "Hey, Doc,

[69]

come take a look, there's a guy up in bed here we want, nothing wrong with him, ain't even scratched." And at one moment, exasperated as he felt, Mitch had to laugh, for they were trying to drag out a post-operative whose chart showed he had been lying in the hospital for two weeks!

He tried to go on with his work. A nurse appeared, at least she was all right, one of those middle-aged ramrods, and she shouted off the police long enough for him to take a blood sample from Emil. Since he had done little surgery lately, Mitch slipped down to a telephone, called Israels Memorial hospital, and asked for an emergency crew. The police were at him again. "Doc, a lot of these guys are faking."

"Let me alone!" he cried in final exasperation. "I won't release anyone!" They evidently hesitated to take people without his consent, and he was nearly mad with the pressure of them, dogging him, pestering him, when relief arrived. Frank Sobol, and with him Sam Eisen—at least Sam was a lawyer. The white-haired man who had made that tourniquet—Gillespie was his name—accompanied them.

Sam Eisen charged into the state's attorney's man, Corcoran. "Haven't you butchers done enough? Even in a war they let the wounded be taken care of!" He went on raving, calling the cops gunmen, murderers. It was the worst possible approach, Mitch felt; why, Sam had become a typical radical lawyer. Calling the cops names would only antagonize them the more.

Now he was quoting law at Corcoran, and Sam did seem to know his law. He was contending that they couldn't take anyone out of the hospital without a signed medical release. Finally Sam and the beefy Corcoran went to a phone and evidently talked to some authority. Sam returned in subdued triumph; all his violence erased; he even cracked a few professional jokes with his adversary from the state's attorney's office. "Okay,

Mitch," Sam instructed him. "Anyone you say has to stay, stays. You just sign a slip saying that's your opinion."

At least that nuisance was over. Police stationed themselves in all the halls and wards, but no longer bothered Mitch.

Sam got him aside, in a corridor. "Mitch, as soon as anyone is let out of here they'll get picked up. They'll be held without booking maybe for days and the cops will do anything to get them to make certain statements . . ."

"What do you mean?"

"If they can stay in the hospital a couple of days until we get bail ready and get some legal machinery going . . ."

"As far as I am concerned," Mitch said, trying to make Sam understand he was talking from a purely medical point of view, "nobody is in a condition to be released."

Sam gripped his hand. Mitch felt annoyed at himself. And at the union. After all Sam was supposed to be a Communist. Wouldn't it be more sensible to get someone without that stamp on him to handle their cases?

He was called to the door. The police were holding up the blood-donors. "Goddamit!" Art swore. "We been here half an hour. What do they think, we want to bomb the place?"

Now he'd have to type their blood. He hadn't even had a chance to complete Emil's analysis. But one of the volunteers touched his arm. "Doctor, thought I'd tell you, I'm a universal. Save you some time."

"You bet!" Mitch grabbed him. The kid was from the university, a divinity student, he said; he earned his way through, partly, by donor work. "But of course this time isn't professional," he said, flushing.

"A divinity student?" Mitch repeated.

"Yep. Professor Ladd took a bunch of us out there as impartial observers."

[71]

Again Mitch had a queer sense of the event as something deliberate, known, foreseen to the extent that "impartial observers" had been arranged for. Then why had it had to happen?

The two abdominals were in the operating-anteroom. Emil's face was drained to a grayish earth-color with a yellow undertint. He was conscious again. Mitch brought the donor over to him. "How do you like this guy, Emil?" he introduced them with attempted lightness. "He's going to lend you a little juice."

But the wounded man was so sluggish he did not even follow them with his eyes.

The other abdominal apparently could stand immediate operation. Gus Lindstrom was his name, a heavier man than Emil, with a roundness about his limbs and chest, contrasting to the bulky toughness of Emil's musculature.

Lindstrom kept asking about his father. "Doc, I saw them club him down. Club a white-haired man, the bastards. Doc, can't you find out, how is old man Lindstrom?"

There was still no surgeon. Hours in this hospital now—no, it was scarcely two hours since the men had walked toward the police. Perhaps he should scrub up and operate. Let the interne handle the transfusion.

Then the crew from Memorial arrived. They'd sent a resident surgeon, Dr. Morey Siegal—pretty young, but Mitch had seen him work: fast and good. He'd brought his own anesthetist. "Where was the fight?" he asked, glancing at the wounded men.

"What fight?" Mitch said.

"Cops downstairs said there was a drunken brawl, Fourth of July, started shooting each other up."

Mitch bit his lip. "It wasn't exactly like that," he said.

"Better scrub up with me," Siegal said. "I've done four majors today."

Now in the familiar relaxed interval of scrubbing, Mitch

[7 2]

Wilner's mind began to come alive: he felt his mind small, like an insect crawling around the edges of the immense fact of the day. He did not know, as yet, what place this day would take in the scheme of his thought, if he ever had had any thoughts before; but his mind was stirring, he felt the stirring, like nerve-movement trying to raise an atrophied limb. The will in the muscles; almost the sense of movement; and yet the arm lies still, immobile. So he felt in him the will toward comprehension. And yet the mountainous thought lay unlifted in his mind.

Talking to Siegal, as they passed their arms under parallel streams, was like restating the event for himself. "Then they marched up there, and after a few minutes all of a sudden the cops began to shoot."

"But why?" Siegal asked. "Did someone give a command?"

That was the central question. A command. "No. I don't know. I didn't hear anything." The picture stood again in his mind; two lines like two rows of Jackie's toy soldiers; move one line up into position, stand the other against it, then the first line goes bang bang bang and the second line is all knocked down. It's a kid's game because it is not like a real war in which some out of both lines get knocked down.

That was the simple picture. Out of that he had to find a meaning.

As they went to operate, Mitch glanced at the transfusion in the adjoining room. The divinity student grinned at him. He was stretched out, fist closed, in experienced readiness for the piercing needle.

In the operating-room the young Swede was going under with difficulty, fighting the ether, all the time asking about his father. His fine torso trembled like a throbbing motor against a brake; then his voice weakened to that of a child sleepily resisting bed. Like a kid trying a last ruse he said: "Hey, Pop, I got something to tell you," and dropped off into raucous oblivion.

[7 3]

The anesthetist nodded. Siegal asked for the blood pressure again. Mitch took it. "Fair, 130 over 90," he reported. "Liter of saline?"

"Yah, keep giving it to him," Siegal said, studying the wound before making his incision. The nurse was good. She had the fluid-rig all set. Mitch started the salt water into the man's vein. "Might want to get at the bladder," Siegal surmised. "Looks like, the way that bullet went through, it may require repair." He shrugged thoughtfully, and made a long midline incision, directly through the bullet-hole.

"This isn't a post-mortem, Morey," Mitch attempted the customary operating-room kidding, though he favored long incisions, gave a man room to work. Siegal slipped the gut out in small sections, careful of surgical shock through too much exposure. Soon he had spotted the first puncture, like a nail tear in the silky amber gut. He stitched it. Mitch, peering from the other side of the table, detected the next hole. They found three.

"Bladder?" Siegal raised his brows; he was sweating heavily under his mask. Mitch checked the blood pressure. A two-point drop. He started another liter of solution into the vein. The anesthetist nodded confidently. Mitch sniffed; ammonia smell was in the wound. He nodded in agreement to Siegal. "Better take a look." Siegal went in deeper.

Just then the door swung open, and a man in street clothes took a step into the room. Mitch raised his arm warningly. The man took another step toward them, staring as if trying to identify them through their masks. Siegal frowned, puzzled and angry. Another plainclothesman, Mitch thought; was there no limit to what they would do! He stepped menacingly toward the intruder. "Can't you see—!" he began, but the nurse intervened. "Dr. Whalen," she announced emphatically, and they knew it was his hospital.

The intruder advanced close enough to see the field of operation. "One of those strikers?" he said with a knowing, almost humorous accent. "Go right ahead. I might as well scrub up and take the next one, now that I'm here. Shot them up, eh?" He backed out.

"Bet he bills for both of them," Siegal remarked. He had exposed a nasty rent in the bladder, which had emptied itself, drenching surrounding organs. The urine smell rose strong, now. Siegal shook his head. "Didn't miss a thing. Nicked the left kidney, too."

Mitch studied the powerful chest, the fine-boned frame in its blanket of fine flesh, so clean, so deceptive, for death was in the cavity. Still, the man might be able to fight down his body's poison. Siegal raised his head. "Gut, silk, anything," he called, ready to close up.

In the next room, the transfusion was going badly. Siegal had completed a major operation while the flustered interne still sought to draw blood from the donor. He had cut the kid's arm open as if for a bone operation; the vein was obscured in the bubbling mess there. The divinity student had finally turned his head away, but as Mitch entered he looked up and forced a smile. "I thought I had good veins," he said. "Maybe they're getting used up."

"Perhaps I'd better try the other arm," the interne suggested. And Mitch pitied him altogether, for being in this hospital, for what he would learn from the showy boss doctor.

"We'll just take one more crack at this one," Mitch said, relieving him of the syringe. The vein was hole-dotted, like a pincushion. But up a little higher he was able to make a firm insertion.

"Nope, she still doesn't come," the interne remarked.

Mitch saw the constrictor, still tied around the donor's arm, to hold back the blood until wanted. "You might try removing

[7 5]

the constrictor," he said. The interne jerked. He'd evidently been forgetting that, all this time. At last the blood flowed into the canister.

Emil's veins were practically collapsed. Mitch didn't even attempt the arm, but used the jugular. The student donor sat up, watching with him for the faint flushing return of color to the dying man's face.

"Well? Ready?" Dr. Whalen stood in the doorway, scrubbed and gloved. He couldn't have taken half enough scrubbing time. In the corridor he paused. "I suppose, uh, Doctor . . ."

"Wilner."

"Wilner. You have some arrangement with—these people?"

"I just happened to be on the scene," Mitch said. "I'm treating them as emergency cases."

"Well, who is—uh—responsible . . . ?"

"I haven't had time to go into that," Mitch said. "But I believe I heard one of the union officials say downstairs that the union would take care of everything; they want the men to get everything they need."

"Yes, hm. They're supposed to have quite a treasury? But now they've got this strike on their hands. Know any of these union people?"

"No. A fellow named Sobol seemed to be in charge. He was here, a little while ago."

Dr. Whalen nodded sagely. They went into the operating-room.

Emil looked eager as he was wheeled under the light; he took the ether almost with relish. Recognizing Mitch, he grinned. "Hey, Doc, we had that boric acid, huh?" He took a breath like a swig of liquor, and was asleep.

Dr. Whalen operated whirlwind fashion. Mitch and Siegal looked at each other, gasped. Once Siegal involuntarily reached out a restraining arm, for the surgeon had simply pulled the

[7 6]

victim's guts out, exposing the entire digestive tract at one scoop. Miraculously, Emil didn't die then and there, of surgical shock. Running the tissue through his fingers like so much burlap, Dr. Whalen sewed up one puncture, and shoved the whole business back with an air of finality. "I believe there was another hole." Siegal pointed to an oozing rent in the duodenum. Dr. Whalen caught it up. "Nothing can kill these fellows," he said.

"If he can't, nothing can," Siegal muttered.

"I handle a lot of them," the surgeon went on. "Get a lot of major accident work from those mills. Had a fellow brought in here pierced through and through with a red-hot steel bar, and in two weeks that sonofagun walked out of here, went back to work."

"Dr. Whalen," Mitch said, "you know we found a bladder rupture in the other case. And as the wounds are almost parallel——"

"Are they?" Dr. Whalen glanced into the wound. "Looks clean to me." He called for the sponge count.

When Mitch went down to see how the Swede was coming out of the ether, Gus Lindstrom's wife was already there, standing by the bed. She was a slight girl, perhaps thirty, with a Polish cast of features, and the fair, almost paste-white skin of her people. "How is he, Doctor, what are his chances, don't give me any false hopes, Doctor, I want to know the truth."

"He's got about a fifty-fifty chance," Mitch said.

She stood still, only her eyes moved, to her husband's face. Mitch was reminded of that other small woman, at Guzman's Grove. Carraway; he wondered whether Jim Carraway had been found.

"Is there anything anybody can do?" Mrs. Lindstrom begged. "Oh, I'd give anything! But I suppose, Doctor, it's up to him, to fight it out now . . . ?"

Mitch nodded. "He was asking for his father, before he went under," he said. "Maybe it would help him to see his father."

"We don't know what happened to the old man," she said. "Unless he got arrested. We don't know where he is."

"Have you any children?" Mitch asked.

"Two kids, a boy and a girl."

Like us, he thought. And, oddly, he wanted to tell her that. It was simply another of the obscure promptings and wonderings of this day.

"It will be a little while before he wakes," Mitch said.

There were a few more patients he wanted to look at, before leaving them to Dr. Whalen. That woman shot through the leg might have bone injuries, she needed an X-ray; it mustn't be overlooked. And in what hospital was that kid he had seen at Guzman's, a kid of seventeen with a forearm wound through vein and artery; he had heard the rushing, whirlpool sound through his stethoscope—vein and artery were short-circuiting into each other. He'd have to ask the union people to call in a specialist on aneurysms, maybe Dr. McVeagh; that kid might lose his arm.

Both Sobol and Jock Kiley were in the corridor, with Dr. Whalen. Do everything that can be done for the boys, everything that is necessary, they were repeating. First Sobol would say it, and then Kiley would say practically the same thing, as though his authority were independent of the other's.

"I've just looked at the woman, the leg wound," Mitch reported. "I don't think we can be certain there is no fracture, without an X-ray."

"I'll look at it, I'll see that she gets an X-ray if necessary," Dr. Whalen concurred, and Mitch saw how the situation stood: the cases were taken over. In a way he felt relieved; the horrible responsibility of the day dropped from him; he had plugged the dike till the repair crew came. Now he could go home.

[7 8]

And then he knew that, beneath his immense exhaustion, there was a kind of dismay. For he was not free. He knew Dr. Whalen's type. There would be plenty of service on the bill. As for those steelworkers, nothing can kill them. Leave them alone; they'll get up, in time.

He saw Sylvia entering the hospital. "I'm leaving now," Mitch said; "my wife has just come for me."

"Well, good-by, Dr. Wilner, lucky you were on the spot," Dr. Whalen said.

Kiley walked down the corridor with him. "Say, we sure appreciate all you did today," the big fellow said earnestly. "And, say, you turn in a bill, you know——"

"Look, Kiley, that part doesn't matter," Mitch said. "I'll tell you—I think I ought to follow up these patients. Do you know this hospital?"

"Sure. I been here a couple of times myself. Doc Whalen is okay, always fixed me up fine. He's a good doctor. My super, in the mill, used to go to him hisself. Handles a lot of accident work for the company." As Mitch stared at him, he seemed to catch the import of his own remark. He sucked his cheek. "He don't work for them though, this is his own hospital."

Mitch said: "I'll tell you, Kiley—I'm not trying to—well, in fact, I don't want any money out of this. But I'd feel better if I kept an eye on some of these cases. I may need you to back me up if I have to say these people are still under my care."

"Sure, you keep an eye on them. You're the union doctor," Kiley said.

Sylvia had taken the children home and then hunted for him in all the South Side hospitals. "They've got three hospitals full, the Burnside, the South Chicago, they even have some at the Jackson Park. Dear, you must be terribly tired. And you haven't eaten."

On the steps, police sat idly now, on relaxed watch. He hadn't realized night had fallen. The air was silken and humid, like a child's breath. A swarm of bewildered people milled in front of the hospital, asking each other: Is Joe in there? Did you hear how is Emil? How many was killed? Two? I heard it was three. They converged upon him—Doctor, Doctor! But relatives had already been admitted to the hospital; these were people he could not help. Sylvia drew him to the car.

Seeing the divinity student, the donor, come out of the hospital, Mitch offered him a lift home. Arthur Main was his name. "I'm sorry he butchered that arm for you," Mitch said.

"Well, even at that I guess I got off easy."

"Do you want to stop and eat something now, dear?" Sylvia asked. "You know you were supposed to look in on Mrs. Margolis; I called and told her you'd be late."

It was the first time he had forgotten about a patient. "Let's stop and eat. This fellow needs some food, too."

They went to a place on Stony Island. Main dutifully ordered liver. Soon they were comparing their stories of the day, precisely what each had seen and done, as though seeking an exact definition, still unbelieving of what they had experienced.

But why had Professor Ladd and the divinity students been out there?

"Well, you know Dr. Ladd has been doing that, being an impartial observer. He was there at the Ford plant when the union men were beat up. He gave his testimony."

How were such things arranged? How did impartial observers know where to be, and when?

There was some kind of church committee on labor relations, and when they thought there might be a clash somewhere, they offered an observer.

To whom?

"To the union, or the employer, sometimes to the Labor Board."

"Well, you observed something all right, today!"

Young Main told how he, too, had wandered up and down the column of marchers. "We must have been right near each other." And when the shooting began, Main had been near the front, a wonder he didn't get shot. "I just lit out of there like a highjumper."

Then what started it?

Main sliced the liver, ate reflectively. "Honestly, I don't think anybody gave a signal to shoot. The police were all nervous and scared. Whoever fired the first shot, the rest of them just fired automatically."

Was it a question of the first shot then, of someone deliberately provoking the massacre?

But why did they keep on shooting, when everybody was running away? Did the cops hate the strikers?

"I was talking to a couple of cops before it started," Main said. "They said they were just working people too, most of them were union men one time or another, some of them have even worked in the mills."

Then what was it happened to them to make them do that? What great fear?

"Maybe a kind of mass hysteria," the divinity student said. "A kind of brutal release; once they started they couldn't stop."

If that were all the impulse needed, a massacre would happen every time police met strikers.

"It does happen. Often enough," Sylvia said. "The trouble with you, darling, is you don't know about these things."

"No, it never happened just like this, I don't think," Main said. "This was the worst. It seemed so—deliberate. It seemed different."

[81]

"It was only the worst," Sylvia said. "But not inherently different."

"I'm not sure," Main said.

"It was like a pure demonstration," Sylvia said. "A law of physics reduced to its simplest essentials."

"It's not so simple," Main reflected. "You know, the boys were going up there for a fight. Some of them. I don't say the cops had any right to shoot. But some of the boys went up with bricks and stuff."

Yes, she agreed. That shouldn't have been allowed. The whole thing shouldn't have been allowed. Everybody knew there was going to be trouble. The march should have been stopped. "What's so brilliant about marching up to a line of guns, when you know you're going to be shot? What does that accomplish? I don't say the union is to blame. Of course only the police are to blame. But the whole thing didn't have to happen. It could have been avoided."

"I suppose in a sense the strike didn't have to happen either," Arthur Main said. "If the men didn't feel like fighting for their rights."

At that moment the kid looked too idealistic. Yes, Mitch thought, you had to discount a certain amount of college-kid idealism. "Well, but did the strike really have to happen?" he asked. "I thought, now there is the Wagner Act, strikes are unnecessary. They can go to law. Haven't they got the majority?"

"Carl Gaul says they've got ninety percent signed up," Sylvia informed him.

"Then why didn't they do it through the Wagner Act?"

"Because it takes too long," she said. "They would lose all the men while they waited for the courts to decide." The minute the men signed up, they wanted results. A contract. If they didn't get it soon, they'd drop out of the union. The Wagner Act way took months. So the only recourse was a strike.

[82]

They were silent when in the car again, except once, while waiting for a red light to change, when Main remarked, as if in continuation of their argument: "But, obviously, if they hadn't marched, the strike would have been broken."

Mitch remembered that Frank Sobol had said precisely the same thing before the march. It was one of those remarks whose truth seemed obvious. But was it necessarily true?

Main lived in Hitchcock Hall. "I used to live here," Mitch said, as they dropped the student. "Better come in and let me see that arm, tomorrow or the day after."

"Oh, that's all right. I'll have the Student Health take care of it. I don't want to bother you."

"No bother."

"He's a nice kid," Sylvia said as they drove off. "But I bet he's a Communist."

Going into Memorial, Mitch felt slightly like an impostor. The nurses, internes, staff men all saw him as the same Dr. Wilner who had come and gone so many times before today. They didn't know what he had seen and done.

Well, what? Taken care of some emergencies. Shootings. Why, when he had interned at County, gangsters used to be brought in, shot; you sewed them up and thought nothing of it. Or suppose you were in a train wreck, the only doctor. You'd take care of the injured as best you could, then go on to your destination.

What destination?

Once when he was still a student, he remembered, he had gone through a cram session, spent an entire week in his room sunk in his texts; carried books with him to meals. And then one evening Joe Freedman had come over; they were chums then, and Joe was thinking of becoming an architect. Joe had dragged him out for a walk. And actually, as he had stepped out of his room, a sort of surprise had spread all through his heart, body, and mind; a surprise, even that there were different rooms in the house, that there were people in cars on the street going to a myriad destinations, and as they walked Joe had made him see things about houses—such as how ordinary flat-faced apartment buildings had pure-styled Grecian cornices over the windows, little things like that.

And today going into the hospital he felt the reverse of that long-ago moment of stepping outside his study-room. The familiars who nodded to him did not know Mitch Wilner contained this new experience, perhaps the germ of total change.

Walking into Mrs. Margolis's room, he could not bring himself to say anything of the day; though by tomorrow she would certainly have found out, and she would chide him: Why didn't you tell me, Doctor, you had such excitement? He'd say he had thought it would disturb her.

"How are you, Doctor? You see I am staying up for you," she chattered. "Did you have a good time today, a good Fourth of July? My son and daughter-in-law took the children to Charlevoix for the week-end. I suppose you went out to the Abramsons'; how is Mrs. Abramson?"

Fine, everything was just fine, a beautiful day, he said; she was in the hospital for deep X-ray therapy, cancer; Lou Margolis was spending money on his mother in her last years. "How do you feel today, Mrs. Margolis?"

She began a long account of her feelings all day. He let her talk.

"I can see you are tired, from the Fourth of July," she chattered. "Everybody comes home tired, after a vacation they need a vacation to recover." She chuckled at her smart remark, satisfied because it was the American thing to say. Like her children would say.

"That's right," Mitch agreed. He dimmed the lights, and left.

[84]

Neither of them could sleep. "I called the folks and told them," Sylvia said. "Just so they wouldn't be surprised."

"Surprised?"

"You might be in the papers, or something."

"Oh." He turned, restlessly. He lay with his eyes shut but with the sense of staring at the ceiling. "What are they striking for anyway?" he asked.

"Recognition of their union."

"That all? Not higher wages or anything?"

"No. Just for a contract recognizing their union."

But he thought that was the law now, the Wagner Act, didn't employers have to recognize unions?

"They're quibbling about it," Sylvia explained. "The law says they have to bargain with them and come to an agreement and the company says, okay, we will agree on a bargain but we won't sign anything."

"Why not, if they are agreed?"

"They say the union is not responsible, or I don't know. Like Mort, you know how he'd get, stubborn on one point and break his head over it."

"It's a point of honor then?"

"I guess so."

He thought for a long while. He heard her breathing but it was not the breathing of sleep. "And they went out on strike over that? On whether or not Otis Speer signs the contract?"

"Well, most strikes," she said, "if you knew your labor history, were not for wages or money but just for union recognition. The men wanted to be respected."

They would risk everything like that, just for a sense of being respected? He lay still, trying to let that be the answer. Of course, he could see, once they had a contract, that would give their organization strength, and as they grew in power they could demand more wages and practically anything they

[8 5]

wanted. So then it was not a struggle over a point of honor, but a struggle for the gate to actual power. And wasn't the day's attempted march the symbol of that struggle? Only let us approach the gate, the strikers said, we won't go in. Only sign a contract, we won't take over power. But if they had reached the gate, wouldn't they have gone in? And would he have been against that? He felt deep doubt and mystery and frustration, as sometimes when observing a surface symptom, a skin rash, and trying to think what deep disturbance in the blood it signified, and the cause, and what cure?

Sylvia reached for his hand and then turned and placed her other arm across his body. "Oh, Mitch," she said, "when you were out there I was so afraid you wouldn't come back." He remained rigid and away in his thoughts, as if he were still out there on the field.

Mob Attacks Police, Four Dead, the *Clarion* headlined. 200 Injured As Strikers Charge. The back page was all photographs of the "battle."

"Your name isn't mentioned," Sylvia said, quickly scanning the columns. Her voice was half relieved, half annoyed. Mitch took the paper. The heroic police had foiled a Communist plot to capture the Consolidated Steel Works, it said. Strikers led by Communists, and armed with pistols, shotguns, knives, clubs studded with razor blades, iron pipes, meat hooks, rocks, had hurled themselves upon the police, pushing women and children forward as a shield in order to keep the police from getting at them. But under the heroic leadership of Captain Wiley the police had repulsed the mob, preventing invasion of the steel mill.

The whole attack, police had learned, was under the leadership of known Communists who had seized control of the union. Strikers had been drilling all week in secret; Communist squads had been strategically placed through the mob, to lead and point the attack. But they could not get through the Chicago police!

There was a telephone interview with the mayor, who was away fishing. "Captain Wiley has upheld the great tradition of the Chicago police department," he said, fully approving the "heroic action."

And Captain Wiley had issued a statement. "The aim of that mob was to get inside the plant and beat up or kill the loyal employees and then hold the mill in a sitdown strike. But we don't let them get away with that stuff in Chicago. If we had allowed that mob to go one step further there would have been hundreds killed instead of a few. We only did our duty."

The dead were listed:

1. Ladislas Wyznowieki, 48, employed in Standard mills, not on strike. Bullet wound in head. Died on field.

2. Hermann Baumann, 37, known Communist. Woodworker, not employed in mills. Died in Steel Harbor hospital of bullet wound.

3. Unidentified man, about 50. Wound severing leg artery.

4. Unidentified Mexican, about 40. Died on field of bullet wounds.

"Look." Mitch pointed to number 3. "That must have been the one with the tourniquet." He told her of the incident. "They pulled him out of Kiley's car. But we had the bleeding checked!" His pulse knocked with anger; the man didn't have to die.

"It may not be the same one, after all," Sylvia pointed out.

Mitch studied the column of names of wounded, looking for one—what was it?—Carraway. That woman with the two kids. The name was not listed. Probably the fellow was safely home by now.

The children ran in wanting the pictures. Sylvia seized the

paper from Jackie. "No, darling, no," she said. "Daddy wants the paper now."

Some of the pictures were all confusion, smoke, tangled legs and bodies. He could not find himself in any of the scenes. "Police Rescue Wounded" was the heading over a photograph of four police carrying a man by his limbs, his body sagging. And there, plainly before him, was the case of the tourniquet. For the cop at the man's leg was hauling him as by a handle— by the strap-end. And thus the sag of the wounded man's body had pulled loose the tourniquet, which was now around the knee instead of around the thigh where it had been placed. The stupid brutes. That policeman's face could not be seen; he was three-quarters back to the camera.

"What's the matter?" Sylvia said, anxiously. He showed her the picture. "Well, dear, you did all you could," she soothed him.

Mitch felt a stab of irritation at his wife's words. He didn't reply. He was thinking he would have to go down to the morgue to make certain it was this same leg-wounded man who was listed as dead. He had to know.

In the Standard Steel mills, a new operator mounted the traveling crane over No. 4 openhearth pit. A burly, confident fellow, name of Giles, been on odd shifts, damn glad to get in a steady roost again. He heard this was the crane that the old Polack ran that got knocked off in that riot there. I ain't saying they had a right to shoot him, but maybe he should have been minding his own business. We ain't on strike. If he'd of stayed home where he belonged, he wouldn't of got killed.

Giles was not a C.I.O. man. I don't need no John Lewis, I can take care of myself, always have, was his motto.

As he took the crane out over the pit, that damn flower pot bothered him, blocked his vision. Sooty, withered geranium. He leaned out of the cab window and once, as a ladle of slag, still sullenly boiling, was hauled away below him, he let the pot drop, a bull's-eye, swallowed with a slight sizzle in the fiery waste of steel.

2. MEX

AT THE cantina of Emilio Perez there was a postcard from Ricardo, the son of Emilio, who was in the United States of America. On one side of the card was a picture showing a great smokestack belching fire, and on the other side was writing. Once more, Emilio Perez told what it said. "Soon he will have many dollars and he will send for his father and mother and we will go there and live with our son. He says tell Jesus Hernandez to come up here also and I will get him a job and he will get so many dollars as easily as sweeping them off the streets!"

Jesus Hernandez wondered again how it could say all those things in just such a few lines of writing, for each time old Emilio repeated the message, it said more. Jesus reached for the card. He showed it to his friend, Pablo Lima. "See!" He pointed with his stubby finger to the word Jesus. "That's me! Ricardo writes of me! That is my name!" He ran to the kitchen, to Ricardo's mother. "See where it speaks of me! Your Ricardo and I, we are like brothers!"

She laughed and embraced him as her son, since her own son

was far away. She came out into the cantina. "See, he sends us American dollars, too!" and from her bosom drew a warm soiled five-dollar bill; they grouped around her and studied the American money, worth many pesos. "Like sweeping it off the street!" Jesus repeated. He turned to Manuel Davila, the three-fingered, and cried: "Here, come and drink with us, you have been to the Steel Harbor of Chicago!"

Manuel Davila approached, as always half asleep from drink, scratching under his sleeve with his three fingers. "Certainly, I have had many such bills," he said. "Five dollars, ten dollars, a twenty-dollar bill is a yellow one, like gold."

"I will go there!" Jesus Hernandez cried. "Surely I will go!"

"I will go also," said Pablo.

"But I don't know. He doesn't mention your name here. He only speaks of me, Jesus Hernandez!" Jesus pointed to his name, and turned the card over again to study the fire issuing from the very high chimneys.

"Anyone can go!" Pablo appealed to the three-fingered Davila. "I also can go!"

"Yes, I could take you there," Davila affirmed. "I am well acquainted. Perhaps some day I will go back." He raised his glass and drank. He told how in one day he had earned eleven dollars there. Only last year. Plenty of work while the Americans went across the ocean to the war. He had unloaded a carload of bricks in record time. "I will go back and make much money and buy the best fighting cocks from San Luis Potosi and bring them here. That is what I will do," he proclaimed.

"When you go back," Jesus said, "I will go with you."

"I am the one that is going with him!" Pablo reminded Jesus. "But perhaps we will let you come along."

Jesus prevailed upon Mother Perez to give him the picture card upon which his name was written, and he pinned it on the wall of the *cabaña*, over his sleeping-mat, and next to the colored photograph of Bebe Daniels which he had cut out of a United States magazine.

During the following six months he was in love with Pablo's sister Rosa, who was fourteen. But she had dreams of a great fiery tender lover, Rodolfo Valentino, beside whom Jesus Hernandez appeared squat like a frog.

One day when Jesus was cutting cane on the big ranch, three-fingered Manuel came by and spoke to him. If a man wanted to go to the Steel Harbor, now, Manuel knew of a way. He himself was going, and might take with him a good young friend.

Jesus meditated. The *patrón* of the big ranch would forbid his going. His father was not strong and was in debt to the *patrón;* who could work but the son?

Three-Fingers chewed on an end of cane. "Who does not ask, does not receive no for an answer," he quoted. Besides, Jesus could send back much money for his family, and thus be more helpful than by remaining. And his brothers soon would do man's work. If a start was made in the night, they could reach the border before the *patrón* lifted his fat behind onto the back of a horse.

As soon as dark came, Jesus went to Pablo's house. Pablo was walking around in shoes, so he knew at once that Pablo was going; and he too would leave. For a long hour they sat in front of

[91]

the *cabaña*. Pablo played the guitar, and his sister sang with him. Over and over again Jesus asked: "Sing 'El Rancho Grande,'" and Rosa, looking into his eyes, sang the song of the young peon who worked on a big ranch, and met a girl there, and how he went away, and how he returned for her.

It was night when they reached Juarez. Three-Fingers took them to a cantina called the Bull of Gold and told them to wait there. He was gone so long they feared he had crossed into the United States without them, but then he returned with a fat one, Señor Rubio, who was dressed like a Yankee with a green necktie. They drank tequila, and Señor Rubio described the glorious life in Steel Harbor, where they could go to American moving pictures every night and afterwards possess beautiful golden-haired girls of the north.

Señor Rubio would advance them sufficient money to take them to Steel Harbor. They made little crosses on paper cards, since Manuel did likewise, laughing.

In the morning, Señor Rubio led them, with three peons from another village, over the bridge to the gringo side, to a store with a name on the window: Francisco Garcia. Inside, men squatted, some still asleep on the floor. Behind a little fence was a desk upon which was a telephone. There sat Señor Garcia. He greeted Señor Rubio and three-fingered Manuel, talking and laughing, and those three went out together. Thus if you were like Manuel, a man who had been to the United States, you could talk and drink with the best of men.

Presently Señor Garcia returned, alone, and took his place behind his desk. Where was three-fingered Manuel? Jesus was worried, but bashful to ask.

Pablo had already made friends with some young fellows who wore new United States overalls. He went out with them and soon returned in similar garb. "How do I look? Now I look like a Yankee workman, hey?" he demanded. He was so happy he danced in the room.

Jesus ran out and quickly bought himself overalls, leaving his cotton suit in the shop. The legs of the overalls were too long, but the shopkeeper showed him how Yankees turned up the bottoms. He bought also a United States cap. He had eight dollars left of the ten advanced by Señor Rubio.

The street in front of Francisco Garcia's place became filled with men. At last Señor Garcia began to call out names. They heard a call—"Lima"—and Pablo rushed to the desk. Jesus pressed after him. "We are together!" he said, and Señor Garcia said: "Yes, very well, together," and he gave each a bit of paper, saying: "Do not lose this." Jesus prodded Pablo, who spoke up: "Our friend Manuel Davila—you have not forgotten him?"

"I could go look for him," Jesus offered. "It would be bad if he missed the train."

"Don't worry for Three-Fingers!" Señor Garcia laughed. "He knows his way about!"

Soon afterward, Señor Rubio led them all to the railway. They swarmed into a train. Perhaps two hundred men were there. "Manuel! Where is Manuel!" Jesus cried. "We cannot leave him, it was he who brought us here!" And at the last moment he would have leaped from the train to find his friend, but Pablo held him as the train started, saying: "In the United States each looks out for his own good."

For two days they rode, and could not descend from the train.

Sometimes their car stood somewhere on tracks, perhaps near by they could see the lights of a town, a United States town with cinemas, but they might not go down. They ate the few boiled eggs and cold tamales they had brought with them. The car was crowded; some stretched in the aisles and slept. The toilet became dirty and stank; when it was occupied, men relieved themselves out the windows. They laughed, watering the rich United States.

At last, in an afternoon, one who had made the journey before said now the train was coming to Steel Harbor. On a wide expanse of tracks, the train halted; the engine pulled away, leaving their two cars standing. They could see only scattered small houses, fields, and, in the near distance, huge factory structures. A road curved, not far away, and on it there passed many automobiles. It was still strange to see so many automobiles.

Soon came another engine, pulling a few boxcars. Men in khaki, like American soldiers, and with pistols at their sides, herded them into those cars. "Well, we are nearly there," the experienced one said. Soldiers stood by the closed door. In darkness the men squatted, while the train pounded a short distance. Presently the door was rolled open. The train stood amidst huge windowless barn-shaped structures of brown corrugated iron. The buildings were longer than any they had seen in their ride across the whole United States.

And there were the smokestacks. But not as in the postcard. No flames leaped from the tops of the stacks.

In a brick building an official at a desk asked for the pieces of paper Señor Garcia had given them. Here, too, guards in khaki, with pistols at their sides, stood by the door; but perhaps this was because the United States was so rich a land.

When the turn of Jesus came at the desk, he asked the official whether he knew of a certain Ricardo Perez who had been in Steel Harbor for many years.

"Who? Ricardo who?" the man barked.

"Ricardo Perez, he is the son of Emilio Perez, the *patrón* of the cantina in our village." Jesus drew out the old picture card with his name on it, but the American was roaring and cursing (keep track of every goddam spick in the place!) and Pablo prodded Jesus to move along.

They were arranged in groups of five or six. A fat bald-headed American who spoke no Spanish took their little group, and they followed him past long buildings full of gloom and **clang**ing noises, until he led them up a narrow iron stairway into one such building. They walked along a concrete ledge, and below them was a track on which were little vehicles with empty hoppers. The ledge upon which they walked lay along huge dark bins full of earth and dust. The American gave them shovels and stationed men at various bins. Talking angrily all the time, words they could not understand, he showed how to direct the flow of red dry earth, iron ore, into conveyor baskets which dumped the ore into the waiting car below. The filled car traveled down the track and dumped into another, larger car which crawled like a great bug up an incline to the top of a high tank-shaped structure; there the car of itself tilted and spilled its ore into the furnace.

"From this earth, iron is melted," Pablo explained to Jesus.

[95]

Behind their bins of red earth were bins containing a white earth, limestone; and in a third place was black coke, and out of these three earths, consumed together in that great furnace, iron came.

The red dust of the red earth was in Jesus's eyes and soon spread over his body; he breathed small in order not to feel that dirt in his lungs. He worked hard, making the earth slide swiftly into the chute, but the fat American began to yell at him, then rushed up and seized his shovel, raging at him in English. Jesus tried to see how the man worked; but when he resumed the labor, the cursing was repeated. At last another Mexican was brought, one who had been long in the Harbor and understood English. "You do too much," he explained. "When he gives the signal with the arm, there below, you must stop the flow of ore."

"But why did he not show me? Why do they first get angry?"

The Mexican shrugged. "That is their way."

They ate in a long yellow-walled restaurant, American food, white bread with meat and potatoes. It cost forty cents. Then they were told to go and work again. Though weary, they labored; the more hours of work, the more dollars.

Jesus was eager to know how much money he had earned this day. Dollars, how many—and pesos, how many? And where would they sleep? And was it like this everywhere in the United States, so many guards with pistols?

As night fell, they saw fire come from the great tall chimneys, tongues of fire against the night, and it was beautiful. "See, as it was in the picture card!" Jesus cried, running to the open end of the building to stare at the sight. And it seemed to promise that all would be as in their expectation. Behind him, the bell clamored for his return to work.

At eight o'clock, other men came to their places, and the bald-headed one guided them back to the boxcars in which they had arrived. Canvas cots had been placed in the cars. "Here you sleep," he announced. The man who had known so much, who had been in the Harbor before, was no longer to be seen.

They went again to eat. And there in the large restaurant Jesus suddenly espied Ricardo Perez, and ran to him, embracing him, clapping him on the back, leaping around him, his friend, his brother! "See, I have come, and brought with me Pablo Lima, too!"

They sat at a table, talking. Ricardo had with him a bottle of an American drink, gin, it was warm and tasted like horsepiss, but he explained that the Americans would not permit themselves to drink good drink, they had a prohibition. Pablo asked him, did he too live in this compound? No, Ricardo said, he had a fine house in the city. But tonight he would perhaps sleep with his friends in the boxcar. Yes! Good! It was generous of him to remain near them. And tomorrow perhaps all could find a house and live together, ah, that would be happiness.

"Not tomorrow," Ricardo said, and shook his head. Just now it was best to remain within the walls. Why? He spat and laughed. He was not afraid to go out! No one could frighten him! Besides, those yellow gringos were even frightened at the cry of a Mexican infant, let alone the sight of a full-grown Spaniard! No. It was that he had no wish to kill any of them, therefore he would stay within the compound.

"These Americans are not friendly, Ricardo?"

He spat. "A man wants to work, let him work!" He eyed them angrily, drunk. Five thousand bastard gringos could not keep him from working, he shouted, if he wanted to make his four dollars a day! No, not ten thousand!

"Is that how much we are earning?" Four dollars, more than would be earned in a week of days at home; though true, it was not eleven dollars as Three-Fingers had promised.

"Four dollars. And those outside there, Americanos, they say a man shall not work for less than five dollars. And only eight hours a day, a man shall work." He laughed. "So they strike. You try to come to work they catch you in the street and kill you. Best thing, stay here, stay inside, sleep here, work and sleep—behind the walls, they cannot touch you!" He eyed them triumphantly.

"The Americans will not work?"

"No," he said. "They strike. Fine. They do not want the jobs. Okay, fine, they do not have to work; we want the jobs, we work!" He patted them on the arms, and laughed happily, slyly. "All the Mexicans come here and work!"

In the morning Ricardo said he would talk to the super, get them better jobs, more pay. That was dirty nigger's work they were doing. He would get them work alongside of himself. He knew the ways, all said hello to Ricardo. He marched them across the great yards to the blast furnaces. There each furnace stood, flanked by three boiler-shaped structures slightly less tall than itself, each furnace like a general among his staff.

Ricardo delighted in explaining to the boys: those structures were stoves, heating up gas that went into the big blast furnace, to make heat, fire hotter than hell, to burn the iron out of the red earth. Oh, he knew everything. And as they approached, they saw the stream of molten iron rushing out of the bottom of that huge furnace, into a great ladle like an inverted bell, but twenty times as large as the bells of the highest church in Chihuahua. There was a whole row of such ladles, mounted on railway carts, with an engine waiting to haul them away as soon as all were filled. Sparks and lumps of fire jumped from the stream of liquid iron. And this was only the beginning, Ricardo explained. This liquid would make iron, brittle and easy to break, pig iron, but if it was cooked again in a different kind of furnace, in those vast long sheds—openhearth furnaces—he motioned to the giant sheet-iron barns with slender smokestacks rising from each like a comb in a señorita's hair—if this pig iron was cooked again in those buildings, in a soup with scrap iron and all kinds of earth minerals, then iron became steel such as the best knives were made of, and guns, and automobiles.

"Here, the boss." Ricardo approached a tall, sour-faced American, and all his ways changed. He spoke as a peon to a señor: "These my two friends, from my home country; okay they work together with me, Mr. Collins?"

Mr. Collins glanced at them and shrugged. "Okay."

They mounted a narrow iron stairway at the base of the blast furnace and came onto an iron floor, and there they saw the source of the spouting metal; it came out of the furnace into a trough much like an irrigation ditch, and from this main trough side runners led, each to a ladle. A half-naked Negro with a long iron tool reached into the seething main trough, breaking the stopper-gobs of clay, guiding the boiling metal toward the waiting ladles.

[99]

Mr. Collins came and shoved a long iron bar at Jesus. He pointed to a section of the trough, still red and trembling with the heat of the gone iron, sparks still jumping from it. As Jesus started to knock out the crusted slag, the heat smote his face, pierced his eyes. Still it was better working here, with air coming to his body, than in that bin of red dust.

For a week they lived in the mill thus. One night Ricardo said there was a girl to be had, in the shed near the warehouse where the Americans and the hunkies slept; they went with him, but there were too many men around the shed, and Jesus saw the girl once as the door opened letting out a man; she was not golden-haired, or even pretty.

Another night, someone brought a Negro girl to the boxcar and she went from one to another, for a quarter a man. Jesus did not know whether he should call her, since Pablo was there and he was in love with Rosa, Pablo's sister. But Pablo called the girl, and when he had finished, invited Jesus: "I will pay for you," and added the word Ricardo had taught them, in English, "my buddy." Jesus had her quickly just like the others.

Jesus, like Pablo, got the leaking sickness. Pablo had known it before, and said it was nothing, it would go away. The other men laughed, though Ricardo swore when he got into the Harbor again he would find that Negress and cut out that with which she had given the sickness to them.

At the end of the third week, more gringos, as well as men of the kind they called hunkies—white men too, but mostly Polish and Italian by birth—these all began to return to the mill. Two came where Jesus and Pablo worked at the blast furnace;

they were sullen and exchanged not a word with the other men. In the afternoon one of these new workers dropped a molten-ended cleaning-iron so close to Jesus that his overalls were singed. He swore angrily at the man, who in return spat in his face, calling him a sonofabitch yellow spick scab. Jesus understood those words, by then. He would have cut the man with his knife, but was held by two other Americans; then Mr. Collins came, and all the men who had lately returned to work stood together yelling at Mr. Collins that they would not work with the stinking sonsabitchn spick finks. Mr. Collins put Pablo, Jesus, and the Negro on the other side of the furnace. Then, in the afternoon, he took Pablo and Jesus from the blast furnace and placed them with a pick and shovel crew cleaning tracks. They learned that here their pay was fifty cents less each day. Labor gang, cheapest wage.

And that was pay night. But for all their work they got only seven dollars and some slips of paper. Twenty dollars was taken to be paid to Señor Rubio, who had lent them ten. And five dollars was taken for their sleeping on the cots. And half the men in the boxcar were told they were no longer needed, they could go away. The rest could now live in the town.

Some of the men spat and fingered their knives, and all cursed the gringos. Why should those gringos get their jobs back? They left, and we worked when we were needed! But at last almost all the men were drunk with ginpiss, and no! they had no fear of going out into the streets of the town, let anyone dare assault them! In a body, they rushed from the gate.

Soldiers were still stationed along the street.

"Walk away from the walls, thus no one can knife you from a doorway," Ricardo cautioned. He led them quickly, almost trotting, to the house where he lived.

In a basement were twelve cots. For fifteen dollars a week, he said, a man could sleep and eat here. On this street all the Mexicans lived, and there were not enough houses.

They did not go much onto the other streets of Steel Harbor, for one time when they went into a restaurant on the main street where the cinemas were, two Americans who sat on the stools beside them began to sniff with their noses, said: "I smell fink," and arose and moved to a table.

They went sometimes to the movies. They went sometimes to a whorehouse but after going a few times to the white girls, they preferred the Negresses. The Mexican girls were so few, all were married. Jesus hungered for Rosa.

Pablo could not save enough money to send for his mother and sister. He bought gin. But Jesus did not care so much to get drunk. He did not even send any money to his own family. At the end of eight months he gave Pablo one hundred dollars and said: "Tell them it is your money. Your mother and sister are alone, without a man to care for them."

The women arrived; now they would live in a house, all together. Up and down the streets they searched; but if there was a good house vacant, it was not for rent to Mexicans or Negroes; and there were only filthy wooden shacks, without bathrooms as in the American houses, without toilets; and the rent was high. At last they found a cottage of four rooms, with electricity and a toilet. This cost thirty-five dollars a month, but Ricardo was willing to live with them and pay three dollars a week for one room. Across the front room they hung a sheet; Jesus and his wife Rosa slept on one side of the sheet, and Rosa's mother on the other side.

The first baby was named Pablo.

Now was a good time for Jesus. Rosa and her mother cooked well; brother Pablo was a friend; more friends came to the house of an evening in the short hour between eating and sleeping, and it was like home, with talk and singing; and Jesus loved each day to know what new things the child could do: now he could pull himself upright by holding onto his mother's skirt—see how he does it, see! And now she, Rosa, the little mother, sat quiet and rounding, with her moist smile, and a new child within her.

In the mill Jesus worked on brick unloading, from car to barrow, partners with Pablo, and sometimes such a passion of content would rise within him that he would seize and toss the straw-pale furnace bricks so swiftly that he made Pablo miss one, and would have to sit down from too hard laughing. Why do you haunt the streets all night like a big cat, Pablo my brother? Marry, and you will have a little pigeon in your bed and be rested every morning and be able to catch the bricks!

Then the rate was cut and it was no longer for joy one worked so fast; hurrying, throwing, wearing through two pairs of gloves a day, a man could make less than four dollars in the twelve hours of labor. And too tired in the evening to hear the singing, or lift his voice with the women, and too tired in bed to be of use to his woman.

He understood and spoke some English now, and once Jesus listened to a group of masons talking, pausing with his wheelbarrow as he fetched them brick for relining one of the great ladles into which openhearth steel was poured. They were talking of the difficulty of life. A man cannot live like this and support his family on so little money. Jesus only stood there listening, in his heart agreeing with them, and wanting to say: Back home, in Mexico, I had nothing, an earthen hut and a handful of corn, but there I did not work so hard as here, and I was not always filled with desire for new things.

"What the hell does a man work his tail off for?" one of them, an Irishman, cried out. "Balls, better knock off altogether, than swallow another cut!"

Jesus, wanting to agree, said: "Yes, no man can live!"

And suddenly they turned on Jesus. You asslicking spick sonofabitch, what do you want? You come up and bust our last strike, didn't you? Sonsabitchn spicks, they can live like Chinamen on four cents a day, ain't got no families, they don't know what it is to be a man. . . .

"I have my wife and kids too," he said.

"Get the hell out of my sight before I—" The Irishman threw a brick at him. He ran, with the empty barrow, and stopped only at the brick pile. He leaned against the bricks, breathing fast, filled with blazing hatred of them; and yet in his heart ashamed of himself.

Soon he was transferred again, back to the blast-furnace stockroom, shoveling the rusty earth down to the empty cars. When he ate the lunch Rosa sent with him, he tasted dirt; and when he drank, the red dirt rusted the water; and when he breathed, he felt it grind in his lungs. He was always weary and, much as he ate, always hungry.

Pablo was laid off. Every day he would borrow Ricardo's

Ford and go into Chicago, where he spent evenings and nights in dance halls. Money he wheedled from his mother, who took it from the household cash.

Then Jesus was laid off. He could not sit in the house. When Rosa asked him to mind the baby—you have nothing else to do —he screamed with anger and almost struck her. He went with Pablo to a poolroom. They did nothing there, but for hours watched others play. Sometimes they got into a card game, playing paco, winning five cents, losing five cents.

Ricardo was the man in the house. Hours of meals were set by him because he was still working. On Sunday he offered to drive the whole family into the country in his car, but the second time Pablo and Jesus did not go. Jesus could not bear to watch Ricardo buy hot dogs, ice cream, for all.

Then Ricardo worked only four, sometimes three days a week. But he did not go out to kill time with Pablo and Jesus. Coming home Jesus sometimes heard Rosa's laughter as he approached the house and knew Ricardo was making her laugh; but the joy ceased after he entered.

That winter was very bad. At last the priest of Santa Ana's church secured a dole of food for the Mexicans. It is the gift of the American churches, he told them. So many had become infidels here, he said, this winter of hunger was the punishment of the Lord. One night Rosa talked to Jesus until he wept bitterly and went to church and repented. But he got no work.

At the Casa Obrera wild ones talked. They brought us here, they must give us work! But others said: Let them send us home! Some had the story: At home things are good now, the revolution is achieved, the land will be given to us now; to each man

[105]

and to his family Obregon is giving ten acres of land. Where have you learned this? Who has received land? In my village men have come with measuring-instruments. It is the truth! Each will receive!

And Jesus began to dream of the warm earth under his bare feet, and of the sight of Rosa, crouching by the stone hearth, in the sun, crushing cornmeal; and the children rolling like puppies on the ground.

Thus, as he ran along the tracks, picking up pieces of coal for the fire at home. He coughed all winter.

Then four of the oldest men went with the priest to see the super. They returned and said: If jobs come they must give them first to Americans. But this they say: they will help us go home. They will send us on a train as far as the border of Mexico, and from there Obregon will take us, each to his village.

Soon the train stood on the tracks, all could see. Those who had nowhere else to sleep went and lived in the train. All that week, landlords on Jefferson Street demanded their rent, or carried furniture onto the street, locked doors.

Suddenly Pablo disappeared. Jesus searched for him in all the poolrooms; at last in Benito's place he heard: "Your brother-in-law, he has gone west with two fellows. They go to look for work in California."

Ricardo would not pay the whole rent; he said he did not have thirty-five dollars. So the family of Jesus also sat in the train. And it was the word that tomorrow, by this hour, they would be on the way home.

And that night, in the train where all could hear, Rosa berated her husband. She did not want to go back to that barren desert where there was not even a movie show, not even a tub for washing clothes. Other men found work, even in these times, only her man was useless! Oh, why had she come to this man who was not a man! At last she cried in her mother's bosom; and Jesus went to the other end of the train and sat by himself and bitterly wept. Behind him, in the train, he could hear the voice of Juan Mendoza singing "El Rancho Grande," playing his guitar, and many singing with him.

The train stood smoking, straining; and all who remained in the Harbor's Little Mexico ran alongside with farewells and last messages. Jesus held the two children in a window, Pablo by a leg, baby Manuela in the crook of his arm; and the grandmother, old Mother Lima, crushed alongside him, pushed herself far out the window to say farewell to Ricardo, for now in the last moment he was so dear a friend they could not part with him. Come with us! they cried. And, Come back! he cried. And the train jerked, and little Pablo bumped his head against the sill and shrieked for his mother. Rosa was not there. Jesus ran the entire length of the train, climbing over bundles in the aisles, knocking on the doors of toilets and calling her name; but she was not there.

He would leap from the train and, waiting craftily till night, come upon them in bed, and slash them with his knife so that their blood poured in one stream.

But when dark came he sat with the baby Manuela asleep in his arms and Pablo curled against his side. And sitting there, age came upon him; quick talk would die before it reached his lips; he would be one of the small men with wooden motionless faces, men who have unending patience in their hearts.

[1 0 7]

Thus they reached El Paso, and he thought perhaps to slip from the train and wring the neck of Señor Rubio, who had taken twenty dollars for his ten; but he had to go find water for the children.

No train waited on the other side of the border, to take them to their villages. Along the road, families were camped; there were soldiers about.

Will they send us to our own village to give us land, or to a new place?

"Ah, my friend, the land is not ready yet, first it must be sliced up with a knife, then wrapped in a paper package, then perhaps they will give it to you if you will pay for it in gold, and pay all the debts you owe to your landlord, and all of your father's debts, and the debts of his father before him. Then they will give you your land."

So on the second day they began to walk, old mother Lima carrying the infant Manuela, and Jesus carrying little Pablo.

At home all was the same; and when he set his little ones down on the earth in front of the *cabaña*, Jesus felt almost a healing in his heart, as though the great plantation were indeed a girl to whom he had come home. His brothers were large, they slapped him and started to wrestle with him, but he was short of breath. His mother shook her head, all her chins rippled. Flat as a leaf he had become, and with this ugly cough, such as Three-Fingers had when he returned, long ago, from Steel Harbor.

Jesus rested much in the sun. He felt a healing coming into his body as into his heart, as though pus-wounds were drying under the sun, and closing.

In the cantina he began to tell of the wonders of Steel Harbor, of the buckets of molten steel larger than the largest beer vats, and how he himself had poured rivers of burning metal as easily as pouring beer from this spigot; and he told, as if he had seen with his own eyes, tales of men who were consumed entirely, falling into such vats of steel.

Three-Fingers, more sleepy than ever, sat in his corner; sometimes Jesus would appeal to him: Isn't it so? and Three-Fingers would come awake enough to lift his head and nod. Yes, it is so. And he would add: Some day we will go back.

One winter a car drove into the village; it was a Chevrolet, bright, shining, with a musical horn. The driver was dressed in snappy American clothes and shoes with intricate patterns of holes punched in them. It was Pablo Lima.

With hat raked back on his curly black hair, Pablo told how things were in the United States. Things were good now. All over the states he had worked, Kansas City, Tulsa, Washington, California; he had picked fruit, he had mended railroads, he had worked in oil refineries. And Chicago too, Steel Harbor—he had only now come from Steel Harbor. He told of this one and that one. Ricardo was still there. As if all were as nothing, he said: "They have children also; two babies. Now, in the mills, a man works only eight hours each day. And for eight hours of labor he earns five dollars, six dollars, even more!" This car was his own; he had bought it!

Pablo remained a whole week, telling wonderful tales of himself, showing United States money. "Drive back with me," he urged Jesus.

And Jesus began to feel young again, a young man. Though

[1 0 9]

he would not go with Pablo. That was not the way to go.

Some weeks after Pablo had driven off, leaving ten United States dollars with his old mother and promising to send many more dollars very soon, Jesus himself left the village. In the United States, he knew, a man has to go alone and make his way alone. That was how it must be.

In El Paso he found the place of Señor Garcia; and, like that other time many years ago, men sat and lay on the floor, waiting.

Men were not needed in Steel Harbor, Señor Garcia said. But he was sending men to build roads. Three dollars a day, and live in a boxcar.

And thus for two years Jesus wandered. Sometimes he was working on railroads putting in new pieces of rail; sometimes he was not working at all, but wandering up and down the Mexican street of an American city, asking where was there work.

Once for a time he had a woman of his own; that was in Pittsburgh; but when the job was ended he moved on, hearing there was work in Gary; and she did not move with him.

One afternoon, for ten cents on the bus Jesus took a ride to Steel Harbor, and inquired around Jefferson Street: where did Ricardo Perez live? It was not the same house but a similar wooden house, unpainted, with the porch rail broken, and newspapers stuffed in a broken window. He entered.

Rosa was in the kitchen. She was fatter, and some of her teeth were blackened; she recognized him at once and called him Michi, their old name of endearment. She said she had heard he was in the United States, in Gary.

One of her children ran in from playing in the street, a boy of four. "See," she said, and patted the child, gave him a slice of bread, and let him run out.

They sat near each other, and she said: "Ricardo is working this shift. You are not angry with me for that time?"

He shook his head. He told her their children were well. She showed him a photograph of the children, which her mother had sent her.

He told her he sent money there, when he could.

Then she watched his eyes, and said: "You are a man now. You have been by yourself."

He nodded, watching her eyes. He knew he could come to her. It would not be as a revenge. It would not be as passion, for he would prefer to have a young girl again, with firm breasts. But he would come to her, when Ricardo was at work, just so.

Rosa often told him they were making a sin. Still, they brought comfort to each other.

D R. WILNER usually got to Israels Memorial hospital by eight-thirty, and put in at least an hour on experimental work. At this time he was working with a resident, Fergis, on a rather prosaic problem. They were trying out peanut oil as a medium for allergen injections; the oil was supposed to slow up the absorption of the proteins and lengthen the effect of the injection. There was practically no theory involved, and the whole thing had to be done empirically, and repeated with each type of pollen, before the correct mixture of oil and protein could be determined. But he had gone into it at the direct suggestion of Dr. Feldner, as Memorial was developing a large allergy clinic, to which Mitch gave a few mornings every week.

The whole hospital knew about his adventure of yesterday; evidently young Siegal had told the story of the emergencies. And of course they had seen the papers.

A couple of the smart young docs kidded him as he passed through the halls: Going in for ambulance chasing, Mitch? You certainly do it wholesale. Next time tip me off, will you?

In the staff room, as he was getting into his white coat, a discussion started. "That must have been an awfully wild mob, Wilner," Dr. Dantzig said. "What were you, right there in the thick of it? During the shooting?"

"Lucky you didn't get hit, Wilner!"

"How did you happen to be there?"

Turk Fergis said: "I don't understand why the police had to shoot, why didn't they use gas?"

And Dr. Stern, who was on the committee for medical aid to Spain, and supposed to be a kind of radical, or maybe just a liberal, said: "That's what bothers me, Mitch. Just exactly what happened there, anyway? You saw it."

Dr. Dantzig answered them: "Why, they tried gas but the mob came right through it. You know those foreigners. A lot of Polacks and Mexicans and niggers too. They rushed right through the gas. According to the *Clarion*, they were led by a lot of Communists. That C.I.O. is full of Communists. Isn't that right, Wilner?"

"Why, I don't know," Mitch said. "I just happened to be there, on the way home from the dunes. My wife said let's stop and see the strike; some friends of hers from the university were interested." Dr. Dantzig eyed him expressionlessly.

Dr. Feldner had come in and was listening to the discussion.

[1 1 2]

"Did you get mixed up in that mess out there, Wilner?" Feldner said, interestedly. "Imagine the crazy fools, going up to attack a line of police. What surprises me is that more weren't killed."

"They're dangerous people," Dr. Dantzig said.

"From the photographs, it doesn't look like they were going up to attack the cops," Dr. Stern said. "Looks more like they were running away."

"As far as I could see, they all started to run as soon as the shooting began," Mitch said. "I ran too." He tried to pass it off lightly, uncomfortable under Dr. Feldner's friendly stare. "I ran too, so if there was any fighting, I guess I didn't see it."

Most of the doctors scattered, still clucking and shrugging over the event. Stern remained for a moment, studying the newspaper photographs. "Looks like slaughter to me," he said to Mitch.

"It was," Mitch replied; and realized he had looked around to make sure the others—Dantzig, Feldner—had not caught his remark.

Siegal came in. He hadn't yet checked with the 117th Street hospital, on the two abdominals. Mitch phoned. The switchboard girl was dense. Who? Dr. Wilner? *His* patients . . . ? Oh, some of those rioters . . . The word annoyed him.

At last he got hold of the interne. The night had been bad for both men, Emil worse than the Swede. Both had to have morphine. Emil was vomiting every few minutes. "What's his blood pressure?" They hadn't taken it. He waited. It was under 90 again. "Line up another donor," he directed; the interne started to stall. Well, he'd have to get an okay from Dr. Whalen. . . .

So that was what he was going to be up against. "Listen, I'm coming right over," Mitch said. "Meanwhile you can at least insert a Levine tube, to fix that vomiting." "Okay, okay, Doctor," the interne agreed.

[113]

Mitch arranged for Turk Fergis to take over his morning allergy clinic. "Let those oil preparations go for today." He hurried out, hoping Feldner wouldn't notice. The old shtunk would expect you to give up your own office hours rather than miss a clinic for him.

They had placed Emil and the Swede in a double room. "Hey, Doc, we're having a race," Emil croaked in a ghastly kidding whisper. "The nurse promised to go out with the guy that don't kick off." Lindstrom's thin mouth pulled slightly toward a smile.

"Maybe you'll have to make it a double date," Mitch said to the nurse with unconvincing lightness.

"Hah. When I go out of here, it'll be feet first," Emil jested. Then he added seriously: "Doc, what chance I got?"

"You've got a chance all right. You've got to fight it out."

"About fifty-fifty, huh, Doc?" Emil's fevered eyes fixed on Mitch, then moved to Lindstrom. "One out of the two of us."

From the other bed, Gus Lindstrom said: "Wanna lay a bet who croaks?"

Emil moved his head in the negative, still keeping his eyes fixed on Gus. "You got a nice wife and kids," he said.

"So what?" Gus cried with feverish bitterness. "Even if we win the strike, what am I gonna do? Watch my kids starve? Hot mills are closing down. They don't need us any more." Then he added: "They must of got my old man, he must be dead. Doc, they won't tell me anything. My wife was here but she wouldn't tell me. Doc, lemme see that paper."

Mitch handed him the newspaper, hoping his memory was right: no other Lindstrom was listed among the dead or injured.

Gus glanced through the columns, then let the newspaper

[1 1 4]

drop on the bed. "Communists, that's us," he remarked. "We went out there to kill the cops."

Mitch bent over Emil. Urine smell rose from his dressing. His pulse was 120. The interne hadn't done anything about the second transfusion. Mitch rose, to find Dr. Whalen. In the doorway, with an expression at once sullen and ashamed, stood a policeman. Still on guard.

Momentarily flooded with bitterness, Wilner muttered: "Can't you at least let them die without the sight of you?"

The cop started, and withdrew into the hall. "I wasn't out there," he said. Looking into the man's disturbed eyes, Mitch half regretted his outburst. Still, it was a thing they had done.

Dr. Whalen was in his office storming at the head nurse. "I don't care what the union guarantees. I want every damn one of those people signed for by their family. I'm not going to be left holding the bag." For a moment he failed to recognize Mitch. Then, half annoyed: "Oh, hello, hello, Doctor."

He didn't think another transfusion would be needed for Emil. "Doing as well as could be expected. Let's wait till tonight anyway, that'll be time enough."

Mitch mentioned his suspicions that the ureter had been severed by the bullet. "The dressing is saturated."

"Oh, well, the wound may be leaking a little urine," Dr. Whalen said. "Just a little leakage. Clear up in a day or so." Mitch stared, incredulous. Obviously there was no use arguing. He'd have to get Emil to another hospital. "They'll pull through," Dr. Whalen said heartily. "Nothing can kill those boys. I know them."

Wilner went and telephoned for the union's okay to have Emil operated on at Memorial. But everybody was down at the coroner's inquest.

Walking into the old familiar building where as a student he had watched so many post-mortems, smelling again the warm, sweetish formaldehyde, Mitch Wilner wondered about the present students who would see these bodies dissected: would they think how these people came to death? We used to get gangsters, he might say, meeting one of them in the hall. We got the St. Valentine's Day massacre. But it looks like you're doing all right, too.

The corridor was cluttered with people; but the hearing-rooms were empty. Perhaps the inquest was over. What could they find but justifiable homicide? The coroner wasn't going to indict the Chicago police.

In the corridor, Mitch saw Frank Sobol and Sam Eisen, and that Negro from Guzman's place. And in another group, Jock Kiley and Carl Gaul and Barbara Macey and Art, the handsome.

"False alarm," Carl said. "They've postponed the inquest, indefinitely. It's fishy."

"They're probably waiting for more to die," Barbara said. Six dead now, instead of last night's four.

He told them of the difficulty about Emil at the hospital.

"Someone ought to check up on all the cases," Barbara suggested. "Carl, why can't you take Dr. Wilner downtown to see Joshua Wheeler and get the whole thing straightened out? There's no sense in leaving those men in the hands of a company doctor."

Mitch Wilner had no desire for such large responsibility; and yet he saw that many of the injured would be left half cared for, or uncared for, unless a central medical authority were established. He'd go downtown with them; but first, since he was already here, he wanted to settle one thing for himself. He wanted to go downstairs and make certain whether the leg-wound corpse was the man of the tourniquet.

A slow stream of people moved along the vault—relatives,

wives, all with the desolate hope of failing to find their own here. The attendant was the same carefully scrubbed, professorial-looking bum Socrates, who since time immemorial had wheeled the stiffs into the anatomy theater for dissection, and had wheeled out the cut-up remains. Mitch greeted him: "Sock! Remember me?" With dignity, as one professional man to another, Socrates offered his hand. "We're quite busy here today," he said.

He conducted the visitors down the aisle between the two series of metal drawers, like walls of filing-cases, and paused to pull a drawer open.

"That's not him!" Mitch heard a quick-taken breath of relief behind him. Turning, he saw among the dozen people fearfully following Socrates that small woman, Mrs. Carraway, still seeking her husband. She was escorted by a young fellow, evidently her brother.

Around the neck of the unidentified body was a tag, as on a ward-born baby. The name space was blank. Mitch pulled the drawer further out, to examine the body: young fellow, well-muscled, over-developed arms.

"They sure killed this fellow for sure," Socrates said. "Reminds me of them gangster machine-gun killings."

There were four bullet wounds; one on the inside of the knee, one sidewise through the chest, and two through the back, as though the man had spun dancing around in the leaden hail.

"I've seen him," Jock Kiley said. "He's a chipper, I think. I can't remember his name. Some Italian name."

Like an auctioneer, Socrates asked again: "Anybody know him?" There was silence. He slid the drawer shut; reached for another.

Mrs. Carraway approached, looked quickly, and quickly stepped back. A round, mild face, the body short, with a paunch.

The man's mouth, fallen open, showed a few decaying teeth, three fillings.

"This one has been identified," Socrates said, showing Mitch the tag, as though sharing a specimen with a colleague. Mitch read the name: Hermann Baumann.

"That's the Communist," Carl Gaul said.

"According to the *Clarion*," Barbara stipulated.

"I guess they got it on him," Carl said regretfully. "He was out there selling *Workers*."

"That's all they needed!" Jock Kiley growled. "They'll put it on everybody on account of him. Bastards couldn't keep their noses out of it."

Mitch noticed that the Communist had been shot directly through the middle of the back.

Socrates drew out another case, and this body Mitch recognized at once. The tourniquet. The dead man looked very wide in the box, his barrel chest touching the sides; his fists were clenched. "I want to see his leg," Mitch said, pulling out the drawer. Yes, there was the wound; and no other serious wound showed on the man, though his head was clubbed. He had bled to death, needlessly. "That's the one; they dragged him out of my car," Jock Kiley affirmed. "Somebody ought to swing for that."

They saw two more. A wrinkle-eyed, stubbly-faced oldish man, his features placid, almost humorous, and his skull split wide open. A bullet had gone through there; but it must have been followed by beating. He had been identified: Ladislas Wyznowieki.

"Wyzy," Frank Sobol said, standing in his little group, distinct from Kiley and Gaul. "Poor guy."

The fifth was unidentified. "Funny thing about this one," Socrates said, opening the drawer fully. The dead man had a wooden foreleg. "Nice job, too," Socrates observed. "Got

[1 1 8]

joints in the ankle, and a spring. Guess they ought to be able to check up on who he was, by that leg."

"Jim ain't here," Mrs. Carraway said out loud, in triumph and yet fearfully.

"Maybe your husband is in jail," Mitch said. "They've got them scattered all over the city."

"No, I looked in all the jails," she replied. "In all the jails and in all the hospitals."

"There's another one—in there," Socrates mentioned, with professional privacy, to Mitch. "A Mexican." He opened the door to the posting-room. Mitch followed him.

The Mexican's body lay in a careless sprawl on the zinc table, arms hanging over the sides. Mitch recognized the doctor who was doing the job: Felix Graham, a classmate of his, who had got himself fixed with a little political spot as coroner's assistant. "Hi, Mitch," Felix said, frowning and ticking his tongue. "Some specimen."

"What's he got?"

"Just about everything in the book," Felix sighed lightly, as a man does over a cheaply made thing, a bum watch, an old car. The Mexican, squat, mahogany-colored, lay there almost as if he would comment to them about himself, about the bum shape he was in, not bitterly, but as a man who understands what happens to men and, for example, to himself.

Mitch noticed an old hernia.

Felix pointed with the knife to a slice he had made through the lung; Mitch bent to inspect the grayish spongy tissue, and saw the small white capsules imbedded there, t.b.

"Seems to have gotten over it," he remarked.

"Yah. Encapsulated. Maybe he went back home for a couple of years," Felix surmised. "The climate up here gets a lot of these greasers."

Kiley, Art, and Barbara had come into the room; but Socrates did not disturb them.

"Identified this morning," Socrates said. "A Mexican woman came and recognized him." He read the name. "Jesus Hernandez."

"What was she, his wife?" Barbara asked.

"You got me. First she was his wife and then she wasn't. You know how those Mexicans are, always switching around with their women; things don't bother them, they don't look at things the way we do."

"They're good union men," Kiley said. "Now you take in 1919, they brought Mexicans up here to break the strike. But now, by Jesus, they learned. They been kicked around. We ain't got a better crowd in the outfit than those Mexicans. They stick together too. If one of their crowd tried to scab, they'd cut him to pieces. They know what's what."

Felix had segregated the heart, and now he cut through the aorta and held it toward Mitch like a sliced fruit; both frowned over the barklike roughness of the inner walls of the blood vessel, which should be so silken smooth. Advanced syphilis of the aorta. Heart would have broken, in time.

Felix piled it all back, shaking his head over the junky remains of the Mexican.

A bullet entering between the shoulder-blades and coursing through the lungs had killed him.

Art, Barbara, and Carl drove downtown with Mitch.

"Look at this!" Barbara read from the *Clarion:* " 'Direct proof that the Fourth of July riot was a rehearsal for revolution was promised today by Captain Wiley.' "

"Rehearsal for revolution," Carl repeated. "Not bad."

" 'Frank Sobol, C.I.O. organizer, who planned the riot, has a long record of Communist Party activity under various names, and was at one time jailed in Easton, Pennsylvania, as Frank Soboloff.' " She laughed.

"That's right," Carl said. "They've got the goods."

" 'Before joining the C.I.O., according to Sergeant Loder of the racket squad, Sobol, *alias* Soboloff, was an organizer for the United Steel and Metal Workers, a Communist organization.' "

"What I don't understand," kidded Art, the dude, "is the difference between that United and the S.W.O.C.? We're supposed to be a Communist organization too, according to the *Clarion*."

Barbara continued: " 'Al Howard, notorious Negro Communist leader, convicted in 1933 relief station riots, is now also in the pay of the C.I.O. and was one of the plotters of the Independence Day assault. Complete Communist plans included invasion of the plant from the lake by a landing-party, who were thus to surprise the protectors of the plant from the rear, driving them into the arms of the invading horde of rioters who were to force their way in through the main gate.' "

Carl emitted a low whistle.

"They've got somebody right inside there," Art said. "They must have some bastard pigeon right inside the Communist Party, even."

"You mean there actually was such a plan?" Mitch asked. Carl chuckled. Art said: "Anyone that would dream of taking over that plant is loony. Why, they had machine guns all through there. We could never of got to first base."

"Then what is all this, a reporter's imagining?"

"Not all imagining," said Carl.

"Where the *Clarion* gets that stuff is from the police," Art decided. "There ain't a thing goes on in the strategy committee the cops don't know."

Mitch was perplexed. For if there was such a wild scheme, weren't the police justified . . . ? "All kinds of plans come up

[121]

in a meeting," Carl said. "You can't hold the organization responsible for every dizzy idea that any member pops off with. The thing is—that plan wasn't carried out, was it?"

"No thanks to *them*," Barbara said venomously; and again Mitch Wilner was disturbed by a sense of meanings existent under the surface of events he had witnessed; as when one examines a patient who withholds symptoms.

The regional office was in the Merchants Building. Carl disappeared into an inner room. From that room, voices mounted.

"Staff meeting going on," Barbara whispered. Mitch was due at his office, but she insisted Carl would bring out Joshua Wheeler in a few moments. The hospital question had to be settled. There was no time to lose, in Emil's case.

They began to make out what was said in the other room. Mitch, Barbara, and Art sat embarrassed at their eavesdropping, and yet together in it.

Sobol's voice rose solid, cannoning. "We all know it. We all know they will defend themselves by attacking, by accusing us, trying to build a conspiracy case. Some of us may be the victims of that frame-up. But I want to say here and now that there are people in our own organization who are aiding and will aid that frame-up, people who from the start of this campaign have played a game of intrigue and sabotage——"

"Name names!" Kiley shouted bluntly. "We don't want any speeches. You can keep that for your fraction meetings."

Much of what they said was obscure. But this Mitch began to understand, that the two factions among the organizers hated each other with a bitterness beyond source in ambition. Kiley accused Sobol of secret meetings, of planning things without letting the other organizers know what he was doing. Kiley yelled: "Those men didn't have to die out there! If I had sent them out there I would feel I had their blood on me! Even like it is I don't feel clean of it, because I didn't stop it! I was there and didn't stop it!"

Sobol replied hotly: "You didn't stop it because you knew you couldn't stop it, you or I or anybody! What are you trying to do, build up a case for the *Clarion* and the Chicago police?"

"You can't accuse me of anything!" Kiley roared. "I am the one to do the accusing——"

The dispute exploded all over the room. A dozen voices took part; some of them Mitch recognized. Now it was Carl Gaul, backing Kiley up, shouting that a couple of days ago he had walked into headquarters where Sobol had some meeting going on, a closed meeting, not even organizers allowed!

"Maybe the men didn't want you at their meeting because they never trusted you!" countered Frank Sobol.

Then they were throwing things up to each other, things from the very start of the organizing campaign. Even trivial things. Sobol charged Gaul with having been insulting to workers, when passing out literature at the plant gate. "You never understood them from the first, you never knew how to talk to them. What the hell is the idea of calling a worker a yellow-belly if he refuses to take a leaflet—that's no way to win their confidence!"

"What has that to do with this!"

"Everything! It explains your whole damn superior approach . . ." And talking of factionalism, Frank Sobol charged, it was Carl Gaul who was spreading dissension, weakening the confidence of the men in their officers, telling them Mike Sisto was unfit.

"Well, he is," Carl yelled, "and just because he is one of your gang is no reason for keeping him in office!"

Perhaps Sisto drank, Sobol responded, but at least Mike would go out and fight on the picket line. At least Mike was no damn spy.

"Who's a spy? Come out with your accusation!" Kiley could be heard leaping to the floor.

"Okay!" Sobol shouted. How was it that the strike had been thrown into confusion by being pulled at 4 p.m. instead of 10, the agreed-upon hour? To whose advantage was that? The company's. Four o'clock was changing shift, the men at work had not yet gone out, the next shift was already mostly on the grounds. At four o'clock the company had two complete shifts to pick scabs from, and the two heaviest shifts. "Why were you at the gate with a sound truck at four o'clock, calling the men out on strike?" he accused Carl Gaul.

Gaul sputtered. "It was your own man did it!" he screamed. "Mike Sisto came running to headquarters at three o'clock and said the strike was on. He was the first man to leave that plant. He jumped the strike himself!"

"That's a goddam lie!" Frank Sobol roared.

There was the sound of scuffling, then a voice of authority, quieting the men. "Boys, are you all gone nuts? We got Speer and the cops to fight, not each other."

Sitting beside Mitch in the anteroom, Art Nowis said: "That's telling them, Alonzo."

Alonzo was Joshua Wheeler's chief outside man, field man in charge of the strike, Barbara explained to Mitch. Like Wheeler, Alonzo belonged to the coal-miners, sent by John Lewis to organize steel. Next to Alonzo in authority came Kiley and Sobol, nobody quite knew which was more important; at the moment Sobol was in charge of the Consolidated local, while Kiley and Carl Gaul had charge of Midwest and Tri-State; the other organizers were assistants on the staff and were shifted around wherever needed.

"No use waiting here, they'll be at it all day," Mitch said.

[124]

But to remove Emil on his own authority might mean a nasty dispute with Dr. Whalen.

"I'll see if I can get somebody out of there, Doc." Art went to the door.

Meanwhile an older voice, low-pitched, but with finality rather than with weariness, spoke. "Nobody sent those people up to the cops, no individual organizer. The S.W.O.C. sent them out there, the C.I.O. sent them out there, every member of this organization sent them out there, and if there was a conspiracy, if the police of this town try to build up a conspiracy, then the whole C.I.O. was in that conspiracy. I did it and John L. Lewis did it because it was part of the strike to establish a picket line. Everything that was done there was part of the strike and the entire organization stands behind it."

"That's Joshua Wheeler," Barbara said.

Art Nowis came back from the council room; with him was a fattish, good-natured fellow, who seemed unaffected by the commotion in there. This was Alonzo. Sam Eisen emerged, looked at Art Nowis with annoyance, almost anger, and then glanced quizzically at Mitch and Barbara.

Inside, Sobol was shouting: ". . . once and for all, if we are going to have some unity in this organization during this strike, I don't want Carl Gaul spying on me——"

Carl interrupted: "You accuse me! You accuse me! When it's you who are on trial here!"

"No one is on trial here," Joshua Wheeler insisted patiently.

Sam Eisen stepped back into the council room. A moment later the transom snapped closed. Art Nowis made a wise face to Barbara.

Mitch explained to Alonzo about Emil's case. "And in general," he said, "some hospitals might have the idea they won't get paid. . . ."

"Okay, Dr. Wilner," Alonzo declared. "You're in charge. We

want all those people that were hurt to get the best treatment. Anything you say goes. If anybody gets in your way you just give me a ring."

Sam Eisen emerged again, and suggested that Mitch obtain a complete medical record of all the injured, as there might be court action. Though he scarcely had time for so wide a responsibility, Mitch realized that he was the logical person for the task.

"Sure, you take care of it, Doc," Alonzo said, and left.

Sam walked down the corridor with Mitch, grasping his arm. "Mitch, how well do you know this fellow Carl Gaul and his pals?"

"Why, I just met him out there. Sylvia took some courses with Barbara Macey; she seems to be Carl's girl friend."

"It's not the best thing for you to be seen with them so much."

"What do you mean, Sam?"

"They're not a good element."

He remembered that Sam was supposed to be with the Communists; but did that necessarily prove he was wrong? "Have they done anything?" Mitch asked.

"Gaul is a disrupter. You can't trust him. He never does anything straight and direct. I don't know why they let that bitch of his come around. Coming right up here in the regional office. She has her nerve!"

"Why, she helped out, out there in the kitchen, and things, didn't she?" Mitch said.

"There are plenty of women in the Auxiliary. They don't need help. Especially from the niece of a board member."

Board member of what? Mitch wanted to ask. And then was appalled at his own stupidity. Syl had often reminded him that Barbara's family were millionaires, the Maceys, one of those names you saw on bank boards and hospital boards and stuff. "You mean of Consolidated? Her folks mixed up in that?"

Syl, too, must have taken it for granted that he would know. And wasn't it typical, in these times, for a radical son or daughter of the boss to turn up on the strikers' side?

"You can't trust those people," Sam said. "She sucks around too much. She's always on the spot, where anything confidential might be going on. What was she doing just now, in Wheeler's office!"

And yet if the girl was sincere, Mitch thought, wouldn't she be around, all the time, showing her willingness to help? "Thanks for telling me," he said.

There were a few patients waiting. And a Mr. Main had called. "He wouldn't leave a message, Doctor," the receptionist apologized, with the guilt she always showed, as if she had lost a possible patient.

Mr. Main? But that was the divinity student, Emil's donor. Probably wanted to know how his blood was making out.

The patients were grass-allergic; one was new, a referred asthma, and ordinarily he would have been pleased that his specialist reputation was growing to this point. But he couldn't get his mind back in the groove. He gave the regular patients their shots, trying to keep up the usual trivial patter.

The newspaper lay on his desk, under the photograph of Sylvia and the kids. One of his patients, Mrs. Lally, a lawyer's wife, remarked on the news: "Wasn't that shooting horrible, Doctor? It looks to me like they just shot them down in cold blood. I don't know why such things always happen in Chicago. You can't tell me all those people were Communists, that's a lot of bunk."

"Of course they blame everything on the Communists," he agreed. "Though there were probably some Communists there, too."

"There must have been something behind it," she said.

"I'll bet that somebody got a good piece of change for this."

He wondered if many people thought as she thought, saw through the newspaper distortions. Perhaps she was a radical. He told her what he had seen. She gasped and gasped. "Something ought to be done," she said. "I don't know why we let those cops get away with murder. They still act as if everybody was a gangster."

Probably she was a radical.

Arthur Main was in the reception room. The kid looked younger than he had remembered; his color had returned completely; he was one of those boys who seem always ablush. With Main was a dour-looking fellow in a wrinkled linen suit. "George Price," Main introduced him, as if Mitch must know the name. Mitch couldn't place it. Price half extended his hand, as though he might jerk it back.

Main was terribly excited. That stuff in the *Clarion!* Strikers attacking the police with guns and knives and razors!

"And meat hooks," Price added dryly.

Well, some of those who were out there, witnesses, were getting together to do something, Main said. Something had to be done. They couldn't get away with this. Killing four——

"It's six, now," Mitch told him.

Main went white. They might have been deaths in his own family. "Not those two fellows . . . ?"

"No, they're still alive," Mitch said. "But if even one of the two pulls through we'll be lucky——"

"That'll make the score seven, eight," Price commented. "Probably be a couple more die in the jail hospital."

"There must be a way," Main persisted. "If the people really knew . . ." He pulled some papers out of his pocket. "Look, Dr. Wilner, we drew this up."

Mitch glanced through the proclamation. "To the People of

Chicago: We are a number of people from amongst yourselves. We saw the Independence Day massacre at the Consolidated Steel plant. Having seen this, we can no longer remain silent citizens of a municipality whose law force is being used as a private army to support violation of the law, of a city shamed all over the United States because its police force is the most brutal and its government the most irresponsibly autocratic in the entire nation. Among us are housewives, students, teachers, a doctor. We became acquainted on the open prairie as we tried to pick up slaughtered men, women, and children. . . .

"The newspapers say this was a mob that attacked the police in an attempt to invade the steel plant. We were there. We saw it. We heard all the speeches. Nobody suggested trying to get into that plant. We marched with the pickets. They were there with their wives and children. They were there trusting the mayor's proclamation that picketing was legal. They were unarmed . . ."

Mitch looked up at Arthur Main. At that moment the clear eager face of the divinity student, white-skinned and high-colored as a girl's, with its purely guileless pale blue eyes, became, for him, the very personification of the idea of a Christian. A Jewish kid would say they were unarmed because they did not carry pistols, knowing he discounted the few sticks and stones they carried because in a fight such arms would be insignificant, and because they had a right to be sore, and because he was on their side. But it seemed to Mitch that the divinity student had come to some faith-idea of the people's being unarmed, as a whole, as a group; even had there been a few pistols among them, this sense that they were unarmed would have been true.

Then there was a description of the long halt before the police lines. "The newspapers describe this as a mob rushing the police lines with everything from sawed-off shotguns to razors. Look

[129]

at the newspaper photographs. They cannot lie so easily. They show people fleeing, people falling, shot and clubbed and gassed. There is not one picture of a striker attacking a policeman. Yet we know that if there were such a picture the newspapers would have spread it over their front pages. There is no such picture because the thing simply did not happen. We have seen the wounded; nearly every one was shot in the back!

"Who ordered this shooting, and why?

"In Detroit, big strikes went on for months, and yet there was not a single fatality.

"Why does this happen in Chicago? We, the people of Chicago, can no longer permit this lawless, murderous use of our agencies of government. We call upon the people of Chicago to initiate a complete investigation of the state of our liberties. Gun rule by politicians is no more excusable than gun rule by gangsters."

Mitch put down the sheet.

"Will you sign it?" Main asked.

For an instant Mitch resented having this done to him. There were already several names scrawled at the bottom of the page; but surely none of those had professional careers at stake.

"It's respectable," George Price reassured him. "There's a sociology prof on there—C. M. Rawley—and this one, Grace Wallen, is a public schoolteacher. Of course a doctor's name always helps."

Mitch could not quite bring himself to hand the sheet back to them unsigned. Yes, a schoolteacher might be risking her job; and Professor Rawley—well, the U. of C. didn't mind a certain amount of radicalism among its faculty. And how did he know who these people really were? If they were active radicals, naturally they took risks of this kind because of their convictions.

"This is one time they can't call it a radical protest movement," George Price said. "We've even got the church federation lined up. Those dumb flatfeet should have known better than to pinch Dr. Maxwell's daughter."

"Who?"

"She was one of our group," Main said. "They kept her in jail all night. Her father was simply frantic, trying to find her."

"You mean, a minister's daughter?"

"Chairman of the interdenominational church movement," Price said, with his humorless grin. "We've got the honorable citizens right behind us, this time."

Mitch looked at the sheet again. Actually, everything it said was true. But there were things, like that line about gun rule by politicians. . . .

"You see," he said, "I have to be careful—if there is the least word they can pick on—you know, in this profession . . ."

"Oh, we could go over it and change anything," Main said hastily.

"I'd have to study it." Mitch tried to see it with his name down there. He felt unhappy. Medically, he was glad to do anything, to give all his time, it made him feel useful. Yet he could not deny to himself that in a way a man's place in society did not end with his profession. If it was his duty to do all he could as a doctor, wasn't it likewise his duty to do a complete job as a citizen?

"Who do you think would print this?" he said in a last hope of escape. "The Chicago newspapers?"

"Of course they won't," Price agreed.

"But you'll print it," Arthur Main said to Price.

"Yah. That sure would set the town on fire." For Mitch, he added: "I run a little sheet called the *Searchlight*."

Now Mitch recalled Sylvia's showing him a copy of the little paper, containing a clever take-off of a certain grafter singing "Bei Mir Bist Du Schoen" to the mayor. And, he remembered,

[1 3 1]

George Price was a Hearst reporter who had started the *Search-light* to "relieve his conscience." Now, Price declared, he had to continue working for Hearst, to keep the *Searchlight* going!

"What we could do is this," he said, "we could run off fifty or a hundred thousand copies instead of my usual twelve hundred, and maybe the divinity students would go around and stuff them in mailboxes." He looked at young Main.

"Sure. I could get the student union to do it," Main agreed.

"That would be quite a printing bill, wouldn't it?" Mitch asked. "And anyway aren't there organizations that should take up a campaign like this? The Civil Liberties, isn't this their kind of job?"

It was, Price agreed. "But if the Civil Liberties or the I.L.D. or any of those organizations sponsor it, the whole thing will be just another radical issue, as far as the public is concerned, with the same old liberals making a holler. If it's handled right this thing has a stench strong enough to wake up even this lousy town. Dammit"—and on his face the cynic visibly battled with the reformer—"if a mass murder can't wake them up, I don't know where there's any hope." But he believed the case might even become a rallying cause for some popular movement like the La Guardia movement in New York, that would finally drive the city hall machine out of office and give Chicago a chance to catch up with the rest of the country. "We might even get back our constitutional rights," he said. "Who knows? It might even become legal for the C.I.O. to organize in this town!"

Main was watching Price with adulation. Mitch Wilner felt he might be getting into things beyond what he bargained for. He fingered the proclamation. "I don't know if I can sign it," he said.

"You think you'd get in dutch with Dr. Feldner and his crowd?" Price asked.

[1 3 2]

"No, that isn't it." Mitch wondered at the fellow's intuition. "If I was sure it was right I wouldn't hesitate." Saying that made him feel a hypocrite; he knew he was now putting himself on the spot where, to annul that feeling, he might have to sign. "But there are certain statements, like this about the people not being armed. Well, I saw a fellow with a baseball bat and——"

Price kept eying him, his head cocked. Mitch felt the shabbiness of his scruples. Medical man's scruples.

"The way we used the word arms, there—" Main began.

"Yes, I know you mean guns and stuff. That's true. As far as I know there weren't any. But this implies—and if I'm going to put my name to it . . ."

"We can change the wording. We can say they had no guns."

Mitch asked for time. He wanted to go over it again, carefully, before he made a decision. They said they quite understood, and withdrew.

He should call up Sylvia, consult her before taking a move of this sort. She would say, Mitch, you're a doctor; as a doctor you are giving them all the help you can. But is it wise to mix in politics?

Perhaps this fellow George Price was a Communist. Main had mentioned the student union, wasn't that supposed to be run by Communists? Probably they were just trying to draw him in, use his name to cover their own mess.

He called the 117th Street hospital. Emil was hanging on, no change since this morning. The news braced him, made him feel like signing that thing at once. If a fellow like Emil could put up a battle like that . . . But the Swedish fellow, Lindstrom, had developed a temperature. Up two degrees since morning.

"Hemorrhage?"

"No."

[133]

"Distention?"

"Yah. Some."

He simply couldn't lose both of them. "I'll be right out."

3. ROLLER, AND SONS

THE years old man Lindstrom worked in St. Louis he was a rougher in the tin mill, and finally worked up to be roller in the Pioneer Sheet and Tin. The mill there stood right on the edge of the street and had scarcely any walls, just a roof on girders, so as to give the men air.

Most of the men brought their lunch pails, but the Lindstroms lived only four blocks away, and old lady Lindstrom used to walk over herself when the kids were at school, bringing Oscar his meal; and sometimes she'd sit there for an hour watching the boys swing the sullen red sheets through the rolls. "Why, I have more work putting my clothes through the wringer," she joked them.

After school she would send one of the kids over with a snack for Big Oscar. Gus, the youngster, was always crazy to go; but Will, getting out of high school, seemed to have no liking for hanging around the mill; he always had "important business" someplace; and besides he dressed too slick. Ma decided he was walking a girl, and paid no mind to his antics.

Gus used to hang around the works till Pa came home with him. Then the kid would be too tired to do his homework. At the mill he used to run errands for the men, especially like when they decided to have a steak fry: they would send him to the butcher for round steak and then they would let him use a roller's iron to scrape off a spot on the floorplate just where the red-hot billets, like red-hot loaves of steel, were dragged when they came out of the reheating oven ready to be rolled down into sheets. His old man would spit to see if the floor was hot enough, and that gob of spit would bang explode. They'd throw water on the floorplate to clean it, and it would hiss up steam; then they'd chuck the steaks down and fry them right on that sizzling floorplate, turning them over with their three-foot tongs. That beat any picnic.

The job Gus was crazy to do was the singleboy's, wearing the wooden shoe with the iron sole and stepping on the red-hot sheets of steel. He knew the job of every man in the crew, beginning with the pair-a-heater, who took those cherry-red loaves of steel out of the long oven, a pair of loaves each time, and dragged them hot across the floorplate by his long pair-a-heater tongs, then gave each billet that final shove-over that sent the burning loaf to the rougher. That was his father, a rougher in those days, the big Swede Oscar Lindstrom, whose long side muscles rippled smooth in their oil of sweat and reminded Gus of the movement of a goldfish at home slipping through water, that's how easily the old man sent the heated billets into the huge revolving rolls of the mill. Gus would watch the catcher on the other side of those barrel-sized, solid steel squashing wringers, the catcher with his tongs waiting for the thick red tongue of steel as it stuck out more and more through the revolving mill-jaws as if through the face of some terrific metal monster. And then the catcher would seize the tongue in his huge nippers, and pass it back through the top rolls, back to big Swede Oscar Lindstrom standing on the other side, who fed it through once more, and each time it went through, the screwboy up there took a turn with his lever-iron on the man-sized doublescrews which each time pressed the rolls closer together, flattening the passing sheet of steel, thinner, longer. Gus would watch his father and the catcher shuttling that steel back and forth through the wringers, two loaves becoming two sheets, feeding them faster, one going through as the other came back over, until maybe after the third pass through, his father, judging it right, held the first sheet on his tongs, waiting for the second of the pair to come over and land on top of it; the old man would jockey those two boards of steel against the guides, matching the pair together, handling the hot steel as lightly as if it were sheets of paper; and then he would shove the sheets through the rolls together, one on top of the other, a pair.

The stuck-together, squeezed-down two-sheets spat on the floor, man-long by now, and that was where the singleboy's job came in. He wasn't a boy but a young squirt of an Irishman, about as old as brother Will, practically a man. With that iron-bottomed wooden shoe he stepped on one end of the pair of red-hot plates, holding it down while he nipped his tongs at the opposite end, got a grip on the top plate and ripped the plates apart with a sizzle and pop like ripping a courtplaster off your back.

That was the job Gus wanted to do: step on it, rip it open, then chuck the two plates over to the doubling-machine, where they would be folded with a middle-crease, like folding two sheets of paper into a four-page book.

Gus knew the rest of the jobs: the heater sticking the four-leaf packs back into the oven, shifting them around in the oven till they were even hot all the way through, then pulling them out to the roller, who'd shove the four-pack through the mill. Then the singleboy grabbing the hot four-pack and tearing it open, like pulling apart sheets of tinfoil. Sometimes when the batch of steel was bad or underheated, the sheets would stick, and then he'd sweat to trick them apart. Singleboy was no cinch job.

Thinner still, the four-pack doubled into eights, and through the heater's hands again into the furnace, and through the roller's hands again, milling down to thirty-two gauge, passing and re-passing through the rolls until it was right, and then the catcher swinging that eight-pack onto the finish pile for the craneman to carry over to the shear-table for trimming and cooling and opening, the opener with his lead-palmed glove flicking the cold thin sheets apart from their packs of eight as swiftly as a bank-teller counting dollar bills. For that was no trick, the sheets were cool then. The trick was the singleboy's stunt with the red-hot doubles and four-packs.

Gus would watch, remembering the time when he was a little kid and heated a piece of tin red-hot in the fireplace, using the fireplace tongs, and carried the metal to the basement and tried to run it through the wringer on Ma's washtub, he and sister Mae together. Ruined the wringer and nearly burned a whole week's wash and a wonder they didn't set the house on fire. Old man laughed so hard he could barely get any force onto that strap, laughing; the kid was a roller born.

Gus was just starting high school when Will graduated and was old enough and big and husky enough to take a job, even though the old man claimed Will's bones were soft and would melt in the mill. The old man said Will could start as screwboy, easy work, just give the lever a turn between passes, and that's where you get the feel of the mill. But Will said he wanted to enlist.

The old man was patriotic but believed Thou Shalt Not Kill. "That's one thing you can't get away from, son," he said. Will replied, hell, the Swedes were all slackers even over there, he was no goddam Swede slacker. The old man didn't get sore. Instead he talked real serious for a whole hour explaining how he came over to this country when he was just a kid, younger than Gus or Mae, about the age of Gerty, here, but still he remembered from his childhood, he had known German boys too, and German people were not bad people. Will cried out that his father was a traitor against the United States! The old man shook his head and said no, he was a citizen, he would go to war for the United States if his turn came; but still in his heart it said Thou Shalt Not Kill, and if others had to kill, let that be, but he would try to keep his hand out of it. He said Will could help his country just as much by staying at home and working in the mill turning out armorplate for ships, this work was just as necessary as being a soldier, and instead of killing men it might protect them. Protect our own boys. "Look at Jack Dempsey," the old man said, "there's a great fighter, but he doesn't want to go over there and murder people."

[1 3 8]

"He's yellow," Will declared.

That night Will got up out of the bed they shared and Gus knew he was running away. Pretending to sleep, Gus watched Will and stifled himself with the sheet when his brother slipped out the door. He was uncertain which of them was right; he was ashamed to think his father was a slacker. A week later the folks got a card from Will in Camp Grant. He had enlisted in Chicago.

They didn't let Gus go to work in the mills though he insisted he was big enough, and to show them, he would always grab and do someone's work while he hung around there. Sometimes when they were fagged they would let him shove the billets into the furnace, or take a spell as screwboy. He got the feel of how much closer together to bring the rolls, after each pass.

Will came home from the war unharmed but a grouch, Gus had to admit. He tried hard as hell to welcome his hero brother, but Will scarcely talked to anyone, and wouldn't even go to see the super at the mill when the old man had a special appointment fixed up for him. "They got niggers working there, it stinks," he complained; for during the war Negroes had been put to work on jobs they had never been allowed to hold before, there being a shortage of men. Now the super was letting the Negroes go, putting back veterans on those jobs; but Will said: "They can take their stinking mill and stick it up a nigger." He talked like that sometimes even when Ma and the girls were in the house. He started being a dude again, insisting on Kuppenheimer suits, always pressed, and two-dollar neckties. "I'm no sucker, I'm going to get a white man's job," he said, and for a long time had no job.

Even his girl didn't like him any more after a couple of months; she came to the house once when he wasn't there and had a long heart-to-heart with Ma, and cried, and Ma cried too. Gus had a good mind to tell his brother, vet or no vet: "Quit bellyaching." First Will would yell the niggers had all the jobs, then he would spit at a job because it was nigger work. And all the time he was cursing about the war. "What did we fight for? I'll tell you what, so a bunch of profiteers could ride around in private trains with their carloads of cuties. All those bastards were in cahoots!" He had an idea there was one crowd up there in the know that was running things, a crowd that had maybe even its secret transatlantic cables and stuff, that ran the whole world including President Wilson. Sure, Wilson wasn't going into the war, but when they told him, he went in, didn't he? And that gang in the know split their guts laughing at the millions of suckers down below. He was going to get up there with the people that knew what was what.

All of a sudden Will went to Cleveland.

They didn't hear from him directly, but a roller up there named Nick Bistella, who used to work at the Pioneer in St. Louis, wrote and told the old man he heard his son had a job in the front office where he could keep his shirt clean.

Later the old man heard from another old-time pal that Will got a break with Pioneer because everybody knew Oscar Lindstrom; but Will always said it was an army buddy got him on as salesman.

The old man had advanced during the war and was a full-fledged roller now, making anywhere from fifteen to twenty-five dollars a day. He liked to talk and discuss, claiming if he hadn't had to labor like a sonofabee twelve hours a day all his life he'd have read more books; but he was going to have his kids read; he was even going to send Gert to normal school to become a teacher. He liked to quote a lot of authorities in his arguments as though he had memorized their books; he was always saying: according to Henry George, all our taxes ought to be lumped together into one single tax, on land; now that's sensible, isn't it? As if he had read Henry George.

He was a union man, a member of the old Amalgamated. There wasn't much of a local at the Pioneer works, except among a few old-time millwrights and skilled sheet and tin men; still, the Swede and Hairy Hank Corrigan and Joe Lamper and about six other fellows used to hold meetings at each other's house and every once in a while a dance at the Odd Fellows hall. When they met at the Lindstrom house they'd drink up Ma's beer, and she would yell and swear at Pa for sending his good money to those no-good union bums in Pittsburgh, but Pa said there was insurance connected with it and the payments were worth keeping up if only for the insurance; that used to quiet her. But just about after Will went to Cleveland, the union boys got all hepped up, talking so long at their meetings that Pa would hardly be fit to work the next day; sure as shooting, one day after a meeting like that he would be so bleary he'd let the rolls catch his tongs and feed his arm through, like Sander Harris did in 1914.

Joe Lamper and Hairy Hank kept running in and out of the house; they talked about a big campaign; they were going to bring that terrific Irishman Adam Ryan, the Chicago stockyards spellbinder, down to address a mass meeting; they had letters

[1 4 1]

and wires from Bill Foster, the main organizer, promising as soon as he could snatch a day he was coming down to help them; they were going to sign up every man in the Pioneer works, the Blainey works, and every man in Standard Steel.

This was the time to strike for the eight-hour day, Pa said, so his kids would work like human beings and have time enough after their labors for a little family life instead of eating and falling into bed like pigs; so his daughters could marry steel men and even see them occasionally in the daylight besides on every fourth Sunday.

The Pioneer plant, being a small plant, didn't go out on strike in 1919. There were men out at the Standard mills; and in Gary and in Pittsburgh the men said it was really murder; the Pioneer men were continually trying to collect money and sending their last dimes for the strikers in Gary. And Ma Lindstrom was scared stiff that any day the Pioneer men would go out and her bread-winner would be sitting home.

But in a couple of weeks it was all over town that the Standard men were going back to work, those that the mill would take back in, for the strike was broken in Gary by the federal soldiers.

That next year nobody was using steel. They weren't building any warships and it seemed that nobody had any money to buy automobiles, and nobody was putting up skyscrapers or bridges; the mill began to cut wages, and there wasn't work enough to go around; the joke was: Hell, you boys went on strike for the eight-hour day, why, now you've got the six-hour day and the four-hour day and the two-day week, you'll come begging for a full day's work of twelve hours!

The mill was doing so poorly the company sold out from the possession of the old Stevenson family that had raised it from a hand forge; it was taken over by some money gang from New York and they put in a fellow named Speer as superintendent. Pa was the first roller to get let out.

"I'll go down there and break that sonofabitch's neck!" he roared, pacing from one room to another, never able to sit down. "Sixteen years I buried in that place. I been there longer than nine out of ten men left in the shop."

Ma pointed out he hadn't been a roller except the last couple of years.

"Yah? Then he could have put me back on roughing. He's got kids in there roughing. Green kids. He's kicking out the union men, that's all it is."

How could he be sure of that? Ma asked. This man Speer was new to the city and to the mill, how would he even know who were the union men, or care?

The old man gave her one of his looks that said what was the use of talking to women. A hundred times he had told her this Otis Speer came from Triton, Pa., the "model steel town" where they had practically killed a couple of union organizers just for trying to get off a train at the town station. Don't worry about Otis Speer knowing who's in the union. Brought along some of his celebrated company police, from Triton.

The old man slammed out of the house. They waited to see if he would come home drunk. He was no drinking man, and if he did that, the old lady said, then it was bad, bad as could be.

Hairy Hank Corrigan brought him home, not dirty, not noisy drunk, but silent; he remained bitter and silent for days, word-

[143]

less at meals; till one night the old lady cried, burst into tears at the table, crying into a dish of ham and hominy. Then everybody got good to each other again.

Corrigan and Joe Lamper were fired.

Pa and they would sit around the basement and talk and swear until they finished all the beer Ma made. Times were so slack, half the men were being let out of the mills. The union local that had swelled to three hundred men during the drive before the strike dropped back to a dozen men that kept meeting in spite of everything, to hang onto the charter.

The end of that year the family was broke; Ma took in three roomers. Young Gus went around to all the mills trying to get work, as there was a rumor things were beginning to pick up. There were no jobs in the mills. He got a few odd jobs fixing cars. Mae married a fellow that ran a garage. Gert quit school to help Ma with the boarding house. Gus knew that on the sly Ma was writing to Will in Cleveland and that Will sent her a money order for five dollars nearly every week. Then one day Ma showed Gus a letter from Will; it was a funny letter, never coming out straight, but full of hints, as if Will had all kinds of secret information.

He was in a position to know, he said, that certain large companies were going to concentrate certain work in the Chicago area. (Hell, everybody knew U.S. Steel was running all its big orders through the Gary works, was that all he meant?) But if his father, because of certain connections, which he did not think it advisable to mention, came up there to Chicago, it might be that he would "find difficulties." The best thing, Will suggested, was for the old man to use a fictitious name and use

[1 4 4]

as reference some mill that had shut down, and couldn't be checked with.

"What the hell's he mean, the old man's on the blacklist?" Gus wondered. And figured it must be bad, if Will knew it up there in Cleveland. That list must be all over the country.

Will had certain connections, his letter hinted, but he would prefer not to call upon them "under the circumstances." Further, he said, it might be possible that he would soon desire to "center his activities" in the Chicago region, and of course that might "make complications."

At first Gus was pretty sore about his brother's letter. Then he dismissed it. "He's screwy."

But Ma repeated: "Will says things are picking up around the mills in Chicago; you know being in the front office he hears things."

The old man said he'd heard that rumor himself, and maybe it was worth taking the chance. So he went on the bus up to Chicago and in two weeks he wrote home that he had a job in the Midwest mills; an old Pioneer employee, Russ Collins, a blast-furnace man, had got him in there; the old man said to sell the house and come up. He thought he could even get a job for Gus if Gus was still crazy enough to want to work in the mills.

"If he knows somebody there I guess he's using his own name," Gus figured.

"Well, what's wrong with the name of Lindstrom!" Ma exploded.

Gus wondered if his brother Will was really screwy, or knew something.

[145]

The Midwest was a hell of a big mill; you could put the Pioneer works into her ten times and still have room, as the old man said, for a ship-building yard and a couple of farms. But rolling sheet and tin was the same job, except they had two stands of rolls instead of one for each furnace, and eliminated the screwboy.

Gus started in as singleboy on Pop's crew. At the Pioneer works he could have walked in and handled any job on the turn, perfectly, but it was funny—here, with Pop watching him and the doubler waiting for him to pull the sheets apart and pass them, he kept getting stuck. He would stagger all over the floor wrestling the hot sheets till the men swore they wouldn't work with him, hell, it was like skipping on ropes of fire all day, keeping out of his way. It made him sore to have the old man come and crack the sheets loose with a twist of his tongs.

The old man was easy on him the first couple of days, till Gus got to feeling the rest of the crew was sore watching the Swede pamper his clumsy kid. Gus worked the week, getting worse every turn, and then the old man changed from being easy and trying to relax him to getting double sore and swearing at him as if he were some lousy greaser. And when he dropped a pack of fours, hitting the doubler's feet so if the fellow hadn't been wearing safety shoes he'd have been crippled, the old man canned him.

Gus left home. He bummed around and landed up in Canton; got a job with the Pioneer mills there under an assumed name, claiming he had experience as a catcher; from the first moment the job came easy, he caught the sleight of it and was sending the finished eights over his shoulder onto the stack as easily as if the steel had wings.

The heater was a Pole who had a room for rent, and a daughter; in three months Gus was married to the kid. Her name was Pauline, she was awfully religious and had sharp biting teeth and a light jumpy figure like a bird. So then he wrote home.

The old lady came on the next train and bawled and was happy and liked Pauline swell and said what difference if her folks were Polish, she had married a Swede hadn't she and her own folks were half-Scotch half-Irish half-French and half-Dutch, she always said that was why there was so much of her, four halves, catch on? Gus got transferred to the Chicago plant of the Pioneer mills; he went back to his own name, Lindstrom, explaining he used a fake name for a while because, you know, like a kid, he didn't want his folks finding him. Once while at work the roller winked, like when the big boss is making the rounds, tipping him off that his old man had sneaked in on a visit to the Pioneer and was watching him perform. Just to kid the old man, Gus streaked the sheets past his nose close enough to clip a cigarette, and gave him the horse laugh. "Throw that bum out!" the old man told the roller. "He can't handle steel."

There were a couple of steady years. They paid up on a Dodge; the eight-hour day came in, the old man claiming it was the union won it after all even if the union was dead, it was the result of the 1919 strike; and in 1926 Pauline had their first kid, Dickie, and in 1928 came their second kid, Wilma; and Gus was a heater then, working regular.

Will never got married. Every once in a while he came

[147]

through Chicago and stayed at some hotel, phoning the family and maybe coming out for dinner at home, then not even spending the evening but rushing off. He didn't like to have them try to get in touch with him at his hotel. Gus said: Goddam the bastard, if he was ashamed of his family there were people in his family ashamed of him. He didn't have to come around at all. Will still acted superior to Gus, ignoring him, or sometimes just asking him how were his hunky kids. Once the old man had to hold Gus back from socking Will for such a crack.

For a couple of years there Will was supposed to be doing all right selling carload orders. It got back to the old man that his son up there in Cleveland was always playing for the big shots; there was some war buddy of his, a big sales executive, and from a money family, that Will used to go out and party with. Then about 1929 when Will came to Chicago he was full of mysterious hints about big things going on, mergers, and he was going to be on the inside, his friend the big man was on the inside, all that kind of bull. And this fellow Otis Speer that had come down there to the Pioneer works in St. Louis, the very same bastard that had fired the old man, he was a super-big shot now in the Cleveland office and he was engineering the deal.

The finish of it was, it came out that some Cleveland gang of bankers did buy up a lot of little plants and throw them together with the Pioneer outfit and call it the Consolidated Steel, so evidently Will knew what he was talking about, that time.

But then a strange thing happened to Will. He had some kind of crackup. Maybe disappointment, or maybe some bad woman stuff, the old man figured. But one night Pop Lindstrom got a call from a hotel clerk and went downtown in Chicago and

[1 4 8]

found his son sick drunk in a hotel on Clark Street, cheaper than the kind he always used to stay in. The boy had been drunk for two weeks. Will wouldn't say what had happened except he was full of vague stories about sonsofbitches and enemies who had knifed him but he would make them pay.

It turned out not to be as bad as it looked. Will still had some kind of job with this new Consolidated outfit, some kind of job in their Chicago office; he still wore good suits, still talked big, only now instead of talk about the company big shots it was talk about the generals he hobnobbed with in his American Legion post. Gus said: "Crap, he's just some kind of order-checker up there in the office," with the pity and scorn a man always showed for those paper-work boys.

First thing that got around about this new Consolidated outfit, they were revamping the Chicago unit of the Pioneer hot mills, putting in a continuous hot strip mill like U.S. Steel had developed in the East. Nothing new about the way you rolled slabs down to strip steel; actually it was still the same process of squeezing the big man-sized chunks of steel through one set of rolls and a smaller set of rolls, and a smaller set of rolls, squeezing it down longer and thinner until it was down to specification for bridges, armorplate, or what have you. Only, the old way, every time the metal went through a set of rolls it had to be picked up or shoved, handled by tongs or overhead crane, placed in the next stand of rolls, caught again as it came out, carried over to the adjoining mill, rolled again. And now the smart sonsofbitches, all they do is hitch up the stands of rolls in long tandem, strung out in a shed a block long, and with automatic conveyors between the stands, everything regulated

[1 4 9]

so that once you dump the slab on the carriers it rides through wringer after wringer until the sheet comes out to specification at the tail end. You don't need a third as many utility men, rollers, heaters, catchers, crane-operators. It's just efficiency.

Consolidated let out two hundred men from the old Pioneer plant.

Good men, too. Men like Al Nees, been in steel all his life, got half his face burnt off in an accident in Mahoning, bar mill there, when a T-rod jumped the guides, never got a nickel for it either; all he got was that taut brown-burnt cheek; Al was making the rounds, looking for work.

"It isn't just that new strip mill," Ma pointed out. "Steel is slack again, every mill is laying off men."

"Yah, but these fellows will never get back on," the old man said. And he started mumbling again about how if they only had a union set up and could get a contract. . . .

"What good would a union be?" Gus said. "You can't stop progress. When they got it fixed so they can turn the steel out without you they ain't going to keep you standing around watching it. Hell, I wouldn't even want that kind of a job if they paid me."

Well, the old lady sighed, at least it hadn't hit them. That hot strip mill could have been expected, any good housewife could have told you to roll the steel through from end to end—just like rolling a chunk of dough, you didn't carry it from one table to the next and use twenty different rolling-pins on it! But, thank God, they'd never be able to roll steel down to thirty-two gauge that way; thick plate was the best they could do on the con-

[150]

tinuous stripper. For sheet and tin, they'd still have to fold and squeeze the metal in four and eight packs, to get it down thin enough. They'd have to use the same old crews, working billets into tinplate.

"What do you mean it don't affect us?" the old man roared. "That's a woman looking at it every time. It makes more unemployment in steel, and we're in steel, and that's gonna hit us sooner or later."

That year, they began working the men faster, in all the mills in the Harbor. For in the Tri-State mill some sap college kid got a summer job and showed them he could roll twenty-two billets a turn instead of twenty, and Tri-State changed the scale, making twenty-two the standard; then Midwest and Consolidated followed suit. The old man raged for a month. Sure he could turn it out, but . . . On top of that, they were rolling more and more thin stuff all the time, thirty-three gauge instead of thirty-two; that meant an extra pass through the rolls for each pack; it sure looked like everything was getting thinner in the world, you were running faster and staying in the same place.

But there was no chance of kicking. It was depression and men were getting laid off in droves and everybody was scared stiff for his job, and then they were running the mill on hardly more than a maintenance schedule; men were getting four days, three days a week, and in Hegewisch, Calumet City, Gary, Indiana Harbor, Steel Harbor, East Chicago, every other family was trying to get relief, from the state, from the city, from the county, from the churches.

Gus still got a couple of days' work a week; but he and his wife and the kids moved in with the old folks; the house was big; why pay two rents?

Then Roosevelt was elected and the old man bust into the house one day shaking the newspaper, slapping it against his palm. "Look at that! A man has a right to organize, now!" It was the N.R.A. and it had a paragraph in it, section 7a, the old man said was labor's Magna Charta, as if he knew what a magna charta was.

The old lady lit in then and there reading him a lecture: the trouble with the male sex was they learned nothing from experience.

But, by Jesus, the old man got up on his hind legs and read her one right back. Nobody ever heard the old Swede talk like he did that time to his wife with Gus and the family listening; and they all got kind of ashamed that they hadn't guessed the things that had been gnawing inside him all these years. He was such an open and big and smiling man. But now they saw what bitterness he'd carried, buried, since the St. Louis days. "Do you think it is easy for a man to sit around the house and let his wife run a boarding house, and his kids are just reaching the age of womanhood and manhood and what have they got for a father —a bum sitting around with his trade dying in his hands? Do you think I am the kind of a man who will let that go by? Who will let the world do that to me only because I tried to do what I had a right to do? Now, God damn them, it's the law! We made it the law, and let them try to stop us now, the sonsofbitches!" Gus had never heard his father use such language in front of the old

[1 5 2]

lady. But the old man was laughing, chuckling, oh, how he and the boys were going to make those bastards toe the line!

When he had got it all out of his system, the old lady quietly said: "Oscar, you went through it all once, why should you be the one to stick out your neck again?"

"Nobody is going to stick out his neck!" the old man retorted. "It's up to the Amalgamated to send in some organizers and sign up the boys. Hell, they're ready for it, it's gonna be easier than collecting signatures for a baseball pool. The electricians are organizing themselves already. Cass Morrison told me they're nearly one hundred percent. All we got to do is give Jim Stacey up there in Pittsburgh a kick in the behind, to get him up on his feet."

"In that case," the old lady said, "I've got nothing to worry about. Jim Stacey isn't going to organize anybody unless he's forced to it at the point of a gun."

No organizers came. The old man groused. Joe Lamper, who was now working in the Gary mills, used to come over and they would sit around grousing. Joe said they had an old Amalgamated local up there in Gary and, Christ, it was a crying shame, fellows all around the mill were asking about unions, what about being taken in, they were taking in a couple of men a week, but they didn't have the authority for a campaign, they kept writing to Pittsburgh how about dropping the initiation fee so as to really shoot up the membership, but they couldn't get any instructions.

At the same time the old man groused about grievances, things on the job that the company could never get away with if there was a union in the joint. Take the other day: the foreman comes around and says the roller has to dress the rolls; why, that was always the millwright's job, dammit, but they're cutting down on millwrights and so they make the roller double up on his work. Not only a roller has to hustle out twenty-two billets in place of twenty, but he's got to spend half an hour polishing rolls every day.

Finally the old man had Gertrude sit down and write a letter to Pittsburgh. Speaking as an old Amalgamated man, I was chairman of the local at the old Pioneer works in St. Louis for seven years, and up here the boys keep asking me how about it, when are we going to get organized now we got this 7a behind us? The company is taking advantage of every minute we are unorganized to speed up and double up on the jobs. Now or never is the time.

There was no answer.

Joe Lamper got the Amalgamated weekly and it was still full of the old crap, personals about how old-timer Josh Summerfield made a trip through the Indian reservations, and crap. Well, lately there was some stuff about men coming into the Eastern lodges fast, but that was just a drop in the bucket to what could be done.

Joe brought along another fellow, Jock Kiley, a big beefy guy that liked his beer, a blast-furnace man from Gary, young-looking but still he could match old-timer stories with the other men, he'd been working since he was fourteen, in mills around Chicago. Jock never said a lot, except to burst out swearing every once in a while.

One night young Gus got down there in the basement with

the men and asked, what about this outfit he'd heard of, the United Steel and Metal Workers? Jock Kiley swore a five-foot string of oaths. Had those sucking sonsabitches started cutting in on Consolidated? he demanded. "Jesus, the Amalgamated better get going or we'll lose every man in the Harbor to those sonsabitchn reds."

"I heard they had a pretty nice little local going at the Lakeside mills," Joe Lamper said. "Pretty near a hundred percent."

"They pulled off a strike in Canton," the old man reported.

"Didn't get anything."

"Naw, but they stayed out four weeks."

"Crap, what do those reds think a union is for?" Kiley roared. "To strike? That's all they got in their heads, sign 'em up and strike 'em."

"The way they seem to work," Joe Lamper said, "is concentrate on the smaller plants, not too many locals, but do a good job where they get started." This fellow at the Lakeside mills, name of Frank Sobol, was a hell of a smart organizer. "You know the Lakeside, they've got about all Polacks there. Well, this fellow Sobol, I dunno, maybe he's a Polack himself, but he goes to all their lodges and picnics and stuff, they're a great people for old-country organizations, those Poles, they stick together, well he's got in there amongst them, all those Polish national societies, he's got them helping him out."

"I know all about that bitchn outfit," Kiley said. "It's a bunch of Bolsheviki. That guy Sobol is a Communist and he's got all those Polack Bolsheviki lined up in his organization."

"It ain't the Polacks that's Bolsheviki," the old man pointed

[155]

out. "That's the Russians. From what I hear the Polacks hate the Russians."

"That's where they got that Paderewski, the pianist running the country, ain't it?" Joe Lamper said. "They're crazy people."

"Those wildcat independent unions ain't any good," Kiley stated. "Where can they get? We got to organize with the A. F. of L., and those red bastards, all they are going to do is split us when we finally get started organizing."

"They're getting the jump," Joe Lamper said. "Lots of men will sign up with them just to get some protection."

"Goddam those bastards in Pittsburgh, what are they stalling for? I'm going to send a telegram to Bill Green!" Jock Kiley cried. "Set him on their tail!"

"Tell them to produce or get off the pot," advised the old man.

Joe Lamper suggested that instead of just Jock Kiley telegraphing Bill Green, let a bunch of men get together and make the demand that steel be organized. Say a bunch of old-time Amalgamated men—that ought to have some weight. He thought of men they could get to go in with them, men in Mahoning, Cleveland, Massillon; Joe knew fellows working all over the map.

Next thing, the company started announcing their representation plan. Started over in Consolidated and pretty soon Midwest and Tri-State were announcing the same kind of thing. Maybe because they knew he was a good union man from way back, men in the mill were always coming around to Oscar Lindstrom and asking him about things. Should we go in for this? they asked. "Hell, plain as the nose on your face, it's just an attempt to forestall us from organizing. I wouldn't even vote in their goddam election," he declared.

But one night before that election, Joe Lamper brought over this fellow Frank Sobol; maybe it would even be better to get the men into Sobol's outfit, if the Amalgamated wouldn't get going, than to let them get set in the company union.

Sobol was a fellow, you couldn't exactly tell how young. He was dark-complected, curly-haired, almost looked Jewish except he didn't have a Jewish nose or Jewish eyes; Gert said she could always tell Jewish eyes; and he had a wide but hard-outlined mouth, as if the lips had been stamped on firm and exact. He didn't talk Communism or try to sell anything; sure, he laid out his proposition, telling why he thought they ought to come into his union. "The old Amalgamated crowd is rotten," he said, "they'll just sell you out. They ain't interested in organizing the men, they're just interested in keeping enough locals in the field so nobody else can organize. They got their little agreements with the bosses to keep the skeleton of a union in steel, so nobody else can come in; why, all they got belonging to the Amalgamated is a few of the higher-paid skilled craftsmen, you know that, the bulk of the men in a mill, even a mill where the Amalgamated has a contract, the bulk of the men are out in the cold." His union was for organizing everybody, from rollers down to labor gang, he declared, all in one union.

But the old man stuck to his guns; he was against splitting the labor movement. "Where can you get with an independent union without the coal-miners and the railroadmen and the electricians and hell, Christ, man, it ain't a union at all unless it

[1 5 7]

is bound up with all the other unions, that's the first idea of unionism."

"Well, we are bound up with a group of unions," Sobol said, "the Trade Union Unity League."

"That's just a Communist outfit to split the labor movement!" Kiley roared.

Sobol said quietly it was not Communist, but progressive. It believed in doing the job the A. F. of L. was neglecting—organizing industrial workers.

Looked like they would get into an argument or even a fight, so the old man tapered it off saying anyway nothing could be done until an answer was received from Bill Green as he figured there was a good chance Green would order the Amalgamated to make a real drive, like in 1919.

Sobol said he would be the first guy to cheer if that happened, but the only chance of it happening was if some of the big outfits in the A. F. of L., like John L. Lewis's coal-miners, got on Green's tail and forced him to take advantage of 7a and organize the unorganized.

But in the meantime some way had to be figured to keep the men out of these company unions, the old man pointed out.

"Why keep them out?" Sobol said, smiling by compressing his wide lips.

"They're just going to put company stooges in there to run those things," Kiley explained hotly.

Sobol said, sure, that was obvious, but since the company was going to establish company unions anyway, why not try to make some use of them? Why not go into those company elections and put up some good men? That was a way to put the company on the spot: elect honest representatives, and have them make some real demands, right from inside the company union!

"Boring from within, huh?" Kiley sneered. Not for him. He wouldn't get mixed up with the stinking company union or with any crapping Communist tactics.

Joe Lamper said, wait, there was no harm in trying out that idea—suppose someone like Lindstrom here stood for election, he could get in, all right, and make things hum! But the old man said no, he didn't like the idea of having a company union job on his record no matter what the real purpose of it was. Besides, he was too well known as a strong outside union man, the company would either tie him into knots or find some way to get rid of him. Finally they fixed it that Gus should run for company union representative in Consolidated. They considered what other men they could get. Gus said there was that white-haired Scotchman in the Consolidated roll shop, Gillespie, he was a good man. "Get all the good men in you can," Sobol advised.

So Gus Lindstrom told a few men in the shop he was willing to put up his name to stand for employee representative, and he never had realized he was so popular—in a couple of days everybody was coming over telling him they figured on voting for him, and already giving him their beefs to take up. He was elected, but there was no chance of accomplishing anything on that job, he saw fast enough. Every once a month or so the company called a meeting, but if any representative brought up

[1 5 9]

things like somebody canned without cause, or adjustment of rates, the super said he'd "take it up" and that was the last you ever heard of it.

When the openhearth furnaces started burning producer gas instead of natural gas and it took two hours longer to cook a heat of steel, the openhearth representative kicked for an adjustment on their tonnage rate as this knocked fifteen cents a dollar off their earnings, but, hell, the super gave them a lot of crap about the company losing money too by increased overhead and all you could get out of them was talk. It took half a year to get a toilet approved for the old wire mill.

But one thing the employee representatives got was a big feed. Come November they all were invited to a downtown hotel, the Del Roi; Gus was a scream when he came back imitating the speeches of the big shots. Hell, they had everybody there from Otis Speer in person down to the last tinhorn strawboss. "Cooperation is the keynote," Gus quoted. "Some theme song, hey, babe? You should have seen Art Nowis, you remember that good-looking dude——"

"I know, he looks like Adolphe Menjou if he was younger," Gert said.

"Kind of go for him, huh?"

"Naw, stupe."

"Well he come up there in a tux. No kid. Hey, Art, I said, are you just one of the hands or do you sign the checks?"

So he told about the speeches, how the director of personnel —that crapper Fred Gash—got up and talked for an hour about the wonderful achievement of the Plan and all it did—"and, honest, when he started out to list what the representatives accomplished, all he could come out with was that can they put in the old wire mill! Only you should have heard him build it up! You'd have thought it was a swimming-pool by the time he got through!"

"How was the dinner, what did you get to eat?" Pauline wanted to know.

The old man and Joe Lamper never let up with the letters and pretty soon they were sending telegrams to Jim Stacey and Bill Green and John L. Lewis and everybody they could think of to come and start an organizing campaign. They had a little group now they called the Committee of Ten, mostly old-timers from the mills around the Harbor, signing all the letters and chipping in for the telegrams. One Sunday the old man was listening to the radio and Father Coughlin, the fighting priest, was on the air talking about the working man; then and there the old man jumped up yelling for Gert; he had an idea. Poor Gert, all she did was write those letters, no rest even on Sundays. "I'm going to join a union and strike," she kidded.

Now he wanted her to write to Father Coughlin to come and organize the steel workers. "Why not!" he said. "That priest says he is for the laboring man, and he has millions of listeners and followers and if he just got on the air and called for every-body to join the union we could sign up the industry inside of a week!"

Gus said he had heard Father Coughlin was a phony, why, even on that church he was building he wasn't using union labor. "I don't believe it!" the old lady declared. "He may be a Catholic but he sounds like a sincere man. Who told you that

[161]

stuff?" Frank Sobol, Gus admitted. "Have you been listening to that Communist?" Anyway they wrote to Father Coughlin, telling him if he meant what he said about workmen organizing, here was his chance to prove it; but they never got an answer to the letter.

It looked like they were never going to get any place, when one day, driving through Gary, Gus saw a big sign over a door, Amalgamated Steel Workers, Come In. The door was open and the place was empty and dim. There was no furniture except for an old broken-down desk way in back. Looked like nobody was around, so Gus drove on home, but at least he could kid the old man. "Say, did you know the Amalgamated was starting a big campaign in Gary? Yep. Opened up new headquarters." And he told about the place. Of course the old man had to rush right out and take a look.

Gus drove him up there. A puzzled lonesome-looking fellow was standing in the doorway. He and the old man kind of sniffed around each other, and finally the old man lets out a name: "Nick Bistella, you sonofabitch! What are you pulling off here!" And Nick pounded him happily on the back to make sure he was real, Swede Oscar in the flesh. Turned out the old man had first broken Nick in as a pair-a-heater in St. Louis, fifteen years back.

"What the hell is this?" The old man pointed to the sign. "Don't tell me they're really going to organize the mills? Why didn't they tip us off?"

"Well, they sent me to Chicago to organize," Nick said unhappily. "But I guess Gary is far enough. I stopped off here." He took out the bus ticket and showed them, paid to Chicago.

"But, Jesus," he said, "I'm on this Chicago bus and I seen in this newspaper——"

"Seen what? When did you get here?"

"Coupla days ago. So we're someplace past Fort Wayne and I get a Chicago newspaper and I see in the headline—Union Organizer Killed. So I said, not for me, I ain't going to Chicago, this here is far enough for me, so I got off here. They got plenty of steel workers in Gary, I'll organize them."

Gus and the old man laughed till they cried. Nick kept showing them that bus ticket to prove he was supposed to go to Chicago and they kept laughing till everybody on the street thought they were drunk, so what the hell, they went into a tavern. And finally they got the story straight, how Nick came there. The long and short of it was, he was out of a job anyway, so one day he gets called into the Pittsburgh office and Jim Stacey says: "Nick, you want to go to Chicago? We ain't got no organization there. Here's fifty bucks, go to Chicago and organize the steel workers."

Just like that. Fifty bucks to organize fifty thousand steel workers.

The thing was, Nick explained, all the Ohio lodges were kicking, why is there no organization in the Gary district?

"That's what we want to know!" the old man chimed in, telling how he had sent all those letters and telegrams and resolutions, begging for action.

Well, Nick said, evidently it was getting too hot for the Pittsburgh boys, so they decided to make a show of doing something, and gave him the fifty bucks. "So I got on the bus, they paid the bus anyway, I got here, I don't know nobody, so I paid

[1 6 3]

twenty bucks for a month rent on this store and I paid a guy ten bucks to fix up this sign, and here I am."

"Didn't they give you any names of people to see or anything? We got a lot of good old-time Amalgamated men right here. Joe Lamper is right here in Gary."

"He just says go to Chicago and organize."

"Looks like somebody was just hoping you'd fall down on the job! Just to give them an excuse to answer us that they sent a man out here to organize, and it was a flop. Fifty bucks!"

"Anyway, I'm here." So they went into a huddle. First thing was to get together with some of the boys, Jock Kiley, Al Nees, Lamper, Gillespie, and Gus said how about calling in some of those company representatives that acted pretty good—like Art Nowis—some of those men sounded okay at the representative meetings. "Yah, but we've got to go easy with them," Nick warned. "Half of them are company spies. That's how I got canned in Cleveland—one of them put the finger on me."

On the way home the old man swore in Gus not to say a word to the old lady, because now things were seriously going to get started and she might not like it so good. A couple of evenings later Nick came over and they went down to the cellar to drink some beer. Gus hung around the corner to steer anybody that came along to the basement, without the old lady's knowing it. The old man had asked a dozen boys over, from the Midwest.

The old lady was wild with suspicion. Four times she bust in on them, offering sandwiches, cake, coffee; but every time the upstairs door opened they started talking baseball. Come eleven o'clock, all of a sudden the lights went off. All they could see was the shape of Ma Lindstrom in that doorway at the head of the stairs. "I know what you're up to," she says, "and it ain't organizing any baseball team. Don't come sneaking around trying to fool me."

"Don't mind her," the old man says. "Just a woman's curiosity."

A couple of Sundays later the old man dressed up in shirt and tie and his best suit, Gus got his shoes shined, and they marched off. In a few hours back they came with Nick Bistella and Jock Kiley and Whitey Gillespie and Art Nowis and about a dozen other men from the mills; they were like a bunch of frolicsome kids, the old lady always described it afterwards, the old man jumped around her kidding her like she was a girl of eighteen, and he kidded Pauline as if he was going to make Gus jealous. "Come on, sweetheart, let's dance!" and he danced Pauline around, with his grandchildren jumping up his legs and tagging onto their mother and everybody laughing like they were drunk.

The old lady took Gus aside and said: "Once and for all, now come and tell me what you have done, all this skulking around in cellars and sneaking around the town as if Fred Gash in the main office don't know every move you're up to."

"Okay, Ma," Gus said, and the old man yelled: "Okay, sure, tell her!" so Gus informed her, they had just come from the Moose hall, just held the first official meeting and signed the charter of the Progressive Lodge No. 1551 of the Amalgamated Association of Iron, Steel, and Tin Workers.

"Oh, God have mercy on this family," the old lady sighed, and brought out the beer.

From then on the old lady complained the Lindstrom home

was nothing but a union hall. Nick Bistella practically moved into the place. He was there so late every night gabbing with the boys, he'd finally curl up on an old cot in the basement. And during the day the men were always popping in to talk to Oscar, especially just after the shift let out; the old lady got so she always had enough in the icebox to feed two or three extra at meals, and sandwiches at all hours of the day or night. Luckily work picked up a little or the union would have eaten the Lindstroms out of house and home.

They soon had a couple of hundred men in the Progressive Lodge, mixing them in from all the mills at first, and then they were setting up new locals in each mill, even the Lakeside mill where Sobol had his stronghold. They debated a long time before moving in on his territory, but Jock Kiley insisted the union had to be in every mill. Sobol stopped coming around.

Then one night he came over and talked to the old man alone. "Listen," he said, the way he had of talking straight, not cold, but straight. "Our union is going to disband and we are going to instruct our boys to join the Amalgamated."

"That's sensible, Frank," the old man said. "You know the Amalgamated has a lot of faults, but after all it is the union in the field."

"That's the way we see it," Frank said, "and we feel our forces can do more good if they work within that union, to develop a healthy rank and file. We have some good men."

Yah, the old man agreed, wondering if Frank was trying to make a deal of some kind, maybe to get some of the offices in the union. But Frank guessed what was on his mind and said, no, his boys would take care of themselves, if they were good men the union would elect them to office, and if not they would be right there building the union anyway. He was full of plans. For instance, the Amalgamated was still very weak in Consolidated, the toughest shop of them all. "But with the nucleus we had there and with the men you have in there, together that makes thirty, forty men, enough to set up a good framework," Frank said. He was all for calling an open organization meeting and putting on a big campaign at Consolidated. He himself would devote all his time and energy to that local. "If we can crack that shop with their army of stools, we can organize any plant in the district."

The old man said, why not talk the whole thing over with Nick and Jock Kiley.

Jock said: "Screw Frank Sobol. We got him licked. He's trying to jump on the bandwagon, that's all. We even got the Lakeside away from him. What's he got? Nothing."

The old man conceded, maybe Sobol was a Communist like Jock claimed he was. Fact, Frank made no bones about how he had been over there to Russia once. Many was the evening, before the competition started and he was still hopeful of getting Lindstrom and his friends into the United Steel Workers, when Frank would sit up past midnight with the old man and Gus and a few of the regulars—Joe Lamper, long-nosed Cass Morrison the electrician—explaining to them the evils of the capitalist system, and how a union had to realize that class collaboration was impossible in the long run and that was the trouble with the A. F. of L. When Cass brought up how the Russian people were still half starved and without shoes, most of them, he would say: "Sure we live better than the workers in Russia, we not only have shoes but cars, but you have to realize they started from scratch, from nothing, and if you measure the amount of progress made in the last ten years they are really going so fast they will be ahead of us in no time."

"I don't care if Frank is a Communist or a Zulu," the old man told Jock Kiley. "I don't give a hoot in hell if his name is Sobolinski or if he killed his grandmother, dammit he's a good union man and he can sign them up faster than any six of us—well, maybe if you didn't booze so much, Jock, you could give him a run for his money. Hell, let him talk all the Communism he wants; I've listened to all kinds of talk in my time, I.W.W. and K.K.K. and every damn kind of crap, never hurt me none."

Jock was still leery about Sobol and his crowd. "That's what they come in for, to bore from within, those reds," he said.

The old man laughed. "Hell," he said, "if we can't take care of running our organization, they got a right to capture it."

So Frank was with them. He worked quiet and good, not sticking himself forward. The main thing he kept harping on was winning over the rest of the company representatives. His idea was, let the companies organize all the company unions they wanted, but the union had to get its own men in there as leaders, and then take over the company unions as a body and make a real union out of them.

"Not bad," Gus agreed. "Especially, they even pay us for the time we put in on meetings."

At the Lindstroms', brother Will began to be heard from again. He didn't come around exactly, but once in a while he would call up and take Gert to a show or a movie downtown, and all the time talk to her about the family, what Pa was doing,

[1 6 8]

and what Gus was doing. "I think he's lonesome but too proud to show it," Gert said. She was always planning to introduce him to some nice girls.

Frank Sobol quit his job in the Lakeside mill and actually got on as a machinist in the Consolidated, under some fake name. Inside of a couple of weeks he had things going well enough so the Amalgamated decided to call an open meeting for Consolidated employees. They called it for the Odd Fellows hall in Hegewisch.

That was an experience Gus never forgot, though the old man laughed and said: "Well, son, now you are initiated, now you've got a taste of the real old-time union stuff." What happened was, they went over there and opened the meeting, and twenty, thirty men that they could depend on who were already signed up and weren't scared to show their faces, they came and took seats. Pretty soon other men began to drift in, new faces. At first that looked good, looked like maybe some new members would be signed up. But Frank, who was standing at the door, came back to the old man and said: "I ain't seen any of these guys around the mill. They look like gorillas to me."

The old man was worried but figured after all it might only be Frank's suspicious nature; he had noticed those Communists got to be awfully suspicious people, maybe because they had to be so careful all the time.

So they started the meeting; Nick Bistella got up and gave a pep talk, he was getting to be a pretty good talker. He hadn't come more than ten minutes along his spiel when bang!—first everybody thought a gunshot, then they realized it was a flashlight went off, and there was a guy standing up on an end seat

[1 6 9]

of the front row, with a camera, taking a picture of everybody in the place. Some of the men made a rush for the photographer, the rest made a rush for the door; at the same time those strangers waded into the crowd with blackjacks; Gus grabbed a chair and socked one of them on the dome; it was a free-for-all, and before they knew it police were in the hall, somebody must have tipped them off in advance.

Gus managed to get away down the fire escape, with Nick, but the old man and Frank Sobol were pinched, and it cost ten bucks apiece, as they were fined for disorderly conduct and fighting; and the old man lost a day's work because they couldn't get him out till late in the morning. Gus had a black eye.

That killed the Consolidated local, for Frank Sobol got canned, and the rest of the brothers were scared even to be seen talking to another Amalgamated man, much less come to a meeting. Somehow Gus did not get fired; maybe because he was an employee representative, and to fire him would cause too much discussion. Anyway the scare got around and even the Midwest local suffered; attendance at meetings fell off.

"It's no use," the old man said, "we can't get anywhere without support from the outside. We need organizers and cash."

The union treasury was bust all the time, depending entirely on what dues the boys could collect, and occasionally a few bucks' profit from a dance. So in 1936 the gang of them went down to the Amalgamated convention in Pittsburgh with blood in their eyes. The old man had a ten-page resolution that Gert had typed up calling on the convention to start a real campaign. Nothing happened.

Nick Bistella stayed in Pittsburgh, figuring he'd just as soon starve at home with his own folks as in Steel Harbor. He was too old a man for Gert, anyway.

Things looked hopeless. Frank Sobol kept yelling: "Forget that old bunch of rats in Pittsburgh." John L. Lewis and his coalminers were going to force the issue, he said. The thing to do was to petition John L. Lewis to come in and organize steel.

Then sure enough the dam broke and the C.I.O. was flooding the field.

The first person Joshua Wheeler got in touch with when he came to Chicago was old man Oscar Lindstrom. Gus and the old man took Joshua Wheeler in their ancient Dodge and spent a whole day driving around the steel district, showing him the location of the three main mills, the Consolidated, the Tri-State, the Midwest, strung along like three fingers into the lake, and then way further up on the lakeshore the Standard mill and U.S. Steel and Gary. They took him around and showed him the smaller mills, the Lakeside, the Wisconsin works, every place. Wheeler was just like the old man, solid, and with a tough grip in his hand, only he was slow of speech and careful what he said; he was soft-spoken while the old man had a roar in his voice. The old man said Wheeler would have made a hell of a fine roller, he bet.

In a couple of weeks things were humming. The C.I.O. put on twenty, thirty organizers. The old man told Wheeler about Frank Sobol, saying there was a good man to put on the payroll. Another was big Jock Kiley. Jock didn't want to quit his job on the blast furnace but Wheeler took him into his private office and gave him a straight talking to and Jock came away saying: "Okay, anything that fellow asks, I'll do." So he walked out of the mill and became an organizer. The C.I.O. wanted one of the Lindstroms, but the old man said, hell, he couldn't make a speech before a crowd, and he was too old to learn new tricks, and all he could do for the union he could do much better right in there inside the fence. And Gus said it was the old man the men followed, and he didn't want a job just on the old man's rep. Besides, he liked his work.

Some men know when they've got the right job, and that was Gus. When they came to the Harbor he had tried out as a heater and even as a roller; he could handle the work but was uncomfortable in it. Catcher was what he did best. Some men know when they've come as far as they want to go and that was how it was with Gus. He had the feel of that job in his hands and wrists since he was a kid; he could handle it easy where another man wore out his strength trying to lift the steel; Gus was proud it was the heaviest job on the rolling crew, though it was not the highest-paying; and when he was working his smoothest, feeding the hot sheets back through the rolls, or snaking the eight-packs onto the finish pile, he felt biggest then, a full man.

So he said, okay, let them get some of those fast-talking college boys like Carl Gaul, let them do the organizing. He just wanted to do his work in the mill.

That year all kinds of talk floated around the Harbor, about the cold-rolling machine U.S. Steel was setting up in Gary. Cost eight million bucks, you heard in Curly's place; cost twenty millions, you heard a foreman say; had fifty million pounds pressure; all kinds of yarns. More and more, the men speculated about that machine. One night at supper when Gus was telling how he heard the damn thing turned out tinplate like one of those mile-a-minute newspaper presses turns out newspapers, the old lady screamed: "For heaven's sake, go and look at the monster and stop building up a fear of it! You can drive to Gary in twenty minutes!"

So one Thursday Gus drove out to Gary. He didn't want to be with the old man, first time he saw that machine. He wanted to be alone, or with someone that didn't count so much. Joe Lamper took him inside the plant.

There she stood, a big square stand, five rolls high, and the steel went screaming through her, winding in and out of the rolls just like paper, winding up on a great spool just like a roll on a newspaper press, and the steel no thicker than paper.

A couple of oilers standing around, and an engineer: all he had to do was pull a few levers and watch a couple of gauges and press a few buttons. Boy, she was a honey.

They don't need pair-a-heaters because they don't have to heat any billets; they don't even roll down billets, they use big slabs on the continuous hot strip mill in the next shed, roll the slab down to a hot strip a block long, coil it up and cool it and then shove the coil onto this cold-rolling press; they don't need catchers because she don't come out in pieces that have to be caught and fed through again, she runs a long carpet of steel; they don't need screwboys to squeeze the rolls tighter together because she runs continuously through closer and closer sets of rolls; they don't need singleboys to tear the hot packs apart because there aren't any packs, and they don't need catchers to feed the sheets back to the roughers because they don't even need roughers; they don't need heaters to shove the four-packs back into the furnace and heat them for rolling into eights; they

[1 7 3]

don't need rollers; all they need is a five-man crew around the machine, and they can turn out as much tonnage as five crews of nine men a crew, working the old hand mills.

Gus watched the wide ribbon of steel screaming through the press and it was like once before marriage when he saw Pauline dancing with a rich college fellow, and a better dancer too. Watching, excited, proud to see your girl dance so swell, and fear tearing you down.

He spoke to one of the oilers. "Hell," the man laughed, "this crap ain't steel. They tried to press fenders out of this stuff and it was so brittle it broke in the press. Well, hell, they finally fixed it up so it would take the shape, but those crappy fenders, if you get a bump in them they'll tear with a grain like a woman's dress. It ain't steel any more when you squeeze it with all this pressure," he explained, "the particles in the steel is all squeezed down flat and stretched, so it tears along a line, it ain't got no cohesion."

Gus reflected. "How about annealing? Annealing ought to fix that. Slow heating will bring it back."

Another attendant agreed. "They claim annealing will do the trick. That's what they're monkeying with now."

"What'd they do with the old mills?" Gus asked.

"Oh, they're still running for the time being. Can't turn out much stuff they can use, out of this machine, yet."

For a change the house wasn't over-run. There was just the old man and the old lady sitting in the kitchen, and Joe Lamper had brought along a bagful of some of that canned beer to make up for the beer he was always lapping up on them, he said.

"You take Gus in to see that new cold reduction?" the old man asked.

"They been having trouble with it," Joe reported. "I figure she won't be running real smooth for a year or so. But they're rolling some stuff with her already."

"They're setting up a new shed over next to the twelve-inch mill in Midwest," Oscar Lindstrom said. "Heard they're going to put in a cold-reduction press cost twenty million dollars. The company is supposed to be broke, lost money these last eight years, but if they want twenty million bucks, they got it."

"They got to keep up with the competition, or close up," said Joe Lamper.

"I'm glad I'm old," Oscar Lindstrom said. "I'd hate to be a young fellow and see those presses coming and know I was gonna be put on the shelf."

"Why, they need men to run those machines, they ain't gonna run themselves!" Ma Lindstrom declared.

"They got a lot of those college boys running around there," Joe informed them. "That's who's going to push those buttons. Got to have a college degree now, a metalloo. Put those boys on there for twenty-five dollars a week, that's all they get."

Old man Lindstrom said the thing to do was to get those boys into the union. "If we get the union built up strong enough, fast, they'll have to take the men in the plant for those new jobs, before they can bring in any outsiders."

"All those metalloos do is handle a calipers or an oil can," Gus said. "With union shop we'd get first crack at their job."

Joe Lamper was easy to switch in an argument. Now he was taking the optimistic view. Sure, he said, and no need to figure

[1 7 5]

the new press was going to put men out of work. Because they could make all kinds of stuff they'd never made before out of steel with those new machines; they could compete with any material; engineer was telling him how they could build entire houses out of steel. "We'll all be living in tin cans!" And look at the way trailers were booming. Now you take the old hand-rolled stuff, you could only make a narrow range of sheet steel, and you had to hit just a certain degree of heat, otherwise the sheets would stick together when you rolled the packs. But with the cold-rolling process and all the new alloys why, you could roll steel hard as glass, soft as paper. "You look all this new stuff they're making out of steel. Now take even all these beer cans, that's stuff we never made before. That's new work."

"They'll have to drink a hell of a lot of canned beer before they can make up all the heaters, catchers, rollers, shearmen, screwboys, singleboys, cranemen that are going to be let loose by those new rolling machines," the old man said.

Ma said: "You can't hold back the world with a pair of roller's tongs."

Joe Lamper lifted his can up to the light. "This stuff right here they rolled on that new machine. We been rolling big orders for American Can."

"We been rolling American Can stuff too," said the old man. He tapped the can with his thick, cracked thumbnail. "I'd say that was hand-rolled stuff. I seen some of that cold-rolled; they had to ship back carloads of it, I heard, it wouldn't take the bend in a can; just crack like cardboard."

Joe studied the can. "Nope, that looks to me like it come out of the machine. See that stretched-out grain?"

[1 7 6]

Old man Lindstrom took a can-opener out of the kitchen-table drawer, and they cut apart the beer can. He felt the lid between his fingers. "Feels to me like the lids and the body are different stuff," he stated. He and Joe studied the materials. They could tell by the feel. The flat lids they concluded were already the product of the cold-rolling machine; the round-bent body was hand-rolled stuff.

"It won't be long now," Joe Lamper predicted. "They'll be rolling it all off that press."

Lying on their hospital beds in that small room, Gus and Emil did little talking to each other; but for long hours they lay facing each other: it helped, to see the other fellow still living.

When the nurse came in—she was young and not bad-looking—they continued their wan kidding, Gus saying: "Yah, I know why you spend all your time on him. You found out I was a married man."

"Sure, why waste my time?" she kidded back.

And with effort he raised himself over the top of the joke, saying: "Yah, sister, but it takes a married man to know his stuff."

Then his temperature shot up and the brown circles spread around his eyes and a film formed over his pupils, and he didn't even notice she was there. Once, Gus Lindstrom said: "Hey, Emil. You still alive?"

"Yah."

"So'm I. What's the use of livin', in another year we'll all be on relief, me with my wife and kids. You tell my wife to keep the kid out of steel. No place in steel any more for a man. No future in it." He waited, and added: "I'd be laid off any-way, soon as they start rolling by machine. Since I was a little kid I worked in a rolling-mill. What am I gonna do when they don't need catchers any more?"

"Take it easy," Emil said. "We're all in it. You do same as the rest."

Gus gave him a haggard look, and a strange, long, sweet smile, like kids' when they go cahoots on a secret. Then the pain caught him again. The pain was as if all his guts were blast-furnace runners and suddenly the tap-hole was opened and the molten iron poured through them. He writhed; sweat broke over him and a shout got loose from him. The nurse came but said she couldn't give him another hypodermic. At last the sei-zure dulled down to a glowing throb, like the burned clay of the runners after the iron has passed through.

Pauline came, and sat by the bed holding his hand, and he dozed in fever.

Once she turned and saw Emil watching her. "We found Gus's father," she said. "He's in that jail hospital but they wouldn't let anyone in to see him yet. Mrs. Lindstrom is over there waiting. We heard he's pretty bad. Don't tell Gus."

Emil watched her, unblinking, figuring should he tell her what Gus said about keeping their kid out of steel.

If he too was going to die, he was glad he didn't have to leave anything like this girl. It was even worth the wasted years of laying around with broads and whores if you had to die young, at least to die without leaving someone like Gus's wife. Then Emil felt dizzy and slipped out of consciousness himself.

[1 7 8]

BOTH were still alive when Mitch Wilner arrived. Young Lindstrom was awake again and in severe pain, though trying to hide it from his wife. The man's abdomen was rigid, his pulse was very weak. It was sickening, after Siegal's neat, slick operation. But the peritonitis had got in too far ahead of them.

The young wife looked up at him and he couldn't keep the truth out of his eyes. She turned and looked back at the body of her husband with a kind of wonder. Mitch had seen people watch death come, and he knew there was a hysteria that arose because they could not comprehend how so great a thing could happen in the bodies of their beloved ones, and not be felt in their own bodies too. Sometimes, and this time, Mitch was impatient with his own cold, organic view of death as only a stoppage of life in the cells.

He could not let her see him turn all his attention to work on Emil, so he beckoned the nurse into the hallway. And yet the woman, the wife, knew everything. She looked at the other bed, where Emil lay facing the wall now, unable to watch the death happening. Then she came out to Mitch in the hallway. The policeman stationed there moved some steps away.

Pauline Lindstrom said: "Doctor, how long—a day?" He shook his head. "Hours?" His eyes assented. "Then, oh, Doctor —he's in such pain. Can't you . . . ?"

"You know I can't," he said. They could shoot a man down, but he might not relieve him of a last hour of torture. Her eyes would not leave off pleading. "I'll try to relieve him some," he said. He administered the morphine himself, not an overdose, but perhaps the organism would cease its hopeless struggle, before this sleep was over.

[1 7 9]

Emil's fevered eyes followed every movement. Then they met Mitch Wilner's eyes, and Mitch could not tell whether Emil even cared to know, about himself.

The nurse brought a screen and placed it around Emil's bed.

"Me too, Doc?" Emil finally asked.

"No. Maybe not," Mitch said.

"It don't make much difference. Only, Doc, I'd like to get a crack back at them."

"But who? Do you know who?"

Emil's eyes darkened; and he looked at Mitch as if to say: "You know the answer to what you ask. Everybody knows."

And Mitch accepted this, as sometimes a man laughs lamely, pretending to see the point of a joke which he does not truly understand, but which everyone else seems to find obvious. "Emil," he said, "I think I can get you through this. You may have to stand another operation."

"Anything you say is okay with me, Doc."

"I have to make an examination. This is going to hurt." Mitch called the nurse to help insert the cystoscope. "Hey, I was hoping it wouldn't be you," Emil said to the young nurse. And to Mitch: "I'm figuring on taking her out, soon as I get better, and I want there to be some surprises left." Then, flushing, he added: " 'Scuse the kidding, nurse, you know, a guy in a hospital thinks he has to kid the nurses." The girl had tears in her eyes.

Part way in, the tube was blocked. Certainly there was a tear or obstruction in the ureter. "You'll have to insist you want me to take you out of here," Mitch told Emil. "The old doc may make a fuss. But he left you leaking the first time and I'd rather have my own team work on you."

"Anything you say, Doc." Then, wetting his lips, Emil added: "Doc, it sure is screwy in this world."

"Yah," Mitch said.

"First they try to knock you off and then they try every damn thing they know to keep you alive."

"They're two different sides," Mitch said. "Like in a war, one trying to kill you, the other trying to save you."

"I dunno about that," Emil said. "The way it looks sometimes, it's all the same people, only they play with two sets of rules."

Mitch Wilner was beginning to catch the fevered man's idea. It was the same confusing thought he had had a moment ago, about the taboo on helping a doomed man die. There was a kind of double image on the page of human ethics that dealt with life and death; society had a double standard for the value of human life. In medical ethics of course life stood as the one virtue; there was no comparable value. All science, all knowledge, all effort, was at the service of a single moment of human life; if a seventy-five-year-old cancer-ridden woman can be given an extra two weeks of life by an operation, try it, an extra three minutes by an injection, do it, you must do it, for beside the least spark of human life there is no comparable value.

And then they stand them up and shoot them down.

But the joke was on the doctors. No, it might be that other doctors, most doctors knew, and that only he was such a romantic fool; perhaps the callousness of a man like Whalen was excusable, was indeed a virtue, for such a man lived in the real world, and treated medicine as a part of the real world, accepting the worldly instead of the medical standard of value on human life, leaving such fools as Wilner to walk in the Galahad illusion.

Sure, there has to come a time when you realize how the world is. He guessed he had retained his virginity longer than most.

So when he told Dr. Whalen he was taking Emil to Memorial, Mitch Wilner understood the cold, almost amused sneer in

[181]

Whalen's voice: "Sure, he's your patient, take him wherever you want." And the calculation behind the sneer: that fellow'd die anyway today or tomorrow, why add another fatality to the hospital record?

Mitch phoned for an ambulance with a transfusion crew in case there was an emergency en route.

When they came for Emil, Gus Lindstrom was in the final coma. Pauline moved from beside her husband, to make way as they rolled Emil out. Touching his hand, she said: "You'll be all right, Emil. You'll make it."

Siegal had come along with the crew. Sitting in the ambulance, Mitch kept the blood-pressure cuff on Emil, all the way; it was a half-hour ride with the siren going. The idea that had begun in Mitch Wilner's mind kept developing, and he felt himself reaching for a new understanding of his relationship to the living world. Once, young Siegal remarked to him: "I was talking to Dr. Waldauer. He had a funny job during the war." Of course Dr. Waldauer had been a German then. "Took care of wounded prisoners. Said he gave them good medical care." Mitch nodded. Neither took his eyes off Emil. So Morey Siegal was wondering about the double standard, too.

They went straight up to the operating-room. Dr. Waldauer, the German refugee surgeon, and Dr. Lewin were already scrubbed up. But Emil looked all right so they waited for Siegal to scrub; he wanted the job, Mitch could tell, to make up for his loss on Gus Lindstrom.

They went into Emil and found, as he had suspected, a severed ureter. Siegal made a quick repair and gave Emil another transfusion as soon as the operation was completed. He was holding up well. Mitch went out with that rare elation a doctor has when he knows for certain that, but for his intervention, a case would have been lost. Of course Emil might still die.

He phoned the 117th Street. It was all over with Gus.

[1 8 2]

As he sat by Emil, a call came from Carl Gaul, at the jail hospital, about the elder Lindstrom. "We can get the old man released," he said. "But, Mitch, maybe you had better come up here first and look at him." Mitch explained he couldn't leave at the moment. "Where is he hurt?"

"The eyes," Carl said. "One eye is out, and he can't see with the other. He's terribly weak. Can't hold any food."

"Better bring him here." Mitch ordered an ambulance.

It was a great-ribbed hulk of a man that they brought from the jail hospital. In the face, though half-masked by bandages, the resemblance to young Gus was instantly identified. Mrs. Lindstrom had come with him, in the ambulance.

Carl was bitter about the jail hospital. Two days Lindstrom had lain there, with his eye untreated!

Mitch called in Dr. Keisler, the optical surgeon. The left eye had been smashed with a club or something blunt; there was no gunshot wound. The eye was destroyed and would have to be removed at once. Infection had reached the sympathetic nerve; saving vision in the right eye was questionable, now.

But he would try.

"Do they know about their son?" Mitch asked Carl.

Mrs. Lindstrom came toward them, seeming to sense their discussion. "I know," she told Mitch. She touched his hand. "You did all you could for him, Doctor. Thank you." She looked toward her husband. "He knows too. I figured, if he was going to die, he ought to know before he died." She had the strange fortitude he had seen sometimes in people who come to an emotional region above grief. "Will my man be blinded?" she asked. "If he lives?"

He explained that Dr. Keisler hoped to save vision in the remaining eye.

"I pray to God," she said.

It was late, and there were still a few serious cases, scattered among the South Side hospitals, that he wanted to check up on. That embolism case was in a crisis; probably amputation could no longer be avoided. Such a young kid, too, a messenger boy, his father an unemployed steelworker on relief. And there was another case just released from jail, someone named Donovan, removed to the Sisters of Grace hospital; Gaul said the man was paralyzed. The jail hospital was evidently releasing people in danger of death, to avoid more fatalities on its record.

He'd never get home for dinner. Then he might as well eat at the hospital, Sylvia said. That divinity student had been phoning all afternoon, wanting him to come to some kind of emergency citizens' protest meeting, at the Stevens Hotel. She'd put the kids to bed and meet him downtown. "Did you hear, they arrested Frank Sobol, the organizer! Barbara phoned me. She's afraid they'll pick up Carl too, and all the organizers. But so far I guess they're only arresting the Communists."

The meeting was already in progress when Mitch and Sylvia entered. About forty people were present. Young Arthur Main was at the door; at the front table, Mitch saw that newspaperman, George Price, and he recognized the liberal Dr. Ladd, whom he had heard speak at a Spanish Loyalist meeting. He saw Sam Eisen.

Barbara Macey wanted them to come up front. "Where's Carl?" Sylvia asked. "They didn't pick him up?"

"No. He didn't come because they want this to be a straight citizens' committee without anyone on it from the C.I.O. It's more effective that way." She began whispering the names of people who had come: "Really a wonderful turnout, on such short notice"; there were representatives from Hull House, and Chicago Commons, from the Lawyers Guild, the student union, the social workers' union, and the teachers' union and the American League against War and Fascism and some youth groups,

[1 8 4]

"and of course the comrades are here but it looks like they are going to take a back seat," she said.

A stubby, elderly woman with a mannish voice was speaking heatedly. "We don't want this to be just another one of those radical protest committees that do nothing but protest," she roared. "We want to rouse the whole city. Six people shot dead in cold blood——"

"Seven," Mitch couldn't help saying, under his breath. But somehow his voice carried: all turned to look at him, a whisper of who he was spread through the room. The speaker lowered her voice. "Is it seven now?" Mitch reported Gus Lindstrom's death. And somehow, to report to this roomful of strangers, strangers to himself and to Lindstrom, was like telling a death to a family. Mitch felt the glimmering of a city no longer cold, of people caring for each other, of people concerned. Or was this again only a group of professional protesters, the sort who could be rounded up in an afternoon?

"She's okay," Barbara was commenting on the speaker. "She's in the teachers' union. Hattie Miller, she ran on the Socialist ticket once."

A bitter-looking man who said he represented the I.W.O. made a long speech with rhetorical excoriation of the murderers in uniform and references to the Haymarket martyrs. Mitch was struck with the thought that he didn't actually know what had happened in the Haymarket; it was one of those symbols he had always accepted, like the Boston tea party.

A man with a Jewish accent got the floor and said talk was all right but let's have some action. He repeated this for several minutes. Sam Eisen suggested that there be a monster picket parade around the mayor's office.

A young woman got up and said what was the use of setting up a new organization, why not use the I.L.D.?

Dr. Ladd, a handsome and ambitious-looking figure, suavely

[185]

explained that, while the International Labor Defense and the Civil Liberties were doing effective jobs, a new committee could draw into this movement groups of citizens who, even though unjustly, had formed prejudices against some existing organizations.

A mass meeting was decided upon. John L. Lewis should be asked to speak. Or Mayor La Guardia. But, no, the mayor of New York couldn't slap the mayor of Chicago like that. Hattie Miller thought La Guardia might be just the guy to do it. Then they went down the list, Senator Gottschalk, Governor Murphy, Governor Olson. And the Gottschalk committee should be called upon to investigate the massacre.

George Price arose to remark that the room rental was eight dollars. The hat was passed and Mitch put in fifty cents.

Committees were being formed. Be sure to put on a Negro; try to get a rabbi, Rabbi Brucker, he endorsed the Scottsboro committee; and can't we get a Catholic priest, well, there is that Father Gillie who spoke at a Newspaper Guild meeting; and the names all began to sound familiar.

Suddenly the meeting was over and little groups were conferring.

They found themselves in a drugstore with George Price and Barbara Macey; Carl had appeared and wanted details of the event.

Mitch went and phoned the hospital. Emil was doing all right. This made him almost cheerful. He returned to the table. Listening to them plan the mass meeting, he felt an insider, almost a plotter.

The main danger, George Price said, was that it would be just another blow-off, with people calling the mayor names, calling Captain Wiley a murderer, and then going home feeling the job was over. But he wanted to make the people of Chicago actually feel they were out there on the field watching the cops turn the guns on the crowd. Maybe that would stir them up enough to find out why.

"What about that movie, that newsreel, can't we show that?" Barbara asked.

"Everyone will have seen it by then," Carl said.

"No. Don't kid yourself. If that reel shows anything, you won't see it in the Chicago theaters, or anywhere," Price predicted. "Maybe they'll flash a few feet of it. But if we can get the whole thing and run it—in slow motion—" He snapped his fingers. "One of the Hearst photogs works for Paramount now, maybe I can get hold of a complete print."

Price turned to Mitch. "Another thing. We ought to have a medical report. See what I mean? Cold. Telling where the bullets entered. They were nearly all shot from the back, weren't they?" He cocked his eyes, apparently ready to discard the idea if the wounds were not in the back.

"I think it would show that they were," Mitch said.

George Price would do the whole job, obviously, it would be on his shoulders. And Mitch wondered what made the fellow so excited, almost elated. Perhaps the feeling of power, of stirring the city. Price was not a Communist, evidently, as he had made several knowing though not unfriendly cracks about the comrades.

Driving home, Sylvia said: "Well, look what it means for that little paper of his. He's going to get this committee to pay for printing hundreds of thousands."

"Oh, I don't think he'll try to make any money off this."

"No, I wasn't suggesting that," she hastily agreed. "But even so, think of what the publicity is worth to him, for his paper."

"I don't believe that's occurred to him, or at least he doesn't calculate on that," Mitch said. "I guess he really feels het up

[187]

about what happened. Maybe a lot of people do. And after working on a Hearst paper so long he must feel he has an awful lot to make up for."

The mass meeting had been called for the following Monday. But who would come? Who would even know about the meeting? As the week wore on it seemed to Mitch that the thing would be a complete fizzle. For although George Price showed fat sheafs of publicity and news stories he had sent to the newspapers, not a line appeared, except for a few paragraphs in the *Daily Times*, the only New Deal paper in town.

And the committee seemed to Mitch to be in touch only with the standard radical and semi-radical organizations. Every day it seemed to him more important that this thing reach into the city, into the average population of the city; yet he was sure the bulk of the population had completely dismissed the shootings from their minds. For instance, say even at the hospital where there should be some special interest because of his connection with the affair and the presence of a few patients injured in the affair, was there any further thought about the matter? Take the average of nurses, orderlies, or even the patients, was the event on their minds, did they wonder how it was that their police would shoot down those people?

On Tuesday, the papers announced that the newsreel company had shelved the film that had been made of the "riot" because it was of such a nature that it might cause disorder in theaters if shown.

Yes, if you brought up the subject, people made wise, even bitter comment. "That movie must show the cops up pretty bad." Or another type of person would make knowing allusions to "somebody getting paid off." But that was all. That cleaned their minds of resentment. Just so they felt they were in on the know.

Wednesday, the *Clarion* carried photographs taken inside the

[188]

Consolidated plant, to prove that all was peaceful and that steel was being made in spite of the strike. The pictures showed rows of cots where men slept, showed men cutely doing their own washing, men shaving each other. "Those fellows have their nerve to let themselves be photographed," Mitch commented to Sylvia. "I should think they'd get their necks broken, after the strike."

The committee met again that day. The tiny office they had taken, next door to the Civil Liberties, was jammed. Professor Ladd presided informally, perched on a desk. George Price sat on a huge stack of the manifestoes calling the public to the meeting.

It was a little frightening to Mitch to see his name at the bottom of the eye-witness statement, among those few other names. Yet the committee members were reading out the call to the people, quoting the words approvingly, and over his fear he felt pride; for it was all true, and he was among the few who had taken it upon themselves to attest.

But how were these stacks to be effectively distributed, in so short a time? Hattie Miller, the firebrand teacher, said she could get rid of a few hundred. The Civil Liberties could mail out a few thousand. Arthur Main said he would get a group of students to stand in front of churches on Sunday and pass out the manifestoes. But the big unions would have to be the main outlet. The big C.I.O. unions, the garment workers' unions, could be counted on. And someone would have to go to the A. F. of L. council meeting on Sunday and try to prevail upon Adam Ryan to give the protest meeting A. F. of L. support.

Still, it seemed to Mitch they weren't reaching the people; the everyday people, who were they? What organizations could reach them? Masons, Odd Fellows, Knights of Columbus, women's clubs—couldn't you get anywhere through them?

A Mrs. Reese, who, Carl Gaul whispered to Mitch, was a society woman who used to give money to the Communists, but was off of them lately, said she would contact the women's clubs and could perhaps dispose of a few hundred leaflets. Mrs. Lally, his patient who had become active on the committee, asked—what about radio publicity?

"Well, we tried to buy time," the Civil Liberties secretary reported.

You mean you were refused!

Yes. All the stations had refused.

"What about WCFL, doesn't it belong to the Federation of Labor?" Mrs. Reese asked.

"It does. That's just the trouble," Hattie Miller responded. "Somebody ought to club some sense into Adam Ryan's head."

At that point, Marcus Olden, the Lawyers Guild representative, hurried in excitedly. "I've just heard from the Auditorium," he announced. "They've withdrawn the hall!"

The radical members of the committee took the news as a matter of course, beginning at once to debate the merits of various halls. The others meanwhile talked about "bringing pressure," about suing the Auditorium.

"But what reason did they give?" Dr. Ladd asked.

"Strobel just phoned me and said he'd forgotten that repairs were starting this week, and the seats will be out."

The laughter was uneasy.

Finally Mrs. Reese was delegated to rush right over and put a deposit on Insull's Opera House. The price was two hundred dollars higher than the Auditorium.

"Did you tell them what we wanted it for?" Dr. Ladd asked when she returned.

"Oh, yes. The manager said he didn't give a damn if all the reds on the continent met there, so long as we paid the rent. They're so much in debt."

As the meeting broke up, the various committee members

took handfuls of leaflets; the gloomy Communist from the I.W.O. lifted about a third of the pile, and the I.L.D. girl took a stack several inches high. Yes, Mitch thought, after all they were probably the ones you had to rely on when there was work to be done in a hurry. But still, wouldn't they reach the same old crowd?

Sylvia had arranged for them to go to Mort's that evening. "But, Syl," he protested, "I'm way behind. I've missed two clinics, and the research is going to hell——"

"You haven't any clinics tonight; and, darling, you simply have to take an evening off and relax. Besides, Ora is having fits, phoning every day, and after all the family is kind of entitled to know what you did out there. I told Ora we'd be over tonight, but of course if you're tired we don't have to go."

As Ora opened the door, Mitch heard a large booming voice in the apartment, and saw her father, Captain Rosen, parked on the sofa.

"Take your coat off, Mitch, and make yourself comfortable," Ora said. Mort and his father-in-law were coatless and had loosened their neckties.

"The hero of the occasion," Mort greeted him. "Will you break down and have a drink for once?"

"It's good wine," Ora said. "Syl, you're a swell one. Why didn't you tell us where you were going Sunday?"

"1921, that was a good vintage year," Mort declared. He had become quite a wine connoisseur lately, collecting books on the subject.

"Just wait, he'll have the gout yet," Ora merrily kidded him.

"I can't tell one wine from another," Rosen said. "Except dago red and Passover wine, I can tell the difference."

"Or would you rather have a Tom Collins?" Ora suggested. "Or beer? We've got it in cans."

"I'll settle for a beer," Mitch said, catching Sylvia's placating glance, telling him she had had no idea Rosen would be present.

"Well, Mitch, how are all your new patients?" Mort asked, smirking.

Mitch told them there was a chance at least one more would die, an old Irishman who had been held in the jail hospital.

Captain Rosen shook his head and finished his wine. "Too bad." He hauled himself to his feet. "Well, kids, I've got to go."

Mitch felt relieved but puzzled. He had been sure Ora had intentionally arranged for her father to meet him this way.

"But, Pop, don't you want to hear the eye-witness account?" Ora said. "And, Syl, next time you know of any excitement you better count me in on it."

"Nobody expected any excitement," Sylvia said.

"Don't be naïve," Mort laughed. "Everything was planned. They all knew what was going to happen." He appealed to his father-in-law for corroboration.

"You've been reading the *Clarion*," Sylvia said scornfully.

"Sure. This is one time the *Clarion* has the dope," Mort said. And, turning to Rosen: "Am I right, or am I right?"

Rosen yawningly struggled into his coat. "They don't slip much past us," he said.

"Good old Ogpu," his daughter said, pulling his coat straight.

"Why, they even asked about you," Mort announced, looking directly at Mitch.

"What?" Sylvia's voice sounded unnatural. She lowered it. "Who asked what?"

Ora reproached Mort. "Oh, darling, you didn't have to bring that up. It was nothing, just routine."

So that was why the evening had been arranged. Mitch was surprised to find himself almost amused, instead of angry.

"He might as well know what's going on," Mort declared, "if he wants to play with the Bolsheviki."

"Who asked about Mitch? What did they want to know?" Sylvia insisted, confronting Rosen.

"Oh, they just gave me a call; I said he was okay, that's all there was to it," Rosen said.

Sylvia looked frightened.

"What is this, Russia?" Mitch asked.

Mort, smirking, coddled his wine.

"What is this all about? What are they trying to do to us?" Sylvia demanded of Ora. "It's too serious a matter to play games with. Mitch's whole future may depend on it."

"Oh, I wouldn't be so alarmed, Syl," Ora said quite sympathetically, though obviously enjoying herself. "All that happened was, naturally, the detective bureau got hold of a copy of that leaflet Mitch signed——"

"He wasn't the only one that signed it. A U. of C. professor—though maybe it was foolhardy——"

"Naturally, they checked up on everyone that signed it. You know: who they were, and whether they were Communists, or what."

Mitch said angrily: "I suppose it was the Communists that shot down those men."

"You don't know what you're playing with," Mort admonished, with that elderly, almost fatherly air he could use when, say, business matters were being discussed.

"Plenty of comrades were mixed up in that trouble," Rosen said. "If two of them were killed, you can figure they had plenty of them there."

"Two? I thought it was only one," Ora said. "He had a German name."

"Baumann," Mitch remembered. "Okay, he was a dangerous red—he was out there selling copies of the *Daily Worker*."

Mort picked up a newspaper and showed them the latest listing of the dead. Gus Lindstrom was now listed, Mitch noticed,

[193]

under the heading, "Seventh Rioter Dies." And down the list he came upon the name: "Dombrowsky, Stanley, Communist, not properly identified as yet."

The name echoed in Mitch Wilner's mind. On the field, as he was placing the stone under the tourniquet, to shut off the bleeding artery: "Dombrowsky, Stanley Dombrowsky, me." Now he read: "Dombrowsky, Stanley, Communist, not properly identified as yet." Mitch turned on Captain Rosen. "How the hell do they know he is a Communist if he isn't even properly identified?"

"If his name ends in *owsky* he must be a Communist," Ora quipped.

"I suppose the cops knew he was a Communist when they pulled him out of the first-aid car and ripped off his tourniquet!" Mitch exclaimed. "He might be a Communist, so let him bleed to death!"

"That's too bad about that case," Rosen said sincerely. "But, you know, in a situation like that, where everybody is excited, accidents will happen."

"What I want to know," Mitch persisted, "is how you can list him as a Communist when he isn't even properly identified. I just don't understand it."

"Well, you know how it is," Rosen said. "Maybe they got a card on file for a Dombrowsky, or they got it listed somewhere that a Dombrowsky signed a party card. So naturally this might be the one."

"What file? What list?" Mitch asked.

Mort regarded him with astonishment at his innocence. "The red squad file."

"I suppose they've got a card for Mitch too, now!" Sylvia snapped.

"Oh, no," Rosen said. "Naw, I told them there was nothing to it, as far as Dr. Wilner was concerned."

[1 9 4]

"What about those other names on that circular Mitch signed?" Mort asked, eying his brother-in-law with satisfaction.

"Well, this professor up at the university, this Rawley, he might be a member of the Communist Party and I think one of those university kids that signed belongs to the Communist Youth——"

"A Y.C.L.er," Ora said.

"But in the main they are just innocent people, like Mitch here. Good-hearted people that are sincere."

"Only they don't know what's what," Mort said.

"Do you mean, if anyone signs a Communist membership card, the red squad knows it?" Sylvia asked.

"Well, they got a pretty good idea."

"What have you got, spies in the organization?" Mort inquired eagerly.

"Well, somebody has to keep track of those activities. They had a lot of old-time reds mixed up in that union. That Frank Sobol, he's been to Moscow for training and come back, his name is Soboloff, we got a record of him when he was running that Communist steelworkers' union back in 1934, and then they disbanded and all went into the C.I.O."

Mitch was watching and listening with all his power; the first antipathy for Ora's father was gone, and he was objective now, for here was the one policeman whom he knew and could talk to without strangeness, and perhaps through him he could come to understand the behavior of the men who had fired the bullets out there. Though Rosen was not a typical sample, being Jewish, an unusual thing for a police officer.

"Why are the police so suspicious of union organizers?" he asked. "Even being a Communist isn't actually against the law, is it?"

"No, but it might be some day," Rosen replied. "Me, I don't give a damn about it, let them be Communists, the hell; only the red squad calls me in a lot because I'm a Hebe, I guess." He lowered his voice. "And I'll tell you—a lot of our yiddles in my district"—he frowned—"that radical stuff don't do us any good. They blame all the Jews for being Communists anyway. So do we have to give them an excuse?" He accepted a can of beer, sat down again. Oddly, the atmosphere had become relaxed, homey.

"I heard someone real high up in the Communist organization was on the red squad payroll," Ora said. "Is that where they get the membership list?"

"Na, once in a while somebody comes and wants to sell the department a bunch of names, or they even want to give them to you, screwballs, but you don't need any of that," Rosen said. "The professional Communists, anybody can get to know them, they work in the open, even if they don't admit their membership, like this Frank Sobol, and a lot of the members, you just cover their lectures and rallies and junk and you see the same faces all the time."

"You mean Communist meetings?" Ora asked.

"Yah, and that American League, and the Spanish war meetings," he half yawned.

"But we've been at some of the Medical Bureau meetings for the Spanish Loyalists," Sylvia said.

"Sure, a lot of innocent people go to them, but if a fellow follows them he gets to know the steady customers."

"But suppose I went to a million meetings. That doesn't make me a Communist member," Mitch said.

"What's the difference if they're signed up or not?" Rosen asked. "To all intents and purposes they're active like Communists."

"I see," Mitch said.

"And a lot of the signed-up members, they put their names in the *Daily Worker* in subscription drives and that stuff. They ain't very smart."

"Then you mean," Mitch said, "if the police can prove some of those people out there on the Fourth were Communists, then it was all right to shoot them?"

"The public will think so," Mort said.

Mitch addressed himself to Rosen. "Look, to satisfy my own mind, what is the feeling among the police about this thing?"

"Well, naturally," Rosen said, "the cops are just as sorry as anyone else, the way it happened. They're just guys like anyone else, they ain't killers. And it makes a stink, you know, it ain't good for the administration."

"If someone else had been there, instead of Captain Wiley," Mitch said, "would it have happened the same way?"

Rosen reflected. "Every officer is different," he said, "still you can't blame so much on him. They had men there from every station in the city. A couple of my men were there."

"Did he actually give the order to fire?" Mitch asked.

"I don't know about that. In a situation of that kind you don't have to give an order to fire."

"Somebody must have collected himself a nice bunch of bucks from Consolidated," Mort surmised.

Rosen shook his head. "Wiley is a pretty honest copper, he never got rich."

"You mean nobody got paid for giving Otis Speer all that protection?" Mort sneered. "Don't tell me. When we had that little strike I had to schmier them every day, cost me over a hundred bucks a day."

"Well, sure, maybe the boys got a little change," Rosen said, talking more carefully. "But that don't mean they acted any different than if they'd got no dough at all. And if there was any big money, maybe somebody might have got some, not Wiley. I'll tell you, in the first place, after a thing like that, a man couldn't take a payoff, it would be like being paid for killing people."

He was talking, Mitch realized, like one outside the department now, as one who didn't know any more than they did, and could only conjecture.

"Suppose you were in charge out there," he put it to Rosen directly. "Would you have handled it any differently? Could the shootings have been avoided?"

"I'll tell you." Rosen finished his beer, his head tilted way back, then carefully set the can on the floor. "I don't like to talk about things if and for instance. I don't know what I would have done. I wasn't there." He rose.

Mitch felt as he did when hunting for some clue in a blood sample under a microscope: Can't see anything on that slide. Try another. But suppose that Dombrowsky were really a Communist? Suppose two out of seven—suppose they all were Communists! How could the police know, when they fired?

4. A DANGEROUS RED

FROM childhood, Hermann Baumann had the habit of using the back door to the house, always going in through the kitchen, for in Cologne, where his father's bicycle repair shop was on the end of their lot, he was always running back to the shop— maybe Father would let him hold the wheel he was repairing —then running into the kitchen for a thick piece of warm bread, with butter and sugar on it. His mother used to laugh and say that he would be a stupid child, for he was such a big eater; but Hermann was clever enough with his hands.

He did not grow tall; he was broad-boned, and in his early teens was buttery-fleshed, having an almost girlish appearance.

His father went to war in 1915, when Hermann, the oldest child, was fifteen. During the next year the boy was always embarrassed, for though he ate no more than the others his fat faded slowly; he was like a plant that persists green, while those all around shrivel in the dust of drought. But finally he became yellow-skinned and empty as a punctured bag; early in 1917, when Herr Baumann returned from the front with a wounded lung, he did not recognize his eldest son in the sunken-eyed youth working in the shop.

Then it became a matter of waiting to see whether the war would end before Hermann had to go into it; that same fall he left for training.

Hermann knew from his father what the war would be like; and through all the years of exhortation against the bestial enemy, who employed Negro savages to slaughter German Christians, he had nevertheless retained his horror-fright at having to kill.

Mostly, young Baumann contrived to sit huddled in a dugout, or to crouch well down below the trench parapet, scarcely aiming. Early in 1918, when it was learned that Americans had come in opposite his company, cold ferocious fighters, with Negroes among them, he allowed himself to be taken prisoner.

A guard named Nick Koscienko, from a city named Detroit, where automobiles were made, warmed to him, and even gave him an occasional cigarette. "Hey, why don't you come to America when the war's over?" Koscienko suggested. "Come to Detroit and look me up." In Detroit, Nick said, he could earn big money as an automobile mechanic, he could own his own automobile.

Hermann could not always tell when the Americans were joking, "kidding" as they called it, but he was sure it was kidding that he could have his own auto. "Honest to Christ," Nick insisted, and showed him a photograph of himself and a girl in a car. "Some baby, huh?" Nick demanded. "It's a Dodge. When I get back I'm gonna get me a Studebaker. That's a bigger car."

After the war, there was nothing to do in Cologne. Everybody talked politics. His young brother was a Communist; Hermann too voted Communist in the elections. As his brother said: Why wait? He enrolled in the party.

The following year he went to Hamburg and found a job on a ship, as second carpenter. In 1923 Baumann was a carpenter on a vessel named the *Wilhelmina*, going to Boston. A shipmate offered to get him two dollars if he would carry some bottles of whisky off the boat; also, the shipmate said, he would take him to a place where there were Negro girls. Hermann Baumann had no desire for a Negro girl; a real American girl like in the movies, that would be wonderful. Viereck thrust some bottles at him just as they reached the plank and he had to slip them under his coat; later Viereck gave him two dollars, laughing, so that Hermann felt Viereck had made more money for himself.

He spent the evening in a movie, and roaming about the streets. The American girls were pretty.

Viereck said: "If you want to jump ship, they'll never find you. Once I spent a year in America, went everywhere, New York, San Francisco, nobody bothered me or even asked where

I came from. When I got sick of it I took ship again. You have to work, even in America."

But Hermann Baumann said, if a man wanted to make a country his home, he should come in legally. Several trips later, he entered as an immigrant.

On a map, he saw that Detroit was far; and when he wandered about the city, among its anonymous millions, he felt the folly of that address of the prison camp guard, which he in boyish faith had kept by him all these years. Now he tore it up.

In 1926 Hermann Baumann was earning an average of thirty-five dollars a week as a machinist in a Detroit wheel factory, and of this he saved fifteen. Whenever there was a birthday or a holiday back home, he sent twenty-five dollars; but it hurt their pride to have him send money regularly. His landlady was always joking that he should get married; but Hermann could not overcome his fear of American girls; they wanted a man to say clever things, such as "the cat's pajamas"; even if he were completely at ease with his English, he would not be able to think of such remarks. And sometimes the boys at the plant would take him along on drunken parties where the girls would get sick with gin and vomit; or else they would embrace their boys, in the midst of company, kissing with their tongues and allowing the men to handle their breasts and thighs. He also tried this, but when the final moment came, the girls would awaken as from stupor, and become offended, and fight away, clawing like cats.

That year Hermann Baumann's mother wrote to him of a girl from Cologne who was now a housemaid in Chicago, as if Chicago were within bicycling distance of a Sunday.

[201]

He wrote to the girl; she replied with a very long letter telling him comical things about her employers; how the mistress spent three dollars a week on special food for her dog, and other crazy things. That summer he drove his second-hand Essex to Chicago.

"As I am the maid," she had written, "you must come up the back stairs." This made Hermann feel at ease at once. Marie Lichtenstein was not a beautiful girl, but she looked all fresh and smelled like new-made rolls in a German bakery, the firm, lightly browned round buns. He did not have to think of clever things to say, because she did all the talking.

The day he was to return to Detroit, Baumann looked at the ads in the *Zeitung*, and saw that lathe-hands were wanted in a furniture factory. The thoughts of a clean lathe and the smell of wood-shavings, the hum of the lathe instead of the clang of the wheel factory, were good to him. The job paid only thirty dollars to start with, but he stayed.

Hermann and Marie were married that summer; and by 1930 they had three babies: George, and Hermina, and Gerda. Hermann had grown fat again, and his cheeks were violently rosy. Though a bald patch was forming on his crown, he looked quite boyish when he wore a hat; he looked like a fat boy of twenty-four. Marie had grown creamy with weight, but she carried her flesh well; there was no blanket thickness on her as around Hermann. Often she folded his loose stomach flesh in her hand and threatened to melt it down like bacon. The child, George, had a game of butting his head into his father's belly.

Baumann was then averaging over forty dollars weekly; they had saved five hundred dollars and invested it as down payment on a two-flat house on Newberry Avenue; in twelve years, by making payments slightly larger than rent, they would own the house. Coming home, Hermann always went up the back stairs because that way he could tell at once what there was for supper; besides, the baby was sometimes asleep in the parlor.

They had a little dog, and Marie, with the American ways she had learned while a housemaid, actually bought cans of dogfood for him; she defended herself, saying this was really more economical as they had no food to throw away. It was strange how, even though she was in the country less time than himself, it was she who made the feeling that they were Americans and theirs was an American home, where people fed dogs out of special cans, instead of leftovers from the table.

Once in the fall of 1932, when Hermann came up the back stairs, he saw a strange man sitting at the kitchen table, eating; the man was middle-aged, with a small head and thin, mottled onionlike skin; he wore a suit not yet threadbare. Hermann had seen such pinch-faced types around Boston, more than around Chicago. Marie, with her eyes, told him the man had asked for food; and suddenly Hermann felt acutely ashamed of being the one to give food to this respectable American. He noticed that Marie had given the man only some sausage and bread, while a large meal was on the stove. He felt ashamed of this, too.

The stranger explained that he was an accountant by profession, a bookkeeper that meant, and, having lost his job in Indianapolis, he had come to Chicago to seek a position.

"It's a shame," they said to each other, when the stranger had retreated down the stairs, refusing to go out the front way.

[203]

"There are lots more people coming to the kitchen door now," Marie explained.

The little bookkeeper from Indianapolis, Wilson was his name, appeared several times that fall. He would wait a few weeks between visits, as though fearful of wearing out his welcome. As it grew cold, Marie gave him Hermann's old coat; it engulfed him, making him look more shrunken and lost than ever.

One time Mr. Wilson came in the evening when Marie had gone to a movie with neighbors, leaving Hermann to mind the children. It was nearly nine o'clock when the kitchen doorbell rang, and Hermann, awakened out of a doze, opened it to find Mr. Wilson, whose haggard face, in the yellowish electric light, struck him suddenly with panic. The little man seemed unable to speak; for one instant Hermann suspected he was drunk. At that time, layoffs had begun in the furniture factory, and the sight of Mr. Wilson awakened all Hermann's fears.

"Sit here, I will get you something to eat," he said hastily, and Mr. Wilson, still strangely speechless, shuffled to a chair. It happened that a grocery order had been delivered and not yet unpacked; there was an entire carton filled with cans of dog-food which Marie had bought at a bargain.

Baumann found a cold chop and potatoes, which he offered to warm; but Mr. Wilson wolfed them down as they were, and refused to let him trouble to make coffee. He too seemed to feel the horrible embarrassment of the absence of the woman. He spoke only once; when Hermann asked whether he still stayed at the municipal free lodging. "I left the lodging," he said.

Hermann asked: "Where are you sleeping?"

"Last night I slept in a hallway."

That week, Hermann Baumann was cut down to twenty hours of work. The furniture manufacturer was trying to keep all the married men on the payroll.

One night a noise awakened Baumann; worry-ridden as he was, he awoke in dark shock, crying out. Marie was also awake. "My, you are nervous." She touched his arm. "It's the kitchen doorbell." Hermann looked at his watch. Just after twelve. Both at the same moment knew it was Mr. Wilson at the door.

Hermann Baumann waded through the dark to the kitchen door; he didn't want to startle himself with the light; this way the horror was in a dream. Through the glass of the storm-door he could make out Mr. Wilson's shrunken form; he was not wearing the overcoat. In the bitter moonlight, snow-reflected, Baumann saw that ghostly face. "What do you want?" He feared the man was crazed, and only partly opened the door, though hating himself for his hesitation.

"I want—I just want to ask you one thing——"

"Listen, Mr. Wilson, are you hungry? Wait, I will find something——"

"One thing. Just give me one of those cans. One of those cans I saw you had for the dog."

"No, Mr. Wilson, don't say that!" Baumann pulled open the door, but Mr. Wilson refused to enter; he simply stood there repeating: "One of those cans. That's all I ask. Just give me . . ." Baumann ran to the pantry, found the carton, and, still in the darkness, took out one of the cans. When he got back to the door, Mr. Wilson was slumped there, sitting in the doorway.

"Are you sick?" Baumann cried. Mr. Wilson seized the can and half crawled, half scuttled down the stairs. Baumann stumbled back to his bed. He lay weeping, his wife for a long time stroking his back.

By 1933, Baumann was worried by the succession of letters, each more terse and formal, in regard to his arrears on the house. He had already borrowed on his insurance. Marie even went to her former employers to try to get a loan.

All that time, Baumann was reading in the *Zeitung* about events in Germany. Sometimes he wished he were there, because in the coming crisis every arm might count. He did not understand this Hitler movement but he felt now was the time for a Communist government to take power. He wrote to his brother. In return he received a strange, vague letter. "For what you say, it is too late, and I beg you do not write to me of such things any more. I am not interested in such letters." Hermann was puzzled. "How can he be uninterested? Martin could always talk all night about politics."

"Perhaps he is afraid the letters are being opened," Marie said.

In those days there was little with which Hermann could occupy himself. To work around improving the house, painting, putting in more electric outlets, required materials that cost money. In the evenings there was nothing to do but talk to people, or listen to the radio. It happened then that the fellow Viereck, once his shipmate, turned up in Chicago, living not far away, on Mozart Street; and as men will who feel no true bond for each other, but a kind of obligation to revive a fancied buddyship of the past, they fell to seeing each other.

Viereck belonged to one of the new German clubs, of the Hitler variety, and he talked much of how Hitler would bring the true socialism to the workingman. He is as we were, a soldier during the war, a worker too, a house-painter. He won't forget us. A few times, Hermann Baumann went with Viereck to the meetings of his club. The members were ordinary fellows from around the neighborhood; they met in a half-basement that Siegfried Scharff had used as a speakeasy until the repeal of prohibition a few months before, when he had opened his tavern upstairs. They bought a keg of beer for each meeting; it came to little.

With the beer-drinking they sang a little, talked; when warmed up, they sang the "Horst Wessel" song; it was funny, about spouting Jewish blood. Hermann Baumann was not crazy about the Jews; Marie's old boss, the Jew-lady, would not even lend her a penny to save their home. Rich pigs. No wonder Jews would not eat pigs—Viereck told the joke—it would be cannibalism.

At one meeting, Viereck arose and said, why dream of what was being done in the Reich over there? Why not get to work and do the same here? Why not bring the awakening and the strengthening force of the Nazi movement to America?

There was applause and yet there was a long argument over this. For some said their work must be only to help the mother country, to send money there, to help sell German goods here, things like that. Others said no, they must bring the new German spirit to the whole world—including America.

At first Baumann thought vaguely this was the same as when he was a Communist, believing Communism would come to all countries; in each the people would rule themselves. But, walking home, Viereck told him: "No, dumbhead. We will rule. We

Germans will rule. God has chosen us! To every country we will bring order and strength. Look how even this rich America is floundering . . ."

After a certain point with Viereck, Hermann never listened to the words, but had a feeling as if he were doing his best to hold onto himself on a rollercoaster that swooped up and down and would whirl him away from himself. Viereck and the others let the words do that to them, he had noticed, at meetings; they became men possessed with this idea of strengthening, strengthening—and he could understand it, almost feel it in himself. For when a man is desperate, when a man feels himself being pressed down, stripped, every day deeper and closer to his barren self, there are moments when a kind of frenzy sweeps his blood and he clenches his fist and all his muscles tighten till they shake, and he can scarcely restrain himself from shouting aloud even if he is alone: No, no, I will not let this happen to me! Life cannot do this to me! I am a man, there is only one way for a man, to be strong! Strong! I will strengthen myself, by my own strength I will lift myself out of this nothingness. . . .

There were such moments. But after them a man looked around and saw he was still alone, without a job, and the printed letter from the finance company threatened to put him out of his house. Then the fever of strengthening collapsed.

But in these meetings, Hermann saw how Viereck and his friends made the fever of strengthening together. And being together they could not let it fall, could not admit it was an empty strength. Perhaps when each was at home alone, the emptiness came, as it came to him.

In 1934 Hermann Baumann ran frantically from one relief agency to another, but everywhere the clerks told him the same story: "You have property, we cannot help you." Not until he was no longer the owner of a house could they give him food.

For some months he had ceased going to the Nazi meetings, because, after that talk about Germany ruling the world, it had all smelled somewhat evil to him; those people were like religious maniacs. But now he even went to Viereck, asking, begging; perhaps the organization knew of some way to save his house.

Let them take this house, then you can go on home relief, Viereck advised him. Let the American government support you. We are not interested in these things here, let it get worse here, then Americans too will see our way is the only way.

"But the house, I will lose everything I put into it—four thousand dollars. I have paid every month, during all these years——"

Viereck snapped: "Now you come to us, when it is something you need. But where have you been these months when the organization needed you? Such comrades we have no use for. Go, go back to your Communists. Oh, I know you well, you are a Communist from the old days, on the boat. I know all about you, and your brother in Cologne."

The expression in Viereck's eyes was such as Hermann Baumann had not seen since wartime, when certain bestialities were committed. He left, remembering that after all he and Viereck had never truly had anything in common.

Another day, when he had gone to the relief office to show his eviction notice, and as he was going down the stairs, slowly, to delay the arrival home, a man began a conversation: "Gave you the runaround, huh?" and finally suggested that he go over to the Unemployed Council. "Maybe they can give you some advice."

The council held meetings in a frame loft on Division Street. A fellow named Mike Burns discussed his troubles with him and said: "I'll bring some friends over when they come to move you out. Don't worry."

On a Thursday morning the eviction was to take place. By nine o'clock Mike Burns and some people had appeared; they sat in the kitchen.

Two men came to move out the furniture, leaving a third in a car. The new friends would not budge from their chairs. The men moved out the loose things, the small tables, things like that. Then together they tried to lift a chair in which a woman sat, spilling her from it. "No, let there be no trouble, let them take everything!" Hermann Baumann cried, but it was no longer as though the cause were his; no one paid any attention to him. Name-calling, scuffling began. In a few moments police came. They arrested Mike Burns and Hermann Baumann and the noisiest woman. The rest of the friends had vanished.

Hermann was in the cell with Mike Burns overnight. It happened often this way, Mike Burns explained. Just now, this was the only tactic. To offer enough resistance to bring the condition to the attention of the people.

In the morning, a harried little lawyer from the I.L.D. put up bail for them and they were released.

Hermann Baumann found his family still in the house. After the police had gone, his wife explained, the friends had reassembled and carried the furniture back. A relief worker had come and said, since the house was no longer theirs, they could be placed on relief, and continue to live in it. The relief office would pay the finance company fifteen dollars a month rent.

"I will join the Communists again," Hermann Baumann said. "This Mike Burns is a Communist." But one thing made him hesitate. To the police, when they were arraigned, Burns had denied he was a member of the Communist Party. "It must be illegal here," Baumann said to his wife.

"No. It is not illegal," Marie said.

And this was something Hermann Baumann could never quite understand. In his unit meetings, he was always suggesting things to which the other comrades responded with whoops of laughter or shivers of fear. If he said: Well, let all the Communists go together to the main relief boss, they would silence him with shudders. If there was a parade against the invasion of Ethiopia, it must not be known as a Communist parade. "But in Germany," he would begin, and they would silence him with laughter.

"In Germany," Mike Burns, the section organizer, explained once when he attended their unit meeting, "you were hundreds of thousands, you had a third of the Reichstag. Here we have not a single Congressman, and if we did have, he could not declare himself openly."

"But the party is legal?" Hermann Baumann persisted. "It is not underground——"

"Yes, but don't you understand, in America . . ."

There was little party work he could do. When there were large meetings he would go and stand on the sidewalk outside the hall and sell *Daily Workers*. Often he went to distribute handbills in the neighborhoods where relief station protests were being called. His unit organizer, Joe Ablin, was eager for him to keep in touch with the Nazi Bund organizations, but this was difficult, as through Viereck he was known as a Communist. However, Baumann sometimes went into Scharff's saloon for a beer, and picked up bits of gossip.

Thus, when the steel strike began the bartender told him: "Your friend Viereck is working these days."

"Yah? Where? Perhaps I can get some work."

"Up there in the Consolidated Steel mills, where they have the strike." The bartender eyed him, teasingly.

"What does he do there?"

"What everyone does. Makes steel. Viereck is a machinist, no?"

At the unit meeting, Thursday, Joe Ablin spoke of the strike, explaining how it was truly a political test, as well as a labor struggle. Volunteers must go out there on the picket line, he said. There should be thousands picketing out there. He was very excited, having toured the strike region only that day. "Two plants are closed up tight; Midwest and Tri-State didn't even try to operate. But the steel bosses are concentrating all their force on Consolidated. Don't think that Big Steel isn't in on this," he said. "They are sitting by and watching, and even helping Otis Speer out by taking care of his rush orders in some of their plants. If he can break the S.W.O.C., the contract Standard Steel made with Lewis will be torn up."

On Saturday, Joe Ablin stopped by the house; he had stacks of handbills in his car, and gave Hermann Baumann a few hundred to distribute in the neighborhood. The handbills advertised a great Fourth of July steelworkers' mass meeting at Guzman's Grove. Hermann agreed to sell *Daily Workers* at the mass meeting, and Joe Ablin arranged to pick him up, early.

Mike Burns was there, too, in the yard, listening to the speakers. When the line of march was forming, Hermann Baumann saw Mike Burns and Joe Ablin talking together; he walked over to them, as he liked to hear what was going on. Joe Ablin turned to him. "Look, Hermann, you too, when the march gets up there near the cops, some of the boys are going to spread out over the tracks." He gestured toward the right. "You go over that way too. We want to spread out the cops. I'll be there."

Hermann nodded. He walked along the line trying to sell his papers. So many comrades had turned up selling literature that he could not get rid of many copies.

Just as Joe Ablin had said, when the column got near the police, it halted; some of the strikers began to spread out to the right, toward the tracks. The police sprinted parallel with them. Hermann walked over the tracks; he had lost sight of Joe, but he was way over, nearly to the boxcars. Between the cars he could see snatches of the high barbed-wire fence. He looked toward the police, and in that moment saw quite sharply the face of a Yank, like all the Yank soldiers he had seen, like the ones that had taken him prisoner, and that taut-muscled war-time look, exactly that look, was on the face of this Yank policeman. Hermann Baumann's heart beat with sudden fear, as in the trench the moment before an expected barrage. The opening gun would sound, and then the chorus of guns.

Looking around for a way of escape, he glimpsed that barbed-

[2 1 3]

wire fence again, and there, standing on a shed or some low building, behind the fence, he saw Viereck. He was certain he saw Viereck, and yet the whole scene was as unreal as the time he had seen Mr. Wilson at the door begging for dogfood. Sharp, and unreal. Viereck was in some kind of uniform pants and shirt, and he was standing together with a big tan-faced American, in army boots and pants, with a pistol belt around his waist. In that moment, Hermann Baumann saw Viereck recognize him and turn to his companion with some remark that pointed him out. Baumann looked back nervously for his column, and saw men waving their arms for the spread-out to return. He nodded as though they could see his obedience; he was going back when a shot sounded behind him, and he felt a punch in the middle of his spine.

MITCH WILNER was the logical person to address the delegates of the A. F. of L., George Price insisted. Every other member of the committee was either ticketed or unimpressive. And there was still time, if the A. F. of L. delegates instructed Adam Ryan to back up the mass meeting, for announcements to be made over the Federation's radio station.

"My God!" Sylvia complained. "Have you got to do everything!" She drove him downtown, leaving the kids sulking at not being taken along, for it was Sunday. He'd have to bring something home for them. "Gosh," Sylvia said, "do you realize this time only last week we were lying on the beach?" He nodded. Such things did not seem strange to him.

George Price met them in front of the musicians' union building, on Randolph. The Loop was deserted. A few men gabbed on the sidewalk. Others came along, entered the building. Two girls whom Mitch recognized, I.L.D. volunteers, were handing out notices of the mass meeting. It made Mitch feel self-conscious that his name was on those circulars.

Carl Gaul and Barbara showed up. "You know who the cops arrested?" Carl waited for effect. "Art Nowis."

"Art?" Mitch repeated. The dude, Emil's friend.

"He's not a comrade, is he?" George Price asked.

Carl stuck out his lower lip. "If he is, it'll be a surprise to me."

"What do they want with him?"

"Well, he's financial secretary of the local."

They were silent for a moment. Price glumly contributed: "Looks like the governor is going to send troops into Canton, so Otis Speer can reopen the plant there."

"Be another Fourth of July," Carl predicted.

"No. That's why they had it here. To scare the guts out of everybody."

"The Ohio boys don't scare so easy," said Carl.

Price reported that he had exhausted his last contact, a big-shot movie company lawyer, in an effort to get the newsreel released for the citizens' meeting. But he had another idea: "Something as good as the movie. Maybe even better." His eyes glittered, mysteriously.

Price and Carl outlined the immediate task for Mitch. He was to request the floor, before the A. F. of L. delegates, in behalf of the citizens' investigating committee. "After all, one of their own members was killed out there. I don't see how they can refuse to come in on this protest," Barbara pointed out.

"Which one was A. F. of L.?" Sylvia wanted to know.

[2 1 5]

"Baumann, the good Communist," Price said, not without his touch of bitter humor. "He was in good standing in the furniture workers' local. The cops found his A. F. of L. card and his party card stuck together in his pocket."

In Mitch Wilner's mind, the question of the second Communist member—"Dombrowsky, Stanley, Communist, not properly identified as yet"—had become almost a testing-point for the truth in the whole issue. Now, half privately, he asked of Carl: "Listen, that other one they said was a Communist, Dombrowsky, what about him?"

"Dombrowsky. Oh, that big Slav they yanked out of Jock's car."

"Sylvia has an in-law, Captain Rosen, who works with the red squad. He claims Dombrowsky was signed up in the party, or someone of that name."

Carl looked wise. "The red squad knows its stuff," he said. And added: "There were plenty of Sobol's boys out there."

"But is there anything for sure, about Dombrowsky?"

"I can't quite place him," Carl said. "Except it seems to me I did see him at one of their fraction meetings. I once walked in by accident, when Sobol was holding a little meeting in headquarters. They tried to throw me out. Imagine excluding a member of the staff from strike headquarters! You had to be a *Daily Worker* correspondent to get into that place! And that's why they get such a bum break in the papers," he went on hotly. "They'd never let the reporters in. Only the *Daily Worker* man. And when I brought it up at a staff meeting, they jumped on me with all that junk about the capitalist press. Sure I know the press is against us, but if we were at least fair to the reporters——"

"Yah, that was a big mistake," George Price agreed, as a newspaperman.

"Still," Barbara said, "the *Daily* is the only paper that gives them a fair story, so why shouldn't they favor the *Worker* reporter?"

"They ought to know—most of the boys covering the strike are Guildsmen," Price said. "Of course we can't do a hell of a lot, once the copy desk gets hold of the story. But we can do something, and there is no sense in antagonizing the boys." He chuckled. "They threw me out, being a Hearst reporter!"

Mitch still wondered about Dombrowsky. Could Carl be sure? He remembered Sam Eisen's advice not to be seen too much with Carl Gaul. Increasingly, he saw himself becoming confused by the partisanships among these people who were supposed to be working together. He sensed how it must be among the strikers themselves, in a struggle in which their very existence was at stake, knowing all the while that amongst themselves, perhaps their very friends beside them, were spies and betrayers. Suspecting everyone, fearing betrayal of every word they uttered.

Going inside, they met the rosy-faced Professor Rawley, whose name had appeared with Mitch Wilner's on the proclamation. Carl drew Rawley aside, on the landing, and explained how Mitch Wilner was to try to address the delegates. "But if they don't let him in, you bring the matter up from the floor."

"I'll request that he be invited in," Rawley said, grinning at them all.

"I think there'll be enough support. The typos will support us," Carl speculated.

"Oh, I don't see how they can refuse," Barbara said. "They can't make a C.I.O.–A. F. of L. issue out of this. Ryan wouldn't be so stupid."

"Don't underestimate Ryan," Professor Rawley bubble-laughed.

"Besides," Price interpolated, "the A. F. of L. boys are not at all sorry this happened. We're barking up the wrong tree here. For them, the massacre was the best thing that could have happened to destroy the C.I.O. I wouldn't be surprised if some of their master minds put a little pressure on the state's attorney to make sure the cops busted up that strike, but good. Maybe they even suggested a little firing-practice. I wouldn't put it past them."

"Oh, they wouldn't go that far!" Barbara cried. "Besides, why should the state's attorney listen to them?"

"The A. F. of L. put him in. If it wasn't for the teamsters' union, where would he be? And you can bank on another thing, he'll go the limit on prosecuting the strikers that were arrested out there, to finish up on the C.I.O. for Adam Ryan. Oh, they've got this town tighter than a drum."

They passed a heavy door with a grated peephole. "Looks like a relic of speakeasy days," Sylvia commented.

Price explained it was the bomb-proof entrance to the office of the musicians' union. "That's how these boys do things."

The door to the auditorium, however, was ordinary, and open. About a hundred delegates were scattered in groups, chinning. Against the rear wall was a haberdashery stand, with a sign: "Wear Union-Made Clothes." Delegates were fingering neckties.

A bright-eyed old man circulated, selling some kind of newspaper. "That's old Griffin," George Price said. "Used to be the town's official anarchist. Now he peddles the Townsend paper." The A. F. of L. brethren seemed quite jolly about buying it.

A ponderous fellow approached and hoarsely inquired if they were delegates.

"No," Mitch said, and explained his mission.

"I'll see." The sergeant-at-arms shuffled toward the dais; they watched him whisper to a triple-chinned official, who peered in their direction, then shook his head. The sergeant-at-arms shuffled back and reported: "Says no." He raised one eyelid. "No C.I.O. committees."

"This is a citizens' committee, it has nothing to do with the C.I.O.!" Price cried indignantly. "How can he refuse when he doesn't even know what we want?"

"Yah, he knows," the sergeant said carelessly. "Said it was all taken up in the executive. All taken care of." Somehow he had backed them to the door. But George Price would not give in. "You let me talk to Adam Ryan," he insisted. "The church federation is behind this. He don't want to make a mistake."

The sergeant, suspicious, but perhaps impressed by the presence of the women, retraced his steps. This time he brought the triple-chinned official, Finney. "We sent you two special deliveries," Price began aggressively.

"Yah, we took it up at the executive yesterday," Finney said, bored. "We can't do anything for you people."

"Dr. Wilner came down here to announce the meeting before your delegates."

"We took it up. That's all there's to it." They had been backed into the hall. The sergeant-at-arms and fat Finney filled the doorway. Mitch shook his head to Price, to give up. It was too sickening, to have to beg.

"After all, I thought we were the ones who wanted to do them a favor," Sylvia said. "Don't the police bust up their picket lines, too?"

"The A. F. of L. doesn't believe in picketing," Carl Gaul remarked.

That was what he disliked about the fellow, Mitch decided. This kind of situation was nothing to joke about.

Barbara suggested they go up to the gallery and wait for Professor Rawley to make his motion from the floor, calling upon Mitch.

The U-shaped gallery was nearly full. "Must be something

[2 1 9]

doing today," Price observed. "The comrades have the joint packed." Mitch recognized a few of the girls he had seen around the committee offices. Carl Gaul said there was going to be a fight about their office workers' union, up for expulsion from the A. F. of L. because its members had refused to go through a C.I.O. picket line.

From the gallery Mitch looked down upon the assembled delegates, representatives of the old-line labor unions of Chicago. How ignorant he was, he felt, in not even having known that this body of men existed and met. But could one really be a citizen in a modern world? Did any man have time to know and to participate in all these things, and must he know and participate in order to fulfill his share in a democratic world?

There were nearly two hundred delegates below, gradually taking seats. The men were mainly of one type: burly, settled in appearance, not sloppy, but few with pressed suits—ordinary folk. Only two women were among them; he recognized Hattie Miller, the teachers' delegate.

The chairman stepped to the rostrum; this must be Adam Ryan. Foreshortened by the balcony view, Ryan appeared wider than tall, with a square, massive head and immense jowls set neckless upon a boulder of a body. "Did you know Ryan was the leader of the 1919 steel strike?" Sylvia reminded Mitch.

"No." He was startled at his own ignorance.

"Yep. Eat-'em-alive Adam Ryan, the big revolutionist of 1919," George Price remarked.

As soon as order was called, the triple-chinned Finney arose and reported the death of "one of our loyal and beloved brothers, Hermann Baumann, of the Furniture Workers Local No. 147, is there a motion that we arise in his memory for one moment of silence?"

The motion was murmurously passed and the members shuffled to their feet while Brother Finney jerked out his watch. His eyes could be seen circling with the second-hand. He pocketed the watch, lifted his eyes; the membership sat down.

Now was the time, Mitch thought. How could the Federation refuse to participate in the people's protest, after thus acknowledging one of the dead as their own? He saw Professor Rawley rise, but the chairman recognized another hand.

The first report was from the pressmen, on strike at the big Casey-Klingman plant. Police had three times broken the picket line, jailing their men. A delegate from the leather workers' union arose with similar complaints. "We can't put out more than two pickets or they throw them in the jug and don't even book them. It costs us nearly fifty dollars every time."

Suddenly there was a motion that the Gottschalk committee be asked to come and investigate the way the Chicago police handled strikes.

"Why, they're right on the same track," Mitch said.

Price patted his hand. "They mean only A. F. of L. strikes," he said.

This time Professor Rawley got the floor. "While we are on the subject of police violence," he said, "there is a big people's protest being organized on this very question. When the citizens co-operate with us, we should certainly co-operate with them. I move we give ten minutes to Dr. Mitchell Wilner, of the citizens' committee, to explain their plans, and that we send a speaker to their mass meeting at the Opera House tomorrow night."

There was a wide clapping of hands. "Second!" several delegates cried, simultaneously. Adam Ryan brought down his gavel. "The motion is out of order," he announced. "The executive committee has already considered a communication from this so-called citizens' committee, and the matter is disposed of."

A hostile murmur went around the gallery. Professor Rawley leaped to his feet. "Point of information," he called, and the chairman with a show of patience recognized him again.

"Are we or are we not sending a speaker to this mass meeting? Certainly this is one issue upon which all labor should be united. One of our own people was killed. We have just passed a resolution on the very same issue of police violence. I understand this meeting of the citizens is to investigate——"

Ryan was pounding the rostrum. "You understand—you know all about this citizens' meeting, don't you?" he shouted. "Well, if anyone else wants to find out anything about that so-called citizens' meeting, go on over down Wells Street to the C.I.O. office, that's where the citizens are that are pulling off that meeting! We are not going to have any part of it!"

Mitch Wilner felt anger choking him. Why, the committee hadn't been near the C.I.O. office! He wanted to leap to his feet and cry out: "That's a lie!" Sylvia's hand restrained him.

Hattie Miller was speaking, her deep voice out-booming even Adam Ryan's roar. "I am on that citizens' committee," she declared, with the antagonism that only a woman can concentrate upon a group of men. "I can tell you there is positively no C.I.O. tie-up. Mr. Chairman, let's not be blinded by our partisan quarrels. We have a common enemy. When the people of Chicago offer to help us fight that enemy, can we turn them down?"

"We'll fight them in our own way," Adam Ryan reiterated. "We don't need any help from the C.I.O. Next order of business——"

Professor Rawley, in a low, penetrating voice, insisted: "I demand that my motion be put. I appeal from the chair."

"Out of order!" Adam Ryan flung at him. Boos circled the gallery. There was a stamping of feet.

Delegates yelled motions; arguments started across the floor. Rawley stood firm; on his face there was still that gamy glow, but without comedy; his eye now held the cold gleam that sportsmen show when fair play is in question. "You cannot refuse an appeal from the chair," he stated. Delegates leaped up to support him. Carl identified some of them. "Regan, the clerks —a Commy. And that's Gerardi, the typos. Good man."

The gallery noise increased. Suddenly, with a savage bull-toss of his head, the chairman pointed his gavel at the visitors. "We're running this meeting, not you!" he shouted, slamming down the hammer. "I don't recognize any appeal from the chair."

The house was aghast. Then cries began to pierce the hubbub. "Parliamentary law!" "Constitution!" "What is this, Fascism?"

Adam Ryan stood there, set as a sea-captain in a storm, listening to the timbers of his vessel strain to the breaking-point. Then he headed right into the typhoon. "We don't need any parliamentary law here!" he shouted, stunning them. "I don't recognize any law but the law of self-preservation. This organization is in a fight for life, and you know it. I have my orders from the national offices. I will go down the line for the organization and so will you. There's not a trick in the world will make me lift a finger to help the enemy that is trying to destroy us. And this is one of their tricks. I am an old hand at this game and I know all those parliamentary dodges. We are in a fight for our life, and that is more important than parliamentary law."

The main body of delegates sat in stunned silence. Only a few stirred uneasily, whispered. But the gallery did not remain silent. "Dictator!" one voice shrieked, and on three sides the cry was taken up. "Dictator!" Then they began to chant: "Vote, vote, vote, put it to a vote, vote——"

Barbara joined enthusiastically. Mitch could not bring himself to participate. True, Adam Ryan's speech was the pure appeal of the demagogue: we are in a crisis, set aside the law, and let me rule. But Mitch could not overcome the sense of intrusion which Ryan had raised in him. He supposed those men felt

[223]

just as delegates to the medical society would feel if the public should invade their hall and attempt to influence their deliberations—rightful as the public, their patients, might be.

"Vote, vote, vote," the chant gained volume, and down there Gerardi, the typographer, was on his feet demanding a vote.

Ignoring Gerardi and Professor Rawley, Adam Ryan again addressed himself to the gallery. "You people ought to be ashamed of yourselves!" he cried. "You are a disgrace to your mothers!"

A sputter of laughter arose, but died under his uncompromising glare. "Oh, I know who you are," he continued. "I know who sent you here. But your tactics won't work. You won't run our organization from the gallery. If you can't show the gentlemanly courtesy your mothers taught you, then get out."

A delegate from the cluster to the left of the rostrum, "the stooge section," Price called it, moved that the gallery be cleared. The entire hall became quiet. At least there would be a vote on this motion; in a sense, a test of confidence in Adam Ryan. There was no debate. It was impossible to tell how many voices sounded in the defiant chorus of ayes. Without calling for nays, the chairman declared: "So ordered."

Delegates were on their feet shouting: "Division!" Many angrily stamped their heels, but Ryan stonily waited out the hubbub; it could be sensed that the meeting was again controlled, the dominant element perhaps felt that good old Adam should win on that last trick. They'd stick with him.

"Clear the gallery!" he commanded confidently.

The sergeant-at-arms appeared at the head of the gallery stairs. "You heard the order," he said, and waved his arms as though to gather in the visitors. "Now leave peaceable."

Girls looked at him and giggled. From behind, Mitch heard a whisper: "Sit down, sit down," and Barbara, delighted, passed the whisper: "Sit down, sit down." What a joke that would be!

A sitdown strike in the gallery of the American Federation of Labor!

The heavy, truculent-looking men in the stooge section turned on their chairs, craning at the gallery. Mitch Wilner felt as he had that moment on the field when Captain Wiley had read the riot act.

Adam Ryan addressed the gallery with bitter calm. "I know what you're after," he said. "You want us to come up and throw you out. You want a free-for-all and the police called. Well, you won't get the satisfaction."

With that, it was plain he had won. He had called the trick. "Is there a motion that the gallery be permanently closed to the public hereafter?" he demanded.

This time it was obvious that the majority voted Aye. Ignoring the gallery, Ryan continued with the meeting. The issue for suspending the office workers' union was avoided. The secretary read an interminable unfair list of magazines printed at the struck Casey-Klingman plant. As the session grew boresome, the gallery began to clear.

Price was the first to rise. They followed him, glumly, filing out, passing the confused-looking sergeant-at-arms, whose expression, Mitch noticed, was exactly that of the cops in the hospital corridor when Lindstrom lay dying—a pathetic truculence that said: "Don't blame me, we had to do this, you know how it is, self-preservation is the first law of nature, we got our jobs to think of."

Once outside, they didn't even curse Adam Ryan, or the A. F. of L. They were too heavy-hearted.

5. NOT ALL IRISHMEN ARE COPPERS

BILL the Little Bull Donovan was a kid of ten when the Donovans lived on Harrison Street near Ashland and his Pop was a bartender in McInerney's place. Bill was the second son, Ralph being ahead of him; and there was a younger sister Sheila and a baby brother Gibney; so being between them all Bill the Little Bull never got anything. He had a wild temper like his Pop. He knew that from hearing his mother bewail his inherited uncontrollable temper; that same temper was what held Pop back in life. Like at the Palmer House it was a calm barside political discussion with the bartender merely putting in his word to agree with everybody, when this ginsoak declared how could Cleveland be anything but a thief he had an Irish grandmother, whereupon Donovan served him a drink in his face, and was out of a job again. A bartender can't afford to have a temper.

So his father was working in that cheap neighborhood saloon. And Bill they called the Little Bull because when his temper possessed him he would assault a grown man with his bare fists; he would challenge the big fellows, Hugh Wiley and Arch Hannigan and the crowd that hung around the alley under the new L; it gave the boys a great laugh to spit close past the Little Bull's face, for in his rage he would scream high like a girl, and they could make remarks about hearing him singing in St. Gregory's on Sundays, the voice of an angel.

When he would get home his big brother Ralph would take it out on him because Ralph wanted to suck around that Ashland Alley gang, especially Hugh Wiley and the Ragen brothers, for old man Ragen was on the force and was in fact a hero of the Haymarket riot. Once they let brother Ralph in on a game they played, hunting anarchists. There was an old wop anarchist lived in a basement on Sholto Street, made bombs there. They were keeping watch on that anarchist in order to catch the other plotters that were going to blow up the Canal Street police station.

It was just like the headlines in the papers, like Captain Bonfield's reports about the anarchist bombs that killed the police in the Haymarket. Those anarchist strikers wanted to blow up the McCormick reaper works and rule Chicago, with blood in the streets. The cops caught those Haymarket anarchists all right and were going to hang them. But others were loose and Hugh Wiley and the Ragen brothers let Ralph Donovan sign a pact in blood, from a pinprick on his finger, not to rest until the entire Blackhand gang of plotters was swinging from the ropes.

From behind a fence Bill watched Ralph lie on his belly two whole hours, in the dark, peering into the basement of a shanty on Sholto Street. That was where the dago bomb-maker lived. Then Bill followed his brother to the secret conclave with the Ashland Alley gang, where Ralph knocked twice on a woodshed, and made his report in the dark.

But by the end of that summer, those fellows would have nothing to do with brother Ralph. When he came with his nightly reports on the anarchist plotter, they just sniggered. Bill Donovan knew those fellows were now watching a certain house on Laflin Street, boosting each other up to the side window sill, watching the girls and men inside. They wouldn't take brother Ralph along after the first time because he puked.

After that, Bill the Little Bull used to spy on them up in the loft of Hannigan's barn, smoking stogies and playing poker for pennies. Once Hugh Wiley caught him and booted him square in the behind, and Little Bull had one of his rages and shrieked he'd get them all for this before he died.

Then those fellows got old enough, and hung around McInerney's saloon where the old man worked.

One night when they were in front of the place, tapping their heels on the wooden sidewalk, and whistling at girls that passed, Sergeant Ragen came along in civilians and Bill heard him have a serious little talk with the boys. "You're old enough to think of making something of yourself," the sergeant said. The force was taking on rookies for the big world's fair; the Ragen brothers always had expected to join their father on the force; and now Hugh Wiley said he'd go into it too; Arch Hannigan said he would like to do it but his father needed him in his harness business.

Bull's brother Ralph was struck pop-eyed by the sight of Hugh Wiley and the Ragen kids in their uniforms, and when Bull derided the tin-star flatfeet Ralph slammed him in the mouth. Ralph tried to lie about his age in order to become a rookie; but finally the year passed, and they let him in. "Not for me!" Bill vowed.

Bill graduated from grammar school and ran errands for Schulte's grocery. One evening the family had a serious talk about him with his brother Ralph in his goddam cop uniform that he never took off even at home, sitting around like the head of a tribe, bragging about the influence he could use to get Bull onto the force. "I can take care of myself," Bull said. Ralph sneered: "Oh, the force ain't good enough for you?" "No, not by a damn sight!" Seriously he had nothing against being a cop —he was even drawn to the work, a man could rise in the force. But Ralph got his temper up, with his air of an archbishop.

They went over a list of possible things. There was the postal service, the force, the cars, or learning a trade. He chose to try the postal service.

Bill Donovan's route was in the old neighborhood, from Racine to Loomis, and it was all full of Jews, and now dagos were moving in on the Jews. Letters came from Russia and Italy with the craziest damn writing, a man had to be educated in seven languages to make out the names and addresses.

On Loomis Street was a Jewish family named Miller and they had a beautiful daughter of fifteen named Hattie. First time she came to the door when he rang the bell, the girl laughed, because he was so young she said, mailmen are supposed to be old; then he said why? which made her laugh again. She was a very smart girl, so when he had a name he couldn't make out, he'd ask her to decipher it. That way he was sometimes invited into the house while she asked her mother did she know of any families by the name of Idskowitz or maybe it was Edlowitz with relatives in Riga? Her mother called her Yetta, and sometimes the Millers gave Bull a piece of brown honey cake they called *lekach*. Hattie explained: "It's so good you lick it off your fingers, *lekach!*" so they laughed. He was terribly in love with her.

[229]

Finally he got up the nerve to ask her to meet him after supper for a walk in Polk Street park; Bill was afraid to call for the girl as her parents might object on account of the religion, so she met him many times and they would walk very thoughtfully around the park, discussing things like religion, and he decided he was a freethinker like that Clarence Darrow. Once sitting on a bench holding hands they talked of the future; she said she was going to be a teacher; she said why didn't he go to night school and study to make something of himself? He said he figured there was no need for that as he would rise in the service in time, and she said: "Bill, you don't want to be a dumb Irish postman all your life!" and he lost his temper and she walked home alone, while he walked a block behind to make sure nothing befell her; when he got home his brother the cop said: "I heard you been going to the synagogue. Why waste your time with those Jewesses, Bull? You have to marry them and get circumcised before you get anywhere with them." So Bill lost his temper again and ran at his brother and got a black eye, and didn't take his route the next day, in fact he wouldn't go back on his route at all, to pass her house every day like an errand boy with letters.

He was drunk for a week and his mother wept all over the flat until one evening he blasphemed the whole family and spent the entire night in a whorehouse. But the next day when Bull got home to the blistering silent gaze of his mother it was with the announcement that he was going on the cars, they needn't worry for his share of the house money.

He only hoped they wouldn't give him the Taylor Street run or any other street Hattie Miller might be riding on.

Bull Donovan was on the cars for fifteen years. It was a miracle how he kept the clamps on his temper; in the first years of his marriage he told everybody the miracle was in the being of his wife, the patient girl Mildred Sykes. He was twenty-two when he met her at the carmen's ball, and she was the sister of George Sykes, a motorman out of the Cottage Grove Avenue barns; Bull couldn't feel her in his arms at all when they waltzed; he said it was like dancing with a sweet breath of air; and then when they stood by the open window and talked, he found she was the sort of girl who made a man tell all about himself; there he was spouting his opinions about politics and Governor Altgeld pardoning those Haymarket anarchists, because they didn't throw that bomb, and men should have a right to think and talk as they pleased; though he wondered, did they have a right to say things that made others throw bombs? She didn't come back at him, or prod him, like Hattie used to; but yet she seemed to open him so that soon he was telling her even the secret things about himself, about his struggle with his temper, and she sympathized, saying it was a wonder any man could contain himself on a job on the rear end of the cars, for people were so stupid! On her brother's run half the riders were Polacks and Jews who couldn't even speak English, and they were always trying to smuggle grown children on for half-fare.

"That's it," he agreed, "and they scream like the devil if you just do your duty." And the cranks! She drew out his rage as heat draws out poison. So they were married; and the boys at the barn sent a baby-bath for a wedding present.

But a year after the baby came, Bull was struggling bitterly, every living hour, to control himself. He never got enough sleep. And he saw himself tied to a wife and kid, a carman all his life. Mildred didn't understand that a man of his energy could do something more in the world. He remembered the Jewish girl, Hattie. Jewish women were passionate, he had heard. Now he and the wife weren't getting together regularly any more, and when they did, it meant using a rubber, which he disliked, but had to use, for Mildred was awfully weak a whole year after the birth; he was dissatisfied and hungry for a female all the time. It was a hell of a life. Times, he couldn't control himself and yelled back at a customer: Come on, get on, we ain't got all day! and sure enough he got reported for discourtesy by some old hen schoolteacher; the super called him in. Then he had a taste of fear; times were bad, jobs were scarce, there he was with a wife and kid.

Bull Donovan got quarrelsome; if supper was a minute late he yelled at Mildred; he hated to stay in the flat, and she complained of loneliness, and if he did stay in, something was sure to make him lose his temper; and she'd cry. And there'd be no woman for him that night, certainly.

But one night they got to bed early and the child was fast asleep and all was still in the house and little by little they warmed back to their old ways and she made him talk again, drew the wild anger out of him, and he said he knew he was being mean, but it was just the strain of people all day, stupid slow people plaguing him with stupid questions, what time was the zoo open, and she had a thought: "Bull, why not transfer to the front end?"

Running the beast, making the car charge down the tracks, or choking it down, feeling it quake to a stop beneath his controlling hand—that was more to his liking. Those middle years were the easiest of his life. Sure, there were times when his temper burned again, when stupid teamsters jammed the tracks, when kids spreading tin bottle caps on the tracks for him to flatten nearly got themselves run over, when drunks rode up in front and spewed; but all in all, it was easier to control himself and keep himself in the rut, during those years.

Then once Bull Donovan got into a mess. He had an evening run, six to ten, and was on his last trip. The streets were slushy. At Thirty-First he stopped to let off a lame man. As the cripple placed his crutch on the street an automobile whizzed by, knocking him over.

Bull got down. The man's good leg was crushed now, too. The automobile had come to a halt; Donovan saw that it was a police cruiser. "Why didn't you stop!" he yelled at the two cops who came out of the car; suddenly, without reason, all his boyhood animosity for flatfeet overwhelmed him.

"Why didn't I stop!" the cop retorted. "You're the one that's responsible. You pulled away before the man was clear of your step."

"That's a damn lie!" Bull shouted. "You lousy coppers think you can get away with murder! You failed to stop, and I'll report it!"

"Go ahead and write your lying report!" the cop blustered. "Report your damn head off! See where you get!"

Two more police came from the auto, and lifted the wounded man.

"Come on," a cop yelled from the car. "The hell with that stupe."

[233]

Bull climbed back to his place, his fists aching. He leaped the car forward. At the barn he turned in his report: police car failed to halt or even slow down.

Next night after the eight o'clock run he was sitting in the car eating a lunch when those two cops, in civs, walked through to his end and said: "Hey, we want to talk to you."

"I'm eating my lunch," said Bull.

"Well, if you like eating regular you better have some sense. What did you do with that report?"

"That's my business."

"Listen, Donovan"—so they wanted to surprise him with his name—"you know, that cripple kicked off."

"Too bad," he said. "Too bad for you too."

"You'd better revise that report, that it was unavoidable."

"What for? It's correct the way it stands."

"You—you— Donovan, it don't make no difference to you what that report says. Now be reasonable. Or . . ."

"Or what? Let me tell you something. I don't like coppers. I never liked coppers. Now get the hell off this car!"

"You'll hear from us!" they said. The cops got off.

Bull charged the car out of the barn, cowboy style.

Next day, his brother Ralph came to the house. "Whataya want to be a stubborn mutt for?" was the burden of his song. "Know who's lieutenant over there at the Town Hall station? Wiley; you remember Hugh Wiley. Well, he don't like to have a mark like that on his men, and besides it might mean a big damage suit."

Sending his brother sucking around. Bastard cops. If they'd been able to pin the blame on him, fat chance he'd have. The dead man's family was suing the police department for twenty thousand dollars, Donovan learned.

Then he was transferred to the graveyard run on Halsted Street. He nearly froze. He couldn't sleep in the daytime. His kidneys were going on the blink, too. His nervous fits were coming back. The kids around the house drove him crazy, and he hated himself for picking on them; little girls had to laugh and make noise. "But goddamit, they're riding me and the only place I can have some peace . . ."

Fourteen years of holding himself in, paying into the insurance, watching his step, solid, every year tied you to the future years, seniority, a man with a wife and two growing daughters, a man nearing forty, if his job went up the chimney what could he do? And for what? What did he get out of life? He hardly touched Mildred any more. He was still a man full of juice. She was going religious on him these last years. Now she had a way to punish him for his temper. If he so much as said damn before his daughters, she would go into silence, not speaking to him for a week. Serving his food on the table but silent as a crazy woman.

It was a winter of horror. He learned the police settled that case for five thousand dollars; but he was sure they were out to break him. He imagined every traffic cop was out to block him, make him late on his runs; he'd get into quarrels with them and each time the cursing got worse. All winter long on split shifts, night runs, and rush hour; his kidneys going bad and they'd stick him on long runs where he couldn't take a leak till the far end, have to hold it for an hour; often in agony he thought he'd bust out, just leave the car standing in the street, never come back.

[235]

One night in March, as he checked in at the barn, everything broke. He had an argument with his conductor, who claimed he'd jumped a starting-signal, knocking some dame off the step. Bull lost his temper and hit the conductor; men had to pull them apart. It was a nasty affair and Bull Donovan got severely reprimanded. Several conductors refused to work with him, saying he was always in a hurry, a cowboy motorman. He got home stewed and Mildred was being silent again. He screamed at her: "Answer me, can't you, talk to me! I'm a man, not a lamp-post!" and finally he smacked her. He lost his senses completely and went on beating his wife, with the girls screaming bloody murder. Then he ran out and got blind drunk.

A squad of cops found him in a basement speak on Madison Street and he nearly tore them apart in his rage; his frig of a cop brother had broadcast him missing on the cop radio, setting the whole force hunting him. Every flatfoot in town had to know Bull Donovan's personal affairs!

The squad took him to brother Ralph's house and there was the frigger with his cop's coat never off. "Mildred tried to commit suicide," Ralph told him. "She nearly killed herself and the girls. The girls are here. They had to take your wife to a hospital."

His wife was insane, that was all. She had to be confined. The cops had done it all to him with their persecution of him just because he turned one of them in. The bastards, how they stuck together!

On top of it all, his kidney trouble got the best of him. The doctor said he must get off the cars. Find a job with less exposure; something he could do sitting down.

Fourteen years shot to hell. His whole life gone to pot.

The older girl Margaret tried to keep house. One evening Ralph and the entire family arrived to lecture him: see how he had let his temper get the best of him and it had wrecked his life!

Then Bull Donovan decided, the hell, he was through trying; he was going to have a woman when he wanted a woman, have a drink when he wanted a drink; things couldn't be worse than they were. Let the daughters go live with their grandmother.

After about a year on the loose Bull Donovan landed up okay with a job in the Tri-State mills running a charging-machine, that was something like running a street car; and he had even got himself hitched again to a red-headed waitress named Marge that had a temper worse than his own but they set up house and took the girls home and after a while even Ralph and his wife consented to come visit.

Bull seemed a younger man. By God, he told Ralph, running that charging-machine was like having a jock twenty feet long, solid iron. You shoved it into the furnace door and fed the raging chamber of liquid steel. The openhearth floor with its seven furnaces each with its five doors was a harem to you, and you rode that charging-car up and down the floor, picking up boxes of scrap and feeding them into one furnace, throwing a box of ore into a heat of steel brewing in the next furnace. Flames sprang out of the furnace door and could lick clear across the floor and singe the beard off the face of the charging-car operator—feeding ore was a trick!

When all the furnaces were going, you had to run your

charger worse than a car through the Loop in rush hour; over-head, the cranes would be lugging tubs of molten pig iron, while, criss-crossing the floor, trainloads of materials came, boxes of scrap, of dolomite, of ore; and all the furnace helpers would be yelling for you at the same time: load my scrap in number six! box of ore in number three! set up the hot metal spout for number one! But when the heats were running long, and maybe a couple of furnaces were down being rebuilt, there were lulls when a man could chew the fat with the furnacemen; and even in the rush times it was a job a man could sit to, and if he had to take a leak, he could always hop off and do so. This job had the cars beat a million ways, paid better too. And Christ, if you wanted to curse out a bloody bitchn furnace, no crossing copper was going to report you for discourtesy.

Bull Donovan's elder daughter married an accountant in her office; couple of years later he was a grandpop; then the other kid got hitched, and it was just he and his old red-head living in a flat way out on the South Side near the mills. He figured he had practically got the best of his temper at last; it had left marks on him; he was stringy-faced, and with eyes that hid behind a shadow: because he knew what the family thought of him—a man who had driven his wife crazy.

Quite often on Sunday afternoons the whole Donovan tribe assembled at Ralph's house, for Mother Donovan lived with Ralph since the old man had died. One such Sunday Ralph started a conversation with Bull about the C.I.O. He wanted to know if Bull had signed up yet with those "Communists In Office." As a matter of fact Bull had not signed, because he was thinking of the long years he had paid dues into the lousy car-

[238]

men's union, with its fat agents selling the men out every time they were in position to strike for a raise. And selling him out in the end when the union might have put up some kind of a fight to get him an inside job, after he had shaken the kidneys out of himself in fourteen years on the lousy cars. But more and more this C.I.O. sounded like the goods to him, and after Ralph made his nasty remarks, Bull went right out the next day and asked for a card.

The last Sunday in June, they were over at Ralph's place again, and Ralph started right in on the C.I.O. "When are they going to pull you out on strike?" he asked. "Next week?"

"You know all about it, don't you?" Bull sneered.

"You bastards go out on strike and take it easy and we're the ones that get hit. All off-days are canceled, we have to stand on duty out there guarding your lousy mills and maybe be blown to bits by one of those Communist bombs."

Bull laughed. But his younger brother, Gibney, now an insurance salesman, said he'd heard from a big executive that they were finding caches of dynamite in the mills, every day!

Bull's old mother cried in alarm: "Bill, don't you stay on inside that plant if the men go out on strike. You're liable to get blown to pieces!"

"Don't worry, Mother," he laughed. "That ain't the only reason I'll be outside the plant, if there's a strike."

"He's joined that Communist outfit," Ralph jeered. And as Bull got sore, Ralph pulled a pamphlet from his pocket and tossed it at his brother. "Here, you might as well get wise to that outfit that's taking your dough."

Bull controlled himself and tried to read the pamphlet. It was headed "C.I.O.—Communists In Office," and inside was a bunch of "facts and figures" about Moscow gold financing the C.I.O., and about a secret agreement of the Communists to make John L. Lewis dictator of the Soviet America.

"Who are they signing up in that union?" Ralph argued. "Hunkies and niggers. Who is signing them up? The Jews. The C.I.O. is full of Jew organizers."

"None of the organizers I seen is a Jew," said Bull. "Where do you get all this crap?"

Ralph's wife said Father Coughlin had announced over the air that he knew of secret documents proving that the Jewish bankers financed the Bolshevik revolution.

"What has that got to do with the C.I.O.?" Bull roared.

"Bill always loved the Jews," Ralph twitted him. "Ever since he was sweet on that kosher girl when he was a postman."

"But a bunch of Jews owns the Tri-State mills!" Bull sputtered, barely controlling his anger. "There's all kinds of Jews, like every other people! You think the rich Jews would organize the C.I.O. to strike on their own mills? Say what you want about the Jews but they ain't that crazy!"

"You should have heard Father Wilks light into your outfit this morning," Ralph said. "He knows a thing or two. And he's for the laboring man. Always was." Father Wilks had held another special mass for the cops, with the officers marching in a body to take communion. "Did the Father hand out this junk?" Bull asked, about the "Communist In Office" pamphlet.

"You may have given up your own soul to the devil, but at least you might speak respectfully of the church in your brother's house!" Ralph's wife snapped.

[240]

Ralph said somebody at the station had let them have the pamphlets.

Bull studied the name printed on the back: Americanism First, Inc. "What is this?" he asked. "An organization?"

"There are organizations keeping tabs on those reds," Ralph stated significantly. "Those criminals won't get away with anything."

"Like the Black Legion they had around Detroit," Gibney said. "That wasn't as black as it was painted, let me tell you. Some of the biggest men around there belonged to it. It ain't dead yet either."

"We don't need any Black Legion in Chicago," Ralph said. "The police can handle anything that comes up."

Bull Donovan recognized a couple of the older men in the line of police facing him on the Fourth, but mostly these were young cops. He saw Hugh Wiley, a division captain now, strutting the length of the line. In that moment he remembered Wiley and the Ragen boys kicking him down from that loft the time he spied on their smoking. Wiley didn't recognize him now, he was certain. But a voice yelled: "Bull Donovan, what the hell are you doing out there?" It was Ragen himself, Chuck Ragen, his boy face still there behind the boiled red mug of a sergeant. One lucky thing, brother Ralph had not been called out for this line.

"What are you doing here?" Ragen repeated.

"Same as the rest," Bull Donovan said.

Ragen laughed good-naturedly. "Same old sucker. Well, this is one time we got you stopped, you goddam motorman!"

[2 4 1]

That crack set fire to all the past. It was the cops who were responsible for his wife going crazy, that year of hell! "This is one time I get a good chance at a cop," he replied to Ragen, without laughing.

"Take it easy," Ragen advised.

And while they were standing there talking, there was an explosion at the other end of the line. Everybody turned and ran; but not Bull Donovan, dammit, he wasn't going to run away from any two-for-a-nickel Irish cops. He walked forward, scornfully.

Up to the day before the Opera House meeting, no big-name speaker had been secured; national figures either couldn't be reached or couldn't come on such short notice. John L. Lewis, the S.W.O.C. reported, felt he should make his first Chicago appearance at a meeting of labor itself rather than of the citizens.

A dozen or more local speakers were scheduled, the usual list: a liberal minister, the liberal rabbi, Hattie Miller, who could be presented as A. F. of L. in spite of Adam Ryan, a prominent Negro, a liberal professor. Father Gillie, originally listed, had phoned to cancel his appearance because he had been "called out of town."

Without a big-name drawing-card, the committee was discouraged. Price took the opposite view. What use were speeches, orations? Truth, the bare truth, was the force with which to shake the city awake. Let the wounded speak for themselves. Let the injured be paraded on the Opera House stage, on crutches, in wheelchairs, and let them tell their own stories to their fellow-citizens, the people of Chicago.

Though heads were no longer bloody, there was still enough horror to display. What about that little boy shot in the foot? Price asked. Could he be brought onto the stage? Yes, Mitch promised, the boy was well enough to be moved by now. The worst cases, of course, could not be shown to the public. That lad whose arm had been amputated was still half-hysterical. And that old Irishman, Donovan, in the Sisters of Grace hospital, with the bullet injury of the spine. He'd be paralyzed for life—if he lived.

Mitch was spending the entire day in the steel district, going to the strikers' homes, dressing their wounds afresh, making sure they would come and show themselves to the people of Chicago. He skipped his clinic again. All morning he drove around the harbor area, Calumet and Hegewisch and all the scattered settlements; he sensed it now as all one place, the steelworkers' habitat, frame houses and some of brick, but always small, with fewer rooms than occupants, sometimes a four-room cottage chopped into three "apartments," with folding-beds to be squeezed past in every hallway. And yet the settlements were scattered over wide, wasted space. And in the most ramshackle unpainted shack there was always the electric refrigerator and the console radio bought on payments, and the parlor set.

Mitch tried to talk with the strikers, feeling a need to get closer, to reach beyond the first excited sympathy that lived between him and these people. They said almost nothing of the strike; indeed, they wanted news from him. Doctor, is gonna do something the governor, Roosevelt is gonna do something? And he told them yes, the President had appointed a mediation board, to make the boss talk to the union. All had the same reaction. They perked up a little with hope, but without relinquishing the

[243]

sour skeptical smile. And about the police, the deaths, and their own wounds, they were unexpressive. Sometimes, a few curses. Only toward the end of his rounds, Mitch Wilner realized what there was in them that was different from himself: they were not surprised.

Very few had ever heard of the Opera building, few even knew the names of the downtown streets. He arranged to have them taken from Guzman's.

The last call circled Mitch Wilner back to the street facing the Consolidated plant. To reach it, he drove over the spot where the massacre had taken place; a squad car was parked alongside the road, and cops in shirtsleeves were pitching horseshoes. He slowed down, thinking they would forbid his passing, but they only glanced at him and waved him on. Cops were sitting drowsily on the steps of a tavern, next to the house he sought. It had a small front yard, graced by scraggy crab-apple trees.

Only half a block further, Mitch saw, was the spot the marchers had wanted to reach: the track-crossing leading to the main gate of the plant. More cops were clustered there. And a group of maybe a dozen pickets walked slowly in a circle, like prisoners at exercise.

So now the pickets were permitted.

There was no bell at the door; he entered, finding himself in a large room occupied mostly by a long table. Evidently a boarding house.

A woman came from the rear. Mitch recognized her; he had bandaged her head at Guzman's a week ago. "Hullo, Doctor," she said. "I don't come back to see you because I am all right now. Excuse me."

"That's all right," he said. "But I was looking for one of the boys. Mike Sisto was shot in the leg. Does he live here?"

[244]

"Mike, yah. He's outside in the back. He's okay now. I change his bandage for him."

"I better take a look."

Mike was the one, he remembered, who had fled, not wanting his wound reported. Mitch followed Mrs. Jugovich through her kitchen; the place was scrupulously clean, the floor scrubbed yellow. It smelled like years ago when he was a kid at home, just after his mother scrubbed the floors. An immense army pot was on the stove.

"Mike, come on," she called. At the end of the yard a group of men were pitching horseshoes.

"Next thing you know they'll be having a tournament with the cops, throwing horseshoes," Mitch joked awkwardly, as Sisto approached. Mike's face went furious. "They better keep away from here. Throw horseshoes! Right at their head! That's where I'll throw them."

Upstairs, a hallway led past a series of cubicle-rooms, in each a narrow bed, a chair, one window. Mike's was one of the two front rooms, facing the mill.

"Some place for a machine gun, hey, Doc!" he slid into the chair by the window, and made a circling sweep with cocked fingers. "Bubububub! I could knock off every lousy copper and every scab going in there."

Mitch looked down at the track-crossing, with its group of cops around the gateman's shack, and the circle of desultory pickets. A few men had come to relieve others in the picket line, who divested themselves of the oilcloth sandwich signs they wore; the newcomers slipped them on.

"Bastard cops, they won't let nobody in that picket line that ain't got a sign," Mike said. He half snickered. "Wiley won't let them carry no signs on sticks. Just hung around your neck. He won't even let anybody say anything. Bitchn finks ride

[2 4 5]

right in past you and you got to keep your mouth shut."

"The boys, when they started to sing, just to cheer up," Mrs. Jugovich reported, "he wouldn't let them."

"I know them scabs though," Mike asserted. "Every stinking rat. I can see them from here. Even the ones go sneaking in at night. I got their number." On the wall he had scribbled a list of automobile license numbers. Mike called to Mrs. Jugovich. "You know that Joe Marusek sonofabitch, I seen him going in there last night. If I had a gun I'd of popped him off."

"Are there many going back?" Mitch asked.

"The yellowbellies, that's all." Mike spat. Yet Mitch felt he was minimizing. "That's all right. When we go back in there, they're going out! We ain't gonna work with them bastards. They're through."

The wound was clean enough. Mrs. Jugovich brought a basin of hot water; Mitch re-dressed Sisto's leg. "Any more of your boarders here hurt? Better let me see them; we want them all downtown, on the stage."

"Sure we got one more hurt, but you can't get him downtown, Doc," Mike said.

"Who do you mean?" He wasn't sure whether Mike was kidding. "What's the matter with him?"

"Stanley Dombrowsky," Mrs. Jugovich said quietly. "He was living here. He was killed."

Instead of deepening the death, this identification for the first time brought life into the thought of that derelict body in the morgue; now Dombrowsky was a man, a being among people, known and spoken to. And perhaps, Wilner hoped, that small mystery of the "Communist, not properly identified" would be solved, so that he might finally dismiss from his mind the persistent hints of conspiracy planted by Captain Rosen, and by that stuff in the *Clarion*, and by Carl Gaul's vague evasions.

[2 4 6]

"In this room, across here, Dombrowsky lived," Mrs. Jugo-vich said.

Mitch Wilner went and stood in the room; it was like all the other compartments on the floor, scarcely more capacious than the body-file in the morgue, a place to lie. A pair of workpants hung on a nail in back of the door, the knee-bulges still molded to the way the man had habitually bent; a pair of workshoes, creased and lopsided, stood by the bed, and a pair of boots. There was an old suitcase upended. Nothing else.

"What did he do in the mill?" Mitch asked.

"He was a pitman. Worked in the pit, in the openheart," Mike Sisto said.

"Didn't he have any relatives here?"

"Dombo? He hardly ever saw nobody. His family is all in the old country, I guess. He used to send over his money. You know he was one of those dumb hunyaks, work and sleep, that's all," Mike said.

"Oh, he was a good man," said Mrs. Jugovich.

"Yah. He was okay. Hey, he had a lady friend," Mike laughed, and screwed with his mouth.

"All the boys used to joke on him," Mrs. Jugovich explained. "Stanley, he had some friend, he used to go to her sometimes to pass the time, that's all."

Often in his work Mitch Wilner had felt this irritation at a mystery that was no mystery at all, but complete simplicity. Like watching a one-celled being: the processes were all the more incomprehensible because they were there before your eyes in the simplest form. And here was the sum of a man's life, a total of nothing: work, and sleep, and maybe talk to a friend. Yet Dombrowsky remained a key he did not know how to use.

"Wasn't he interested in anything? Politics or anything?" he asked, placing Mike now as one of Sobol's group, probably a

Communist. Living in the same boarding house, Dombrowsky might indeed have signed a card.

"Stanley? Naw. He didn't know from nothing." Mike Sisto shook his head. "He was a good-hearted guy, though."

"One time he got nineteen weeks' layoff," Mrs. Jugovich recounted. "Stanley he said, Mrs. Jugovich, I owe you so much money, I cannot pay. He will go live in the street. But I said, Stanley, I know if you get job you will pay me. So every day, Stanley he says he got to wash the dishes. He washes, every night!" She laughed. "But when he has job, he paid me anyway every cent, he gave me the paycheck every week. He says: Give me only for tobacco, till he paid all."

"That was a funny thing," Mitch commented, "how the *Clarion* put down he was a Communist, only not even identified!" He watched Mike Sisto; maybe they even had a right to plan something, out there. But he wanted to know.

"The sonofabitchn *Clarion*," Mike said hatefully. Proving nothing, about him or Dombrowsky.

They had come down to the dining-room; as they talked, Mike pawed through some letters in a bowl on the table—evidently the mail for all the boarders. "Lessee if I got some more of those love letters from Mr. Speer," he jested. "Hey, Dombo got one!" He extended one of the envelopes to Mitch. "Seen one of them, Doc?"

The fat letter was addressed to Mr. Stanley Dombrowsky. In a corner was the seal of the Consolidated Steel Corporation. "Go on, open it," Mike Sisto said. Mitch hesitated. "Shouldn't you give it to his relatives?"

"Naw, he got nobody. Anyway that's the same crap we all got; go on, open it."

The envelope contained a letter and a pamphlet. "Dear Fellow-Worker"—he glanced down at the signature, Otis Speer. The thing read like intimate advice from a friend. Mr. Speer

[248]

knew that Mr. Dombrowsky was a good American. "You are a good workman, otherwise you would not be working for Consolidated." Mr. Speer did not blame Mr. Dombrowsky for staying away from the plant these few days. Mr. Dombrowsky had been misled by false statements spread by men who had their own selfish reasons for confusing him. Those men were professional organizers. They made a living that way. Mr. Speer had nothing against unions, "and you know that, for as an employee of Consolidated you have shared for several years in our employee-representation plan, which has benefited the company by benefiting you." But Mr. Speer was going to see that Mr. Dombrowsky was protected from outside professional agitators whose sole purpose was to make money at the expense of both the workmen and the owners of the steel companies. "What are they after? Your dollar a month. Figure it out for yourself. A dollar a month from the forty thousand employees of this company alone is a lot of money. It will buy a lot of fine automobiles for high-living labor-union executives with fat expense accounts. And what do they offer to do for you? Raise your wages? No. You are already getting the best wages in the industry and they admit it. They just want your money. They want a closed shop so that every worker will have to pay them a dollar a month to keep his job. Nobody that works for me has to pay tribute to any individual or organization to get or keep his job. This is a free country and you and I are going to keep it free. . . .

"Come back to work," Mr. Speer said to Mr. Dombrowsky. "We realize you have been kept out of the plant by unlawful mobs and force. Your job is waiting for you."

"Too bad Stanley never got that letter," Mike Sisto said. "He'd have run right back in there, huh!"

The other item was a pamphlet entitled "C.I.O.—Communists In Office." On the cover was a crude drawing of John L. Lewis placing a hammer and sickle over the American flag.

Mitch glanced through the pages. Every paragraph started with "facts and figures." "It is an undisputed fact that the C.I.O. coffers have been filled from Moscow." "Look at the C.I.O. leaders. Who are they? Why has the legitimate labor federation expelled these unions? Because these men are known to be agents of a foreign government which plans to seize control of our great basic industries, steel, and coal, and automobiles, our very life-blood in time of war. That is the gigantic plot behind the Communist C.I.O." Then there was the usual stuff about Earl Browder, head of the Communist Party, giving orders to John L. Lewis; more stuff about Lewis and Roosevelt introducing "piecemeal Communism" by such projects as the T.V.A., and revealing plans of how one fine day the country would run with blood and John L. Lewis would be dictator of America!

On the back of the pamphlet was printed: "Issued by Americanism First, Inc."

At Guzman's, Barbara Macey was sprawled on the kitchen table, exhausted; she had been rounding up the families of the deceased, for the meeting. They sat all together, waiting, talking little, except perhaps to ask again: Who's going to be there downtown? The mayor?

Two huge girls were there, the daughters of Wyznowieki, and an Italian family he recognized from the mass funeral; they were relatives of young Nicoletti, the youngest of those bodies he had seen at the morgue.

"They found another one," Barbara said, sitting up; her face was greenish.

"Dead?"

"Out there in a ditch on the other side of the mill. He must have been trying to run away through that swamp."

[2 5 0]

"Is he identified?"

"He had a union card on him. A Greek name, Damon something. From Steel Harbor."

There was more news. The company was starting a back-to-work movement in the Harbor, she informed him. "That fat whore what's-his-name—used to be a liberal—you know who I mean—goes around making speeches about the American way now—he's in from Cleveland. George Price said he contacted the newspapers, trying to take the stink off the massacre. They'll probably try and hold a fake vote to get the men back to work."

Mitch showed her the pamphlet and the Dombrowsky letter. Yes, she had seen them, every striker had received a copy. "'Americanism First, Inc. Kansas City.' I bet they're hooked up with the Silver Shirts."

"Why?"

She just had a hunch.

Mitch glanced again through the pamphlet. It was effective, in its way. "The American workingman is the highest paid on earth," it proved, with a table of figures.

Though it was before eight when they got the witnesses to the Opera building, people already swarmed on the sidewalk. And this seemed quite a well-dressed crowd. "At least it won't be the same icky gang of comrades," Barbara remarked, elated.

"Not a cop for blocks," Mike Sisto observed. There wasn't even a traffic policeman on the corner. The police seemed to have deserted the Opera House area to the people, as a token of minor victory.

George Price came rushing toward them, nervous as an impresario. All day he had been after Mitch to permit the blinded Lindstrom to appear at the meeting, while Mitch insisted that the risk of shock was too great. Jesus, everything was falling down! Price cried. That little boy who had been shot—even he couldn't be secured.

"But he's all right," Mitch said. "I saw him yesterday. He was all set to be released from the hospital. He still has a limp, but that can be treated at home."

"The sonsabitches won't let him out," Price swore. "I sent my wife down for him and the cops threw her out of the hospital. The house would go wild if we brought him on." For a moment, he regained his knowing objectivity. "I guess they figure on letting us blow off steam, but not enough to bust anything open." Espying a *Daily Worker* salesman, he rushed him from the lobby. "For Chrisake, those people have no sense. They'll crab the whole thing. We agreed, no revolutionary literature to be sold inside. We shouldn't even allow them within a block of the place."

They herded the witnesses backstage. George Price had even remembered to rent a wheelchair; he had put white coats on Arthur Main and another student. "I thought we'd bring the kid on in the chair," he explained. "Have to use a woman now, I guess." He searched the group, to select a wheelchair patient.

A lanky, bucktoothed young man eyed the strikers, with their bandaged heads, crutches, arms in slings. "These your actors, Price?" he inquired. Price glanced at the fellow, annoyed, and warned everybody: "Watch out for this bastard, he's from the *Clarion*."

"What are they going to say?" the reporter asked. "I've got a nine-o'clock deadline."

"What's the difference what we say? You'll lie about it," Mike Sisto spoke up.

The reporter approached Mitch. "You the doctor? How did you happen to be out there that day, Doctor?"

"We drove by, returning from a picnic," Mitch said.

"Just happened to be driving by, eh?" The *Clarion* reporter's lip dropped suggestively.

"That's right." Mitch told himself if the fellow's manner weren't so insolent, he'd have added that his wife had an interest in the strike. It might be better to say it now, as the fact would probably come out.

"Getting paid for all this work, Doctor?"

"I intend to put in a bill to the union."

"You—uh—don't practice among these people, regularly, do you, Doctor?"

"I haven't been in practice in that neighborhood, no."

"I see." Always with that inflection of seeing much more. "Now, uh, what are these witnesses going to say?"

"They're just going to tell what happened to them."

"You've been over it with them, I suppose. It would save me some time if——"

"Nobody has been over anything with them."

"No? What if they say the wrong thing?"

"As long as they tell the truth," Mitch declared, "there is nothing wrong they can say."

The *Clarion* reporter eyed him amusedly and walked away.

The hall filled. Extra rows of folding-chairs had been set out on the stage, and these filled. There was an overflow crowd on the sidewalks; George Price rushed around trying to get loud-speakers set up out there.

From the wings, Mitch, Sylvia, and Mrs. Reese, the society radical, surveyed the stage crowded with nearly a thousand people, the lighted swanky Opera House with its four thousand filled seats. "It's not the usual radical crowd at all," Mrs. Reese repeated delightedly. "I believe we really got the city out." Sylvia excitedly pressed Mitch's hand. She was no longer worried about his connection with the affair. Here, in the fine Opera House, it looked dignified and unobjectionable.

[253]

"We brought them out!" Price crowed, and Mitch caught the gloating feeling the fellow had, of having made this, of holding the city by the ears. The newspapers would have to report a meeting of this size. It really might start something.

The Reverend Dr. Maxwell, head of the interchurch committee, was opening the meeting with a calm speech about seeing both sides of the question; if the police were wrong, let them be punished, if the strikers were wrong, let them be punished. "Who let him in?" the I.L.D. girl whispered wrathfully. And there was a heavy, resistant silence from the audience. Yet wasn't that the proper tone for the meeting? Mitch wondered. A true spirit of investigation by the citizens, rather than a meeting of agitation? The minister finished, with some remarks about protecting our new laws regarding labor's rights, as well as our old. Just then Mitch was handed a telephone message from Jock Kiley. Bill Donovan had died at the Sisters of Grace hospital.

George Price went out onto the stage and read the message. "That makes nine, so far."

A frightening roar, as of some powerful machine jolted into operation, rose from the house. Then the first group of wounded started single file to the microphone; Price had placed the instrument clear across the stage. They made their way: an aged stubble-faced Croatian, hobbling, his pants-leg turned up to show a leg wound; a grinning husky lad with bandaged head; a woman with her arm in a sling; Mike Sisto using one crutch. Amazingly, they had no bashfulness before the microphone. Each approached and spoke with freedom and naturalness, a citizen telling his townsmen what had happened to him. Professor Rawley stood beside the instrument, and asked each a few questions, skillfully guiding their talk so that it did not last too long.

Mike Sisto rested on his crutch, and with his free hand seized the microphone.

"Your name?" Rawley asked.

"Mike Sisto."

And the second stock question, "Now tell us, why were you out there?"

"Why?" Mike paused. "I'm a striker."

The auditorium resounded. These people had come, knowing what they wanted to hear, Mitch realized. You couldn't convince anyone of anything. Yes, he was on their side; but, still, with him there was a need for some finite proof, some visible germ, some cause of what had happened.

"What happened to you?"

"Well, we come to the line and ask the police to let us through like the mayor said we could picket." Being an officer of the local, he had demanded to talk to Captain Wiley. "No soap. Then all of a sudden bingo they start shooting and I turned and started running and I get hit in the leg." He spoke with surprise, and raised his leg as if to make sure he was really hit.

The next witness stepped forward.

George Price had done a skillful job; within the body of that theater the citizenry could be felt sitting in judgment, perhaps as in a town meeting of the settler days of America, all come to partake in government. But would this spirit spread from this hall to the entire city?

The Negro speaker, representing the Pullman porters' union, followed the first group of wounded. Grave-voiced, deliberate, he made the Fascist charge. What is there under Fascism? he demanded rhetorically. First, destruction of labor unions. What have we in Chicago? The police attack the union. What happens to the press under Fascism? It is the organ of the Fascist gang, all true news censored out. What is the Chicago press?

Boos and howls against the *Clarion* arose.

And what of the radio, the cinema? he demanded. Could time on the air be bought, to announce this meeting? No! the air is

[255]

controlled. And what of the movies? They took a complete record of what happened out there. Can you see it? No. Censored. That's Fascism.

Hisses, applause, whistles shook the hall. Mitch noticed how the comrades wore beatific smiles, it took a Negro speaker to sound the truth!

"Our turn," Price said, and half-pushed Mitch onto the platform. The medical report.

One by one, Price read names of the dead, and after each name, Mitch was to recite, in simplest terms, the cause of death.

"Hermann Baumann," Price called out.

"Hermann Baumann died of the effects of a bullet wound entering his body about two centimeters left of his spine, fourteenth vertebra, and perforating vital organs as it went directly through the body."

"Stanley Dombrowsky."

"Stanley Dombrowsky died in a police ambulance due to loss of blood from his right femoral artery, severed by a bullet which entered from the rear and passed diagonally forward."

"Jesus Hernandez."

As they went on, Mitch was conscious of a rising and glowing sense of fulfillment in himself; surely what he had done was no medical achievement; any interne, any doctor would have been his equal in the emergency; rather it was what he was doing now that fulfilled him. For this was a part of medicine that he hadn't been taught, and that he had never thought about. This was responsibility, this was where a doctor could fit into society, perhaps losing that separateness doctors generally felt. Maybe after tonight he would be finished with this whole business (though inwardly he sensed that he had more to discover), but certainly now, standing before the people of Chicago, as a citizen and medical man, he was filled with the thrill of usefulness.

[256]

"Gus Lindstrom."

"Gus Lindstrom died"—and of this one he felt he must say something, say something of the man. After the medical report he added: "I knew him all last week, he was a wonderful specimen of a man, husky and young and he put up a great battle to live—"

A short cry sounded from the hall. Someone hysterical. And a wilder sound came, of sobbing spreading.

"Al Nicoletti."

"Randy Carey."

"Mr. Carey had four bullet wounds. And it might be added, this man was a cripple, wearing an artificial right leg."

"Of these nine dead, Doctor, how many were wounded from behind?"

"I should say nearly all were shot from behind, though with varying angles toward the side. Perhaps Nicoletti and Hernandez could be said to have been hit more from the side than the rear."

"Then you would say at least seven of the nine were rear wounds?"

"I think we might classify them as such."

Mitch was conscious of flashlights exploding around him.

He concluded: "In total, though I cannot say this is a complete list, I can report forty-six bullet-wounded, nine of whom have died, and at least three others are still in danger; there were, in addition, approximately sixty patients treated for wounds of various sorts, chiefly scalp wounds from clubbing; and the most serious of these is the case of Oscar Lindstrom, who has lost one eye and may lose his sight completely."

"Thank you, Dr. Wilner."

He sat down in the first row, between Joshua Wheeler and Hattie Miller. The old unionist put his hand on Mitch's, and gave him a restrained smile of thanks.

[2 5 7]

But what had it been? Only a recital of the dead and injured. Did it prove anyone's guilt? Mitch wondered whether he as a doctor was insensitive to bodily harm. For the people in the hall seemed more affected by this medical report than by all the scorching speeches that had been made, more, even, than by the parade of the wounded. But couldn't these same devices— a parade of injured, a roll-call of dead—arouse a public in any cause? He looked to the wings, and saw Sylvia waiting, her face slightly unhappy. He knew she was worried about those news- paper photographs; thus far he had had no publicity.

George Price was concluding the meeting with the stunt about which he had been so mysterious. A large screen was let down onto the stage. Price had had a number of stereopticon slides made. He drew Mitch down to the orchestra pit. "Hand me these slides one at a time. I'll work the machine."

The theater was dark now, only the screen glowed, a huge white square. Down there in the pit Mitch could feel the entire audience converging on them, a palpable warmth, a weight.

From the pit, Price spoke: "There is one question that has been unanswered about what happened there on the Fourth. Who started the trouble? Was it a riot or a massacre? Was it planned, on either side? Did someone give the order to start?"

Each side had made charges, but there was one kind of evi- dence that could be trusted, he said. The camera didn't lie. A motion-picture camera had its eye fixed upon the whole scene, and recorded it. "Why won't they let the public see that film?"

Murmurs of anticipation began. Was the suppressed film actually about to be shown? "No. No. We do not have that film," Price stated, "but we do have a photographic record of what happened out there. Dozens of newspaper photographers were there and they shot it from every angle. There were also some private citizens with cameras, and they had their cameras taken away from them, and were jailed for taking pictures, yes, friends, right here in the United States. But, remember, it's Chicago.

"The newspaper photographers, however, were not jailed. And we have made a complete chronological record of what happened, using the pictures they took. Where did we get them? Right out of the Chicago newspapers. Even out of the *Clarion*. You've all glanced at these pictures; but in the papers the captions told you what they meant. Now look at them, without captions, and draw your own conclusions!"

Mitch handed Price the first slide.

On the large screen, augmented as under a microscope, the photographs proceeded like a series of specimen slices into a growth. Here was the gathering in Guzman's Grove, with that monkey-jumpy little speaker Szutak on the truck, and behind him Frank Sobol. Did Frank Sobol already know, at that moment, of what might happen; did he then contain the fixed and secret determination to fight his men into the plant? Was that ever his real purpose?

George Price pointed out in the crowd a kid eating a Good Humor, a couple of fellows with their arms around their girls, a little group of women, gossiping, not heeding the speaker. Mitch was reminded of old Professor Nyquist, in his histology course, pointing to cluster formations on a slide. Yet in any one section, particularly at the beginning of a growth, ninety-nine percent of the activity seen is normal.

There were photographs of the line of march, of the waiting police, of the two lines face to face. And then came the key photograph, of that disputed instant when the fight had started.

Now, Mitch reflected, how easy it was to fall into the fallacious assumption that the person who struck the first blow in a fight was the one in the wrong. But wasn't more sought here than the proof of which side sprang the release? The start of the fight was not due to someone who, in final exasperation, threw a rock or kicked a cop, or to some cop who shoved or conked a striker; the search was for an evidence of concerted intention, of planned attack on a given signal, from either side.

The photograph now on the screen had been published over a double page of the Sunday *Clarion*, with arrows, captions, and explanations proving that the strikers "started the fight."

It was a crucial photograph, complex, again, as a slice of tissue under the microscope, in which a million different actions may be going on at the same time, and the student must determine which of these is the action significant to his purpose.

For in that crowd, could a thousand different wills-to-action be patterned into someone's plan, into the guilt of someone perhaps absent from the scene?

And suddenly Mitch remembered Carl Gaul's accusation of Frank Sobol—why was Frank not in the march? Wasn't his withholding a sign of foreknowledge that trouble would happen? Wasn't he perhaps directed to stay out, so that there would be no chance of his being caught, arrested, and produced as a Communist?

But on the other side, what dark contrivance had set off a concerted line of fire from the police?

The photograph, taken from behind and above the police line, showed the double line of police facing the line of marchers. But toward the middle of the picture, heads of police and people were turned, evidently, on that instant, to see what had happened to the right. There, the facing lines of police and people had split, leaving a circular open space, upon which lay a beginning gas-cloud; through that cloud, the shapes of fleeing people could be seen, and the stretched-out leg of a falling man; and stepping into the cloud was the figure of a policeman, not running, but on a stance, his right leg forward, like that of a man set to fire a pistol, his right arm outstretched. Since his back was to the camera, it could not be certain that the outstretched arm held a firing gun.

But adduced against the strikers was an object caught in the air in this same photograph. Either a tree-branch or a piece of pipe, the thrown thing sailed just over the police line; a small group of police were seen ducking, their elbows up to protect their heads.

"Now," Price pointed out, "the police claim that someone yelled: 'What are we waiting for?'—that this cry was an agreed-upon signal for an attack, that the thrown branch was the first missile in a barrage of stuff, and that the police in retaliation threw tear gas and then fired to protect themselves.

"But from the photograph, showing one policeman already in a cleared space firing a gun while the striker's missile was still in the air, it would seem that, at best, the thing was thrown simultaneously with the firing of the first gas bomb; actually it was perhaps tossed by a striker as he turned to run away from the exploding bomb.

"And could it have been a signal," he asked, "when we see these strikers right next to all this happening, still standing, puzzled, looking over to the direction of the sound?"

If this complex instant proved anything at all, Price concluded, it proved the failure of the strikers' plan, if there ever was such a plan, but in either case, it proved the total lack of necessity of gunfire from the police.

The next photograph showed the missile, clearly a stick now, landing near a ducking cop; and the bomb-cleared space still greater, and a man in plain clothes and gray fedora running into that space, reaching to his back pocket as for a gun. The whole line of cops was moving into action; and the following photographs showed several police firing, some in the air, some with their guns forward; and all the strikers running away, except in

[261]

the center, where there was a pile-up of people. Now it was difficult to keep the time-order. There were photographs of police leaning over huddled groups, clubbing, photographs of police chasing fleeing figures, photographs of people struggling up from the ground, with their arms stretched back in pleading gestures.

A strange organic noise was forming out of the audience in the vast dark hall behind Mitch and George Price; it came as if out of one great beast. And as the pictures grew in horror, this sound augmented, became like a cry of an entire city in rage; it rushed down upon them in the pit. Mitch became frightened. "Quicker, cut it short," he whispered to Price, "they'll riot," for from all corners of the hall individual cries pierced over that general rumble: "Kill the bastards! Justice! Hang the cops! Murderers, murderers!"

At that moment Price flashed the photograph of the four cops carrying Dombrowsky, and pointed out the tourniquet used as a handle. "Murderers, murderers!" the roar heightened to a scream, and Mitch felt the crowd must rush down and destroy even the effigies of the police on the screen.

You could do anything with these people, he realized. You could lead them out and march them four blocks east and they would tear down the city hall with their bare hands.

Yet what was it? A flame that shot out like the flames in those Bessemer furnaces he had seen around the mills, great tongues of fire consuming the sky, lighting the whole steel area; but in twenty minutes they were burnt out.

Price flashed a photograph of "injured police" now, showing three sheepish cops: one holding out a bandaged finger, another with his arm in a very clean, fake-looking sling, the third with a courtplaster on his cheek.

"That was what the strikers did to the police in their pre-meditated assault with shotguns, nickelplated revolvers, meat

[262]

hooks, etc.," he said. He ended with a photograph of blinded Oscar Lindstrom, whose son had been killed.

"We could not bring Oscar Lindstrom here to talk to you," he said; "he is too weak. But there is one of the Lindstrom family present. The widow of Gus Lindstrom." From the wings, Barbara urged Pauline onto the stage. She stood, momentarily unable to speak. At last she said: "Our family don't want any revenge. All we want to know is why is it? Why does it have to be?" She stood for an instant longer, uncertainly, made an incomplete sound, and then seemed to realize where she was, and that she was before strangers. She walked quickly from the stage.

What could be done with this great, accumulating rage? The audience arose to resolve that Captain Wiley should be tried for murder. It arose again to the resolution that the Gottschalk committee be asked to investigate the connection between Consolidated Steel and the Chicago police.

In the wings, Jock Kiley was talking with some of the wounded. "Sure, that's fine, all those people come downtown," Mrs. Jugovich was saying. "Do you think that's gonna help us win the strike?"

Watching the auditorium empty itself, George Price remarked: "If there was an election coming we could kick over the town with this. . . . But by fall, I guess it'll all be lost."

In the *Clarion*, the following morning, there was no story about the meeting of citizens, except for a single short paragraph at the end of a general story about the steel strike. Leftwing and radical groups, it said, had drawn in with them some church and social service organizations, and met in the Opera House and called for an investigation of the strike riot deaths.

[263]

The other morning paper, however, devoted space and photographs to the event. Dr. Wilner's photograph appeared, with the headline: Strikers Shot from Behind, Physician Charges.

Jackie asked, why wasn't Mama in the picture too? Judith ran away with the paper and was using Sylvia's cuticle scissors to cut the picture out. Sylvia stopped her. "Judy, I've told you a hundred times not to use my scissors. You'll hurt yourself!" Judy whimpered and came to him; he knew Syl would be annoyed at the child's obvious trick, and rightly so. But just to quiet things—there was so much tension in the room, he couldn't yet tell how Sylvia felt about the whole thing—he cut the picture out with his pocket-knife for Judy. Then Jackie was after him again, for a Boy Scout knife. "Okay," he promised, "for your birthday."

"I never see Daddy any more, so now I have to have his picture," Judy announced, with that amazing adult manner she sometimes adopted. Sylvia looked to him, and they touched each other. He guessed it would be all right. Now that business was all over, he would be home again.

"Taking your clinic this morning?" Sylvia reminded him.

"Yes. Of course." He realized he had snapped the words.

"Well, you missed it all last week——"

"I know. I couldn't help it." They looked at each other, and stopped their goading. Of course she was worried about the effect of the publicity at the hospital, and on his patients.

He had to say it: "The damned *Clarion*. Not even to report the meeting! After all it was news, it was something they should report."

She shrugged. "It's better to have them say nothing than to report it badly." She shoved aside the other paper, with the story about him. "At least, people won't pay much attention to it in a Hearst paper," she said.

He dreaded walking into the hospital. Though he had only

[2 6 4]

done what a man should. He hoped he wouldn't run into Dr. Feldner, that was all.

The morning passed well.

He went up to see Emil. The newspapers were spread on the bed. Emil was having a good time kidding about the pictures of those he knew: "Jees, look at Mike Sisto, the terrible wop. Old Pop Wheeler sure looks like a senator or something here, don't he, Doc? That's one fine guy." Then: "Hey, Doc, I feel pretty good, lemme get up and get out of here."

"What's the matter, don't you like the nurses?"

"This is costing too much dough."

"The S.W.O.C. will take care of it."

"Yah. We can't throw out money like this."

He might be let out a few days early if he could get decent care, at home. "Where do you live, Emil?"

In a rooming house. Mitch envisioned one of those cells, airless, as at Mrs. Jugovich's. "Anyone there that could take care of you?"

"I'll be all right. Art lives there too. My landlady can fix me soup and stuff. Say, what did they throw Art in the can for? Did they let him go yet?"

"I heard he got out yesterday," Mitch said. "They just picked him up for questioning, I guess."

Emil's eyes darkened. "Art's okay though," he repeated. "Hey, I got to get out of here."

"Remember you were going out feet first."

"Yah. That's a funny thing, Doc. When you get pulled back from the edge like that, you get to figuring: what are you going to do with it? Gus Lindstrom had a wife and kids, but me . . ."

"You can get a wife and kids too."

Emil brooded. "I never did nothing with it before. When he gets it handed back, a guy gets a funny kind of a feeling like it don't even belong to him, for himself."

[265]

Mitch nodded, watching the man's face. Religious feeling often came to people who made near-miraculous recoveries. But certainly Emil wasn't being drawn to give his life back to God.

"Haven't you got any family?" Mitch asked.

"I got some brothers and sisters back East, but you know how a fellow bums off by himself." His eyes withdrew. Mitch went about his work. He didn't run into Dr. Feldner.

At Mitch Wilner's office, that day, the girl phoned in that a Mr. Flint wished to see him. As the man entered, with the wary, hesitant air characteristic of new patients, Mitch attempted a sight-diagnosis. The fellow was middle-sized, with good color and clear gray eyes. He walked with a straight bearing but was unathletic. Well dressed. Charge him five, anyway, for an examination.

"Dr. Wilner?" the man said in a slightly aggressive voice. His mouth looked peculiar, infolded. Perhaps he was a g.u.; they often sought strange doctors. Flint; he wondered through what reference.

"What can I do for you?"

"I—uh—just want a checkover."

Mitch drew out a card. Still might be a g.u., they often asked for a checkover, then got around to admitting a certain fear.

"Anything special wrong lately?"

"No. Well, I had some insomnia, don't sleep so good."

"I see. Who was your doctor before?"

"Fellow on the North Side but he moved away. I don't get sick much. I like to get examined about once a year."

"That's a good idea," Mitch agreed. He asked the routine questions. Occupation?

"Well, clerk, just say clerk."

The man's hands, Mitch noticed, were newly callused.

[266]

Directing Mr. Flint to remove coat and shirt, he made the usual examination; heart action okay, respiration good, pulse a little rapid and pressure a trifle high. "Been having any nervous strain lately?"

"Well, I been working a little harder than usual."

"Maybe that's it. Married?"

"No." The fellow answered all of the questions with a touch of resentment.

There seemed nothing wrong with him.

"Did anyone recommend me to you or did you just happen . . ."

"Tell you how I happened to come to you, Doctor; I saw your name in the papers."

"Oh, I see." Mitch tried to pass it off lightly. "I really didn't expect that type of publicity to bring me patients."

"Well, as a matter of fact, Doctor, I saw you up at that citizens' meeting last night, over those strike killings. I attended that meeting and heard you make that speech."

"It wasn't exactly a speech. Just a report."

"That was a pretty terrible thing out there, all those people killed." Could the fellow be a cop? But what for?

Mitch waited. Mr. Flint was buttoning his shirt. "I certainly sympathize with the families of those men that were killed," he said. "They're the ones that really take the rap. A man can go around and be a Communist or any the hell thing he wants and get himself in trouble, but his family has to suffer."

"Their troubles are over for the dead ones, that's one way of looking at it," Mitch Wilner agreed, playing safe.

"That Swedish name, what was the name of that family, they sure took it on the chin, the young fellow dead and the old man blind."

"Lindstrom," Mitch reminded him of the name. "Yes, they're fine people. I treated the young fellow before he died."

[267]

"Has the old man got a chance, with that other eye?" Mr. Flint asked.

"He may have. It's hard to say, right now."

"Be tough if he was completely blind." The stranger took out his billfold. Mitch decided to prescribe a sedative. And five dollars was about right.

"Look, Doctor. Tell you what I'd like to do. I'd like to contribute a little dough to that fund you were raising at that meeting. I didn't have it with me last night." He produced an extra ten-dollar bill. "But that Lindstrom family, I think they're gonna need it most. Can you earmark it for them?"

Well, Mitch said, all he could do would be to turn it in with that request.

"I see. Well, you go ahead. . . ."

In the reception room, Mitch instructed the girl about the contribution, and insisted that Mr. Flint take a receipt.

If he wasn't a dick, Mitch couldn't figure it out.

6. GREEK IN THE OPENHEARTH

THE older he got, the sourer Damon got, so even his partners on Number Five furnace hardly talked to him or asked him how he felt. Before, they used to kid him: "How's the demon?" but now he knew they only called him demon behind his back, because now they meant it bad. Yah, I am devil, I am sourpuss! Okay! What the hell I got so makes me so happy, you tell me?

My old lady? Ten years ago already she is no good. You want my old lady you can have her. Thanks. Pha!

On his left side, he had arthritis; on damp days that leg was stiff as a wooden crutch, except that in a crutch a man does not feel pain. The only place Damon felt not so bad was when he was around the furnace. "Heat, she goes inside and she melts the sore in the bones," he explained. The men said: "Sure, you old bastard—that's the demon in you—wants to crawl right inside the furnace!"

In winter sometimes he would have to chase to the end of the floor, where the biting lake winds blew into the huge tunnel of a building, chase there after the stock-loader, and it was agony. The first helper, Cannonball Loomis, was a sonofabitch; his idea of a joke was to send the limping Greek on every conceivable errand into the bitter wind.

At home, the old lady was cranky sick; she hardly even cooked any more, and the girls were always out, the sons were married and gone, and nobody had a word of talk for the sour old father. The old lady fed him lamb stew till he could bleat. "What I need her for? I go get me a good sheep like those shepherds in the old country. When I am finish with the sheep's tail, I eat him." That joke still made sonofabitch Cannonball laugh. Times when the steel was cooking good, when they were waiting for the moment to take the first sample, Loomis would make some talk: "Hey, Demon, how you coming with your old lady these days?" and he would make that joke.

Or he would talk of old times. "Twelve hours day in the old times, what was that so bad? You don't work so hard all the time hurry up quick. You go around back furnace, you take a snooze.

[269]

When was that strike, we go on strike what for? Work eight hours, that's what they say, and I get kick in the asses. Sure, that was 1919, I was third helper, openheart, Gary, in the big mill. Me, I strike too, I go on strike. Next day, comes to my house, he was the big shot, foreman in the Number Three openheart, Mr. McManus, you know him? Hey, Greek, you want you can be first helper, you come on go back to work, fifteen dollars every day. Boss, I tell him, I don't give a damn to go and work, this is a strike. I'm gonna fix you, he say. So that time, pretty soon I go outside to buy some grocery. Outside my house, all these 'goddam soldiers fill up the street. Three, four soldiers, they grab me quick. You, Greek, you don't want to work, okay! Here is a broom, you sweep the street! They kick me in the asses, out on the street with the broom. Boss, he is in his automobile, yah, my boss, right across the street, and he laugh. How you like your new job, Greek? So we go back inside the mill that time, we don't get nothing, just I get fine big kick in the asses."

"But now you got the eight-hour day, you bastard, you can lay all you want now."

"Nah, I got no use for that now, I am through with that in my life!"

Though his shift didn't start until seven, Damon Antinoous dumped himself out of bed at four-thirty and shoved himself on bare feet, neglecting to use the slippers the old lady provided but always raising a howl if she put them back in the closet. "What do you try, she-ass, to kill your spouse of pneumonia? Whom will you have to plague when I am dead?"

And she would cry: "No such fortune is mine, as long as I

am alive to be plagued, the plague itself could not kill you. You will live through fire and fever, only to keep on torturing me."

Then would come the ancient quarrel: what need for her to rise out of bed before dawn? Couldn't a man light the fire under his pot of coffee? His lunch was already prepared and in the box. But, no, the nature of him was perverse. "Why should I labor all day, and the she-ass stink in bed at her ease?" he would demand.

"No other man rises before six!" she would screech. "But this one will go without sleep at night, for he can snore all day behind the furnace, but he must rouse me at four, to light the fire under his coffee! No man, but a devil, this is!"

But sleep no longer came to him, Damon complained. He would lie with the twitching, grinding pain in his joints, and if he dozed, pain would wake him, as though she-devils with tongs pulled at each muscle in his leg, pulled him out of sleep. And where had he acquired that pain? Slaving, working year after year in front of the furnace, his face roasting, and the wind whipping the frozen flesh off a man's back. And for whom this labor, this slavery? For himself, a man needed little. A woman, indeed, a ton of woman, a limitless, expanding bag, into which he must shovel food all these years; a woman, a family, children, and what were they to him? What good? They spit on me, tpoo!

His pains were real, the woman knew; and when they were worst was when he ceased his whining grumbling and crawled onto the bed, curled like an infant in belly, his limbs contracted to make his pain small. Then she would come with olive oil and rub and soothe his electric-tortured flesh, her fat watery-cool hands soothing him. "Turn, Damon, lie on the other side,

[271]

I will put pillows under you"; and he would grudgingly accept these ministrations: small enough pay for what a man endured.

Every morning she made his coffee; her white-streaked hair chunked around her shoulders, and the long body-greasy nightgown molded to the bagfolds of her flesh. He might ask about her pains, but did not. Only sometimes when she returned from the doctor with new medicines he would let her talk, telling what the doctor said was needed and what it would cost. Damon would rarely comment except to say they had no money for such fancy doctor foolishness.

Sitting in the woolen underwear he wore to work, he would slup the coffee in long drafts, while he tore off hunks of bread. He ate slowly; for when he left she would crawl back into bed, time enough for her to stink in bed all day.

On the street there was no movement, except sometimes a long-haul truck pounding by.

At the mill the gateman was scarcely ever around, the odd hours Damon arrived. Antinoous would walk past the night-silent merchant mills, looming black and dead, but on the other side of him the openhearth sheds were alive, their fires apparent through the half-walled pitsides, buildings like great shells of uncooled steel, aglow. And above, he would count the trails of smoke as he approached: six furnaces going, only Number Two was down, her stack dead, Number Two was being rebuilt.

In the deserted washhouse, Damon changed to his burn-pitted dungarees, leaving his shirt. Then he climbed the sooty iron stairway to the openhearth floor, peering into the long vast cavern, with its gleams of light from around the edges of furnace doors on the left, and maybe a yawn of light from one open door

[272]

of a loading furnace. The floor always seemed deserted on night turn, though the traveling-crane rolled slowly overhead, its warning bell deliberately clanging; and at the far end a loco-motive pulled a chain of buggies laden with emptied charging-boxes, out onto the highline, out to the scrap pile.

His glance went instantly to his furnace, to estimate what stage the heat was in, and thus forecast his labors on this turn. A dull flare was still visible behind Number Five, making a red-dish aura around the furnace; she had just been tapped. If no time was lost in fixing bottom, and the next heat was charged at once, that heat might be ready to come out at the end of his shift, and he'd have the crappy stinking job of blowing out the tap-hole. A half-hour's difference would put the job safely into the next turn.

Gregory Pryzowitz, second helper on the night turn, was already dancing along the track yelling for the dolomite-blowing machine, hurry up to make backwall, already yelling for stock to load the furnace again, goddam those hurryuppers, like a man already pouring down a new drink before he has finished stream-ing out the last, his glass in one hand, his other hand guiding the stream.

Pryzowitz spotted him. "What's the matter, Demon, the old lady kick you out of bed again? She got somebody better there?"

"Naw, I just come from your wife, she got a whole line waiting," he feebly joked back. "She is always hurryup, hurryup, just like you, hurryup a new load, don't take time to do the job good." Pulling his blue glasses down on his nose, he peered through the middle door-port into the emptied furnace, the heat dancing rosy and porous in the football-shaped interior, pink and clean as the inside fleshwalls of a sheep. But over on the right, by the fourth door, Damon thought he saw like a round stain, a slight indentation in the furnace bottom; not enough to call a hole, yet toward the end of the next heat that might make trouble, especially if some brass or stuff from the next load of scrap should melt into that spot and begin to burn through.

"Hey, Pricky," he called Pryzowitz, who was squatting to adjust the dolomite-blower, "why don't you fix this bottom?"

"I'll fix your bottom, you old crab-ass," Pryzowitz responded, wiping dolomite dust off his caked lips.

Damon circled to the fourth door and peered at the sore spot from close. He had seen spots just like that develop into trouble. He scolded the third helper, a youth named Whitey: "Look at this here, she's gonna make a hole in the bottom. Whole damn heat is gonna go through! You never saw that! Holy sonofabitch! That's when you're gonna catch hell!"

Whitey brushed his arm across his sweat-running, smeared face, and went for a drink of water. "What do I care, Demon? If the crapper goes through, that's next turn, she'll go through in your lap."

"You got to rabble out, this!" Damon screeched. "Blow her out good with the air hose and fix this bottom."

The first helper, Al Bemis, came from behind the furnace. "Christ, who let you in?" he complained. Peering at the bad spot, he decided: "That's just a little slag left over." He spoke to his third. "Throw some dolomite on there."

"You got to rabble out!" Damon demanded, fearing they would just cover up the wound with dolomite, and leave the residue of metal underneath, to boil its way through the furnace bottom. He had seen a heat of steel go through bottom once, the whole potful running out like through a bath-drain, freezing into a horrible inextricable mess on the pitside, one terrible hell of work and a fortune of loss, maybe over $30,000 loss, they said, every time a heat went through the bottom, figuring the cost of rebuilding the furnace in addition to the loss of steel. "You got to rabble out!" he insisted, standing over the twenty-foot iron used to scrape out holes in the furnace bottom.

Bemis grabbed him by the shoulders. "You rabble the hell out of here! I'm running this heat! Why the hell don't you stay home till your turn! Honest to Jesus, I'm gonna have the super lock you out of the grounds. Why the hell don't you stay home and sleep?"

"I can't sleep," Damon said, pitifully. "I go crazy, try to sleep, can't sleep." He tapped his arthritic leg. "Just, I go crazy, she hurts so bad."

Without anger now, Bemis said: "Well, get the hell away from here, you don't punch in till seven." He seized the shovel and himself threw in the dolomite, hitting the sore spot precisely, like an expert spittoon-spitter. "I had enough trouble," he grumbled. "That north end is plugged up tighter than a consti-pated whore." He gave Damon a friendly shove, and a pre-tended kick in the rear.

Damon went around to the back of the furnace. The crane was just hoisting away the great pot of brimming steel, and the last dollops of slag were drooling out of the tap-hole, into the pit. He went down the steep iron flight, slippery with night-gleaming graphite. Each step twinged his paining knee. Below, he peered into the north slag pocket: mucked and plugged up, much worse than the last turn he had worked on her; with this end clogged so bad, it was only half a furnace. About time to tear her down and rebuild; she had made nearly two hundred heats since the last repair. Still there was something about a furnace running old: you knew just how she cooked, and she was all welded together solid. She was like an old car, cranky, but you knew all her troubles, and hated to trade her in. With the north draft plugged up like this, the limestone and scrap had better be dumped almost entirely in the south half of the furnace, he had better make sure of this or he'd never get the next heat melted; that old Irishman on the charging-car was a street-car conductor, what did he know about spreading stock in a furnace?

Damon clambered painfully back to the monkeywalk; the second helper, Pricky, was already plugging the tap-hole, all hurry, hurry, tonnage, tonnage, she had not had half enough time to leak herself clean. "Scrape her out good," Damon demanded. "You leave some slag in there and this whole heat is gonna come crapping out that tap-hole!"

Pryzowitz flung a gob of loam at him. "Demon, some day I'm gonna stick you in there head first for a tap-hole plug, if you don't stop telling me what to do."

"Too much hurryup hurryup," Damon grumbled. In old times, the twelve-hour day, the heats took longer, too, and a man did not rush so hard, there was time to do everything right. All down the line of furnaces now there was not a properly cleaned and fresh-lined spout.

Pricky straightened up a moment, from the hell-hot job of plugging the hole that still breathed out the torrid afterfumes of the molten heat. Damon noticed that the young fellow wore a C.I.O. button on the side of his cap. Pryzowitz caught his glance and said: "Hey, Demon, you signed up yet?"

"I got no use for this union business," Damon replied. "I belong to unions one time. Pha. Strike. That's all; union, strike."

"You go out on strike, Demon? When was that?"

"Was 1919. I get kick in the asses, that's all I get from this strike."

Pryzowitz half listened, working and laughing as he heard once more the tale of how the Greek had been forced to sweep the streets. "In those days we still have plenty horses, lots of horses, I sweep it up."

"Yah, but now we don't need any horses to give out the crap," Pricky said. "We got you."

"Okay, you see what you're gonna get from this strike! First thing, right away, they call the soldiers." Damon made the gesture of a bayonet, jabbing. "Back to work, you dirt, you!"

Young Pryzowitz looked at him without laughter now. "Yah, I know all about that 1919 strike. My old man was in that strike too."

"He sign up now with the C.I.O.?"

"Damn right, or I'd break his goddam neck."

"Well, what you gonna do? Strike? Be the same thing we had in 1919."

"No, it ain't gonna be the same thing," young Pricky said. Pulling a card from his pocket, he shoved it at Damon. "Here, sign this."

Damon took the card, as he had taken half a dozen others in the last few weeks. "I got no dollar," he said.

"Gimme the buck whenever you got it. Just sign the card," Pryzowitz replied, slapping on the outer clay, now, with his shovel.

Damon, sighing, put the card in his pocket. "Don't can sleep no more," he complained, rubbing his leg. He would go talk to that charging-car Irishman, for he already heard the regular in-and-out rumbling of the loading-beam, shoving the boxes of limestone into the furnace. If he didn't watch out that stuff would all be dumped in the cold end.

Donovan happened to be dropping the lime in the south end anyway. "Don't tell me what to do, you Greek fart; where the hell do you think I'm loading it, can't you see!" He spat. "You working this turn?"

"I can't sleep. I come early," Damon said. "I got arthritis, can't sleep. Terrible pains."

The Irishman softened. "I get spells of that myself. Gets you in the joints." Then he talked about the kidney trouble that had forced him to quit his street-car job. He said he had heard there was a nigger over in the sixteen-inch mills that had the power of healing in his hands. Wouldn't take any money, either. "I don't believe in that superstitious stuff but maybe what he gives you is some kind of massage that does the trick."

"Can't be no good if it don't cost you nothing," Damon said. A train of scrap rumbled onto the floor. Big chunks of old machinery, locomotive wheels to melt down. Why didn't they break it down more, Donovan grumbled, it was hell to feed such big hunks through the furnace doors. Damon reminded him to pile the scrap behind the three north doors. "Get the hell out of here, damn it!"

It was still an hour before he was due to work. Damon went down to the pit again, crossed the tracks, and clambered up on the teeming-shelf opposite his furnace. They were finishing pouring. On the narrow shelf, Damon bumped into one of those college boys who ran around the mill with battery-boxes slung to their sides, taking heat-readings through some kind of contraption like a stereopticon. He had tried it once: all that could be seen was a glowing reddish line. The boys were supposed to figure out the temperature of the pouring steel, through that machine, but he could guess it closer, just looking at the color of the molten stream.

"Watch out!" the college kid yelled, nearly stumbling against the pouring ladle. Recognizing the Greek, he cursed. "What the hell are you doing on the pitside, can't you stay where you belong?"

"Shut up! You don't tell me nothing!" Damon bawled, all his anger and strange fear of these college kids mounting in him.

The young fellow, tired from lugging that heavy box around, angrily swore he would report him for violating safety rules. Damon spat and turned to the back of the shelf, where there were some bales of hay, used to cover hot-top ingots. He lay down on the loosed hay.

Here he could sometimes sleep. The sulphurous smells of the mill mingled with the odor of hay; heat pulses from the furnaces could be felt across the pit like warm regular breathing from a woman; drowsily he watched the long string of fuming and sparking ingots drawn out through the open end of the pitside, into the yard; dawn was coming, like light from under a lifted skylid; he could see way off to where slag was being dumped

[2 7 9]

at the tip of the lake against the light-turning sky. He slept for a while.

About a quarter of seven, Damon rose, went to the clock-house, and punched in. He returned to the openhearth floor; his first had not yet shown up. Damon peered into the furnace. The flame was blasting through there, roaring like a tornado. Al Bemis was running the bejesus out of that old furnace; the roofbricks would melt any minute.

Scrap charge was nearly melted down, though several jagged red hunks of steel stuck up above the level of the melting-bath. "When you throw her over last?" he asked Al Bemis.

" 'Bout five minutes. She's nearly melted down," the first said, with satisfaction.

"Yah, the roof she's nearly melted down," Damon sneered.

"That's just sweat. She's sweating good," Bemis said, but the Greek noticed him easing down on the controls so that the first helper on the coming shift might not see how badly he had been racing the furnace. "I been giving her twenty minutes on the south end and ten on the north," Al reported, by way of turning over the heat to Damon instead of waiting for the first helper to arrive. Then Al checked with the melter and went off the floor.

Those few minutes, before his superior arrived, Damon felt good. He could turn out a better heat of steel than any of these first helpers. He looked at the automatic needle scratchings on the fuel chart. Every twenty minutes—bullcrap, that crazy Bemis was turning her over twice as fast as he said, feeding fuel to capacity. What for? Why burn the top off a furnace? Plenty of furnaces were standing idle, let the company light up a few more, give work to some more men. He throttled down further on the fuel flow.

Then his superior arrived. Cannonball, an American from the South, was all the time playing jokes on niggers. He was a skinny, tall sonofabitch, younger than Damon, whored all the time, drank all the time, and, like Al Bemis, was always in a hurry for tonnage, always reminding Damon it cost a hundred bucks an hour to run that furnace, get that steel out of there, ten-hour heats, nine-hour heats . . . some day he was going to have the roof cave in and lose a whole bitchn heat, with his rushing.

Loomis glanced into the furnace, came back to the controls, and upped the fuel. "I was here early," Damon offered. "Al was running the crap out of her, only just now before you come he eased her off, better leave her cool a little, huh?"

Cannonball glared at him. "Go on and spoon up," he ordered. "I'm gonna give her the hot metal in a half-hour."

That was crazy. The half-melted steel wouldn't be ready for the addition of iron for another hour. Damon walked off to get a drink of water. He moved slowly, his joints paining. He came back, picked up a shovel, and waited. Cannonball peered into the furnace again. "Spoon up," he reminded Damon.

Damon grunted. He had seen ten thousand heats made before Cannonball ever set eyes on an openhearth furnace. He didn't have to be told when to spoon up. Anyhow his third helper was over at the next furnace with the rest of the cinder-snappers, poking through the tapping-hole. Couldn't spoon up alone. Damon took another look inside the furnace. The walls and roof were a bilious white; a couple of stringers of molten brick hung from the roof. Damon looked so long and worriedly into the furnace that the head melter, coming down the floor to superintend the tapping of Number Four, stepped over and glanced into Number Five, then said to Cannonball: "Better ease off, huh?"

Cannonball spat, went to his controls, and eased down the fuel. Damon knew he was going to catch hell all day now. "I didn't call no melter!" he wanted to protest.

The third helper—Sandow they called him because he was always showing how much weight he could lift, his name was Kapp, father's name Kapusta—Sandow saw him struggling to lever the ten-foot iron spoon onto the first doorhook; the young fellow grabbed the end and swung the iron up, the hard way. As Sandow almost playfully flung shovelfuls of dolomite into the spoon, the Greek dumped the stuff against the front furnace wall. They had only finished spooning up around the first two doors when Cannonball started yelling at them to wheel stock, weigh out manganese; and Damon had scarcely replenished the piles of silicon and manganese in front of the furnace when that crazy bastard was yelling for him to go order up the hot metal.

"That bath ain't melted yet," Damon protested. "You got to watch out, I see a spot there, Number Four door, bad spot; before they loaded in the scrap I see that bad spot in the bottom. Sonofabitch Al Bemis, I told him and he just covered it up. If we get her too hot that stuff he left in the hole there she's gonna melt right through the bottom."

"Go on, go on, get that metal," Cannonball ordered. "The lousy crap is gonna take all day to cook anyway, might as well start it in there now."

[2 8 2]

It was true, there had been a run of lousy metal from the blast furnaces these last few days, the stuff was lousy with silicon, full of phosphorus, and took hours to purify. The blast men blamed it on the ore.

Phosphorus or no phosphorus, Cannonball was going to get himself a cold heat, sticking that pig iron in there before the scrap had a chance to melt. Damon let himself get lost for a quarter of an hour, spent another ten minutes discussing his ailments with the checker, before taking his hot metal order over to the mixer. By the time he was through jawing with the mixer operator he figured the scrap in the furnace would be good and melted. Cannonball came down the floor screaming for his hot metal, claiming everybody was stalling him. The scrap was melted all right, maybe even melted too far, the way he had had that heat on.

The whole day was like that. When they poured the hot iron into the furnace, the level of the soup rose so high it over-ran the door-banks, looked like half the goddam bath would puke out that middle door. Cannonball cursed Damon, though it was the Greek who plugged the flow with a few quick shovel-fuls of dolomite. The half-cooled spillings formed a crusty pan-cake on the floor. They tried to force the point of a crane-hook under the pancake and peel it off the floor, but the iron chunked off every time they got a hook into it. Finally, standing with one foot on the sizzling steel, Damon planted the small hook in a fissure right in the middle of the pancake, and the craneman jerked the whole thing loose from the floor and hauled it away.

It was a little after eight; the heat had scarcely been in the furnace three hours; his left side, the whole side, throbbed. He squatted on a bench near the water-cooler; the hell with washing his hands; he dug out a sandwich from his lunch, and ate.

The soup of steel was beginning to form now in the vast pot. Damon peered through the center door: the bath was several shades darker, heavy with carbon. Pretty soon the action would pull that limestone up from the bottom, fluxing the steel, drawing the phosphorus and silicon and sulphur and all that crap out of the iron, bringing it up like scum on soup. Then they would work her to the .65 carbon point, seasoning with a box of ore, a dash of lime, a dose of spiegel. That was the best period, the couple of hours of seasoning and purifying the soup, before tapping.

Now was the hour when they felt best toward each other, Cannonball knowing that without the grizzled old Greek to hold him back, he'd rush every heat through so fast it would tap cold and freeze up in the pot before it could be teemed. "She's gonna be a hell of a thick slag," Damon observed. "Awful bad iron, got to stew a long time," so as to blame the blast-furnace men, and get Cannonball to resign himself to a little time of waiting. Meanwhile give the bath a chance to soak some heat into her.

Soon the boiling bottom-lime rose to the surface, floating to the front edges, the breast of the furnace: a heaving under the scum, then a bubbling. Damon watched the boil spread, and come to a fairly even action over the bath; he had feared the plugged-up north end would lag. Still, if he were running the heat, he would wait before beginning to work her; give all that bottom-lime a chance to work up to the surface before adding new lime. He believed in adding ingredients when the boil was good and strong instead of right at the start of the boil.

But Cannonball called the charging-car man himself and had more lime dumped in there; probably throw the ore in next and knock the carbon down so fast they wouldn't be able to stop it at the required .65, and would have to bring it up again.

That was just what happened. It was scarcely noon when Cannonball had him take the first sample. Damon stuck the testing-spoon as far as he could under the surface to get through that blanket of slag; he stirred it once around, and backed away, pulling out the long already-melting rod, the red-hot endweight of the spoon bending it down; he barely managed to hold it high enough from the floor to tilt the sample brew into the waiting boxmold. Then he swung the spoon away, banging it on the floor to loosen the skull of residue metal.

Cannonball grabbed the mold with a pair of tongs, turned it over, broke it open, picked out the sullen-red brick of test metal, dunked it in the rusty tub, and laid it on the floor again. Damon pounded it twice easily with a sledge, then swung hard and broke it for the fracture test. Cannonball picked up one piece, and the Greek picked up the other, studying the patterned striations of the carbon lines in the broken surface. Cannonball handed his half to the third helper, to take to the floor lab; but they didn't need to wait for the lab results. Damon knew from the feel of that metal under the sledge, the carbon was already going down too fast.

"Give her some pig iron to hold her," Cannonball muttered; pig iron would keep the carbon up. All that rushing, Damon growled to himself, and then you have to stick in pigs to slow

[285]

her up; why not let her take her time in the first place? She takes so long to cook and you can't make her cook faster.

After the next test, Cannonball added hot metal, to bring the carbon up faster. Then he got the carbon too high, so the damn fool throws in some ore to knock it down.

Over at the next furnace, the first helper, a Pole named Jastrow, was having his laugh at Cannonball. Jastrow let Number Six take her time, his heats were never under ten hours, sometimes ran eleven, twelve, but somehow at the end of the month on the tabulation sheet it all evened out; Cannonball and Al Bemis ran the crap out of their furnace and then had to waste hours fixing the pitted bottom; Jastrow had longer cooking time, less time spent on bad bottom. And always at work he seemed to be taking it easy, perched on a stool behind his door-controls; and his second helper took it easy too. That was the way to work.

Just past noon, Damon detected a rolling movement in the bath, right there over the spot where he had seen the bottom-flaw. He watched it, worried. Cannonball took his place at the peephole and watched the whirlpool for a moment, silently, then began to curse that lazy bastard sonofabitch Al Bemis for trying to highball the hole in the bottom. He raised Number Four door, and Damon spat a few shovelfuls of fifteen-percent silicon at the sore spot, hoping the stuff would settle into the hole. They watched anxiously. The swirling increased.

"Try spoon some dolomite?" Damon suggested, and set about to swing the long spoon over the spot and dump some dolomite there. The dolomite, at least, seemed to ease the sore. But pretty soon she began to bubble again, even to geyser a few inches

[286]

above the surface of the bath. Only thing now was to speed the metal out of the furnace as quickly as possible. She'd be a slightly cold heat but maybe she'd pour.

They began taking fingerling samples and running them to the lab. The melter came over and stood by as if his added presence would force the faster purification of the steel. The lab test showed her still rotten with phosphorus. Best thing was to give her a shot of spiegel, work up more action.

"Dig her out," the melter decided. He'd toss in manganese as the steel ran into the ladle; let the final purifying action take place in the pot.

Sandow was wheeling the air cylinder behind the furnace, to burn out the tap-hole. The big boy was proud of managing the heavy cylinder without help. It was still an hour to the end of their turn; the rotten tapping job and mending bottom were fallen to their lot. Damon took a rake, knelt, and began to scrape burnt dolomite from the tap-hole. Soon the green putrid fiery fumes cracked through, choking and blinding him; any instant now the rush of steel might catch him in the face.

He seized the iron airpipe and poked it into the hole, nodding to Sandow; the hiss of air shrilled over the hiss of escaping gas, and suddenly his long knowing told him: he jerked the pipe back through the cinders and muck; the white burning steel came, fist-thick, and then log-thick, filling the trough and plunging into the waiting ladle.

"Under nine hours," Cannonball crowed when the steel was out of her. The crazy hurryup fool. Then they slaved and sweated, their eyes boiling, staring for the sore spots on the furnace bottom, scraping and splashing the remaining scum out of those pits; six men together struggling to direct the heavy raveling-iron that melted and bent after a moment in the furnace. Eight ravels were burned up, one after another, hauled out wilted and thrown to the floor. Still that puddle-hole near Number Four door was unclean of muck.

The cindermen from half the furnaces on the floor labored with that long iron ravel like a gang on a battering-ram. As they backed, pulling the ninth ravel from the furnace, red-hot and twisted corkscrew-shape from their efforts to work it around, Damon knew he was actually holding on, supporting himself as on a railing, instead of holding up his share of the iron. His legs felt molten and twisted, like that rod. Yes, he was getting old for this job. He let go his hold as the men pivoted with the iron and threw it clattering onto the heap of wilted metal. They lifted a fresh bar. He went around to the rear of the furnace and stared at the tap-hole. He still had to clean the hole. Then it would be time to go home. His knee throbbed. Home, here, there was no place he felt good any more.

Sandow clapped him on the back, walking beside him on the cindery path toward the gate. "Hey, Pop, you gonna come out on strike? You sign up yet with the C.I.O.?"

"Strike, pah!" He spat. "What for, what you gonna strike for?"

Six-hour day, Sandow said.

"Six hour, eight hour, what's the difference to me?" Damon cried. "Used to work twelve hour was better than this, we was taking it easy, that time. Six hours, we are gonna have to make six-hour heats, you're gonna see!"

[288]

Sandow laughed.

As strike talk heightened, Damon was uncertain what he would do. First he thought he would stay and work, the hell with everybody, he hated everybody, he would remain inside the mill and be a first helper, make steel himself, after the strike he would be the one to sit and pull the furnace door-controls, let some other damn fool wheel the eight-hundred-pound barrows of manganese.

Then he heard talk, better go out with the C.I.O., they got bombs planted all over the mill; when they go out on strike, they're gonna leave those bombs; you stay inside and, bang, some day the furnace will blow up in your face.

The best thing to do would be to go out with them, and wait maybe a few days. Then if they did not win—by that time the bombs would have exploded—then if the foreman came to his house offering him a first helper job, why, he would go back to work.

That was Damon's plan.

And if the C.I.O. was winning, he would sign one of the cards that had been given him, and turn it in with his dollar.

The strike was called at eleven at night, when Damon was at home, trying to sleep. He woke early, and though he had heard the C.I.O. men would be out that day, he made his way through the night streets to the mill.

"You C.I.O.? You come to picket?" voices yelled at him. In the middle of the night, they were picketing, thirty, forty of them, there by the main gate. "The mill is closed, nobody goes in!" they yelled. An openhearth man recognized him. "Hey, Demon! What'd you come here for? To scab?" he demanded.

"No, I just come down to see. I don't sleep. Me, I can't sleep," he whined.

The next week he nearly went crazy. He hated to be in the house, with his old wife. He could find nothing to do. Better even if he could be lying on the pile of hay, on the teeming-shelf, with the noise and the stink of the mill around him, and the smoke in his eyes. It was too quiet; his ears were not used to it, the entire Harbor was quiet; he could not rest; he could not sleep.

Any day, he expected, soldiers would come, and then the strike would be over. He sat for hours in the Athens Café, and listened to the speculations. Himself, he had never talked much, and he did not play cards. He sat near the window and stared into the street, waiting to feel the twinges in his leg. Sometimes one or another of the older Greeks would ask him: "What you think, Damon? We gonna win?" He would shrug.

There was one young Greek, Skourakis, talked English well, a fellow red-hot for the C.I.O., always putting up signs in Greek to join the C.I.O.; he even spoke against the priest for signing his name in the ad in the paper, like all the American priests and the business men signed that everybody should go back to work. Once this young Greek started on Damon. "Hey, old-timer, you are on strike anyway, you better sign up in the C.I.O."

The whole crowd came around, plaguing him, so he cried: "I am sign up! I got my card! I got all kinds of cards!" He pulled out the blank card Pryzowitz had given him, pretending he thought that was all there was to it. But Skourakis laughed out loud. "You old bastard, you don't fool nobody! You have to sign it, sign your name, sign it in Greek, I will fix it up so they wait for the dollar."

With all those C.I.O. men around him, Damon had to sign the card. Well, maybe C.I.O. would win, and it would be a good thing he had signed.

Over in the Consolidated plant, he heard, work was still going on. Men stayed inside and were making steel. An idea formed in his mind. Some said, now, that the strike would last a long time, perhaps months. He would only go and look at Consolidated, to see whether they were really working there. Hundreds of police surrounded the plant, men said, and the strikers could not come near, with their picket line. Cars full of men drove into the plant with police on the running-boards. Well, he would only go and look.

If he became a first helper in Consolidated, and the strike was broken as in 1919, he would be making steel, a first helper. And if it was not broken, who would know he had worked inside there? For it was said all the men working in there were strangers.

On Sunday, there was a big meeting, and everybody from the Harbor was going to march outside the Consolidated mill. That would be a good time to go, with all the others, Damon reasoned; then he could just take a look, and see for himself.

He saw a crowd of men standing behind the fence, inside the plant, and worked his way over toward them, thinking, perhaps while all this shouting and excitement was going on, he could talk a few words with one of those men inside there, ask a few things about the rate of pay, and did they need first helpers, and how one got inside.

He was sidling closer, through the grass, when the shooting started.

ATTENDANCE shrank at the citizens' committee meetings. The big show was over, and what had it accomplished? Raised a thousand dollars, got some newspaper publicity. Dr. Ladd was satisfied. "We mustn't expect too much from these things," he said, speaking from long experience. "Under the circumstances, I think we did a good job. We filled a need."

But, the I.L.D. girl pointed out, the strike was on, picketing was still restricted. And the cases of the sixty people arrested at the massacre were still pending, though all were by now out on bail. "The cops keep postponing the trial, to keep our funds tied up."

The young sociologist, Rawley, was for continuing the committee until the job was cleaned up. He was for holding neighborhood meetings, showing George Price's stereopticon slides, sending speakers to clubs and groups all over the city, keeping the thing hot.

Barbara reported that a back-to-work movement was being pushed in the Harbor. "We've got to keep the committee alive, or there'll be another massacre when they try to open Midwest and Tri-State."

Marcus Olden, hurrying in late as usual, produced a wire

from the Gottschalk committee. They were coming to investigate the massacre.

George Price immediately phoned his paper.

Dr. Ladd pointed out that they should all be proud their work had brought this about.

Dr. Feldner dropped his arm on Mitch Wilner's shoulder with the friendliness that, from some people, awakens apprehension. "You seem pretty busy these days, Wilner," he said.

"Well, I've had a lot of extra work."

"I'd heard," Feldner said, in a voice that didn't show which way he felt about it. "Say, did you get anywhere on that peanut-oil stuff?"

Mitch didn't dare meet Feldner's eyes. The whole project had slid out of his mind. He didn't even know if Turk Fergis was continuing the work. "We've been slowed up on it," Mitch said.

"It might be useful right now, with the pollen season starting," Feldner remarked. "I notice you've practically given up the clinic."

"I asked Dr. Fergis to sub for me a couple of times," Mitch said, "but that won't be necessary any longer. I think most of the pressure is over, on that emergency I got into." Perhaps this would be a good time to bring up the subject of checking that Kansas City experiment on the relationship of intelligence to allergic susceptibility. Though maybe that was too big a thing to start on, just now.

Dr. Feldner had walked him into the office. "Sit down, Mitch; I'd like to talk to you for a minute." The "Mitch" scared him, too, like the arm on the shoulder. "Mitch, did you know you were being investigated?"

"Who's investigating me?" he asked, steadily.

"There was someone here yesterday from the state's attorney's

[293]

office. He wanted to go over your complete record. Every patient you ever treated in this hospital." Feldner edged his tone with levity. "Looks like they're trying to get something on you."

"They're welcome to all they can get," Mitch said. His entire career tumbled through his mind. He reassured himself: he was safe. He had always been kidded about his super-carefulness. Now it counted.

"I heard they were going back all the way through your interneship at County."

"I don't think they'll find anything," said Mitch.

"No. I didn't think they would." Feldner patted his desk with his large hand, and said, paternally: "Mitch, I am going to ask you something personal and I'd appreciate a frank answer. If you want the answer to be confidential, I'll respect your wish."

"All right," Mitch said. He realized that for the first time he was entirely without awe of Dr. Feldner.

"Are you a Communist?" Feldner asked, looking him straight in the eyes.

"No," Mitch said, trying to keep his voice solemn.

"All right. I am going to believe that. Now, Mitch—if that's the case—is it worth while to let yourself appear to be one?"

"I never thought of it that way," Mitch replied. "These things came up; first it was a medical emergency and I happened to be there, so I did what I could. And then I was called upon for a report."

"Aren't you doing a little more than you have to do?"

Mitch tried to get the meaning behind the remark. Feldner was smiling queerly, his mouth slightly open. From under a blotter he drew some papers, clipped together; he handed them to Mitch. There was young Arthur Main's manifesto, and in the group of printed signatures, the name Wilner had been circled with a pencil. Was this the sort of thing referred to in the newspapers, and even in histories, when there was talk of revolutionary pamphlets distributed to the people? Perhaps the other signers, Main, Rawley, the schoolteacher Grace Wallen, were after all Communists. But wasn't his suspicion as simple as Dr. Feldner's suspicion of himself? Was it based on anything more than their activity over the massacre, parallel to his own activity!

Putting down the pamphlet, Mitch said: "Did someone take the trouble to bring this to your attention, Dr. Feldner?"

Feldner smiled. "Mitch, when you get to be my age, you'll know there's always someone taking the trouble." Mitch went over the possibilities in his mind. It was probably Dr. Dantzig, tattling to teacher. "In this world, Mitch, you don't have to have God to note the fall of every leaf off a tree; some busybody in the human race is sure to be on the job."

What was he supposed to do now? They wouldn't press him so far as to make him resign from the hospital staff? He felt a rhythm in his veins, of fear.

"I just thought you ought to know these things," said Feldner, still smiling, as he placed the little sheaf of documents back into the folder. "A doctor has to be careful what he puts his name to."

"The Gottschalk committee is here," Mitch said. "They've subpoenaed me."

"They don't subpoena you to make speeches, do they?" Mitch had to lower his eyes. "Mitch," Dr. Feldner said, "every time a doc sticks his nose into the world he discovers medicine is a pretty good little hideout. You can do all the good you want, for humanity, right here in medicine." He arose. "I thought we might let Dr. Dantzig take over your clinic, say temporarily, till you can give it all the time it needs."

Mitch knew he wouldn't be able to tell Sylvia about this interview.

"Striker Confesses Riot Plot," the *Clarion* headlined. Sylvia had already read the story; an expression almost of bitter satisfaction was around her mouth.

Art Nowis, Mitch read with astonishment, was the one who had confessed. Confronted by Assistant State's Attorney Corcoran with evidence, Nowis, union officer and member of the strike strategy committee, had admitted the details of the plot by which the Communist-led strikers expected to capture the Consolidated Steel plant, drive out the loyal workers, and establish a sit-in strike.

The state's attorney's office, the paper declared, was in possession of a signed statement from Art Nowis, detailing the union plot.

"At a secret meeting of the strategy committee, attended only by members of the revolutionary clique," the story went, "it was decided to organize a 'marine force' which was to land at the ore-docks of the Consolidated plant; this picked force was to attack the plant from the rear, while the general body of strikers and Communists attacked the police lines in front. One member of the strategy committee was placed in charge of the task of securing boats for the 'marines,' and the plot would have been carried out, but for the vigilance of the police."

"It's a wonder they don't accuse them of using submarines," Mitch said, putting down the paper.

"I don't think it's so funny," Sylvia said. "We ourselves know Sobol and his gang did have secret meetings. Even Carl couldn't get in."

"All right," Mitch agreed. "So they had some fraction meetings. But this crazy plot is too much. And how could Art Nowis confess to it? He'd know damn well he'd get his neck broken.

[296]

The whole thing must be invented." And he pointed out that there was no direct quotation of Art's "confession" but only the implication that Nowis had admitted the things that were asserted in the story.

"Oh, Mitch," Sylvia said, "why waste any more time on this whole affair? It's all right to be idealistic, and I still sympathize with the strikers of course, but it's all mixed up with things that we never bargained for, and when it comes to such things as supporting every plan that Frank Sobol might have had, I don't know why we should sacrifice ourselves."

"I don't feel that I'm sacrificing anything," he said.

"Oh, no. Only your practice and your clinic, and by the time you get through they'll even drop you from the staff. Don't think I don't know what's happening even if you don't feel your family is important enough to be confided in, about these things." Her voice was dry in her throat. He felt a warm, intimate pity for her, but he could not help her.

"Sylvia," he said, "all I'm doing now is only for myself, to get things clear in my own mind. They don't ask anything of me. I just feel I have to know about these things; I've—I've neglected all this side of living."

"But, Mitch, you don't have to risk your whole career and your family's welfare just to satisfy your curiosity; can't you be more discreet and—well, why should we be involved any more? Can't you see they're just using you to shield themselves? Look what a mess it is." She pushed away the newspaper. "I don't even know if I blame the police any more."

"You haven't come to the point of believing what you read in the *Clarion?*" he asked.

"Oh, if everything was only straight and aboveboard. You don't know what to believe any more."

That was it. That was exactly what he had to find out. What to believe. Perhaps this kind of newspaper story, like a whis-

[297]

pered rumor, like gossip, was in the class of an unfilterable virus; there was no way of building immunity to it.

"You know Art," he said, "he's a showoff, he likes to be smart, he probably thought he was fooling the police with a crazy story."

Less than a half-dozen showed up at Guzman's that day, to have their dressings changed. A bitter silence pervaded the place. Even the game of hearts that had gone on ever since the strike started was being played without words, out of a spirit of dogged persistence. The standbys were on hand, like Al Nees, who hadn't budged out of the place since the strike started, except to march in the parade; his voice was lower, softer, more patient every day, he was on the go every minute, all the details passing through his fingers: Mike needs some gas, for driving pickets back and forth, here's a ticket for two gallons; better get somebody else to go to the stores for food donations today, Gillespie's got to stay home, his wife is sick; hey, Al, that Carraway woman—you know Jim Carraway, he's still disappeared, one of her kids got to have some medicine. . . .

Mitch had felt a coldness toward himself, and wondered whether it was because he was identified as a friend of Art, through Carl Gaul. When he had come in, they had scarcely nodded to him. But now Al Nees asked him if he could maybe stop over some time and take a look at Mrs. Carraway's kid. Sure, on the way home, he agreed; and their need of him eased the atmosphere slightly. A huge fellow, of course named Tiny, who was around headquarters all the time, giant-framed and with a genial farmboy face, came in carrying a newspaper. "Whatayaknow what it says about that sonofabitch Art," he remarked. "Turned out a rat."

Mike Sisto, like a pressure stream at last released, shot out a streak of curses: that c—— s——, c—— e—— bastard fink, if he ever shows his face again——

"That's the last we'll see of him," Nees predicted.

The card-players continued bitterly with their game. They began to recall the intimate councils to which they had admitted him. "Why, he was right here when we——"

Mike suddenly decided: "Art's the sonofabitch that tipped them off we were supposed to pull the strike ten o'clock."

"Sure, Art was out there in the sound truck four o'clock, calling them out. That's what bitched up the whole thing."

Mike Sisto looked testingly at Mitch. "Know who was with him? Carl Gaul."

"I never trusted that sonofabitch either——"

"What I don't understand," Tiny said, "why did they have to pick him up and pinch him, couldn't he of just give them all this dope on the q.t.?"

"Sure, but this way it looks like they made him do it."

"I known Art a long time. I worked next to him two years in the spike mill."

"He was always sucking around. He was even a representative in that company union, always sucking after the super."

"Gus Lindstrom was a company rep too. So was Gillespie."

And in the midst of this, Art entered. He was sportily dressed as ever, his collar starched, his white shoes spotless. He wore his characteristic wise-man smile. The fellows stared at him, and then looked down at their cards. Mitch sensed his own thought in them: Art wouldn't have dared show up if he had really betrayed them.

"Hey, I called Tannen's South Side office and put the bee on them," Art reported to Nees. "They're gonna send over one of them big cans of milk every day."

Nees grunted.

[299]

Art began to recount his experiences in the jail, talking to Mitch, but for all to hear. "Doc," he said, "if you ever want a good vacation, you want to get inside that fifth-floor jail; it ain't a jail, it's like a hotel; I heard they fixed it up that way, when they built it, in case they ever had to entertain big shots like Capone."

"That's what they call the stool-pigeon's paradise, up there," Mike Sisto remarked, but disregarding Art.

"They put me up there in a suite of rooms, radio and everything, the nuts." Art laughed self-consciously. "The guard comes, only he acts like a valet or something. What do I want to eat? What can I have, I says. Anything, want a steak? So he brings up a swell steak. . . . Finally this Irish kid, this state's attorney shows up, Corcoran. I know him, he used to live on my block, but I ain't seen him in years. He starts asking me a lot of questions. I said, I ain't telling you anything that could hurt the union—and I didn't. All that crap that's in the papers—that's all crap that he told me, not what I told him. He asks me who is on the strategy committee, then he starts giving me names, Nees, Vikulik, Mike Sisto—he had all you guys written down there on a piece of paper—Gillespie, Emil—everybody. 'What do you want me for?' I says. 'You've got all that stuff from your spies.' So he says: 'Then you admit it's correct?' Well, I seen I slipped up, but I said I don't know anything, so he says: 'Okay, Art, see you tomorrow!'"

They listened with open interest now. Art described his three days in the paradise, the showers, the meals. "I could of even had a broad up there." All this time, while Corcoran was pumping him, Art said, he himself was trying to get a clue to who might be the spy within the union. "The way I saw it, they got this dope from their spy, but they couldn't prove it, so Corcoran was springing it on me to see if I would check with it. So I didn't know from nothing. So finally Corky pulls this old-pal stuff; he knows I got an old mother and father to support. 'Art,' he says, 'Consolidated got plants all over the country. You just play ball and they'll give you a lifetime job anyplace you want to go; hell, you can even move your folks to California, they got a plant out there.' " Art laughed. "Pretty soft, huh?"

But after three days, Art said, he got tired and decided his mother would be worried, he wanted to go home. "So I sent my valet—I was calling the guard my valet—I sent him for Corcoran. And I told him: 'Listen, you got no reason to keep me here, let me go home.' So he says: 'Sure, any time you want to go, Art, just sign a little statement that we didn't coerce you or anything!' So I says: 'Sure, I'll sign anything to get out of this joint,' and that's all I signed, and they even drove me home in a squad car."

"What statement?" Pete Vikulik was the first to address him directly. "What was in that statement?"

"Nothing, nothing that could hurt the union, all stuff they had already, like Al Nees is chairman of the strategy committee. They know all that, that stuff was all in the papers."

The group froze on him again. Art picked up the newspaper and, reading the report of himself, burst out explosively, at every other line: "I didn't say nothing like that! That's all crap. I'm gonna sue this sonofabitchn paper!"

Art sat there, pretending interest in the paper. The men let him alone.

The fellow who was supposed to go out among the stores, soliciting supplies, reported and asked if anyone was going with him. Art volunteered. "Sure, go ahead," Al Nees said, "that's one job we need a smooth talker."

As Mitch was leaving, Pete Vikulik asked for a lift; and when they had gone a few blocks, Pete suggested stopping for a beer.

[3 0 1]

Mitch was about to pull up in front of a tavern, but Pete said no, that place served scabs, and directed him to a place called Curly's in the next block.

A few strikers were at the bar; and beyond a half-partition Mitch saw a scattering of men, among them Jock Kiley; they were listening to race returns. Many said hello to him.

He paid as the beers were served; Pete introduced him to the bartender, who shook hands with friendly formality.

The bartender asked Pete how it was going, and on his side confided the names of a couple of men who had gone back to work. Mitch didn't recognize the names. But up and down the bar strikers mouthed them bitterly. One fellow announced: "Assface Donahue, he's my foreman, twelve-inch mill, he come around my house last night. He wants give it twenty dollars a day. He say, police going give it protection, I go to work. My wife, she tell him go jump in the lake." The men laughed, and ordered another beer, for his victory.

"Some of those bastards are gonna need protection all right," another of the boys said dourly.

"Art Nowis is one guy they can start protecting right now."

"He been in here yet?" Pete asked the bartender.

"Yah, he was in here an hour ago crapping about how he didn't say any of that stuff they had in the paper."

"I wouldn't trust him further than I could throw a larrycar," said a blast-furnace man.

Pete Vikulik turned to Mitch. "Doc, if you don't mind my asking, I seen Art hanging around you a lot, you didn't know him before, did you?"

"No. I only met him on the Fourth. With Emil"—Mitch hesitated, and refrained from adding—"and Carl Gaul."

Pete said: "You want to be careful of that guy."

Mitch was half-sure Pete Vikulik was a Communist; he seemed always to be with Sobol and Mike Sisto. Now Pete tried to

[302]

pump him. How well did he know Carl Gaul? Just from the strike, Mitch said, finding himself tending to minimize his friendship. If there was factionalism in the union, at least he didn't want to be identified on either side. The bartender set up a free round of beers. Mitch felt he had passed Vikulik's examinination.

A serious-looking man entered, stood by the end of the bar, ordered a shot and a beer.

Word passed down the bar; the men left their drinks and went into the back room, as Curly silently served the newcomer. Mitch, puzzled, slid off his stool and followed Pete.

"Cop," Pete said.

It was a policeman named Braden, lived on the street; they all knew him.

"I seen him out there on the line, I told that bastard to watch himself; I can swear he pulled his gun," Mike said.

The officer tossed down his whisky, gulped the beer chaser, and stalked out.

"First time he come in since the strike," the bartender said apologetically, as the men drifted back to the bar.

"You don't have to serve him."

"He won't come back," Pete Vikulik predicted.

One of the men opened the door to look after the cop, and they heard a couple of kids yelling: "Yellow cop, get off our block."

"Hey, you know that copper Emil kicked in the nuts? He's never gonna use them again. Young fellow too."

Some said if that happened to them, they'd kill themselves. Some said it was impossible from just a kick. They asked Mitch; he explained that it was improbable, but possible.

The crew from Washington was officed in the Opera building. Going over there was like resuming the feverish activity of the mass meeting; but now the job would be finished. Mitch felt relieved, in a measure, of the responsibility that had somehow come to rest upon him and George Price and grinning Rawley and a few others: to identify the cause of this wound in society. He felt a return of trust. There was still safety in the system in which he lived; there were still defending phagocytes to cope with infection. If the local government failed, the federal government remained with power to probe and correct the failure.

The federal government was like a staff surgeon standing behind the interne during an operation; true, there were times when an interne's knife slipped, and a patient died; but at least the superior was there to investigate and expose the error, and, if of negligence, to punish, if of incompetence, to eliminate the doer. Now it would become known how the knife had slipped on that Fourth of July.

Price, Rawley, and Frank Sobol were there. Rawley seemed to have some previous, personal basis of acquaintance with the men from Washington; he introduced Mitch rapidly. There were four or five investigators; the room was bright with an atmosphere of quick teamwork, and in the conversation there was a certain knowingness, as among newspapermen.

One fellow, extremely young-faced, was at the phone and remained there constantly, working from an endless list of numbers; he simply waved acknowledgment of the introduction. Another, named Sproul, apparently a classmate of Rawley's, had a huge, bulldog head, and the indefinable but instantly recognizable manner of the young liberal sprung out of some aristocratic, wealthy American family. Then there was a long-headed Jewish kid with a blotchy skin; and a slight, ill-dressed, insignificant-looking man with the kind of face that is easily forgotten and the kind of voice that is scarcely listened to, name

[304]

of Mussetti—they called him Musty. No one seemed to be in charge; the men worked well together.

They were discussing the status of the strike. It looked bad in Ohio. "Consolidated is putting the screws on in Canton and Warren," Sproul reported.

"Johnstown has gone berserk. The mayor has deputized the whole American Legion." The Jewish kid tossed a newspaper clipping onto a trestle-table that had been set up in the room.

Mussetti was looking through a letter, which he now handed to Mitch. It was from a lawyer in Ironville, evidently a friend of Musty's, telling how the sheriff and the mayor had been putting up a stiff fight against the Chamber of Commerce, but "the thing may bust wide open any day now. Speer has sent his right-hand man, Bert Field, down here, to put the bee on the Chamber. Told them if they didn't break the strike Speer would close up the mill for good. Said Ironville will be nothing but a junction between Routes 20 and 74, if they don't bust that picket line. All they yell about at the Chamber is, look how they handled it in Chicago, that's the way to handle things! They're just begging for another Chicago massacre here, and they'll get it too, unless . . ."

The Jewish kid, Tannenbaum, read from an editorial in a Mahoning paper. "No one is happy over needless death, no one will applaud the death of nine strikers in Chicago. But neither can lawlessness be applauded. To deny men who want to work the right to work is anarchy. Wars have been fought for liberty, and if blood must be shed again, in the cause of law and order——"

"As I see it," Sproul said, "we haven't got time to make a full investigation here. Even if we had the funds, they'd pull three more massacres by the time we nailed them on Chicago. We've got to make some kind of a flash to scare them."

They planned. There were two stories to stress, Sproul said.

First, the fact that nearly all were shot from behind. "That depends mostly on you," he informed Mitch. And, secondly, the story of that fellow who had been killed by what he called "aggressive negligence"—Dombrowsky.

"What about the Lindstroms?" Price put in.

Could the old man stand the trip? Then he must tell his story in Washington. That would make every front page in the country, and ought to make Otis Speer hesitate before pulling another Chicago.

Price wondered about the money-passing angle. "There ought to be some way to crack it," he said, repeating how he had overheard a cop in the plant beefing: " 'Dammit, the sergeants got theirs today, but a copper doesn't even get a sniff.' There must have been a big payoff at the top, too," George insisted. "Joshua Wheeler claims it was a hundred grand."

"We'd have to check every bank account in the city and probably then we'd never find it," Mussetti said wearily. "We haven't the dough or the time for a job like that."

"Does it matter so much if they were corrupt for money?" Rawley put in with his characteristic unmeant laugh. "It might even spoil the picture, to prove they got bribed."

"How?" Price asked.

Frank Sobol half smiled, with bitter appreciation of Rawley's remark.

"Well, what are we trying to stress here?" Rawley said. "We want to prove that the attitude of the Chicago police toward the strike was one of war. They were ready to shoot, at the company's behest. Now if we go and prove the cops did it for five bucks apiece, or even that somebody got fifty thousand bucks for ordering them to do it, we only prove that they were corrupted by money, and people will think, well, if they don't get bribed next time, they won't kill anybody."

Mitch felt dense. Sproul was smirking, in anticipatory agreement with Rawley's thesis. "What we have to show," Rawley concluded, "is something much deeper and more threatening than corruption in terms of money."

"But in the last analysis it all boils down to a question of money," Price said.

"Does it? Does it?" Mussetti blinked, lively.

"Doesn't it?" Sproul smiled.

"Well, maybe we'd better not get into it all the way," Tannenbaum remarked dryly.

"The only way it makes sense to the public is to show they were bribed," Price maintained.

"Exactly!" Rawley saluted the paradox. "That's just what I'm saying. The public expects to discover a bribe and to dismiss it as a bribe. But if there was no bribe, then the dumbest man will wonder—why did they do it?"

"Well, why?" Price asked, and answered himself: "Okay, so they got no monetary bribe. So a cop's salary is a bribe, if he wants to go on getting it, and a mayor needs donations to maintain his political machine—he gets bribed that way. The whole system is bribery."

"There is even the possibility of something more sinister," Rawley said. "There are things about this that you can't explain except on the basis of a deliberate plan for government by terror."

"Let's get down to cases," Sproul cut him short. "What about this cop that pulled Dombrowsky out of the first-aid car?"

"Gillespie can recognize him," Sobol offered.

"I'd recognize him," Mitch remarked, remembering the bull-wild man.

Gillespie would be a good type of witness to call to Washington. They considered what other witnesses to call, from the union. Frank Sobol?

"We'd have to go into your history with the United Steel

and Metal Workers, to forestall their springing it on us," Sproul said frankly. Mitch decided he was not a Communist, but maybe sympathetic to them.

"They can't bring up anything," Sobol stated with quiet confidence.

"What about this fellow Art Nowis? Is he a stoolie, or what?"

"I don't think he's an operator," Mussetti said. "If he is, he's the smoothest I ever ran across."

"Well, what about this statement he signed for the cops? About the landing-party and all that crap?"

"I can't quite make up my mind on him," Sobol said. "Art thinks he's such a smart boy, the cops might have foxed him or bulldozed him into signing anything. Maybe they had something on him that made him sign. His story is that they had all that stuff cooked up and sprung it on him for confirmation. We don't want to do anything about Art until we're dead certain. A lot of the boys know him since he was a kid. That's the trouble with a case like that; it's hard to get the goods on him."

"He's financial secretary," Mussetti reminded them, speculatively. "That op we caught in Warren, he was a financial sec. They go for that job."

"We've got him boxed in now so he can't do anything," Sobol said. "If we kicked him out or tried to expose him just now, it would weaken the morale."

They agreed it might prove worth while to talk to Art and see if he could give any testimony that would take the curse off the story about the "marines."

"I figure if he was really an operator he'd have blown town after that," Sobol said. "If he gets caught now"—he shook his head. "No, I think he's just an irresponsible fool, got in with some of those smart boys. He's not under the best influence, in the organization."

[3 0 8]

Sproul brought up the name of Carl Gaul: should Carl be asked to testify?

"That's what I mean," Sobol said bitterly. "Leave that gang out. They'll screw up everything."

Tannenbaum suggested Barbara Macey as a witness. He had heard she was a relative of a member of the board. That might be a juicy angle.

"Her uncle is a director, all right," Mitch informed them.

"We haven't played it," Price said. "I thought it would be a swell surprise angle to save."

Sobol looked at the wall, silent.

"Would she testify?" Sproul inquired.

Mitch could picture Barbara enjoying herself in the limelight.

"Is she okay?" Musty asked. Sobol shrugged. "Well, we can talk to her anyway."

Sproul was going out to Captain Wiley's station in the morning to take depositions from the police and to select cops to testify in Washington. Mitch agreed to go along and see whether he could pick out the Dombrowsky case bull. Besides, he had to examine their reports on police injuries on the Fourth.

At the station they were received with grinning bravado. Sure, come on in, ask us anything you want, we've got nothing to hide, you sonsofbitches, was the feeling in the air. The sergeant ushered them to the lieutenant. Captain Wiley was out. But the lieutenant said: "Talk to anybody you want. A lot of the boys are in the locker-room upstairs. They were all out there the Fourth, I guess, all those that are here."

He himself had already made a deposition about his activity on the Fourth. Roughing through some papers in his old roll-top desk, the lieutenant found a carbon of his deposition. While

Sproul and Tannenbaum attempted to requestion him, Mitch glanced through the report. It was cut and dried: how he had marched out his men, lined them up, how they had been attacked. . . . And as he read, Mitch heard the lieutenant giving the same answers; he knew his story and stuck to it. Did the police eat in the company cafeteria? Well, they had orders not to. Were the orders obeyed? "Well, I got no reports of disobedience." No use calling him to Washington.

Upstairs was a long room, locker-lined, furnished with a few tables and folding-chairs. Maybe a dozen cops were in the room, coats shed.

"These fellows are from the Goshall committee——"

"Gottschalk," Sproul corrected, genially.

"Yah, this committee in Washington, investigating the riot on the Fourth. Tell them anything they want to know." The sergeant shuffled out.

The men looked unsure of themselves. One arose and started to put on his coat. Sproul approached a group playing cards and said, generally: "We just want statements about what happened out there on the Fourth."

"I already made a statement," said one card-player belligerently.

"Yes, we have those. We want something more detailed."

The policemen stared at Sproul, at Tannenbaum, at Mitch, and remained silent. Then one who had been at his locker came toward them. Mitch recognized the man. It was that policeman—Braden—who had come into Curly's place for a drink. "I'm a union man myself," he stated. "I was in the bricklayers' union before I got on the force. Six years in good standing. Lots of the boys were union men. Most of us, one time or another. We've got nothing against union men."

There was a murmur of corroboration.

"But those people out there the Fourth"—he shook his head,

like a man who regretfully finds it necessary to reveal the immorality of his neighbors. "They were led by a lot of wrong guys. You know a lot of Polish people and Italians work in those mills—now I got nothing against the foreign element— but you have to admit they don't always understand so good. Anybody can come in there and stir them up."

A group was forming now, of men ready to talk in this same vein, if, as it seemed, the investigators were willing to hear their side of the story.

"I can tell you I lost some sleep over what happened out there," Braden continued. "Nobody likes to see people killed. We seen a lot of slander and bad words about the Chicago police, like we was monsters or something. I live right around there and some of those mill people on strike live right down-stairs of me. They got their kids in the street hollering dirty names when I come home off my beat, but that don't influence me. I don't hold it against them. They don't know any better."

"The lousy sonsofguns were laying for us! They were drill-ing out there all week!" another cop burst in, thrusting him-self between Sproul and Braden. Instantly, Mitch recognized him as the one they had hoped to find: the short, beefy-faced cop who had pulled Dombrowsky out of Jock Kiley's car. "Those bastards were marching around drilling like for a war!" he asserted.

"When was that? Did you see them?" Sproul asked.

"MacFadden saw them. He put it in his statement. Three hundred of them drilling."

"MacFadden? Is he here?"

MacFadden was not there. But the bull-cop, Bill Gorcey, continued: "What about them guns? I seen them shooting, right at us."

"Did you fire your gun?" Sproul asked.

Braden interposed: "Just before we marched out, the cap-

[311]

tain ordered us: 'Don't use your guns, don't fire unless your life is in danger. Only to protect your own life.' "

A vigorous movement of corroboration passed among the men, many repeated the statement.

"The first shot was fired from that mob," Gorcey declared. "I seen it. The sonofabitch was wearing one of them white armbands, he had an automatic in there and he was dodging around in there, taking pot shots at us, the lousy bastard. I arrested him; he was trying to get away afters, in one of them ambulance cars they had all set for the battle, but I spotted that guy and arrested him."

So that was going to be their story.

"Who was that, with the automatic? Do you know his name?" Sproul inquired.

"Yah, some Russian name, some Communist."

"Where is he?"

"He's dead."

"He must mean Stanley Dombrowsky," Mitch put in.

"Yah, sky, that's the one. That Dombrowsky, he was in there with an automatic, that Communist."

"Did you know he was a Communist?"

"They found that out after they got him to the morgue."

"Did you get hit?" Sproul passed on.

"Naw," invincibly. "But I seen fellows—that sonofabitch Bolshevik was shooting out of that gun. And all this time our captain was pleading with them"—almost tearfully, Gorcey quoted: " 'Get back, folks, for God's sake get back, let us have no bloodshed'—and then"—Gorcey's eyes bugged—"I seen a hand reach up from out of that crowd, four rows back it was, and he had a revolver, and he fired point-blank straight at us."

"Did anybody get hit?" Sproul asked.

"No. He didn't hit any of us. Then all hell let loose. They let loose with rocks and milk bottles and hunks of scrap iron,

[3 1 2]

it was all coming over in a barrage, and I saw MacFadden go down." He was acting it out for them now, and the rest of the police sat back watching the performance, partly in amusement, partly in approbation, like soldiers admiring a bull session long after a war, not bothering to remember how it really was.

"They were coming at me—this fellow with the gun—I got set, and just as he comes up I sidestepped and let him have it. Then I seen this nigger. He was on top of MacFadden and he was pulling a razor. I rushed up on him and knocked him over."

Tannenbaum was taking shorthand notes. Gorcey waited patronizingly for him to get every word down.

"Did you use your gun?" Sproul persisted.

"Naw. I don't need no gun. I can take care of myself." A large round sweat area was spreading on his shirt, over his belly. "Then is when this Communist come at me. We was skirmishing around and it was every man for himself, then. He come at me but I give him the old one-two."

"You didn't shoot him?"

"Naw. We couldn't shoot. That's what they had those women and children in the mob for, so we couldn't shoot."

"Who did the shooting then?" Tannenbaum interjected.

"That was their own people, shooting," Gorcey explained, as to a nitwit. "They hit their own people, see? They had the guns hid in there in the second and third row, in back, and when they started shooting they hit their own people that was in front of them, that's how come they shot them in the back." He looked to the other police, triumphantly.

Tannenbaum glanced at Sproul, with an air of apologizing for having unwittingly opened the way into a stinking bog.

"They was all set for us," Gorcey concluded, his pig-eyes gleaming knowingly at Mitch. "They even had their own ambulances! They come out on the field with those ambulances and I stopped them. I got that lousy Communist bastard out

[3 1 3]

of there, they were trying to help him escape. I took him prisoner."

"That was Dombrowsky, who you didn't know was a Communist at the time?"

"They was mostly all Communists, we knew that, they was reds. They was out to get us and it was every man for himself." He sat down, pulling his sweated shirt away from his belly.

"Thanks," Sproul said.

Gorcey grinned. "They can't put nothing over on us."

The other police were tame in comparison. But as their testimony progressed, none admitting firing, none admitting carrying the non-regulation bludgeons they were shown carrying in the photographs, a fright of hopelessness grew in Mitch, for what could be done with men like these?

Stopping for a beer, Sproul and Tannenbaum checked over and assembled their notes. Sproul often clucked at a choice phrase, as a pathologist might gloat over a beautiful malignant neoplasm: what a specimen was Gorcey! They ticketed material for the hearing: about the bludgeons, which Price would testify were the same as those carried by company guards; they checked denials of firing against photos showing police firing. . . .

Tannenbaum, more and more depressed, circled his beer glass on the table. "Okay, we can show them up for a bunch of liars," he said.

"And killers."

"Yah."

Mitch caught Tannenbaum's despair. It was like his own feeling, sometimes, at the sight of some incomplete, idiot life, which, as a doctor, he knew must continue living.

"You have to figure," Sproul speculated unhappily, "these

[3 1 4]

men were practically all in the army. Did you notice, they all speak of it in terms of a war engagement? We met the enemy, and conquered."

"So what?"

"Bad as they are—I don't believe they'd ordinarily have that attitude. Somebody pumped them up. During that week. Somebody fed them that bull about the strikers drilling in secret, somebody scared them."

"Aw—they're just Chicago cops," Tannenbaum said. "And all Irish. So they wiped out a bunch of foreigners and niggers and Jew reds. That's all it is to them. Where does it get us, to show they are what they are?"

"Education, my boy!" Sproul said mock-cheerily. "Educate the public, and changes will come of themselves."

Tannenbaum made a disgusted mouth. They started to draw up a list of police to call to Washington. Gorcey first, of course—what an exhibit!

Mitch Wilner heard, next day, that Barbara Macey had begged off from testifying in Washington. No one could understand this. "She's just afraid her old man will cut off her allowance," Sylvia said.

The Gottschalk boys were chagrined. "It would have made the banner of every paper in the country," Sproul declared.

"I had the impression she was a showoff; I thought she'd jump at the chance," said Tannenbaum. "There's something fishy about her refusing."

But aside from the publicity value, what would the girl's testimony be worth? Mussetti pointed out. "She'd have been more useful playing on the other side; she might have got some inside stuff there," he muttered.

Just before noon, Barbara called Mitch. "Come have lunch with me." She insisted he pick her up at her "office."

[315]

"What do you mean, office? Are you working?"

"Not exactly." He heard her chuckle. "I'm volunteering."

"Volunteering what?"

He'd see, she said. The office was on the sixteenth floor of the *Clarion* building. The door was locked. There was no lettering on it, but written on a card stuck in a corner of the frosted pane were the words "Citizen Volunteers."

He heard the catch click; and, trying again, found the door open.

"Oh, here you are, Mitchell, you're late!" Barbara called in her most Eastern manner, arising from behind a desk where she was sorting newspaper clippings. "I'm all ready!"

The office was a typical one-room setup, with a small railed entry space, two desks, a safe, some filing-cabinets. Behind the larger desk sat a square-faced, mannish-dressed woman with a tallowy complexion, stringy hair, and startling, heavy eyebrows. She stared expressionlessly at Mitch. Perhaps it was for her benefit that Barbara put on the Boston accent.

"I think that finishes up to today, Martha," Barbara said brightly. "See you tomorrow morning."

"Thank you," the woman replied, watching them go out.

They walked to the elevator in silence, Barbara obviously relishing her mystery. He gave in. "Is that why you can't go to Washington?"

"Mmhm!"

"What does a citizen volunteer for?"

She gave him a shushing glance as the elevator door slid open. Not until they were settled in an alcove in a bar-restaurant to which she steered him, some fancy hangout on the lower level of the boulevard, did Barbara resume the subject.

First she pledged him to secrecy. "Mitch, you're the only person I felt I could trust. Even Carl doesn't know what I'm up to."

[316]

"Well, what are you up to? Who's that woman?"

"I thought you'd enjoy having a peep at Martha, that's why I asked you to the office. Also so someone could identify her in case my pretty corpse is found stuffing a sewer."

"Cut out the comedy."

"No comedy." She ordered a cocktail, and was silent until the waiter was a safe distance away. "That woman, my dear, is Martha Cross," she informed him.

"What am I supposed to do? Salute?"

"Exactly." And covertly, against her side, she angled her palm upward as in a Fascist salute.

"What is it? A female Fuehrer?"

In zigzag fashion, Barbara told her story. Some days ago she had been sitting in the lounge of International House waiting for Carl; a copy of Father Coughlin's *Social Justice* was lying around, so she had picked it up out of curiosity, and come upon an article that was practically word for word the same as the pamphlet Consolidated had mailed its employees— "you know, that 'C.I.O.—Communists In Office' thing. I had one in my purse and I was comparing them, so I must have looked the picture of a little Fascist literature-peddler." And behold, a very tall and blond and handsome young man had approached, making some remark about what was she reading. Since he had a very cute German accent, and International House was full of Nazis sent over on some sort of scholarship arrangement, she had pretended to be fascinated by some anti-Semitic junk in that same issue of the Coughlin paper, and thereby gotten into quite a friendly discussion with the Nazi. About how the Jews financed the Russian Revolution, and Jews in the C.I.O., and pretty soon they were practically soulmates. Heinz—that was his name—was delighted when he found out that she was related to a member of the board of Consolidated, "and of course that made me kosher with a Nazi

right away." He had offered her all sorts of fascinating literature, and suggested that he help her read it, in German. And
next thing she knew, he was eager to introduce her to some
fine people, especially to "a very brilliant woman doing some
important work," who needed secretarial assistance, just typing
letters, and in fact sometimes a few corrections in her English.
Perhaps Barbara would volunteer a few hours daily to the
cause? That same evening he had taken her to a meeting.

"Nazis?"

"Silver Shirts. Sort of half and half, Bund members and
Silver Shirts."

"Weren't they suspicious of you?"

"Say, I gave them a wonderful line about how the University
is swarming with Jews and is run by a Jew Nathanson who
sleeps with all the gentile faculty wives by threatening to can
their husbands if they refuse, and I told them how I personally
spied on the Communists in the student union. . . ."

Then she had got that gang to talking about the strike.

Barbara spoke in an excited sub-voice, intimately, her head
angled so she could look into his face. And as she talked, Mitch
felt a sense of chimera, of unreality, coming over him. Nothing was certain any more. What was this girl? You knew nothing of anyone except the phase a person presented. To the steelworkers she presented herself as a rich man's daughter in
sympathy with the workers. To those Fascists, she was a mag-
nate's daughter, working against the union. On which was she
spying? Where was the truth?

Amongst the men themselves, within their own councils, they
knew they were being betrayed. There was no trusting anyone.
All relationships were diseased with suspicion. That was perhaps the most horrible effect of all; he could see this force of
suspicion working like an enzyme, breaking down the cohesion
between the men, destroying their mutuality.

[3 1 8]

She was saying, laughingly: "It's silly how careless these people are. Anyone can get in with them. They don't know me from Adam and yet Martha Cross takes me right in to work in her office. It made me think—the comrades are the same way. Anybody that comes around and acts sympathetic can get in."

And what did this Martha Cross have to hide?

Well, she had only been there a few days, but the whole setup was fishy.

"Who are the Citizen Volunteers anyway?" Mitch asked.

"There aren't any, I guess. It's one of those organizations on paper, you know, just a name; and some one person is it; and every once in a while they change the name. I guess Martha is the Volunteers; only her name isn't even Martha Cross."

Her real name, Barbara suspected, was Emily Schwartz, for the other day a package of stuff had come, from the German consulate, and Barbara had started to unwrap it and inside was an envelope addressed to Emily Schwartz, and just then Martha grabbed the whole mess away from her.

"But what is she supposed to be doing?"

"They're going to do something about the strike—some kind of a mass meeting. That's why Handsome Heinz put me in touch with her, seeing how I am a little daughter of Consolidated. You know they work the same as us, get a bunch of fancy names on a committee, and then they get in touch with clubs and churches and sympathetic organizations, only they're on the other side."

"What organizations?"

Well, she had seen Martha Cross's list—the Knights of Columbus, and Daughters of the American Revolution, and Chambers of Commerce and service clubs and the Legion, and women's clubs and young people's groups. Martha sent out stuff to them, like that anti-C.I.O. pamphlet, and stuff against lifting

[3 1 9]

the embargo on arms to Spain, and stuff against aliens—junk like that. "And she writes to all kinds of prominent people, congressmen and whatnot, exposing Communist organizations and activities like the American League, stuff like that. Her English—I have to rewrite all her letters. But she only lets me do the innocuous ones so far—anyway you can see they're not so innocuous."

Another thing, Martha Cross was in touch with all the American shirtmakers, as Barbara called them: Pelley and Gerald Smith and Winrod and other people whose names sounded familiarly sinister. "Her main idea is to get them to kind of work together through her, you know, like a central exchange for them. The reason they haven't gotten together into one movement so far is I guess they're as bad as the Lovestoneites and the Trotskyites and all those splinter groups—each leader has his own little outfit and if there's going to be a united front he wants to be in front. So she wants them to exchange information through her."

Another thing, this Martha Cross was a sort of one-woman red squad. "Yesterday she had lunch with Miss Gosling—you know, that society dame that got out that book, *Red America*. Well, apparently Gosling and Martha get together every once in a while to add to the list. But Martha really knows her stuff."

"Where does she get her money? The German consulate?"

"That's what I wanted to tell you!" Eying him excitedly, Barbara drew an envelope from her purse, and smoothed it. "I fished it out of the waste-basket." On the back flap was the engraved monogram of the Consolidated Steel Corporation. "A fellow came in with this, and right after he left Martha sailed out, said she had to go to the bank."

That was all she had found out so far. She glittered. What did he think she ought to do?

He supposed she should give her information to the Gott-

[3 2 0]

schalk boys. But there was probably no law against Consolidated Steel contributing to a reactionary organization.

"Listen, they don't throw their money away," Barbara said knowingly. "They get something for it."

"Well, they're getting all this propaganda."

"I think they're getting something more tangible. I'm going to find out what it is if I have to sleep with her."

She agreed for him to tell one of the Gottschalk men, confidentially, about the Citizen Volunteers office.

Sproul and Mussetti were at Guzman's Grove taking depositions from strikers. " 'Citizen Volunteers,' " Sproul repeated. "That's a new one. Ever heard of it?" he asked Musty. "Heard of a Martha Cross?"

"Martha?" A faint amusement went across Mussetti's deadpan face. "What's she up to? Last I heard she was working with the Bund crowd in Los Angeles."

Mitch explained.

Mussetti shrugged. She didn't have much on the ball, he said. A fanatic, who got tangled up in her own feet, most of the time. Her real name was Schwartz, Hilda Schwartz or something. "Speer giving her money? I wouldn't be surprised."

Mike Sisto stalked into headquarters; over one arm, he carried a stack of posters. "Sonsabitches, look at this, they got the town plastered!" He spread one of the posters on the floor. "They even tried to stick one in Curly's joint! He told them where they could stick it, all right!"

The poster, a many-colored, expensive-looking job, showed a beautiful girl in flowing white robes floating cloudlike over a parade of men heading for a mill gate. She was like Montgomery Flagg's Columbia, of wartime posters; but instead of a flag, a banner unfurled behind her, with the words: The Right to Work. In her left hand, she held the eagle-tipped

[3 2 1]

staff of the banner and, under her right arm, a gilded governmental emblem—a thing like an umbrella-stand.

A group of men gathered around the poster.

"Sonofabitch! That's the Fascist emblem!" Pete Vikulik swore, pointing to the gilded fasces under the girl's right arm.

"I don't think they can have used it intentionally," Sproul said; "after all it's on the back of every dime."

"Yah, but that's what they mean all right, they showed themselves up without knowing it," Mike insisted.

Several of the men had to have the fasces pointed out, the symbol being unfamiliar to them. "If you was a wop, you'd know it okay," Mike told Tiny Jardine.

Below the picture was an announcement of a Big Americanization Meeting in the high school auditorium, Friday.

Al Nees, in his laconic way, produced a stack of tickets from his littered desk. "Some of the boys picked them up." The tickets carried a thirty-cent price but were all stamped complimentary.

Mitch took one.

It announced the Citizen Volunteers sponsoring a big Americanization meeting, program including winners of the high school patriotic oration contest, and Colonel Gordon Roper of the American Legion, Nationally Famed Speaker.

"Bastards, getting the high school kids in on it," Jock Kiley commented.

"Where do they get the right to use the school auditorium for their meeting!" Nees exploded. "That belongs to the taxpayers. That's taxpayers' money built that place!"

"Roper, huh?" Mussetti said, with his glance of a shared joke, to Sproul. "The California boys are getting their little cut, too."

"Who is he?" Mitch asked.

"One of the Legion's red-hunting committee. He has a name for himself—what does he call himself, Musty?" Sproul asked.

[3 2 2]

"Guardians of America, Incorporated," Mussetti responded. "Used to be hitched up with Gerald Smith, but they split."

"I know that outfit! Guardians of America"—Kiley smacked down his fist. "That Indiana fink—Tiny Jardine's brother—contracting gorillas down there in Terre Haute—he was affiliated with that organization. Guardians of America. I remember kidding Tiny about it."

"Is this Jardine supplying any men to Consolidated?" Sproul asked.

"Naw, he beat it the hell out of here. Tiny nearly killed his brother himself when he found out he was peddling scabs in that carburetor strike down there."

But the links began to form now, in Mitch's mind. To these others, evidently, the chain was long familiar.

And why should it be astonishing to him that the same people who broke strikes were the people who agitated against aliens and who printed anti-Semitic stuff and who distributed literature supplied through a German consulate? This should be no more astonishing than that the people who organized unions were the same people who agitated for unemployment relief and for racial tolerance and eventually for some kind of socialism.

Only, what was proved? Because some kind of American Fascists were busy in the strike, did it mean they were running it, did it mean that they had stationed that firing-line? Because some Communists were in the union, did it mean they ran the union?

There was one hint of hope in the papers. Old Joshua Wheeler had thought up a good one. He was demanding that the health department close up Consolidated Steel, forbid the scabs to live inside the plant, as the buildings had no sanitation. The mayor had ordered immediate inspection by the health department. Looked like the mayor was going to have to order those scabs out, maybe to square himself for the Independence Day massacre. And once they were out, most of them wouldn't dare go in again. The plant would have to close down.

The men asked Mitch Wilner's opinion about the health department stunt. "That's right," he said. "According to health regulations, they have to send those men out of there." It looked like a cinch.

Emil had moved out of the hospital to Mrs. Jugovich's place, instead of his old boarding house, and often of an evening, now, Mitch found himself sitting around the place with his convalescent patient and some of the other boarders. They had only speculations, rumors. Consolidated was losing five hundred thousand dollars a week on the strike. Consolidated had lost a two-million-dollar government contract because it could not comply with the labor specifications.

Often Mitch wondered how long the boarding house could hold out, with all the roomers on strike.

One fellow moved away. A sluggish, middle-aged Pole. They cursed his guts, swore he'd gone back to the mill to scab; others said he'd gone to Mahoning to scab.

Art came around to see Emil. He seemed to be accepted again.

"Did you get one of those lousy cards, to vote if you want to go back to work or not?" Mike Sisto demanded, picking his card out of the fruit-bowl used for mail.

"Yah, I got one," Art said. "Watch out, they can take those cards and check up how you voted."

"How are they gonna check up on you?" Emil demanded. "It's supposed to be a secret ballot."

"Yah?" Art pulled out one of the cards. "Look at that." He pointed to a little serial number next to the printer's trade-mark.

"Sonofagun"—Mitch noticed that the men always modulated their swearing in the presence of Mrs. Jugovich—"I figured that was the printer's job number or something."

"There ain't no printer's union label on that card!" Mike discovered, indignantly.

"That number is different on every card," Art explained. "That way they can check up how you voted." He compared his card to Mike's. The numbers were different.

"Screw them," Mike tore up his ballot. "They know how I vote without any lousy cards."

Barbara phoned Mitch's office. She had been rushing around all day with Martha Cross. "This will kill you. We're using the private car of one of the vice-presidents," she said. "He loaned Martha his car and chauffeur." They were driving all over the steel district, and Martha was interviewing ministers and a Greek priest and superintendents' wives, clubwomen, and Rotarians, getting them all to sign up as Volunteers. "She even got a rabbi," Barbara reported. "Poor old soul, he was so scared he didn't know what to do. Martha pulled that stuff about what a shame to have it said that Jewish agitators were causing all this C.I.O. trouble, and how using his name would show that the real Jews were against the radicals. Rabbi Shiffman, or something like that. I'm trying to keep out of sight, but if Emil or any of the boys see me riding around on this committee they'll probably cut my throat."

Al Nees had clipped out the full-page ad about the Citizen Volunteers, from the *Steel Harbor News*. He stuck it on the wall, under the photographs of the massacre, and next to the union card taken from the body of Damon Antinoous. Someone had tacked that up, and drawn a black border around it.

The men gathered, reading the names signed to the Right to

Work ad. Groves, the realtor, old Judge Hines, Sam Marcus of Marcus's Big Store—catch me going in there again—Fred Vlasek, the Ford dealer—no union man would buy a Ford anyway— the Reverend Theodore Holmes, Father Wilks—and suddenly a ferocious voice cried: "Sonambitch! Father Stephen Antonidas of the Greek Orthodox Church, that stinking crappot! I'm gonna break his neck!"

"Keep your pants on," Jock Kiley kidded the Greek, Skourakis.

"What's the matter, we go build him a new church and he signs up with this stuff. We're gonna show him where he gets off at!" The Greek beat it for the coffee house, to gather a committee.

The Gottschalk crew had to return to Washington to prepare the case. "I don't think much will happen at that citizens' meeting," Sproul speculated. "But it would be well if someone outside the C.I.O. were there." Mitch arranged to go with Arthur Main. Sylvia said she was tired; Judy had been peevish all day, and worn her out. She had hoped they could spend an evening together quietly at home, listening to some records. He was sorry he had even mentioned the strike. Could have told her he was going to a medical society meeting.

The high school occupied half a block; he noticed that an extension was being built by the W.P.A. A row of state police cars was parked near the entrance. Mitch knew, however, that the union had decided to stay away from the affair. Half a dozen more cops were in the lobby.

Nobody asked for the tickets. But just inside the auditorium was a group of men in white shirts, ushers. One of them looked familiar. It took Mitch a moment to place him. The name came to his mind—Flint. That strange patient who had given him ten dollars for the Lindstrom family. The man recognized him, too, he was sure, but turned away.

Up in the front row, Mitch saw Barbara, notebook in hand, sitting with Martha Cross.

The main floor was about two-thirds full; the balcony was empty. Very few in the audience looked like workers. Most of the men wore coats; even the coatless wore ties. The women looked as if they worried too much. But toward the rear, in one row, sat an obvious C.I.O. section. Mitch recognized some of the fellows; about half were leering, the rest were solemn.

Half a dozen men were seated on the platform, before a huge American flag. A boy and a girl, the winning school orators, sat tensely to one side.

Of the men on the platform, a few had the easy authoritative look of superintendents, who might have been workers in their time but were living evidence that every man had a chance to become a big shot; there was a ministerial type, pudgy-faced, with spectacles and a gray suit; then a president of something, a man obviously used to going out from his small town to hobnob with importance in New York.

But it was the man on the end seat, separated from the others by a few empty chairs, who drew attention. He was obviously the speaker of the evening, Colonel Roper. A distinctly American type, large, fattish, jowly, nearest to the mill superintendents in style, but suggesting more of urbanity in spite of his ruggedness—a man like, say the successful ranchers who once went to Europe and showed hotel-keepers they couldn't be fooled; a man who could probably still suck in his gut and bulge out his huge chest and look fit as a fighter; his large red cheeks were bursting with vitality, a man of the West, bold and free, with great arms and huge fists.

[3 2 7]

First—just as in that meeting in the Opera House—the minister spoke, about peace, and reason, and an end of strife in the community.

Mitch wondered about the kids. "Folks must be scabs," Arthur Main surmised. "Or foremen." Still, they might be workers' kids, ignorant that this was a strikebreaking event.

"All those Americanization outfits are trying to work in the schools now, nabbing them young," Arthur Main informed Mitch.

The girl was introduced first, and she delivered her little oration about the Constitution with elocutionary gestures obviously rehearsed before the mirror. Our forefathers, who shed their blood that we, their children, might have freedom . . . Nasty, to use the kids.

The boy was apparently from a richer family. Something in his ease of manner, in his voice, in the way he wore his clothes. Most of his oration was a sonorous paraphrase of the Declaration of Independence.

And then the minister introduced Colonel Gordon Roper, president of the Guardians of America, nationally famous speaker, who had flown from California to address them on this occasion.

Colonel Roper, smiling genially at the high school orators, stepped to the rostrum and began to talk in an easy way, his voice redolent of the West and yet with a touch of warm Southern inflection, his words informal and tangy, starting like philosophy in a country store, rising sometimes to the pitch of gospel-preaching in a tent, and yet full of humor, like a speech before a Rotary Club. He began by saying every time he had to make a speech he was reminded of the advice of his good friend Will Rogers. " 'Will,' I said to him one time, 'you've talked to folks all over the country, now what is the best way to win their confidence?' 'Colonel,' Will said to me, 'the way I always start in is by telling them something they already know. That way they figure I ain't a liar, and after that they'll believe anything I tell them.' "

The audience warmed to him, and he threw in the next chunk. "There are only two kinds of people in the world," he said, "the kind that see what they believe, and the kind that believe what they see. Now we Americans are the second kind, we're all from Missouri, facts is what we want, and I am going to give you facts tonight. And let me tell you people, the time has come to wake up to the facts!" He slapped the rostrum with his thick palm, and with his other hand drew from his pocket a sheet of paper, to which he occasionally glanced, as a man referring to facts and figures.

Arthur Main was shaking his head, worried. "Damned skillful," he murmured.

"Now I tell you the hour has come, in our country . . . yes, I say, we are going to have to pay the piper!

"We have lived pretty well over here. Oh, yes, I know we have unemployment and we have our mother-in-laws, but, folks, when we look at the rest of the world, we can thank God for America! The people over there in Europe are already paying the piper; they have got Hitler and they have got Mussolini and they have got Stalyin! And, folks, the same thing is going to happen to us unless we get hold of ourselves right now!"

He was like a radio tube coming to a glow; the huge red cheeks suffusing with blood, as the excitement of his manner mounted. For nearly half an hour he developed his ominous generalities, now thundering grave, biblical phrases, now propounding the "four main principles of history." Then he would lighten his speech with a Mark Twain joke; you almost expected him to say his old friend and buddy Mark Twain. And still he didn't come out with anything definite; Mitch was be-

[329]

ginning to feel relieved, maybe it was just a pointless pep talk; but there were hints, hints, and after the intense respectability he had built up, upon his intimacy with Will Rogers, with Cecil De Mille, with senators and governors and that great humanitarian Cardinal Mundelein, whatever he advised would be fact and gospel. Such seemingly careless, dangerous skill. And you could see him, day after day, and a hundred florid-faced orators like him, a thousand, pounding the rostrums of high school auditoriums, pounding pulpits, and, between biblical parables and Will Rogers jokes, slipping in the business, for now Colonel Roper was slipping it in, tying it to a drawling joke about a schoolboy and a frog.

"—The frog makes a noise like it can almost sing, but all it really does is croak; it hops around like it can nearly fly; and it spends most of its time squatting on what you might call it's hind end—nearly—and that's a pretty good description of some folks in Washington. Yes, sir, they can nearly sing and they can almost fly but most of the time . . ." He rode the laughter again, and came out saying there were twelve principles of citizenship and liberty, and he had been over there to where they had those dictatorships, Italy and Germany, and he had been over there in Russia, three times in Russia, and studied it first-hand. "Those people are falling deeper and deeper into slavery, and what we have to watch out for here in the United States is certain elements that are starting us on the road to dictatorships, I don't care if they are Fascist or Communist!"

He had climbed up there and now he was on the plateau, chasing game. Arthur Main leaned to Mitch and quoted: "American Fascism will come under the guise of anti-Fascism." Mitch nodded; he could hear for himself.

But certain Americans were on the lookout, Colonel Roper cried. The Legion was on the lookout. "We in the Legion committee have a complete file and a complete record of all those subversive agitators and their fake organizations. The Communists have 645 organizations; they mask themselves under the names of patriotic organizations and peace organizations and certain labor organizations——"

"What about the Silver Shirts?" one of the boys in the C.I.O. group called.

Colonel Roper leaned forward courteously, while in the rear the white-shirted ushers took a few tentative steps in the direction of the heckler.

"I'm going to take care of them all," Colonel Roper promised. He wiped his glowing red face. "Now those Communists know there are two ways to attack a government, from within and from without, and you will find them everywhere like termites boring at the foundations of Americanism. We had one of them out there; in Arkansas they have a college, Commonwealth College—that is one of their Communist institutions—a fellow named Jellicoe ran it but we rode him out of that state, no reds allowed in Arkansas, but do you know where he is now, my friends?" He wiped his face again. "In Washington!" he thundered. "Getting our federal government money."

Down the line he went now—Federal Theater projects preaching Communism . . . Madam Perkins protecting a Communist alien, Harry Bridges, from deportation . . . and the National Labor Relations Board full of young Communist lawyers . . . and who is the first one invited to the Soviet embassy in Washington when they throw a banquet but John L. Lewis and family.

"And what are those Communists talking now? Democracy; progressives they call themselves; Communism is democracy, they tell us, and, folks, that is the kind of democracy we do not want, because every time it was tried in history it has failed; they had that democracy in Greece and it failed, and in Russia they are starving. We are not that kind of democracy, folks, in the words of President Madison, we are not a democracy. . . ." To his puzzled hearers he shouted out the next words: "We are a representative republic! We are not and we never were a common democracy, that is not the American ideal! . . . Our ideal is to be represented by the best of us! That is a republic of representatives!"

"The new Fascist line," Main whispered. "The difference between a republican and a democrat."

The speaker was pounding home the point, pounding in the republican word wherever he could; democracy, that is government by the lowest common denominator, by the ignorant and the unfit, but in a republic the most fit are chosen.

"The basis of our republic is that a man has a right to work and to own property. . . . Twelve million unemployed and the C.I.O. is trying to make more unemployed, men sitting down on their jobs, forcing industry to close down, and those people in Washington, those relief departments that are honeycombed with Communists, they will pay people to quit their jobs, they will put strikers on the government relief, because they want to be dictators, they want to fix it so one man can say when you can work and when you can't work, and that is too much power for any one man in this country and we don't have to call it Fascism or Communism or democracy, we know a dictator when we smell one!"

He had sweated through his coat, and now he removed it, standing before them, a huge torso so big of bone that his fat seemed flesh: a wide belt creased his belly. The sides of his white shirt were wet. "The way to solve unemployment," Colonel Roper announced, "and I have talked about this matter with a man who knows working conditions better than anyone else in this country, I refer to my old friend Bill Green, head of the A. F. of L., the way to solve unemployment is to work with industry, not against it, to encourage business, not to tax

[3 3 2]

it out of existence, to put our shoulders to the wheel instead
of to walk away grumbling because we haven't got perpetual
motion yet. No, sir. We still have to work to make the wheels
go around!"

Mitch looked at the audience. The faces were attentive but
impassive. This was the face of America listening, always that
solemn expressionless face, and it occurred to him that he was
a stranger to these minds, he simply could not tell what was
going on in these people, whether they were believing this
stuff or not.

It was time for another joke and Colonel Roper told one
about his good friend General Pershing making a surprise inspection of the front-line trenches and there were the doughboys
grouching like hell, cussing out everything from G.H.Q. to the
cooties, and the captain got red and embarrassed but Pershing
says fine! that is a soldier's privilege, to grouch, just so long as
he stands there in the trenches at his post! "And that's us!
What we need in this country now is a spirit like we had in the
war, all working together to win through this terrible crisis!
Grouch, hell, yes, that is American liberty, to grouch and kick
and you know damn well if G.H.Q. has any better grub at the
docks they will break their necks to get it to us boys in the
trenches, so let's all work together, and pull through!"

There was some applause. He pulled out a bandanna to wipe
his face. The high school boy orator was leaning toward him
with rapt admiration.

"What we need is that wartime spirit of unity! Why, with
that unified discipline we can put everybody to work! Remember in wartime there was no unemployment, why, wages were
high, everybody was making more money than he has ever
made since!

"And we have a war on our hands right now. It is an internal war, an internal scourge we must fight, folks, the twin

[3 3 3]

scourge of Communism and Fascism. There would be no Fascism if there was no Communism. No, sir! What brought on Fascism in Italy and Germany? It was the Communists, that is a known historical fact. Let us wipe out the danger of Communism and we have nothing to worry about from those Hitlers and Mussolinis!

"For already we can see the effects of Communism in our land. All over the country we see mills shut down, people starving. All at the behest of a labor dictator whose organization is filled with known and proven Communists. . . . Look at the facts . . . our big industries most necessary in wartime, our steel industry, our coal mines, our automobile factories that we depend on to turn out airplanes and tanks—that is where the Communists seek to gain control. We have their names and records on file, hundreds of them. We know who they are! And it is up to you. I tell you we are in a war and fighting a big battle right now, and every decent American citizen will do all in his power to break the hold of these foreign agitators and open these mills, bring back the first great God-given principle of liberty, the right to work, to produce and to create and, as the Good Book says, to enjoy the fruits of our labor. And there is no better way to conclude this meeting than by singing our national anthem."

He stood suddenly at military attention, his stomach sucked in, his sweat-shining face composed in resolution and power.

Excited, Mitch felt the desire to discuss what he had heard with someone intimate, wanted Syl to have been there. The way it was done—that last appeal to the war spirit, to the idea of unified command, and that clever bribe—remember how high wages were during the war—and the careless skill of it all!

On the seats were Back to Work resolutions for signatures; the ushers came down the aisles to collect them. That fellow

Flint was in the next aisle. Mitch saw Martha Cross stop to talk to him.

All the way back to Guzman's, young Main was depressedly silent. Some of the C.I.O. boys who had been to the meeting were already back, reporting. Several Tri-State and Midwest strikers had come over; there was a rumor of trouble brewing.

Half a dozen men sitting around the table went on calmly playing hearts; Jock Kiley had a hand in the game, and Carl Gaul was kibitzing.

"They won't get anywhere," Pete Vikulik stated confidently, talking to Cass Morrison, the long-nosed electrician, an officer of the Midwest Unity Lodge. "They didn't have more than three hundred people in the place, supers and their families, and storekeepers, that's all."

"They say anything about opening up Midwest?" Cass inquired.

"They can't pull anything like that!"

Al Nees said he had heard Tri-State was going to open up, on Friday.

"Sonofabitch, they'll never do it!"

"That's what they had this meeting for, to warm up the public," said Carl Gaul.

Tiny Jardine arose and stretched his huge form. "They ain't going to open that place! We'll show them a Fourth of July; we'll bring our firecrackers too, this time."

"How are they going to open it?" Vikulik reasoned. "That's over the Indiana line and it's a different story there. The Chicago cops can't help them. The governor made a promise not to use the militia in a labor conflict and he's kept it so far."

"Wouldn't do him any good if he wanted to use the militia," Nees said. "Who the hell is the militia, in the state of Indiana?"

"Okay, Captain!" Tiny mock-saluted.

Nees defended himself. "If you had any sense every man-jack in the C.I.O. would go down there to camp. Get a couple of weeks' free grub and the more men we have in there the surer we are they don't pull anything on us."

"Listen, the governor could order out the boys from down-state and ship them up here and where would we be?" Carl pointed out. "Those farm boys don't give a hoot in hell what happens to you guys."

"There is only five thousand militia full strength in the state," Nees said. "Couldn't muster more than three thousand of them any time, and in a situation like this"—he shook his head—"they couldn't find five hundred of them downstate to send up here. And they ain't going to get the federal army like in 1919, not with Roosevelt in. And they haven't got enough state police to handle us. No, sir, they won't try it."

"What about the Legion?" Mitch ventured.

"Too many of us belongs to the Legion, in the Harbor," Cass Morrison said. "They ain't going to get any of our posts out."

"Don't be so sure," Carl said. "They got them out in Johns-town, and that's a workers' town."

"It shows up in a time like this all right," said Pete Vikulik. "Every man that's eligible ought to get into those things. There's no reason why we shouldn't run the Legion and the militia, instead of those bastards."

Tiny said, disgustedly: "Ain't going to catch me drilling around in any Boy Scout suit."

"Go on, laugh, you dumbbell," Vikulik kidded him half angrily. "You notice every foreman and all them college boy engineers and metalloos they're hiring, they all go into the state militia and work to be officers. We ought to beat them to it."

The Greek Skourakis came in laughing. "Hey, you didn't see that Greek priest up there on that stage tonight, huh? No, sir, you didn't see no Greek priest, by God! Not in those ads any more neither! By God!"

"What did you do to him, George?"

"I don't do nothing myself. No, sir. I bring a committee."

They had to laugh at his wily expression. Skourakis told his tale. He had gathered a committee in the coffee house, that night the priest's name appeared among the back-to-work sponsors. And the Skourakis committee had marched over there to see papa priest. "We got plenty on him! Who's giving him the money for that church? There ain't no rich Greeks in this town, just chippers and maybe a couple of second helpers, that's all we got here. We come over to the priest's house and, by golly, he is so scared he don't even talk to us. 'Here's the key to the church!' he says, and good-by, boys. We got no more priest in that church, he's one thousand miles away!" The Greek, laughing, reeled off in search of someone else to tell the triumph to. "Next priest we get, he's gonna be a union priest!"

They were laughing like that when Barbara Macey came into the place, agitated. Carl went aside with her. Barbara had information that Midwest would open day after tomorrow. She'd got it from the fellow who was Martha Cross's go-between for Consolidated.

Carl was alarmed. Those bastards might even try to run scabs into the plant tonight. He rushed to the phone, to get hold of Alonzo.

Sobol came in, with white-haired Gillespie. Both looked tired. They took Al Nees aside, and talked; Vikulik joined them. They were still conferring when Carl came hurrying out of the phone booth, only to stand there, wild with the kind of fury that has no object upon which to spend itself. "I was just talking to downtown," he announced. "They got a long-distance call from Ironville; deputies just shot up the union head-

[3 3 7]

quarters, they surrounded the place and shot it up. There's two killed."

Tiny Jardine and several others jumped up from the table, as if to go, to do something. Then, like Carl, they stood, futile-handed.

"What's the use of exciting everybody!" Frank Sobol cried. Evidently he had come with the same news. He glared at Carl, for spilling it so crudely. "Take it easy, boys, don't lose your heads. That's just what they want." Nees sat down and dealt out the cards. "It's three hundred miles away and there isn't a damn thing we can do."

Someone turned on the radio, trying to find a news broadcast. All he could get was "Stay as Sweet as You Are."

After a while some of the boys came in with the news in the paper. It was another Fourth of July massacre; already they were charging that a secret, Communist-led faction in the union had planned to capture the plant that night; so the deputies had "prevented it." But one of the papers said there was a dance going on at union headquarters when a whole gang of newly deputized civilian police started shooting, from across the street, then charged and wrecked the place.

"That's the follow-up on Chicago, sure, they got away with it here, why shouldn't they pull it everywhere else?" Sobol said.

A bitter, helpless silence fell. The card-players went on with their game, inattentively.

Carl drew Cass Morrison aside and repeated Barbara's information. "They're going to try to bust open Midwest. That attack on Ironville was just the beginning."

"What do you want to do, start a panic?" Sobol broke in on them. "They ain't gonna open Midwest. I was just over there. Two hundred Mexican boys are reinforcing the picket line. Don't worry, nobody is gonna get past them."

[338]

Mitch wanted to know where Barbara had got that Midwest story—from that usher at the back-to-work meeting?

She nodded.

"Who is he?" Mitch asked. "He came to my office once, name of Flint." He told how the man had left ten dollars.

"Flint?" she repeated. "Martha never mentioned his name." He had stopped Martha Cross in the aisle, there after the meeting, and whispered something about a "promise from the gentleman from Indiana" and "thirty-six hours." Martha, elated, had confided in Barbara that the Midwest would be opened.

It was nearly twelve o'clock, time for the change of Consolidated shifts. Pete Vikulik arose. "Who's going over?" he asked. "We want a big line over there; they may come out this shift." The health department order was supposed to go into effect.

"They won't come out," Carl reminded him. "Consolidated ran a whole bunch of Pullmans in there, for those rats to sleep in."

"They ain't got enough for all of them," Nees said.

The men were too angry to jest about scabs in Pullmans.

"If they'd come out, one sure thing, some of those guys would never get back in." Tiny flexed and unflexed his fingers. He went to the counter for a cup of black coffee before doing his turn on night picket.

Just then the door was kicked open, and a policeman stepped in, with a tommygun pointed at them. A squad of cops poured from behind him, all with revolvers drawn.

The strikers looked up from their cards, stared openmouthed. In his own mind, and in every mind, Mitch could feel one thought—what they did in Ironville. It's here. Walk in and shoot up the union headquarters.

The protective backstop that had always been in his mind, the citizen's sense of safety in government, was gone. If police,

[339]

the agents of that protection, could walk in and shoot up people—the inversion whirled him beyond nightmare. He only felt—and knew he shared the feeling of all there—trapped.

Perhaps this was happening everywhere, tonight, in all headquarters of the strike, all over the United States. Wipe out the union.

"Line up," one of the cops commanded.

The men, still holding their cards, arose, lifting their hands in the air.

Maybe these weren't even police. Maybe they were disguised company gangsters, like the time on St. Valentine's Day when a gang of bootleggers, dressed as cops, rushed in on their enemies and mowed them down.

"All right, look them over," the cop ordered; two of the police went toward the strikers, and frisked each man, thoroughly. An officer approached Barbara; Mrs. Jugovich, who had been working in the kitchen, stood beside the girl.

"Leave us alone, you don't have to go feeling up the girl, you cheap cops," Mrs. Jugovich said.

The cops searched the kitchen and returned, shaking their heads.

Pete Vikulik had found his voice. "What's the idea of busting in here like this? You got a warrant?" he demanded.

"What is this?" Jock Kiley asked, in an easier tone. "What's up?"

"We got a call," the officer replied. "Heard you boys might have some plans for the change of shifts tonight, so we came over to protect you."

"Thanks," Carl said, with an effort at sarcasm.

The police backed out, as in a movie bank raid, the one with the tommygun keeping them covered until all the others had left. They heard the police cars pull out of the yard.

Nees sat down at the card-table. The long burn on his face

[340]

quivered like uncovered flesh. "Come on, boys, I'm dealing," he said.

The air was sultry with their anger. Occasionally a curse flared like flame licking out the door-crack of a shut furnace.

"That's one thing they can't pin on Art Nowis," Carl remarked, on the way home. "Tipping off the cops."

"Why? Was anything really going on?" Barbara asked.

"Some of the boys were going to have a little reception party ready if those scabs came out. But there weren't six guys knew about it. Art hasn't been here all day; he went out to his brother-in-law's farm. There's a pigeon right in their own crowd."

"After all, the police could have guessed the boys might try something, if the scabs came out," Mitch said.

"Yah. I suppose. But that cop said they had a tip."

The strike seemed to have reached its crisis. The papers carried stories of militia in Canton, Mahoning, Johnstown, where "invasions" of C.I.O. rubber workers and miners were feared. There were fuller stories now, about what had happened in Ironville. The sheriff had taken the day off and gone out of town, as "things seemed quiet." Actually, it appeared he had been sent out of town by the Chamber of Commerce group, who, under pressure from Consolidated, had finally deputized a Major Carter Ross, and sixty men of his selection. Major Ross declared he had received information that the Communists in the union plotted to take advantage of the sheriff's absence and invade the Consolidated plant. He charged they had assembled a mob at headquarters, ostensibly for a dance. So he and his men had surrounded the headquarters and "prevented an attack on the plant."

The same story, Chicago all over again.

And now, the Tri-State Corporation definitely announced it

would open its mills. The governor of Indiana was still making last-minute compromise efforts, but Tri-State would open tomorrow. Midwest would probably open late in the week, depending upon the success of Tri-State.

As Syl was going to have dinner with Mort and Ora, Mitch Wilner didn't bother to go home. Out at Guzman's, things were quiet. Every extra man was over at the Tri-State headquarters, on the Indiana side.

Mitch stopped in at Mrs. Jugovich's for a look at Emil. He had one of the front rooms, and sat by the window with a notebook, recording the license numbers of the cars entering the plant. Art was there.

"Bastards are really making steel in there now, no crap." Emil said, pointing his chin at the smokestacks.

Mitch stared with him at the smoke streams coming red, yellow, white out of the chimneys, the colored streams mingling in the cloudless sky. "That brown smoke," Emil said, "that's where they're charging up a furnace. That white smoke is the working period, and that real thin smoke, that pot is ready to tap."

"Did you see, they may try to open Tri-State?" Mitch remarked.

"Huh? That's my shop!" Emil cried. "They ain't going to open that up," he added ominously. Art said he'd drive over to take a look, and Emil insisted on going along. "Okay—if you stay in the car. No running around," Mitch stipulated. He went with them.

The picket line was swollen to a huge circle encompassing the entire parking space in front of the main entrance to the plant. A couple of Mexicans carried guitars, and the whole crowd sang.

Alonzo himself was on the spot. There was some fear that

Tri-State would attempt the old trick of bringing scabs in by boxcar. Mitch followed Alonzo's Buick to the picket-posts at the freight entrances. Mexicans were there in force. "Never saw anything like it," Art Nowis said. "All you have to do is whistle and they come up out of the ground. Last night, when it got around the plant might open, there was fifty of them here inside of five minutes. Boy, I'd hate to run into them on a dark night if my name was Speer."

Back at the main gate they saw Carl Gaul and Barbara. "Going back to work?" Carl kidded Emil.

"They ain't gonna run this plant," Emil repeated, ominously.

"Got any ideas?" Carl asked.

"Yah. I got an idea."

They all sat in Carl's Chevrolet, and watched the pickets circling, like an enchantment in front of the huge, inert steel plant. It was hard to believe this little band of people, or any little group of men in front of a gate, could keep the monster paralyzed.

"There's one place, if it goes out of commission, they can't run a mill," Emil said.

The power house, Mitch thought.

And Art said: "You can't monkey with the power line; they tried that in Canton; hell, it was operating again inside a couple of hours."

"I got a better idea."

At first, Mitch had thought Emil was merely finding some sort of release in talk. But then he realized how the man had a necessity to return force for the force he had suffered. Mitch found it strange that Carl didn't discourage Emil at once. Emil had dropped his voice; they sat in the car, bunched conspiratorially. There was a water-pump shed, isolated from the rest of the plant, Emil explained. Down there by the shore; the water came through two intake pipes, and was pumped to the entire

[343]

plant, water being essential to almost every operation in the mill—the furnaces were water-cooled, and in the rolling-mills water had to be sprayed on the moving slabs of steel, and in the sheet mills . . .

"But you can't very well remove the lake," Barbara said.

If that pumping-station were shot, it would take several weeks to replace the equipment and get the water system going again, Emil explained.

"There's nobody even works down by those pumps," he went on enthusiastically. "You could blow the whole damn thing to hell and there wouldn't even be a chance of hurting anybody."

"Emil, I thought I checked up on everything, but I guess I better have your head examined," Mitch said, deciding to pretend he thought it was all a joke.

"The reason I'm telling you, Doc," Emil said, "is I figured you could get us some of the stuff."

"We could get dynamite from the miners," Carl pointed out. Evidently this idea was not entirely new to him. "But dynamite isn't the best thing for this and it would mean involving some of the miners. Alonzo can't afford to get mixed up in anything."

Mitch still couldn't believe they were serious.

"Look, Mitch," Barbara was saying, "if you could get me a condenser to use, maybe in your office-lab, I could distill enough nitro—you know, there's nothing to it, we made some for a gag once, in the lab."

"A joke is a joke," Mitch said, in a last faint hope.

"We've got to do something, and quick," Carl declared. "The Harbor can't hold out much longer. Everybody's bust. And they can see Speer has got Consolidated going full-blast now, they're scared. If this place opens up, a lot of them will go in. They've been beat down, that's all."

It was no use telling them bombing never worked; they knew labor history better than he did; they knew it always accomplished more harm than good; and if someone should get hurt . . .

"You heard about the times it didn't work," Emil said. "There's times it worked, too."

"The organization would never stand for it, you know that," Mitch insisted. "Why, it's just the kind of thing that provocateurs would be doing. You plant a bomb and that gives them an excuse to demand the militia." He looked directly at Art.

"That's okay, too," Art said. "They can call out the militia to keep the plant shut down, like Murphy did in Michigan."

"The organization will stand for anything that'll win the strike," Carl said. "There are lots of things Josh Wheeler don't know about and don't want to know about."

"I can't help you," Mitch stated. "The whole thing is insane. For Chrisake, get it out of your minds."

"I could use the university lab," Barbara went on. "It's vacation and most everybody is away. Only a couple of those idiotic grad students are around and might get curious, so it would be better if I could find a condenser someplace else."

"Forget it!" Mitch cried. "Your nerves are shot, all of you. Get some sleep and you'll wake up and realize what a lot of crap you've been talking." He stared at Barbara. Her mouth twitched up into her wry smile; she looked at Carl, then at Emil.

"Anyway don't mention it to anybody," Carl said.

"Of course not. But forget it."

"If something goes up, it's a surprise to you," Art said.

Mitch stared at them; all laughed uneasily. He decided they had only been playing with the idea, and would drop it. There was nothing more he could do. Mitch drove home.

He began to feel that he understood now how things happened. How a few people could dare and excite each other into a thing of this kind, after living weeks in an atmosphere of

[3 4 5]

mounting tension. At least for tonight things were safe; they had no explosives. He'd have to find a way to stop them. Going to Joshua Wheeler with the story would be unfair. That would have to be the last resort.

It was after twelve; but the apartment was still light. As he came toward the door, Mitch heard the orthophonic going. He hoped there was no company.

Sylvia was sitting alone, listening to Brahms. He felt troubled at her obvious loneliness; yet she could have been with him. He stood for a moment listening to the music. Perhaps if he told her of this new worry, in discussing it, the estrangement that had been growing between them would dissolve.

"Tired, dear?" she asked.

"Yes. Been home long?"

"Since ten. There were two calls; I told them I didn't know when you'd be back, and I guess they got someone else. One was a new patient, the other was Mrs. Becker." He was irritated by the undertone of accusation. He went to phone Mrs. Becker, who had frequent inconsequential attacks of asthma. Syl shut off the victrola and went to sleep in the separate room.

The morning papers said the governor had persuaded Tri-State to delay the opening of the plant another forty-eight hours. The news affected Mitch like a personal reprieve.

Luckily, too, he had a South Side call to make after dinner; but then he was shocked to realize he felt lucky to have a legitimate excuse to be away from Sylvia.

Barbara lived at the Mansions, on Blackstone; it was one of those fountain-in-the-lobby places, with apartments arranged like stalls, down a long corridor. Handy for the girl, he imagined, as it was near enough to the University, and yet a place where a co-ed might live as she pleased.

She wore lounging-pajamas. "Come on in, I was just moping."

"I was looking for Carl," he said awkwardly. "But he wasn't around Guzman's; and I don't know where he lives."

"He only lives here part of the time," she said with her perverse grin; "he's supposed to live at the Harper Hotel. What do you want him for? Won't I do?"

"Maybe." He couldn't pick up the manner; felt too old. Though he had the usual share of half-invitations that fall to a doctor, Mitch realized this was the first time in years he had made what might amount to a social call on a girl; and Barbara was one of those females who, especially in a setup like this, inevitably aroused speculation.

"Listen, maybe you and the boys were just joking last night," he came directly to the point. "But I'm terribly literal-minded. You haven't gone ahead with it, have you?"

"With what?" she teased him, sprawling on the couch.

"That crazy idea. The nitro."

"Sure," she said cheerfully. "I spent the whole day in the lab." Stretching, Barbara picked up a test-tube that lay carelessly among some books, and offered it to him. The tube contained about an inch of colorless fluid. "With my own little hands, Doctor," she boasted. "I haven't tried it yet."

He didn't take the tube. "If I work all day tomorrow," she babbled, "I think there'll be enough to blow up the whole damn plant. It's perfect this week, the entire building is deserted." Trailing over to the window, which gave onto a court, she suggested: "Shall we try the sample? The worst that can happen is it'll break a few windows." She hung out the window, her buttocks, in the neat-fitting slacks, confronting him. He might take the opportunity: what she needed was a good walloping.

"Listen, why are you getting into this?" Mitch demanded. "To impress Emil?"

[3 4 7]

Barbara withdrew from the window and turned around to him. She wore that essentially feminine expression of pleased curiosity. "I don't really know why I do anything, Mitch," she said. "Look, you think I'm just a little rich bitch playing with the woikers because it's fashionable now. The boss's daughter on the picket line." She sat down beside him, still holding the damned test-tube.

"Put it down." He took it from her and carefully placed it on the table.

"I just want to be with people," she continued, "people who are flesh and not paper. To do things their way."

"Whose way? This isn't anybody's way of doing things. Whose idea really was this, to begin with? Art's?"

"No. I think it was Emil's."

"Well, Emil isn't responsible for what he does, he's still woozy. And probably Art put him up to it, made him think it was his idea. After all Art Nowis still isn't clear of suspicion. And this is just the sort of thing a provocateur would do."

She looked directly into his eyes. "And after all I'm the boss's niece, why shouldn't I egg the boys on to their ruin, too? Look, Mitch, don't you realize that it's just when people are under suspicion that they will do something desperate, to prove their sincerity? I can understand Art."

"The one I can't understand is Carl," Mitch said. "The rest of you might go off your heads but he is supposed to have some responsibility in the organization."

"Carl is ready to try anything," she declared. "That gang is forcing him out. Frank Sobol has complete control there now. It's the craziest thing, instead of being blamed for their blunder, they take credit, they're proud that nine men were killed, and you'd think Carl was to blame for everything because he tried to stop it! They've undermined him, started all kinds of stories about him so the men won't trust him——"

[3 4 8]

"So now he's willing to go into a senseless stunt that will wreck the whole union."

"He's willing to take a gamble, that's all. It might work."

"But it can't work. You're just being romantic—bombs, conspiracies—if it wasn't so dangerous it would be silly."

"You're the one who's silly," she said. "You see everything, and you don't see anything."

He wondered at the penetration of her remark, for it was what he often felt of himself. He was in the midst of this, and yet could not understand why people did what they did.

"But Carl was the one who was opposed to violence," he argued. "His whole fight with Sobol and that crowd was because they were the ones who tried force."

"Force? Who tried force? When?" she demanded.

"Out there. On the Fourth."

She laughed. "Force is just what they didn't try. They sent people out there like sheep. All those people had was a few sticks and stones they picked up. What force was that against a line of guns?"

Mitch didn't dare follow the implications of her remark. Yet she and Carl were evidently ready to act upon them, justifying their own use of force if they could do it successfully.

"Listen, you can't play around with things like this!" he cried. "Thousands of people are involved. Barbara, you're nothing but a dilettante. You have no right to risk the strikers. You don't represent them."

"Isn't Emil a striker? And Art? I don't think you know the men, Mitch. They're not playing at this. They know what they're risking."

"You have no right. None of you have the right to assume so much responsibility."

She arose, picked up the test-tube, and leaned out the window again.

"Why don't you keep out of it, at least?" he insisted. "The best contribution you can make is to find out what's going on on the other side. Mussetti said you were in a swell position to do that. Why don't you come to Washington and testify about that Volunteer Citizens stuff?"

"In the first place, it's not ready, Mitch. I haven't half found out what's going on there. All I could do now is expose Martha, and she isn't much. I don't think I'd even want to expose her—you know I've kind of gotten to like her, poor old girl. It's her whole life. She may believe a lot of insane crap but she's absolutely sincere——"

"Sincere!" he cried. "Everybody is sincere! Hitler is sincere! Speer is sincere! That doesn't excuse being wrong!"

"Yes, I know," Barbara agreed, with an air of pained helplessness, her underlip thrust forward in a little-girl look of dismayed irresponsibility. "That's what's so hellish about the world." She leaned far out; he waited, knowing she would drop the tube this time. The explosion reverberated in the enclosed court. Panes rattled. In a second, windows went up, all around, and voices cried: what happened? The explosion of life out of all those inanimate window spaces was like kicking a dunghill, starting an insane confusion of bugs, flies, running and flying in all directions.

A man's voice finally decided: "Nothing, somebody must've thrown an electric-light bulb." The man repeated this over and over, reassuringly, as excited females kept sticking their heads out of the windows.

"You goddam baby," Mitch accused Barbara. She looked at him with her eyes large, impish, and disgustingly amused. She'd go through with anything, he decided, for the thrill.

He couldn't sleep. At breakfast, Sylvia noticed his eyes twitch-

[350]

ing. "Dear, what's the matter lately? Are you worried about something?" she asked. He told her.

"Imagine those fools! Thank God, you didn't get mixed up in it!" she cried. "Mitch, do me a favor, don't go near that mess again."

But something had to be done to stop them, he insisted; if there was only someone Carl would listen to.

"How about Professor Rawley?" Sylvia suggested. "Carl respects him. But, Mitch, don't let them get you mixed up in it any further. If Rawley can't stop them, tell Joshua Wheeler and let that be the end of it."

"I see. I see." Rawley listened with sparkling anticipation, the same kind of zest, Mitch sensed, that a medical man feels as a perfect set of symptoms is unfolded in the progress of a disease.

The boys really meant to go through with the plan, Rawley agreed, but he thought he could talk Carl out of it.

"I simply don't understand such irresponsibility," Mitch said. "It begins to look as though the Communists were justified in distrusting him."

Rawley eyed him amusedly. "Why shouldn't they distrust him?"

"What do you mean?"

"Didn't you know Carl Gaul was kicked out of the party?"

"Oh," Mitch said. "What for?"

"When he was doing graduate work here. I guess it was because he wouldn't hew to the party line on every occasion. I'm not a party member, Wilner, I'd tell you if I were. But I often work with them; I find they're all right to work with."

"But what right has Carl got, or the party got, to carry their quarrel into the S.W.O.C.?" Mitch demanded. "After all it is the union that is suffering because of their disagreement."

Yes, Rawley said, but of course neither Carl nor Sobol could be made to see it in that light, as each would insist he was devoting himself entirely to the building up of the union. "And they would mean it. They're absolutely honest, in that sense. To Carl, keeping the union free of what he'd call party domination is a major service. And of course the party people can only think of Carl as a Trotskyite snake."

"Well, is he a Trotskyite?"

"Carl probably knows a few of their local people, and discusses things with them. But whether he's technically a Trotskyite doesn't matter. To the comrades, any revolutionary opposition is Trotskyism."

Mitch wanted to know, did the Trotsky group have any real policy?

"Like all zealots," Rawley said, "they of course believe that they have the one and only truth, that they are the only pure revolutionary party left. But in practice it seems their one policy is to be against anything the Communist Party favors. They're purists. In Spain, for instance, they insist on a pure workers' revolution. Well, that places the Trotskyites in direct opposition to the government which is actually at war with the Fascists." He bubbled, in fascination at the strange forms, the boomerang tracks, of social forces.

If being contradictory was the mark of the Trotsky group, Mitch said, Carl was certainly eligible. "One day he burns at Sobol for trying to use force to break up the police line, and the next day he himself wants to use bombs! It doesn't make sense."

"But it makes exquisite sense," Rawley insisted, as one pointing out the group-marks of a seemingly irregular strep specimen. "And don't get the idea that contradiction is patented by the Trotskyites. The Commies can be just as perverse. It's often

[3 5 2]

a necessity of revolution. Just now, they call it flexibility. The river may have to backtrack, but it gets to the sea. The genius of revolution is the person who recognizes the precise form of force to use, and I don't mean only physical force; also the precise moment at which it will be successful. Carl was against the force Sobol used because he believed it was damned obvious it would fail at that moment. There, he was right." Rawley had lost the laughing character of one examining curiosities, and spoke with some passion now, the passion of participation. "Why, you never, even in a revolution, send a crowd of a thousand unarmed people up against a trained army with guns and machine guns! If you are going to try to knock over the Chicago police you don't do it at one plant, you do it at twenty, at a hundred industrial plants, simultaneously——"

"That's revolution."

"Of course. And the time for it has not yet come. And when it does come, you try to have the police with you. But Sobol wasn't thinking in terms of starting a revolution there. I suppose he figured he was using the situation to develop militancy in that mass of people. That would be the orthodox idea of how to use a strike."

"At least," Mitch said, "it's preferable to terrorism."

"Is it?" Rawley questioned, in his purely objective way. "The Irish revolted by bombing and sniping—there was a successful use of terror in a widespread, prolonged campaign. Probably economical, in deaths, as against what mass war would have cost."

For a moment, Mitch feared he had come to the wrong place. But it was incredible that Rawley could agree with that insane plan.

"No, no," Rawley reassured him. "The boys are crazy. Terror never works in isolated instances of this kind. And in this country"—he shook his head—"the McNamara business finished that.

[353]

In the long run here, mass militancy may work, terror never will. In other words, in this instance Sobol was half wrong but Carl is all wrong. He's lost his head," Rawley concluded. "He's no longer thinking of the strike, but is simply in competition for leadership, against Sobol. He's at a great disadvantage because Sobol is experienced and really a hell of a good organizer, which makes Carl all the more ready to accept this wild scheme, just on the chance of success."

"How will you stop him?"

"He still listens to me."

Why? Mitch wondered. Was it only an ex-teacher relationship, or did they belong to some organization?

Rawley guessed his thoughts. "I can't actually give him orders," he said. "I do happen to belong to an organization; Carl isn't in it; he respects our ideas, though."

A revolutionary organization? Mitch tried to ignore an insistence in his own mind, that if he encountered a group whose attitude coincided with his own, it would be morally wrong of him not to join.

"Well, most people confuse revolution with bloody revolution. But suppose it is expressed as a change to an accelerated system of distribution. It can be bloody or bloodless, depending on luck, and on planning. Blood is only a surface, not an inevitable mark of revolution."

"You think it's coming?"

"Oh, it has to."

"Well, if you're not Communists," Mitch said, "how is your outfit going to bring it about?"

"We're not bringing anything about," Rawley laughed. "We're more interested in analyzing, in arriving at a precise understanding of the movement of social forces. We're not a revolutionary group to the Communists, because they think we're so damn intellectual—we believe too much in education."

[354]

Did he mean, then, that the revolution could be accomplished by education, and not by force?

"That's a force, too," Rawley said, laughing. "But, sure, in the end there has to be some clash; it may come by blood—as status-quo propaganda wants people to believe, for such a belief frightens people out of doing anything—or it may come by perfect preparation, by organizing your forces so well that the show of strength alone is enough to bring victory. That's one technique we could borrow from the Fascists."

"In that case," Mitch wondered, "couldn't the revolution come by vote?"

"So far it has. But look, in Spain it was coming by vote and the other side saw it coming and started the war of blood themselves, the counter-revolution. And as for us over here, well, wasn't the Fourth of July massacre the same thing? We did something by votes, and they started shooting. You see, they're not dumb. They recognize it, any way it comes, and they'll fight any least step with every savage means at their disposal. They'll not hesitate to shed blood, though we may. They know that organization on a large scale, whether it is the C.I.O. or the A. F. of L. or the Communist Party, can be an instrument of revolution."

Then it was pretty hopeless, Mitch felt, for if the opposition was so ready, and the people themselves were handicapped by such internal fighting as between Sobol and Gaul——

"Wait a minute. Those splits aren't final, or fatal. You've got to understand what's going on with the men, more than with their leaders. In the first place Carl isn't a significant factor, except that he's hooked onto Jock Kiley, who is the natural leader of the steelworkers here. Ever since Sobol's old union, the United Steel Workers, went into Kiley's local of the Amalgamated, those two have been wrestling for control. You see, Jock Kiley is the old-fashioned, simple unionist with absolutely

[3 5 5]

no political program. He'd probably agree with the eventual desires of the Communists but he's afraid of them in his union. Well, mostly because he reads the Hearst papers, and *Liberty*. He's like a lot of A. F. of L. guys. He kicks like hell every time a party stooge introduces a resolution to back Loyalist Spain, complains the party boys fill the union meetings with so much twaddle about international issues there's no time for union business."

Mitch had heard that complaint.

"In the long run, of course, the men will realize that the union is just the place for such things, that everything in the world concerns them."

Did he mean, then, that the Communists should dominate, in the long run?

"No, nobody should dominate!" Rawley cried. "Don't you see? You can't depend on leaders. Especially when they are way ahead of the people. You've got to bring up the people so that they really know what's going on, so that they tell the leaders, instead of having the leaders tell them what to do."

But wouldn't that mean an awful lot of disagreement?

"Sure. That's our system. Democracy is the most difficult, but the most rewarding form of control. It is the essence of democracy that there should be some disagreement. As long as you have factions you can be sure of a powerful demand for expression, at least by the weaker group. Of course one danger is death by dissension, and the other danger is suffocation by one side's getting strong enough to build a machine. That's what happened in so many A. F. of L. unions, and the same thing often happens in our two-party system, in the government. As in the city government of Chicago."

"But then," Mitch said, "you just mean using the system we have."

"That's right. But using it. All the way. In economic life, too."

"And that would lead to socialism?" Mitch ventured.

"Wouldn't it?" Rawley laughed again, and for the first time Mitch began to perceive his equation. "What does your organization do?" he asked.

The sociologist looked a bit vexed. "We try to spread a few facts of life. I'm afraid, though we've got the right ideas, we don't know how to spread them, as yet." Rawley pulled open a drawer and handed Mitch a sheaf of mimeographed stuff, headed "Toward a New America." "I'll talk to Carl," he promised. "Don't worry."

Mitch glanced at the mimeographed pages. There were lots of charts and diagrammed statistics of production and consumption and consumer goods and capital goods. The text was academic. Imagine Mike Sisto wading through stuff like this. Rawley's revolutionary movement, he guessed, was a head without a body.

Mitch Wilner awoke with a sense of fear; the bombing might have taken place in this night. If Rawley had not reached Carl.

While he was in the shower, Jackie came marching into the bathroom, carrying the *Clarion*. Judy was directly behind him.

"Pop, I got a present for you," Jackie announced.

"From Mom," Judy said.

"Wait, don't come in here, kids, you'll get wet."

"Mommy said look in the paper." Jackie reached out the *Clarion* to him.

She wouldn't have sent it if the news was bad. He held the sheet damply outside the shower curtain.

Steel Mills Open . . .

Not that the strike was broken. Agreement reached. Tri-

State at 3 a.m. had consented to sign an agreement, not with the union, but with the governor of Indiana. Thus, in compromise, the company had saved face, maintaining its position of refusing to sign with the union. And the strikers could point out two items of "victory." All strikers would be taken back to work. Grievances henceforth would be decided by arbitration, instead of by the company alone.

The whole thing seemed to slide off him. Undoubtedly Midwest would accept the same sort of compromise. And perhaps even Consolidated. A kind of tired truce.

Syl was waiting in the bedroom. "Isn't it wonderful, darling? It's all over." And the way she looked at him, almost with the touch of forgiveness of a woman for the man who has erred but come back, made him realize that there would be no complete understanding between them, of what had been going on inside of him these weeks, what distrust of himself as a being. She would never be able to understand that part of it, for she was too proud of him in his possible career.

"All they got is permission to come back to work, it looks like to me. So much struggle, for nothing." She sighed. "I bet they have a big celebration out there tonight, to make it seem like a victory."

"Imagine if Carl and those idiots had gone through with that crazy idea yesterday!" Mitch shuddered. "It would have spoiled everything."

"Well, they ought to thank you for stopping them."

"Rawley stopped them. He certainly must have influence over them. They wouldn't listen to me."

"You know what I feel like, darling?" Syl said, taking his hand as they went into breakfast. "A vacation. Just to go somewhere, just the two of us, if only for a few days."

He remembered. "The hearing in Washington starts Monday. I have to be there."

[3 5 8]

"Take me too. Let's make a holiday of it. We could start to-morrow morning and drive down. Let's leave the kids, huh, dear?"

It appealed to him. Yes, he would clear up everything today. And when he returned, maybe he could get into research again. Maybe even something related to occupational allergies. He'd noticed quite a bit of skin stuff among the boys.

7. LIFETIME JOB

WHEN Randy Carey was nine, the farm was sold off from under the family, at an auction. There was a secret hiding-place he had for himself, in the barn. An old buggy stood there, with broken shafts, and rents in the black leather top; a buggy never used, the years he could remember. The back of it was built out to a trunk box; he could lift the lid, curl inside, and cover it down on himself. Randy bedded that box with straw; there he hid when he was mad. The buggy was backed against a par-tition, and on the other side were the stalls of Pa's pair of mules. When Randy lay hiding, he could hear the old mules bumping their noses against the wood as they licked the last grains from their feedbins.

When the auction started in the house, and men carried the plush rocker from the parlor onto the porch, and sold it, and he saw them carrying other things, coming nearer and nearer to the bed he slept on though his mother had promised the bed would not be sold, Randyboy fled to his hiding-place; but after a long while in the warm dark he heard the pack of people nearing the barn; he curled himself smaller; men passed so near that the buggy quivered; but they went beyond, and led out the old mules, and sold them. They dragged things from the barn, harness and the old grindstone, all those things he heard being sold; and at last he felt the buggy jarred; he felt hands against the wood of his box like hands seizing hold of his own body; he put his fist in his mouth to hold from hollering. They pushed the old buggy into the yard; strains of light came through the joints of the box in which he lay.

He heard his father say: "Used to be a smart contraption."

And his mother telling: "Ben took me riding in her, 'fore we was married. Sparked me in that buggy."

People shook it on its springs, said the shafts were broken, said the roof was tore, said nobody wanted with buggies nowadays; and his father in his whispery voice said: "Wouldn't take much fixing up, easy fix her up, good springs, good box in back, good for carrying feed and groceries."

Randy heard Mr. Ritchie, the toothless old buzzard, say he'd give a dollar for her, maybe. And someone was pulling at the lid of the box where he lay; in one last frantic panic Randy tried to hold it shut, but it was yanked from his hands. The sun came in on him, and all the people saw him there, huddled in the box, his face pressed against the wood so his crying wouldn't be seen.

His mother, lifted him out, saying: "You can't stay there, Randyboy. She belongs to Mr. Ritchie now."

They took up a place in the next county, cropping for Mr. Gladstone, but the furnish was scant; all year they had hardly enough meal to make out, clothes were tore and Ma couldn't even get calico cloth from Mr. Gladstone for a dress for older sister.

They didn't make out there with Mr. Gladstone, and moved again, and it seemed like every year they had to move; Randy was always switching from one school to another, and he wasn't smart for school anyway, he was behind in grades.

His mother died when he was thirteen; the old man got shiftless drunk; there were five kids, the oldest sister, Penny, being then sixteen. She married herself to a fellow that had his own place, and took the two little sisters to live with her, and that left Randy and his brother Hank with the old man.

Hank tried to keep the place going, and Randy sometimes tried to cook; but the end of it was an aunt came over once and screamed how filthy they were and took them home to her place. She told her husband the boys could earn their keep, but he was sore and threatened to kick out the thieving bastards and her with them.

Randy was seventeen when he and Hank tried going up north to Chicago where there were jobs for good money. They had twenty-five dollars that was their share of the crop, worked all year for that money and their keep—only kin would treat you that stingy, Hank said.

Hank got himself a job pushing stuff around a warehouse; but for a long time Randy couldn't find anything to do, and was ashamed of living off his brother. When he did get a place he just had bad luck. Worked as shipping-clerk but turned out they just wanted extra Christmas help. Found a job in a box factory at a stamping-machine, but the place went out of business owing him two weeks' wages.

Hank was all the time wanting to move. No sooner they'd get a room than he'd want to move to some other end of the city where he'd seen a girl. Then he wanted to go to Detroit. Met some fellows in a crap game, fellows been to Detroit, said it had Chicago beat twelve ways. Make more money, get girls easier. Randy was against going. "How you know we're going to find work in Detroit? We'll come up there where we don't know nobody and get broke."

Hank said they'd find them jobs in the Ford factory, and anyway Detroit was a place you could buy good cars cheap. They'd get a snazzy used little roadster and fix her up and go all over the United States, California and Florida.

The Ford factory was down, just special men working setting up new machines; everybody said Ford was coming out with a new model. Pretty soon brother Hank was broke. Randy had five dollars hid away from the time he had a job himself; now he didn't know whether to let on to Hank, or use the five alone. He decided to buy groceries for it little by little, telling Hank he borrowed the money.

Then he got dishwashing work in a restaurant, meals and twelve dollars a week; he sneaked enough food home for his brother. Told Hank the wages was ten dollars, and saved the other two. Randy wanted to go home.

"What for? We got nothing there," Hank said. "Who you going to?"

Randy said, Christ, it would even be nice to walk behind a pair of high mules, on the dirt. Maybe they could take up a place, the two of them.

"Yah, walk behind the mules and watch the crap come out of them," Hank said. "Not me no more, boy."

But Randy thought, what was wrong with that? Hell, it even felt good seeing a good mule manure the field, sometimes.

Hank said: "Go on yourself, if you want to." But the thought of making his way down there alone, and who would he go to down there? frightened Randy.

Next thing, Hank heard from some married woman he had monkeyed with in Chicago and right off wanted to go back there. He said a man could make good money in the steel mills back in Chicago; there was jobs there now.

"You want to hang around doing nigger work washing dishes ten bucks a week all your life!" he accused Randy. "Okay, you stay here; I'll get set in Chi and you can come on after I get set."

When Randy was twenty-one they were living in a boarding house in Gary, Indiana, working in the steel mills, averaging around thirty dollars a week each. Hank was always borrowing some from his kid brother by the end of the week. Sometimes he would take the kid along on a beach party or to an apartment a couple of girls shared. When it came to girls, Randyboy was no good; he either got foolish drunk and tried to push a girl into bed before even dancing with her, and that would insult a girl,

[363]

or he got sick drunk and couldn't do anything. Hank gave up telling Randy how to do. Often went off by himself, didn't come home to sleep. Wouldn't take the kid along, said he queered his style.

Best Randy could do for himself was go down Washington Street. First he went to the two-dollar places but afters he went further down the street to where the nigger girls did it for fifty cents. He was saving his money.

Summer of 1929, Hank and another fellow from the boarding house got two girls to go with them and shoved off to spend a couple of months fishing, as one of the girls had the use of a cabin on a Canadian lake. Randy wouldn't go because he was afraid he'd never get back his job.

He was groundman, then, in the stripping-shed. When the train of ingots pulled over from the openhearth pit, with the steel still sizzling in the gray line of upright coffinlike molds, it was his job to help strip the molds from the ingots. The stripping-machine was like a huge pair of pincers that clawed onto the ingot casing, and lifted, and when the work was going good the casing would rise up clean, gradually revealing the glowing pillar of steel, like a dress being slowly and lovingly raised up revealing the glowing body of a woman, all aburn inside.

Often enough, the mold would get stuck and fail to come off, the entire ingot rising with it as the mold was lifted from the ingot-buggy, then sometimes the ingot would begin to shake out; that was when the stripper-operator needed a man below, to signal him, or the naked ingot might drop onto the ground. Times, when a mold was fast stuck, Randy would have to crawl with a hose and try cold water on top, to loosen it from the ingot; coming that close felt like swallowing inside him the heat from the entire train of liquid steel.

He had to work around the tar-vat too, where the ingot-molds were dipped for a coating of tar to ready them for the next pouring; and around other jobs, as hooker, dragging and attaching the heavy cranehook to machinery that had to be lifted; heavy work, dragging and shifting stuff.

Hank didn't return at the end of the summer; he sent a postcard saying he and Chuck had decided to try a season of fur-trapping, big money in it. Said Randy could come up there too. They figured on coming out with five, six hundred dollars apiece, in spring.

Randy figured and figured. Even if he made that much money, he would come out with no job. He discussed it every evening with the landlady, Mrs. Reade, and then when he went up to his room he discussed it with Mac, an old-timer who was a switchman in the mill. Mac said jobs were getting scarce. Said layoffs were coming. He mentioned this with a kind of satisfaction, having a lifetime job himself, for losing his leg in the rail mill.

"Think I'll get laid off?" Randy asked.

"Dunno," Mac said. Used to be last come on, first laid off. But nowadays they were laying off the old-timers. He told a story of a man he knew, worked in the mill thirty-seven years, just coming up to his pension time, got laid off. "Nobody is safe," he said.

An engineer was going through the whole works, making measurements and calculations; and one day they started to re-build the cab of the stripper-operator, lowering it so he would

[3 6 5]

be sidewise to the ingot-buggies instead of above them. That way he could see for himself everything he was doing, and needed no groundman to signal him.

All the time that was going on, Randy was worried stiff. He hardly went out, even to a movie, saving his money. He sat in the dining-room a lot, listening to the radio; he liked the hill-billy singing programs.

There was one person in that house who paid some mind to him. She was a niece of Mrs. Reade, and helped out with the cooking and cleaning, in exchange for a home for herself and her child. Louise was her name, a young woman, could be called still a girl if you chose, though being rather large, and having a child, you thought of her as a woman; she was bust up some way with her husband, divorced or maybe the man just lit out; the child was two years old and the pet of the house.

When Randy was so worried about should he go up to Canada with Hank, Louise told him she had just read a story about fur-trapping in a magazine, describing how trappers were snowed in all winter, that was a terrible life to lead, being all by your-self, and what if your food gave out? She let him have the magazine to read. She said her policy was, hang on to what you've got, don't go chasing the rainbow.

When he was worried about their not needing him any more on the job, Louise said, best thing was to ask for a transfer to some other department of the mill, before they finished fixing that stripper-machine. Like the slab mill, the bloomer—if there were any orders at all you could be pretty sure the blooming-mill was working, because those ingots had to be rolled into slabs before they could make bars or sheets or anything. And, besides, he could get a chance to pick up the way of some higher-paying job, there; he might learn how to set the rolls, or run the shears.

His job was four cents more an hour than what he had been getting in the stripper. It was a harder job, too. He had to stand beside a conveyor at the end of a series of rolls that crushed the ingots down to fat slabs of steel, three inches thick, and big as table-tops. As the slabs came from the shears, Randy had to mark each one. He did this by swinging a sledgehammer against the edge of the hot slab; then he would have to change the number-die that was set into the hammer. Then he had to go up a few steps onto a bridge that passed over the conveyor, and poke a chain around the piled-up red-hot slabs, hitch the chain to a hoisting-hook, and wave the overhead craneman to take it away.

They said two men had been on this job before; one to swing the marking-hammer, the other to prepare the hoist. Each had refused to double on the job. One man could handle it, though, if he hustled.

That first evening, Louise figured out his new scale with him; it would amount to thirty-two cents a day, $1.92 a week more in his pay envelope; and being grateful to her, he asked her to a show.

She washed up and fixed her hair and put on just a little lip-stick on her lips, and it was fine, being with her. She looked real fine. Not like those dizzy girls Hank was always chasing, but fresh and neat-looking like sometimes in the morning you saw young wives coming out of the markets, saw one stooping to give an all-day sucker to her baby.

The State Theater was thirty-five cents; save your money, she said, they'd have the same pictures at the Adelphi in a couple of weeks for twenty cents. Walking back from the Adelphi they stopped and looked in the windows of Sears Roebuck at a wonderful streamlined new gas range, and in the next store you could furnish a four-room house for a hundred and fifty dollars, easy payments.

"I don't believe in buying on payments," Louise said. "Might come a time when they take it away from you. Best is cash, even if you have to buy cheaper things. But then you own what you got."

One day the boys at Mrs. Reade's egged on Louise's little Howie, and he marched up to Randy and climbed on his knees and called him Daddy. They all had a laugh, but the feeling of those small limbs twining around him and the little kid leaning against him made Randy funny happy like as if it was his own kid.

Louise found a little house, a bargain, only twenty dollars a month because it was frame and it was up at the end of the street where you got the cinders from the mill if the wind was blowing the wrong way, and the plumbing was old-fashioned. Randy had two hundred and fifty dollars saved; and they spent half of it for furniture. A lot of things, like linens and dishes, Louise had stored away.

It was nice with her. It was real nice. When they got in bed she told him how all the men in the boarding house had always

[368]

tried to come into her room, some boys even got mean, she wouldn't tell who. But a woman was for one man, she said. She made him feel so good, like he was newborn every time. He never thought of the man she had had before, like he never thought to be jealous of the father or brothers she had had; it was as though the way he really wanted and needed to find her was a grown woman with a baby for them.

In 1932, business was so bad, the blooming-mill was down, days at a time. Then Randy was laid off altogether. Call him back when things picked up.

He saw how Louise was trying to save every penny. She stopped buying milk in bottles, for it was a couple of cents cheaper bought in bulk. But he was laid off for a long time. He got so frightened he could hardly eat. When she said, if worst came to worst, she might get her job back at Mrs. Reade's, he was like sick; this home would be lost to him.

Every time he went to the bank and drew out five dollars, it was a knife cutting a strand of the rope of his life.

He went to all the mills. Louise said, the Tri-State mills were busier than any, because they were taking the business away from Standard, because they handled smaller orders and made the newer kinds of metal. Randy had his name there, and went there every week, to see if anything was stirring. After he was four months laid off, he got a job at Tri-State.

He couldn't stand anything like that again. It was the biggest scare he had had in his life.

Then the thing began again. The rush order was over; lay-offs, two days a week, three days a week, a whole week layoff; another rush order.

[369]

Louise wanted to move to the Harbor to save him carfare every day to Tri-State, but how long would he be working there? If only a man could somehow bind himself to something, if a man could be sure of going on!

Once Randy had a piece of luck. He was working as hook-man in the blooming-mill; the craneman started a lift before the hook was set; Randy's middle finger was caught and pulled right off at the root.

While he was in the hospital, the company adjuster came. He was a friendly, chatty sort of a man, said: "Tell you how it is with these things. Some fools go ahead and make a battle of it, try to go to law and get all they can out of the company for the accident. Well, you know the company is bigger than most fellows works in it; company got a big bunch of lawyers all the time, don't cost them nothing extra to fight a case. But, see, the company will play ball with you if you play ball with them. Now you got to expect some accidents to happen, you know how the company is trying all the time to make the safety rules tighter, but you can't make a hundred percent on the human element. Sometimes a man gets a little careless—sometimes something busts—it's all in the day's work. Now you take a thing like yours. That finger missing. All depends on the job you do, what that means to you. Some jobs, hardly means a thing; some jobs, like if you was a piano-player, huh, that might mean your whole living to you."

The adjuster said, company would pay all the hospital and doctor bills, so he wouldn't have to worry about a thing. Also pay him seventy-five dollars; "and I'll tell you what, you won't even lose a day's work. Fix it up so you can just punch in, you

[3 7 0]

won't have to do anything but stand around and look wise till that hand is all okay again, and that way you won't lose any working time."

Randy didn't want to sign anything until he had talked to Louise. But Louise said, yes, that was the best way instead of going to court. She was there when the adjuster returned, and she got him up to a hundred dollars.

The doc did a real neat job on that finger; first look at the hand, you'd never guess a finger was missing. And funny how a man could do just about with four fingers as he did with five. Maybe, Randy joked, that extra finger was a waste, people just ought to have four.

Back in the mill, standing around with nothing to do, those next few days, he got into a conversation with an Irishman named Donovan, ran the charging-car on the openhearth floor.

A hundred bucks, Donovan said, why, he knew a man in sheet and tin got two hundred fifty, and only lost his finger down to the second joint. It was all in the compensation laws, Donovan said, how much they had to pay. "That's why they come around getting you to sign a release, because if you go to court, it's in the law how much they have to pay you. Anything down to the second joint of a finger is two hundred and fifty bucks, but that middle finger is worth more, that's three hundred for half, and six hundred bucks for the whole finger."

"They got all that in the law?" Randy asked.

"Sure. Now you take if you lose your thumb, that's nine hundred bucks because a thumb is like all the rest of your fingers put together. Everything you do, you got to have a thumb. Try to hold a fork without a thumb."

Randy had never thought of that. He moved his thumb, in a grasping motion. Yes, the thumb was important.

"How much, if you lose a hand?" he asked.

"Depends, if you lose it below the elbow, that's three thousand smackers," Bill Donovan said. "And if you lose it above the elbow, that's worth thirty-seven hundred fifty."

"And a leg?"

A man's leg wasn't worth so much as his arm, Bill Donovan said. It figured three thousand dollars for the whole leg. "The way they get around paying you that much cash, they offer you some kind of a job, so you won't fight the case." And Donovan told how the other day a young fellow, just a kid, an oiler, working up there by the hot metal mixer slipped and fell so his leg went right into the pouring stream of pig iron, burned off to the ankle, you could hear him scream higher than the emergency whistle. "They didn't give him a nickel, said it was his own carelessness; but if he wouldn't fight the case, he had him a lifetime job."

"How about, suppose something happens to you so you can't even do no work. Suppose you lose your eyes?" Randy asked.

"One eye is two and a half grand," Donovan informed him. "A man can buy a chicken farm for that and take it easy. Both eyes is the top, five thousand bucks, that goes for both legs or both arms, too. Hell, they got everything figured out on you. They even got it figured out how much a man's nuts is worth."

"And how much if you get killed?"

"That ain't so much," Donovan informed him. "Maybe around four thousand bucks; you get more if you lose a couple of legs, or, like we say in geometry, the whole ain't equal to the sum of its parts. Nope, that don't pay."

Then, they had their own kid. The hundred dollars from his finger just about paid for it; so when the baby came, Randy saw her like a part off himself; and Louise liked to hold her mouth to the gap in his hand saying, Eve was made out of Adam's rib; so they called the girl Eve because she was made out of her father's finger. It was their private family joke.

What if he should get laid off now? Two kids and a wife; and men were being laid off all the time. There was a story the whole sheet mill was going down, since the new continuous strip was coming in; all the new men back to 1933 would be laid off because the old sheet mill hands had to be given other jobs around the works.

1933 meant him too.

There was union talk; fellows saying if there was a union, the company couldn't just lay off anybody, anytime.

A fellow named Emil in the spike mill started signing up people for a union, and he got canned. A fellow in the blooming-mill came around wearing a union button on his cap, and nothing happened to him for a week; but the second week the foreman canned him for coming to work drunk, he said.

Randy was down to two days' work a week again.

Every time he came into that mill, a great wish came over him, if he could only tie himself to that job, bind himself to it like a man married a wife, if a man could only know where he stood, so he could plan ahead for a while in his life.

[373]

And one day Randy knew what he had all the time been thinking. It happened while he was going to work, past the soaking-pits where the ingots came out red-hot ready for rolling; just as he passed, a fellow named Steve lifted his hand off a pit-lever, waving to him. Fat-faced, always cheerful, hunyak Steve. Walking on, Randy for no reason remembered the hand coming off the lever, and thought—if he had two hands he'd have waved the free hand, kept the other on the job. Lucky Steve, lost his arm in the mill; lifetime job. No wonder that hunyak was always laughing.

From then on, Randy could not rid himself of the idea. When the order-checker came through, he noticed that the man limped on his wooden leg; in the pulpit was an operator with a hook on the end of his left arm; and wherever he looked, he saw the hook-armed, the stump-legged; all the old timekeepers, all the crippled switchmen, goddammit, they were safe, they had lifetime jobs.

And he thought, what was better to lose, an arm or a leg? An arm showed more; but then, he already had a finger gone. A leg, if you were lucky and lost a leg just under the knee, nobody could tell, a man could learn to walk damn good with one of those trick artificial legs.

Once they went to a ten-cent movie and Louise happened to remark, see that actor, the star, well she had read in a magazine, that star had a wooden leg. It never showed. They even had that actor dancing.

But in bed with your wife. Did a man take it off, first?

When you thought of that, a lost arm was not so bad as a lost leg.

[3 7 4]

He would never do it. A man could not bring himself to do anything like that. He wondered if any of them could have done it on purpose. He remembered old one-legged Mac at Mrs. Reade's boarding house. If he could only find out from Mac how it felt.

Maybe next time he got a day in the mill, he would do the thing, for soon now the long layoff would come. If a man's hand got caught under a hot shear—clean off in a second, and the stump burned neat, flat, ready for the hook thing.

He could never do it.

The way it happened, Randy didn't do it willfully. Though he never was free in his self from feeling that maybe he had made it come. Maybe if he hadn't wanted it to come he wouldn't have been back-turned, or he would have somehow jumped out of the way.

The conveyor jammed and one slab rode up on top of the other, and slid onto the floor knocking him over so that his leg was pinned under the slab of hot steel.

When Randy awoke, he was already a stump below the right knee. He waited for the toes to itch, like they said they'd itch when a man's foot was lost.

The same adjuster came. He was like a father. Tough accident, he said; didn't happen once in fifty years, for the conveyor to jam. Still if a man was alert he might have jumped back in time.

Randy was all set with what he had to say. He didn't want to hold up the company. He wanted to work. Plenty of sitting-down jobs. Like pulling a lever in a pulpit. Or on the circular saws.

That was what the company wanted, too. Wanted to keep its men working. The company would buy him a damn fine artificial leg, with a spring in the ankle, so he could even go dancing. How about four hundred dollars? And knowing his job was safe?

He took five hundred.

They made him a shearman. He sat operating the lever that sent the big knife crashing down slicing through inches of steel.

Once, as Randy was limping from the plant, that fellow Emil met him on the street and said how about signing a card with the C.I.O. Lots of men getting laid off. With a union, a man had security.

"They ain't gonna lay me off. Not me, no more," Randy said.

At home, he always undressed in the dark and slipped into bed alone, first; almost always he stayed on the far side, and slept untouching his wife.

He couldn't figure what to do, if there was a strike; he guessed he would have to stay in and work. He couldn't take any risk of getting on the outs with the company. Where could a cripple get a job?

He couldn't bring himself to talk of it, at home. But at last, the week when the whole town was talking of nothing else, Louise's kid Howie brought it to the table. "Pop, you gonna strike or you gonna scab?"

He couldn't say a word. But Louise said: "You can't stay in that mill, Randy, if the men go out. The neighbors is all C.I.O. If they go out, you've got to go out, too."

"Sure, it's all right for them, they can go out!" he cried bitterly. "But where would I ever get another job! You're the one I did it for! I did it so—" He burst into tears, like a baby.

She never said a word more.

But when the strike was pulled, luckily Randy didn't have to stay and scab; Tri-State closed down completely.

He didn't know what to do with himself. He could hardly talk to Louise any more; since that other day something bad had come between them; he always felt ashamed of himself before her, and yet felt angry at her for causing him this shame.

If the C.I.O. won, maybe they'd only let the union members back into the mill; maybe they wouldn't let him in because he had not joined.

Fourth of July, their neighbors were going to the big meeting in Chicago, and asked if they wanted to ride along. Randy decided maybe it would be good to be seen among the men, like as if he was a member; maybe he would even join, if it looked like the union was winning.

Louise and Mrs. Reade were standing there listening to the speeches; some of Mrs. Reade's boarders, on strike, came and talked to them. Louise was standing against the sun and her figure could be seen plainer than in a bathing-suit.

She called over and said: "Honey, let's all go on a beach party after the meeting." Randy didn't refuse, but he hated the idea; he would have to stay dressed, when everyone else got into their suits; they would all be reminded about him.

"Wait till after the parade," he said. "I'm gonna march in this parade." Louise looked at him strangely, for a moment, as though she was going to say something against it, but she didn't.

When the cops began shooting, Randy couldn't run as fast as the others; one thing he couldn't do with that artificial leg was run.

AT lunch, George Price insisted that the compromise reopening the mills was actually a defeat of the strike. "Those three companies are controlled by the same money crowd, in Cleveland," he pointed out. "And as I see it, they realize that, so far as the public is concerned, Consolidated has become the symbol of the strike. Tri-State and Midwest might as well open and do business. Actually they did not give the union the contract for which they struck"— Rawley attempted to interrupt, but Price went on—"and their earnings will help support Consolidated, which will fight the battle to the bitter finish. Speer is only the front they're all using against the C.I.O."

"But where did you get the idea the men went back to work without gaining anything?" Rawley demanded.

"What did they gain? Oh, I know the company co-signed with the governor, but to the public that doesn't mean a thing. Actually it smells like defeat."

"But the union won the main point!" Rawley insisted. "They've won compulsory arbitration on grievances. The boss can't push the men around any more, as a complete autocrat. If the union feels a man has been fired unjustly, or discriminated against, it can press the case, and the state labor board's decision is final. That's an immense concession. That's the basic

[3 7 8]

concession. Sure, in the eyes of the public, the dramatic controversy was over whether or not Mr. Speer could be forced to sign his name on the same sheet of paper with John L. Lewis. But the practical issue involved is the break-up of industrial autocracy. And in those two plants, the break-up has begun."

There was a small silence. The others didn't concede the importance of the point. "The public will overlook that entirely," Price insisted. And as he viewed it, the effect on the public was all-important. The strike was simply a battle for prestige: the union winning meant C.I.O. couldn't be stopped; if Speer won, even though he conceded a few practical points, even though he lost millions in business, still, if he ran his plants without giving in to the union or to the Wagner Act, the C.I.O. was cooked.

"I wouldn't say it was as clear as that," Rawley stipulated.

And anyway, Mitch pointed out, even if Price were right and the strike was now narrowed down to the Consolidated plant, it was not yet lost. The men were still out, and public opinion was on their side. The Gottschalk committee hearings would undoubtedly give Mr. Speer a couple of jolts, too.

Right, Price said, and he had an idea for putting some punch into the Gottschalk testimony. In order to stress the way all those people were shot in the back, he wanted Mitch to mark all the bullet wounds on a composite figure, a statuette of some kind. Put holes right through it.

Mitch thought the stunt would be too undignified. Besides, there would be no time to arrange it as he hoped to leave in the morning for Washington.

"Driving?" Rawley asked.

"Yep. Sylvia and I decided to make a sort of vacation of the trip."

Rawley said he had a notion to drive, too, and spend a day in the strike area in Ohio. He understood Sobol and some of the other witnesses were driving; perhaps they could all arrange to go together.

"Sure," Mitch said. It would be stimulating, going in a gang. Of course, if Sylvia didn't enjoy it, they could easily separate from the others.

Before leaving, Mitch had one more case to check. Jim Carraway had finally been found. He was in the asylum, at Dunning.

"Go out and see him, will you, Doc?" Jock Kiley kept asking. "His wife wants a doctor to go out and see him."

"But what you want is a psychiatrist," Mitch insisted.

"Just take a look at him, Doc. It would make her feel better. You remember, that little woman."

He felt he ought to do it, for completeness in his Washington report. If there could be such a thing as completeness. For how could one report the scattered, uncounted, unknown effects, the submerged mental bruises that would not show up for years, and the emotional scars, and even the bullet-wounded who had sneaked away? How could there be a total report?

At the asylum, a Dr. Geer had the Carraway case. "Oh, that Fourth of July guy," Geer said. "He might snap out of it; might take a year or so. Seems to have been a pretty deep shock. What are they going to do about that business anyway? Did they ever put those cops on trial?"

Mitch explained he was going to Washington for the Senate investigation. "That's the only hope of getting at the root of the thing. You can't expect the city politicians to investigate the cops."

At least, people were still interested.

They had reached the second in a row of long brick cottages. Dr. Geer unlocked the door; they entered a ward. Inmates were standing around, pajama-clad.

"Here's our friend," Dr. Geer said, approaching a thin, long-faced fellow who leaned by a window. The man eyed them untrustingly.

"How are you, Jim?" Geer asked. "Here's Dr. Wilner come to see you, your wife sent him out."

"You know my wife?" Carraway said suspiciously. "What's her name?"

"I know her just in a professional capacity," Mitch began.

"You're a cop." Carraway drew back a step, and his lip trembled as he stared, with betrayal-fear, at Dr. Geer.

"No, Jim, I've been acquainted with the doc here a long time," Geer reassured him. "He's okay."

"Say, listen, take a message back to my wife for me, will you?" Carraway demanded.

"Sure," Mitch said.

"I seen a plane go over. It passed over here. They're gonna bomb the house. Tell her to watch out. Tell her to get the kids out of there, quick."

"I'll tell her," Mitch said.

"Tell her I'm okay. They can't find me here," Carraway said.

"Sure. Jim, you work at Tri-State, don't you?"

Jim looked from him to Dr. Geer, without answering.

"The plant is reopening," Mitch said. "All the boys are going back to work. The strike is over. You get well and you can go back on your job."

Jim shook his head knowingly. "They want to get us all in there and blow it up." He stared out the window. "I seen the airplane going over."

Mitch looked to Geer, and they left. Jim Carraway stared after the psychiatrist with the anxious, trembling look of a dog whose master has shown him to a stranger.

"Say, I've got another of your people here, come to think of

[381]

it," Geer said. "She's okay though. I'd send her out, but there's no one to take her."

"Who is it?"

"Sophie something, one of those Polack names. Witco. She was a girl friend of one of those guys that got killed. Tried to drown herself, in the Calumet River by the mills there. The cops fished her out; we get all the suicidals. Nothing wrong with her; just hysterical for a couple of days. Only when we have to discharge them, it must be to a relative or somebody. She seems to be a lone soul."

They were going down a graveled walk toward another of the cottages. Inmates wandered on the grass.

"She tried to kill herself over one of the men? Who?"

"One of those hunky names. Owsky . . ."

"Dombrowsky?"

"Yah. That's it."

That wide-chested, hairy body. Who would have wanted to kill herself over him, for love?

Over a dozen women were in the large, screened living-room of the cottage. Several rocked; one was sewing, peaceful-looking. A nurse approached the doctors. "Where's Sophie?" Geer asked.

"Sophie's helping in the kitchen. I'll get her."

One of the patients sidled past the psychiatrist, to the piano; she began to play, a sentimental tune; the room changed; the senseless rockers slowed their eternal movement, and a giggler quieted. The nurse returned with a diminutive, mild-faced woman, Sophie Witco. Mitch realized that the idea of suicide-for-love had led him to expect a young girl; this woman had graying hair.

He was introduced: "Dr. Wilner, from the union."

"I am glad to know you," she said.

He didn't know just how to proceed. "You're a friend of Stanley Dombrowsky?"

"Yes. I am his friend."

"I know some other friends of his—in the boarding house where he lived."

"By Mrs. Jugovich?"

"Yes. They all feel bad about him," he said.

"I nearly go crazy that time; I want to kill myself," she said. "But now I feel all right again." She raised her eyes.

"You want to leave here?" he asked.

"I can go," she half said, half asked.

"I can let her out if you sign for her," Geer explained. "I'm terribly overcrowded."

"I can work," she said. "I call up Mr. Borland and tonight I go work."

What sort of work? Cleaning, she said, downtown buildings, Field Building. Then Mitch understood what had seemed so familiar to him in this woman: she was one of that army of night scrubwomen, creatures with dry lifeless hair and doughy cheeks, in shapeless bundles of skirt and lopsided shoes, all with the same timeless look of weariness.

Where did she live? Alone in a basement room. Dr. Geer advised she be moved, for the suicidal impulse was the mate of loneliness, more than of any hunger. Mitch agreed to move her to Mrs. Jugovich's boarding house, where her friend Stanley Dombrowsky had lived.

She was timid about taking the front seat beside him in the car. And driving with this woman by his side, he had more than ever the sense of holding the answer to the indefinable mystery that had troubled him these weeks; like holding a long-sought book that treats of a haunting problem, but finding it to be in a foreign language. She could tell him of Dombrowsky, and yet with her, as with the Lindstroms, even with Emil, he did not quite know how to ask, to reach what he wanted. Perhaps it was the barrier of being a doctor.

After they had driven for some time, she said: "Doctor, is showing the moving picture?" No, he said, it had been forbidden. Maybe in court, in Washington, it would be shown. Would he see it? Yes, he was going there. Please, Doctor, if she could only know—if it showed Stanley, if it showed how Stanley was killed. He agreed to tell her if he saw Dombrowsky in the film. She settled back into another long silence, but she was no longer frightened, and often looked at him with a solemn friendliness, as though she knew she was no longer with officialdom but with a friend. He wondered whether he might suggest to Sylvia having this woman help out around the house, watch the kids. Better not, for a while.

The place where she had lived was one of those weather-gray frame houses, chopped into tiny apartments; they went around to the back and into the basement, passed several doors. "Here I live," Mrs. Witco said. The room was filled by a heavy old dresser, a brass bedstead, a table covered with an old-country tasseled velvet cloth, such as he remembered his mother having when he was a child. There was a drape over the half-window that craned to earth-level.

"You like, I have a glass of wine, Doctor," she said with a dignity of being in her own house, having a fine guest. From the dresser, she took a fancy cut-glass decanter, obviously the remnant of a real home. "For Stanley, I keep some wine for him to drink. When my husband was living, Stanley he came all the time to the house, they drink my wine, I make every year good wine. Stanley was good friend my husband; he is dead five years." She placed the decanter on the velvet cloth; a worn pack of cards lay there. She put away the cards. "Stanley and me, we play always some casino."

[384]

In his outpatient years at the hospital, Mitch had seen West Side poverty and the deepest slums; and always the sight alone made everything explicit: so things were; but here, over the death of Stanley Dombrowsky "not properly identified as yet," he was involved in a sense of things inexplicit. What could be plainer? A laborer, a pit-cleaner, coming to play casino, to pass the hours with the widow of an old friend, she a scrubwoman now. Here they sat, said little, played cards, drank a glass of wine. That was all, all. Perhaps, through this Mrs. Witco, he would yet come to know the thing in its meaning.

At Mrs. Jugovich's, Sophie wanted to live in Dombrowsky's old room. Where his workpants had hung, she hung up her scrubbing-dress.

The door at the hall-end was open; Mitch saw Emil sitting by the window. He hesitated to go in; the big fellow might be angry at his having told Rawley of that bombing scheme. But it was best to make clear he had not blabbed it all over town.

He walked into the room. Emil did not stir; he was watching the Bessemer flames, two erect banners of fire, rising with bitter laughing spite against the sky, showing the whole damn world that Consolidated was making steel.

"You sore, Emil?" Mitch asked.

Emil shrugged. "Naw. We got excited, that's all. It's a good thing you made that guy stop us."

"Did he talk to you?"

"He came over here with Carl. That professor can talk all right."

"It's lucky you didn't do anything. They opened the plant anyway."

"Yah." He added: "This here is the one we ought to fix."

Hadn't he given up the thought of violence, then? And yet within his own disapproval Mitch could feel the same itch somehow to smother that challenging flame, to cut off whatever fed it.

Emil said: "But once you stop to figure those things out, you don't do them. You can't take a chance for anybody except yourself."

"Listen, Emil," Mitch said, "the first time that idea came up, was it yours or Art's?"

"I guess everybody has that idea, Doc. In a thing like this a man gets so he has to try and do something."

"But when you were actually planning to do it?"

"The way it was, we got to talking. And it just came up that way. . . . You mean about Art? Doc, I know Art a long time. We played on a ball team. Doc, if it ever comes out that he was guilty of ratting on us, I'll bash his brains in." He arose, solemnly, staring at the Bessemer flames.

"You think it might be true? that he is?"

"Doc, they got it so you'd be afraid to trust your own brother, any more. . . . Listen, Doc, I want to ask you something. Am I okay?"

"Why? You feel all right, don't you? Just a little more rest——"

"Yah. I feel good as new. But I mean—is it that way? Am I as good as I was?"

"What's the matter? You want to get married or something? You're all right. Just don't strain yourself. And, if you mean about women——"

"Too late to advise me about that, Doc," Emil kidded morosely.

"Well, what do you mean? Going back to work?"

Emil shook his head slowly. "They ain't going to take me back."

"But I thought Tri-State agreed—"

"Not this guy. They canned me before there was a strike. I got a labor board case. But I wasn't thinking about that."

[386]

"What were you thinking?"

"I was thinking, if I could take a trip?"

A trip? Why, sure, it might do him good. What kind of trip?

Emil motioned with his chin, toward the factory. "No fun fighting where you can't shoot back. I was thinking, maybe I could go over and take a couple of pot shots at those guys."

Only then, Mitch caught on. "You mean Spain?" But what for? From what he heard, they didn't need more men over there. They needed food and munitions. They had plenty of men.

"Maybe they don't need me, Doc. But they got something I need. That's one place a guy can shoot back. The way I figure, it's the same sonofabitchn bastards against us, there as here."

But he could never make it. Why, there was a hike over the Pyrenees, Mitch had heard, thirty or forty hours through the snow, before volunteers even got into Spain. "You're in no condition for that. It'll be a year before you really get your strength back, and then you'll never be completely like you were, Emil. A man doesn't go through a thing like you had——"

"Yah, I know, Doc. I figure by rights I should have kicked off. I figure I got this second life for nothing anyway so it don't count if I throw it around."

"You don't want to go over there just to get killed? There are simpler ways."

"No, don't get me wrong. I'm not looking to die. But I mean, what have I got to lose?"

"Better get it out of your head, Emil. Anyway, I thought they only sent Communists."

"No, you don't have to belong to that," Emil said.

"The Communists run it, don't they?"

"That kid, Arthur Main, he can get an okay for me."

Did he mean Arthur Main was going? "But that's insane! What does he want to go for?"

Emil stared at the two flames, roaring up furious with life, purple-centered, illuminating the sky.

"Well, Emil," Mitch joked, "a doc just hates to see a good job like you get mussed up."

"I'll try to take care of it, Doc, just to show I appreciate the job you docs did on me," Emil replied.

The day was nearly shot but he still had to make a call at St. Cyril's hospital to examine a Negro, Ephraim Law, the last of the wounded to be let out of the jail hospital; a hopeless case of septicemia—a miracle the man had hung on this long. He stopped at the Lindstroms' to check on the old man for the Washington trip.

Pauline was sitting with her father-in-law, reading the Bible to him. Lindstrom could feel light and dark, in his remaining eye now, but the house was kept in a shade-drawn twilight, as the sun pained his senses.

In the kitchen, Ma Lindstrom was preparing boiled chicken for the invalid; he could stomach only the blandest foods, and the diet was costly.

"How are you getting along?" Mitch asked.

"The union is giving us fifteen dollars a week for a while. We still have my son's car to sell," the woman said.

"But doesn't your husband have some kind of disability insurance? I thought I heard them talking about it."

She lowered her voice. "I don't like him to think about it. They're holding it up on account of the case."

"What case?"

Everybody that was arrested, she reminded him, in the hospitals and in the riot—that case.

"But didn't that come up long ago?"

No, it had been postponed again. And the insurance company

would not pay until the case was settled; there was some legal tangle to it.

Lindstrom gave only the simplest responses, during the physical examination. Did this hurt, did that hurt, was he dizzy; he would answer with a slow considered yes or no, never enlarging upon his symptoms, and would end with a careful "Thank you, Doctor." It seemed impossible to draw him into conversation; and Pauline too was silent. In a way, Mitch felt, it would be sheer cruelty to exhibit them in Washington.

"What do you read him, from the Bible?" he asked.

"Different parts. Wherever it opens, he don't care. Sometimes I think he never listens, but sometimes he asks me to read something over. I was reading what Jeremiah said, how everything would be destroyed, the cities sit in ashes, and he said to read it over."

"Have you read to him from Job?"

"He made me stop."

He wanted to ask about herself, about her own feelings, but could only ask questions of health. "Do you sleep any better? You've lost weight, haven't you? Maybe this trip to Washington will do you good."

The look of scorn came onto her face.

"Why don't you invite your girl friend too, isn't she going along?" Sylvia demanded stonily when he told her about driving along with Rawley and the others, and spending a day in the Ohio steel towns, en route.

He felt bad about spoiling her idea of a vacation. But she had no right to pull stuff like that about Barbara; it was crazy; it wasn't like Syl at all. "What's got into you?" he demanded.

"What's got into you is what I want to know! Mitch, you're absolutely obsessed with this whole business. It's a wonder you

[389]

didn't bring that crazy old woman home with you to leave with the kids!" How had she known that thought had crossed his mind? "You might as well give up your practice altogether and just go and live out there and be on strike yourself! Mitch, you know I'm as much interested in justice as you are; after all it was I who wanted to go out there in the first place. . . . If there was any good you could do by all this . . . ! Tell me, what good can it do, what good can it possibly do?"

He couldn't explain. He wasn't interested in doing good. He was never interested in doing good. He just had to know all, all there was to know about a thing, once he got started. "Look, Syl," he capitulated, for the sake of peace, "we can meet the rest of them in Washington. There's probably nothing we can see in Ohio anyway, in a single day. . . ."

But now she didn't want to go. She had calmed; but honestly she didn't want to go. "It'll just be to sit in a stuffy hot court-room all day. And the drive is too long to be fun." And she really oughtn't to leave the kids; Judith had a cold. "You go, dear. No, really, I don't mind. You do want to see those steel towns for yourself—and it wouldn't have worked out, as a vaca-tion, anyway."

Then she gave him Barbara's message. Barbara had left word for Mitch to be sure and come over tonight. "She said you had to help her with some data. She said you'd understand."

"Oh, it's some silly idea of George Price's," he began to ex-plain, but Syl was distant.

Instead, she might try to be helpful. Here he was, worried stiff over having to appear as an expert on ballistics, the course of bullets, junk outside his field. During the last few days he had tried to read up on the subject, but it would be horrible to pull a boner. What worried him most was classifying wounds as rear or side. Knowing they were so eager to emphasize how many were shot from the rear, he found himself stretching every doubtful case the other way. In Dombrowsky, for instance, the bullet had taken an oblique course through the leg, entering the thigh on the inner side and going forward and downward, as though it had hit while the leg was raised, running. The bullet must have come half from the rear and yet it could be called a side wound, and as it was actually in the forepart of the thigh, it might even be called a front wound. He wished there were some standard method of classification, to take the matter out of the realm of opinion.

Barbara had bought anatomical outline charts, poster-size, front, side, and rear; they were spread all over the floor. The chart idea was at least more dignified than George Price's original plan of using a manikin. Barbara, George, and Carl were sprawled on the floor, penciling names of wounded on the charts, at the points where bullets had entered bodies. Long disputes arose, as to which chart certain wounds belonged upon. Several times Mitch made them erase markers from the rear-chart, and transfer them as side-wounds. It was after one o'clock when George Price hoisted himself from the floor, pridefully studying the completed rear-wounds chart. It was arresting enough, peppered with crosses marking "wounds of entrance, fatal," and circles marking "wounds of entrance, non-fatal." Mitch was satisfied that the classification was as conservative and accurate as could be made under the circumstances, though that chart was really a frightening thing, spotted like a sieve. There were thirty-one bullet-markers on it, compared to five on the frontal chart.

Barbara had made a separate series of charts, showing only fatal wounds, that was even more striking. Seven on the back view; three on side views. And Price insisted on including the front view—a blank.

Leaving the car at home for Syl, Mitch went along with the others. Gillespie drove. Mike Sisto sat beside him. Mitch was in the rear with Rawley and Frank Sobol.

They drove out, passing through the entire steel-mill and oil-refinery district, to hit Route 20. Calumet, and Hegewisch, and East Chicago; he knew those places now.

Driving past Gary, Mike Sisto counted the plumes on smoke-stacks. "They got fifteen pots going," he said, and Mitch knew that meant openhearth furnaces, in the long, seven-stacked buildings.

"They're way down under capacity. About thirty percent," Rawley remarked.

"It was up to sixty in March," Sobol said.

"They got plenty of orders piled up," Mike asserted. "They're refusing to roll stuff. Big business is on strike."

"Don't let them kid you with that," Rawley said. "That's no way to look at it—to imagine that the big boys get sore and say the hell with it and tear up orders. They're in business for orders and profits and they won't tear them up on a peeve."

"It's a fact though!" Mike Sisto insisted passionately. "I seen it myself! They had a whole bunch of rail orders in there and just refused to roll it."

Rawley looked to Mitch and smiled.

"Well, maybe they don't tear up orders," Sobol put in, "but they've got ways of going on strike. They hold back on enter-prises they might go into if there was a quick fat profit, but if it just looks like they'll break even, though they'd give jobs to a lot of people, they figure the hell with it."

They passed a roadside poster showing a handsome fellow with a beautiful girl and a couple of apple-cheeked kiddies sup-posed to be theirs, driving a red sedan that was at least a Buick; it showed a city and some kind of mills behind them, and beau-

[3 9 2]

tiful country roads before them. "The American Way," it said. "What Helps Business Helps You."

"Crap!" Mike Sisto announced. "Look at that broad, she looks like she never even been laid, and she got two big kids already."

"They must be spending millions on those ads," Gillespie said. "Who puts up all that money?"

"The manufacturers' organizations," Rawley informed him.

"They got it wrong," Mike sang out. "What they mean is, what helps business screws you." He squirmed around to get appreciation from the back seat. "How about it, professors?"

"Maybe they ought to try it the other way around for a change," Frank Sobol suggested.

"What helps you screws business?" Rawley tried it.

"It just depends who's on top," Mitch put in, surprised he could do all right in this kind of jabber. Mike Sisto, howled, and looked at him like a pal.

They stopped for hamburgers and beer at a joint that had a small dance floor attached and smelled of the night before. Mike stuck a nickel in the music box. Rawley began to play the marble machine. "I'm having a steak," Mike informed Gillespie. "What the hell, the government pays for this! How much we get, three bucks a day?"

Sobol said expenses were by the mile.

"Better make that jackpot," Rawley advised as Mitch put a dime into a slot machine, "the Gottschalk committee is practically broke now."

"That sonofabitch Jock Kiley," Mike remarked, "he's a lucky sonofabitch, I seen him hit the jackpot twice in Curly's."

"He ought to on the law of averages," Frank said, taking a turn at the marble game, which scored like a race, with bells and lights if you hit the winner. "He spends all his time there."

[393]

"At least that keeps him away from headquarters," Gillespie offered.

Mike said, hell, what good were organizers, anyway? What good were any of those miners, sitting up there on top? What good was Wheelchair, all he did was sit up there in his skyscraper and think. What was needed was a scrapper. "What he should have done was bring ten thousand miners, march them up from the coal fields and close up the whole damn Harbor, after our guys got killed!"

Sobol said, the trouble with Wheeler was he was a little old-fashioned and too slow-moving. He didn't understand how to use the political power behind the C.I.O. He could have scared the mayor into really closing up that mill, after the massacre. The national scandal scared the pants off the mayor, and that was the time to put the screws on. "But Wheeler thinks the way to win a strike is by starving."

"After all, he has to take his orders from Washington," Rawley pointed out.

Their talk had a different tone now, in his presence; he felt they were no longer withholding; Sobol talked at times with a "we" that was admittedly the party, though Mitch was still uncertain whom it included—Gillespie? Mike?

All day they drove through Ohio towns, a whole area where the buildings were of old red brick, even farm buildings and roads of this red brick; and towns with the conventional central square surrounded by five-and-tens, banks, movies, Sears stores. "I played basketball here once," Sobol said as they went through one such town.

Sure, he had played basketball all through here, and football a little, just a hick-town team. "My home town is near here," he mentioned. He told things of himself, more to Rawley than to

Mitch, but mostly as a man turning up bits of the past for his own retasting. Mitch put it together: a miner's family, nine kids in all, seven still living. One terrible period when Frank was about fourteen, his oldest brother had his back crushed in the mine, and lay at home dying for a year, in the bed Frank shared. A big fellow when he got hurt, two-hundred-pounder, and no one could handle him but the old man; the old man had to stay home from work to tend the cripple, while kid Frank scrambled around trying to earn nickels.

Sobol told bitter jokes about trying to go to high school; running a paper route in the dawn, then tending the school furnace, working after school too. But there was not enough to eat at home; he had to quit school, take a job in a mill.

As they neared Canton, the car was stopped by a state trooper. The fellow was just a pimply-faced kid. "Where you men going?"

"Washington," Gillespie said, as Mike said: "What's it to you?"

Sobol asked: "What is this, buddy, some trouble around here?"

The trooper looked into the car as if searching for cannon. "All right." He waved them on.

"They're scared of an invasion," Rawley surmised.

"Step on it, I bet we see some fun there," Mike cried.

In Chicago, Mitch Wilner now realized, he had had no idea of the proportions of the strike, for back there the strike had been something happening in a corner of the city, a conflict after all smothered under the vastness and the indifference of the city as a whole.

But in these small industrial centers—Newton, Canton, Ironville—Mitch began to know the pattern of the conflict and, thinking back, he could detach the same pattern from the con-

[3 9 5]

fusion of Chicago, for the Harbor towns too were such communities as these, distinct from the city which had sent its police to rule them.

In each town, there was the plant. And it was striking how universally the plants were located on sites chosen as if by strategy of war, moated by rivers, isolated behind tracks.

That could be accidental, Rawley pointed out. A large industrial plant such as a steel mill had to be situated on cheap land and would therefore automatically tend to place itself outside the city; it had to have transportation facilities, hence the tendency to locate on rivers, or lakes, and obviously there had to be tracks.

"It isn't all accident. They figured on it in Gary. When they laid it out they figured in case of strikes," Sobol declared, reminding them how only a few company-owned bridges gave access to the Gary plant. And here, look at this in Ironville: the plant on a river bend and a hill, like an old-time castle, and only one long narrow bridge going to it.

Familiar, too, in every town, as in Steel Harbor, the plant lying huge and inert, and near it the shack or empty store or crummy upstairs meeting hall, with a makeshift partition or maybe just a desk in the corner, and around it three, four guys that were the heart of the strike, an organizer and the union president or secretary or whatever office the local leader happened to hold; and though of all ages they seemed to look the same: fellows with bitter strength in their tired faces, maybe yellow-toothed, wiry little guys or big lumbering slow-spoken men with solemnity of responsibility, but always men about whom you instantly felt they were okay.

In Ironville the main S.W.O.C. headquarters was in an upstairs meeting hall on the city's busy street. Sobol asked for a fellow named Taylor, and it was a narrow-shouldered guy who somehow reminded Mitch of Al Nees; this fellow had an old burn too, but on his arm. Taylor said the headquarters near the plant was abandoned, since the place had been completely wrecked. But if they wanted to take a look he'd go out with them.

Once in the car, his pep sagged—as though he had had to keep it up, in the hall there, for the men.

"How's it look?" Frank asked.

"No so good."

"I thought the labor board was finally starting on your case?" Rawley asked.

"Yah, we had a good case. We had them signed up ninety percent. But now how are we going to prove it?"

"You've got the signed cards, haven't you?" Rawley asked.

Taylor looked at him and shook his head. "That's what they bust in there for. Those cards were in there. All I had a chance when they started shooting was to grab what was on the table in one of them little files. The rest we had locked up in the desk. When I come back that desk was chopped to firewood."

They drove through the town, to a spot where the bridge spanned from high bank to high bank. A police car parked near the bridge followed them across. On the other side, to the left, lay the plant; to the right was a workers' settlement, frame houses, mostly unpaved streets. A block down, they came to an empty store, windows broken, door unhinged. A couple of police guarding the ruins allowed them to enter.

It was still a shambles, the floor littered with torn posters and old handbills. A long table, which Taylor said had been used for the commissary, lay overturned, one leg off. Taylor pointed out bullet-marks in the wall.

He repeated how it was: a few hundred people around, the Sunday night dance, and then the squad cars sneaking up, and suddenly the firing beginning, and firing down there by the bridge, too, at the pickets. And all through that night, squads

[397]

going through this entire district, pulling men out of bed, searching rooming houses, dragging people to jail—people who weren't even Consolidated employees—just so long as they looked like strikers or had foreign names.

"They sure cleaned up on us," Taylor said wearily.

Mitch picked up a copy of a local newspaper, lying on a chair. Taylor was a Communist, Major Ross charged. The plot, Major Ross revealed, had been to wreck two cars on the bridge, thus isolating the plant from the city. Then the union mob was to attack the loyal workers in the plant. Sure enough, the Major claimed, at the scheduled hour, two cars driven by strikers had collided at the bridgehead. . . .

Same stuff . . . Communist plot, attack from behind, assembled mob . . . then shoot them up, break into homes, drag everybody to jail.

Rawley sat beside Mitch on the stoop, reading the newspaper. "Notice how concerted their movements are?" he said. "The same night they shoot them up here——"

Mitch had noticed. "They raided us in Chicago."

Rawley puzzled. "I wonder if there could be anything more to it than just . . ."

"Just what?"

"Just the company." Then he shook his head, laughed his burbly laugh. "Have to put Dick Tracy on the case."

On the way back, Rawley asked Taylor about that Major Ross. "Wonder if you could find out if he might be connected with some organization?"

"Naw, all he belongs to is the veterans. Gets a fat pension, so he's got nothing to do but horse around."

"There's a big California Legionnaire, Colonel Roper, has that organization called Guardians of America," Mitch reminded Rawley. "He's the one that was in the Harbor making the back-to-work speech, and Barbara is trying to find out if he's hooked up with the Silver Shirts. I'll bet Consolidated sent him into these other towns too."

But Taylor said the local Major would not have needed any organization behind him to tell him how to shoot up a place. "He just acted natural."

Like Captain Wiley, Mitch concluded. They believed in what they were doing. And there were people who knew how to use them.

It was mid-morning when they drove into Mahoning; and here at last Mitch felt the heart and source of infection. From the hillroad spiraling down into the city they saw the river, cutting like a lifeline across a palm, yellow and sluggish, the yellow not of a river at all, but of some refuse duct. Encrusting both sides of the river, the gray and black factory masses; and beyond them, on one side a few tall buildings, the business town, and on the other side the homes of the workers, on a clifflike hill directly over the river and over the mill.

The edge-street of this hill was called Slovak Avenue; it was beyond all nightmares of decay. A long, endless stretch of dump-heaps interspaced with wrecked-car lots; and shacks, old unpainted boards long lived in, crammed habitations oozing children—Negroes, whites, no slum-borderlines here; buildings crooked-perched as if they would at any moment topple on the metal-roofed mills below; a few starved-looking taverns and ramshackle gas stations; a street of torn windowblinds and broken panes; and below it, Consolidated's main plant, sending up green fumes and black smoke. They drove the length of Slovak Avenue in silence. Only once, Sobol remarked: "I lived here, three years."

At the far end was a hut scarcely larger than a hot-dog stand;

"C.I.O." was on the one window. Inside, on the walls, were newspaper photos of the massacre in Chicago, of the gutted headquarters in Ironville.

Here, too, Sobol knew the fellow in charge. "Jesus, Frank, glad to see you!" the man cried, like a beleaguered general at the arrival of reinforcements. He took them into a back room to talk. The strike was going strong. Plant was shut tight. But the last week things were getting pretty much on edge. Rumors the plant would be opened, any day. Thugs being brought in, maybe a couple of hundred inside there. The National Guard was due any day. Only waiting for an excuse to call them in. Something might break any minute. He had a feeling after Chicago and Ironville, Mahoning was next.

And hell would break here. "These boys aren't going to take it," Jamie said, his voice low. "They'll scrap. We got the screws on tight but if the lid is blown off from outside there'll be hell to pay. You can't tell the boys any more to lie down and be shot full of holes like in Chicago."

He offered to take them around to the picket-posts. Anxiously, with the anxiety of a man who can't quite believe things are holding up as well as when last he looked. On the way out, he showed them a snapshot pinned on the wall, marked: "Joe Lurie alias Joe Lambert, No. 1 Rat." "He might show up around Chicago, they might ship him up there, watch out for him."

The story he then told seemed incredible to Mitch. This Joe Lurie was simply and actually a company policeman, a guard who had worked for Consolidated in Cleveland. "Six months ago they ship him down here and give him a job in the pipe shop. He come sucking around and wanted to organize for us. I smelled him from the first day but Nick says I've got spy fever, so before you know it Lurie is financial secretary of the local."

"Yah. We got one," Frank said. "How'd you prove it on him? We got one but he's pretty smart so far."

"He even had his wife in the ladies' auxiliary. Nice kid, too. Being he was secretary, he had the names of every last man that was signed up. So when they began picking off our guys, I told Nick: watch that bastard."

One day a fellow who had worked in Cleveland recognized the former cop. "Even then he wouldn't admit. it. We put him on the spot and he said, what of it, he used to be a company cop but he was clean now." By then, they were on the verge of striking, so, to avoid breaking down morale among the men, the whole affair was hushed up for a time. The books were taken away from Joe Lurie but he was not read out of the union.

"He still around?"

"He was back in a guard's uniform in Buffalo a couple of weeks ago, last I heard."

They sat in the car and watched the picket line, circling in front of an underpass which led to the mills. From a sound truck parked in an adjacent lot someone was yelling out wise-cracks to keep the strikers in good spirits.

"There ought to be open season on those spying rats, when this bitchn strike is over," Mike Sisto muttered wishfully.

The address Barbara had given them, of one of Martha Cross's "contacts" in Mahoning, was of a Neal Hollis, who proved to be the manager of a fair-sized Ford agency. Rawley introduced himself as Mr. Gray, and Mitch as Dr. Huyler. "We're friends of Martha Cross," he said.

Mr. Hollis showed no sign of recognition. "We're making a survey of the situation in the strike towns," Rawley went on. "Just been through Newton, Ironville, and Canton. I'm writing an article for the *Guardian* on it."

"I see," Mr. Hollis said, evidently familiar with the name of the paper. He looked them over again, seemed to make up his mind, and walked to his private office. They followed.

"How does it look in those towns?" Mr. Hollis asked.

"Pretty good," said Rawley. "They did a beautiful job in Ironville."

"Yah. That's what we need here," Hollis said. "The sheriff is scared of those bastards. They got that whole hill fortified. Slovak Avenue. Got bombs up there, they could bomb the plant. But all we need is, deputize the citizens. We'd clean them out quick enough. Why, they're holding that side of town by force. It's revolution."

"That's what it amounts to," Rawley agreed.

It couldn't go on much longer, Hollis declared. Unless that situation was cleaned up inside of maybe a week at the out-side . . .

Mitch marveled at the skill with which Rawley led him on, topping his every statement with an even more horribly re-actionary cliché, until like old cronies they were cursing Roose-velt and the Jews and the reds. Hollis asked if they were going to be in town that evening. There was a meeting they might attend. He gave them his card, it would get them in.

Emerging from the agency, Mitch Wilner and Rawley looked at each other, half scared, half amused. It was the first time Mitch had used a fake name; he saw it written on the back of the card: Introducing our friend Dr. Huyler. Aryan enough.

"We might get our necks broken," Rawley said, with his bubbly laugh.

That same "Right to Work" ad, but with local sponsors, lay on Jamie's desk, clipped out of the *Mahoning Press*. Yah, just like in the Harbor, he checked with them: mass meeting in the high school, fancy speeches. "Who was it, Colonel Roper?" "That's the guy. But there wasn't many fooled by that crap." And there were a couple of names, used to be on that back-to-work committee, that weren't there any more, he informed them proudly. A couple of ministers, and a rabbi took their names off. "That rabbi come right out and said: 'This isn't a committee to investigate the strike, it's a committee to break the strike.' Took off his name."

Rawley ran his finger down the list of sponsors, and stopped at one. "Our friend Neal Hollis."

"That sonofabitch!" Jamie exploded. "Run for sheriff last year. Good thing we beat him. If he was in office now they'd come out on us with tanks."

"What is this outfit, tonight?" Sobol asked. "The stooge committee?"

"No," Rawley said. "This is some organization that Hollis belongs to. Something kind of secret, I gather."

"He's a Silver Shirt," Jamie asserted.

"They active around here?"

"They had a whole damn convention here a while back," Jamie declared. He was so overwrought that Mitch wondered how much of what he said could be believed. "Those Silver Shirts met right in Adams Hall. District convention for the whole state. A couple of our boys tried to get in there but they wouldn't let them in. Had cops protecting for blocks all around."

"That was before the strike?"

"Yah. Couple of months before."

"This a Silver Shirt meeting tonight, Dr. Huyler?" Sobol wanted to know.

"Watch out they don't pull your pants off, Doc," Mike jested. "That's one way they got of checking up."

"I don't think it's Silver Shirts, not from what he said. They're probably trying to work up a Fascist united front," Rawley replied, but Sobol didn't seem pleased with the quip.

The meeting was in the city's best hotel. On entering the chrome-shiny elevator, with its ad for Sky Room, dinner and dancing, Mitch felt a chill in the very typicality, the very anonymity of the people against whom he rubbed, for even these might be folk who contained the purpose of destroying such as himself; several got out with them, went down the corridor with them to the same meeting-room, and how could they be told apart from people everywhere, and how would he know, from now on, who and how many walked the streets or sat in restaurants beside him, and contained planned readiness to destroy?

A middle-aged woman, bridge-club type, was taking tickets, but hovering around the door were a few hefty, fattish men, well enough dressed, but they could probably slug, too. The woman took the card, glanced up at them, squeezed a smile: oh, yes, Mr. Hollis had mentioned them. He was already here.

They went inside.

Some thirty or forty people were in the room, a small hall which reminded Mitch of that room in the Stevens where George Price's committee had first met. Except that these were mostly men; there, the majority had been women. And these were older folk.

People stood in clusters, talking. He realized that he had half expected a first glimpse of shirters, silver or brown. There were none in evidence. From one group, he caught a German accent.

At the rear of the room was a table with little piles of newspapers and pamphlets. A fairly good-looking girl was in attendance. He was reminded of left-wing meetings, like those of the Medical Bureau for Spain. Only this was the opposite pole. *Social Justice* and the *Guardian* were most prominently displayed, alongside the *National Republic*, also a pamphlet bearing a cartoon with a Shylock face and octopus arms, entitled: "Jewish Conspiracy to Rule the World (containing the authentic Protocols of Zion)"; there was the "C.I.O.—Communists In Office" pamphlet, beside a pile of "Red Roosevelt"

[404]

booklets, and there was a volume containing the anti-Jewish stuff that had been in Ford's *Dearborn Independent;* and there were pretty books about Germany.

Neal Hollis greeted them, dropping his arms heavily on their shoulders. He would introduce them around. Some big people here tonight. Some of course had to remain kind of incognito but—he winked. Indicating a hollow-cheeked fellow with a big Adam's apple he murmured: "Good contact in the sheriff's office." He pointed out a young, bland individual who was "right up there in Consolidated," practically Speer's personal emissary.

Mitch felt himself flushing, crazily remembering Mike Sisto's joke about certification—and was it so far away impossible?

"From Chicago?" a calm, respectable-looking man with a slight and distinguished German accent asked. "And do you know our group there?"

Rawley glibly replied that he had attended a Bund picnic at which Fritz Kuhn spoke. Mitch felt sweat run under his arm. Fortunately, the meeting began. He was certain they'd have soon given themselves away.

Hollis, acting as chairman, opened the session by calling for the singing of "The Star-Spangled Banner." Then he made a short speech. "Friends, we are met in a grave situation, a crisis. Many of us here fought and bled for America and we are not going to see America taken away from us now by a bunch of foreign reds." A million dollars' worth of business was being lost every week. The government was stalling so as to give John L. Lewis more time to wreck the steel industry. What was wanted was action.

He introduced a speaker from the Guardians of America, a Reverend Mr. McCullough. The church denomination sounded obscure. The Reverend rattled forth words of fire; his high clerical collar became drenched. The words spat out in long rhetorical bursts like machine-gun chain-flashes, all about red

[4 0 5]

America, and bloodthirsty nun-killers in Spain, and Russia running red with the blood of purges, and suddenly out of the confused mess, like a torso in a slaughter pile, he was shouting: "In Chicago we knew how to do it and in Ironville we knew how to do it and we can do it in Mahoning too. We can stop them. Our organizations everywhere are preparing to stop the red tide of blood and revolution and this strike is the first test. We must stop it now, for they are trying to capture the steel industry, the heart of our country, so that they can paralyze the nation at one stroke, they are trying to capture the mines and the automobile plants so that in time of war . . .

". . . and in Chicago, besmirching our great national holiday, Independence Day, and hiding behind women and children, the Bolsheviks tried to capture that steel plant and drive out the honest and loyal American workmen. But they got what was coming to them, a hail of bullets! And over there on Slovak Avenue we have the same type of agitator and radical, the same Communists, and let it be a warning to them . . . !

". . . the time is coming," he cried, "when every good American should know how to handle a gun, and I mean just that! For any day, life and liberty and the sacred right of property might have to be defended. . . ."

This was not a stolid audience as in the Harbor. Men were wiping sweat from their foreheads. Others sat with clamped teeth and an enlistment stare.

". . . no use putting them in jail because their Jewish lawyers will get them out . . . we'll not be safe until we are rid of them, until we have cleaned every last subversive snake out of our land!"

A man in the audience leaped up, crying: let all the organizations represented here muster their people to march in a body upon the sheriff's office and demand the right to clean up the situation.

In this connection, Mr. Hollis called for a confidential report from a certain party. The man he had pointed out as a contact in the sheriff's office arose and, with the intimate air of dispensing inside information, said the plain fact was the sheriff was a coward, scared of his skin, scared those reds would get him some night, if he did his duty and went out after them. But, the contact promised them, certain men on the force would know how to take care of things, if they only had a chance!

A bald-head arose and cried: "In Ironville they had that kind of sheriff but they got him out of the way, all right!"

A committee to "work together" for "immediate action" was formed.

Mitch and Rawley ducked out quickly so as to avoid Hollis. Rawley said he needed a drink; they went into a tavern. The place was ashout with swing from a nickel record machine.

Rawley appeared deeply depressed, all the bubble gone out of him. "There'll be shooting up here," he said. "Same thing as in Chicago and Ironville. We know it's coming and we can't stop it."

Mitch, too, felt the dark presage. And yet, what was the precise source of the coming violence? They had seen an actual point of infection. But was there proof that Consolidated was the source? Was there a clear link between the company and these half-formed Fascist councils? "But we know that Consolidated gave money to Martha Cross," Rawley reminded him, "and she's tied up with nearly every Fascist gang in the country."

"That doesn't prove anything except they paid for propaganda. It doesn't prove they engineered any shooting."

"I didn't say these guys pull the triggers. Lord knows, some of them may. Why shouldn't a few company cops and maybe even city cops belong to the Guardians or the Shirts, or some

[407]

other gang? But this, these people tonight—they provide the basis of social justification for the shooting. The propaganda furnishes the impulse, and the respectable names behind it remove the inhibitions to murder. If a cop or a deputy shoots, he can tell himself he carried out the will of the citizens—and we just saw what citizens . . ."

Suddenly Mitch isolated the key to his quandary. "Didn't one of the union boys say Hollis ran for sheriff, and was defeated?"

"Yah."

"But now, if Hollis and the people he represents can pressure the sheriff into acting against his own conception of his duty, then Hollis is really the sheriff. He, or his kind, can command the sheriff's office."

"Exactly!" Rawley lost some of his gloom, in following the analysis, like a teacher watching a fairly bright pupil.

"Then that means the election is perverted? The citizens knew what Hollis stood for and defeated him, yet he can put through his policy."

Rawley nodded. "That," he said, "is what has us worried about the way our democracy works."

Mitch felt the same excitement as in his own science when at last a long-searched-for organism comes into focus under the microscope.

"Here, in an industrial city, where the vote is really in the hands of the workers," Rawley pointed out, "if their vote is nullified even here, what can we hope for, out of our elections? And all over the country, if the few labor reforms that it took twenty years to build into law, if these can be nullified—what's the use?"

"But why does there have to be shooting here, in Mahoning, too? Why can't it be prevented, after the experience of Chicago and Ironville?"

"The answer is, why couldn't it be prevented in Chicago by

[4 0 8]

what was learned from the general strike in San Francisco in 1934? Or by what was learned from every strike that has taken place in Chicago since 1887. The answer is exactly the same as in Spain. The answer is a question: whether a true democracy which in the long run means economic as well as political democracy can be established under capitalism."

Mitch bit. "Just what do you mean, economic democracy?"

"Look," Rawley squared off, "this is the democracy we've got: democratically, more or less, we make laws about sex crimes and cleaning the alleys and bathing suits on beaches and making left turns. Until recently we thought, if a Vanderbilt could be fined for speeding, that proved everybody had equal rights. Now, there is a kind of suspicion growing that political forms cannot be separated from economic forms. Hence the confusion about democracy."

"Then you mean, we can't have a real democracy until we break down capitalism?" Mitch asked.

Rawley listened with a rapt smile to a spiraling trumpet passage. "Old Bix himself. Listen to him mount the stairs!" His eyes followed a couple dancing, leaden-faced. "Capitalism is an emotional word," he said. "Say what's wanted is a way to increase production, widen distribution of goods, forever and ever—a widening instead of a narrowing spiral. Undertakings have to be tremendous in this age—well, look at the steel plants. You have to assign big chunks of wealth. Well, if the people who do the assigning, under our present system, are stumped because they can't find ways to reinvest wealth and make it profitable, then we have to devise another kind of management. There are a dozen plans; any one, or the combination of several, might be correct. But the general idea is to have a continuously rising standard of living, instead of to burn mountains of coffee to keep a price up. Well, Otis Speer says he is only a manager anyway, money doesn't mean anything to him, he just wants to

[409]

make steel. So let the banking of all enterprise revert to the people. That would be a kind of economic democracy."

"You mean, no private ownership?" Mitch asked.

"Hell, you could even have private ownership. Run things just as they are today, but with a few more wage controls, and the government as the banker."

"Doesn't the American people resent the idea of so much government control?" Mitch objected.

"That's a propagandized superstition. And where would the control be apparent? The mechanism of life would be the same. Look, we don't even dream of questioning government control of currency, do we? Yet not so long ago money was issued by feudal lords or private banks. First, the government had to guarantee their currency, and finally the natural way was for the government to take over the whole job. Well, currency is the token for wealth, so why not do it with the real thing?"

Yes, since the crash the government was at the stage of guaranteeing bank deposits, so . . .

"Oh, Joseph, Joseph." Rawley drummed on the table.

"Is this the program of the group you were telling me about?" Mitch asked.

"There isn't any pat answer to things," Rawley said. "The people themselves have to make whatever they get. All we can try to do is clear the bunk out of their way. The Commies try to tell them they belong to the lower classes and have to fight the capitalists. But it's in the Constitution that we all are born equal. We all have the vote. Well, my outfit wants to show how, the way it is now, outside of the bathing suit laws, American life is a dollar vote, and Mr. Speer has a couple of million votes to your one. So we figure, one thing folks will understand—and you don't have to call it the class struggle—is democracy on the economic level. It doesn't matter just what mechanism is used to realize it. Only, there isn't much time."

The leaden-faced couple paused by the nickelodeon to choose a new record.

Stay as sweet as you are . . .

Rawley grimaced. "There you are. Democracy. You pays your money and you takes your choice." He tossed some change onto the table.

Going south, all the next day, up through the mild Appalachian Mountains with the sudden wide views of farmland, and then through the neater older towns with their ease and peace, and touching towns only at bright clean brisk gas stations, the threat of Mahoning receded, seemed unreal. Space brought a sense of safety. And coming into Washington this was buttressed by the dignity and solidity of government materialized in blocks and blocks of stone buildings.

And when they came into the Senate building, into the busy and purposeful atmosphere of Senator Gottschalk's office, Mitch felt again that the whole revolutionary view was a nightmare; there still was government. What had been done wouldn't go ignored. Here were the Chicago police, from the topmost chief, and Captain Wiley, down to cops on the hoof, brought to judgment in the nation's capital. The people could not be utterly disregarded or betrayed.

In a back room of the senator's office, the crew held their last quick conference before the start of the hearings. Sproul, Mussetti, Tannenbaum, and a young lawyer named Kahn who spoke with a Southern accent. They had a stack of folders, one for each witness, containing questions planned to bring out facts they already knew. Mitch realized that for them the main part of the job was over. The actual hearings would only serve to dramatize the facts and put them into the official record. Still, they hoped the police might let something drop.

The medical charts were splendid, Sproul said, a swell idea.

[4 1 1]

"We won't get to your testimony today, Wilner, probably to-morrow afternoon." But he wanted Mitch in the hearing-room at all times, if possible, as points requiring a physician's verification might come up.

The first morning was to be devoted to the chief of police and his assistant, who, the boys knew, had held conferences with Superintendent Chesney of the Consolidated plant as far as a week before the strike. Tannenbaum shook his head pessimistically. "Just be luck if we can shake something out of him. He's tight."

"The afternoon papers will play a general story anyway," Sproul said. "If we can get to Captain Wiley by tonight, that'll give the morning papers their break."

Their central concern seemed to be to arrange the evidence so as to keep the hearing in the headlines. At first this irritated Mitch. But then he realized: what other weapon did they have, but exposure? Their one hope was to excite people enough so that they would take part in government.

Apparently, though an educator like Rawley might be apprehensive, these fellows believed there was still time to educate the public.

The high-ceilinged ponderously decorated chamber was already crowded with spectators. Half of the long room was railed off, for them. The rest was cluttered with long heavy tables, in a T-arrangement. At the top sat senators and their staff. Longwise, the press; George Price waved to Rawley and Mitch. His paper had sent him down after all. His wife was along, too. At the bottom of the T was the witness chair. Against each side wall were rows of chairs, as if for two juries facing each other. The far side, Mitch noticed, was already occupied by the union people. Opposite them, on the door side, sat members of the Chicago police. However, most of their chairs were

[4 1 2]

vacant, for the police seemed to dislike sitting in the room; they congregated in a pocket of the corridor.

Even in their plain clothes, the cops were an obvious type, bulky men, not as young-looking as you somehow remembered them in uniform, and with their skins coarse-grained from exposure.

From his first glance at the senators, Mitch felt reassurance. An oddly special sense of security came from the idea that Gottschalk, sitting there alert and solid, was already second in the line of such men; little as Mitch Wilner had occupied himself with political affairs, there was alive in his mind, he now discovered, a complete picture of Gottschalk's father, the late Watchdog of the Senate, embodying a powerful and unquenchable spirit of democratic zeal. Hadn't old Gottschalk been some sort of a Socialist? And wasn't his state still the model of progress in the United States, of rational steady progress toward co-operation? For the first time Mitch felt himself in the presence of an American tradition, here a family tradition of career, and honest career, in government; at the very moment that he felt shamefully ignorant of the operation of the land in which he lived, he felt a pride that it did breed traditions of responsibility.

The son was youthful without being young; and established an immediate dignity without being formal. He could make a joke or a quip, insert a word of slang, but always as if extending permission to his own very human person to do so, while remembering the office he represented. Even more; Mitch came to feel that this man had to reserve his behavior to that of one who recognized the possibility that he might some day be President of the United States: not a recognition by ambition so much as by a respect for a potentiality.

The elder senator, as if selected by a showman, was precisely the correct counterweight for Gottschalk. He had a soft murmurous voice like—who was it that played tender fathers in the

[4 1 3]

movies?—H. B. Warner; and his role, as it developed during the hearing, was to question not so much for details of fact as for attitudes, for morality; when he took a witness it was always with a kindly agreement on fact: yes, let's leave it at that, you don't know who broke the window, sonny, but now let's see— naturally, you want to play ball and you have a right to play ball but . . . And he would lead and sweetly lead his man, seeming to be a garrulous old senator putting in his oar, until suddenly, after nearly dozing to inattention, the house discovered that the old boy was getting off something good, that he had led his witness around to an inescapable admission of injustice, or negligence. And that he had done this through such a labyrinth that the witness could not backtrack.

Now the parade of police began, in order of superiority.

"Watch them pass the buck, right down the line," Rawley predicted.

The police chief was a man with a look of concern and candor. He wore a banker's gray suit, and wore his vest, though all sweltered. In stature, the chief appeared smaller than the rest of his group; his voice was modulated, executive.

The chairs on the police-side filled as the men filed in, their presence lending moral support to their officers, and among them Mitch recognized Braden, Gorcey, and the big-cheeked young lawyer, Corcoran, who had come, that Sunday, to the hospital. He looked like just one of the cops.

The chief was expressionless under the flashlights. He looked toward the senators with the air of a man whose own conscience is at rest, and who, too, seeks truth. When asked for any document, he made a point of repeating that he had turned every- thing over to the committee's investigators. "They asked for it and I gave them everything I had, my complete file."

What could be learned from him? Whether there was any

direct tie-up between the police department and Consolidated? He had heard of the impending strike three days before it broke, from the head of the South Side district, Captain Simmons. Of course, too, it was "in the air" that a strike was coming.

And did the chief of the Chicago police stay awake nights in touch with what must have been the most ticklish situation in his career? Did he go out in the district? Did he instruct the strike leaders and the company managers as to how to conduct themselves, to keep the peace?

"From your long experience in police work," the senator asked, "you knew strike situations create difficult and delicate problems of policing?"

"Oh, yes."

"And didn't you anticipate that a major strike in the steel industry would give rise to a particularly difficult situation for the police?"

"Yes, of course."

"How, then, did you prepare for the situation?"

"I told Simmons to check up on the situation."

"And that was all?"

"That was all that was necessary at that stage."

On Wednesday, Simmons had phoned to say that the men would go out either at 3 or at 10 p.m.

A murmur of excitement went through the row of S.W.O.C. witnesses. How did Captain Simmons know the strike might be pulled at three o'clock? That information certainly could not have come from the union side, even through a spy, as the union plan was for 10 p.m. So the company itself must have been planning the three o'clock trick, and told the cops to be ready. That was how they had started the strike in confusion.

And what, the senator asked, had the chief done when Captain Simmons reported the men would go out that day?

"I told him to make the necessary detail, and see that life and property were protected."

"That was all?"

"And preserve the peace."

"And that was all?"

"Yes, that was all," the chief said calmly.

Couldn't it be said, then, that he had handled the strike in routine manner?

"Oh, no, it was not a routine matter." The department knew what to do. He had full confidence in his men.

Did he hear of the trouble on Wednesday night?

Oh, yes, some twenty-two men were arrested, he had a report on it.

Did he investigate the situation then?

He had the report, that was enough.

Did he hear of the trouble on Friday?

Yes, he heard a column of strikers tried to march on the plant and, as a result, six police were injured.

"Any strikers injured?"

He had heard some strikers were injured too.

Did he inquire into that?

No, he didn't think it was necessary.

"Sonofabitch," Mike Sisto muttered. "They nearly killed my brother."

Did the chief of police know there was a meeting planned for Sunday?

Yes, it was in the papers.

Did he discuss preparations for this meeting with anyone?

No. Didn't think it was necessary.

Mitch couldn't take his eyes off the witness, so contained and confidently righteous. Suppose the man were truly on trial, with all these citizens as jury? Mitch felt there were only two possible views to take. The man was either admitting a negligence which, having resulted in ten deaths, was criminal, or he was lying, to cover an even more criminal complicity.

"And we pay that guy," Art Nowis sneered.

"He ought to be shot," Gillespie said, seriously.

"In Russia, he would be," Rawley remarked.

"Damn right," said Frank Sobol.

As a matter of fact, the chief was saying, the union had sent a couple of lawyers to him, Thursday or Friday, wanting to know how many pickets they could have. "Have all you want, I told them, so long as they are peaceful. They asked me, can we have fifty, and I doubled it. I said you can have a hundred, for all I care."

Mike Sisto squirmed as if to jump out of his seat. "They wouldn't even let eight guys—" Sobol silenced him.

Now the elder senator took up the questioning. "And what is peaceful picketing? Who is the judge of that? . . . What I am trying to get at is the responsibility involved. Perhaps you can help me, Commissioner. The police are a disciplined body of men?"

"They are."

"So that, anything a policeman did, his superior would be responsible for?"

"Well, up to a certain point," the chief hedged. "The human element enters into it."

"That is what I am trying to get at. You feel your men were well disciplined? Under control all the time?"

"Yes. Certainly."

"Then, on the Fourth, if the captain had whistled, they would have retired in response to his order?"

The chief wasn't sure.

"What I am striving to determine," Senator Starrett con-

[4 1 7]

tinued with philosophic calm, "is who is responsible for a man's action, the individual policeman or the organization? Who initiates a man's action?"

Well, in a case like that, in a fight, every man was responsible for himself.

Then it was no longer a disciplined body of men?

Rawley nudged Mitch, in appreciation. Yes, it was neat. The chief was pinned. Either he had to accept responsibility or admit his force was poorly disciplined.

The chief made a speech about how fine the force was, and how he approved of everything they had done on the Fourth.

The younger senator snapped back into the chase. Did he approve of shooting people in the back? Was he aware that seven of the ten dead had died from bullet wounds in the back?

No, he didn't know that for a fact.

It was in the coroner's reports, hadn't he called for the coroner's reports?

No, he hadn't.

Why not?

"I'm waiting for the inquest. That is the legal procedure."

So it was no accident, Wilner realized, that the routine inquest had been so long postponed. Delays came in handy.

Would the chief take the senator's word for it that the reports showed seven shot through the back? And if so, could he explain such shooting?

The only shooting he knew of was from the reports of a few officers who were knocked down and who, with strikers on top of them beating them, fired their revolvers in self-defense.

How could a man on the ground firing at someone on top of him hit his assailant in the back? What sort of marksmanship was that?

[4 1 8]

Well, the chief retorted, in that situation a man couldn't think of his marksmanship.

The senator arose, anger in his voice. "You show me how it is possible! How could all those people be hit in the back?"

"Well, they might have been shot by people in the crowd, their own people."

Was that all they could do to him? Make him squirm for an hour in a chair, only to let him retire smugly into the midst of his men, whose grinning showed their contempt for these entire proceedings, their confidence that nothing could be done to them?

Now came Captain Simmons, the man who had been in contact with the superintendent, days before the strike; was he the man who really knew what deals had been made; was he the link between the downtown declaration—have all the pickets you want, have a hundred, we don't care—and the eight pickets chased from the field?

A heavy, inscrutable face, ponderous jaws, a bulky body crowding the chair. Listening, Mitch felt that here was a cunning concealed in bulk, like a heavily insulated wire, or say like a bacillus active through its insoluble layer of fat.

Why, he was a friend of labor, started as a foundryman at sixteen, carried a union card, as had ninety percent of the Chicago police, at one time or another, he could assure the senator. Yes, he'd gone out there to talk to the super. Mr. Chesney was afraid of a sitdown, so he had told Mr. Chesney: " 'We don't allow sitdowns in Chicago, they don't get away with any of that stuff here.' And that was our policy, Senator."

"Well, what did you allow? How were the strikers to know what you did allow?"

"Senator, if I was a laborer in a situation like that, I would

[4 1 9]

come to the police. I would make it a point right off to discuss things with the police, so everything would be peaceful."

"The police go to the boss," Rawley commented, "but the strikers are supposed to come to the police."

Mike Sisto growled, in an agony of self-restraint. "What the Christ were we doing all week but going to everybody from the mayor to the janitor! And Wiley. Wednesday night me and Jock Kiley went and talked to Captain Wiley there in that shack by the gate. How many pickets can we have? So finally he says eight so we put on eight pickets. So by the time we get back to headquarters they shag them. Thursday, Friday, we try to talk to Wiley, we try to find Simmons, and they won't even talk to us. 'Why didn't you come and ask us'! Jesus!"

The senator rapped for quiet.

The second police chief went off the stand. They had got nothing out of him beyond the admission of his early conferences with the mill superintendent. Mitch noticed Corcoran's grin to Simmons, in congratulation.

But now it was Wiley's turn. The two others had not been on the actual scene of slaughter, on Independence Day; no one could charge them with immediate responsibility. The buck was passed to Captain Wiley.

He was an old man, probably around retirement age, but still strong in appearance; tall, well fleshed, a man who might have been handsome in his time. As the captain took the witness chair, Mitch Wilner recognized in him the officer who had read the riot act, out there, the moment before the shooting began. And Mitch felt again the frightening wall of the man's personality, a deadly negativism extending all around him. The man had a gloomy, colorless face, with pouchy, darkened tearsacs; his eyes were kept almost closed, and there was a catatonic immobility about his features. His voice was monotonous. He moved with the air of a man convinced that the world was evil.

[4 2 0]

In a droning, pessimistic voice, he testified for hours, and it seemed to Mitch that the hatreds he revealed amounted to manic fears; it seemed as if the miasmic marshes of a mind were being uncovered, and what was revealed there filled Mitch with the same sickening hopelessness as when, during an exploratory operation, the seat of disease is found to be some spreading, malignant neoplasm in a vital organ, untouchable with the knife, ineradicable; nothing to do but close it, quickly, hide it again; no hope, just wait for death.

Mitch remembered some story of Wiley's having been mixed up in a relief station riot; Sam Eisen had mentioned it.

"Yes, a couple of years ago." Rawley knew the story. "He told them to go ahead and hold their meeting, even brought out a chair for the speaker to stand on; then, as soon as they got started, Wiley and the cops bust in and started clubbing."

Sobol nodded. "Mike Burns got beat up in that, and Al Howard."

"Wiley got beaten up too," Rawley said. "He's really been a terror since then."

Obviously, a man filled with such hatreds was the last man to place in charge of a strike situation, unless to make certain the strikers got no chance. And the horror was that a man like Wiley might be purely honest, Mitch thought; his very hatreds were honest; he was a hundred percenter, even if it might be one hundred percent prejudice.

A week before the strike, it developed, a subordinate of Captain Wiley's had been out to the plant to confer with the superintendent, Chesney. They had kept in touch with Chesney, and on the very hour the strike was called, one hundred policemen were inside the plant; by four o'clock Captain Wiley himself had arrived with reinforcements. There he had found "some C.I.O. fellow, Jack Kiley he calls himself, he says to let him call out his men. I said all right. So he climbed up on a stack of slabs there, and started making a speech calling everybody out. Oh, no, you can't do that, you can only talk to your C.I.O. men, I said. He was trying to get out all those men, to agitate in there, so I put a stop to it."

"Did you make clear to Mr. Kiley or to any of the strikers what extent of picketing would be permitted under the law?" the young senator asked.

"I knew, Senator, what was permitted under the law."

"Yes, but did you discuss it with the strikers?"

"The need had not yet arisen."

"Why not, had they not started to picket?"

"No, there was just a mob of them out there," Captain Wiley said, "with a sound truck by the gates, insulting the police, yelling: 'You scabs in uniform, come out of there!'" So he had ordered the sound truck silenced, and the crowd dispersed, and those that wouldn't move, like that fellow Kiley, he had them arrested.

The row of strikers listened stonily. Arrested all right. They had picked out every C.I.O. organizer and union officer in the crowd, and thrown them into the can, paralyzing the strike until Friday, when the leaders, out on bond, tried to organize the picket line.

"On Friday they came marching on us, three, four hundred of them," Captain Wiley testified, "and there was a fight. One of them pickets went to the jail hospital, well, I wouldn't call them pickets, members of that mob——"

"That was my brother," Mike growled. "They put him in the jail hospital."

"And we arrested some more, and their cases are pending; they are booked for conspiracy and committing an illegal act, that is chapter 38, section 139."

Then, the captain reported tonelessly, he got a phone call

[4 2 2]

tipping him off that the strikers were planning to invade the plant on Sunday.

Who had made that call?

Some newspaperman.

Did he know his name?

No.

Did he often get such tips?

Newspapermen were pretty good fellows.

Did he say what paper?

No.

Wasn't the captain curious as to the source of so grave a report? Did he recognize the voice?

No.

The courtroom tittered as the captain bluffly stuck to his story. Finally, the senator passed up the point.

Wiley told how, after receiving that tip-off, he had called out extra reserves for Sunday. He had instructed them that those reds were going to try to break through into the plant. "But they will not pass our lines. I told them, don't use your guns unless you have to, to protect yourself."

With those words, Mitch felt the whole event becoming understandable. For suppose he were a cop called up from some West Side station, knowing he was in emergency reserves, knowing there had been "bad blood" all week, with a scrap on Friday, and hearing, first thing he got on the scene, tales from the other cops of how a buddy was in the hospital kicked in the testicles and maybe never use them again, hearing that the strikers were wild and out for blood today, then hearing the captain say don't use your gun unless you have to—surely he would have felt he was going to have to use his gun.

And in such a state of fear, certainly the first explosion would have jerked his own finger on the trigger, whether that first explosion was the tear-gas bomb that Wiley now told of ordering released, or a rifle shot the boys claimed had been fired from a mill roof, wounding that Mexican woman, who had disappeared. If the cops had been set off by such a shot, wouldn't the next few moments of shooting and wild advance be accomplished in a mass war hysteria? They'd have accomplished a massacre before coming to their senses and realizing there was no opposing force.

Where did the gas bombs come from, that the police used? the senator asked, since a check-up proved the department's own supply was intact. Could those bombs have been from the Consolidated supply? Perhaps, the captain admitted. He hadn't stopped to inquire.

And were the police trained in the use of gas?

No. (In fact, in the confusion, one officer had discharged a gas bomb in his own face.)

Even more certainly, Mitch sensed how, had he been one of those police, his fears would have overcome him. Not knowing how to use the gas bombs, his gun his only protection, wouldn't he have drawn, and fired?

For now Captain Wiley, his head drawn back, his eyes closed to slits, like a man speaking through visions, was painting the enemy. Just so, he must have painted him for the men in his charge, before they went into line. The trouble-makers, the reds, the Communists in there, they were in there to assault the police, to knock the police down and overcome them and wrest their guns away from them, and then invade the plant. "If we had allowed them to go a step further, there would have been hundreds killed."

(Don't let them through our lines, men! They can't get through the Chicago police!)

The elder senator gently asked: "Then you believe these trouble-makers, reds as you call them, are against the police?"

"They are against the police and against the government," the captain firmly stated. "I have had very serious trouble with them before. In 1933 it was the Communists in a relief riot, they assaulted us, and there is an officer walking in my district now with a metal plate in his head, an object of pity, all done by Communists. And there is another, limping on a stick, they did it to him. I put six of them in the penitentiary for that, chapter 38, section 139, conspiracy to do an illegal act, and that was the assult on the policeman."

He blinked his eyes slowly.

Were these assailants still in the penitentiary? the senator asked.

"No, one of those lawyers got them out on an order for a new trial on a technicality, saying the judge showed prejudice, and they are at large, Communists, and some of them were out there on that day, free to assault the police again."

Morosely, he repeated: "All they are doing is undermining this government, and they are sending money over from Russia to do it."

High laughter came from the audience. But as more and more of the poison poured from the officer, Mitch Wilner felt concern instead of scorn. For this was the same as the ranting in Mahoning, these were the ideas Colonel Roper had expressed in the Harbor; only there was no longer any bulwark between the thought and the act. One could not listen and take cover in the reflection that the law is still between them and us. For here was the officer of the law. Here the thing had happened. Captain Wiley had not seen himself as a policeman in a strike, but as a defender of his America against a revolution.

"Do you think there was anyone in this disturbance that was in Russia's pay?" Senator Starrett asked.

"I wouldn't be surprised."

"Do you think there was?" the elder senator persisted.

"I saw some Communists locked up there after the riot."

"How did you know they were Communists?"

"I have seen them around demonstrations, and when they parade downtown. Once or twice a year we give them permission to have a parade."

Were people who walked in such parades, the senator said—he presumed the witness meant such occasions as the May Day parade—were they all Communists?

"I call them reds," Captain Wiley responded. "I will give you my definition of a red. He is here to undermine the government and assault policemen."

The tittering broke out again.

"I am an American!" Captain Wiley asserted. "My grandparents were born here!"

There was a shout of laughter.

But Mitch saw Rawley frowning, and he himself felt angry at the stupid laughter. This was the powder behind those bullets.

The young senator asked: "Do you think the disturbance on the Fourth was a fight between the police and Communists?"

"It was brought on by red agitators to march down the police and go into the plant and take those men out of there. I told every platoon commander to hold those lines."

The elder senator re-emphasized the question: "You think this affair——"

"The riot?"

"I called it trouble, in the beginning, and I still think it is a good word—do you think this affair was primarily between the police and the persons whom you call Communists and that it was not incidental to the industrial troubles?"

"It wound up between us and the Communists," Wiley maintained. "But their real objective was to get into the plant and take those men out of there. But it was my place as a sworn police officer and the commanding officer of the policemen

[426]

there, and my duty to find out about it and to prevent it, and if I did not do that I could have been indicted and put in prison. I could not let them get by those lines."

The courtroom quieted. The man was sincere, passionate in his belief. And was he entirely without justification? There had been Communists out there and they had had some plan to get through the police line. If Captain Wiley had guilt, wasn't it for believing exaggerated reports of this plan? Weren't the spies, as he admitted, "the people we had in there," equally culpable, for spreading so wild an alarm? And wasn't the guilt also upon those who had put a known red-scare sufferer like Wiley in charge of such a situation? The bland chief, and stolid Simmons. But this made a full circle, for their choice of Wiley could not have been accidental.

"So if they had got in and accomplished their purpose," the senator continued, "if the purpose was to bring the men out—as Communists, what would they have accomplished?"

Captain Wiley responded with conviction: "They would have accomplished killing a lot of people in there."

The elder senator inquired: "Do you think the people you call Communists want to kill people? That is one of their objectives?"

"Not all of them. But all that I have met. Maybe there are some I have not met."

"Do you think that murder is just inherent in their natures?"

"Those that I met, it seems that way."

"They want to murder more people than just the policemen, do they?"

"I am a policeman and I don't know what they done to others."

"I just can't understand that situation, just the desire to kill, because generally you kill for a purpose," the senator reflected. "If the fight is just one between the Communists and the police, we would know how to legislate against it."

[4 2 7]

"We represent the law," Captain Wiley said. "The uniformed police represent the law of the state of Illinois and the city of Chicago, and that is why the Communists go after the police. I don't think it is anything personal. It is the uniform."

"Do you think Communists are against uniforms?" The question produced laughter. But the police officer was fixed to his idea; his face remained immobile, his eyes heavily lidded, he seemed completely oblivious of his surroundings, sunken within himself; Mitch thought of faces he had seen in the asylum, a few days ago, possessed people, who obviously were not even aware of other beings in the same room with them. "Could I make a recommendation to clarify the mind of this committee?" Wiley asked.

"Yes, sir," the senator replied.

"Deport every one of those Communists and all the reds out of the country and then we will get along; they won't be assaulting policemen and dynamiting buildings and then we will have a good nation."

"Where would you send them?" the senator asked soberly, through the laughter.

"Back to Russia, over there with Lenin."

"Where would you send the Americans?"

"I didn't know there were so many American Communists."

"You actually think they are paid agents of Russia?"

"I know some of those in my district, they went to Russia for instructions."

"What part of Russia?" the elder senator persisted.

"To the capital."

"Where is that?"

The officer moved his head slowly, as a man coming out of a vision. "Well, where Lenin is," he said.

The audience shrieked. Oh, better than a play. The young

senator permitted himself a wry smile, but banged the gavel and warned the spectators that they were present as guests of the committee and must maintain order. But how could they laugh! Mitch clenched and unclenched his hands, nervously. How could anyone laugh! For since this man believed these things, and had power in his hands, all those others had been killed!

"They called themselves anarchists and I.W.W. during the war," the captain declared, "but now they are in this new movement, Communism."

"How did the Communists come out at the last election?"

"I did not look at it," the captain said.

"As an orderly process, then, they are not much of a problem for us, are they?"

"I think they are a bigger problem than we have ever given a thought to."

"Have you any Communist city councilmen in Chicago?"

"I am glad to say we have not," Wiley retorted.

"Anyone running for city council on the Communist ticket?"

"He did, but he didn't get four votes. Nobody bothered with him." A new strength was coming into the captain's voice.

"He didn't get any votes, you said?"

"No. Communists are not very strong there. They have about thirty units there in Chicago. Maybe around thirty thousand all together, including the colored."

"There are a lot of colored Communists?" the senator asked with concern.

"Oh, yes."

"Did they come from Russia?"

The spectators could not repress themselves. The beautiful trap! The logic of that old boy!

Yes, Mitch thought, Wiley had been thoroughly shown up. And to what end? When they were through with him he arose, blinking his heavy lids; he made his way to the corridor where the gang of big men with big shoulders absorbed him. They stood together. They could hold their own against these red senators and this crowd of laughing hyenas, Washington reds. Let them laugh. Let them have their fun. Only a day more of this monkey business and, back home in Chicago, they'd still have their stars, their clubs, their guns.

"I don't care if Wiley belongs to an organization or not," Tannenbaum snapped. His wife watched apprehensively, for he was doing a sloppy job of carving a shoulder of lamb, while excitedly replying to George Price. "What difference does it make? He talks a pure Fascist line and he acts on it. When the time comes, such guys will be polarized instantly. For that matter, I wouldn't be surprised for a minute if he does belong to the Silver Shirts or something."

"Darling," his wife said, "don't get so excited. You're tired as hell." Then she said to the guests: "The boys haven't had a minute's rest for a week. They've been working day and night."

Tannenbaum said he'd have to go off right after dinner. Fact, he should just have grabbed a sandwich at the committee rooms.

They couldn't get off the subject of Wiley. Rawley thought there were statements in the captain's testimony which indicated delusions of persecution. "To put a man like that in charge of such a situation, with power over life and death—that's where the real crime is."

"Couldn't you say some element of accident entered into that?" asked Mrs. Tannenbaum. She reminded Mitch slightly of Sylvia, managing a group of guests in her orderly, modern apartment.

"Can there be anything accidental in such a setup?" Rawley countered.

"Not in Chicago," cracked a young labor board lawyer,

[4 3 0]

Victor Fuchs. The Tannenbaums had introduced him, saying he would probably be coming to Chicago on the Consolidated case.

"I don't pretend to condone Wiley," Mrs. Tannenbaum said. "But when he said it wound up between the cops and the Communists—well, there were a lot of comrades there."

"Sure there were Communists there, and sure they had some plan!" Tannenbaum cried. "Their plan was to establish a picket line."

Mitch said: "Remember, Wiley admitted he had spies in there because, he claimed, it was his business to know the union's plans. Well, didn't Art Nowis admit the union had some kind of idea of getting into the mill, that time the police had him in custody?"

"We'll have him on the stand," Tannenbaum promised. "We've got a little surprise coming out of that guy."

"Does he deny it now?"

Tannenbaum remained mysterious.

"Anyway, even if we don't believe that story, the fact remains that Wiley believed it. So from his point of view, he had to do what he did." George Price's wife sided with Mrs. Tannenbaum, in her effort to understand Wiley's behavior.

"Except for one thing," Rawley pointed out. "No matter what you say, he still didn't have to allow the men to shoot. There's absolutely no excuse for that. They can't get around that. Gas would have been enough."

"I don't think you did anything to those guys today," Price told Tannenbaum, pessimistically. "What they said sounded funny to us but in the papers it'll sound convincing. They just got a chance to shoot off a lot of red-baiting speeches. The thing to do is, at least one of those cops has to break down and admit he did some shooting."

"We're going to nail one of them tomorrow. You watch,"

[4 3 1]

Tannenbaum promised. "We've got this one by the short hairs, all right."

"Put him on for the morning papers," Price advised.

"Yah. We figure on breaking the spy story in the afternoon."

"Spy?" Price caught his slip. But Tannenbaum would say no more.

"Ernest Braden," the senator called, and the policeman who had come into the tavern, that time, took the witness chair. Tannenbaum slipped up to the young lawyer, Kahn, who sat beside the senator, and pointed something out, on a photograph. Kahn looked at it with a magnifying-glass, nodded; Tannenbaum returned to his seat.

Braden told of having been a union bricklayer once, told of his war service. He spoke in hurried snatches, gulping his words.

"Are you nervous?" the senator asked.

"Yes, Senator, I am nervous," the man admitted, but with bravado.

"You don't have to be. This is not a trial."

"Yes it is, Senator. The police department of Chicago is on trial here before the whole nation." His forthright speech startled the room.

"I am glad you take that attitude," the elder senator said. "We too believe this inquiry should be regarded most seriously."

Perhaps through this man, Mitch felt, he might come to understand that isolated group of men—the police. Of course he knew one police captain well enough—Mort Abramson's father-in-law. But Rosen was that odd thing, a Jewish cop, as a Negro cop or even a Polish cop would be an odd thing.

Braden told how he had marched out his platoon and deployed his men across the tracks. He told of the strikers approaching.

[4 3 2]

"They came toward us in military formation," he asserted, "it was a marching column, with file-closers."

"Were they in step?" the senator asked.

"They didn't have to be in step. In my judgment they advanced like an army. They were under discipline."

He grew angrily red as the crowd laughed.

"They came to a turn in the road and did a right oblique," he related; and told how "a detachment deployed across the field on the double, attempting to outflank our lines. Then their color-bearers halted, and when they saw they could not complete their flanking movement, they made a direct front attack. I ordered my men to stand firm. . . ."

As the man spoke, Mitch felt his blood run cold. To the police, all war veterans, this had been a military engagement. They had seen the enemy advancing. So they had mown them down, and counter-attacked, chasing the routed enemy, shooting and beating.

Braden concluded his testimony: "I ordered my men to help pick up the wounded, and when that was done we reassembled and marched back to the plant."

Relief was in his voice. He had stood his ground. He was nearly through. He had upheld the honor of the department; and, indeed, Braden had made a convincing witness. At this point the senator handed Braden an enlarged photograph. "Will you tell me what you see on that photograph?"

"Why, that is a photograph of some action, when we were clearing the field."

"Could you describe what you see? In the foreground?"

"There are a lot of people on the ground," the officer said cautiously.

"Any women among them?"

"Yes."

"How many women can you count?"

"Well I can count one, two . . . four."

"I see six," the senator said. "Look, in the melee there."

"Yes, six, I guess."

"How many police?"

"Well, there are a lot of us, all in through there."

"To the right, on the picture, what do you see? A separate little group. . . ."

"Well, there is a man fallen there, with some police there."

"Does the man appear to be injured?"

"He does."

"What position is he in?"

"On all fours, kind of like he was trying to get up."

"Is there any blood on him?"

"There is that black stain, I guess that is blood, on his shirt."

"His shirt appears to be torn?"

"Yes."

"Now, the two policemen bending over him, have they got clubs in their hands?"

The officer began to sense the goal of the questioning. His voice dropped. "Yes, sir."

"The one on the left of the fallen man, what is he doing with his club?"

"Well, it looks as if that club just landed on the man's head."

"And the other officer?"

"Well, he has his club raised."

"Would you say, as if about to bring it down?"

"It might be."

"It looks that way?"

"Yes, but he might be only trying to help the man up."

"Now, Mr. Braden—would he be trying to help the man up by swinging a club over him?"

The officer squirmed, and remained silent.

The senator persisted: "Two officers beating a man who is down, and wounded with what appears to be a bullet in his back, and a third officer standing handily by—do you think this picture does credit to the Chicago police?"

"No, sir. But, Senator, I don't think it is fair to say that is a typical picture of the Chicago police. Some of the men may have got excited in there—and lost their heads."

"Do you think a man who loses his head in such a situation belongs on the force?"

"He is not a credit to the force, no, sir."

"Mr. Braden, please look closely at this photograph. The officer with his club raised—he has his back to us. His coat is hanging open. Do you see that?"

"I do."

"His star is visible in the photograph."

"It is."

"With the aid of this magnifying-glass you can make out the number on that star."

There was a dead silence as the glass was passed down the long table to the witness, as he examined the picture, and looked up. He did not speak.

"Did you recognize the number on that star?" the senator asked.

Braden nodded.

"Whose number is it?"

His mouth opened once and closed, without uttering a sound. Then the words squeezed through his compressed lips. "That's me, all right."

"Mr. Braden, are you ashamed of your conduct there?"

"I am. I am, Senator." His head was jerking from side to side like that of a collapsing fighter blindly trying to avoid blows. From all angles photographers pointed their cameras at the breaking police officer. Among the other cops, there was a

[4 3 5]

tightening, an anxious extension of force, like a physical movement of going to his aid. In a husky voice, Braden stumbled through the next few questions. No, he didn't remember doing that. No, that was not the way he usually behaved, he must have lost his head in the fight; true, it didn't look like a two-sided fight but he must have lost his head there; no, an officer shouldn't lose his head, he was ashamed, he was sorry. No, nobody gave orders to behave like that. No, nobody gave orders to fire.

He made his way, glassy-eyed, from the chamber.

There were few other police. A cocky, youthful patrolman declared that the first shot had come from the strikers, hitting the open door of a patrol wagon by which he stood. But the senator produced photographs which showed that very wagon-door to have been at an angle that made it impossible to hit, from the strikers' side.

Then Gorcey was called. The bull-cop stamped to the witness chair with the obvious intention of avenging Braden. His manner varied from a sanctimonious innocence, in denying he had used a gun or seen any officer use a gun, and in repeating how the captain had "pleaded and pleaded with them to go home like peaceable citizens," to a bloody-eyed belligerence, when he shook his finger at "that man sitting there," charging he had seen Mike Sisto assault an officer.

Nothing could budge him from the story of how he had seen that Communist Dombrowsky, with an automatic. How did he know the man was a Communist? He knew it. He just knew it. Laughter of scorn or disgust only made him more adamant. And supposing the man had been a Communist, and known to him as such—did he have orders to shoot to kill Communists on sight? No, Senator, but them Communists were vicious people, and against them it was every man for himself. Did he believe Communists were deserving of less mercy than other people? It was just like a criminal to him, he said. He wouldn't shoot no criminal, unless he was attacked and defending himself for his life, then he might shoot. And that Communist Dombrowsky, he was in there with a gun, grappling with an officer, and that was how he got shot.

But, the senator pointed out, Dombrowsky had been shot in the leg, from behind. How could a man be shot from behind by someone with whom he was fighting, face to face? Furthermore, medical analysis of the wound, from the coroner's report, indicated that the leg was in running position.

"I saw what I saw," Gorcey said.

His stubbornness had ceased to be funny. It was on that higher plane of blind insistence in the very face of fact—as in Germany, Mitch reflected. And Rawley whispered a quotation: " 'The boldest lie, if repeated often enough, will be believed.' "

Gorcey went on to describe how the strikers came onto the field "with their own ambulances, it was premeditated, Senator, they tried to snatch that Communist away from the law."

"Did you notice there was a tourniquet on his leg when you pulled him out of the so-called ambulance?"

It would not be beyond him to deny the existence of the strap that was visible in the photographs. But Gorcey did better. "I helped tie that strap around his leg myself," he asserted, "seeing the bleeding was so bad."

"You did? Then how do you account for the man's being carried in this manner, by the end of the strap? It seems to me this led to his death."

"Well, sir, it was the only way we could carry him. He struggled with us, Senator," Gorcey said in a shocked tone.

"He struggled?"

"Yes, sir. Them Communists are hard to handle, they are dangerous."

"This man was mortally wounded as it proved."

"They will fight to the last drop of blood, I'll say that for

[4 3 7]

them." Gorcey announced. "He tore the bandage loose himself, struggling against us."

The senator produced a newspaper photograph, taken just after Dombrowsky had been removed from Kiley's car. It showed Kiley and Gillespie gesticulating, obviously remonstrating, while Dombrowsky, between two police, seemed to be sliding toward the ground. "Is this what you mean by struggling?" the senator asked, identifying the photograph as from the *Clarion*.

"That's where he wouldn't come out of the car, yes, sir, he fought with us," Gorcey said. "That says so right over the picture, Striker Struggles with Police!"

"Indeed, so it does," the senator read the caption. "However, we must view the picture itself, and not what the newspaper tells us it shows. It looks to me as if that man were slumping, unable to stand on his feet."

"That's your opinion, Senator," Gorcey replied.

"And you have yours," the senator snapped, losing patience. "And it will stand in the record, with the photograph." He produced a series of pictures, all from the *Clarion*, showing police carrying the sagging body of Dombrowsky, showing them tossing him into the patrol wagon. "Here are several pictures of the incident. Do you see the wounded man struggling on any of these pictures?"

"No, Senator, not on the pictures, he wouldn't be struggling if he saw them taking pictures of it."

"Do you mean to suggest that this man, wounded to the death, deliberately posed for newspaper photographs?"

The shock and disgust in the room was becoming unbearable. Gorcey was silent a moment, and mumbled: "No, Senator. But them photographers wouldn't have taken his picture until he was still."

"Were you not told by anyone that this man needed immedi-

[438]

ate medical attention? That he was in danger of bleeding to death?"

"Yes, sir," Gorcey said, "I could see that, and that is why I took him to the police ambulance, so they could take him to the emergency hospital."

His tone had changed from defiance to one of sober concern and duty.

The senator called Gillespie to the witness chair. The white-haired Scot replied briskly, coldly, with his eyes never leaving Gorcey.

Had he assisted in placing a tourniquet on the leg of Dombrowsky? He had. Dr. Wilner had come up and helped him finish the job.

Had officer Gorcey aided in this operation?

"No, Senator. We didn't see anything of Officer Gorcey until we had the wounded man in the back of the car. Just as we were starting away, this officer, brandishing his gun, ordered us to halt. We did. He looked in the car and said he wanted that man, that man was his prisoner. We explained the condition of the man and said he could place him under arrest if he must, but to let us take the man to a hospital. He and another officer dragged the man out of the car."

"Did the man struggle with them?"

"No, sir, he was practically unconscious."

Gillespie was followed by Kiley, who repeated the story. "The officer swore at us and said he would arrest us all. We had to leave him take the man."

"Dr. Wilner, will you please take the stand?" the senator called.

This was not to be his main testimony, Mitch knew. He took the chair. Gorcey's eyes were upon him, fierce, furious. He could not look into the man's face; it was frightening.

He repeated how he had placed the stone under the strap,

checking the bleeding of the artery, and how he had been chased off the field by Gorcey. "The last I saw of the wounded man, he was being placed in Mr. Kiley's car."

"Would ordinary caution have kept the tourniquet in place?"

"I believe so, although I would not care to put my statement in that form. As we see from the photographs, there was apparently an extraordinary lack of caution, in carrying this man."

"In your opinion, Doctor, might the life of this man Dombrowsky have been saved, by prompt medical attention?"

Gorcey's stare was so intensely hateful that Mitch felt an actual fear of replying; as though this were a trial for murder, and he were called upon to utter the definitive, incriminating word. Yet there could be only one answer.

"Yes, Senator," he said. "The man need not have died."

There was a short silence.

"Thank you, Doctor," the senator said.

Gorcey's eyes followed him until he took his seat. Then the tension relaxed. The bull-cop settled back in his chair. For suddenly it became apparent—nothing would be done. It was not, after all, a court of judgment. There was no court of judgment for such murder.

Gorcey looked toward the senators, defiant, brazen.

That was all, then, for the police. Their lawyer, Corcoran, submitted a long statement quoting ordinances and citing cases to prove that a policeman had the right to shoot practically anybody, anytime. The senators politely but professionally questioned his every reference, and soon had Corcoran flustered and twisted; that smart young lawyer Kahn produced from a pile of books in front of him the very volumes containing the cases to which Corcoran had been referring, showing that the senate staff had anticipated all the citations, and had taken pains to show they were non-applicable. It was neat, neat. And even when

[440]

Corcoran had the cops wheel in a trunk full of "strikers' weapons picked off the field," rocks, milk bottles, iron pipe, sticks, the Gottschalk boys proved they had anticipated him again, for they placed on the stand an old Pole who lived in the house nearest the massacre-scene, and who testified that he and other residents used the field there as a dump, that pieces of iron, sticks, rocks were always to be found there; also he had a little garden right out on the prairie—it had been trampled, on the Fourth— and he had seen the police going around immediately after the shooting, picking up everything on the field, including some sticks he had placed out there to hold up his tomato plants, and a milk bottle he had carried out there with drinking water, one day when he was working in his garden. The garrulous Pole identified the milk bottle among the police trophies.

Then the police slammed the evidence back into their trunk, and wheeled it away. Their ordeal was over. Yes, the senators had made the chief look incompetent, handling a steel strike by telling his subordinate to "take care of it," and they had got some laughs on Wiley because he didn't know the geography of Russia, and they had sweated poor Braden, and they had pulled their smart tricks on Gorcey, and they had proved Consolidated provided some free meals—so what? Where was the force supposed to eat, in that wilderness out there? And they had proved the company's gas was used, so what? First they kick about no gas being used and then they kick because what was used belonged to Consolidated.

They didn't pin any shooting on anybody or any orders to shoot, or any money passing, did they? When a bunch of men stick together, how are you going to pin anything on any one of them?

In quick succession now the senators called good citizens, and had them relate their eye-witness stories: the divinity students,

[441]

who scrupulously but in a condoning manner reported having seen the strikers carrying stones and baseball bats; a social worker who told of her harrowing ride in a patrol wagon, and how one of the men died in the dark wagon with his head on her lap; George Price, who repeated how he had seen the men fed in the plant, how he had seen ax-handles, like those carried by the police, stacked in the plant, how he had stood on a porch during the actual encounter and seen the strikers approach, and seen no shot, no violence at all from their ranks. And then Art Nowis was called.

Art had taken off his coat, like the rest of the strikers; but his crisp tie was fitted precisely into the arrow of his collar. Smiling, he wriggled around and eyed the police.

The questions established that he was Chicago-born, that his father had been a steelworker, that his parents now lived on a farm in Michigan, that he had worked in the Consolidated mills since he was twenty-two.

Then the questions turned to his career as company representative. How had he happened to run for that office?

"Well, to tell you the truth, Senator, that was the superintendent's idea."

"The superintendent?"

"Yah, Mr. Gash, the personnel man. He came around and says, Art, you get along with all the boys, and I said sure, girls too—"

The senator made a show of suppressing his laugh.

"So he started telling me about this employees' representation scheme, that's the company union, and he says I ought to run for election."

"Did he offer any inducement?"

"Well, you know, get paid for time you spend at meetings, and all. So I figured like, I'm the kind of guy always wants to be in on everything, so it's okay with me. So I said what's the

[4 4 2]

strings, and he said no strings, so I said if the boys want me, okay I'll run."

He told of the company representative meetings: "Naw, we never got anything out of it, if anything serious come up like a raise or a real grievance they always said they had to take it up with Cleveland and that was the last they ever heard of it."

Were the men satisfied with this plan?

"It didn't mean anything one way or the other, it was just a gag, except, the fellows that were wise, they knew it was to keep out a real union. Except when the C.I.O. come around, Gus Lindstrom and me, and some more of the employee representatives, we told the boys it was a fact the company couldn't keep out a real union; it was the law."

Did anything happen between him and Mr. Gash when the C.I.O. came around?

Art smiled. "Oh, yah. Sure. One day when Mr. Gash is walking through, he comes over and says how would I like a little talk with him in his office; so I told my partner to take over the machine. I went over to his office."

"Was anyone else present?"

"There was two other fellows, I seen them sometimes around the main building there, I think they belong to the personnel department, that's how he introduced them."

"What were their names?"

"Well, one of them had the name of Linn, because I saw him again. I don't remember the other."

"Continue."

"Gash says, what did I think of the C.I.O. So I said, it looked like a pretty strong outfit to me. He laughed and said, yah, but the bigger they come the harder they fall; then he says he didn't see me wearing a button yet.

"So not knowing what was coming I said when I figured that was what I wanted to do, he'd see me wearing it. Well, we

[443]

boxed around there for a while and he says, he don't care if I join the C.I.O., in fact that's just what he wants me to do. And then it come out, he says they want somebody in there in the C.I.O. just to keep in touch with what is going on and how the men take to the idea and he wanted me to get in it, and every once in a while, he said, this fellow Linn would meet me someplace, because it wouldn't look good for me to be reporting in the office."

The strikers were leaning forward, their eyes riveted on Art.

"Did they offer you anything for this additional service?"

"Yah, he said there'd be something in it maybe thirty, fifty bucks extra a month, maybe more."

"Did you accept?"

Art looked over at the boys, then, grinning, said: "Well, I figured I would play along with them and see what they were up to, so I told them I would do it."

Mitch saw Frank Sobol jerk erect, saw Mike Sisto nearly jump out of his seat as if to attack Art; Frank restrained him. Kiley looked worried. Art was smiling as if in anticipation of a joke he knew would go over big.

"Did you then carry out your agreement?"

"I met this fellow Linn a couple of times. I never told him anything secret, just stuff they could have found out for themselves, reading the papers."

"Where did you meet him?"

"Well, in a—kind of a tavern."

"Any special one?"

"One of those places in Calumet City."

"And what sort of information did you give him?"

"Well, like when Mr. Joshua Wheeler met with a lot of us representatives from the company union, and gave us an argument we should try to bring all our members into the C.I.O.—

that was all in the papers, in the labor papers, but I told him that."

"Was the company satisfied with this type of information?"

"I dunno. He said they wanted more stuff, names, like who was joining the union. I told him I didn't know who was signed up. Except some fellows were wearing their buttons around the shop, so I figured they didn't care who knew they were signed up, so to play along with him I gave him their names."

His purpose in all this, Art said, was to "get inside their confidence, 'cause I figured they had some real spies in there spying on us, and that way I would get a line on who they were."

"Did you suceed in this?"

"Well, no, I guess they were too foxy for me."

"They out-foxed you?"

"That's it, I guess."

"How much did they pay you?"

Just a couple of times, Art said; he had received thirty dollars once and another time twenty-five.

"So this spying work doesn't pay very well?"

"I figure, whatever it was it was gravy because, the way I figured, the company was paying me and all the time I was spying on their spies."

What made him so sure there were such spies?

"There must have been somebody because they had all the dope on everything; they just used to ask me things to kind of check up on their spies, I figured."

Did he have any specific instance of the company's knowing of the union's plans?

"They knew when the strike was called for."

How did he know that?

"I saw this fellow Linn, the night before. And he knew the men were going out. He even knew what time."

"Was this common knowledge among the membership?"

"Only the officers were supposed to know, we had a meeting in the afternoon, the officers and the organizers, and it was that we would take the strike vote next day and call the men out at ten o'clock."

"Then one of those people must have told Linn?"

"I figured either that way or they had somebody in the union way up, in Pittsburgh, that tipped them off what Pittsburgh wired us. Or besides, when maybe ten, twelve fellows know something, it leaks down, they are bound to tell their pals, in confidence. Or maybe their wife."

"So that makes it difficult to find the informer by the process of elimination," the elder senator concluded.

Art nodded.

And yet, why could it not have been himself? What certainty was there, with a fellow who admitted he was playing both sides? Those company people were no fools. They wouldn't have paid him for stuff that was already in the papers. And after he had accepted the first check, they could have threatened to expose him to the men as a spy unless he really came through.

"The strike was set for ten o'clock. And yet it was called shortly after three. Do you know how that happened, Mr. Nowis?"

"First I knew was when I heard the big whistle. Some of the boys in the spike mill came up to me and said: 'Is this it?' and they were kind of mixed up because by then the word had leaked around it was for ten o'clock. But I figured, the company knows we're supposed to go out at ten so they are all set for us, and maybe it is better to surprise them and pull it off early. So I said, okay, this is it, and we marched through the mill calling people out."

Or else, couldn't it be said that Art and the mysterious Mr. Linn, meeting the night before the strike, had decided that a

[446]

mid-afternoon walkout would be more advantageous to the company, so at 3 p.m. some company official had pulled the big bell, and Art himself, as a double-crosser, had started the confusion of the walkout?

Only his supreme self-assurance, his confident smile, was there to guide belief in him. And in his favor was the supposition that no man could be so crazy as to confess this sort of deal unless he were sure he could prove himself loyal, or was asking for his own murder.

Did he confide in anyone in the union, as to his activities with the company?

No; he was waiting until he had the goods on the company.

Then Art related, in long and comic detail, his sojourn in the stool-pigeon's paradise. "I figure the cops picked on me because the company put the finger on me; they could never get the real information out of me and maybe they figured the cops could scare something out of me."

"But the police didn't succeed?"

"The cops or nobody could make me say anything that would be harmful to the union." He settled back, self-satisfied.

Now, Mitch wondered, would they pin Art down on that story about the plan for the "marine squad" to attack the mill from the rear? Sproul went up and conferred with the senator and his young lawyer Kahn.

"You signed a statement for the police?" the senator asked.

"Sure, I told Corcoran I'd sign anything, just to get out of there."

"Even though it was a paradise?"

"Well, a jail is a jail no matter if you get steaks and showers; I figured, suppose they don't want to let me out? So Corcoran says just sign a statement and you can go any time you like. So they made up this statement and I signed it."

The senator offered him a copy of the document; Art identified it, and they marked it "for the record." Then, Mitch realized, the senators were not going to open up that whole matter of the "marines" by reading the statement and cross-examining him. Was there something to the story of the "marines," after all? Was the committee protecting the strikers? Or did they figure Art was so completely discredited that it was unnecessary to go into further detail?

Excused, Art started for his place next to Kiley, then seemed to change his mind; he sat down at the end of the row.

Why had he admitted all this spying business?

Just then, Sproul sidled over and asked Mitch to go down to the committee room and see if old man Lindstrom was okay to come up. In the hallway, Mitch Wilner met Mussetti hurrying along with a sheaf of documents. "Listen, do you mind telling me—how did you find out the company was paying Art Nowis?"

"Simple as hell," Musty said. "It was in the payroll records. We usually check on all the union officers and leaders. Showed he got a couple of extra checks. So we asked him and he told."

"Do you think that's all there was to it? Do you think he really held out information on them?"

Mussetti shrugged. "Maybe, maybe not. Anyway this proves they were paying men to spy on the union, doesn't it? That's a violation of the act." He added: "Looks to me like there might have been a big operator around Chicago, besides Nowis. But maybe not. Maybe not."

"Well, what about this man Linn that he mentions?"

"That guy who used to meet him in the gambling-joint?"

"Is that what it was?"

"Yah. And then some. That Calumet City is quite a place. You should know your city, Doctor. Linn was evidently a fake name. There's none on the payroll. The company denies having anyone assigned to such nasty tasks. Consolidated does not practice industrial spying. And you try and prove that they do."

"I was wondering why you haven't put on anyone from the company. The superintendent. Or even Speer."

Musty blinked. "No use putting people on to deny things. We've got to have the goods on them first. In your science, you don't make a report until you've found something, do you?"

"Some of us do, I guess." Mitch laughed.

"But sometimes you make a preliminary report to let the field know you're working on a problem."

"That's right."

"That's what this is. We'll take that whole damn company apart if they give us some dough. But it looks like we're going to have a tough time getting another appropriation." He made a sour mouth, and hurried into the hearing-room.

As Mitch walked the block-long corridor, past all the high dark doors with names of senators upon them, he was trying to fetch up something from his mind. Something he knew about a Consolidated employee, and as he turned the corner into the second long stretch of corridor, the name came up to him—Flint. That phony patient who had left the donation for the Lindstroms. And then, at the back-to-work rally, Barbara had identified that same fellow as the contact who brought money from the company to Martha Cross. Flint and Linn, they could be the same person.

He was getting detectivitis. But perhaps he had better give this information to Musty—in a casual way, so he wouldn't appear too ridiculous. It might be something they'd want to follow up.

A wheelchair had been provided, but old Oscar Lindstrom insisted upon walking; and now Mitch followed the Lindstroms in their slow progress toward the hearing-room, the tall man between the two women—his wife and the wife of his son.

As they neared the chamber, Mitch heard the senator call

[449]

the name, Oscar Lindstrom; yes, in perfect time, for the spectators would have this moment of suspense, while the attendants cleared the doorway.

The Lindstroms entered: an emaciated man with gaunt frame and face, his clothing loose, large, indicating a recent suffering; the black band around his eyes as on a man blindfolded; the powerful steelman's hand on the shoulder of the elderly woman, her head erect, her smooth plaincombed white hair peacefully framing her composed face; and on his other side, dropped back slightly, the younger woman, Pauline, her hand on his sleeve for assurance both to him and to herself. At the sight of them the room stilled; and even the photographers withheld for a moment, turning to Sproul as if to ask whether their flashlights might not shock the injured man.

Sproul nodded permission, and the trio halted while the photographers stepped in front of them, some kneeling, and, at a concerted signal, one flash bulb was released for them all. Lindstrom was led to the witness chair, a seat placed beside him for his wife. He reached for her hand, and she held his hand in both of hers. Pauline sat in the row of strikers; Sobol gave her his chair.

Mitch noticed Sproul glancing at his wristwatch, and then over toward the press section; yes, just in time for their editions.

"Mr. Lindstrom," the young senator said, "this committee realizes you have been under great physical strain; it will not be essential for you to testify orally; we can read the deposition which you have already made, and you have only to corroborate it for the record."

"I want to speak," Lindstrom said.

His voice was deep and resonant, and his words, as he unfolded his story, were slow-spaced, as though in his weeks of darkness he had chosen every word, preparing himself for this hour. As the blinded roller launched into his experiences of the

[4 5 0]

Fourth, his voice became ever deeper, his speech slower, but not as though his physical weakness impeded him; rather with slow care for defining his inmost knowledge of his Job-like experience, for giving it forth with meaning exact as gospel.

"I had two sons," he began, "Gustav and William, and, like their father, they worked in the mill. When the strike came, one son, Gustav, was on strike with me, but the other son, William"—the old man waited, then spoke the words—"remained in the mill, a scab."

Even Gus, dying, had not spoken of the other brother who was a scab. And in all the time he had tended Oscar Lindstrom, Mitch had heard no word in that house of a second son. This, then, was the reason for the old man's long brooding, and for his reticence. And Mitch could understand now how in his darkness during these weeks the old man must have been trying to salvage, to reconstruct, his hope of morality in the universe, for now Mitch saw that Lindstrom's experience was not only like the experience of Job, in which the innocent and the good suffered evil; he had seen wrong-doers go unharmed.

If he were ready now to speak of his experience, then he had surmounted it; but had he found any reconciliation?

"And on that fateful Sunday," Lindstrom said, "I left my wife at home, she not feeling well. 'Mother,' I said, 'you remain at home,' as she was worried for our son, that they might be holding him there by force. 'I will go to the mill,' I said, 'and find out if William is in there, and I will bring him out and bring him home to you!' I went with my young son Gustav, and with his wife and their little children. We listened to the speeches, and we bought ice cream for the children."

Then he told of the march, with the complete detail of a man still seeking meaning, who fears that in the omission of the slightest detail he may drop the clue to meaning. He told how, coming close to the police line, he saw, over behind the mill fence, a group of men assembled upon the low roof of the new washhouse, like spectators: those were the scabs. "I tried to recognize if my son was among them but the distance was too great, and I could not see." He leaned forward, as if straining with his blind eyes. "So I spoke to the officer before me. 'Officer,' I said, 'I have a son who is in the mill, and I want to speak to him. Take me to the gate, send men with me if you wish, surely you can see I have no other intention.' The officer shook his head. I asked him again, but it was just a shaking of the head."

He paused; Mitch knew it was to gather force before plunging into the violence that must come now, for to tell it was to live it again. "Then my son Gustav standing beside me spoke to the officer saying: 'My father is telling the truth, my brother is in there, let my father talk to him'; and the officer responded" —all saw his wife stroking his old hand rapidly—"the officer shouted at my son: 'Shut your mouth or I will fill you full of lead!' "

Oscar Lindstrom quoted the words without passion, reflectively, seeing them now as prophetic. A murmur traveled around the courtroom as those who knew told those who did not know, how Gus Lindstrom was among the dead.

"At that moment I looked at the officers' faces to my right and to my left. Their faces were drawn tight, with their muscles quivering. They seemed to be like sometimes you see on the field, football-players, set tensely waiting for the signal to charge the line. And my expression must have reflected what I saw, for one of the officers said: 'What are you afraid of?' "

He rested on those words, weighing all that had happened to him, and whether all this was to have been feared. He slowly shook his head. "Then all hell broke loose. It seemed like the blast of a whistle, and then the shooting. Immediately I was struck in my face, the left side. It was like a thing of fire. I felt the blood coming down my face over my mouth. I went down

[452]

and fell on my hands and knees. I had vision in my right eye, then, but no vision in my left eye. I saw men going down, it seemed to me like they were being mowed down by a scythe. I could not see my son. I saw officers with their revolvers shooting into the crowd. I called: 'Gus,' but there was no answer. I scrambled a little further and fell into a shallow ditch where I thought I would be safe. A voice called: 'Help me, I am shot,' but I could not help him. . . . Then a green ball of fire fell to my right, a few inches from my face, and smoke came from it, burning my right eye. I tried to move away from this but a trembling came all over me and a sickness in the pit of my stomach. I fell. I could not see at all. I called for help." Each sentence, now, was produced with effort. "At last someone grabbed me under the arms. I was carried. I was placed in a machine. I could not see. After a long time it started. It was a patrol; there were other men there. One was begging the driver to go to the nearest hospital. 'We must have first aid,' he said. The driver called back: 'Shut up, you sonofabitch, you got what was coming to you.'

"There was a man who was shot in the leg. He was on the floor of the patrol, and another tried to help him, I could feel them moving. 'He is still breathing,' he said. We drove a long time. The driver did not seem to know where he was going. He kept turning, I could feel him making many right turns as though going in a circle. I thought he must be lost out there in Hegewisch, as many streets do not go through. It seemed like three hours. One man said: 'He isn't breathing any more,' then I knew the man on the floor was dead.

"At last the car stopped. The door was opened and the driver said: 'Take these,' and they pulled me out by my legs, and some others got out. Then the driver said: 'No use bothering with these, we will take them to the morgue.'"

A smothered gasp was heard, where a woman in the room

had fainted. The senator intervened, saying he would complete the testimony by reading from Mr. Lindstrom's previously made affidavit. Lindstrom, whose voice had become unbearably labored, now halted, he sat listening as the senator read rapidly, monotonously, in an effort to reduce the effect of horror upon the listeners.

Of how, in the hospital, the blinded man had been dragged up and down stairs, then left naked for a long time, on a bench, the congealed blood unwashed from his face; how at last, bandaged, he lay on a bed. He could not eat solid food, begged for milk and did not get it; begged that his wife be notified, but no one came. How on Tuesday they tried to stitch up his torn eye; and at last on Wednesday his wife learned where he was, and came and got him released on bail. Of how he was told then that Gus was shot on that field, and dying; and of how at last he was taken from the jail hospital to Memorial, where the doctors said his right eye was infected owing to those days of lack of care, but might still be saved.

The senator hurried to reach the end of all this horror, for what could be learned from horror? And at the end he said: "Is this a portion of the affidavit which you made and signed?"

Old Oscar Lindstrom rose to his feet, pressing himself upward by his hands on the table, the force making his fingers tremble.

"Yes. That is so," he said. "But, Senator, there is one more thing I wish to say.

"Out of fairness to my wife and family, and the children of my dead son, I want to say, though I am not a church-going man, I have feared and trusted God all my life, I have never been an unbeliever, and I have raised my children to believe. I want to say, when they took my clothes from me in the jail and left me naked, I heard them cry, search for Communistic literature. In my wallet was my name, and it said to notify my family in case of accident or injury, and I called their attention to this, but they ignored me, and said only search for Communism. In fairness to my family, let me state, I am not a Communist, we are not Communists, my son who died was not a Communist, we were just union men."

His voice became powerful again, with judgment. "As I believe in the Lord, I believe also in the Evil One. The Lord says, Thou shalt not kill, and the Evil One destroys. I worked many years in St. Louis, and was a union man, a roller, and there came a new superintendent there, named Speer, and when he came, he discharged all we union men, we had to leave our homes, and find new places to live and work. The Evil One has pursued me, for what have I done that he should cause my son to be shot to death, and my eyesight to be destroyed? And my living son, William, he has sold himself to the devil."

On the right side of his face, there were tears.

Men offered help, but he leaned upon the two women, who led him from the room.

All the police had cleared out; they were not even in the corridor.

One more day would complete the hearing. The union leaders had still to testify—Sobol, Kiley, Sisto—then the famous suppressed newsreel would be shown. Toward the last would come Mitch Wilner's turn. He had decided to take the train home instead of driving back with the others. He wondered if Syl would bring the kids along to meet him at the train, and he was puzzled by a lack of longing, in himself, for Sylvia, though he got pleasure out of anticipating how the kids would jump around him, sticking their hands into all his pockets, to find what he had brought. What he felt about Sylvia was perhaps the continuation of the worry about the way things had gone between them just before he left; his being away these few days should have cleared the air, but if it had not, he would not know just how to proceed. He wished for someone to talk to, a friend who could give him advice. Perhaps he could talk to George Price, if he could get him away from his wife for a while, tonight. Syl liked the Prices.

On the way to the hotel with George, Mitch saw a toy shop and they stopped in, for Mitch wanted to find things to take home; better get some presents for Sylvia too: he thought of going later to some fancy lingerie shop, buying her something intimate and clinging, a nightdress perhaps; he had never bought things like that for her but he found himself thinking of making love to her, of somehow destroying that coldness between them, after this was all over.

In the toy shop, he selected a calico rag doll for Judy, and was trying to find something that was manly and yet not military for Jack. There seemed to be only tanks, gunboats, cannon, soldiers. He found a terrific jackknife, complete with scissors, saw, file, and can-opener; the kid would be tickled because he wasn't expecting one until his birthday; he'd probably take the house apart with it. On one side was a name-plate, so he had Jackie's name engraved. That would give him a bang.

"Look at this." Price came toward him with the grin that presaged an idea. He held up a cowboy manikin.

"Boys don't want dolls." Mitch shook his head.

"No; this is for you, Doc," Price said. "We'll take the clothes off, and we'll get a long hatpin or something for you to stick through it, demonstrating the direction of the bullets."

Mitch balked. But George paid for the doll, and said he would fix it all up real dignified, in white.

Mitch decided not to talk to George about Syl. But maybe to Price's wife, if he could get to talking with her. . . .

"I'm going out chasing with Art tonight," Price said. "I got an idea if I get him drunk enough he'll spill something. There are four females to every man in Washington, Mitch; want to come along?"

"No, I think I'll take care of your wife."

"Noble fellow."

They all had dinner together; then George went off with Art. Mitch took Mrs. Price to a movie. Afterwards she suggested a drink. She was nice; but it was she who asked, with vivid interest, why hadn't Sylvia come along? And he found himself suddenly unresponsive, and at the same time that he feared her too sharp interest, he felt a possibility of attraction between them; he couldn't tell her of his trouble about his wife. Nor could he bring himself to ask her help in selecting a gift of lingerie.

During Sobol's testimony, Mitch waited eagerly to see how the senators would treat the whole charge of Communist conspiracy. Would they avoid the entire Communism question? And if so, wouldn't that indicate Communist influence, at least sympathy, in the staff of the committee? Or, might they not go easy simply out of fairness to the C.I.O., since the least breath of a Communist charge would be exaggerated by the opposition, out of all proportion to truth?

Sobol told how he had been chairman of the meeting. He summarized what each speaker had said, and stressed the fact that there had been no suggestion of getting into the plant.

"Did you, at any time, have such an idea in mind, Mr. Sobol?"

"No."

"Was such an idea discussed at any of the meetings of the staff or of the strategy committee?"

"Naturally all kinds of ideas pop up, some of them pretty wild, and the wild ones are stepped on. Somebody, just talking, might have said something like that sometime but nobody would take it seriously, except maybe if some spy was there and reported it as an actual plan."

"Can you remember specifically someone suggesting this idea?"

"To get inside the plant? No."

"To land men on the shore side?"

He smiled. "No, Senator. Not at a strategy meeting. As I said, wild talk of all kinds may have been going on around the strike area, even provocateurs might have been suggesting a scheme like that in a tavern someplace, but we'd have put a stop to it if anything like that came to our attention."

As for the "military formations," and "drilling" reported by some of the police, he laughed. There wasn't any.

And when the parade started, what had he done? Had he marched in the parade?

"No. I had to take my superior, Mr. Szutak, back to the district headquarters, as he wanted to discuss some matters with me. We didn't anticipate anything could go wrong with the demonstration."

Frank Sobol made an impressive witness, open, responsible in manner. The elder senator took over the questioning, gently. It was not the policy of the senate to question a man's politics, he asserted, but since some peculiar charges had been made in this connection, he wanted to ask Mr. Sobol a question. How had he voted in the last election?

"Well, I'm a registered Democrat," Sobol said. "I voted the straight Democratic ticket."

The question left Mitch Wilner unsatisfied. Wouldn't it have been healthier to thrash the whole thing out, directly? But then, obviously, if asked directly whether he was a member of the Communist Party, Sobol would have had to answer no. Mitch realized he was still confused on this issue, perhaps because the nation was confused. Nominally, to be a Communist was legal, but in the minds of the majority of the population, Communism was illegal. It seemed, therefore, just for the senators to preclude the awakening of prejudice, on this issue.

While Sobol was testifying, a message arrived for Kiley. Jock swore, and passed it to Al Nees. In a moment, the word was up and down the row of strikers: union headquarters had been broken into, last night. About half the signed-up membership cards were stolen.

Kiley, Nees, Sobol rushed out into the hall, to discuss the theft. The cards had been locked in a steel file cabinet. Art Nowis remarked: "At least this is one thing they can't blame on me."

Mike glared at him. "You watch yourself. You ain't getting away with anything," he said.

Kiley told them to take it easy.

Tannenbaum came out of the hearing-room. When he heard the news, he whistled. "You'll have a hell of a time proving majority before the labor board now. The company will claim the burglary story is a fake; they'll say you never had the cards signed up in the first place."

"That bastard Carl Gaul," Mike Sisto complained. "We should of never left him in charge."

For the afternoon session, the medical charts were on the wall. "Looks professional, huh?" Price bragged. Mitch felt nervous. This was different from reading a few notes on the platform of the Opera House. This was for the permanent record.

His name was called; he took the chair. On the table directly in front of him lay the doll which Price had bought, and beside it a long desk-spindle.

Senator Gottschalk led him through the routine questions: his first-rank internship, his post-graduate studies in Vienna, his publications of research.

And in the course of his experience, had he dealt with gunshot wounds?

"I have." As an interne, in County hospital. "That was in 1930, and we often had gangsters brought in, shot."

There was laughter; photographers snapped his picture. He saw Corcoran whisper something to Captain Simmons, who nodded.

Now came the key question. Could one tell what direction a bullet came from, by the wounds it made?

Mitch found himself replying with expert ease. He explained the ways of various types of bullets, how musket balls might be deflected in the body, but round-nosed police bullets took straight courses.

"In other words," the senator said, "a line projected through the wounds would point the direction the bullet came from?"

"In most cases, yes."

"Dr. Wilner, did you see many of the people who were wounded on the Fourth?"

"I did. I believe I saw more than any other one person." He explained how he had attempted, at the behest of the union, to make a summary of the cases.

"Have you made this summary?"

"I have." He directed attention to the charts. Photographers took pictures of the senator standing before the charts.

"According to this classification," the senator said, "sixty-eight percent of all the gunshot wounds were rear wounds."

Mitch noticed Corcoran making notes swiftly, his tongue protruding between his lips. "That is correct," Mitch said, "though I should like to explain my method of classifying rear

[460]

wounds." He picked up the doll and the pointed spindle. "For instance, in the case of Stanley Dombrowsky, this was a leg wound, severing the artery." He sought the point on the inner thigh, approximating the wound of entrance, and pushed the spindle through, frontwards. As he did so, he had a strange sensation, as if he were really running the steel through a living body; and as he held up the spitted doll, it swung slowly forward around the spindle, like a man pitching forward.

Half a dozen photographers leaped to flashlight him in this pose. He regretted the stunt instantly. It would look undignified.

Drawing out the long needle, he explained that he had classified the wounds in quadrants, counting as rear wounds only those which projected at more than forty-five degrees to the lateral midplane of the body.

"Al Nicoletti, for example, I have classified as a side wound, though the bullet came at quite an angle from behind him; still, it was less than forty-five degrees." He pierced the image as for Al Nicoletti, from left to right, just below the ribs, going upward and forward.

Name by name, just as when he had stood on the Opera House platform, Mitch Wilner went through the roll of the dead, only now he felt that all America listened; this was full proof that such a happening could not go by unheeded. Now it was a senator in Washington, instead of George Price, who called out each name.

"Gustav Lindstrom," the senator called.

Mitch looked directly at Corcoran, who leaned forward, pencil poised. "In this case," Mitch said, "the coroner's report does not specify through which wound the bullet entered. The report states that the wounds were obscured owing to operation after the injury, so that it was no longer possible to distinguish

[461]

accurately the wound of entrance from the wound of exit. However, I have classified the wound of Gus Lindstrom as a rear wound."

"Upon what evidence, Doctor?"

"I saw him upon the field, I saw him again in the hospital, I saw him operated upon. I talked to Lindstrom many times before he died; he told me he was shot from the back, and my own observation is that the rear wound was the wound of entrance."

Corcoran's eye glinted; he made another note.

Now the senator asked whether he knew anything of police injuries.

"Only from the official reports," Mitch stated. He read: " 'Officer Gorcey reported an injury described as an abrasion of the knuckles of right hand, suffered while breaking up an unpermitted parade.' " Through the laughter, he saw the bull-cop, furious, his lips moving in suppressed cursing. He continued with the police report, a few sprains, a few gas cases, two head contusions, a report of an officer who "turned his ankle, getting into a car on the way to the scene of conflict." The laughter flared again.

"There were no gunshot wounds reported among the police?" the senator formally inquired.

"I found none," Mitch stated.

"Thank you, Dr. Wilner."

His hands were shaking slightly as he put his notes back into the briefcase. He was in the record now. But he had been so careful, there couldn't be any mistakes.

There was a recess while the room was prepared for the showing of the suppressed newsreel. Down in the committee office, the boys ganged around him, telling him that his testimony cinched the story. Senator Gottschalk hurried in. "Dr.

Wilner"—the senator's hand was extended—"I want to thank you for an excellent report. I think you've done a real service."

Mitch remembered only one pleasure like this: the time old Dr. Nyquist at the University had congratulated him on his first paper in the *Medical Courier*. But that had been entirely his own achievement, a piece of knowledge wrested from the unknown. This was no comparable work. Any doctor could have assembled this routine information. And yet the gratification that welled up in him at the senator's praise was more pleasurable even than that other joy. This was no peak of excitement, but a fullness of goodness. He felt himself to be among good people.

Word had gone around the senate building that the famous film was about to be shown, and now several senators arrived, while all the stenographers and clerks in the building seemed to converge upon the hearing-room. The chamber overflowed; people stood in the doorway.

"I want to make sure that the representatives of the Chicago police get a good view of this film," the younger senator said in his most blandly biting manner. "Will the ushers please arrange seats for them?"

The ushers, carrying chairs over their heads, threaded through the crowd to set a special row for the police officials, directly in front of the screen. "Never mind, never mind," the police chief protested, from where he and his group sat, along the side wall. "We can see all right from here."

"Oh, no, I insist," the senator replied with utmost courtesy. And finally, sweating under the eyes of the crowd, the police took their places.

The newsreel photographer testified. He had been filming the scene, and as he saw nothing to indicate an immediate outbreak, he was changing lenses for some closer shots, when the violence started. How much time did he require to change lenses? Not more than five seconds. But during those seconds he still had his eye on the crowd, as he changed lenses automatically, and he thought he had seen someone in the crowd throw something. Before he was filming again, a tear-gas bomb had exploded.

The film itself, after such great anticipation, was in many ways disappointing. Even though the committee had arranged parts in slow motion, and made still-stops at crucial points, and even though the whole thing was run through twice, the net effect was one of confusion. For, first, there were the two groups standing face to face. And then suddenly (skipping those critical five seconds) there were the rising clouds of gas and the backs of people running and the backs of police advancing, crackling and sounds like static on the sound track, and occasionally a voice, a garbled word. Was some order to fire recorded there among the scratchings on the track? Might it be disentangled from all the other sounds, settling specific guilt? For even during the disputed five seconds of lens-changing the sound track ran on; surely a clear order to fire would have been recorded. But equally significant, there was no order to cease firing, and full minutes after all were in flight shooting was still heard.

The total effect was of horror and mounting horror, true, but what specific accusation could be taken from this? The second time through, the eye began to follow single figures in the crowd, rather than to watch the entire surging movement; a figure suddenly leaped up and there were two police on that figure, beating it down to the ground again, and another cop came and swung his stick on the figure when it was down; there was a woman struggling to her feet, falling again; and then came scenes of wounded being picked off the field, dragged to the wagon, a man, his hand to his bloody head, being shoved into a wagon; a policeman standing over a fallen man who had a growing round dark spot on the back of his white shirt, the policeman

[464]

shaking his head; then two policemen lifting the man and turning him over and placing a fallen placard, People Versus Consolidated, under the dying man's head.

"That's Al Nicoletti!" Mike Sisto excitedly remarked.

Now it was over, and people sat with sickened or stunned expressions; the police sat rigid, their faces hard. Mitch felt he must see it again and again, watch each figure separately in those scenes of confusion; others might find enough in the first total effect of horror and revulsion, as operating-room visitors found shock enough in the first sight of opened flesh. But the man with the scalpel had to seek in that flesh for each pathological detail.

There was a last gesture. One by one, the senator called each of the police heads to the witness chair again. First the chief. "You have heard the testimony and witnessed the evidence. In the light of this, do you wish to change your testimony in any way?" The chief shook his head, negative. "Do you still fully approve of the conduct of the Chicago police in these events of Independence Day?"

"I do."

"You are excused. . . . Captain Simmons."

The formula was repeated. Everyone knew what the answers would be, and yet there was suspense in the hope that someone, perhaps, would waver, would break.

"Do you still approve——"

"I do, absolutely," Simmons replied belligerently before the senator could finish his question.

Captain Wiley, in his turn, answered gruffly: "I do."

The hearing was over.

It was over; and a train going into the dark gave a man a sensation of detaching himself, leaving the last set of things behind him. Perhaps he and Sylvia would meet as in a resumption

[465]

of their life before this strained interval, but with an added richness of understanding. All his recent concern had perhaps seemed naïve to her, as he absorbed all in one lump the things she had come to understand during the last years, in her university courses, and in the committees she attended. For though he had always thought of himself as being a liberal, he had left that political side of their thinking to her, much as he left the social side of life to Sylvia.

Now he could see she might have been worried that he would become so involved as to lose his perspective, even injure his career. But in a way he resented her holding such fears for him. She should know him well enough, being his wife, to know that what drove him into this investigation was the same impulse that made a man stick to and complete a piece of research: the need to trace causes down to the final cause, the need to discover the entire cause of observed phenomena. Syl should have realized that he would not feel free of this problem until it was resolved in his own mind; indeed she should have bolstered him in his need to keep on searching, as she had so often done when he was engaged on a medical problem.

And was it so different? Wasn't it pretty much like a problem in allergy, in anaphylaxis? Couldn't the sudden, convulsive action of the police, in shooting into that crowd, be compared to a convulsive reaction of the human organism, at contact with a specific protein which it would not tolerate?

Yes, he should begin to think again of medical things, become reabsorbed in some phase of allergy, or anaphylaxis. The oil injection he had been piddling with at the hospital was too mechanical, no wonder he had been so easily distracted. What he wanted was some problem that led back into the fundamental enigma, through new avenues, which might contain clues.

But as he tried to set his mind into medical channels, it kept jumping over as if into a parallel track, and he could think of

[466]

allergy only as an analogy to this situation in the social organism.

Rawley came back into the compartment they shared. Nothing interesting on the train, he reported. "Except our friends the cops."

"The hell with them," Mitch said. "Thank God I'm through with the whole business. I've let my practice fall to pieces. . . . What'll happen now? Will the hearing lead to anything?"

Why, what could happen? Rawley asked. "The Senate committee can't indict anybody. They can just take testimony as evidence on which to base new legislation. They'll probably try to introduce some laws limiting the use of armed forces in strikes. They want to complete their job on employer associations but they need some more funds. At least, I guess they got enough headlines this week so Congress will come through with another appropriation."

"And nothing happens to the cops?"

"That's up to what we do in Chicago."

"I see."

"This made a pretty big stink. The least that could happen is that Wiley should be retired. We might even be able to force the mayor to liberalize the whole police department handling of labor. I don't know."

"So what did it all prove?" Mitch asked.

Rawley poured himself a drink, and this time Mitch took one also; why had he always been so abstemious? People talked better when they drank a little.

"It proves what we knew all the time," Rawley said. "You mustn't look at this as an isolated incident. You don't take a single case to establish a rule in your work, do you?"

"No," Mitch said. "Of course not. But can you really apply the scientific method in this type of problem? Isn't the human element too unstable?"

[467]

Rawley laughed. "Isn't there a human element in medicine too?" Of course, he said, it was dangerous to assume a complete parallel between the human organism and the social organism. But some parallels could be followed out, to possible advantage. "Look, you're an allergist. Okay . . ."

Mitch felt anticipatory excitement. His mind, and Rawley's, worked the same way. "I was just thinking of it in those terms," he confessed. "How there is a similarity to an anaphylactic shock in the way the police reacted. I did a lot of work on anaphylaxis, in relation to serums. That was when I was going to be a researcher."

"Anaphylaxis—that's like an allergic shock, isn't it?"

"Something like it," Mitch explained. "Many regard them as having the same mechanism. But there is an important difference. In allergy, individuals are sensitive to specific substances which are harmless for most other people. Say you are or become allergic to horses, you can't go near them without getting an attack of asthma. Well, most of us can take horses or leave them alone. We're not bothered. Still, this sensitivity is a natural reaction on your part. Something in you, and in a small proportion of the human race, but certainly not in the entire race, has made you react to horse dander."

"Maybe I'm a natural reactionary," Rawley cracked, anticipating the analogy.

"But in anaphylaxis," Mitch went on, "you have a different condition. You have an induced sensitivity. Injected. Suppose you have never been allergic to horses. One day you get an injection of anti-toxin made in a horse. The first injection of this horse serum does not trouble you, but something in you begins to work on it, and by the time you get a second injection you are sensitive to horse serum and you shock. You can't tolerate succeeding doses."

"Aha," Rawley said. "The Haymarket case was a first injection, and ever since then the Chicago cops have been sensitive to horse sense."

Mitch groaned. Rawley summarized: "As I see it, your allergy is a kind of natural sickness—individuals, through no interference by man, are allergic. But anaphylaxis is man-made, even with the best intentions, even in the act of preventing disease. Then an anaphylactic shock is an artificial allergy, only more deadly."

"Yes, it can be more deadly."

"And Fascists or super-patriots who want to save us from the reds may be people who, themselves allergic, or naturally sensitive, are trying to inject others with their own sensitivity, which is unnatural for the majority."

Mitch smiled. It was perhaps one of those strained analogies between the sciences. But if it were illuminating, why not?

"And what have you found out, medically, that may save the social organism from being destroyed by these lads? Have we no universal anti-copsin?"

Mitch had to laugh. "We never have found out the precise mechanism of shock. But we can prevent deadly reaction by injecting anti-toxins in very small doses, developing tolerance, or by changing to anti-toxins made in some different blood-stream —for instance, to anti-toxins developed in human blood—convalescent serum—instead of from sheep or horses."

"Very nice. So we get some human police?"

"That might be the parallel," Mitch said.

"It's nice to play with," Rawley agreed, taking another drink. "But you say you still don't understand just what happens in the body when this shock reaction takes place?"

"It's something at the very foundation of the life process," Mitch said. "It's some instant and sharp reaction in the cells; it has something to do with cell-metabolism; histamine is produced in larger amounts than normal—that's about all we know."

"Americanism is produced in larger amounts than normal," Rawley murmured. "So the next question is, what produces it?"

"Well, as I said, metabolism. That's the living-dying process of the cell. The cell is composed of various proteins which decompose into the amino acids of which they are formed. Histamine is just one of those amino acids."

"Aha. The social being is a compound of various ideas, beliefs, religions, of which patriotism or Americanism is one component."

"What must happen," Mitch said, "is that something changes the equation of metabolism, so that the process becomes unbalanced; then we get the overproduction of some one substance, like histamine, which may then act as a poison."

"And what can unbalance this process of metabolism? What activates this collection of beliefs and ideas and prejudices that we call a human being?" Rawley answered himself: "Why, social forces activate us—economic, religious, historical. So perhaps when your cell comes into more than normal contact with one of these activating forces, these—" He paused for the medical parallel.

"Hormones," Mitch supplied. And suddenly he was excited. He was reaching deep back for an idea. "You know, that analogy may not clear up anything on your side. But it could start something on mine." For he remembered that Kansas City study, which had indicated that allergic people had higher intelligence activity than non-allergics. It was a good thing he had not put in time checking that theory, as a counter-study had appeared almost immediately, a more careful study, in which several kinds of intelligence tests had been used, and which showed no difference between the mental capacities of allergics and non-allergics. Now suddenly it seemed to him that both contentions could be right. Suppose the first set of tests had measured mental activity, the other, mental capacity. Activity might show an in-

[4 7 0]

crease; capacity, none. Well, of course! Mental activity was directly related to metabolism. Certain hormones must be stimulants of that activity. If allergy spells were accompanied by stepped-up mental activity, then there might be something common in their hormone-picture. If a man could find out which hormones stimulated mental activity, he might be on the track of some hormones that were involved in allergic shock. And people in whom that hormone-picture appeared might include the allergy-susceptibles. And then, if a man could somehow find a way to control the ductless glands which produced those hormones . . .

"I'll tell you something about yourself," Rawley said. "You made the error that most people make; they get isolated in their own little field of work, and they tend to apply their methods to all problems, like Henry Ford trying to apply the assembly line method to international politics. But then, Mitch, if you crawl out and sit in the world for a while, you may reverse the procedure. You may find there are ideas and methods in the outside world that can be applied, that can enrich your thinking, in your own specialty."

"Yes. I know. I was just noticing that," Mitch said abstractedly. His mind was busy, wondering whether this idea that had just come to him would lead into a major study of the allergic mechanism. To study the gland factor. To find by elimination what hormones were present, then to try to normalize . . . It felt good to be thinking in medicine again.

A boy came through with papers. "Let's see what play they gave us," Rawley said, buying one of each, and tossing the *Post* to Mitch.

There he was, on the front page, holding up that doll with the spindle stuck through it. Doctor Shows How Cops Killed. Bad, terribly cheap. Feldner would not like it. It was a stunt. And yet Mitch could not help a feeling of gratification in

[471]

the effectiveness of the device; George Price certainly knew his business.

Before reading the story under his picture, Mitch Wilner's eye was caught by an item in a box. The newsreel company had announced that, owing to the wide public interest in the film of the Fourth of July strike disorders, the film would after all be released, as a "matter of public policy."

At least that much had been accomplished. He was about to make a remark to Rawley but, looking up, saw him shaking his head in a kind of sorrowful disbelief; a low whistling sound came from him. "What's the matter?" Mitch said. For answer, Rawley indicated the banner headline; Mitch realized that in his eagerness to find news of himself he had overlooked the main headline.

"Three Dead in Steel Riot."

Police had "clashed" with pickets at the Consolidated plant in Mahoning, killing three.

8. IN A PERFECT BODY

In 1926 Mrs. Teresa Soriano made a visit back home in the old country to the village of Spesa near Turin. She went there to see her sick mother before she died. It cost nearly five hundred dollars altogether, with the bus to New York, and the boat, and bringing them some presents, and showing herself off as the wife of Achille Soriano who did okay in Chicago, America.

Her own people were the Nicolettis in Spesa and they were

just like she remembered them, struggling along barefoot year after year with their couple of olive trees and some grapes and their chickens and their donkeys. Only, they said, bread was dearer every year and there were now four police in the village where there had been none, but they wished not to talk of those things; people live, people live, they said. Tell us, better, of America.

What tore her heart was the ill fortune that dogged her cousin Vincenzo Nicoletti, who had so often wrestled with her under the vine when they were children; yes, once, and she sixteen, he had almost caused her to break her pledge to Achille Soriano, who had gone away to America to find riches and send for her. Luckily as she wrestled with Vincenzo it had begun to rain.

But now how badly life had dealt with Vincenzo! That arm that had held her locked against him, till luckily the rain made them laugh and brought her release, his left arm Vincenzo had lost in the war. He received a small pension for the arm, a few lire a month—enough to feed a donkey. One-armed, he labored in the fields, as other men.

His wife had borne two sons and a daughter. And of the children, only one was perfect. The first son was crippled from birth, with a clubfoot. The second son was good; but the poor girl, born a beautiful child, was stricken in her first year with scarlet fever, and had remained a deaf-mute thereafter. It was two years since the mother had left her burden, run off.

At home in Chicago, Teresa Soriano had been as loud as any other in complaint of her hard lot, standing in the store from early morning and running back to the kitchen to get her two girls ready for school, and running back into the store if the bell tinkled. But now in Spesa she could sing of the wisdom of her husband's twelve years of stinginess and struggle, sing how she had tended the grocery while Achille was a bricklayer in the mill, how they had lived in the two rooms in back of the store till only last year, when the last note on the mortgage was paid and they owned the house, the store with the flat upstairs; yes, now the season of gathering was come for the Sorianos; yes, now at last Achille himself tended the store, no longer worked in the mill, and now she too had her reward for the long years of struggle, five hundred dollars for a trip to go home and show herself off to the old folks.

Yes, in Chicago she could complain of her two lazy daughters and no son, but here, seeing the fate that might have befallen her had she married her cousin Vincenzo and mothered his imperfect children, she shuddered at what she had escaped.

"Ah, here," the old folks said, "everything grows tighter, tighter every year." They squeezed their hard-boned hands into tighter and tighter fists, to show how life was dry without marrow, as under a consuming sun.

That very first evening, in her mother's earth-floored kitchen, the plan was born—how to nurture the kernel of good that remained in the evil fate of Vincenzo. Suppose the one perfect son should be taken to America? There let him learn to make a fine living, and, grown, he would save money and send for his lame brother; in America, who knew, there might even be healing for that lameness? And even the deaf sister might be made to hear, and taught to speak. So eventually, through his one perfect son, Vincenzo might reap joy out of life.

Early the next day, Teresa went to her cousin's womanless

[4 7 4]

house, and her heart wept at the sweet eyes of the mute girl; but when at noon the strong child, Alfonso, came storming into the house, she was overcome with sudden love, as in waking after giving birth. The boy was like a sponge that had taken into itself all the life, all the health, all the energy of this miserable home. Yes, it would be better for the others if he were far away, that they might not see their pale selves alongside him.

So Alfonso came to America. He was nine years old, the same as her elder daughter, and those two fought from the first day. Al soaked up this America so quickly, in two weeks he was running around the house saying American dirty words, she had to wash his mouth with American family soap. The girls would hear him.

He never quite caught up to Nina in school and she teased him because he was the same age and a grade behind her. Then in high school he was a baseball star, a pitcher. Mrs. Soriano went with her daughters to the games and, my, Alfonso was handsome out there with his white teeth flashing in his dark smile, and his curly hair, the kind a girl would want to curl around her fingers, his long hard limbs; yes, like his father before he went to war and lost that arm, he was perfect. Nina was in love with him and, poor kid, she starved herself reducing, but there was something, glands she said it was, so no matter how she starved she was fat; and to make it worse Al never caught on she was in love with him, he was just a healthy young fellow kidding her like a brother, always pretending he saw her sneaking into the store to eat candies after making off she was reducing at the table. Nina couldn't stand kidding and afterwards she would cry.

[4 7 5]

So when they were graduating from high school, only half a year apart, Nina said Al should be the one to go to college because it was more important for a man, but Al said, the hell with it, he was going to get a job, and if the family had dough to throw away sending anybody to college, let Nina go and sit on her fanny another four years, "I got things to do." He didn't mention about the family back in the old country but Teresa knew, yes, it was like he was in a hurry to work off a debt. To them back there.

Achille took the boy over to the Midwest mill and talked to Mr. Schute, and they put Al on as a chipper right away. Nina wanted to know exactly what he did. The old man said, a chipper, that's nothing, he chip, all day long he chip. What did he chip? The steel, what do you suppose he chip! What do they want to chip the steel for? So Al explained, they take these big ingots of steel, big as a man, and they got to break them down, rough them down into chunks that can be handled in the rolling-mills. So they send these ingots through the roughing-mills, the bloomer, and they come out maybe slabs, maybe heavy bars like for girders; right now he was working on slabs, four, five inches thick, a yard wide, and as long as this room. "Okay, when that slab comes out of the roughing-mill, it has imperfections, say like little tiny cracks on the surface, you can't hardly see them, but those inspectors, they come along and mark those cracks with a streak of chalk. Now that's got to be chipped down because, if you leave that crack in there, when that slab goes to the rolling-mill to be rolled down into sheets, that crack is liable to spread in the sheets and make a defect. See? So those surface cracks got to be chipped out."

[4 7 6]

"You mean you chip the steel with a hammer and chisel?"

"Naw, dummy, it's an automatic hammer," Al explained. "A big automatic, you couldn't hardly even hold it, it would jump out of your hands."

"So that's what you have to do all day?" She studied him absorbedly, as though she were there in the mill, watching him on his knees on the slab, leaning on that hammer, racing his partner, a Mex called Ricardo, to see who could chip the most inches. They were getting paid by inches then, and above 2500 inches was bonus pay. He had to laugh telling about that Mex. Ricardo would carve up a slab as if it was some guy that had stolen his girl. He'd leap on a slab and chew it up regardless of the chalkmarks. "Inches, inches," he would sing, and go a foot beyond the mark on each end. There was a lot of Mexicans on there, chipping. He was a hell of a guy, that Mex, he could really spot the cracks, thinner than hairs. He wanted to be an inspector, marking the cracks, seventy cents an hour—I mark with the chalk, you sweat with the hammer!—but no chance for a Mex. He told Al: "You got to get that inspector job, sure, wops can get that inspector job, I'm gonna show you how you catch the cracks, then, sonofabitch, you're gonna be the inspector, you're gonna give me all the inches, huh, my pal?"

"Sure, I got to give you inches," Al would kid. "You tamale, two inches, that's all you got!" And they would kid like that with the hammers rattling in their hands.

Al was the kidding kind of a guy, always with a joke or a song on his lips, he'd work all day singing Christopher Colombo ta-da-da, a happy-go-lucky type, looked like, though maybe inside, like Nina sometimes said, discussing him with her sister

Bella, inside she said Al was not happy all the way, because he had, like an iron lump in his heart, the knowledge of that family of cripples he came from, and sure he was gay all the time realizing how lucky he was to have nothing wrong with him, but all the time he knew he had to make it up to that family, sometime, for being perfect himself.

Al used to bring home his paycheck and hand it over unopened to the old lady, Mama Teresa; and when he needed spending money he would ask her for some, but otherwise she took care of everything.—Al, you know I am putting your money in the bank, she told him; and once in a while, even though he never asked, she would tell him how much money he had in the bank, just so he should know. He was making thirty-five, forty bucks a week, then, making bonus every week the way that Mex showed him to eat up the inches of steel. "You've got to take out for my room and board," he insisted to Aunt Teresa; "take out ten bucks a week at least." And though the old lady objected that he was just like a son to her, and anyway lots of evenings he helped out in the store, Al still insisted, and the old man Achille said: "Well, even so it's you got your own son, when he's grow up, you're gonna let him pay room and board, at home." So Teresa took out ten dollars, every week.

Once she let Al take sixty dollars out of his account to buy himself a car; one of the boys at the mill was selling it, a bargain, a Studebaker sports model only six years gone; and that summer Al was chasing around with every girl in the neighborhood and a couple of times he stayed out all night and Nina knew it. She would hardly speak to him for a week every time that happened, but the old lady said: "Nina, don't pay no attention, boys are

[4 7 8]

different, Nina baby." To herself, Teresa felt like she was young again.

All of a sudden Al made up a song. He used to pick out tunes on the piano, and one night he said: "Hey, Nina, I made up a song, listen to this, is this hot!" It was funny how he respected her opinion though he was always kidding her. His song was all about cruising in the dark looking for a place to park, in front of your door baby is there room for one more maybe; and he had a cute idea there, the words would break and he would make a nose-noise like an auto horn, aunk aunk, it even made Nina laugh. She told him the sang was terrible, lousy, but she wrote down the notes for him and even made up chords on the piano, to go with the tune.

Then Al got very much interested in the mailman, going to the box twelve times a day; and one day he bust in with a letter: "Look, they like my song, they say it ought to be a hit!"

He had sent the song to the Cosmopolitan Music Publishers, having seen their ad in *Wild Stories;* and here was their letter saying his song had the makings of a novelty hit, like the "Peanut Vendor," which had grossed two million dollars; all it needed was an arrangement—whatever that was—and a little professional polishing which their staff would supply for a special price of twenty-five dollars and twenty-five percent of the rights; they were willing to take a gamble because they believed in the song.

"Don't be a sucker," Nina said, "it's just a racket to get your twenty-five dollars."

But Al said: "Oh, yeah—look at this!" They had enclosed a folder with a list of their hits—everything from "Yes, We Have

[4 7 9]

No Bananas" to "Minnie the Moocher." "A company like that is no gyp outfit!" Al declared. So even though Nina insisted he was throwing away money that ought to be sent to that poor family in Spesa, the old lady gave Al the twenty-five dollars—after all, it was his money—and he sent it away.

About a week later he got Teresa in the store when there were no customers and said: "Listen, Ma, listen, babe." He didn't want Nina to know, but he wanted to invest another fifty bucks in his song because the company would get another fifty percent of the rights, making seventy-five percent they'd own, unless he wanted to share fifty dollars in the printing costs. Why, that fifty dollars might amount to tens of thousands if the song was any kind of a hit! The old lady got dizzy trying to figure out the deal, but it was his own money and he was so happy and excited, so she gave him the fifty dollars. And then one morning a big envelope came registered mail for Al Nicoletti, and there was a whole stack of copies of his song, "Looking for a Place to Park," by Al Nicoletti, with a cute picture of a couple in an automobile gazing at a full moon. Al dragged Nina into the parlor and made her play his song while he gave out with the words. "Oh, boy!" he boasted. "You'll be hearing that on the radio, all day long, from now on!" He sure was happy.

All the fellows in Calumet kidded the pants off of Al. They claimed he bellowed that song at work until you couldn't hear the goddam chipping-chisels, all you heard was Al.

The C.I.O. was organizing in the mill, and at home once the old lady asked: "Al, you ain't going to join that C.I.O.?" "Why?" Nina asked. And the old lady explained, well, in church the priest said the C.I.O. was Bolsheviks against religion

[480]

and they killed the nuns like in Spain. Then the old man Achille said: "You tell the priest C.I.O. don't bother with him, so he got no business, what for he's gonna bother with the C.I.O.?"

Al said, na, as far as he knew, it was nothing like that, what did the C.I.O. have against the nuns in Spain, that was a laugh, and anyway all the fellows were signing up, it wouldn't look right if he didn't sign up too. Next thing you know he was on a union dance committee and he gave the whole family tickets like when he used to play baseball; he gave tickets for Nina and Bella and the old lady and the old man, even though he took another girl himself. Right in the middle of the dance the orchestra leader, Pinkie Sisto—he had a couple of brothers working in the mills—Pinkie stopped the music and announced they would now play a big new hit by that popular chipper and song-writer, Al Nicoletti, and all the fellows in the orchestra held their noses and made aunk aunk, like automobile horns, it was a riot! Al was blushing pink as an infant, so Nina said: "You know, Al, that song don't sound so bad after all!" So he said: "Come on, baby elephant, let's see if you can dance to it!"

One day Al came home kicking because the mill got wise about all the extra inches, and suddenly the chipping was shifted to tonnage pay. It was just luck if you got a slab full of cracks and hacked away at it for two hours, or if you got a run of clean slabs and built up tonnage in no time. Mr. Schute said it would all even up in the average, just like everywhere else in the mill where they worked on tonnage, but "Sonofabitch!" Al complained. "You know what them guys are doing, if you wear a C.I.O. button, they stick you on the bum stuff, it's all cracked up like an old Indian's face, but Schute got some guys that suck

[481]

along with him, they're all set to scab when we go out, and he gives them all the clean stuff to chip, they're making bonus every day."

For a couple of weeks after chipping went on tonnage Al's pay fell, down to twenty-five dollars, twenty-seven-fifty, but then it began to go up again. "Mr. Schute, he's treating you better now, huh?" Mama Teresa said, but Al winked. "There ain't nothing you can't get wise to. I got to hand it to that Mex, he's smart." Why work your guts out to make tonnage? All you had to do was wait until the inspector was over at the other side of the chipping-yard, then just get a hunk of oil waste and rub out half the chalkmarks on your slab. Chip down the rest, call the hooker, pull it away! And, boy, you sure could add up tonnage with that piece of oil waste!

Nina worried. "Don't they find out?" she said. "If some of the cracks aren't chipped down?"

"Sure, when they roll it they get defects and then they got to scrap it. Sometimes they inspect it again before they roll. So if they catch the slab with some cracks, they send it back to the chipping-yard."

"Can't they tell who did it?"

"How they gonna know the chalk was erased? Maybe the first inspector was asleep and missed those cracks!"

So then after a while the mill put the men on a straight hourly basis, sixty-two and a half cents an hour. "Okay," Al said. "This way we don't rush our guts out on that hammer. They got to know, every time they try to beat the boys, the boys are going to figure something out to beat the company."

Even in spite of the seventy-five dollars he had invested in the song, and the five dollars a week Teresa was sending to the folks for him, Al had two hundred and fifty dollars in the bank at the end of that year, working steady all year; but in spring work got spotty. They were laying off men from the chipping-yard. The company had a new trick that was tried out up in Gary: burning the steel instead of chipping it. One day a guy came out to the yard with welding-goggles and a torch, and he zipped the flame right down the chalk-line, burning out the defect in less time than it took to set a hammer to it. It was as fast as wiping the chalk off with oil waste.

By the end of the week there was a crew of burners on the job. They still used chippers on the low carbon steels and the stainless steels, but at least half of the steels they burned, "scarfing" they called it.

Al was worried because he was a new man there, and if they laid off according to seniority he was cooked. Besides, they knew he was C.I.O., even if he wasn't wearing the button into the mill.

Nina talked about it with him. "What is it, skilled work, that scarfing?" she asked. "Do you have to get training to be a burner?"

For Chrisake, there was nothing to it, he said; he had handled a torch lots of times down at Benny's garage, just for the hell of it; sure, you had to be careful regulating the air and all that stuff, but there was nothing to it.

And the next day he had a bright idea, what the hell! Why knock his arms off on a hammer when he could handle a torch, and even get more dough! They needed scarfers, too, were putting them on as fast as they could get them. So in the middle of the afternoon he asked one of the boys: "Hey, lemme a hold of that for a minute. Lemme your goggles." And when Schute came along, there was Al Nicoletti, burning up the chalk-line fast as the rest of them. "How about it?" he asked, and Mr. Schute said: "Okay, better get yourself some goggles and some gloves."

Al felt kind of funny splitting with his partner, the little old Mex, but what the hell, chippers were getting only four days a week by then, and he had to send money home to the old country.

When the plant closed up with the strike, the old lady didn't want to take his money for board till the strike was over, but Al yelled he was no different from anybody, she had to keep on taking out ten bucks a week. At last she settled to take out only five, as long as the strike lasted. It was kind of lucky, for he was using up more change than when working; a fellow had to have dough in his pocket, knocking around all day, buying beers, gas, and stuff.

Once he went out to the picket line, but he couldn't go for that picketing stuff, walking around like a bunch of monkeys in front of the gate, when the plant was closed tight anyway. In fact he was thinking if the strike lasted he'd take himself a vacation, maybe him and a couple of the boys go up to the Wisconsin lakes, fishing.

Saturday night about 2 a.m. the old lady heard Al come home, carefully closing the downstairs hall door. But instead of tip-toeing to his room as usual, he came and knocked on her door and whispered: "Ma." The old man grumbled in half-sleep: "If he don't keep still I'm gonna throw that kid out," but she

[484]

shushed him and struggled into her wrapper in the dark, and waddled out. "What's the matter, Al? You in some trouble?" She sniffed but smelled no liquor. He laughed. "No, honey, I ain't been drinking, just a couple of beers; we been dancing in one of those road joints. Ma, gimme ten bucks."

"Ten dollars, Al? This late? Aw, go on, Al, take your girl home and you come home go to sleep, don't be such a bum."

But, no, he has to have ten dollars right away hurry quick, his girl is waiting outside in the car.

"But, Al, what do you want ten dollars for? Where are you going? Remember you can't throw away so much money, you are on strike."

"Well," he said. "Ma, we're gonna drive to Crown Point and get hitched!"

He was so jolly and happy she could hardly go against him, but she sat him down and said: "Al, you crazy? Who is this girl? How long do you know her?"

"Come on, Ma, I know her all right; look, I haven't even been drinking."

"Al, you're just a kid, you're only twenty-one——"

"All I asked you was for ten dollars," he said.

"Al, it's your money, and I ain't even your mother. I'm going to give you the money," the old lady said. "But, Al, you're gonna have lots of time to be married all your life, so you can talk to me for one minute, huh? What girl you wanna marry? Alice?" she guessed, as that was his Number One girl friend just then.

"No. Winnie," said Al.

"Winnie?" She didn't know no Winnie.

"You never met her, sweetheart. She's a swell kid. I'll bring her home tomorrow——"

"Al, you got to realize you're on the strike, you don't even know when you're gonna go back to work——"

"All right, all right, you let me do the worrying; come on, honey, give me the ten bucks." He grabbed her by the elbows, laughing, and turned her around and started her down the hall. She didn't know what to do next, so she went slowly to the dining-room, where she kept money in a jar, but, passing her daughters' room, she slipped inside. Nina was sitting erect in bed. "What's the matter, Ma?" she whispered in an awful, knowing voice. So the old lady told her: "Al, he wants to go to Crown Point and get married."

"Oh, that damn fool, that's all he's had to do all week, run around chasing chicken." Hopelessly, she asked: "Who is it?"

"Some girl, her name is Winnie."

Nina's voice was utterly sad, so sad and loving for Al, just like a wife's voice forgiving a husband's foolishness. The old lady could have fallen on the bed and wept for her daughter. "Oh, that sucker, that poor sucker," Nina was saying, still careful not to wake Bella. "Why, that little bitch, she's slept with every fellow in Calumet; even when she was in school she was letting half the fellows jazz her in the basement; she used to tell me; she was even pregnant last summer and had an abortion. Oh, stop him, Ma, oh, that poor sucker!" Nina wanted to come out, but Teresa said: "No, you wait. You stay here. I'm gonna try and handle him." Then she went back to Al, with the ten dollars.

He was standing at the window signaling to his girl down

there in the car. Teresa gave him the money. "It's your money, Al," she said, "and you can go. Only, please, now you gotta listen to me a little. I have been like a mother to you and I am worried like you are my own son."

"Sure, Ma," he said, and sat down, but dancing his feet impatiently.

"Al, marriage is a most serious thing," she began, "and if you and this girl really love each other you can go and get married tomorrow just as good, in the daytime is better than the middle of the night."

"Yah, but we feel like doing it now," he said, "and that's the time to do it!"

"Al," she said, "now you are going to be a married man, you better start thinking what's gonna be. You know how much money you got?"

"Sure, I guess about two hundred bucks, you said, huh?"

"Well, Al," she said, "right now you got two hundred and fifty-four dollars in the bank but that ain't even gonna furnish a house and, Al, you know you been sending five dollars a week to the old country. How you gonna keep on doing that if you gotta support your own home and a wife?"

"Well, Christ," Al said, "I'm gonna get married sometime, I'm not going to be carrying a bunch of cripples on my back all my life! . . ."

The way he said that word, and somehow because it was in the night, when two people can talk to each other with no barriers between them, it struck Teresa that she had never let herself know, all these years, what was in the boy when she took him from that terrible house in the old country. She had never

[4 8 7]

let herself know how all this time he had carried in his heart, like a closed poison sac from his childhood, the poison of the malformed and the sick and the miserable, and it was as if he had sealed up that sac but now in one spurt, like a pressed-upon boil, the ugly fluid had burst out of him. She knew how it was, just from living she knew how the thing in health hates the thing that is diseased, and now she knew this feeling was what had made her take him away from that house of sickness; and he was right, he should have a life altogether free of those cripples, free; he should take a healthy girl, and have good luck and breed fine strong children, ending the curse that was on the Nicolettis.

So it hurt her, like it would hurt her to stick needles into his fine young flesh, to have to be the one to say to him that his duty was a sacred thing, his father and his sister and his brother had given her a sacred trust to raise him in America so he could help them. If at least he would wait and earn money for a few years and perhaps bring over his brother to America——

"And have him on my back all my life! Why, they'd be better off dead!" Al cried, but instantly caught his awful words and hung his head.

Yet shame didn't make him change his mind. Oh, if it was only for a good girl, Teresa thought, she would have been happy to see him strong and grand in protecting the right of the healthy. "Ma," he said, "take that dough, whatever I got, and send it to them. Winnie and me will get along, we don't need no furniture, we can rent a furnished place. To hell with the strike. I'll get a job, maybe welder in a garage. And if I can spare a few bucks I'll send it to them, when I can. But I didn't say I'd be responsible for them. I didn't make them sick. They got no right to keep me tied, to keep me from my life."

"All right, Al," she conceded. "You got a right to be a man now and make up your own mind." But seeing Nina's door open, she made one last desperate try. "Al, it's so late now, half-past two, why don't you go down, Al, and bring your girl upstairs and I'll make some coffee, huh? And she can even stay here tonight and tomorrow you can go get married, get married nice, in the church, on Sunday, so you won't ever have no shame for your marriage, Al, and then, we're all gonna feel good. Huh, Al?"

Talking that long about such serious things, he was cooled off, she could tell, and he said: "Okay, Ma, I'll leave it up to her. You know, when you tell a girl you're gonna marry her you can't renege, so if she wants to wait till tomorrow, okay, but if not, then good-by, sweetheart, I'm on my way to Crown Point!" He finished with a little kick of fun again, laughing, as he hammered down the stairs.

Nina came out and asked in a ghastly voice: "Well?" and the old lady shook her head, defeated, and tears came down Nina's cheeks; but then they heard Al on the stairs again. Nina rushed to her room. Al came back laughing and half swearing. "She ran out on me!" he yelled. "I guess I left her waiting too long. Can you beat it, the bim ran out on me!" And he wasn't sore at all. He gave Teresa back the ten dollars.

The next morning, Sunday morning, they pretended nothing had happened. He got up real late and he went and phoned this girl, but she wouldn't even talk to him; and when he hung up the phone he said: "Hey, there's a big strike meeting today over at the Consolidated; they wanted all us guys over there too. Gimme a buck will you, Ma? I wanna take a girl over there, I might wanna buy a hot dog or something."

She gave him the dollar, and said: "Who you taking, Al?" and he said: "I dunno," and pulled out his address book.

"Take me over, Al, I want to go over there," Nina said, and he kidded her as usual: "Hey, you think I want to break the springs on my jalopy?" But he stuck his address book back in his pocket. When they drove off he started singing his song, "Looking for a Place to Park," and Nina gaily pushed the horn-button, aunk aunk, and he looked so handsome, his black hair shining in the bright sun, she even said: "Al, you know you've got a nice voice, all you need is a little training."

"Training, hell!" he joked. "It's perfect!"

THE Citizens' Committee met to consider the results of the Senate investigation. A very good job had been done, in Dr. Ladd's opinion; and now having served its purpose, the committee might as well disband.

Why, the committee had not begun to do its job! Hattie Miller protested. The strike was still on at Consolidated. In the public mind the picket lines had been broken and Speer had gotten away with it. The police might have had a few bad hours in Washington but, rest assured, they would stage their rebuttal. Those sixty arrested strikers had not yet been tried; the police could make that trial into a witch hunt unparalleled since the Haymarket. The committee had to carry on, to enlarge, to become a political force.

"Right. But how?" George Price posed the question. The newsreel of the Fourth, though released all over the country, was still banned by the Chicago censors. The public had practically forgotten the case.

"It's our job to keep them from forgetting, until justice is done."

"They haven't forgotten!" the I.L.D. girl said. "The real people haven't forgotten."

So they arranged to hold more meetings, in neighborhood halls. But twice halls were withdrawn after placards had been printed. And when meetings went through, Mitch, attending them to repeat his medical report, found himself dispirited by all the effort put forward, each time, only to gather a few hundred people in a hall and to make speeches and collect a few dimes. And each time the Communist zealots were more and more obviously in charge; no one bothered any longer to keep them from selling their literature in the halls. Sure, they were the only ones who would do the work and arrange the meetings, but were these meetings of any use, except for them?

Once when Mitch Wilner went out to see Oscar Lindstrom he found the little woman, Dombrowsky's friend, sitting in the kitchen. Sophie was wearing her scrubbing-clothes, the old rundown shoes, and the shapeless wash-worn dress. Another scrubwoman was preparing to go out with her, a younger woman. Until she said: "Hello, Doctor," Mitch failed to recognize Pauline, for already she had assumed the colorlessness of all those little bundled women who trudged through office buildings at night.

"You going to work too, Pauline?" he asked.

"Yah, looks like it. Sophie is taking me over there to get me started."

He was about to ask, wasn't there anything else she could do, but checked himself; she certainly must have tried every other possibility. He could see how it formed now, that army of night-time scrubwomen, and the idea of this still-young Pauline resigning herself to such an end of life was hard to swallow.

"Doesn't the union give you any relief?" he asked. "I thought they were going to sue the company, too."

"That's gonna take a couple of years," Pauline said, "and even then who says we're gonna get anything? I don't want to take the money from the union, so long as I can go out to work."

Drawing him aside, she lowered her voice and spoke of Sophie. "Doctor, Sophie is crazy on the subject of seeing that movie. She thinks she's going to see her boy friend, that Dombrowsky, like he was still alive. I don't think it would be so good for her to see that picture though, huh, Doctor?"

"But it isn't showing anywhere in Chicago."

"She says they got it showing in Indiana. She ain't so dumb. She finds out things like that. You think it's all right if she goes to see it? You think it wouldn't—maybe—give her ideas again?"

In one way it might be good for the woman to see the film; perhaps it would finish the trouble in her mind, give her an image to put away. Or suppose, instead, these last images became indelible, carried forever in the forefront of her brain?

"If she can't be talked out of going," he said, "at least somebody ought to go with her."

Sophie had approached them, sensing the subject of their discussion.

"Doctor, the movie, you can see Stanley?" she asked.

"You can hardly see him, Sophie; he is in the crowd."

"You can see who is shooting him?"

"No, Sophie."

From her purse, she extracted a newspaper clipping, unfolding it before him: the photograph of the police carrying Stanley. Sophie put her finger on the image of the cop who lugged the wounded man by the strap around his leg. "You can see, Doctor, who is this one?"

"I don't think so," Mitch said. As he remembered, the film, too, showed only a back view of these police. "You can't see their faces, Sophie."

"I will see," she declared, staring at the picture of that policeman as if the other side of him must exist in the recorded image, as if she would somehow see inside the piece of paper, and discover the guilty man's face.

The massacre newsreel was showing in a little dump of a theater on the outskirts of Gary; evidently the larger movie houses were under the control of Chicago firms, who played ball with the police and refused to exhibit the film. The theater smelled of twenty years of sweat and spit. A movie about the Foreign Legion was running. Pauline relaxed, he could almost hear her small weary bones unflex into ease; but Sophie sat tense on the edge of the seat and kept asking: "When they show Stanley, Doctor?"

Presently the film ended; there was an excerpt from a coming attraction, kissing and shooting from speeding cars, and suddenly the Independence Day newsreel was on the screen. "What it says?" Sophie demanded with the same panic ignorance that patients showed when they turned to you after an examination and begged: What is it, Doctor? "What it says?"

"It says they are showing the picture for the good of the public," Pauline repeated, tonelessly.

Even though he knew the film, the impact of it was sudden and again unexpected, like an airplane, long heard in the sky, suddenly bursting into sight, and gone before quite seen. And

[493]

this audience made it different, for here all were steelworkers and families of workers; many were here like Sophie, to search for the instant flash of some loved one, or even of themselves, in participation there.

Sophie half lifted out of her seat when the film showed the crowd advancing, lifted as though she would any instant meet her friend Stanley Dombrowsky and pull him away from that bad place. Voices throughout the theater read the signs, and the stale air of the theater was electrified as they read out: "Be Men, Don't Scab," "Win with C.I.O.," "Come Out in the Open"; and now, Mitch knew, the sudden break was coming, the changing of lens, as when a train rushes from smooth fields into a tunnel and the experienced traveler knows it will come out upon precipitous crags. "Watch now," he warned Sophie, and the clamor of the cracking guns sounded, and there on the screen was the dust and gas cloud and the tangle of figures running, thrashing, groping. Sophie stood in an agony of anxiety, seeking her friend, as if she might actually call a warning to him there: Stanley! As if she might cover him from harm with her own body.

"Up in the corner, look!" Pauline said, and there it was— the chunky figure bursting into an open space, like a football-player finding a hole, and there was the figure dancing across that space, with his hands in the air, hands up to show he was peaceful, and see how he turned his head, his arms still raised, turned his head to see if they were after him.

"Stanley!" Sophie screamed, and the whole theater shook with a hysteria she had ignited; people were calling names, and some were cursing, and then, like a malaria-seizure, their fever was over, and they sat back, exhausted; and Pauline was exhausted in her seat. Right there, in the instant after Stanley Dombrowsky turned to look back, just there where he ran off the screen as a man might run out of life, into the endless space of death—at that instant he must have caught the bullet in his leg.

There were the dazed moments now of cops standing over fallen bodies, the horror moments of cops clubbing the fallen; and then, like the dead returned, was the scene Sophie needed; there was the bull-cop Gorcey, with his unbelievably demented eyes, pulling Dombrowsky away from the ambulance car, and: "Look, Doctor, that's you!" Pauline said, and Mitch saw himself on the running-board of the other car going into the distance.

"Stanley, Stanley," Sophie moaned now, for this was the scene of the procession of four police, each holding him by a limb, like a sack by its corners, while his sagging body scraped the earth. But the policemen's backs were three-quarters to the camera, and their faces could not be seen.

"Stop, stop," she muttered, "they are killing him," but already her voice was controlled, in futility. And there was, like the very instant of death, the sight of the carried body jerk-slipping closer to the ground; that must have been the instant when the strap came loose. And then the four police, with a concerted heave, let the body fly into the dark interior of the waiting patrol wagon, a corpse flung into the darkness of a waiting grave.

The camera hung an instant longer upon the police, and they were just turning, turning their faces toward the lens, when they were blotted into a following scene.

"That man killed him, the one by the strap," Sophie said quietly.

But who could say? Certainly in that moment the cop who took the strap had willed no death; indeed, he might have thought he was helping rescue the wounded man. If any individual was immediately to blame, wasn't it Gorcey, who had dragged Dombrowsky from the rescue car? But could even

[4 9 5]

Gorcey be blamed for the maddening ideas that had been pumped into him? You did not blame a wound; you tried to clean it up.

But what could be done with the carriers of this infection? He saw now how cold reason alone brought world-changers to conclude that some extermination was inevitable. Yet after a crisis perhaps even the Gorceys could be cured. The danger was that in the meantime, unisolated, unchecked, their fever would become epidemic.

Sophie wanted to remain to see the reel again. "I'll watch her, Doctor," Pauline promised. "I'll get her home. I know the bus."

He left. Even if Sophie should somehow discover the identity of the policeman who carried Stanley Dombrowsky by the strap, what could she do? Would it give her rest?

Now it was Corcoran's turn to stage a show, for the local politicians had to erase the effect of the testimony produced before the Senate committee. Directly on his return from Washington, Mitch Wilner was served with a subpoena to appear for the coroner's inquest. He phoned Rawley. The sociologist had not been served. Nor had any of the divinity students. Nor had George Price.

"They can call anyone they want," Price explained, pointing out that the city would certainly not call witnesses unfavorable to the police, just as the Gottschalk boys, too, had been careful in choosing their witnesses.

It was as if each side were holding its own trial.

"Then what did they call me for?"

"To try to ball you up and discredit what you said in Washington."

Mitch was determined not to worry. His testimony in Washington had been drawn from the coroner's own autopsies, upon which this long and mysteriously delayed inquest would have to be based. How could the coroner discredit facts taken from his own reports?

But as Mitch Wilner approached the scene of the inquest, he became apprehensive. The subpoena ordered him to appear, not in the familiar, commonplace inquest rooms in the county morgue, where so many accidental deaths and deaths of violence were droned into the records, but in the main trial room of the Criminal Court building.

The halls were ominously clear of loiterers. Pauline Lindstrom was just arriving by another corridor. "Wait a minute, sister." A cop halted her at the courtroom door, while he called into the room: "Hey, Matron." Mitch watched, astounded, as a muscle-wadded matron emerged, and proceeded systematically to search the young widow, running her hands over Pauline while the cops made the inevitable good-natured raw remarks about how they would be willing to relieve her of that job. Finally the woman took Pauline's purse and, rooting through the contents, extracted a long nail-file, which she handed to the first cop. "Okay, dear, you can get it when you come out," she said, opening the courtroom door for Pauline. The widow had suffered the entire search mutely, but with an obviously mounting horror; Mitch noticed the pulsation in her throat; she seized the outheld purse, and hurried blindly into the chamber.

"I'm Dr. Wilner," he said, showing his summons.

The cop acting as doorman hesitated, but his partner nodded; shamefacedly, the doorman ran his hands over Mitch, then stepped back, opening the door. "Okay, Doc," he said.

The large, imposing room was scantily occupied. Apparently the public was barred. On a few rear benches sat union folk— Mitch recognized several strikers—and older people who might be relatives of steelworkers. Toward the front, circulating in the aisles or sprawling on benches, were many of the police whom he now knew by sight; newspaper photographers were

[497]

busily flashlighting a pretty young girl who sat in the witness chair. In the judge's seat was the coroner, Paul Gambetti, a small-headed, amiable blank, the type of man often seen behind a cigar counter, shooting dice for the price of a handful of Garcias. He was staring out the window, letting the photographers take their time.

At the counsel's table Mitch noticed Sam Eisen, with an elderly man, probably another C.I.O. lawyer. George Price was among the newspapermen; Mitch felt less alone.

Corcoran, coatless, and looking much bigger in his ballooning white shirt, elicited from the girl on the stand that her name was Grace Dalrymple and she was a student at the North Shore High School. With well-bred candor, she related how her civics teacher, a Mr. White, had offered to take his pupils out to see the steel strike. "I believe in seeing both sides of a question," she said, "so I volunteered to go, even though Mr. White is a radical."

"How do you know he is a radical?" Corcoran asked blandly.

"Because he was always after us to join the student union," she said.

"Where is Mr. White now?"

"He is visiting in Russia."

Corcoran acted surprised.

So Mr. White had taken several of his pupils out to "a place called Guzman's Grove or something," the girl testified. "It looked like a saloon. And some woman there put me behind the counter to serve water to the strikers."

"Just water?"

"That's all we served them but a lot of them had whisky bottles in their pockets and were just using the water for a chaser, I guess."

Had she seen anything of interest?

"Well," she said, "some of the men had guns."

[4 9 8]

"Guns?"

The flashlights popped. Reporters scuttled out to telephone. North Shore Girl Saw Guns on Strikers.

Mitch remembered that girl now. On the Fourth. This was the one who had come through the kitchen, as Sobol was handing out the picket signs. And he remembered the instant of shock when she had glimpsed, in the drawer of the kitchen table, some pistols Carl had taken away from hot-heads.

"Who the hell let her in Guzman's?" muttered Alonzo, at the strikers' table.

"Gaul," Sobol said. "That's some more of his university stuff. He was gonna get all the kids of the rich to win the strike for the boys."

Miss Dalrymple chattered on. Yes, she had been in sympathy with the working men but when she saw those guns her opinion changed. Now she thought those men were to blame for their own troubles.

Mitch realized he had another day of waiting before him, and went to telephone his office. Price was just coming out of the booth. "That's terrible stuff," Price said. "I had to phone it in. They'll play it all over the front page."

"But why don't they cross-examine her and bring out that the guns were confiscated?" Mitch asked. "And on the Fourth of July, everybody that owns a pistol has it out to make noise, anyway." Another thing—why didn't the union put Barbara Macey on the stand, to make a counter-sensation? And bring out all that stuff about Martha Cross, and the tie-ups with Silver Shirts and other Fascist groups?

Price shook his head. "Eisen won't do it. He's saving all that stuff for the trial."

"What trial?"

"There's still got to be a trial," Price reminded him. "All the boys are still under arrest—including the dead."

"Then what is this?"

That was where those bastards were clever, Price explained; you had to hand it to them, they knew the publicity angles. In the public mind, this was the trial. "First, they move it to the Criminal Court building, so every news story with the court building mentioned in the lead makes it sound like a criminal trial. But, Jesus, in an inquest like this they don't even have any rules of evidence. Why, the C.I.O. lawyers are here only by courtesy, the coroner can even kick them out if he wants to. Then, when he renders his verdict, it even comes as a jury verdict!" Price grinned at the smartness of the maneuver.

"What jury?"

"Those three stumblebums, the legionnaires."

As far as Mitch knew, coroner's juries were supposed to consist of any three citizens, chosen off the street, near the undertaker's, or wherever the scene of an ordinary inquest happened to be. The citizens were simply supposed to endorse the coroner's verdict, as witnesses.

"Sure. That's the laugh," Price said. And told how Gambetti had made a practice of giving the coroner's jury jobs, a dollar a hearing, to unemployed members of the American Legion; a little gang of professional coroner's jurors had developed. Naturally, as the men valued their jury calls, they couldn't be expected in any case to question a coroner's verdict.

"But suppose he starts in on me?" Mitch became worried. He thought of getting his own lawyer, perhaps Lou Margolis, who had certain connections among city politicians.

Price advised him to rely on the C.I.O. counsel. "They won't let Corky get too raw," he said. "He just has to get back a couple of innings, for what they did to him in Washington."

Mitch phoned home, too, telling Syl he'd probably have to lose the entire day. He returned to the courtroom. The police frisked him again as he went in.

Sam Eisen, cross-examining that butter-faced high school girl, brought out that her father was a stockbroker, and opposed to unions. Also, she had discussed her testimony with a friend. A boy friend. And gradually, Sam Eisen uncovered the fact that the girl's boy friend, who had helped her "change her mind" about the strike, was nothing less than the son of a police captain.

Price rushed for the phone again, but the other reporters only shifted in their seats. They knew what their papers wanted.

After Grace Dalrymple, Corcoran produced his second sensation. A freckled, bespectacled young man took the stand; him, too, Mitch had seen in that compressed hour at Guzman's, on the Fourth; and Mitch had a curious, uneasy sensation, as of having before him a puzzle he had laboriously fitted together, and now watching an adversary across the table take the pieces and turn them over and fit them together into an altogether different pattern that he knew to be wrong—but nevertheless the pieces fitted.

For this witness was the reporter who had rushed up to Jock Kiley, just before the people marched, and begged him to halt the parade. Lindeman, of the *Steel Harbor News*. He testified that he had begged Sobol to stop the march, but that Sobol, handing out clubs with signs loosely tacked to them, had declared: "Our plans are all made, we can't stop now." Then, Lindeman said, he had rushed back to the police lines and had observed the clash from a porch.

Had he observed the beginning of hostilities?

Yes. After the strikers had faced the police for several minutes, he had heard a voice yell out: "What are we waiting for?" and at the time he had had the impression this was an agreed-upon signal.

How did he get that impression?

Because of the manner of the voice.

Mitch caught himself snickering; and yet, on the other side, hadn't he felt that Captain Wiley's reading of the riot act was a signal, just from the manner in which it was reeled off?

And after this signal? Corcoran asked.

"I heard a shot, fired from the ranks of the strikers."

The newspapermen went out to telephone again, and the coroner obligingly suspended proceedings until they had delivered the sensation.

A lanky fellow with horseteeth, whom Mitch by now recognized as the *Clarion's* labor expert, paused on the way out and winked delightedly at George Price. "At last we're getting the truth," he chortled.

Price was quick on his come-back. "It can't be the truth," he said, "if it gets into the *Clarion*."

Sobol was explaining to Alonzo: "I know that punk Lindeman. He was always sucking around. That stinking sheet of his was printing a full-page ad for Consolidated twice a week. They ran all those back-to-work ads. This punk got a ten-dollar raise."

"How about asking him about that?" Alonzo suggested to Sam Eisen.

"Yah, but I'll tell you"—Sam and the other lawyer seemed in agreement—"why take it seriously? This is Corcoran's show, let him make a fool of himself. The more opposition we give him, the more it'll look like a victory when that stooge jury hands in their verdict."

From then on, Mitch noticed, Sam and the other attorney confined themselves to heckling Corcoran, rarely questioning facts. It worried him, to see them let the wildest statements go undisputed, particularly as Dr. Whalen had appeared, and he foresaw medical testimony in some way aimed to invalidate his own.

Corcoran was busily pursuing his red conspiracy now. In

rapid succession he had called relatives of the deceased. They took the stand, some bewildered, some stolid, some subdued; they spoke in foreign English; a woman named Wyznowieki, who, at every question, kept begging that he call her daughters —"they are American, they can talk"—admitted that her husband, the dead Ladislas, had often brought out to the house a young man, Pete Vikulik. "He come to see my girl, too, but now he don't come no more."

Did she know that this Pete Vikulik was a Communist?

Pete? No, she didn't know nothing. "Maybe, please, you ask it my girls—they can talk American good——"

Did she know that her husband was a Communist?

"Ladislas? No, he got no time for that, he is always busy, by the house, we have a farm, we have all the time work——"

Could she swear her husband was not a Communist?

She looked at him, frightened, mute. "All right, Mrs. Wyzowaksky, that is all," and still she sat there, bewildered, till a bailiff half-shoved her off the chair.

Then Corcoran proved that the Mexican, Jesus Hernandez, was not an American citizen, and had once been deported from the country, and had re-entered illegally.

"Marie Baumann," the clerk called. A sallow-faced woman, with lifeless blond hair, took the chair. This was easy sailing for Corcoran.

Yes, she admitted, her deceased husband had been a member of the Communist Party at the time of his death. In Germany too he had been an active member of the Communist Party.

And had the Baumann family been on relief?

Yes, she admitted. After they had lost their home, they had received home relief.

And what was her husband doing out there, on the Fourth?

"He went there to sell *Daily Workers*," she said. With each answer, she looked directly at Corcoran; then she would lower her eyes, in repose.

Was her husband a veteran of the World War, a trained soldier?

"He was conscripted in the war," she said, "but he was not a good soldier; my husband believed in peace."

"A Communist, and he believed in peace?"

"Yes," she said.

The laugh was unsuccessful. Corcoran dismissed her.

A letter from the detective bureau was read into the record, stating that no relatives of the deceased, Stanley Dombrowsky, had been found, and that there was evidence that said deceased had been a member of the Communist Party.

"Pauline Lindstrom," the coroner called.

George Price came over and whispered to Eisen. "Aren't you even going to make them put on the old man? If they refuse you the right to put on witnesses, we'd play it up." Sam shook his head.

To Pauline, Corcoran spoke in a gentle, sympathetic tone, as if regretful of disturbing the young widow in her sorrow; and yet his whole bearing suggested an even greater regret, that so fine a young woman should, perhaps, have been deceived in the character of her husband.

She had lived with her husband in the home of her husband's parents, had she not? And were there not strangers often congregating at this home?

"I don't know what you mean by strangers. They were our friends."

But had not their home become a meeting place, so to speak?

"Some of the men from the mills used to come there, about the union."

Was she present at the meetings?

No, not often.

[504]

Then she could not say for certain that union matters were the only matters discussed?

Well, maybe they talked about the races sometimes, and baseball.

"Very subversive," Sam Eisen cut in, at Corcoran's expense.

Where were these meetings held?

"In the basement," she said.

"And did Mr. Sobol come to many of those meetings?"

"Certainly, lots, he was the union organizer."

But even before the union drive, was it not a fact that Mr. Sobol had spent a great deal of time at the Lindstrom home?

Sure. They were planning to organize a union then.

Did she know that Mr. Sobol was a Communist?

Sobol's lips moved in a slight smile. No, Pauline said, she didn't know if he was a Communist or not.

Had she heard talk of his being a Communist?

Yes, she had heard such talk but she never paid any attention to it one way or another.

Had she ever discussed it with her late husband?

Yes, she and Gus had talked about people saying Frank was a Communist, but Gus said if he was that was his own business.

Gus did not object to the idea of a Communist coming to their home?

"I have even heard of people who didn't object to the idea of an assistant state's attorney coming to their home," Sam Eisen interjected.

"Yes," Corcoran snapped, "and I have heard of people who breed skunks and Communist shysters in their cellars."

"Boys, we are trying to conduct an inquest here," the coroner said mildly, without turning his gaze from the window.

"I would like to know when the inquest is going to begin!" Sam Eisen shouted. "All we have had so far is inquisition."

"Maybe that's just what we need," Corcoran retorted, leaving the defense gasping. He turned again to Pauline. "Now, Mrs. Lindstrom, did you ever hear your husband discussing the government, or politics, with Mr. Sobol?"

Eisen flung his arm over the back of his chair and laughed. "How about the weather, did you ever hear them discussing the weather?"

"Answer the question," Corcoran insisted.

"This is preposterous," the elder C.I.O. lawyer declared. "Hearsay and generalities! What sort of evidence is that?"

"We aren't sticking to any rules of evidence," the coroner said. "Just trying to find a few things out."

"We're just following those rules they have in Washington," Corcoran sneered gleefully. "These are the Senate committee rules." He turned on Pauline again. "Did you ever hear them discussing the government?"

"Sure, lots of times," she said. "They used to sit around and talk."

"Who?"

"Well, Frank Sobol and our folks, Cass Morrison and——"

"Pete Vikulik?"

"Sure, Pete used to come sometimes."

"And what did they say about the government?"

"Well, my husband was for Roosevelt because Roosevelt is for the workingman and made the law so they could organize their union."

"He was for Roosevelt, eh? . . . Did you ever hear Sobol discussing Russia?"

"Yes, they talked about Russia sometimes."

"What did they say?"

"Well, Frank used to say they had a good government, for the people over there, and things like that."

"Did your husband agree with him?"

"Well, Gus used to say maybe that was right but why were

they always having those trials and shooting their own people? Gus said there was something fishy about those trials."

"It's too bad he isn't here," Sam said, earnestly. "He'd learn something about fishy trials. Here they shoot them first and try them afterward."

"If you don't like this country, why don't you go where you like it?" Corcoran roared at Sam.

"I like it fine!" Sam Eisen cried. "I'm just going to make damn sure it doesn't fall into the hands of people like you."

"Boys, boys," said the coroner peevishly.

"Mrs. Lindstrom," Corcoran resumed gently, "maybe your husband was just an innocent victim who got into bad company, but it makes a pretty bad picture, doesn't it, agitators and radicals coming to your house and holding secret meetings in the basement, coming there before the regular union meetings—they did that, didn't they—to hold their fraction meetings and figure out how to dupe the members——"

"I don't know anything about that, and Gus wasn't anybody's —dupe—you can't say that! just because he was a worker in the mill, he was no dummy."

"I made no such suggestion," Corcoran said smoothly. "But, Mrs. Lindstrom, your husband was killed in a very unfortunate affair, and we are trying to find out who was responsible, and punish them, and I am sure you will help us do that."

Pauline Lindstrom stiffened, her hands gripping the sides of the chair; her face grayed. Mitch Wilner had the immediate impression that he was watching a shock, like anaphylactic shock. He was on the point of interrupting the hearing to declare the woman in no condition to continue testifying; but she had risen above her shock, and was shouting, dry-voiced, at Corcoran: "Oh, I don't care what you find out or who you punish, is that going to bring Gus back? Is that going to help me feed his kids? . . . You took my nail-file out of my purse," she

[507]

laughed hysterically, hoarsely, in her throat, "you thought maybe I'd try to put the eyes out of one of your cops for killing my husband! You know who murdered him and all those men! You don't have to ask any further. Oh, let me go!" She rushed from the stand. Old Joe Lamper sat her down and quieted her.

The coroner called Frank Sobol.

There ensued an hour of struggle that was like a wrestling-match, in which the aggressive fighter circles and circles his opponent, making sudden rushes, seeking a hold, while the opponent with irritating calm takes care always to keep his face toward the circling adversary, never to leave a part of himself exposed.

Sobol confined his answers to courteous monosyllables, so far as possible. Mitch found himself attempting to determine in his own mind at exactly which points the witness found it necessary and justifiable to lie. He had been born in San Francisco; birth records destroyed in the earthquake. "That quake was very convenient for a lot of foreign comrades, wasn't it?" Corcoran sneered, but Sobol calmly answered: "I don't know." Corcoran flashed the records of several arrests, in 1930 and 1931, in Ohio, of one Frank Soboloff.

Yes, Sobol admitted he had often been arrested for distributing handbills, picketing; and, yes, he had changed his name from Soboloff to Sobol. "Why?" "I like it better this way." Yes, he had been an organizer for the United Steel and Metal Workers. Wasn't that a Communist-controlled union? Not to his knowledge. Didn't he receive orders from the Communist Party in 1935 to disband the United Steel and Metal Workers and have the members join the S.W.O.C.? No, he received orders from no one. The union voted to disband when it became apparent the S.W.O.C. would start an organization drive, for the men in the United did not wish to foster dual unionism, he explained. Did he know Al Howard, a Negro organizer for the Commu-

[508]

nist Party? He knew a Mr. Howard who was an organizer for the C.I.O., but had no impression that Mr. Howard was or might be a Communist. Had he ever been to Russia? No.

Until finally, after pounding and pounding and stating his question a dozen different ways, Corcoran demanded directly: Was he a member of the Communist Party? Had he ever been a member of the Communist Party? To all of which Sobol answered, coolly: No.

If, as he thought was the case here, a man had to lie to protect what he believed in, then how could one determine truth? Mitch was not troubled at the possible fact of a lie, but at the necessity for it; he could imagine that in a few years, if things kept progressing in the directions already noticeable, the record of an affirmative answer by Sobol here today might mean his death then. And more; such a lie would seem justifiable in the name of justice, for, if a man were permitted justice, it would be no crime to admit he was a Communist. And yet something in Mitch wished that this would be put to the test, that once and for all Communists would openly say they were Communists and what of it?

Corcoran was badgering Sobol now, about his precise activity right after the march started. Wasn't it a fact that he had attempted to drive to the other side of the slip, where he was to take charge of the "landing party"? Wasn't it a fact that police had stopped his car and that the plans for the landing party had only then been abandoned?

No, Sobol said. He had driven Mr. Szutak to the regional headquarters in Steel Harbor and had been there when someone phoned, telling of the massacre; whereupon he had rushed back to Guzman's.

Was he at present out on bail?

"Yes," Sobol said.

What was he charged with?

[509]

"Conspiracy to commit an illegal act."

"The punishment," Corcoran announced ominously, "is one to twenty-five years."

"I am aware of that," said Frank Sobol.

"He is not being tried for it here," Eisen interposed.

"Boys, let's have some lunch," the coroner said.

There was only one restaurant near by, the corner place famous for its last meals for condemned; it was jammed, noisy, as convivial as a onetime speakeasy. At a large round table Corcoran and his group were established; among them Mitch noticed Dr. Whalen and the *Clarion* reporter. Corcoran was examining the headlines of the early afternoon papers. "Strikers Fired First, Says Reporter." "Girl Saw Guns at Strikers' Headquarters."

Sam Eisen paused at Corcoran's table. "Doing pretty good for yourself, Cork," Sam said, indicating the headlines.

"You're not doing so bad either with those crappy cracks of yours," Corcoran replied with professional tolerance, showing where the story quoted some of Sam Eisen's heckling remarks, such as the one about inviting state's attorneys to one's home.

"Cork, will you put Dr. Wilner on next after lunch?" Sam requested. "He has to get back to his practice."

"Sure, Doctor." Corcoran looked up at Mitch, and grinned. Then he agreed with Sam to try to wind up in one more day. "I've got that damned ax murder around my neck. How many witnesses you calling?"

"I'm not calling any witnesses," Sam said. "I'm saving them for the trial."

"Oh, so there's going to be a trial?" Corcoran eyed him speculatively.

"Is there?" Sam countered.

"I want to talk to you about that," Corcoran said.

Sam hesitated, then said: "Okay. When?"

[5 1 0]

Corcoran's manner became almost jovial. "Anytime. Anytime, Sam! After tomorrow."

Mitch followed Eisen toward a booth, where Gillespie, Al Nees, Sobol, and the elderly lawyer, now introduced as Philip Garvey, were eating.

Sobol was discussing the police evidence. "If this is all they got, we haven't anything to worry about."

"That reporter's stuff wouldn't stand up for a minute before a jury," Sam said. "All they've got is Art's affidavit about the marines."

"Maybe he was crazy when he signed it," Sobol suggested. "He was beat up on the head and he had crazy spells a long time after."

Sam Eisen and the elderly lawyer exchanged glances. Sam asked Sobol: "Do you think he'll testify to that?"

"That sonofabitch, he'd better," said Frank.

"Corcoran wants to make a deal," Sam reported. "But I'll take it before a jury any day."

The elderly lawyer wearily cut at his meat. "If we go to trial, that means two hundred thousand dollars in bail money tied up another three months at least. And the expense of the long trial. A really heavy expense."

The men looked worried. Mitch recalled a remark Gaul had made lately, about drastic cuts in organizers' salaries—to half; and several men had been dropped. Dues collections were down to almost nothing. The thousands of men who had signed cards and paid their initial dollar had never been integrated into the union, never become active, attending members. Even the Gary local, where there was a contract with the mill, was shot to pieces, demoralized by the strike in the Harbor.

"But if we go to trial and win, we'll have a cinch on the damage suits," Sam Eisen pointed out.

"In Chicago? . . . What kind of a deal does he offer?"

Sam said it would most likely be the usual thing. A few convictions at nominal fines so the police couldn't be sued for false arrest. "That would knock hell out of the civil damages. We could never recover a dime on the dead or injured."

The elder lawyer said a guilty plea in the criminal court would make the civil suits more difficult of course, but at least the cases of the dead would not be affected since dead men couldn't be convicted of crime; besides, their families might sue the company instead of the police.

"What about the disabled?" Sam insisted. "Take a man like Lindstrom. He ought to get a pension for that eye."

Garvey pondered. Perhaps they wouldn't all have to be pleaded guilty, he suggested.

"You don't know these Chicago bastards," Sam said. "If you have to make a deal with them, you might as well make up your mind you won't get a thing."

"I'm willing to fight it out as far as my case is concerned," Sobol offered.

At this Sam Eisen shook his head, worried. "We would be taking a hell of a chance, on you. Look at these papers, already. They'd work it up to another Haymarket case."

"They can't hang me, that's a cinch."

"Yah. But twenty-five years is no joke. Do you want to be another Tom Mooney?"

Sobol was silent.

Mitch felt an intruder. He wished they had not discussed the deal in his presence. And then he realized, this wish came not from disapproval, but from a reluctance in himself to know about the thing, a desire still to preserve an illusion. Only now he was not clear as to which illusion he wished preserved: the illusion of the workability of the democratic system of justice, or the illusion about idealism in radicals. If Eisen and his crowd would compromise with the city hall on this issue, were they not in a sense selling out the strikers in order to protect their own clique? Even if from a witch hunt? Or were they in a larger sense protecting the union, too? He saw, now, the dilemma in which the revolutionist might find himself, the type of situation in which it might be charged that he gave allegiance first to his revolutionary organization, and only secondly to the union in which he was active.

As they passed Corcoran's table on the way out, the Irishman eyed Sam archly. "Well, how about it, Sam?"

"I don't know," Sam said. "I don't see what we've got to gain."

"No?" Corcoran glanced significantly at Sobol, who had passed on. Then, as to a man who is foolishly passing up a bargain offer: "Okay, boy. It's your funeral." And as an afterthought: "I'll call the doc first thing." Mitch thought he caught an innuendo there. The deal is off, the gloves are off.

He was placed on the stand as soon as the session began. Corcoran, armed with a thick folder, worked over his entire record, in school, in County, cited every paper he had published. "I notice," Corcoran said, "that all your work has centered around the specialty of allergy; is that correct, Doctor?"

"I have specialized in allergy and anaphylaxis."

"Would that make you an expert on gunshot wounds?"

Mitch looked to Eisen for help.

"Answer yes or no."

"Expert is not a scientific term," Mitch said. "I have recently made some studies and had experience which I believe gives me special knowledge of gunshot wounds."

Had he ever done post-mortems on gunshot cases? Would he put himself in the class of a coroner's physician who had handled

[5 1 3]

thousands of such cases? Had he, personally, treated bullet wounds surgically?

Mitch realized his replies must sound like evasions. Waving a sheaf of coroner's reports at him, Corcoran demanded: "Now, Dr. Wilner, you have stated that seven of these wounds were in the back, and three in the side?"

"That is correct," said Mitch.

"We'll take one that you ought to know about," Corcoran said. "Take the case of Gus Lindstrom. Was that a rear or a front wound?"

"Rear," Mitch stated, describing the wound of entrance and the wound of exit.

"What makes you so positive it wasn't the other way around? I don't see anything here on the coroner's report indicating which was which."

Again, Mitch explained that usually the entrance wound was about half a centimeter in diameter, and indented, while the wound of exit was three times as large. Besides, the wounded man himself had told him he was hit from behind.

"Okay. Will you step down a minute?" Corcoran called: "Dr. Whalen."

The 117th Street hospital surgeon testified that in thirty years, he had treated hundreds of gunshot wounds, that he had at one time been on the coroner's staff and performed autopsies.

"Dr. Whalen, on July 4, did you see an operation performed on Gus Lindstrom?"

"I did."

"Did you examine the patient afterward?"

"I did."

"Would you say the bullet entered from front or back?"

"It was impossible to tell. Both wounds can be quite similar, as is often the case, in my experience of such wounds. The patient said he didn't know what hit him. As it couldn't be

[5 1 4]

stated with accuracy, I made no finding of the direction of the wound."

"It could not be stated with accuracy?"

"No."

Mitch felt himself flushing. He must look awfully young beside that imposing windbag. "Make them call Dr. Siegal, he operated Lindstrom," he whispered fiercely to Sam Eisen. Sam made a calming gesture.

"Dr. Wilner, will you take the stand again? I wasn't through with you."

Brushing by Dr. Whalen, who eyed him with kindly, elderly knowingness, Mitch returned to the witness chair. Now Corcoran began a detailed grueling on each of the cases. "Take the Dombrowsky case, you call that a rear wound?"

"Yes."

"But as I understand it, the wound was in the forepart of the thigh!"

"It went from the rear, forward."

Corcoran called to the stand Dr. Felix Graham, of the coroner's office. Graham winked to Mitch, took the stand, and testified that he had posted the one, Stanley Dombrowsky. The fatal wound was in the forepart of the thigh.

"The front of the body?"

"Yes."

"Dr. Wilner," Corcoran returned to Mitch, "do you still insist that you, as an allergist, are more of an expert on gunshot wounds than Dr. Whalen, a surgeon, and Dr. Graham, who has handled thousands of cases of this type? Do you dispute their opinions?"

"I said the wound went through the forepart of the thigh but that the angle of the shot was from the rear," Mitch insisted. "You can call them all front wounds if you classify as rear wounds only those that were dead center shots in the back!"

[5 1 5]

"And you can call them all back wounds, no matter what the experts testify, evidently!" Corcoran retorted. "What about Ephraim Law?"

"Rear wound," Mitch said doggedly, of the Negro, the last to die.

"But Dr. Graham's report states that the body showed evidence of two operations and a drain, so that it was impossible to distinguish the wound of entrance," Corcoran cried.

"Ephraim Law told me before he died that he was shot in the back."

"It is certainly fortunate these men all confided in you before they died."

"It is," Mitch said, remembering, as though the corpse had been dragged into the room, the miserably butchered body of that Negro, the botched operations, the infected drain, the long weeks of battle Ephraim Law had put up, and the needless death.

Corcoran asked Dr. Graham for his summary of the ten cases.

"I find four front wounds, five side wounds, and one wound in the back," the coroner's physician reported, with an amused glance at Mitch. He went down the list. The only admitted rear wound was that of Hermann Baumann. "The Communist," Corcoran put in, as if this made it permissible for the man to be shot in the back. Even Ladislas Wyznowieki, shot in the head from behind, was reversed to a frontal classification. And of course rear wounds of the slightest sideward angle were called side wounds.

"I don't care what you call them!" Mitch shouted, aware that he was losing control, but intent on hammering home his point. "The places of these wounds are matters of factual record. I didn't say those were seven wounds in the back, I said they were shots fired from the back! Mark the wounds on a dummy and you'll see which way they came from, all right!"

"We know your weakness for sticking pins in dolls," Corcoran said. "But these are human lives we are dealing with, Dr. Wilner, and we will take the coroner's word, instead of your demonstration on a doll."

"But the coroner's records don't classify the wounds. They tell you where they were. Now Dr. Graham comes in here and calls them all front wounds——"

"He ought to know! He did the autopsies."

"And I am using them. And where they are inconclusive, I take my findings from my own records of these patients. I cannot permit you to slander my reputation by attempting to contradict my testimony without an examination of the facts. I saw Wyznowieki in the morgue. There can be no doubt he was hit from behind."

"Then it is a case of your word against Dr. Graham's and Dr. Whalen's and everybody else's."

"It is a case of the facts against your wishes!" Mitch snapped.

"Dr. Wilner," Corcoran suddenly switched, "how did you happen to be out there that day?"

"I told you. I was driving home from a picnic. My wife wanted to stop at the strike. She said I might be needed."

"You thought you might pick up some business?"

He had difficulty controlling his voice. "If you are trying to insinuate that I——"

"I'm not insinuating anything," Corcoran shouted. "I just want to know why you were there. Whether it was out of sympathy for the strikers or for professional reasons."

"Why not for both?"

"You are sympathetic to the strikers?"

"Why shouldn't I be?"

"Dr. Wilner, isn't it strange that your wife should have known a physician might be needed? Wouldn't you say, if people thought a doctor might be needed, they were intending to start a fight?"

"They might be afraid someone else was going to start a fight."

"Wouldn't you say there were certain plans made in advance, if they even arranged for a doctor to be there?"

"After the way they were beaten up on Friday, they expected only the worst from the Chicago police," Mitch replied. "It turned out they were right."

Corcoran slammed down the folder, in complete exasperation. The prosecutor's shirt was a mass of sweat-spots; he took a gulp of water, then turned on Mitch with fury. "You know all about the Chicago police. You know all about everything, more than all the experts, don't you, Dr. Wilner!" he shouted. "Now, Wilner, Mitchell Wilner, isn't it?"—he seemed suddenly to recollect something.

"Yes. You needn't shout at me. That's my name."

"Has it always been your name?"

"What?" Mitch was too startled to feel immediate insult.

"You say your name is Mitchell Wilner. Were you born in Chicago?"

"Yes."

"What date?"

"February 10, 1904."

Corcoran looked into his folder. "Apparently at that time your name was Moses Wilnowitz," he said. "And your father came from Russia."

Vaguely, Mitch had the impression of Sam Eisen rising, yelling. . . .

He too, stood up. "Are you trying to emphasize the fact that I am Jewish?" he demanded.

"I only asked if your name was originally Moses Wilnowitz."

"I can see no purpose in these questions except to bring out that Dr. Wilner is of Russian-Jewish extraction!" Eisen roared.

[518]

"You have investigated everything he ever did in his life and not been able to find a single point of attack. You failed to break down his medical testimony so you are trying to arouse racial feeling."

"Are you ashamed of being a Jew?" Corcoran demanded of Mitch.

"I am not, I never hid the fact that I was a Jew——"

"Fascist! Race-baiter!" Sam Eisen shouted at Corcoran. "To stoop to bring such issues into this hearing . . . !"

"You are bringing them in yourself!" Corcoran retorted, almost leaping at Sam across the table. "I only asked if his name was Moses——"

Mitch Wilner felt his whole being white-hot; but in an instant he was out of shock, he had control, not of his usual self but of a feverishly accelerated being, with a blazing, pulsating clarity of mind. Corcoran had over-reached but had touched off a streaking flash of truth that had illuminated the whole pattern of the long affair. Now Mitch knew the murders almost as an experience within himself, rather than as events seen objectively.

"My name has been Mitchell Wilner ever since I can remember," he stated as sharply as he could. "Most immigrant Jewish families Americanize their names as they become Americanized. We have no intention of disguising our race. I am a Jew and I am proud of it. I am a born American, but you make me wonder whether I am in America!"

He was conscious that the whole atmosphere of the room had changed. The change could be seen in these big men with their fleshy faces, the cops. Something had happened, a signal word had been uttered. As when people, talking in the presence of children, accidentally utter the grown-up word; an ugliness stands naked in the room, a fact of life is bare. The whole organism of which Jew hatred was part was naked here; this was

[519]

the enemy. And at the same time he knew in himself the straining, hammering pulse of shock; the Jew-word was the agent of this wild reaction.

With lowered voice, Corcoran backed out of the situation he had so carelessly ignited. "I am sure, Dr. Wilner, you will believe me when I say that I did not mean any reflection upon your race by my question. The question was simply a matter of routine. Perhaps we are all super-sensitive on the subject."

Mitch accepted the apology silently. He sat down. "No further questions, Doctor," Corcoran said, his tone edged with irony.

He was in the headlines, all right. "Experts Refute Dr. Wilner." "Coroner Contradicts Dr. Wilner on Shooting in Back." "Doctor Admits Partiality for Strikers." "Autopsy Findings Prove Strikers Not Shot in Back." The only report which treated him decently was Price's, and even there the headline-writer had taken the fervor out of George's story by captioning it: "Doctors Disagree Over Where Front Ends, Back Begins."

There were photographs of himself, of Dr. Whalen, of Dr. Graham, and scores: "Wilner, Strikers, Claim Seven Shot in the Back; Inquest Proves Only One Shot in Back."

The stories quoted Corcoran's allusions to an allergist setting himself up as an expert on gunshot wounds, against older and more experienced men; and then, he read in one paper how Dr. Wilner, contradicted with expert medical evidence by Drs. Graham and Whalen, lost his temper and charged the state's attorney with attempting to arouse racial prejudice, when Mr. Corcoran in a routine inquiry brought out that Wilner's family had changed their name from Wilnowitz. Mitch dropped the sheet, and went into his study.

Sylvia came, a moment later. So far, they had been unable to talk together of the sickening subject. "Look, Mitch, this isn't so bad."

She showed him a box headed "Doctor Calls Corcoran Fascist."

" 'I am a Jew and I am proud of it!' Dr. Wilner cried when the state's attorney, unable to shake Dr. Wilner's testimony that seven of the strikers were shot from behind, started to question Dr. Wilner on personal matters, and for no apparent reason brought out that the Wilner family name had once been Wilnowitz. 'I am an American,' the infuriated physician shouted, 'but you make me wonder whether I am in America at this moment.'

" 'This is America,' Corcoran said, 'and the law does not discredit a witness because he is a Jew or a Negro or a Chinaman. That is what makes America America.'

" 'The thing that makes America America,' replied Dr. Wilner, 'is that people do not ask people what they are in order to prejudice someone else against them.'

"Mr. Corcoran stated that he had no intention of arousing prejudice, but cries of Fascist and race-baiter were heard in the room."

Sylvia said, comfortingly: "At least he didn't get away with it."

"That's just George Price," Mitch reminded her. "And anyway"—why should he have to point this out? she should understand—"the question isn't how much he got away with. The whole thing is that he should even try it!"

"It just shows they're desperate. They'll try anything," she said, "because they know they're in the wrong."

He was startled at the almost complacent way in which she uttered the words. But didn't she understand, she was naming the very core of danger?

[5 2 1]

This time Mitch was no longer apprehensive of how they would take the publicity at the hospital. They did not crowd around him for details. Drs. Fergis and Lewin held a short discussion with him about a case, but avoided the racial subject as if it were one of those instances where a man, through indiscretion, got his private affairs into the papers: the polite thing to do was to abstain from reference to the matter. Dr. Stern, the radical, approached him with a smile of partnership; and he noticed a resentment in himself, he wanted to insist—no, it's not the same with me as it is with you—for he felt that Stern was almost glad when horrors happened in the capitalist world, proud when evil events confirmed his accusations. Mitch did not want to have to get his moral compensation out of a knowing superiority to the society in which he lived, or to have to flee for self-justification into Stern's attitude of non-participation in that society. He didn't feel it right for himself to be grouped with Stern.

Then Dr. Waldauer, the refugee surgeon from Berlin, sought him out, meeting him alone in the locker room, as if through conspiracy. In Dr. Waldauer's eyes was that vibrant, peculiar expression he had noticed on refugees—an expression at once shrinking and accusatory, it seemed to beg intimacy, and yet to refuse all intimacy in the fear that any human contact contained the seed of betrayal.

"Dr. Wilner," Waldauer began almost formally, "this I see in the papers, is this correct?"

"How do you mean?" Mitch said. "The reports are not all accurate."

"I have seen, in this testimony, they have brought out in the court that you are a Jewish doctor."

"Yes, they did that," Mitch said. At the same moment he felt an unreasonable resentment against the refugee, an impulse to declare this was still not the way it was with them over there.

[5 2 2]

Dr. Waldauer's voice became whispery, incredulous with fear. "Are we really come so far, already, here?" he asked.

Their eyes met, and Mitch could not bear the shame in Waldauer's, a shame he knew to be reflected in his own eyes. "Looks like it," he said huskily.

Waldauer shuffled away, shaking his head, a man frightened and confused.

In mid-morning, Mitch Wilner abandoned all hope of freeing himself from his preoccupation. He could not go on as a human being until he knew how he must act.

Almost aimlessly, he left the hospital; then found himself driving to the court building. All day he listened. The captains and the cops recited their litany against the reds again, but this was not to a sophisticated and jeering audience of Washington liberals; here what they spoke was solemn gospel, and as the stream of phantasmic convictions flowed unchecked, the fear that he had felt while listening to the leaden recital of Captain Wiley increased to practical terror.

And from this, the inquest took flight into realms of what might have seemed amusing fantasy, but that the men who uttered these fantasies were armed with revolvers, and had pulled them out to fire wildly at the images their minds had evoked. One sergeant mounted the stand to testify that the strikers had "come at us and I could see their pupils of their eyes dilated, and I knew they was drugged and like maniacs they would attack us with the wild strength of maniacs."

"You mean they were drugged?"

"Yes, sir," the sergeant stated. "Their leaders passed out marijuana cigarettes to them before the march and they was all smoking marijuana. I picked up lots of butts on the field right after the riot. I used to be on the narcotic squad and I know marijuana."

The papers banner headlined, "Strikers Drugged to Assault Police."

Coming home, with the accumulated horror of the day still beating in his mind, seeing crowds on street corners buying papers and glancing at the headline, "Jury Exonerates Police," remembering Price's explanation of the trick of calling the coroner's witnesses a jury, so that now the headlines had the effect of finality, of an issue settled in court, of deliberate judgment by the people themselves, Mitch Wilner felt in his very muscles the frustration of that whole citizen self, perhaps that most important element in social man, the part of him that acted to achieve a life of order, a community security in justice. Why, if things like this could pass, then the entire foundation of society was insecure. And these hundreds of people, glancing at the announcement of their own betrayal, and turning to the sports pages! He felt an impulse to tear the papers out of their hands, to make them know, somehow to make them know!

The second headline was of Franco's army closing in on Oviedo, where the dynamite-throwing miners, trapped, would have to make their last stand.

At home, he found the Abramsons all come to dinner. Instantly upon entering the house, Mitch sensed that it was a feast of forgiveness toward him; an atmosphere that said, maybe he should never have become tangled up in this mess, but certainly the other side should not have hit below the belt with the anti-Semitic attack.

The kids came rushing toward him to show what Gramma Abramson had brought—Jackie had a toy fiddle, and Judy dragged him into the living-room to show a toy grand piano, actually large enough for her to play upon. At least fifty dollars, he estimated. The Abramson hat business must be doing well.

Jack and Judy gravely arranged themselves like professional concertists, and the old lady sighed with joy.

Jackie wanted to know why the lid of the fiddle couldn't be raised up like the lid of the piano, so you could see what made the music inside.

"Just like his father!" Mrs. Abramson decided. "He has to see the inside of everything."

"Don't worry," Syl joked. "He will. Just wait, tomorrow he'll have the top off! Jackie, darling, be careful, for once; it's a very expensive toy, like a real violin."

It was really almost pleasant, except that he was disturbed by the way they avoided the main topic, like folks avoiding allusion to a recent derangement. Only, after the kids were in bed, Mrs. Abramson herself brought up the subject. She started by referring to the Washington trip. The government ought to pay Mitch for being away from his patients, in the middle of the season. What patients? Sylvia joked. And how were things at the hospital? Mother Abramson asked with concern. She plunged: "How did they take it?"

Sylvia replied for him: How should they take it? Naturally, the doctors could understand what Mitch had been through. Mother Abramson brightened. Yes, she herself had reasoned that the best doctors at Memorial, being mostly Jewish, ought to be proud of Mitch. It was as though he were talking back for all of them, when he told it to that rotten state's attorney. "You told him good!" she said. "That cheap Irishman! Imagine bringing up a thing like that in a trial!"

"Dear, did you see Feldner today? Did he say anything?" Sylvia asked. He detected strain in her voice and was certain she had found some cause for anxiety. And Ora was being strangely quiet, watching the game as if she knew something.

"I didn't see Dr. Feldner," he said. "I wasn't there, most of the day."

"I know," Sylvia said. "I called."

"I was at the inquest."

"Again! Honest, you should make them pay for your time, the city ought to pay for it!"

"I didn't have to be there today," he said. "I went of my own accord."

Sylvia looked at him stonily, worried. Ora relieved the strain by interjecting loudly: "Oh, did you see that stuff about marijuana! Syl, after this, take me to all the strikes. If they pass out marijuana on the picket line I want some too."

Mort said he would prefer hashish. Or he had a better idea, why not give everybody morphine and then there wouldn't be any labor trouble.

Mitch couldn't stand it. Pretending he had to phone about a patient, he escaped into his study. In a moment Sylvia came in. Now her worry was not hidden. "Mitch, didn't Feldner talk to you at all?"

"No. Why should he? This has nothing to do with the hospital."

"You know they have that reception for Dr. Counselman tonight," she reminded him of the visiting British urologist. "We weren't invited."

"I don't especially want to meet him. It's not my field."

"Yes, but Mrs. Feldner always invites us. . . . It's no accident, Mitch."

"I can get along without her ptomaine salad," he said. "I only hope she forgets us permanently." But Sylvia was actually trembling. Being off Mrs. Feldner's list was practically being off the hospital staff.

"If Ora makes any crack about it—" Sylvia said helplessly. "You know the reception was announced in the paper."

He was silent. He couldn't help her at all, just as she couldn't help him, now.

Returning to the living-room with her, Mitch said he had to

[5 2 6]

see a patient, and left. He didn't know exactly where he was going. Perhaps just to sit in his office. Merely being in the car, in motion, was of some help. A car gave a man a sense at once of power, security, and direction. Yes, he was at this moment a scattered atom, incapable of choosing the way he should go, eager for the car, for any force to take initiative away from him, and carry him; yet at the same time the mere necessity of holding the wheel and regulating the mechanism tied him to the use of will. Abstractedly, he wondered whether this was not the essence of man's freedom of will, and of the mechanistic, all-caused world which he conjured up in order to rid himself of the burden of will.

The office would be too lonely. Now he wanted to talk to someone, but as he cast over in his mind the possibilities—Price, or Rawley, or Barbara Macey—he knew how each would view his situation. Perhaps he should drop in on union headquarters, or Mrs. Jugovich's place; but he would feel he needed to offer some excuse for his presence; he had never truly found the bond to those people; he had to admit he was another sort. Like Carl Gaul: undoubtedly that was the failing of Carl as an organizer; the men would never accept him as one of themselves.

Wilner passed through Grant Park, and along a lakeside stretch of drive; lanes of cars were parked there, of young couples necking, he had always thought, but now he noticed that in some of the cars just some man would be sitting alone, looking at the water, at the mast-tips of yachts riding in the harbor. He drew into a slice of space, and sat there, also, one of those men, each of whom like himself must have some incommunicable problem, each sitting in his little box, his car, as in some expansion for his cramped self, a space bounded by himself, but with, because of its possibility of motion, the potentiality of escape.

[5 2 7]

To go somewhere, to do something.

Then Mitch Wilner tried to attack his problem logically. Granted he had come to a realization of the war in the world, and of his need to take active part. Was the same war not evident in his very own field of work? Wasn't the medical profession itself one of the battlefields, most active today? Yes, that would be Sylvia's suggestion: if he must do something, to do it in medicine, take part in the movement toward, not exactly socialization, but toward providing more medical care for more people.

He thought of Rudy Stone, one of his old gang on the West Side and all through medical school; Rudy was doing well in the co-operative clinic he and some of the boys had set up a few years ago. Perhaps Rudy was on the right track; certainly it must be a satisfaction to have pioneered. But after all, wasn't the clinic just another way of getting started in practice and earning a living?

What if he were to join the Committee of Three Hundred, sign the manifesto against the clique that was running the medical society, attend meetings, add his little weight on the side of progress? What would it all amount to? Yes, those were things he should do in the ordinary course of events; those were things, really, like going to vote on Election Day.

And Mitch remembered wryly that he rarely voted, figuring it was a waste of time, a farce, for could a citizen control the selection of candidates? It was always either one gang or another.

Granted, he was to blame for failing to participate in his government and in the government of his profession. But it was no remedy of failure merely to vote in the next elections. He had to find a hope of action.

He thought of one person, Emil, whom it might be good to be with, tonight. Yes, Emil had found the front of action.

Unconsciously, responding only to a sense that he had come to the terminal of his thoughts, Mitch Wilner started the car, drew away from the lake, and pointed it south.

Now as he drove he was filled with fear, a kind of physical fear, and even pity for himself for a decision he had had to make. He could picture himself taking leave of Sylvia and the kids; he could picture himself swaying in some ambulance on a pitch-dark shell-holed road, going to perform candle-light sutures in a tent behind the lines. He had heard nurses and doctors, returned from Spain, describe such experiences at meetings sponsored by the Medical Bureau, and always he knew that every medical man in the audience, like himself, was touched by a guilt, a feeling that he too should be over there doing just what these speakers had done; and always after the lecture came the whispered debate with Sylvia as to how much they could donate to the collection—five dollars? ten?—to buy back a man's conscience.

Rationalization came soon enough, as one reached the street, as one met friends. After all, not all were needed over there. Let those who were more purely convinced, who were perhaps Communists, let them go. It was equally important to create sympathy here at home, and to send funds.

But now the need seemed to be upon him, to find a pure action for himself. He even reflected: there was a completion in having children; if a man were killed, what special thing he might have for the world would not be lost; his continuity was assured. He was free to go. And then he realized he had no right to dramatize himself, unless he were surely going.

Mitch had driven the car to the Harbor. He passed Curly's place, and glimpsed a row of men at the bar; but, much as he needed companionship, he could not fix on anyone, he shrank from specific contact.

He parked a little farther up the street, got out, and walked along. Passing the tavern again Mitch identified Jock Kiley, Mike Sisto at the bar, but went on.

He went into the tavern on the next corner, sat at the far end of the bar, and ordered a beer. The same sort of men were in the place, but none he knew; a group were discussing parlays.

An allergist would not be of much use in Spain. But what about immunology? Once a Dr. Coleman, coming through on a speaking tour for Spanish relief, had got down to shoptalk with a group of physicians, after his lecture at some North Shore home Syl had been anxious to attend; and then Coleman had told some pretty bad stuff—lots of typhoid, why, the hospitals were choked with sick rather than with wounded; jaundice, dysentery, and stuff. They'd need him all right.

Even if he went for a little while. Now would be the best time to go, for his practice was disorganized as a result of the weeks he had put on this case. And the unnamed strain at home. Perhaps an absence would bring him clarity of mind; the trouble was in himself, not in Sylvia.

"Remember me, Doctor," a fellow said, mounting the stool beside him. It was Braden, that cop who had broken down with shame before the senators.

"Hello," Mitch said.

"I saw you up there in the inquest today," Braden said. "Yesterday too when they had you on the stand."

"Oh," Mitch said.

"Have another beer, Doctor?" Braden offered.

"All right. Thanks."

"You don't live around here do you, Doctor?"

"No. I come out here sometimes, to see patients."

"I lived here most of my life. They got us moving now. Pestered the life out of my wife and kids, kids couldn't go out on the street without these Polack punks yelling lousy names

[5 3 0]

at them. My kids always getting into fights. So we're moving."

"That's too bad," Mitch said.

"You was there that time I came into Curly's, that tavern over there," Braden continued, in a tone more morose than aggrieved. "I used to go in there for a shot every day, coming home."

"Well, I suppose men get terribly sensitive in a condition like this," Mitch said.

"I don't hold any hard feelings, I can see how it is," Braden stated. He drank half of his glass of beer. "Look here, Doctor. I'm going to show you something." He pulled out his wallet, extracted a postcard, and handed it to Mitch.

In awkward lettering were the words:

"What for you kill Stanley Dombrowsky?"

Mitch felt the man watching his face intently. "Where did you get this?" he asked.

"That come to my house. My wife, she was scared sick. . . . That's interference with an officer in performance of his duty," Braden declared. "Whoever done that might get themselves in a hell of a lot of trouble."

Mitch handed the card back. "It's probably some crank," he said.

"They were going to spring these at the inquest," Braden informed him. "But then I guess Corcoran figured it would be too much of a warning to these people. If there's a conspiracy trial, that's where they'll spring it."

"Have you any idea who might have sent it?"

"I checked up with the other boys. The way I figure, every officer whose name and address was in the paper, in the list of injured, that's what they used to send these out. Outside of that list they never could of got our home addresses, they don't give out police addresses."

"Then you are not the only one who got one of these?"

"No. Some of the other boys got them too." He put the card away. "Dombrowsky, that was that Communist."

"They claimed he was, but never proved it," Mitch said. "I asked some of the people where he boarded. They said Dombrowsky was just a dumb Polack, never had anything to do with that kind of stuff."

Braden looked at him, directly. "Doctor, are you one of them people, do you believe in that stuff, radicals?"

"I'm not a Communist, if that's what you want to know."

"I think you're a square-shooter, Doc. I studied you up there on the stand and I got nothing against the Jews; that was no good that stuff Corcoran pulled. That smelled. That's why I figured I could talk to you." Mitch Wilner saw now that the policeman was deeply troubled.

"Who would do this," Braden said, "if not those Communists trying to terrorize me?"

"You don't feel you killed Dombrowsky, do you?" Mitch asked.

"No. I didn't kill anybody. Look, Doc, this is between you and me." The pain was like spears of light, in the man's eyes. "I didn't admit this anyplace. My own wife don't know it—I shot off my gun there, on the field. I emptied it."

"Did someone order you to fire?" Mitch asked.

"No, that's a fact, Doctor, there was no order to fire. I'm not bulling you. I'm talking to you as one man to another because I think you got no interest in this thing outside of you want to do what's right."

Mitch nodded. He felt immeasurably better. "I see," he said. "In the excitement, like that, when one fired, you all fired."

"Yah, it was like that. You lose your head. We were scared those strikers were really wild, Doc."

"Then maybe the first person who fired started the stampede."

"The guy that did it might not even know himself that he was the one. Hell, Doc, one of those company dicks might have shot off his gun. Somebody might have shot off a firecracker. But, Doc, why blame it on the first guy? We didn't all have to fire because we heard a shot. We should of been able to hold fire, no matter what happened. Doc, I'm asking myself, didn't I want to shoot at those people?"

"Did you?"

"They had us scared. They worked on us all week." He lifted his eyes again. "Doctor, you think I ought to quit the force?"

"I can't judge anything like that," Mitch said. But why should the man quit, when he was just learning his work?

Braden went on: "Everybody makes a mistake sometime. I was thinking, suppose it happens to a doctor, he makes a mistake, and a patient dies . . ." Mitch looked at the man swiftly, but there was no hint of guile.

"It happens," Mitch said. "Some quit, I guess. If they are scared they might do it again. It's not so simple a thing. The main thing is to know what is right, and what is wrong."

"I could have refused to have gone out there." The policeman brooded. "Some of the boys refused." He shook his head. "I figured that was running away."

"You quit," Mitch said, realizing that in seeing for others, a man sometimes comes to understand himself, "only if you are convinced the setup is such that you can't possibly work right, that you can do more good by quitting than by sticking to it."

Braden eyed him with slow-rising, uncertain relief. "They picked the worst ones to show up in Washington," he said. "We ain't all like Gorcey. Though I guess I didn't make such a good showing myself."

"What would happen if they sent you out there again?" Mitch asked.

Braden took a long time to answer. He was evidently trying to

[5 3 3]

be completely honest. "It was the way they had us sore and scared," he said. "Maybe more of the boys wouldn't go. Or they'd have to handle it different. But I can't say it wouldn't happen again, Doctor," he admitted sorrowfully. "The way things are, it might happen even worse." They sat side by side staring at their beer glasses as at finite truth. Then Braden, sighing, gathered up his change, and lumbered out.

The few beers had stimulated Mitch; and now all his misgivings were sharpened. "It might happen even worse. . . ." For, certainly, what was changed? Braden's remorse, and even the remorse of all the police, if there were that many sensitive men among them, could not alter the way things were. "They had us scared . . ." and suddenly he saw the whole thing deliberate and clear:

Chicago, then Ironville, then Mahoning, the same pattern of slaughter. In this night, with his entire psyche still quivering from that last question, wasn't your name Moses, it seemed to Wilner that the entire world was laden with conspiracy, that fools like himself and maybe earnest men like Braden were the greatest laugh to the Gorceys and the Corcorans and Ford dealers and colonels in the Legion and Martha Cross and Speer. The general conspiracy was clear; what did it matter who pulled a trigger? Why seek for the finite carrier, the final louse, when as with yellow fever it was only necessary to clean up the stagnating pools, the generative morasses?

Yet something in him as ever demanded the pinning down, the specific, the detonator.

Driving again, but unready for home, and being south, he thought of dropping in on Barbara.

The door buzzed open to his ringing; and, as that other time, she came out into the hall to see who was her visitor. She was pajama-clad. "Well, hello, stranger." Barbara took his hand and

[5 3 4]

led him in; the wall-bed was down. "I was in bed already. Yes, alone, damn it. Carl has deserted me since Sobol got him shifted to North Chicago. God, that was a noble speech you made, Mitch; you certainly didn't let him get away with anything! Imagine, coming right out like that! Have a drink?"

He let her bring out some beer. "But that's what I've been wondering," he mused. "It couldn't have been unintentional. Can't you find out through that Martha of yours? Is Corcoran hooked up somewhere in any way?"

"But, honey," she said, "they don't have to belong to anything; they think that way and act that way already."

He repeated to her, how there must be some link, Chicago, then Ironville, then Mahoning. . . .

"But sure. The company. Consolidated. What more link do you want!"

"But Martha and her crowd, didn't you find out any more about them?"

She shook her head. "I guess that's all there is."

"Why don't you expose her, then, if you think you've got all you can get?"

"George Price wants to write some articles exposing her. He wants me to give him the dope."

"Well . . . ?"

"I don't know. I've gotten to know her so well; in a crazy way she's like a friend. She's just got religion, that's all. It seems like exposing—some poor suffering imbecile."

"That goes around killing people with hatchets, because he doesn't like the shape of their noses."

"Oh, sure, I'll do it all right," she agreed unenthusiastically. "I mean if George can keep me out of it some way."

"Then you don't think they engineered those things?"

"Martha? No. Mitch dear, she just isn't important enough. The company can get its own hatchet men."

"But suppose they hired them from these organizations?"

"The shirters? They probably did. Naturally, they'd give such folk preference."

"Then it's here. It's all here complete."

She nodded gravely, and her eyes widened as if she hadn't quite realized the fact before. "Yes. It's here. But you can't put your finger on it yet. It's all loose. Exposing Martha won't do much good because there's always the Bund and Deatherage and Coughlin and Gerald Smith and Winrod . . ."

Like the pneumonias, the thought occurred to him. Not one variety of germ, but thirty, forty. And each required a specific serum. He shuddered at the safety he had felt in the idea that in America there was no single leader, no single organization expanding Fascism. Why, this was worse, because it took a hundred different names, it had a hundred different varieties; if one was exposed, the others remained and the ferment of them grew. They all fed on the same broth, and they would all invade the same organs, yes, as here they had invaded labor.

"She took me to a Bund picnic Sunday," Barbara confided, recovering something of her excited, adventurous manner. "I met Fritz Kuhn. He was real chummy. And she's written to Ford for an interview; she's going to ask him for a hundred thousand dollars, to expand the Volunteers."

"But don't you think it's time to do something?"

"I'm giving all the dope to George; he's going to write it up as if he got it out of me by pretending to be sympathetic to the organization. He says if he doesn't do it that way I might get bumped off. Anyhow his articles ought to put the kibosh on the Volunteers," she said, almost regretfully. She smiled, a personal smile, at him. "You're all disturbed. Don't let it get you down."

"I'm getting to feel, like Emil, that the only real thing a man

[5 3 6]

can do is go to the front where he can take a pot shot at them."

She squeezed his hand. He wondered if he had said that to create an intimacy between them. Then, staring at him, she cried: "Mitch, you aren't really thinking of going?"

He sensed himself a fool, but said: "I might," solemnly.

"What about Sylvia, and the children?"

He was silent, as if to say, such things had to be. "If I could do anything, I'd go," she said. "Maybe I could be a nurse? After all, look at the experience I had, on the Fourth."

But her wanting to go was already invading him, cheapening the plan with the color of adventure. Unfair to her, because she did risk herself, she did offer herself, she did work. Yet he could not help feeling Barbara's main drive was a lust for excitement. Even though she was on the right side.

She was studying him. "You're a strange man, Mitch," she said, her mouth rising just a shade, at one end, in that almost pathetic smile so characteristic of her. "I suppose one never understands a Jew." She leaned to him and kissed him fully, almost solemnly; then drew away as if to study the effect on him, and on herself. Not with passion, but for the first time with an unreserved friendship, he liked the girl, for now she was all the more pathetic, a confessed kid. Whether they got into bed or not, he would like her from now on. It was some weeks since he and Sylvia had made love.

"Friends?" Barbara said, and squeezed his hand.

"Okay," he said, with a nervous laugh. And all the time there was a kind of dismay in him, a sinking of the whole elation he had been building in himself, to free himself, in kidding himself about going to Spain. That was what kids like Barbara might do.

As they sat there, letting the moment draw them where it might, the phone rang. Smiling back at him, she answered. "Oh, hello. Yes, darling . . ." He gathered it was George Price. Kind

[5 3 7]

of late to call. Feeling he had been altogether silly, Mitch arose, but she waved to him to stay. "He just wants to come up and finish on that stuff about Martha. Stick around."

Yes, probably that was really all George was coming for. But this wasn't his kind of life. Mitch shook his head. She kissed him again, at the door, and pressed her body to him, saying: "You're a darling."

He wanted to sleep anywhere but home, not to go home at all. But in the end it would be harder to explain the state of mind that kept him away than to endure the familiarity. What was it he felt anyway? he asked himself. An unnamable shame. Perhaps a shame for the world, become so powerful that he dreaded to look into the eyes of any other human creature, even his own wife.

It was after one, late for him, when Mitch Wilner reached the house; and though he sensed that Sylvia was lying awake waiting, he went quietly into his study, to sleep there, with the pretense of not having wanted to awaken her when he came in late.

In the morning the kids were subdued at breakfast and Syl was sharp with Judy, who burbled in her milk. Judy began to whimper.

"Dear," Sylvia said, when the maid had gone into the kitchen, "you didn't have a call last night, did you? You just wanted to get away."

"No. I didn't have a call," he admitted.

"I'm sorry; I guess I shouldn't have asked the folks over." She was trying so hard to reach him; perhaps Syl was the one he could talk to. "What did you do, go to a movie?" She attempted lightness.

"No. To a bar." He might tell her about meeting Braden, and how the policeman was remorseful. But all the time, sitting

[538]

in this comfort with the maid bringing in the eggs scrambled to the perfect degree of loose-firm, he remembered his half-resolve to test himself with the utmost deed—Spain. If he just said that to her now—What if I should go to Spain for a while?—it would sound like stupid bravado. He couldn't speak.

His office hour was about over; there had been very few patients. The girl called to say his wife had come in. Mitch arose to meet her at the door, though usually he just kept on with whatever he was doing when Syl arrived. He noticed she made an impression of a remarkedly well-groomed woman, as he sometimes noticed of a new patient entering. She sat down just like a patient at a consultation and said: "Mitch, I know you're upset, but please, dear, let's try to talk it out. It means so much to me."

He looked out the window; it gave upon the yellow brick, almost windowless wall of a skyscraper.

"Is it anything about me?" she asked.

"No," he said. "No, that has nothing to do with it."

"It's this thing about the strike, still?"

"I don't know. It isn't that so much as . . ."

"Dear," she said, "I hope you won't be angry. I talked to Rawley about you this morning."

He flushed.

"Mitch," Sylvia went on, "remember that first research you did on anaphylaxis? You once told me the story of old Dr. Meyerson and how the first time he knew what it was was when he was injecting a little kid and it turned out she was sensitive to horse-serum and he started running to the hospital with her and she died right in his arms? And he wanted to quit medicine right then and there because he felt so helpless?"

He remembered the cop last night.

But he resented her speech; moralizing, as if for the kids.

[539]

"But then when you got into studying and analyzing anaphylaxis you thought maybe if enough research was done——"

"But it never was," he said.

"Look, dear, will you do me a favor, will you read a book?"

"What book?"

"Rawley gave me a book he said you ought to read. It was pretty heavy, I left it in the reception room." It was a huge tome, a bound thesis, over a thousand typewritten pages. The title was *Violence in Strike Situations in Chicago*. The name of the author seemed familiar. Victor Fuchs.

"Rawley said you met him in Washington," Sylvia said. "He's with the labor board now. In fact he is supposed to come here to take charge of the Consolidated case. I thought it might be nice to have him to dinner. I think he's a West-Sider but he was a little after our time at school."

It seemed that from the day the Chicago police force began, the pattern began. Or rather it was then that Chicago took up a pattern that reached back through centuries into other cities and other lands. Mitch Wilner, alone in his office that evening, his feet on his desk, and the heavy volume balanced across his thighs, read the monotonous records but with the same excitement as he got from watching slide after similar slide under a microscope when he was in search of the determining single factor.

In 1877 the pattern appeared in Chicago, with a strike of railroad men. . . . "The mob fled pellmell before the bluecoats, who fired a perfect hailstorm of bullets into the retreating rabble, and hammered the heads and shoulders of the lagging ones with their batons and revolver stocks." The police "threw hand grenades into the group"; twelve were killed then and there, three more fatally wounded, and fifty seriously wounded.

An explanation offered at the time was that the police force

[5 4 0]

was small and frightened of the mob, which had gathered at the Sixteenth Street viaduct when strikebreakers and office workers tried to run the trains.

Ten years later, in the dispassionate text of the graduate student in sociology, the pattern was repeated. This time the scene was the McCormick reaper plant. A crowd gathered to prevent strikebreakers from entering the plant. And the papers said: "The crowd broke and scattered over the prairie, the police pursuing hotly and firing and clubbing mercilessly." Six dead.

But that, Mitch for the first time realized, was the cause of the Haymarket riot. All these years, he had accepted the Haymarket as a byword, as the symbol of some explosive, crudely revolutionary disturbance in which police had been heroic. Then, during the last few months, because of the scathing way in which labor leaders referred to the event, he had come to regard the Haymarket as a symbol of injustice, knowing vaguely that several innocent men, martyrs, were hanged because of that riot. He became irritated at his unbalanced education. Why weren't these things taught in schools? Surely the Haymarket had been an epochal event in this city, where he had been born and raised. Yet it was like so many names and symbols clouded in history, things which intelligent folk were ashamed to ask about, because they were things a man ought to have known. And so instead, he supposed, most Chicago citizens, like himself, went about with their knowledge of the Haymarket taken from an occasional anniversary paragraph in a newspaper and from the sight of that statue of a helmeted tight-pantsed cop standing in Union Park, with a dried decaying wreath covering the inscription. Why, he had not until now realized the irony of calling that place Union Park.

For here in the record the Haymarket was nothing but a citizens' protest meeting such as he and his group, a half-century later, had held at the Opera House, a meeting to protest

[5 4 1]

the shooting of strikers by police. And suppose some hate-maddened fool or provocateur had thrown a bomb at the Opera meeting? Would Mitch Wilner and Rawley, Arthur Main and the other kids who signed the first eye-witness statement on the massacre—would they have been tried as anarchists —Communists, today, Wiley had stated before the Senate—and would he and Rawley and Main and Sobol and perhaps a few others have been sentenced to execution?

For there in the Haymarket, just as a few weeks ago in the Opera House, the citizens' meeting had been an orderly affair. The mayor himself had stood in the crowd to make certain everything was under control. And it had begun to rain, and the mayor, seeing the crowd breaking up, had gone home. It was then that a Captain Bonfield, prototype of Captain Wiley, an old man with a devil-ridden mind and a hating fear of the public he was supposed to serve—then that this Bonfield had marched his police into the crowd, and they had started clubbing. And someone, unknown to this day, had thrown a bomb, killing police.

There undoubtedly was Chicago's root infection, for from year to year as new police came into the department they must have absorbed the traditional fear of labor trouble, the story of cops blown to bits by an anarchist's bomb in the Haymarket, because of the McCormick strike; old-timers must always have filled the new men with advice: shoot first, boys, if you don't want to get what they got at the Haymarket.

Several evenings, Mitch Wilner sat in his office with the unwieldy volume opened across his propped legs. And as he followed the record through more than half a century, the pattern began to contain patterns within itself; he saw that it was not a picture of a simple antagonism between police and laborers, but rather of a sensitivity constantly stimulated.

[5 4 2]

For there, in the Pullman strike, was the record of police-men discharged because they showed sympathy to strikers.

And in the streetcar strike, two cops suspended because they tried to disarm a strikebreaker.

Thus the lower ranks of police, not normally antipathetic to strikers, were constantly stimulated toward hatred.

And in 1910, in the clothing workers' strike, five dead, and "the police seemingly obsessed with the idea that they were there to break the strike."

And in 1915, "the right to peaceful picketing was in the police book of rules and regulations, but the chief of police didn't even know it was there."

Where had he heard that echoed? How the strikers, that Friday, had marched to the police, carrying newspapers head-lining the mayor's statement that they had a right to picket. For which they got their heads broken.

And in 1915, when strikers beaten by company sluggers asked for warrants, police told them: "We don't serve warrants for strikers, nothing doing for strikers."

And in 1924, out of twelve hundred striking garment work-ers arrested only two were convicted of anything; "arrests in a strike don't mean a damn thing," the police officer said.

And citizens investigated always and sometimes they proved the price was a dollar a day for a cop and two dollars for a mounted cop and five dollars for sergeants (during the mil-liners' strike, Mitch remembered Mort Abramson beefing about that envelope for the cops, every day), and citizens' committees recommended, and the church federation recommended, and the city council even adopted strike plans—and the police depart-ment went on slugging and shooting, chapter after chapter, generation after generation, the same bloody routine, strike, slug, shoot, churchmen protesting, citizens sympathizing and

[5 4 3]

getting slugged and sometimes shot, unions getting laws passed on the books . . . police chiefs instructed by law to meet with union leaders at the outbreak of their strike (the senator asked Captain Wiley: Did you attempt to meet with the union leaders? and Captain Wiley said: It wasn't time to discuss it with the union) . . . and the city council said there should be peace, and the regulations said the police must not send spies into union meetings. . . .

Thus, after a thousand pages, the social scientist concluded that "heads of departments have clearly shown a bias against strikers, but in several cases the attitude of patrolmen changed almost overnight when the attitude of their superiors changed. The police bias is never so clearly shown as when race prejudice enters. His Irish or American blood boils at contact with hunkies and Negroes. . . ."

And again, proposals and recommendations for boards and committees of reform. . . .

Sylvia had invited the newly arrived Fuchs, Barbara, Rawley with his current pleasant, smiling, always silent girl, and the Prices. Fuchs was different than he had been in Washington, much younger and more excitable in manner, and at the same time given to almost comically imposing speeches, in which the Harvard Law School smothered the West Side manner. At dinner he was enthusiastic over the genuine sour tomatoes in the manner of one who has acquired a taste for them at some ghetto slumming party rather than by living on Roosevelt Road.

Maybe he was trying to impress Barbara.

But later the conversation steadied down, and Mitch could see in the fellow the kind of single-track brilliance that he realized must have characterized himself in his own field; maybe that limitation was a trait of the Jewish mind.

"So far as I can make out from your thesis," Mitch said,

[5 4 4]

"your findings indicate two methods of approach toward the police. First, the police are a selectively sensitive group, all micks. Do you think it would be much different if the Irish dominance were reduced?"

"Look at New York," George Price cut in. "There are probably just as many Irish in proportion on the force, but they learned how to behave."

"Fiorello was using that Chicago movie to show them how not to behave," Fuchs chuckled, as though this were something his own department had accomplished.

"The second point you made was that the anti-labor attitude came from on top."

"Don't be naïve, Mitch," Barbara said. "We've all been through first grade."

"We may have forgotten some of the things we learned there," Syl said.

"Well, obviously, the people that own industry usually own the government," Rawley said, "and in Chicago they happen to show their control through the police department; in smaller cities, where people can sometimes elect true local governments, the industrialists may have to work through the state militia, or special deputies or the American Legion—it all comes to the same thing in the end."

"Except if the people regain the control of all government by democratic process," Fuchs announced.

"You believe in gradualism, gradualistic reform?" Rawley half accused him.

"Well, they did it in New York; why can't you get someone in Chicago? The crowd in Washington is sick to the guts of the Chicago machine and if you could get a candidate who had any chance at all they'd back you."

Price agreed, insisting that the massacre issue was still hot enough. You could build a whole populist movement around a

[5 4 5]

man and a cause. Take Chicago, call it America's most backward city—"America's Shame City"—he was already thinking in slogans.

Get a man. If you could get a man like President Cavanaugh of the University to run, you might really knock over the machine. In any case labor would be tremendously strengthened by realizing itself as a political force.

It was exciting to hear them talk as if the next mayoralty campaign was being born in the room; yet Mitch knew the thing was not entirely new. All during the strike, and in the framework that remained of the citizens' committee, talk had been going on of the eventual necessity of using this issue to clean out the machine, to bring the New Deal to Chicago, and even to extend the progressiveness of the New Deal. With some New Dealers, Mitch now saw, progressivism was the only prevention of a revolution; while with the radicals, progressivism was the kind of feeding that increases the appetite.

Rawley even had a rudimentary plan; he had had a little talk with Dr. Ladd.

"Ladd wants to be mayor himself," Price said. "He's got the bug."

"Okay, but he knows he wouldn't stand a chance in this election. The idea is to get the committee together again, and enlarge it, and put pressure on Cavanaugh to become a candidate."

"He won't," was Price's opinion.

Rawley wasn't sure. Cavanaugh was getting mighty sick of the University, he thought. "The old guard has him hog-tied. He can't even begin to realize his educational ideas." Rawley confessed that he himself was shopping around for an appointment elsewhere, as the entrenched element of the faculty would never let him get beyond his present minor rank. "So Cavanaugh might bite at an opportunity like this. If he could clean up

[546]

Chicago, he'd be perfectly set up for Washington in 1944, maybe even by 1940."

"If he couldn't beat the system at the University with practically a free hand, how is he going to beat it as mayor? And for that matter what has Roosevelt been able to do? They've torn down practically everything he attempted," Barbara said. "The trouble with reforms is that you get the habit of compromise and compromise yourself into the status quo. Look what happened in England. Okay, so the bobbies don't carry guns in strikes, and they don't shoot workers down any more, and they even had a Labor government—and the workers are absolutely helpless. They have gentlemen's agreements. That's what happens to labor as soon as you start to play politics. Well, for that matter look at the A. F. of L. Unions don't change the political machines, they just get to be Tammany Halls themselves."

"Well, what do you want them to do?" Fuchs asked.

"Learn how to shoot," she said. "Like they're doing in Mexico. At least there, they learned something from Spain."

"So next Fourth of July they'll go up against the cops with guns?" Fuchs asked.

"Why not?"

Fuchs offered a better way. All labor needed was to learn how to be smart. The laws were enacted. Unions simply had to learn how to use them. "This whole strike was unnecessary, here; all they had to do was ask the board for a separate bargaining contract."

"That's easy to say," Barbara sneered. "Did you ever try to organize a bunch of men? As soon as you sign them up they want to strike." Mitch recognized the quotation from Carl Gaul. "Every day they come around and say, when are we getting a contract? When do we strike? The organizers had all they could do to hold them back as long as they did."

[547]

Yes, but the mistake was made by the S.W.O.C. attorneys in Cleveland, Fuchs insisted. "They should have asked for exclusive bargaining rights in each plant where the S.W.O.C. had a clear majority—as here in Chicago. Instead, they asked Consolidated for a contract similar to Standard Steel's, lumping all the plants together. That gave Speer a chance to claim they weren't entitled to anything at all, because in certain plants they had no majority. That's how they gummed the thing up."

"Well, why can't the board handle the plants separately?"

"Because they're just getting around to filing charges now, on separate plants. And now they are going to have a hell of a time proving majority here because I understand they haven't got the cards."

"They were stolen," Mitch said. "Headquarters was broken into."

"Can't they get the men to sign up again?" Sylvia ventured.

"It won't be so simple now. A lot of the men have gone back to work. A lot have scattered, out of town." What he would advise the union to do, Fuchs said, was to send all strikers back to ask for their jobs. Then, if the company refused, the board could slap an 8b on them: refusal to reinstate being discrimination against the men for striking.

"You mean you want them to call off the strike?"

"The plant is operating anyway. The strike is beaten. Their only chance is through the board, and if they can prove a real case, they can get an order for reinstatement and stick Speer with back pay that'll run into millions."

"But if they had gone to you in the first place, the whole thing wouldn't have been necessary," Sylvia said gravely, with a kind of horror.

"That's right," Fuchs maintained.

Barbara laughed scornfully. "They'd have waited about three years for the case to go through twenty appeals, and by that

[548]

time the Republicans would be in again. That's gradualism."

Fuchs, offended, started a long recital of cases in which the board has secured thousands and tens of thousands of dollars in back pay for dismissed unionists. After all, even plans for revolutionary societies were based on the idea that laws were enforceable, he insisted. "You're not even a Trotskyite, you're a plain anarchist," he accused Barbara.

Sylvia suggested they listen to some records.

And finally the massacre was come to court. Not the solemn, imposing Criminal Court building, where the inquest had been held, but the Eleventh Street bureau to which petty thieves and prostitutes and speeders were taken; there, on the eighth floor, Mitch found the men clogging the narrow corridor and jamming the doorway of a bench-filled room occupied by the usual assortment of habituals, onhangers, and scared citizens in minor trouble.

"I been here four times," Al Nees complained. "If they don't hold this bitchn thing today, I ain't coming down again; they can come and get me."

"They'll hold it today," Sobol assured him.

An elderly Pole complained: "Sure, come down, sit all day, spend carfare, then judge he says, continue, come again."

"They're supposed to pay your carfare," Mike Sisto said. "Ain't you been getting your carfare?"

A whole circle formed, confusedly discussing how about gas, how about last time sat all day spent two bits for lunch. Pete Vikulik was running around with a list of names trying to check up who was there, sonsofbitches, we're gonna lose the bail we put up. "Where's Gabby Markonitch, anybody seen him lately?"

"He won't come down here," Nees reported. "That bastard is in that plant working."

The dark blood spots were gone off their clothes; the dead

[5 4 9]

were long buried, and those who had lived had new flesh and new skin where their wounds had been. But even now, with their anger divided, and tired as they were by repeated court postponements, the call to trial made their old fury flicker. Can you beat it, we're the guys they got to try! Did we kill anybody? And a few, in whom the irony had sunk deep, so that their fury was each time more sulphuric, muttered wildly about next time, sure, knock off a couple of those lousy coppers, they arrest you anyway, might as well give them a reason.

"Inside, inside," the bailiff herded them; there were not enough seats, and they thronged the aisles. A shingle over the door carried the name of the judge: Pacelli. Heavy, but energetic, the youngish judge stood leaning over his desk after the clerk had mumbled the now-in-session-be-seated rigmarole and the bailiffs had barked, find seats, find seats, you can't stand in the aisles.

"Come on, come on, let's get that mob out of here," Pacelli said. "Can't breathe in this place." The clerk began to read down the long list of names. Antonio Dalpino, Harry Chase, Alfred Nees, Mrs. Anna Jugloitch—Jugovich—whatever it is—Peter Zloto . . .

"Answer when called." The judge rapped on his desk. "Step up here when your name is called."

"Frank Sobol, Thomas Fuscarin . . ."

A few men were worming their way toward the bench. The clerk continued, yelling the foreign-sounding names with an air of annoyance. "Damon Antinoous . . ."

"Step forward, step forward," the bailiffs repeated.

"He's dead," a voice shouted.

"Ruth Falls, Mike Sisto, Oscar Lindstrom, Ephraim Law . . ."

"Dead," the voice repeated.

"All right, all right." The judge made a short-armed clearing motion, as if sweeping a whole lot of junk off his desk. "Don't bother calling them all." He raised his voice. "Hey, all you men, everybody mixed up in this Fourth of July riot, come up here . . ."

The men gravitated frontward, filling the railed enclosure. Sam Eisen and the elderly lawyer, who, Mitch now heard, came from the miners' union, downstate, were squeezed up against the bench. Beside the judge stood a young fellow who had been with Corcoran at the inquest; he was smiling in a bored and cynical manner.

"Okay. Everybody here?" the judge shouted. "Now, let's get this over with. You all plead guilty. Right?"

"Guilty?" There was a confused questioning and babbling among the men. Guilty, what's that? What do we get if we plead guilty? And all the while worried elderly Poles and Italians were trying to give their names to the clerk, or shouting up their names to the judge: Hey, Nick Pappos, you got that name? Hey, Tony Magliore couldn't come, his wife is sick. But through this confusion, Al Nees's voice suddenly reached up, hard: "What is this? We ain't guilty of nothing. I don't want no record . . . !"

The judge rattled on: "Listen, we can't take all day. Now I want to know, plead guilty or not? How many of you plead guilty?" He lifted his belly over the desk and stuck his head out toward them. "Put up your hands. Plead guilty, put up your hands." Several hands were raised. Pete Vikulik and Frank Sobol, with their hands raised, were busily urging those around them to do likewise. Sam Eisen kept saying angrily: "Yes, yes, plead guilty, that's the best way." The movement spread, but still the bulk of the men were dubious, hesitated.

"Okay," the judge cried, as though he had counted the hands. "The majority pleads guilty. Majority rules here. Plea of guilty."

"I ain't guilty of nothing! I want a trial!" Al Nees yelled.

"Majority rules here! You don't want to hold things up."

[551]

Judge Pacelli banged his gavel, good-humoredly. "One and one, pay the clerk," he announced, and banged the gavel again, completing the case.

A churning movement began as some of the men tried to reach the door while others remained rooted, unable to believe the whole thing was over. What had happened? Four times they had come down for a trial, and now, all of a sudden, bingo, the trial was over. "It's okay, it's okay," Sobol was reassuring them. "We'll pay the fine."

"Yah, but that's our dough, union dough," Al Nees protested. "Two bucks apiece, sixty guys——"

"They got us off as cheap as they could," Vikulik maintained.

"What the —— are we guilty of?" Nees insisted. "I wanna understand about this. I didn't enter no guilty plea——"

"Clear the court, go on home," the bailiff yelled, shoving people. Gradually the men squeezed toward the corridor, still confused, but the feeling was spreading, well, we got off, the lawyers know how these things work, leave it to them.

Word had got around that things would come out at this meeting, and the main Harbor headquarters was filled with Consolidated men. Groups stood on the landings leading to the second-floor auditorium, the men asking each other what was what. There was a rumor that the labor board man was coming to explain their case. "Frank said the board guy was coming up tonight." This gave the men an excited expectancy, a hope they had not shown for weeks: at last we get some action. By eight o'clock the rows of folding-chairs were filled. Mitch stood around, in the rear.

In the hallway, a few Mexicans still leaned against the wall, under a "Ford Is Unfair" poster, talking in their low, long-paused manner. Carl Gaul had come up with Jock Kiley, Al Nees was with them, and now they engaged white-haired Gillespie in an argument. Al's bitterness over the trial had deepened in these few days until now it seemed like another burn-mark, on his very soul.

"Why couldn't we go to trial? I'll tell you why," he drove at Gillespie. "Because they were protecting a couple of their boys, that's all. They were afraid Frank might be put away for a while. Now, listen, maybe you are one of them for all I know, Whitey, you're always sucking around with those boys, but I don't give a goddamn who knows it, I'm going to bring it right out on the floor, they got no right to plead us guilty and give us a record."

"What did Frank have to be afraid of?" Whitey Gillespie argued coolly, his shrewd eyes going from Nees to Jock Kiley to Carl Gaul. "They tried to pull all that red stuff on him at the inquest. They didn't get nowhere."

"You're not putting any of that crap over on me," Al replied. "That inquest was just a warning, it was fixed up to scare the boys into making some kind of a deal. That's what they done."

"All they did was to follow the lawyers' advice," Gillespie maintained.

"Sure," Kiley put in contemptuously. "That shyster Eisen. He's one of their crowd too. That's all he was looking out for was to protect their boys, to hell with anybody else."

"I wouldn't be so sure," Gillespie said. "I walked in there one day up in Alonzo's office and Eisen was the one that wanted to fight it out in court. That lawyer from downstate, the miner, he was the one said to make some kind of a deal and hush it up."

"Maybe." Nees was momentarily taken aback, but Carl Gaul stepped in for him. "Damn right, they had to hush it up. If the case ever came to court, that inquest was only a beginning; the state's attorney would put it on so thick about the reds, the whole C.I.O. would be smeared. You think it would be good for the union to have it in court that a bunch of Stalinists are running the show? Alonzo had to hush it up."

[553]

"I don't care if they are Stalinists or Chinamen," Gillespie said. "That lousy *Clarion* was just aching to make another Haymarket case out of it."

"Who gives a damn?" Carl cried bitterly. "Maybe it would do some good if they hung a couple of those bastards."

Whitey Gillespie's face became rigid. He seemed about to answer, but turned, contemptuously, and walked off.

Kiley laughed. "That old bastard. He's one of them."

Mike Sisto presided, taut and solemn, with the rigid sobriety of a fellow accustomed to slight tipsiness. Pete Vikulik, the financial secretary since Art Nowis had been suspended from office, made a routine pep talk about all those on W.P.A. better pay their dues as they were not exempt. At the first opportunity Al Nees stood up for the floor. "What is it, old business or new business?" Mike said, wavering with parliamentary uncertainty.

"It's about the trial. That comes under old business, I guess," Al said. Pete Vikulik leaned to Mike, whispering, and Mike said, maybe they could discuss it later, right now there was a lot to take up about the labor board case.

"This comes right in under the case," said Al Nees. "How are we going to have a case if they're gonna make us ineligible for re-employment?" The men stirred, startled, scared.

"Where did you see that?" Mike asked.

"What about Midwest?" Al Nees challenged. "They made a deal with the governor to take everybody back to work, and they took them all back—except three guys that were convicted in the courts. They didn't have to take those boys back, because they had a court record of conviction."

Alarm spread. Mike banged the gavel. "Those cases got nothing to do with us," he said, confused.

At the back of the room, Sobol arose and said: "Mr. Chairman, I can make that clear. Those are three cases of men that committed small offenses in the strike; one of them socked a company union man." There was a laugh. "A couple of others, I don't know what crimes they did, if that is a crime. But those cases are before the labor board now and those men will be back to work."

"Well, they ain't back to work," Al Nees retorted. "What I want to know is who and by what right did anybody decide we were all pleading guilty? This is supposed to be a democratic organization, we hear a lot of talk about democratic procedure, but we come there in court and it's all fixed in advance, we are all a bunch of criminals for going out there and having the cops bust our heads open. That ain't all. The company is in cahoots with the politicians, we know that, and that ain't no accident they made us plead guilty. Every man that is down there guilty is going to have a hell of a time getting back to his job, and I want to know who is responsible for making that decision."

"That decision was made by the legal counsel of the S.W.O.C.," Frank Sobol informed the meeting. "That's what we have lawyers for, and they figured that was the best way to handle the case."

"What's the idea of springing it on us in court? Don't we have nothing to say about a thing like that?" Nees persisted. "I ain't guilty of anything except standing for my rights and I ain't going to have a record against me!"

"Well, what do you want? You got a motion to make or something?" Mike asked.

Gillespie took the floor. "Brothers, as far as I can see there was nothing else to do but plead guilty there to a small offense of disorderly conduct. Sometimes you have to deal with skunks and that is what we had to do. This is not the last strike the C.I.O. is going to have in this town, and we've got to work with those politicians while they are in. Our job is to build up ourselves so we are strong enough to kick them out and put in our own men, then we'll tell the police department how to behave——"

[5 5 5]

The young Greek, Skourakis, jumped up. "I don't care to talk politics what we're gonna do. I come downtown four times I'm gonna show them they broke my head, and what I get, guilty, kick in the pants, good-by."

Several men raised their voices—Croatians, Poles, all the foreign who had been puzzling, feeling unfree to complain because maybe the court was something the Americans understood; but now their anger burst. Mike Sisto rapped and tried to yell them down, Gillespie cried that he still had the floor, and Nees wrathfully shouted that he wasn't through.

Kiley walked from the back of the room and held up his arm, quieting the meeting. Momentarily, Mitch Wilner wondered whether Jock Kiley would take advantage of this opportunity to step on Sobol. Carl Gaul looked eager, pleased.

"This ain't going to get us anywhere, brothers," Kiley said. "Okay, we took another beating in that court, like we took out there on that prairie. You can't bring back the ten men that were shot dead there and you can't change what happened in the court. But we're still in this scrap and what we got to work on is our next move. Now we got a man come down here to talk to us, from the labor board, to tell us what we got to do on our case. If you don't mind, Brother Chairman, I suggest we hear from the representative of the labor board."

Mike Sisto bobbed his head and sat down, then jumped up, saying: "Is that a motion, somebody make that as a motion?"

"I move we hear the labor board man, like whatever Jock Kiley said," Tiny Jardine spoke up.

Mike shuffled the motion through and Fuchs walked solemnly up to the platform. He said he had not yet had time to go into the case thoroughly, but certain things he knew already would have to be done. Every man on strike would have to file a formal reapplication for his job. They ought to have a committee to see that this was done.

[556]

Questions popped from all sides. Would they get back pay? When would they go back to work? Would the scabs be allowed to continue in there? He answered without making commitments. All he could tell them was that each striker's case would be stronger if he asked for his job back, for if the company refused to give it to him, while a new man was on that job, then it was discrimination. He advised each man to find out who was working on his job, get the name, and find out if he was a newcomer to the plant.

"You mean, we got to go and ask for our jobs back?" Tiny Jardine said.

Yes, that was it.

"How we going to do that without going through our own picket line?"

Fuchs said he couldn't advise them on that.

Al Nees arose. "I move we all march down there in a body and ask for our jobs back. They ain't going to give them to us, but that'll put it on the record."

But Fuchs explained such procedure would not be practical, as there had to be a record of each individual case with the reasons given for refusing the job. Besides, it might be that some of them would be re-employed.

Art Nowis got the floor. "Sure," he said, "we got to figure the company is on to all the tricks of this game. What they are going to do is take some men back and some they won't take back but they ain't gonna say it's because we are union men; they're gonna say it's because they ain't got work for us or some excuse like that. But the fellows that get in, they've got to make a list of every man inside that plant that wasn't there before the strike."

Uncertainty toward Art was obvious. Mitch had the feeling the man was talking simply out of boldness.

"I made a motion on the floor," Al Nees insisted. Either the strike was on or off, he said. If they marched down in a body, it was on, but if every man went crawling back by himself, better call the strike off and be done with it.

The Greek jumped up and challenged Nees. "Sure! You can go, stay on strike all the time. You are on W.P.A."

A side argument developed, the W.P.A. men yelling they didn't want to be lousy shovel stiffs forever, Gillespie pointing out that if the complainers had taken the trouble to become citizens they could have gotten on W.P.A. too, and Pete Vikulik rising to defend the aliens, while insisting that the union had to pep up its naturalization program.

Fuchs said he had to leave.

The Greek arose again. "I make a motion that we do like the labor board said."

Al Nees insisted he had a motion on the floor. To march down in a body. Mike Sisto, in a troubled way, said all right, and put that motion. It was defeated. Pete Vikulik quietly reminded the chair that there was another motion, to carry out the suggestion of the labor board, each man going by himself and asking for his job back.

"How about going through the picket line?" Tiny Jardine asked.

Art Nowis suggested each man should phone, or maybe go to his foreman's house. But that way, it was objected, there'd be no record.

No one seemed to have the face to make the obvious suggestion. At last Mike himself mumbled: "Looks like we either got to call off the picket line or go through it."

A feeling of fatalism pervaded the room, tiredness, and relief. Sobol asked for the floor. Don't think the strike is lost if the picket line is called off. Consolidated already spent two million dollars' cash on the strike, outside of what they lost in canceled orders and in spoiled stuff. Speer ain't going to get away with it even with his own stockholders; they are going to kick him out for the losses and the bad name he gave the company. Besides, there is a strong labor board case and every union man is going to get back pay for all the time he was out! The C.I.O. is going back into that plant and make it a hundred percent union shop! We showed them we could go out, and we'll show them they have to take us back in! They will have to sign a contract too. Consolidated is one company that is never going to try to break a union again.

Gillespie put an amendment to the previous motion, the amendment being that the picket line be called off.

There was a scattered murmur of ayes. But only Al Nees came out sharply with nay. Three or four followed him. Then silence.

"We've still got the motion," Vikulik reminded Mike Sisto.

"Yah, read the motion," Mike said.

Pete read: "That we follow the advice of the labor board, and every man ask for his job back."

"All those in favor," Mike said, and paused. "I guess we ought to put up our hands on this one."

Hesitantly, with men looking around to watch each other, hands went up. More and more. Nees and a small group directly around him were keeping their arms down. But it looked nearly unanimous.

"The motion is passed," Mike said, and in silence the hands were lowered.

A Slovak voice said: "That's finish, huh? Strike is finish."

As men began to rise heavily from their seats, Kiley reminded them: "Wait a minute, Brother Sisto. You've got to have a committee for the labor board to work with."

Mike rapped and said: "This meeting ain't adjourned yet."

There was a moment of uncertainty, but then almost all the men resumed their seats.

[559]

Fuchs and George Price occasionally met Mitch Wilner for lunch. Men were coming in every day to make their depositions, Fuchs said; the case was fair, but not nearly as strong as he would have liked. Plenty of petty instances of foremen making derogatory remarks about union buttons, plenty of evidence of company unions organized by company stooges and reorganized under changed names as fast as the government tightened regulations. But technically it was hard to prove refusal to bargain. The men were gradually being taken back to work; Consolidated, cagey and clever, was giving as little evidence of discrimination as possible. The situation played into their hands, as steel production was low, and there was very little employment to offer in any case. Chippers were the worst out of luck; scarfing had supplanted their craft—there were a couple of hundred guys out of this mill alone who never would get back to work as far as he could see. "That was one of the best unionized departments, too."

He had one funny story, though, of how you couldn't get those boys down. When the Independents—the latest version of the company union—had called an open meeting, the C.I.O. had jammed the hall, elected their own chairman, unanimously passed a motion that the Independents be officially disbanded, and held a funeral for it in the street! What a bunch of guys!

What percentage of the strikers were back at work, Mitch asked.

Maybe about a third. A couple of hundred men.

How about the sixty who had been arrested?

No direct refusal to rehire. "They just smile and tell the boys to come back and ask around Christmas. Once or twice a foreman slipped up and told somebody to ask the C.I.O. to get him a job."

"Did Art Nowis get back in?"

"Nowis?"

"That fellow suspected of being the spy."

"Not yet. But that wouldn't prove anything."

Mike Sisto, or his brother? No. They were chippers. How about Al Nees? No. There was a pretty strong case of discrimination there, as he had the name and proof of a new man on his job. Gillespie? Yes, he was back on; skilled man, evidently they needed him.

One day the following week, Mitch received a call from Pauline Lindstrom. Would he come out to the house? The address was new, around the outskirts of Hegewisch; he found the unpaved, unmarked street with difficulty. The house had tar-paper walls; but there was a large, pleasant vegetable garden in the front yard.

"We had to move," Ma Lindstrom explained. "But anyway this air out here is better for Mr. Lindstrom."

"How is he? Did you want me to look at him?"

"Oh, he's fine," Ma Lindstrom said. "He's getting strong. Wants to go back in the mill but I guess they won't take him on account of the physical defect. He says he can see clearer with one eye than with two."

"How is Pauline? Are her kids all right?" He was momentarily worried that Pauline had broken down, doing that scrubbing work, but Ma Lindstrom smiled, saying Pauline and the kids were fine, too. "It's for my boy," she said, "Doctor."

"Your boy?" he was puzzled.

"Yes. You know we have another son," she reminded him nervously, as she opened a bedroom door.

After a moment Mitch recognized the man inside. It was the man who had come to his office long ago: Flint. Dressed in shirt and pants, he half reclined in an old Morris rocker. He appeared a much smaller man, shrunken, desiccated. Pauline sat there with a dish and spoon, attempting to feed him, like a baby.

[561]

"Will!" his mother called sharply. "Here's Dr. Wilner come to see you."

There was no response from the man. "He's kind of paralyzed, Doctor," Ma Lindstrom said. "He hears. Sometimes he talks, like a baby, learning."

"He got hurt in the plant," Pauline explained. "They had him in the hospital a couple of days; then they brought him home, here. They said there was nothing they could do for him. He fell and hurt his spine, they said."

"How long has he been here?" Mitch asked automatically, approaching the patient.

"Just since yesterday."

"Can he take care of himself at all?" he asked the mother.

"No, Doctor. He's just like a baby," she said. "Except he don't move. He's paralyzed."

The man's eyes followed him now.

"You say he fell on his spine?"

"Yes, but there's not a mark on him, Doctor. Maybe it hit a nerve or something," Pauline ventured.

"He was working in the office there up to the strike," said Mother Lindstrom. "He was using the name of Flint, I guess. Will always liked to be kind of mysterious, you know, like boys like to play detective. . . . Well, the strike come and they put him in the sheetmill, his father being a roller, he knows the trade. That's where he worked, all that time. When the men started coming back into the mill, Will had something to do with the employment records, that was his regular department, and he had to go all over the mill, registering the different men. My daughter Gertrude told me this; he saw her awhile back but swore her not to tell us."

There was a slight pupillary reflex. The others failed. No use going further. He was no psychiatrist.

[562]

"You know how the men are," Ma Lindstrom continued. "Things started falling near him. Pa used to tell me; the men know ways of—little accidents and things, in a mill, with all those tons of things passing overhead, and the hot metal every-place. Seems like, this time, there was one of those big ingots lifting out of the soaking-pits, burning hot, and they travel them overhead and bring them down to a conveyor. Will, he was standing there alongside this conveyor, and the lift-chain slipped, so that ingot come down all but on top of him. He jumped just in time, but fell over a track, and that was how he come to hurt his spine."

"I see," Mitch said. Her face was calm, making no accusation. "Do you know if they made X-rays, in the hospital?"

"They said they did," Pauline reported. "They said there was"—she quoted—" 'nothing organically wrong.' He was just scared. Like shell shock, I guess."

Mitch Wilner finished his examination; they retreated from the room. Old man Lindstrom was waiting in the parlor. He had been provided with an artificial eye, and appeared well. Pauline's children, shyly in awe, watched the doctor.

Mitch said he'd try to get a nerve specialist to come out. "We can only pay a little, you know, Doctor," Ma Lindstrom told him. "Gertrude is working now, but that's about all we have is what she and Pauline make."

"I don't think he'll charge," Mitch said. But they insisted they wanted to pay something, to him as well, for his trouble.

"I lost that thousand dollars' insurance I had through the company," Lindstrom said. "They won't pay it, account of I was guilty in court, in that case when they hauled us all up there, all us they arrested on the field that day. So now they say the injury was received while committing an illegal act, and the insurance company don't have to pay." He smiled, not bitterly, but as a man in scorn of lack of honor in the world. Arising, he towered alongside Mitch, a powerful-looking man again, imposing with his curly white hair. He walked out with the doctor, and they stood together for a while on the earth path from the door. "You know, Doc, I don't feel any bitterness toward that son," Lindstrom said. "I guess this struggle is the same as all the other wars in one thing, it's the working people that have to do the fighting on both sides, and they are the ones that get killed and maimed. So they might as well fight on their own side, it seems to me. That is one thing I failed to make both my sons understand: what side they were on. Maybe, in those days, I didn't realize myself the way things are."

"Yes," Mitch agreed. "We are slow in learning."

"I take it on myself as a responsibility," Lindstrom said. "I always figured my kids should get educated, go to school, but this is something they wouldn't of learned in school and should of learned from me. I used to shoot off my mouth about the single tax and stuff, when I was a younger man. Well I don't believe in any trick way to Utopia, Doctor. I guess I understand a little better what is practical, now." He gazed solemnly back at the house, as if he saw there all the homes he had earned in his life, the one in St. Louis, and the one in the Harbor. "It cost a lot but maybe some way I can return on the investment of that experience. I ain't dead yet."

"Have you seen Frank Sobol lately?" Mitch asked, remembering that George Price had lately hinted that Lindstrom had become a Communist.

Lindstrom caught his meaning and said, quite simply: "I'm not with those people either, Doctor. I don't hold against them. Maybe they will prove out to be right and their way the best way, but I personally can't see it. I'll tell you what I object to, Doctor." He sat on the stoop, and as the words poured out of him, Mitch realized that he was perhaps the man's first audience; Oscar Lindstrom, after long self-examination, had come to examine those around him, and was now ready.

"What I object to is, they don't really trust all the men. There was secrecy there, things planned in secret, right or wrong things; yes, I know, Doctor, sometimes in a war your tactics have to be secret, for the effect of surprise. But in a union we know the company has their spies in among us, and no matter how few on a committee, if so much as five men get together, it seems there is going to be a leak somewhere. So the only ones you are keeping a secret from is your own brothers in the union, instead of the company. Frank knows that like I know it, but, Doctor, I think maybe from those long years and habits of getting into a huddle and having secrecy in their own party, they can't help continuing some of those ways. And that is the first deep thing I disagree with. I have seen them educate good men, real workers, fellows like young Pete Vikulik, I guess that is the enlightened proletariat they talk about; but at the same time it looks to me like they kind of distrust the mass of the men; they meet in their own caucuses and figure out how to move the men one way or another. I want everything open and aboveboard. I believe everything should be put to the men."

"But there has to be some leadership," Mitch pointed out. "Some people have to plan what to do."

"Sure! But put it all up to the boys to decide. Keep no secrets from them. Look, here is an example, how the strike went off half-cocked right from the start. The strategy committee voted to call it at 10 p.m. but kept it a secret from the men. The company knew all about it, though, so they jumped the gun at three o'clock, the best time for them. Well, now, if the men had all been told it was for ten o'clock, they wouldn't have been fooled or thrown into confusion. That one mistake alone was responsible for killing that strike there in Consolidated, because in our plant and in the Tri-State plant everything went off like clockwork."

But the Communists were not the only people in the strategy committee, Mitch pointed out. Did they control it?

"No," Lindstrom said. "But that is another thing. There was a bad situation of political rivalry in there and it became a factional fight. Certainly that ain't Frank Sobol's fault any more than it is Kiley's or Gaul's, except, when that kind of thing starts, they should all go out and squabble amongst themselves instead of fighting it out over control of the union. I have seen unions where the Communists did a swell job of building a strong labor organization. Maybe it depends on the individual party member that is doing the job. Some of those party boys, even though they say to you building the union is first and foremost with them, still they can't wait for the proper time to inject their party issues. Maybe not Frank Sobol, here, but some of the younger ones, even boys like Pete Vikulik, they get over-anxious with their campaigns for Spain and the United Front. Doctor, I believe that eventually every workingman has got to see that his fate is bound up with the fate of all other workingmen all over the world. But we have to make union men out of them first, before we start to feed them all those issues.

"Take, in our campaign here. Most of the mill workers around here are Polish and Italian—Catholics. First thing you know a man comes to a C.I.O. meeting and half the meeting is devoted to issues about Spain and China, and he comes home and mentions it to his wife, and she tells it to the priest; then there is hell to pay because the priest says the C.I.O. is a lot of nun-killers because they want to send arms to Spain. Now, sure, some of the men are educated by that process, and they tell the priest to go to hell. But a lot of the others get mad and quit the C.I.O.

[5 6 6]

There is a case of conflict between what they have to do as party members and as builders of the union. They have got a few hundred postcards sent to Congress to lift the arms embargo, but they have weakened the union."

"But then," Mitch said, "if the men are not to learn of such issues from their union, where will they ever learn the truth about them?"

Lindstrom nodded. "I agree that those things should be brought up, but in special educational meetings, not on the union floor, until the union is much farther along. Sure, some locals, even some S.W.O.C. locals may be ready for it. And if plain union men have control of their organization, they will know when the boys are ready for it and how much they can take. But when a political organization is trying to spread its program all at once, giving its members directives to bring up those issues everywhere, it will bring trouble in some places."

The way to rebuild the locals in the Harbor, Lindstrom said, was to go in there and bring back some bacon. "When the men see results, they will come back into the union. Now, Cass Morrison is the kind of a man I mean. He came over here the other day, about the question of lapse of seniority. They've got a rule in Midwest, if a man is laid off more than three months, he comes back as a new man, all his seniority is gone. With those long layoffs they got now, they can ruin anybody; you put in years, and what have you got for protection? Not a day's seniority. Cass and his electricians have got a tight little organization there, they could go in there separately and get that three months extended to a year, for themselves. But Cass is willing to hold off until he can go in there with a committee for the whole mill, not just the electricians. That is the way to work. We've got to show the men they have the power to go get something. Those other issues, those international issues, we can't be in such a hurry about them. It takes time, time."

Then, Mitch asked, did he feel that Communists and other political workers had no place in the union?

"Hell, no. They're the most active and hard-working element we have, if they just don't overdo it. And that is sometimes our own fault, for letting them do all the work. I think, you take most of the Communists, they got no selfish motives; what are they working their heads off for if not for us? But the way I feel, their approach is wrong in this country. They are all the time trying to make us feel like the underdog that has to revolt, or else like we are superior to anybody that owns some stocks and bonds. The way I feel, I am as good as anybody else, and he is as good as me. If there are going to be any changes, it has to be through making people understand how to run things better, not through raising hatred. We've got a good system, democracy. If we really put into effect what it means, why, we don't need any revolution here. The way I see it, Doctor, no other system of government is going to give us any more democracy so long as we ourselves don't use it. A Communist government could go in tomorrow, but if the whole population wasn't active in it all the time, it would still be a few of the people running the rest of the people. The vote is all the revolution we need, if we make every man's vote count equal."

Yet hadn't he just said he should have taught his sons the meaning of being in the working class?

"Sure I said that, Doctor. We've got the upper class, the rich. But we don't feel like any lower-class scum. I am as good as the next man. That was the mistake my son made, in there; he thought he had to go crawling into the upper class. He thought he was born wrong."

"You think we are all born equal?"

"Sure. And why start to teach anything different? The thing to teach is that we should live as equals."

It seemed to Mitch that Rawley, that time in Mahoning,

had been trying to say the same things. But how could they be put into effect?

"I think maybe we've got a start," Lindstrom said. "That is my job now, to work on that. I've been thinking, what were we after when we marched out there? Not a few extra cents an hour, hell, no. Why did every man say: Speer has to sign his name on the same paper with our man, John Lewis? Why, because we had a feeling that would give us a kind of equality, a share in running things. The management can go out and sell the stuff, but we make it, and we have to have our share of the responsibility for that. That's self-respect. And once every man knows for certain he has a right in the mill, from that point there is no end to how far we can go." He looked back into the house. "You see, Doctor, that was what was the matter with my son Will. It started with him as a soldier in the war—he got that feeling that the common man has no say in anything, in the way things are run—and when he came out of the war, he wanted to be up there with the officer class, in civilian life. With the people that run things. No son of mine should have to go sucking around in the personnel office to get the feeling he has a share in making things go. He's got a right to that feeling, in the shop or anyplace, if he's an American."

This was the end of his thoughts. Lindstrom arose and walked with Mitch to his car. They shook hands. The steelman's grip was powerful and young.

Cavanaugh had, discreetly and privately, steered the draft-a-mayor committee away from himself, pointing to John Heiser, the fire-eating cabinet member in Washington, as the man for the job. Heiser was old enough to have nothing to lose politically; if elected, he could really shake Chicago by the heels, and set it upright on its feet again. And so the committee, frequently mentioned in the papers, owing to a rattling publicity campaign in which Price had dubbed it with a dozen slogans, from the Shake-Up-Chicago Committee to the Put-Chicago-Back-in-America movement, now looked toward Washington. The *Clarion* had helped with a few nasty editorials about "Professor Ladd's Reformers." And further, Price had astutely started a rumor, fed through national columnists, to the effect that the citizens had the secret backing of New Dealers who would be pleased to toss over Chicago's Tammany. Apparently the only remaining necessity was a vote-drawing candidate.

A delegation was to journey to Washington to appeal to Mr. Heiser to come home and save Chicago. Price wanted Mitch Wilner to make the trip—at his own expense. A doctor's name always lent dignity.

Just then news came out that Otis Speer himself was to testify before the Gottschalk committee.

"But, dear, it'll cost at least a hundred dollars for the trip," Syl said. "Do you have to go? If they need you, can't they pay your expenses?"

"They don't need me," he replied. "I just want to go. I need to go."

Though he had been such a short time in Washington before, the committee room seemed a familiar place to him, and the staff, long and intimate friends. They fell upon him with enthusiasm; Tannenbaum asked after Vic Fuchs; Tannenbaum and Sproul took him out for a quick beer and regaled him with tales of the progress of the investigation. Yes, the publicity on the Fourth of July massacre had brought another appropriation, so they had expanded into a really complete investigation of Consolidated, didn't he know? Been on it all this time. Probably would be the committee's last job, as the funds were nearly used up again. But the stuff they had! Papers hadn't been playing it; Consolidated was using a fancy advertising firm to smother the story. But, Jesus, the fun. They'd finally landed the chief of the Consolidated police force on the stand, after chasing him all over the United States and Canada. Damn fool had been so crap-scared he'd traded in his car in some Michigan town, and left a whole raft of evidence under the seat—copies of hectographed spy reports on union meetings, copies of black-lists sent not only to Consolidated but to other mills. They'd traced munitions which had been supplied to strike towns, with the company paying the bills; they'd traced criminal records of a dozen regular Consolidated guards—everything from petty larceny to rape. And, boy, the way those company police had tossed money around! Blind vouchers—a thousand dollars, two thousand dollars—just chunks of dough handed to the private police, and never accounted for—you should have seen their superintendents squirm, trying to explain those blind vouchers! Hawk Musty had caught one cold. A thousand bucks that the chief of the Consolidated police in Wilton, Ohio, had given to some mysterious bird that kept phoning him from Detroit with tips about when the auto workers were coming down to invade Wilton and help the steelworkers win the strike.

"That's a neat way to get yourself a thousand bucks," Sproul said. "Anytime you run short, Mitch, just call up Consolidated and sell them a few tips. Boy, you should have seen that stupe's face when the senator asked him—he imitated Gottschalk's bland poker-voice—'And did the auto workers ever come down to invade your town?' 'No,' he says, 'but they might have.'"

They laughed at the recollection. It seemed to Mitch that they were so overwrought, so overworked, that any trifle could trigger their emotions, and their work had perhaps created for them a whole new category of values, so that things were comic or ironic to them, which were not so to an outsider.

"And the job Musty did on Machine Products," Tannenbaum took up the song. Mussetti had simply walked into the main of-

[571]

fices of the Machine Products Association, and for once realized his dream of catching a gang completely off guard. Come away with a truckload of impounded records. "There was a list of a hundred and twenty-five spies, itemizing every goddam job they had been on—neat and complete as a library index! You never saw anything like it. Twenty-five years of it! Those guys just rotated from one company to another. Fellow named Blackstone was at it year after year, two or three different assignments a year. Company sticks him in the plant on a phony job, he's a good mixer, joins the union, pretty soon he's secretary, pretty soon squabbles begin in the union, and all the time he's the righteous one holding it together while membership drops. Jesus! What that guy did to a machinists' local in Akron! From 348 paid-up members down to eight in four months.

"Why, half the machinists' locals in the country must have had Machine Products operatives as secretaries, according to that record," Tannenbaum declared, gloomily.

Was Consolidated in the Machine Products? Mitch asked.

"Sure, a lot of their small manufacturing plants, tubes and stuff, hold memberships. . . . Say, you should have been there the day we had the Ironville major on the stand! You'd have thought he had a decoration coming to him for shooting up the union!" Yes, they'd had blood-eyed legionnaires, and comical Chamber of Commerce fatheads by the ton, but they still remembered with affection those hours with Captain Wiley, the expert on Moscow and Lenin, how was the old boy doing?

"Still on the job as far as I know," Mitch said.

Sproul whistled. "You *have* got a town," he said.

Tannenbaum muttered: "A fine lot of use we are."

"Coming to the show tomorrow?" Sproul asked.

"That's mainly what I came down for," Mitch said. "Have you got a show?"

Sproul shrugged, with the gesture of a man who, if he fails, at least knows he's done his best. "We hope the star won't disappoint us."

There was one new element to the scene. In that double row of chairs near the door, once occupied by Chicago police, there now sat a species of men quite different from all others in the room. They were like characters in movies, yes, the tycoon and executive type. Something about their suits, of quiet-patterned, distinctive cloth, fresh-pressed without being over-creased; something about their shirts; but mostly a quality of their very skins, worked over, tended, set them apart so completely that they might have been made of different flesh from other men. And though they were not alike in manner, there was a unified effect of abruptness as they sat together, a frontal impatience with this annoying situation which they had consented to suffer from a poorly conducted world.

Speer was recognizable from newspaper photographs, without his actually resembling the photographs. For no picture could reproduce the bone-smooth hardness of the man. It was no accident that he had become the symbol of intransigence; he suggested not only a rock that would not budge, but a slippery rock.

To see him was almost enough. For if one could not understand before how any man could allow such havoc to happen in his name, the sight of him explained. Mitch Wilner was well acquainted with callousness, in his world, but not with irresponsibility; responsibility for human life hung over all the medical world as the one measure of good, and though there were doctors enough who valued money, or position, or ease, there was none who in the last analysis could shake from himself the imposition of responsibility.

But here was a nature of command to all appearances divorced of responsibility. Even the military nature, one read, was never

[573]

free of the knowledge that human life was a material of war. Otis Speer, it seemed to Mitch, was a being full-charged with the power of command, to make, to combine, to direct—not a single quality else.

In the men about him was reflected a striving toward this same unity, but distracting traits appeared; there was one with a thick lapping skin, like an old bulldog's, who proved to be an attorney, and he was full of subtlety and caution; and there were others who were obviously lieutenants and minor executives; none bone-pure like the chief.

Opposite, where the strikers had been, sat a group of men who, in dress and general scale suggested workers, small and middle-paid men. But they had no ease toward each other. Mitch was going to sit among them when Tannenbaum caught his hand and whispered: "Uh uh . . . stinks, over there." They found a place for him in a row of folding-chairs squeezed against the rostrum. Thus, he faced the witness chair and, by squirming and arching his head, he could see the senators.

In this special row, a few seats from him, sat old Oscar Lindstrom, his glass eye fixed directly upon the witness seat, while the well eye moved, now examining the tycoons, now swerving to the group of spies and guards, their own employees, who sat opposite them.

The senators immediately called Otis Speer.

Facing each other across the long table of newspapermen, lawyers, investigators, the questioner and the witness were not greatly dissimilar; in size and round shape of head they were the same; the senator, too, had that executive alertness so noticeable in Speer. Only the very element of human responsibility, whose absence Mitch had so sharply felt in Otis Speer, was their differentiation.

A man could not help but think that here were the two governments of his country, in apposition.

To the senator's first question, Speer responded by reaching forward a document. "I have prepared a statement regarding my position in this whole matter, Senator," he said, with respect and self-respect. "It will save us both a great deal of time if I may be permitted to read it now."

The senator replied smoothly that the witness would be given opportunity to make any statement he wished, at the close of his testimony, but that in the meantime the chair preferred to continue with the method of inquiry established with all other witnesses.

The corporation lawyer pointed out that, since Mr. Speer hoped to be able to get away at the end of this day, the prepared statement might make the best basis upon which to begin.

The senator refused again, and Speer settled back with the air of a man who resigns himself to an expectedly stupid obstruction, after having made all decent efforts to remove it.

Now came a series of questions bringing out Otis Speer's background in the steel industry.

Around Otis Speer, since the beginning of the strike, had grown the obvious newspaper legend. A tough self-made steelman of the old school, a blustering swear-mouthed guy up from the mills, the old American legend. But now Mitch Wilner saw what was changed about that American story. Any young fellow from an owning family, going into the business, could of course be sent "up from the bottom"; he'd put in a few weeks observing or maybe even doing each task, and in a year he would rise from cinder-snapper to superintendent, a "meteoric career." And his biography could truthfully say that he had once shoveled dirt.

Speer was no untaught youth of brawn who had studied metallurgy in his two-dollar-a-week room after twelve-hour shifts in the openhearth, but a graduate of Cornell Engineering School. By 1919, he had had six years of experience as super-

[575]

intendent of a mill in Triton, Ohio; the mill was a unit in the old Shelling Corporation, and Otis Speer had already given Triton a national reputation: by some with bitterness and by some with pride, Triton was referred to as America's model steel town. It was a company town. The Shelling Corporation owned the homes, and sold them on long terms or rented them to the workers. The company believed in the "personal relationship" with its employees.

"Would you explain that to us, Mr. Speer?"

"My door was always open, and any of the men knew he could come in to see me with any problem, and they did come. I knew and could call hundreds of those men by name. That was a model steel town because the men had the best working conditions and the best wages of any steel center. And I still believe that is the best relationship between a company and its men."

"How many people do you, or does the Consolidated Corporation, have in its employ now?"

He didn't know precisely. Upwards of forty thousand.

"And can any of them walk into your office, and do you know them all by name?"

"Any of them can walk into my office," Otis Speer insisted, impervious to the laughter. "Naturally we have a big organization with foremen and superintendents of varying degree, and they have direct contact with our employees."

"You also have a system of police?"

"To protect property against theft and things like that." Again he offered his prepared statement, saying it dealt fully with the company police, and would save time. The senator politely demurred.

Were company police in Triton, he asked, also instructed to watch certain activities of employees?

Speer didn't understand the question, unless it referred to

[5 7 6]

watching out for drunks and men who were otherwise undesirable; naturally the police had an eye out for them.

By "otherwise undesirable" what was meant?

"Men that might interfere with the work, trouble-makers."

Could union organizers be regarded as such?

Let it be understood, explained Mr. Speer, there were men in
the Triton works who belonged to unions, and he had dealt with
them, he had nothing against unions; but sometimes outside
agitators would get into a plant with no other aim in view than
causing trouble and forcing the men to pay dues to some organization in order to keep their jobs, and it was his policy and
always had been his policy that no man who worked for him
had to pay tribute to anybody or any organization to keep his
job. He had a prepared statement to that effect——

"We'll come to that." A supplementary witness was called,
taking the chair beside Otis Speer. A stringy, elderly man, he
reminded Mitch Wilner of Whitey Gillespie.

The witness said he had been an organizer for the Amalgamated Steel Workers in the unionization drive preceding the
strike of 1919 against the twelve-hour day and seven-day week.
He had been sent to Triton. "We organizers used to call that
the Siberia of America."

Speer chuckled appreciatively.

The senator asked the organizer, had he accomplished anything in Triton?

"I got as far as the railroad station. When I got off the train,
two company police come up, searched me, and marched me
right back onto that train again."

"Were they armed?"

Armed.

The witness was excused. He resumed his place, in the little
row in which Mitch Wilner sat.

Mr. Speer said he did not know the witness or any incident

similar to the one to which he had testified but he could say and would say that all during the 1919 steel strike the Triton plant had worked at one hundred percent of capacity and that there had not been the slightest vestige of discontent among his employees.

Following 1919, Otis Speer had become general superintendent of all the Shelling works, and as more plants were added to the chain, he had spent some time "welding them into the system."

Had he, for instance, occupied himself with the Pioneer plant, in St. Louis? Yes, he had spent some time there.

Oscar Lindstrom was called to the supplementary witness chair.

This time, he was no personification of a biblical figure, no blinded Job. He did not look at Speer. Yes, he had worked sixteen years in the Pioneer plant, risen to the position of roller. He had belonged to and been an officer in the union. They had not been called out in the 1919 strike. Shortly afterward, however, the plant had been absorbed by another company and Mr. Otis Speer had come out as superintendent.

"Did you experience any change in the nature of your employ?"

"There were changes right away. More guards were added and they were put in uniform."

"Had there been guards before?"

"Hardly guards, you would call them, just watchmen, mostly retired employees."

"Had they carried arms?"

"No, Senator."

"Did these new guards carry arms?"

"They carried pistols strapped around them."

"Was there any noticeable change or effect upon the employees?"

[5 7 8]

"It was different right away. It was like we weren't trusted any more. When you see a man with a gun going around, watching you."

Had there been any change in his own status?

"I was fired."

Lindstrom related how almost all the union leaders lost their jobs, how the union dwindled to half a dozen men, how his wife had to take in boarders, how he finally had to move from the city to find work.

"Thank you, Mr. Lindstrom." The old roller resumed his place at the other end of the long table, facing the witness. Speer did not comment upon his testimony. No reference had been made to the Chicago massacre.

Rapidly, now, the senator sketched the formation of the Consolidated Steel Corporation, which had absorbed most of the Shelling and the Pioneer plants, with Otis Speer receiving $150,-000 a year to help form and then to direct the new company.

Now a huge chart was unrolled upon the wall. Tannenbaum approached it with a pointer. He glittered. Undoubtedly this was his work.

The chart was in the form of a wheel of chain-links, with lines interlacing the links. The hub was marked Groves Rogers Corporation.

Tannenbaum read out the names of some of the links. Consolidated Steel, Midwest Steel, Tri-State Steel, Acme Shipping, Mahoning Groves Bank, Acme Ore—all interlaced, through board members who were in turn laced to the board of the Groves Rogers Corporation.

What was the greatest stockholder in Consolidated Steel? Groves Rogers Corporation. Third largest stockholder in Midwest Steel? Groves Rogers Corporation. Fourth largest stockholder in Tri-State Steel? Groves Rogers Corporation.

With a few quick questions, the senator confirmed Speer's

[5 7 9]

personal interest in the various companies: strongest in Consolidated, secondary in Midwest, and minor in Tri-State.

And was the labor policy of the new Consolidated Corporation similar to that of the firms with which Mr. Speer had previously been connected?

Exactly, Speer said. Except, of course, some things, which an employer was allowed to do in 1919 and even praised for, like taking an interest in the welfare of his employees, were against the law now, for if you gave your employees advice, why, that was an unfair labor practice, so naturally the company confined itself to those things which were not against the law, but still tried to be friendly to its men.

And now, the senator said, since Mr. Speer seemed to prefer to read prepared statements into the record, he would offer him one to read. It was a statement of policy issued by the Consolidated Steel Corporation shortly before the strike. It was signed by Otis Speer.

Speer's smile conceded the neat trick, but promised to top it. He accepted the document and read: Consolidated Steel Corporation believed, as the Wagner Act and the Supreme Court had guaranteed, that every man had a right to choose his own representative for collective bargaining, or to represent himself if he so chose, and it was the policy of the company that employees should be permitted to make their choice free from any form of interference, intimidation, restraint, discrimination, or coercion. Therefore—Speer raised his voice, with the anticipation of finessing the trick—therefore the company would not sign any agreement with the C.I.O., but would continue, as it always had, to bargain collectively with its own employees.

The senator asked: Was that a correct statement of his policy?

It was, said Mr. Speer.

Quickly, the senator called a series of supplementary witnesses. Taking the chair right beside Otis Speer, a man named

[5 8 0]

James Ardley related how he had worked in the company police of Consolidated Steel for three years; how he had been instructed to get any information he could find on things that would be "detrimental to the company," such as union activities; how members of the police force tapped wires; and how outside men attended union meetings and phoned in reports, including lists of union members. He named a dozen men who had been assigned to such espionage, and then told how during a strike in 1935 he had been sent from the Cleveland plant where he worked to the Grovespoint plant, which was on strike.

"What were your duties there?"

"We bust up the picket line."

"How?"

"They rode us out the gates in an armored truck, and we unloaded on the street and come up behind the pickets and opened up on them."

"What were you armed with?"

"I had a steel pipe, gas gun, revolver, and some gas bombs." After that, he said, the strike was broken.

Then he had returned to Cleveland. All job applications, he testified, were sent to the police department for checking; if they proved to be from union members, the police department marked the cards and jobs were refused.

With the air of a man resigned to having his time wasted, Otis Speer watched Ardley testifying. When the man had finished, Speer said he didn't know him from Adam, and a company official took the supplementary chair to state that Ardley had in fact been a member of the company police, but was now a disgruntled employee, having been fired because he deserted his wife and family and was a man of "bad repute."

Ardley was followed by a series of trapped spies: John Fay, *alias* John Hall, who had actually got himself on the union payroll as an organizer; Peter Moscaro, who had become secretary of the S.W.O.C. lodge in Buffalo but betrayed himself by constantly suggesting bombing parties; Joe Lurie, whom, Mitch remembered, the Mahoning boys had caught, and, finally, Captain Howard Crawford, who had left the telltale hectographed records of spy reports in his traded car on his flight to Canada. Crawford, with the squirming sheepishness that only overlarge men can suggest, seemed to be trying to get as far as possible from his boss in the next chair, and held his face stiffly averted as though ducking a blow. Otis Speer, however, only looked at him with faint amusement.

For an hour, these men, brazen, sometimes slimy, sometimes shamefaced, related their double-dealing, and when they had finished, the senator asked Otis Speer whether he considered labor spying a violation of the company's statement on collective bargaining, for instance the statement about freedom from intimidation, signed by himself and read into the record by himself that same morning.

"I have a section in my prepared testimony, dealing with this very point," Otis Speer replied, and this time the senator permitted the document. Labor spying was a vicious and ignoble practice which Consolidated Steel would not countenance, Speer read; specific orders had been issued against it, and if any such activity had gone on in the company, it was without his knowledge and certainly without his approval.

His voice was solid, there was not the slightest color of embarrassment on his face as he pronounced his denial for the record.

Could it be, the senator asked, that such a practice could go on in the company without his knowledge?

It could, Speer said, and the senator let the amazing statement rest unchallenged.

The buck was passed to a member of the personnel department who took the supplementary chair and admitted he had paid out money for certain spy information, though he "knew it was against the policy of the company." Then why had he done it? He stared at the senator, as though shaken out of a dream. "I can't imagine why I did it," was all he could find to reply.

Mitch Wilner realized that in this realm, the realm of tycoons, as in diplomacies between nations, odd gentlemanly immunities were preserved. A contradiction might be laid bare, shining, glaring; but none would call it what it was.

All through the morning, visitors of importance had been slipping in to sit for a few minutes, in a little alcove just behind the flagstand. Many were recognizable, senators, congressmen, officials of one sort or another whose photographs were often in the papers. They would sit there half screened, watching the senator play his hooked tarpon, and in a few moments they would leave. Sometimes, as a visitor was spotted, a murmured name would go around the room; and now Mitch heard the name of a cabinet member and, turning almost completely around in his chair, saw a stooped but springy old man, with a humorous, partly open mouth, nod to the senator and take a chair. Wilner's excitement rose, as once, years ago, when he had gone to Rochester and shaken the hand of Charles Mayo. This was the man they had come from Chicago to see; this was the man who might cleanse the city of its long disease.

The senator had started on a second series of questions; Mitch recognized the technique now, of getting the witness first to make a statement of policy, then producing evidence which proved the statement to be untrue, and leaving statement and contradiction bare, for all to see.

What did he think of company unions, the senator asked the tycoon.

Speer said he knew nothing about them.

[583]

What of the employee representation plan?

Ah, yes, he had some knowledge and experience of that. In his opinion, it was the best form of collective bargaining.

Did his companies participate in the formation of employee representative plans?

No, of course not. Such organizations were formed only by the employees. The company had given them an infinitesimal amount of financial support, until that too became illegal; since then employee groups had supported themselves.

Now, said the senator, he would read from the minutes of the board of directors of Consolidated Steel. He read how: "The chairman recommended an employee representation plan worked out by the Eastern Cement Corporation, and was authorized by the board to put such a plan into force as promptly as possible."

Would it not seem from this report, the senator asked, that the company did have something to do with forming employee representation organizations, or company unions as they were commonly called?

"Our personnel director can give you full details on that subject," Otis Speer passed the buck. "I am not entirely familiar with the details."

"But these minutes state that the chairman of the meeting made this report."

"Yes," Speer admitted. "I was the chairman."

The visiting cabinet member made a long, laughing face of applause at the senator, glanced amusedly at the hooked tycoon, and left.

The investigation spiraled upward with amazing rapidity; Mr. Speer was a director of the American Iron and Steel Institute, which was in turn affiliated with the National Association of Manufacturers, which had, in 1934, suddenly branched out on an "educational program," needing a special $50,000 fund, to which Consolidated Steel had contributed heavily. Otis Speer was vague on this point. Consolidated belonged and contributed to hundreds of organizations, he didn't even know how many——

"One hundred and eighty, officially," the senator helped him, pulling out a record sheet.

"That many?" Mr. Speer said. "Wasted money. We'll have to cut it down."

"Of course these were only the officially recorded memberships and donations," the senator pointed out. The committee had no way of knowing how many or what specific organizations had received unrecorded financial support.

Martha Cross and the Citizen Volunteers, at least, Mitch reflected. Evidently the senate committee was not ready to press this point.

"I don't know what use we got out of those organizations. It's just goodwill," Otis Speer declared.

"I think I can remind you what use you got out of this special educational campaign," said the senator suavely. Now, the inquiry proceeded with a series of don't remembers and don't knows from Otis Speer, while the senator, like a magician, each time responded by pulling out as "refreshener" a copy of a letter out of Mr. Speer's own files, or his company's files, or from the files of the Iron and Steel Institute, or of the National Association of Manufacturers.

Tied together, the documents showed that Otis Speer had evidently been very much interested in the N.A.M.'s "special educational campaign," for the subject was employee representation; the documents proved that hushed conferences of companies sponsoring such employee organizations had been held in Chicago, publicity being avoided because "employee representative organizations would be discounted generally if it was found they had been originated through the National Asso-

[585]

ciation of Manufacturers." The Iron and Steel Institute, with Otis Speer as the driving force, had approved all this and, in a resolution, extended its thanks to the N.A.M. for its work in developing company unions.

But the development of company unions was not all. Energized by special funds, the N.A.M. had attacked the problem of strikes. "Now more than ever," the senator read from a pamphlet which it had issued to its members, "strikes are being won or lost in the newspapers or over the radio . . . the settlement of strikes has been thrown more and more into the laps of public officials . . . and it is public opinion—what the voters think—that moves those elected to action along one course or another. . . . Machinery should be set up in every community to cope with the issue of unscrupulous unionism and radicalism both in its immediate aspects and in its long-range potentialities."

From another pamphlet, also issued by the manufacturers, the senator continued: "The breakdown of law and order in many communities as a result of the impasse between labor and industry has caused a third party to interfere in the struggle. This party is composed of merchants, professional men, farmers, white-collar workers, and other groups which are known as the Public. This activity has been expressed principally in two directions: a spirit of Vigilantism in different areas of the country, which seeks to maintain Law and Order where Chaos and Anarchy threaten, and, secondly, the formation of Citizens' Committees in communities afflicted with labor difficulties." The pamphlet pointed out events in the Little Steel strike as examples of the citizens' movements.

The senator asked: Did Mr. Speer think citizens' committees played an important part in the strike?

Citizens' committees? Speer repeated. He didn't know exactly what they might be, but he would say that the substantial citizens of the strike communities finally got together and got some semblance of law and order.

At first Mitch Wilner could not see what the senator was driving at. For he, himself, had helped form a citizens' committee as a result of the strike. How far had they got? They had held one big meeting, after having the Auditorium denied them, and then had found their movement smothered by small obstacles, and by the apathy of the vast public. But they were a true citizens' committee; they had acted spontaneously, on conviction born of events which had aroused their civic indignation. And, he realized, they were not the kind of committee the senator was talking about. What chance did they have against the "machinery set up" by the manufacturers' association, what chance against the vigilante committees organized in Ironville and Mahoning? Against the citizens' committees manufactured for the steel company by Martha Cross and Neal Hollis?

The senator was pointing out further passages in the pamphlet which described the Mahoning Valley, the steel strike area of Ohio, as "seething with the spirit of vigilantism." This spirit had "failed to materialize into a formal organization," the pamphlet pointed out, only because there was "no machinery set up for it as yet."

Was the machinery later set up, the senator asked.

"What machinery?" Otis Speer demanded. A lot of coal-miners, outsiders, and bums were keeping the men from going back to work, and when the substantial members of the community realized it, they corrected such a situation.

And how had the substantial members of the community come to realize this, the senator asked.

Speer looked up cautiously. Why, as anybody would realize it. They had seen the facts.

[587]

And who had selected the facts for them to see? And what kind of facts? The senator offered in evidence the records of payment of nearly one hundred thousand dollars by Consolidated Steel Corporation to the advertising firm of Norris Crane, for services rendered during the strike period. Evidence of five-thousand-dollar fees paid to speakers at meetings in steel towns. The senator reminded Otis Speer that the National Association of Manufacturers had spent a million and a half dollars in its educational campaign to "acquaint the public with the problems of industry." What chance, Mitch thought, did a few liberals collecting dimes have against such machinery? But Otis Speer coolly professed to see no significance in all this. He sat, calm, answering in bored corroboratives, as the senator briefly documented the strike, showing how every effort toward negotiation had been met with blank refusal; how the President of the United States himself had telephoned Otis Speer, to no avail; how the President's special mediation committee had finally given up, declaring Consolidated Steel's attitude to be "not the way to industrial peace."

Then he read into the record Otis Speer's letter of thanks to the mayor of Chicago for the splendid work of the Chicago police. "Have you seen the photographs of what happened in Chicago?" he asked.

"Yes, I have seen the pictures," Otis Speer said with the same glacial calm, staring, Mitch noticed, not at the senator, but directly at Oscar Lindstrom.

"Do you see anything in those pictures which you would disapprove of?"

"It is very deplorable," Otis Speer said, "that things like that have to happen."

The following morning, the Chicago committee entered the office of John Heiser. The cabinet officer greeted several whom

[5 8 8]

he knew by name—Professor Ladd, and the stubby, clear-eyed head of the garment workers, and the head of the teachers' union; he shook hands all around.

He asked if any of them had been in town yesterday for Gottschalk's show, and when Mitch said he had, the secretary grinned, with mutuality. "Beautiful job, wasn't it? Beautiful," he chuckled, and rubbed his chin. Then coming to attention: "Well, folks, we all know what you're here for and we might as well get to it. The answer, much as I hate to give it, is no."

They were stunned. All had expected assent, since he had allowed the delegation to come to Washington.

He grasped this at once. "I let you come on," he said, "because until yesterday there was a chance I could do it. I'm all for it personally. End my career in a blaze, if not a blaze of glory. But your mayor was in town yesterday. So was your state's attorney." He rubbed his chin again. "Frankly, and this is just between us, here's how it is: if a cabinet officer goes back there to run for mayor, it comes as a kind of rebuke from Washington. We just can't do it that way. Reform has to come from the people of Chicago, not from Washington."

"But we are the people of Chicago, asking you," Rawley said.

He chuckled again. "Thanks, but you've got to ask somebody back home. No matter what, if I'd run, it'd look like a slap from on high. If we permit the atmosphere of a row, the Republicans will work the Washington dictator gag to the limit, and it may throw the election into their lap."

Then what remained? Either find a candidate at home, or back the mayor for re-election.

"So far as I can see," he said, before they had assimilated the shock of the second possibility, "you've got to back him. Nineteen-forty is too close for us to risk the breakup of the Chicago organization. Now, they talked turkey to your mayor here yesterday, and I can tell you the man is honestly terribly disturbed by that July Fourth business; he'll never forget it—has it on his conscience. And he promises certain reforms. Maybe you'll get them quicker by backing him than by fighting him. Of course I know it's an election promise, and a machine is a machine." He appeared momentarily very weary. "What I would suggest," he said, "is infiltration. Get some good men into the city council. You can demand a couple of places on the slate. Then at least you'll have a voice. The way it is now there's not even a voice to protest, in that sink-hole." He turned to Professor Ladd. "Why don't you run?"

Dr. Ladd frowned.

"Hell, you're a young man. Run for the council. Kick up a fuss once you're in there, and next turn you can run for mayor."

"I really haven't any political ambitions," Ladd said.

"You'll develop them." The secretary laughed. "That's the trouble with this cock-eyed country. The good people have no political ambitions." He half sighed. "Well, that's the way it is."

As they left the building, Rawley quipped feebly: "It may be the New Deal, but they're making the same old deals, all right."

"Phew. That stinks," Price said.

"Yah. Everything stinks."

That fall, in Chicago's municipal elections, Mitch Wilner was for the first time aware of the candidates and what they stood for. In the primaries, two men sought the Democratic nomination for mayor, and two, the Republican. On the Democratic side, how could a man vote to re-elect the mayor who had blessed the Fourth of July massacre? The alternative was to vote for the state's attorney, Corcoran's chief, who now sought the mayor's chair, and was attracting attention to himself as a "reformer" by sending police squads out with axes to wreck bookie joints.

But that egg was twice as reactionary as the mayor, George

Price declared. Plenty of unions had taken an awful bouncing around from his office; besides, he was lined up within the Democratic Party with the old guard who were simply waiting for a chance to knife the New Deal, the people who would even combine with Republicans, if necessary, to beat Roosevelt.

Nor was the attorney clean of the massacre, for wasn't it his office that had staged the phony inquest? And forced the guilty plea?

What a choice!

And look to the Republican side, for after all La Guardia had run as a Republican.

The Republicans advanced an upright, handsome stuffed shirt whom they were trying to build up as a Dewey because he had helped send Al Capone to jail. But the man's every utterance was reactionary, and slippery. He believed in less taxes, in less relief, in leaving business alone, and in a general program of reaction, which was only a milder and more evasive statement of the things Otis Speer openly stood for.

Against him, old Big Bill Thompson suddenly appeared, Big Bill the wild man of Chicago's twenties, risen as from the dead, campaigning with vague battlecries that were like ghostcalls of his heyday slogans—Put Everybody Back to Work, Down with War—but underneath all was a rumor that his comedy acts covered a Hitler complex.

Four candidates democracy offered to the people!

If it was true that, in such circumstances, some underlying force, perhaps the surge of popular resentment, inevitably pushed to the surface a candidate for the people, this was a time such a thing must happen, Mitch Wilner felt. For surely there were tens of thousands like himself who could not put a mark opposite any of those four names. If at least there were some candidate through whom they might register their protest, even though there was no chance of electing him. Surely such votes,

[5 9 1]

for candidates certain of defeat, were not wasted when they gave voice to the thousands who otherwise had no true way of voting, and gave warning to the machine-elected.

He received an invitation to a luncheon for Dr. Ladd.

It was at the Palmer House; Marcus Olden, the lawyer, presided. Fifty, sixty people were present, the usual progressive group. But to Mitch Wilner's surprise, he ran into old Professor Nyquist among the lunchers.

Of course, he had long known Nyquist was liberal, having seen his name on letterhead sponsor lists for such groups as the Medical Bureau to Aid Loyalist Spain, and amongst that great group of Nobel prize-winners and other topflight scientists who headed relief organizations for exiled German scholars. Nyquist grabbed him and, ignoring politics, began a theoretical discussion referring to that work Mitch had done on anaphylaxis while still at school. "What have you been doing with yourself these days besides patching up gunshot wounds?" Nyquist demanded, and Mitch admitted he had branched off into some practical applications of his research, in allergy. "Sure, you have to eat," Nyquist said, stowing away a huge mouthful of steak. Mitch brought up a thought he had had some weeks ago, while returning from Washington with Rawley—the idea that it was time for a comprehensive investigation of the whole field of hormone activity in relationship to allergy. Nyquist agreed at once: "Yah, it is the long way around but it's the only way we know how to do it, yet. And some hints we do have." For instance, he reminded Mitch that, since men are more prone to shock than women, the male sex hormone might be mixed up in the problem, somewhere. They embarked on a whispered discussion, disregarding the speeches.

Marcus Olden was outlining the political situation, with which they were all familiar. It would be altogether too dangerous to introduce a progressive candidate for mayor, even in the primaries, he said, for that candidate might split the New Deal following and allow the reactionary state's attorney to win.

Therefore the best thing to do was to stay out of the mayoralty campaign. However, a great deal would be gained by having a progressive voice in the city council, a whip, so to speak, to hold over the city fathers. In this connection he was pleased to announce that Professor Ladd had consented to run for alderman, for the university district.

Even that would not be an easy race, for the present alderman was rich, and a part of the county political machine. Progressives would have to concentrate all their energy on the fight in that district. Labor's Non-Partisan League, the Labor Party, the liberals in the Democratic Party, the student union, all would work together to elect Dr. Ladd alderman.

And—who knew?—perhaps next time a mayor was voted for . . .

When Mitch got home, Syl asked if he had seen the news. About Dr. Ladd.

"But of course. I went to the lunch."

"Yes, but—" She held the paper out to him.

Mayor to Support Professor.

Mitch read on, as though immune, by long endurance, to further disillusion. The same old game of alliances. The mayor welcomed the candidacy of Dr. Ladd for alderman of the fifth ward, and promised him every support. "I can accept this support only on condition that I promise absolutely nothing in return," Professor Ladd had said. If elected, he meant to press for reforms in the school administration and in the handling of labor problems. The mayor must fully understand this. The mayor had repeated that he understood, and there were no strings attached to his support.

[5 9 3]

In a parallel column the headline read: "State's Attorney's Aid Deserts to Mayor."

Corcoran was now also on the mayor's ticket, running for judge.

"Damn it, I'll vote Communist, or anything!" Mitch snapped.

"But the C.P. is supporting the mayor too," said Sylvia.

He thought she was joking. "No, dear, it's a fact. Barbara told me. They're afraid the New Deal might be defeated, so all of a sudden the mayor is a real progressive."

The campaign was loud and bitter enough. Yet no actual issues were raised. The mayor kept pointing with pride to his record of streets paved and bridges built, and the state's attorney kept reminding the public that all those achievements had been accomplished with federal relief money, and that gambling was rampant in the city until he gave it the ax. It was too sickening. Neither man stood for anything at all. Neither man uttered a word that might indicate he had a thought in his head about the function of government. It was just a question of power and patronage. Yet they did represent, as chance-chosen generals, the clash of left and right, within the Democratic Party, and on the outcome of this primary, national auguries might be based.

A few days before the election, the Wilners were having dinner at the Prices'. At eight o'clock George turned on the radio. "Mitch, you want to hear this."

A deep, familiar voice came into the room. "A month ago, even a few weeks ago, I might have hit anyone that said I would be on the air talking for the re-election of the mayor. Yes, you might well have thought I would be the last man to advocate his re-election, after what happened out at the Consolidated Steel mills. I am not speaking of what happened to myself or even to my family, though we got it as bad as any. I am thinking of all of us who worked in the mills and tried to exercise our right to strike and picket, and were stopped, and shot down by the police. Now here I stand asking labor to vote for the man in whose administration that happened."

"Shut it off," Mrs. Price begged. "It's too horrible."

"How can he do it?" Sylvia wondered.

"Orders," Price said.

"Don't tell me he's in the party?" Sylvia demanded.

Price grinned. "Sobol got him on the S.W.O.C. staff, as an organizer."

"That doesn't make him a Communist!" Mitch said. He remembered the way Lindstrom had talked, that last time. He was certain the old man was doing only what he believed had to be done.

Old man Lindstrom was continuing: "I am going to vote for him myself, and I will tell you why. I went with a labor committee and talked with the mayor, and I believe the mayor is deeply and sincerely regretful of what happened, and that to re-elect him is the best guarantee that labor's rights won't be trodden on again. The mayor knows the shame of it, on Chicago. A new man might let something bad happen, before he knew. The man who has made a mistake and understands his mistake and is on the lookout to avoid repeating that mistake, is better than a green hand. But that isn't the only reason I am voting for this mayor. Look at the other candidates. Every one of them is a positive danger to labor. Labor wants the New Deal, and the one man who will go along with the New Deal is the man we will vote for. The mayor asks us for another chance and I for one am willing to give it to him."

"God, that must have been torture to him, to do that," Sylvia said.

"He wouldn't have done it unless he believed it," Mitch said.

"It gets them like religion," was Price's conclusion.

"I don't understand the party; why didn't they put up a progressive candidate?" Mrs. Price suggested. "Is the election really so close that the New Deal needs their support?"

"No, darling," Price said cynically. "The mayor will get in by a runaway. That's why they're trying to get a grip on his shirt-tail." Didn't they understand? The old bandwagon tactic. After the election they'd claim he could not have won without labor's help; labor could then make demands of him.

But surely, Mitch pointed out, an old political gang like the mayor's was not that naïve. If he won by a landslide, he'd laugh at them all, afterwards.

They were silent, most of the way home. Mitch couldn't speak, for fear of the wrong response from Sylvia, fear that she might make some remark that would increase the strain. She might say, look at what he had given himself to.

And again he realized he was being unfair, thinking meanly of her. How far apart they had come, that he could no longer tell how she would think, that he feared to talk to her about things.

Crossing a viaduct to the outer drive, they faced a billboard with a big colored poster of the mayor. "The Citizens' Choice," it said. "One Good Term Deserves Another."

Sylvia said, with bitterness: "I suppose we'll have to vote for him." He realized that she was feeling as bad as himself.

"Not me," he said.

"What else is there to do?"

"I don't know. Write in Mickey Mouse, or anything. . . . I went this long without voting, I can wait till there's a real election."

"That poor Lindstrom," she said. "I can't get over it. What it must have done to him, to have to make that speech." She shivered with repugnance. "Ugh. It's so ugly." He remembered, in that instant, a time when Syl as a girl had come into the lab where he was operating on a depancreatized dog; that expression of repugnance.

Their silence now was like that of a sickroom, both knowing mutual sympathy. After a while she touched his sleeve. "Dear, don't you want to stop by the lake for a minute?"

They were near the place where he had stopped by himself, a few weeks ago, after that horror at the inquest. He drew over and parked. Neckers were on both sides of them. It was a cool, simple night, with few stars.

"It's nice," Sylvia breathed. They both looked southward, and the whole sky there was saffron-tinged: the glow of the mills. Her voice, when she said: "and it looks so beautiful," made him feel nothing had been lost between them; she had been with him all the time.

"I guess Lindstrom must really believe the most useful thing to do right now is to help re-elect that guy," he said, beginning to feel that his own wish for a protest candidate was more an emotional than a practical response. But a man had to have iron guts to be able to stomach so bitter a dose. "Anyway, he couldn't have done it on party orders. Last time I talked to him he criticized the Communists."

"Oh, you know George. He would suspect an angel from heaven. . . . I think Lindstrom meant exactly what he said, that under the circumstances there is nothing else to do."

To start in at the very bottom of the morass, and work with what there was. "He's got something more than I have. . . . I couldn't do it."

"Mitch," Sylvia said, and he felt she was braver than he, in this moment, forcing open the slight beginning they had made. "What's wrong? Where did I fail you?"

He kept his eyes fixed on that sky glowing with the fire

[5 9 7]

of steel. "You didn't—I don't know; maybe that time I went to Washington, the first time, and you were against it, I thought——"

"I was frightened," she said. "Mitch, I was afraid—oh, when you go into things . . . And what's the use? What's the use of torturing ourselves, when those men are dead?"

He recalled Pauline Lindstrom's hysteria at the inquest.

"But we have to find out. Someone has to find out. . . ."

"Yes, I know. But I—I guess I'm too squeamish, about the ugly things of life." She was trembling, and like a girl; he saw, suddenly, that, perhaps because they had been married so many years now, and with children born, he had made her into a cold adult in his mind, and much of what he had thought was selfishness in her lately was this fear of the hurt that ugliness still gave her.

"And lately," she said, "you don't tell me anything that's happening to you. I don't know what you're thinking, or what you want to do. Mitch, I even began to feel that you didn't want to be with me. . . ."

It was not easy to tell her, but he felt that he must make the effort, he owed it to her, the way she was trying, now. "I did think of becoming a hero—going to Spain." He laughed deprecatingly, for the foolishness of the gesture seemed so apparent, now. She grasped his hand. "Oh, Mitch," and laughed slightly too, with nervousness, and sympathy, and relief, as if at the foolishness of both of them.

"Did you go to see Nyquist?" she asked.

"Not yet."

"Why not? He asked you to."

Actually it was because he was afraid it would turn out too good: he'd get all fired up about that ductless-gland research and before he knew it would be devoting most of his time and energy there. "I've got to get the practice back in shape. And I ought to finish that oil-solution stuff to make Feldner happy."

"Oh, Mitch, but this is the kind of thing you really can do! And anyway Feldner would be impressed, if you were working on a problem with Nyquist."

Soon she had him talking about the theory itself, about a report he had seen on the prevalence of allergic reaction in blondes as over brunettes, so perhaps the hormones that affected pigmentation . . .

Only one thing remained, like a stone. It was as though they were coming together through a defeat, through a failure.

When they were going to bed, Syl appeared in that lacy nightdress he had brought back for her, that first time, from Washington.

On election night, Mitch Wilner had an impulse to drive out south and see how the fellows were taking it. Guzman's had been abandoned, since the picket line was off. He drove to Harbor Hall. About a dozen men were hanging around the office; a few more drifted in as a committee meeting let out.

Al Nees had a paper with early election returns. Looked like the mayor by a big majority.

Tiny pawed at the newspaper. "Sonofabitch. Shot down ten of our men and they want us to go and vote for him."

"Who else you going to vote for?" Skourakis piped up.

"S——, I don't vote."

No discussions started. The men were mostly sullen.

"Old Oscar Lindstrom going on the radio. I'd wish I lost my tongue, instead of my eye, if I had to do that. I'd kill myself first," Nees said.

They were silent, as if ashamed for the old man.

"Screw 'em," Kiley said, thumping an imposing stack of

cards. "We're going to have one hundred percent in Midwest by November." There was an increase of nearly two hundred dollars in dues over last month, he announced. "You Tri-State bastards stop crapping and collect some dues and we'll get our contract. We don't need to elect no mayors." The last remark was pointed maliciously at Sobol, who passed through the hall.

The door to Sobol's little office was open. Mitch went in. "Looks like the election is over," he said.

Frank snorted, and made a gesture as if flinging off dirty water.

"I heard old man Lindstrom on the radio the other night," Mitch said. "I couldn't understand why he had to do it. I mean, I know all the answers about the political situation, but I still can't understand how he could bring himself to do it."

"Why don't you ask him?"

"Well, because there are a lot of things that have been bothering me about this whole business, Frank, and I thought you might be able to answer some of them for me."

Frank eyed him curiously, with a smile in the back of his eyes. Sticking his feet on the desk, he said: "Okay."

"This is just for my personal edification."

"I know."

Mitch found he couldn't place the questions in very good order. "Did anyone tell the old man to make that speech?"

"Well, Wilner, you know him. He isn't the kind of guy anybody could tell to do anything like that."

"I heard it was a party order." He felt foolish using the phrase.

Frank Sobol, smiling, shook his head. "Lindstrom isn't a party member." He enlarged: "It wasn't a staff order either. He didn't have to do it. We talked to him, and after a while he thought it was a good idea, too. That's all."

"It must have been a hell of a thing to have to do."

Frank's voice dropped to a tired monotone. "Do you think

[600]

we enjoyed supporting that sonofabitch? Or telling people to support him?"

"Then why did you?"

"It's not just a local affair, Wilner. He was the New Deal candidate. We're supporting the New Deal."

"You mean you got your orders?"

Frank smiled again. "They're not exactly orders. And they're not from Moscow. We discussed it and it seemed the only practical thing to do under these conditions."

"But what I can't understand about the party is this," Mitch said. "If it occupies the place of the main revolutionary party, doesn't it have to fulfill that function? Doesn't a situation of this kind demand a protest vote candidate? Wouldn't you have scared them more by piling up a big protest vote than by being a part of a majority—but who can tell what part?"

Frank said, but rather wearily: "We don't believe in conforming to an idea of revolution. We believe in making it effective. That means we have to be flexible. We have to throw our strength wherever it will mean the most. We're not sitting in a corner and being pure intellectual revolutionists. We're taking full part in the people's movements, in Amercia. Sometimes for a moment that might seem to put us on the wrong side. This time, locally, it might have looked better if we put up an outside candidate for a radical vote. But if you look at it from a national point of view, I don't think so. Christ"—he shook his head—"you don't think I enjoyed this, do you?"

They were silent. Mitch decided perhaps this was the time to ask all the other questions. Maybe Frank would get sore. But he had never been able to dismiss from his mind some fragments of the "plot" charged by the police. He asked, were there any things that had come out during the investigations that would indicate the police had an informant right inside the party group in the union?

[601]

Frank shook his head. "We don't have so many people out here; we know who they are."

"What about Art? Was he ever in the party?"

"No. Art was never a party member."

"Well, did you hold meetings or caucuses he might have gotten in on?"

"We didn't hold caucuses, Mitch. A couple or three or four of us sometimes went over to Curly's after a meeting and talked things over, or maybe to my house."

The thing was becoming simpler now, in Mitch Wilner's mind. He asked about others, directly. Was Mike Sisto in the party? No, Mike was too unstable—drank too much. But he wasn't a bad sort, he listened to advice. Gillespie, though, he was a member, surely? Yes, and Pete Vikulik, and Mrs. Jugovich.

"What about that fellow that was killed, Dombrowsky, who lived at her place?"

Frank shook his head. He had never known him. "She got pinched once and I guess the cops came out to her place and wrote down everybody that lived there."

There were a couple more, Mitch guessed, among the organizers and officers of the lodges. But naming them no longer seemed necessary. He asked, directly, what about that business of a plot to get into the plant? About all that strategy, and the landing party?

The strategy of spreading while coming up to the police line, that was planned, sure, Frank said; it was planned to draw out the police lines, thin them out, so the crowd could get through to the gate. That was all decided at the strategy committee meeting. "That was no party decision, that was a union matter. We were fighting in a strike, that's all." So the night before, a couple of the boys went out and strewed a few extra rocks in handy places on the field, in case the cops got tough. "But nobody ever planned to get inside that plant. That would be crazy. They'd have slaughtered us."

What about the boats, for that landing party?

"There's always a wild element with some wild ideas. Some of the boys have those boats; they go out fishing in the lake, from there. They brought up that cock-eyed idea at the strategy meeting and we voted it down, and then when I heard some of them were going to try it anyway, I went around there to stop them." Frank looked Mitch directly in the eye and spoke impersonally, disinterestedly, merely as though he wanted to help Mitch.

Sure, it could all be the other way. Like the question of who called the strike at 3 p.m. Carl Gaul charged it was Mike Sisto, a Communist; Frank said Mike was no Communist, to begin with, and claimed Gaul himself was responsible. . . . Carl claimed the Communists had an invasion-from-the-rear plot, and he had stopped it; and here Frank claimed some hot-heads planned the landing party, and that it was he who had halted them.

What was proved was simply that, in a large complicated action with so many people involved, complete control was impossible. But certainly these things were small things that had gone wrong, he saw now; their importance had been exaggerated because they were unexplained; and because they were unexplained it had been possible to imply that they were the ultimate cause of the massacre. No, that was no divide grown out of a crack; no conflagration whose cause was an accidental spark. Cathode and anode had been approached, closer and closer; the charge was in them and would break through at the point of least resistance, but the identity of that point was of little consequence, there would always be such a point; and the fire would leap the gap, and burn.

[603]

"When Wheeler first came here to start the campaign," Frank said, "he didn't have any contacts or knowledge of the place. We went to him and told him what we had, contacts with the I.W.O. and other organizations, the old United Steel Workers. We offered to come in and work; we didn't ask for anything because we don't want anything from the C.I.O.; we believe in building the union. They know the ones of us they have in. Gaul and some other fools tried to work up a movement against us, just to elevate themselves; they even held fraction meetings in a lawyer's office up in Gary, a Trotskyite louse, but we can take care of ourselves." But now Mitch felt his interest slackening. Yes, this was why he could never join them. It always came down to a factional fight, and faith.

The winter was quieter for Mitch Wilner. The project upon which he had embarked with Dr. Nyquist proved to be one of those experiments that opened into wider and wider reaches, so that soon he had a dozen graduate students working under his direction, and was himself back at the University nearly every morning. It was possible to relate the research project to the clinic at Memorial, through his tests there upon allergy patients for suspected hormone deficiencies; but it would be a long, intricate job of elimination or combination to find, if ever they would find, the hormone-picture related to protein sensitivity.

But the work gave him a sense of continuity which he had lost that summer; even the atmosphere of continued crisis which existed in the world was bearable under this hope of progress.

He was not back where he had been, isolated in a lab; that he knew. But he tried to find the balance that Nyquist seemed to have found: a full interest in the significant events of the world, an ability to participate in them without losing himself there, and without insistence that the relationship between medical research and the world crisis should be apparent.

Once Nyquist warned him: "To be a radical if you are a good established scientist is easy. The world accepts a certain number of radicals. You will find them in the stuffiest institutions. 'Oh, that fellow, that is our radical,' they say, and they pat you on the back and pay no attention to you. You have been around a long time and haven't changed anything, so they have no fear of you."

So the influence of important people on the left was not so useful, Nyquist maintained. "In fact, sometimes I think maybe we are a harmful element because we lead to compromise. I don't know. It is an interaction. But the main thing is for the plain citizens to know what is what. Important people's votes are unimportant. The idea when we started this democratic system was that each citizen should control only one vote." Perhaps that was indeed all a scientist could do: be a citizen.

The sense of strangeness and almost of suspicion of each other was gone, at home. There was not the unconditional acceptance of each other that, Mitch now realized, had existed before; but if something of the ease of that relationship was gone, he knew, too, that he and Sylvia had ridden over a danger that comes when people who have taken each other for granted see anew. They had discovered some differences of basic attitude toward the world, but discovered, too, that this difference would not break their relationship. The differences made a slight bitterness in him at times, especially times before other people; most badly, times with her family, when he saw how the fear for their personal family safety could operate in Sylvia strongly enough to make her withhold from other things she believed in. Perhaps women had to be like that.

By degrees, through the winter, the people whom they saw, exchanged dinners with, became medical people again, though they still saw the Prices, and Victor Fuchs came around on Sundays, always bringing presents for the kids, till Sylvia decided she had to get him married so he could have his own. The Consolidated case was stalled; he was now working on the Hearst strike. Consolidated, he said, was being tested on the Ohio cases. If the labor board order to reinstate the Ohio strikers with back pay was upheld in the higher courts, the corporation would perhaps consent to much the same arrangement for the Chicago strikers, without a separate labor board trial. So the men were waiting. Meanwhile, slightly over half had been taken back to work.

But another time, months later, Vic Fuchs bitterly declared the Consolidated attorneys had stalled them with that talk of consent, while Speer was behind the whole immense lobby in Washington, attacking the labor board, calling for revision of the Wagner Act. "We've been going easy, trying to get the men back to work, but the only thing to do with bastards like that is to sock them with every charge we've got."

That was early in June. That same week, Sylvia called Mitch's attention to an item in the paper: Arthur Nowis, steelworker, found dead. The body had been found on a street in Calumet City early in the morning; Nowis had apparently been killed by a hit-and-run driver; there was a skull fracture. Nowis, the item recalled, had testified in the Consolidated Steel case.

Mitch phoned George Price. Yah, Price said, it looked fishy to him, too, and he had checked on it as best he could, but nobody seemed interested in Art any more, and there was no evidence. The hit-and-run story was plausible enough, since Art was found in the street up there in Calumet City where plenty of drunks skittered around; he had probably been drunk himself. Later, George saw the body at the inquest and reported: "My theory is, it was a hit-and-run driver disguising his car as a hunk of steel pipe." The company might have thought Art knew too much about its spy system. Or some union man might have thought he talked too much. . . . What was the use of going into it? George concluded. Art Nowis was just too smart to live, that was all.

The meeting to plan the massacre anniversary was held in a gloomy third-floor chamber known as the recreation room, in Harbor Hall. About fifty persons had responded to the call, signed by a half-dozen of the usual names, representatives of the Workers Alliance, and the I.L.D., and the American League for Peace and Democracy. Oscar Lindstrom was chairman. And the usual people had shown up to plan the anniversary, all the comrades in their different coats, Price said.

The more polished, more middle-class effect that the citizens' committee had achieved last year was missing. Of course the bright-faced secretary of the Civil Liberties was there, and a scattering of liberals and even a Socialist or two had dutifully shown up. But on the whole, the people that stuck were the people actually affected, and the party people.

And what could they accomplish?

The call had been broad enough: to all the unions, to all church and civic organizations, and this was the meager response. Chicago had forgotten, or Chicago didn't care.

The heavy-browed girl from the I.L.D., whose name Mitch could never remember, was explaining the plan for a gigantic mass parade, over the route the crowd had taken last year, over the very spot of the massacre, and on to the gates of the plant.

But from where would the thousands come, for this gigantic

mass parade? Who would bother to come out to the edge of the city, and walk over the route of death?

And will they allow us to do it? a representative of the office workers' union arose to ask.

Oscar Lindstrom answered: "We have an official permit for the parade, from the police department." A cynical murmur went around the room. Yes, now the permit was to be had.

Lindstrom went on, saying one thing must be made clear about this memorial; let it not be directed at the police or at the city officials, for they could be made to understand how they had been wrong, they could be made to understand that the people owned them. But Consolidated had made no mistake, Consolidated would do the same thing again tomorrow; and this parade must show Consolidated that they could not get away with it again, tomorrow, or next year, or any time in the future. "Only then can we say, those ten dead did not die in vain."

The man's energy and faith roused something almost of melancholy in Mitch Wilner. For who would come, but a few hundred, perhaps a thousand party-followers? Here they were as usual, making long speeches, talking in big terms, of the "estimated twenty-five thousand" who would throng the streets and cover the prairie, making elaborate plans for handling the tremendous traffic problem. And who would come?

He kept wanting to leave, and yet waiting, as though for some one clue that would give him optimism. The usual suggestions that he had heard so many times in committee meetings last year all came out again—publicity committee, pictures in the papers, radio publicity—still with enthusiasm, still kidding themselves that they would get more than a paragraph in any paper except the *Daily Worker*. Sure, the *Daily Worker* would print a special anniversary edition on the massacre. And it occurred to him that party people already lived in their enclosed world, with their own complete circle of organizations and

[608]

their press, and to many of these representatives, as to the I.L.D. girl, it really was a minor matter whether publicity would get into the "capitalist press"; a special edition of the *Daily Worker* was the complete publicity goal, in her mind.

Or, she had probably been in this stuff long enough not even to waste thought or hope on getting into the regular papers any more.

But then, how could their movement expand? How could it ever affect any but those people who already agreed with them, to the extent of reading their press?

A Negro woman had arisen. She identified herself as Mrs. Law. "Please, Madam Chairman," she said, "I have come to this meeting, I am the widow of Ephraim Law that was killed out there, and I have been trying all I could to get a stone to put on his grave." She had a little money, she said, could maybe raise fifteen dollars, but the cheapest stone she could find, they wanted forty dollars. Maybe she could get some help for the remainder?

After a long discussion a motion was made that any profits of the memorial meeting should go first to the milk fund for strikers' children, especially children of the dead, and that the artists' union should petition the W.P.A. authority for a project to put up a statue on the spot where the men had fallen. The delegate from the artists' union said he happened to know that Joe Freedman, the sculptor, had already made some sketches for such a memorial.

"But doesn't Consolidated own that land?" the Civil Liberties representative asked. "How can we erect a memorial there?"

Sam Eisen arose and said: No, Consolidated never owned that piece of land, it was just a rumor the police had started to justify their action with the claim that they had to keep strikers off company property. The C.I.O. had finally traced the deed; that land had been subdivided, and the actual spot of the massacre was on a lot owned by a Mrs. Belfiorno; the union had leased that lot for fifty dollars for the day of the parade, so there would be no chance of trouble. And doubtless Mrs. Belfiorno might be induced to sell, if the memorial project could be put through. A committee was appointed.

The I.L.D. girl said last May Day they had cleared two hundred dollars selling flowers for a dime apiece, and if twenty thousand red carnations could be sold—they went into estimations of the profits. A committee was appointed.

The I.W.O. representative suggested it would be a good publicity stunt for women in mourning to picket the city hall, carrying signs announcing the memorial meeting.

Lindstrom said, yes, that would be a good idea, but suggested the widows picket the downtown offices of Consolidated, instead of the city hall.

Right, it was finally agreed, everybody was always picketing the city hall.

The hat was passed for temporary expenses, and Mitch gave a dollar.

On the way out, Mitch stopped at the union office, downstairs. There was a completely changed atmosphere. Nothing like the gloom upstairs, among the weary liberals and radicals. Maybe it was the physical appearance of the office that gave the new effect of purposeful activity. For it had been entirely reconstructed. A new partition stretched across the room, with dues-payment wickets, one for each local. And at the window of the Al Nicoletti lodge there were actually several men in line, waiting with their dollars.

Oscar Lindstrom came down from the meeting. "How do you like it, Doc?"

"Pretty fancy," Mitch said. "It sure gives some life to the place."

"Yep. We're going to paint the hall, next. Looks like we'll have the dough, this month." He opened the partition door. "Come on in, Doc."

Behind were three new metal desks and filing cases. An enlarged photograph of the last C.I.O. convention and a calendar with a photograph of John L. Lewis dominated the wall.

"You remember Cass Morrison?" Lindstrom introduced him again to the solemn-faced, thin man who was taking dues at the Nicoletti window. They shook hands. Mitch greeted Pete Vikulik, who was busy with the files.

"You sure have them coming in," Mitch remarked to Cass Morrison.

"Damn right. They better come in," Cass said. "July first is closing. After that it's gonna cost ten bucks initiation, fifteen for reinstatement." He slapped a stamp onto a dues book, punched it with his fist to make it stick, and handed the book back to a Mexican at the wicket. "Okay, Pedro, don't forget your button." He marked the card and stuck it back into the file, put the dollar on a thick stack in the till, and reached with satisfaction for the next dues book.

"How did you do it?" Mitch marveled.

"That ten dollars, that's what does it," Lindstrom said. "They know they got to come in some time; soon as that case goes through the Supreme Court that the company has to sign with us, we're gonna get that contract, and anybody that don't come in now it's gonna cost them ten bucks. We had a hell of a time getting permission from the national office to slap on that initiation, but now Gary is putting on a campaign with the same thing. We're showing them the way," he said proudly.

"We got a loophole too so it don't cost them so much," Cass Morrison said. "After the deadline, if they come in by groups of five, we charge them only ten dollars for the group; that way, it makes them organize themselves."

[611]

The results hadn't exactly come overnight, either, Lindstrom explained. They had put on a slam-bang campaign, dragging every member out on the dues inspection line so that it looked as if there must be thousands of active men signed up. "Why, we had dues inspection lines of three hundred men out there," he recollected, chuckling. "That ain't interfering. We're just inspecting dues. Out with your book, brother, and plenty of the boys that didn't have any books, they signed up, before they got to work."

"Had a hundred oil workers out there on that dues inspection once," Cass Morrison recollected humorously. "Those boys are all right. Come over whenever we need them."

How was employment generally, Mitch asked. He had noticed in the paper that steel production was up. Were they calling men back to work?

"It's up, all right. Up to seventy percent; that's twice as good as last year," Vikulik said.

Then, Mitch supposed, lots of men were being called back off relief.

"There's three thousand men at the employment office every day asking for jobs," Cass Morrison said. "Experienced men."

"More than half of the men in this town will never get back to work in the mills," said Lindstrom. "Now is a good test of it because we've got a boom going on now. Steel production is high, but they don't need the men back to work. Why, you can figure it out for yourself. First there was the continuous strip—that let out thousands of men from the hot mills—then there was the cold rolling—that let more than half of us out of sheet and tin—now they got that scarfing operation that does away with the chippers——"

"Hell, you go through the yard and the place looks deserted," Cass Morrison said. "Used to be men running around everywhere but now you have to go a block to see a man."

[6 1 2]

"Even in the openhearth," Vikulik said, "where the process didn't change, they're making bigger and bigger furnaces, hundred-and-fifty and two-hundred-ton furnaces instead of the seventy-five and hundred-ton, but the same number of men to operate them."

Mitch remembered the pessimism of young Gus Lindstrom, before he died, seeing no future in steel work.

"Future?" Oscar Lindstrom said. He was sitting on a desk, and had picked up a copy of *Life* magazine, with a layout of modern housing. "Why, hell, there's no law says we all have to work on our old jobs in the mills. We've got to make more things, that's all. There's plenty I want. Look at those cars." He flicked the magazine. "Look at this stuff in the ads, radios, air-conditioning; look at that electric stove—why, there ain't enough houses in the Harbor, there ain't enough anything, thousands of people need clothes and stuff, shoes—we've got to make all that, don't we? If new machinery takes a man's job, okay, there's still plenty to do, if we only open things up."

He went to the Tri-State wicket and helped a welder make out a grievance form. The man complained that the welding rates in the pipe-shop were three cents an hour lower than the rates for the same work in the rolling mills.

"Wait till they start their war over there," Cass Morrison said. "I don't like to see it happen, but anyway that's going to put some more men back to work."

"Don't kid yourself," Vikulik commented. "They can step production up to a hundred percent without reducing unemployment so you could notice it. The last war is what started all these efficiency methods we got now, all this unemployment is the result of the last war. You get going so fast and you can't slow down. But that isn't an evil in itself——"

"That's why the company is stalling on the contract," Cass said. "That's why they're dragging it through every court.

[6 1 3]

They're stalling us, hoping the war will start, because in a war labor has to pipe down and play along."

"And after the war we get it in the neck," Lindstrom said. "Like in 1919."

"Not this time," Morrison declared, punching another stamp. "This time we're gonna cinch it so solid they can't take it away."

At lunchtime Friday, Mitch Wilner went out of his way to LaSalle Street to pass the building in which Consolidated Steel was housed. Near the corner he saw the I.L.D. girl and Mrs. Jugovich and Stanley Dombrowsky's friend, Sophie Witco. Only Sophie had taken care to dress in black, like a widow.

"Lots more were supposed to show up, from the Auxiliary," Mrs. Jugovich said. "It's half an hour late already."

Mitch asked if any of the newspapers had sent photographers, and the I.L.D. girl responded, oh, yes, the photographer from the *Worker* had been there already.

"Pauline said she can't come," Mrs. Witco reported. "She got to take care of her brother-in-law."

"We ought to have brought him down here too, as a lesson," the I.L.D. girl said vindictively. "Well, I guess we might as well start. I thought Mrs. Law was going to show up, but all she wants is a tombstone."

The three of them took up their signs, and began walking along the edge of the sidewalk, in single file. "They Did Not Die in Vain," one sign said.

Sophie Witco carried a sign reading: "Mr. Speer, Why Did You Kill Stanley Dombrowsky?"

The last sign read: "The People vs. Consolidated Steel."

The street was thick with lunchers, girls in groups and men in groups, walking slowly back to work, some window-shopping; and there were hurried people darting, weaving,

[6 1 4]

through the crowd; people came out of office buildings, hesitated, and walked one way or another; people got out of cars, and arranged to meet, and the cars drove away; people got into cabs, into street cars—and none paid any attention to the picketing women.

Mitch Wilner stood and watched. He listened for comments in the crowd. Nearly all went by blind to the women and their signs, as though the pickets were a part of the daily scene, sandwich signs for two-pants suits, nothing out of the ordinary. He caught a girl's voice once, reading: "They did not die in vain—who?" she asked her companion. And the reply: "Search me."

Another remark he caught from a man: "Oh, I thought that strike was finished long ago."

Mitch went on to his office.

9. A SINNER, LORD!

OVER in France was the first time Ephraim Law got the feeling of wanting to be a respectable man. Got Paris leave, one time, together with his buddy Andy Revere, a Harlem boy. Andy could parlez-vous, almost; let that boy loose in a town and in five minutes he knew where was the best crap game and girls. Ephraim wasn't sure where it was okay for them to go in, especially the fancy places; he said maybe they ought to follow some of those Senegalese boys because they belonged to the French and knew the ropes. But Harlem Andy laughed and

[6 1 5]

pushed him right past the doorman of a swell café, the kind he wouldn't have dared go around to the back entrance of, even, at home.

"That little old bullet don't ask the color of your skin when she comes along the trenches, boy," Andy said. "And those folks over here, they know one man is just like another. Specially the mamselles!" He wouldn't have nothing to do with those Senegalese niggers. "They're just niggers," Andy said, "just wild men swishing around in their red capes," and Eph had to laugh even though he thought the regalia was kind of hotsy.

Andy said, hell, those niggers were dirt to the French people, and not to associate with them, but an American soldier was different; the froggies had respect for the U.S. uniform—you watch!

Sure enough, those frogs ran out bowing and dusting off chairs just as if a couple of Pershings had walked into the place, and damn if some of those high-class French dames didn't start giving them the eye and smiling like to limousine millionaires. It took Eph a couple of days to get over the feeling of wanting to ask, before going into a place, if it was a place where you could go in. And then that whole feeling was gone, where can you go in and where can't you go in was gone, and he was just a man walking around.

The second night they went in a taxi driven by a hot mamselle, up a hill, and there was a café with a darkie band. The place was crowded with officers, lots of American white boys and some English fellows too, but Andy got a table next to the band and began talking big talk to the band-leader, a Northern

[616]

boy called Satchel Jones. They were all Northern boys and they began riding Ephraim about being from the South. They drank some green stuff with a kick like a plantation mule and Ephraim showed his dogs like old times on the levee feeling good with a pint of corn. Slap your feet, smoke! a white boy called. Set that floor on fire!

They went home with Satchel Jones and he had a swell flat and a French wife living with him; some more people came up to whittle down the night and there was a girl cuddled up to Eph and kept saying he was *beau*. Took him back to her hotel and didn't even charge him anything. Made him feel kind of funny though, 'cause she acted like times he'd seen a woman talking lovetalk to a beautiful horse and stroking his neck. He never had any yearning for the white stuff.

Finish of the war, he couldn't go back to New Orleans. A man was supposed to miss his family, long for his wife and kids, but Eph, he felt no longing except to go walking around. What'd he come to war for? He was no drafted man. Had a wife, three kids. Came to war because he was tired of pushing bales around with his big hands. Look at those grabs on him, big as steam shovels, boss always said; so sure enough he'd get the heavy load off any ship. Tired man needs a woman to rest him. Kids come along fast and Del was no fun no more.

Two weeks after the armistice they were still in camp, everybody talking about home, and Andy was telling him: Hey, Eph, come on and live in Harlem, and all of a sudden he knew he was going to Paris right away. "Can't do that, boy!" Andy said. "You're still in the army, fella." But Eph had to do it, and one night he slid under the tarp of an empty truck; when it hit the town of Senlis he jumped out, took a train for Paree.

Two days he went around there, feeling wrong. He couldn't find that spot where Satchel Jones was playing, didn't know the frog lingo enough to try to find some kind of job; he wished he'd see a colored man someplace to talk to, somebody out of uniform.

Third morning, the old Frenchie in the hotel started to talk to him in a kind of English. "Mister Law, you are very happy now you go back home, yes?"

"Me, I like this country, maybe I'll stay here," he said.

"You wish to remain in France?"

"Yes, sir, if I could find me a job here, this is where I'd stay."

"But in America, you have your family, no?"

"No. I got nobody there," he said. "I like it here."

"Ah. Thank you. That is very nice for you to say so."

But when he came to the hotel that night, a couple of M. P.'s were waiting for him and they jugged him for a.w.o.l.

In 1920 in Chicago Eph was making sixteen dollars a week, washing cars in a garage on Sixty-Ninth Street, also cleaning up floor grease and making himself useful all around, from eight in the morning to whenever they were through with him, after supper. Next to the garage was a laundry, and in the back, by the alley, colored girls stood doing ironing. In those months of heat, the big rear sliding doors of the laundry were left open and the girls stood there working, some in just their shimmies because it was so hot. Couple of the white mechanics were always stepping out in the alley to get a look, telling him they liked colored mamas best, and wanting him to fix it up. Even offering a buck. Sometimes a man had to pretend he was just a dumb nigger fool, didn't understand how to go about a proposition.

One of those girls, she wouldn't even open her dress at the neck, no matter how hot it was in the laundry. She was a pretty girl; one time he took out a car from the garage and drove her home; Angela was her name.

Sometimes he thought he ought to tell her about his family; sometimes he thought he ought to write to that family, write to Del and say they were divorced, to make it clean and straight, like Angela was always saying things should be, clean and right.

Sundays she took him to her church; it was in a store on Cottage Grove Avenue, and the walls and the platform was painted white, and the preacher had a singing choir of kids up there with white gowns on them. The service was everybody singing "Walls of Jericho" and hallelujah songs but standing up respectable to it, not like in prayer meeting back home where the spirit got hold of you and rolled you on the ground. Then the preacher preached. We are all sinners, he said, let each look into his heart and he knows he is a sinner; and Ephraim knew that was true of himself. Angela held his hand and her hand was hot and the preacher kept working up the fires of hell and Ephraim said to himself he would repent and send money back home, five dollars for his family and children. "The way to the Lord is repentance!" the preacher cried, and was like to shake the walls and windows of that store; more and more folks jumped up crying: Amen! Yes, Lord! and repenting; now it was like home, only respectable.

Except he did not have the feeling like back home, when after

[619]

he got the spirit of the Lord a man felt born anew, a babe; after this preaching all Ephraim felt was fresh clean like after washing his face of a morning.

Angela said, would he take her to visit her aunt in Gary, Indiana. Though he had got over the strangeness long ago of climbing into a street car and sitting anywhere, Ephraim still was surprised when in a train a man could sit him anywhere, on any vacant seat. The way to Gary, Indiana, was on a train; it cost ninety cents apiece, round trip. Angela's folks lived in a brick apartment on Adams Street, and they were very proud of a new furniture set and rug, which Angela didn't cease admiring. Her uncle worked in the steel mill, and he said that was what Ephraim ought to do, get him a good steady job and settle down.

Angela showed him she had forty dollars in the bank. She was real sweet going to picture shows with him, but she wouldn't marry him or love him right until he had the same amount in a bankbook; he sure was gone on that girl.

The first job he got in the mills was in a labor gang, making four dollars a day, but the strawboss pretty soon sent him to help out different places in the mill when they needed an extra man, because with those big mitts Eph could handle most anything, and he caught onto the way of most any job, fast enough.

Then he was making five dollars a day as a utility man in a bar mill; those bars of steel would come through the rolls like snakes on fire, and he would have to catch each bar in his pair of tongs and give it a turn onto its side before it fed into the next set of rolls. That was a hell of a hot job; when he told Angela she stroked his big hands, and even let him come up and

[620]

sit in her room. It was a respectable rooming house and she left the door open when she had a caller.

Pretty soon Ephraim had the forty dollars in a bankbook; she had sixty dollars then, but she didn't wait for him to catch up with her. They were married in her church, with the kids in white gowns singing, it cost fifteen dollars. They bought two hundred and fifty dollars' worth of furniture on payments.

Angela didn't have any children, though she wanted them so badly, and sometimes she got the blues and cried and cried. Often Eph got the feeling it was a punishment for the family he had run out on; the Lord wouldn't trust him with another family because of that. Many times he was going to tell Angela, but she would surely say for him to go back there and find his folks. Angela had a mind for what was right. And he couldn't bear to break her heart.

He worked real steady. He was made a deacon in the church. Angela paid every week on insurance and a radio and a car and a vacuum cleaner, and after she got the cleaner paid up she paid on a washing-machine and after that she paid on a fine new rug. She belonged to a women's Thursday circle, and when they met at her house she always told Ephraim in the evening how all the ladies were envious and said what a wonderful husband she had to make her such a home, and some of the girls had worked in white folks' homes in the best sections of the city and said those folks didn't have such nice rugs as the Laws.

He could have handled any job in that merchant mill, guide-setter, even roller, and the super knew it. But it looked like there was only so far a colored man could go, and there was even a limit for how far a hunky could go, though Mr. Zarach the head roller was one of them foreigners. But the difference was, you take Mr. Zarach, he had a son and sent him to college, and that boy could rise to be a super or anything, but now if a colored man had a son, college or no college, there was only so far he could go. Six years Ephraim worked as utility man.

One time, Angela got rheumatism. It threw her in bed; she lay with her knees drawn up, and to move her joints was a terrible pain. First they tried all kinds of liniments. Then they got a doctor, who said it was arthritis and to buy an electric heat lamp, so they paid on it, but the pain continued. One night Angela said: "Honey, you give me a massage." She still was crazy about his big hands, with the lines deep-marked in black from the steel dirt that could never be washed out.

Ephraim massaged her back gently, strong, and pretty soon she relaxed and straightened out her limbs and said she felt all better. Then whenever the pain came on her, he would massage her and she would feel better. Once Angela got a terrible seizure of pain during the day while her aunt was visiting, so Angela had her aunt massage her back, but it did no good.

"Ephraim must possess that power of healing in his hands!" Angela's aunt declared, and would not budge from her belief. Angela said maybe Eph was the only one who could help her because he was her husband. But her aunt said, no, Ephraim was such a good man, he had the holy power in his hands, like an elected of the Lord.

When Angela told him this, Eph said, no such thing, it was just the massage that was good for her. Angela said he'd better not go around stroking every pretty girl that had a rheumatism or she'd come after him! The way it was, though, her arthritis

[622]

kept getting better every time he stroked her, and then it was gone altogether. All the women in her Thursday circle talked of the miracle, and soon many were asking Angela to have Ephraim lay on his hands, and cure their ills. He refused, saying he wouldn't presume of the Lord.

Then Aunt Louise took sick with a big growth coming out on the back of her neck. She set herself down in Angela's front room and said she wouldn't budge out of the house until Ephraim cured her by laying on of his hands. He was ashamed and felt foolish to try it, but Angela said he had no right to hold back his gift if it was truly a gift of the Lord, and by that time he had a strange feeling inside himself, like a stirring, a feeling maybe it was so that there was a power in his hands. So he worked on Aunt Louise, stroking that thing on her neck; every day she would come and he would put his hands on it, and by the end of the week that thing was going down, and in a couple more days it was gone.

Angela said they ought to talk to the preacher about it, and Sunday they stayed after service and told him. Reverend Stone said perhaps indeed the Lord had entrusted a great gift to Ephraim, and that Ephraim must be worthy of this gift; he warned him of one thing, never to take money for his healing, because if it was done for money, it would not prove efficacious, and also be a sin.

From then on, Ephraim did healing. He could not do it with everybody. But some people, when he talked to them, he would get that feeling of power in his hands, and if they believed in him, he would try to work on them, and after a time, many of them got healed.

[6 2 3]

There was an operator in the mill, an old Polish fellow, must have been sixty years old, operated a shears. And he got a stiff hand. Got so he could not bend his fingers; they stayed curled like for grasping the lever that controlled the huge knife that slid down like a guillotine and sliced butt-ends off the slabs of steel. Every day he complained, almost weeping with the pain in his fingers, and he could hardly keep on working, but if he worked for another year he was due for pension, so he would not quit. Some of the smart fellows said his twisted hand was from grasping that lever all those years, and he ought to get a lawyer for compensation, and if there was a union such matters would be taken care of, but it looked like there was nothing to do.

One day Ephraim was listening to the old man moan, and said: "Let me feel of that hand, maybe I can straighten out that hand." He felt the power coming up in him. And after work he kind of admitted to the old Polack, how he had made some cures. The old Polack offered him twenty dollars if he could fix his hand. But he said, no, he couldn't take money for it.

Every evening for two weeks that old Polack came to the house, and Ephraim worked on his hand. It was getting better, he could flex his fingers, and the third week he said, by Jesus, he could even play the piano like Paderewski if he knew how! His wife sent over all kinds of presents, a baked chicken, and some bottles of homemade cherry brandy, and a beautiful hand-embroidered blouse for Angela. Those Polacks were very nice people.

The story about his curing the old Polack went all over the mill; sometimes people kidded him, others came and asked for

[6 2 4]

his wonderful massage. One day Mr. Massey, the super over Mr. Zarach, approached him and said: "Well, Eph, I hear you are a miracle healer." Mr. Massey was from the South and Ephraim never felt easy with him; it was like, underneath, Mr. Massey knew he was an impostor, a nigger escaped from below; and always when Mr. Massey came by he had to fight with himself to keep from lowering his eyes and stepping back out of the way.

"No, sir, I don't do no miracles," Eph said. "Seems like some-times I can help people. But I wouldn't make any claims."

Turned out Mr. Massey had some arthritis too, not much different from what Angela had had, and nothing helped his miseries. Ephraim was scared because this was the boss, and be-cause he wasn't sure he had the power, in this case. He worked on Mr. Massey several times, and in himself he felt it was not like real healing, but the funny thing was how Mr. Massey believed in him. Mr. Massey had real faith, Angela said, and that was why he was beginning to be cured. Yes, Mr. Massey would say with a little laugh, you people always sure had something, maybe it's voodoo, but you sure have something we folks ain't got! It didn't please Ephraim, it made him feel cheap and maybe like a savage nigger; it didn't do any good to tell Mr. Massey that their church was a regular church of Christ, he just laughed to himself, like he was sure they were voodoo, all niggers were voodoo.

One time the job operating the kink-straightening machine fell open, and Mr. Massey, still like he was joking, said: "How about it, Ephraim, do you think you can handle her?" Ephraim said he knew he could. And still like it was a big joke, Mr.

Massey said, okay, go on and try it, and winked; so in himself Ephraim felt this was a kind of reward for the cure he had done, as otherwise Mr. Massey would never let a nigger have a chance at so good a job. Ephraim wondered if it was all right with the Lord for him to take this reward; but still, it was not a reward of money, and he had not done the healing with any thought of pay.

He sat in a metal pulpit, beyond the hotbed where the bars lay cooling after rolling; the bars were sheared, and then they reached the bulldozer. By keeping his eye on the edge, not the flat, of the bars, Ephraim could detect the bumps and bends that had escaped the straightening-machine; he would release the twin hammers of the bulldozer, and by the touch of his hand regulate the strength of each blow, not too much or too little, to straighten out each kink. In a couple of days he had the feel of the machine. The job paid ninety cents an hour plus tonnage, and some days he made as high as two dollars on tonnage.

Once some college boys came to study the mill. Now those boys were graduate metallurgists. Mr. Massey brought them over to the pulpit and said for Eph to let them sit with him and see how to handle the job. Mr. Massey gave him that special kind of wink he had, and went away, and the wink made Ephraim feel like it was a boss back home wanting his darkies to show off before some visitors from the North.

After work, though, he told his wife how he showed those young metalloos a thing or two. "Now I ain't a college man, never went to school at all," Eph said, watching Angela cook on a big new fancy pot she had, a pot with all kinds of indicators and gadgets, called a pressure-cooker, they were paying

[626]

installments on. "But that college boy is sitting next to me, watching that steel come through, and I says to him, is that high- or low-carbon steel?" He laughed, imitating how the college boy said he would have to take that steel to the laboratory and test it before he knew how much carbon it contained. " 'Why, that's a high-carbon steel,' I told him. Any man working in the mill knows that, without running to no laboratory. All he had to do was look where the shears were cutting through those bars, red sparks flying thick as fireworks. They go to college but they don't know carbon makes red sparks. 'Have to take it to the laboratory'!" He laughed again. "What do they learn in those colleges? Those kids don't know which end of them came out first!"

She said for him not to talk so coarse. But he knew she was proud of his intelligence. He could tell a white college boy a few things now. Yes, there he was sitting in the mill in just about as good a job as a colored man could get. And look at this fine respectable home. He had proved all a man needed was a chance.

Just outside the mill gate, nearly every day, those union organizers were passing out circulars announcing their meetings. A kid named Monty, a white boy that had Ephraim Law's old job as utility man, walked out beside him one day and said, did he know Al Howard, showing him that name, Al Howard, as one of the principal speakers at the C.I.O. rally. Who was it, Ephraim asked, somebody worked in the mill? No, Monty said, this Al Howard was a C.I.O. organizer. "I kind of thought you might know him, he's a colored fellow. I heard him last week. Best speaker they got."

That made him curious, so Ephraim went up to the rally that

[627]

evening, and listened. Al Howard was a hot speaker all right; he could rouse a man, even better than Reverend Stone. He didn't speak especially to the colored in the audience. He didn't say a word like that. He talked like any of the white speakers on the program, to everybody together, and there he was, a colored man talking to everybody, even the whites, and they certainly listened to Al Howard, and gave him a big hand.

The first time that young fellow Monty took him to a closed meeting of the lodge, where he had to show his membership card at the door, Ephraim Law still felt unsure of his right to go inside. Like when he went on trains, and felt unsure he could sit with the whites; or like, in downtown restaurants, a man was never sure it was a place he could go in.

Once Al Howard came to speak at a meeting of the Progressive Lodge, and after the meeting Howard took Ephraim Law aside, and discussed how to get more of the colored men in the mill to join the C.I.O. Al Howard said he wanted Eph to be on the membership committee, because he was one of the solid and respected men in the mill.

Mr. Massey never said anything; maybe it was just something in his eyes. Ephraim Law had a feeling that Mr. Massey knew all and was always laughing at him, like white folks laugh when colored folks get big notions.

Just once, when some rods that had slipped through bad, on another shift, came back charged to him for restraightening, and he started to explain to Mr. Massey that it was not his error, Mr. Massey gave him that quick, mean look, a look that jerked him back twenty years. "Watch yourself, boy! Don't talk back to me, when I tell you you made a mistake!"

He let those rods be checked against him.

The year 1936, after he and Angela had given up all hope of a child—fifteen years they were together; he was a man with curly white sprigs in his hair, and Angela was turned thirty-five—that year she got with child. But in the sixth month she just turned terribly sick and lost the baby and lay near death herself.

Ephraim was all broken up. He knew it was his own arrogance and pride and sin. His being big, his being on committees, his taking the power of healing. "Lord Jesus! I been presumptuous!" he prayed. "Lord Jesus, I been no good. I took unto myself the power of Your hands, I know that is a sin!" He twisted his thick strong hands over each other and saw the fingers like live independent things that did not belong to him, maybe devil-inhabited things. "I don't know how I dared." Yes, he had been tempted, the power was devil-born. "But I never did it for money, Lord; that's where I am clear. Temptation for Your Glory, Lord, that's what tempted me!" He knew why he was punished. He had come too far. He had come too big. He had a job as good as many a white man. He had gone into places where a man would never have thought he could go. Long ago, there was the wife and family he had walked out on. That was his life. That was all the life he was entitled to. A man could not run away from what he was. Mr. Massey knew. Mr. Massey had him spotted. At last, Ephraim begged the Lord for a bargain, only to let Angela live, because she didn't have anything to do with his sin. She was innocent. "Take me, Lord, and let her live."

When the police picked the wounded strikers off the field, they loaded Ephraim into a wagon with other wounded, and

[629]

that wagon stopped at a hospital, and some of the worst wounded were lifted out, but when it came his turn, he heard them say: "Uh-uh. Better take the jig somewhere else." They kept him in the wagon and drove a long time. He knew he was getting weaker. But that hospital was not a place where a man like him could go in.

SUNDAY was the twin of the one the year before, a perfect day, clear, cloudless, with a hot pale sky. From the lake, not quite a breeze, but movement of the baked air.

"We might as well stop on the way," Sylvia agreed, as the Wilners drove off for the dunes. "If it looks like there's any point to it we can stay for the parade, if not we can just drive on."

As they turned onto 18, feeding into Steel Harbor, the traffic thickened; and within half a mile of Guzman's Grove, the going became slow as downtown. The roadside was lined with parked cars.

Sylvia said, with pleased surprise: "A crowd must have turned out, after all!" They couldn't get within three blocks of Guzman's. Busses and festooned trucks jammed the street.

Droves of people circulated among the cars, spotting friends, helping each other fasten signs and placards to their autos, taking snapshots. Mitch parked, and they got out. The kids were excited. Jackie remembered: "Isn't this where we were last year, Daddy, and there was all the shooting? Everybody shot off their guns, all the cops, gee, that was something! Are they going to shoot again today?"

[630]

"No, dear, they won't shoot today," Sylvia said, and Mitch knew she would repeat Jackie's clever remark to her family.

"Aw, why not?" he insisted. And Judy said: "Because today ain't the Fourth of July. Today is only the third."

They laughed. Jackie insisted, people were shooting off fire-crackers anyhow, that made it the Fourth, didn't it!

A girl approached with carnations, and Mitch bought four. "How's it going?" he asked, recognizing her vaguely, American League or something. "Oh, fine, I don't think we'll have enough flowers," she said. "We only ordered five thousand."

"There's George and Beth," Sylvia cried, seeing the Price car.

Inside the Grove stood Al Nees, with his pretty young wife. "How goes it?" Mitch asked. Nees shrugged. His scarred cheek looked darker than ever. "What are you doing these days?" Mitch asked. "Still on W.P.A.?"

"No, they got me off," he said.

"Al's not a citizen," said his wife. "He came over here from Canada when he was five years old."

Somebody must have told on him, Al declared, because the W.P.A. came around wanting proof of citizenship. "I used to go and vote all the time and nobody ever bothered me for no proof of citizenship, but now they got it on me."

But who would do such a thing! Then Mitch remembered the meeting after the trial, when Al had been so bitterly outspoken against the leadership for making a deal with the cops. From Al's glance toward the door of Guzman's, Mitch knew that was what the man meant.

But how rotten it was, after all these men had gone through together, that in this long waiting they should be driven to augment every distrust amongst themselves, to split and quarrel. That was the result of defeat: the search for blame among themselves.

[6 3 1]

"How are you living then?" he asked. "Get your job back?"

Al snorted. "Not me, they won't take me in that mill."

"Getting any relief?"

He nodded, and added shamedly: "Living with my wife's folks."

"Well, the mob certainly came out," Mitch observed, trying to cheer him.

"Yah. They come out all right."

"I happen to know the labor board man on your case," Mitch said. "He said there's a good chance of everybody getting back pay. They'll have to pay out millions in back wages if the higher courts uphold the board."

Nees pulled his upper lip taut, in the made smile people have when they tell kids, oh, yes, they believe in Santa Claus.

"We could get our own flat back, then," his wife said, smiling in farewell and drawing Al on into the crowd.

Mike Sisto and Pete Vikulik hailed him. "Hello, Doc!" Mitch complimented them on the turnout, and then made a remark about Al's being shoved off W.P.A. "That sonofabitch, serves him right!" Mike Sisto cried.

"Why, what's the matter with him? He worked day and night during the strike."

"Aw, half the money he handled, we don't know where it went," Mike growled. "He got enough to dress his wife up awright. My old lady saw her going into Field's. That's the kind of stuff she buys, at Field's."

"Don't you believe he was honest?" Mitch asked Vikulik, directly.

Pete shrugged. "If you take his word for it, he was."

Guzman's had been opened again, for this one day. The floor was littered with signs, volunteers from the artists' union were feverishly tacking banners onto sticks, the I.L.D. girl was phoning, trying to order more red carnations. Mitch glanced into the "hospital" room. By some weird chance, that little box of boric still stood on the sill.

Outside, horns began to blare. Perhaps they were starting. He went back along the line of cars; someone yelled: "Hey, Mitch!" It was Carl Gaul, in Kiley's sedan.

"Where've you been?" Mitch asked, realizing he hadn't seen Gaul in several months. He was up in Detroit now, Carl said; the U.A.W.; been there since January, when the S.W.O.C. had to let out so many staff men.

"Hear anything from Barbara?" Mitch asked. "We haven't seen much of her all winter."

"Oh, I guess she's still around. Heard she was sleeping with the Stalinists now," Gaul remarked.

The horns were blowing incessantly, like the trumpeting of an immense conclave of elephants.

Then word drifted through the crowd: "It's starting!" and people hurried for their cars. But it would be half an hour, Mitch figured, before the long line could unsnarl itself and actually get into motion.

Syl was still at the Price car. George was telling about the department store strike he was covering. That bull-cop Gorcey had shown up in the police detail yesterday. As soon as the pickets saw him, they knew trouble was afoot; and sure enough there was a whole squad of goons in the lobby, strike-breakers armed with crank-handles, all set to bust up the picket line, with the assistance of Gorcey and the cops' picked anti-labor squad.

"Well, of course our papers wouldn't play it but I got a New York paper to query the department on Gorcey, and they got so scared they hauled him off of strike duty permanently.

They've even transferred Wiley someplace where he can't do any harm."

"Some victory!" his wife hooted. "The strikers got beat up and arrested anyway."

The horn-tooting was rhythmical now, folks were amusing themselves sounding shave-and-a-haircut on their horns while others in the line responded six-bits; Mitch stepped onto the running-board of George's car; for blocks back, as far as he could see, the road was jammed.

"Where did they get such a turnout?" he asked, still incredulous.

"C.I.O.," Price said. "They really got them out, packing workers, electrical workers, thousands of oil workers from the refineries—everything."

"Looks like mostly steelworkers to me," Mitch said. "From around here and Gary."

Slowly now, the parade got rolling. In the lead car rode Lindstrom, Sobol, Alonzo; their car bore the banner, "Steel Workers Memorial." Then without any effort at order or display, the parade unrolled itself, jalopies and old respectably washed cars of the steelworkers, and newer cars, and trucks from Hegewisch, from Gary, a truck full of girls from the office workers' union, making an effort to sing "Solidarity" but laughing and chattering too much, cars half covered with signs, all the old slogans, strike slogans and shall-not-die-in-vain slogans; there were no bands; there were no marchers, only this endless train of cars, winding back down Route 18 to Steel Harbor, and through the main street of the Harbor, all the horns blaring incessantly, down Indianapolis Boulevard through steel-town; street cars were halted, all traffic halted for the miles-long parade.

Not a policeman was to be seen anywhere; even the traffic cop at Ninety-Fifth Street was missing. And all along the route,

[6 3 4]

people filled the windows of houses, and waved flags and hand-kerchiefs at the paraders.

A sense of complete but good-natured mastery spread. Now for this hour the city was their own.

Over the bridge they drove, glimpsing briefly the rust-red jungle of blast furnaces and smokestack rows, the hills of coal and limestone and ore piled alongside the slip, dust to be burned into iron; then down into the heart of the steelworkers' district, and through the Mexican slum, and over the tracks through streets of barrack-like cottages, and past the dreary little hotels, each window a room, a man; and forward, the circle completed, forward on that little stretch of road toward the Consolidated plant.

From their spot in the parade, blocks behind the head of it, and with cars stretching endlessly behind them, the Wilners could see the lead car as it went up the slight rise where the road turned to parallel the tracks: the precise spot where the police line had stood. It was a strange bitter thrill, to see the first car make the turn and move up that blood-forbidden stretch of road, and themselves to arrive, and make the turn. From there the cars spread out over the prairie, people parking and getting out, converging toward a speakers' stand.

More and more cars flowed into the prairie, with people end-lessly augmenting the fanwise crowd that spread in front of the speakers. The crowd was an inundation, swelling over the ground, oceanic. From all sides Mitch Wilner heard people marveling at the numbers of themselves, knowing and yet astonished that the same impulse could bring them all out. "It's the biggest turnout since Armistice Day," he heard. And: "Big-ger! There never was a turnout like this in Steel Harbor!"

There was a restlessness among the people; they did not stand long listening to speeches, but would wander over the prairie in clusters, come back and listen, and wander again. Many

[6 3 5]

squatted on the grass, or lay with their arms folded under their heads, staring into the pale hot sky, half hearing the words of the speakers.

All over the place, zealots were selling radical literature. "Quite a field day for the revolution," Price observed, and it did seem almost comical, for every group and every splinter group was represented. Communist Party literature of course dominated the scene, with dozens of hawkers of the *Daily Worker* and the *Daily Record* constantly circulating; but Socialists were plentiful, and there was an old geezer standing over a cartoon handing out anarchist tracts, and somebody was selling the *Catholic Worker,* and there was a Labor Party paper, and a thing published by a Revolutionary Workers Party. There were a dozen others—Townsendites, Epic-followers, pathetic, almost comical little hawkers of Utopias.

The crowd, the mass, seemed impervious to them all. Here and there people stopped, sometimes with amused smiles, inspecting a pile of literature, or glancing through one of the odd papers; here and there squabbles broke out among venders of competitive brands of revolution; but surely, the crowd, the mass, was uninterested. Or did the people feel they already knew? They knew what was what, when it was time to come out, they came out.

"Hey, Doc!" called a big fellow, as Mitch passed. Turning back, he recognized Emil. The fellow looked well, bronzed, bigger and more powerful than ever. He was wearing the usual workshirt and black workcap.

"You sonofagun!" Mitch greeted him. "When did you get back?"

"Couple of weeks ago," Emil said.

"All in one piece?" Mitch ran his hand down the powerful arm, and touched, poked at the torso, as if expecting to find it full of holes.

[636]

"Yep," Emil said. "I stopped a couple of hunks of scrap iron in my leg, but I can still navigate all right."

Mitch fell in beside him and they walked slowly on the grass, on the fringe of the crowd. The man impressed him as more impenetrable than ever, and awfully lonesome now, somehow; a man who had found out everything, but knew there were things he could never communicate, things he just had to carry within himself. "Well, fella," Mitch said, "how was it?"

"Not so bad."

"Think they can hold out?"

"Naw," Emil said. "We'll lose. It's the same every place. We got the men, they got the guns."

All the usual questions about Spain seemed futile; he'd heard and read the answers. "Did you get what you wanted, Emil?"

"I guess so. I got satisfied," Emil said. "I dunno."

"Where were you? In Teruel?"

"Yah. I was in there. Just after I got over. I was in Gandesa, too."

"You saw plenty of action," Mitch remarked; the talk was heavy; he couldn't reach the man, somehow. They had slowed, and now they stopped and faced each other. "Tell me," Mitch said, "in a war—do you know when you hit someone? Do you know if you yourself kill anyone?"

"Not mostly," Emil said. "You just shoot and even if they're coming at you and some of them fall you don't know if you hit anybody, or who you hit. Unless you're a sniper, then you see what you hit. But in Teruel, we had some streetfighting there, it was you against the other guy."

"And did you kill anyone?"

"Yah," he said, without emotion. "There was three times there, twice in Teruel and once just before we crossed the river that last time there, I saw when I hit them. . . . That don't mean nothing though," he said quietly. "Even if I tried to figure

[6 3 7]

they was Chicago cops, or Otis Speer. I guess there's a limit to a man's feeling or he couldn't do what he does."

By saving this man's body, Mitch reflected, he had somehow shared in those distant deaths. He asked: "What happened to that kid who went with you? Arthur Main?"

"He got killed," Emil said.

After a moment Mitch found something else to ask: "Are you back working?"

"They didn't call me back yet." Emil gazed at the crowd, and then at the slow curling smoke from the mills.

"You're being away, didn't that matter?"

"Naw, the hot mills are down anyway; they're putting in a new strip mill to do the job. I'm a hot-mill man. They're trying to find us some other jobs there; they got the 1930 men back to work now. I guess that lets me in pretty soon."

Away, and kill, and come back, and resume a place in line. "Well, Emil, I'll be seeing you," Mitch said, but feeling there was still something inexplicit between them.

"Yah."

"Quite a turnout," Mitch filled in. "It's tremendous."

Emil's gaze went slowly over the crowd again. "Yah, they come out now." He nodded.

Then Mitch said: "Say, you heard, your pal Art Nowis got killed a couple of weeks ago?"

Emil looked into his face, and nodded again. "I was back already," he said, "when that happened."

"Oh." He didn't know how far he wanted to ask. "There was some talk it wasn't an accident. You know Art testified in Washington that he actually did turn over some information to the company, though he claimed it was nothing they could use."

"Yah," Emil said. "We got some of those Gottschalk reports over there. I seen his testimony. . . . That sonofabitch, I used

[638]

to go with him, to that canhouse in Calumet City." He continued to look directly, calmly at Mitch.

"I'm going over to hear the speeches," Mitch said.

Emil showed no desire to hear the speeches; he remained standing there, a blade of long grass in his mouth.

". . . and make them realize there is a law in this land, and they are not above the law, money is not above the law, corporations and heads of corporations"—old Joshua Wheeler's arm pumphandled his every emphasis.

On the grass near the car, Mitch found Syl and the children and Barbara Macey. Barbara was telling how she had undertaken the job of hunting up the wives or relatives of the deceased, and getting them here for this meeting. It was appalling, she said; the union had completely lost track of practically all of them; it had only last year's addresses. That Mexican's family—what was their name?—Hernandez, she had spent a day trailing them. God, how those people lived, they had moved, and the grocer gave her an address, but after asking a million Mexicans there, somebody sent her to another Hernandez family altogether. . . .

"It's strange how they can just vanish as if off the face of the earth," Sylvia said. "Didn't they have kids? I wonder how the woman takes care of herself and the kids."

"Did you find what had become of the Baumanns?" Mitch asked, remembering the clear-voiced German woman at the inquest.

"They were moved too but I found them." She described the place, a paintworn shack, with hardly any plumbing. "The mother goes out to do housework. The oldest kid watches the others."

". . . let them realize," Joshua Wheeler was saying, "that

this is no defeat like after the 1919 strike, when the union lay smashed . . . today . . . a great organization, shown itself capable of going through a major strike unshaken, and growing . . ."

That Mrs. Donovan, Barbara said, could not be found, either.

"It makes you feel," Sylvia said, "like you're watching a piece of driftwood swirl and struggle to keep afloat, and at last it's sucked under and lost."

Well, with some of them it was pretty discouraging, Barbara said. They just weren't interested. They didn't want to come. That Polish woman, Wyznowieki, had practically kicked her out of the house. What a place! Simply swarming with dogs. . . .

". . . and I won't say we won everything, but right now in two out of three of those plants, the union is practically one hundred percent, and as for Otis Speer—the fight is not over, and we won't give up until we . . ."

"But you should hear that young Nicoletti's cousin!" Barbara cried, recounting her most successful search. "She knows what it's all about. Poor kid, I guess she was sweet on him."

Mitch arose. He wandered through the crowd again. A priest was talking now; Father Gillie had come through this time. It sounded all right, too, snatches of it, about the right to labor being as important as the right to own property. He espied Rawley, standing with Vic Fuchs.

"Where did you blow from?" Rawley was supposed to have a job in some Western state college. He still had that young, boyish laughing face, looked more of a kid than ever.

"They caught up with me," Rawley said. "I am a victim of the Independence Day massacre. Behold the eleventh corpse."

The eleventh corpse, he explained, was his career. Finished. Dead. The academic life of Rawley was over. What had happened? Very simple. The head of his department had found out he had signed a revolutionary pamphlet.

"A what?"

"Remember that leaflet we signed, right after the massacre?" That had been enough for the faculty, out West. They had refused to renew his appointment for the coming fall, on some polite and impeccable grounds about its having been a trial semester, and his not fitting in with the scholastic plans of the department.

"Well, what are you doing?"

"Going to be a professional revolutionist," Rawley said, still laughing in his nervous way. He was going to work full-time for that organization he had talked about, New America. Write pamphlets and stuff, maybe a book.

Mitch had a feeling the man ought to remain in sociology, that it was wrong for him to take so drastic a step. "Look at all the pamphlets they got already," he half kidded, indicating the hawkers all over the grounds. "What good is all that stuff? What does it all accomplish?"

Sometimes he thought it was nothing and sometimes he thought it was the whole thing, Rawley replied. After all, the written, organizational propaganda was the core of any revolutionary program. The people that went to work in unions, in mass organizations, they weren't working at random, they were all politicalized. And look at this mass of people; if it moved, it would move through some such leadership. "They don't have to belong to anything, be party members, any more than the guys on the other side all had to be signed up with Father Coughlin or Martha Cross. You've had a clash here, already. What you had here," he said, as though it was a point upon which he had long deliberated, "was the first outright clash between the people and Fascism in this country; active agents of both revolutions participated, and gave direction to men, to forces, which had become, to various extents, impregnated with their points of view. Sure, not every cop was a Fascist and not every striker was a revolutionist, but they were willing to go along and take direction from leaders who were pretty much the one or the other."

"You mean, this is the way it will be? You think it has to come to a complete war?" Mitch asked.

"Well, where did you get with the election here?"

"Then you believe the democratic system is a failure?"

"Jesus, Mitch, don't fall for that stuff!" Rawley cried. "We haven't had a democratic system. That's the whole idea. You've got to have economic democracy too. That's what we've got to make them see. . . ."

Wasn't he just trying to solve things with another phrase? Mitch wondered. "It seems to me the main element of democracy is a feeling of direct responsibility, in all the people," he said. "And that's what gets me down, it's the people, that whole damn city, it's so indifferent—the people just don't care."

"There are lots of people here," Rawley observed.

"Yah. Sure. Because it means something, directly, to these people. But I mean the millions of Chicago, the damned indifferent. . . ."

". . . that this shall not happen again, because labor shall become strong," Oscar Lindstrom was thundering, "united and strong, and know how to secure its rights—not only the right to picket but the right to work, to produce, to have a full share of what we make, to have a full share in the control of our destiny, to live as Americans . . ."

There was no band, no sound. The crowd strung out, on foot

[642]

now, an undefined column, just as it had been a year ago, in ranks of two, in ranks of four, eight, swelling, contracting, but lengthening, this year far longer, three, four, perhaps ten times as long as that column that had walked here last year. The Wilners walked in the parade. The people walking around the block of houses that faced the plant, heading up to the very gate of the mill, and rejecting it, turning to walk on the street that paralleled the tracks, walking down the street where the police had walked a year ago; thus, as over conquered territory, the people quietly paraded, until they came to the point where the police had stopped the strikers. There, now, a mammoth floral wreath stood, and over it was a banner:

TEN DEAD MEN WILL PICKET HERE FOREVER

Across the wreath was a scroll with the names of the dead.

As the people approached the wreath, the column narrowed to a single file, and, passing slowly, one by one they dropped their dark red flowers, like great swollen beats of blood augmenting the spreading red pool on the ground.

A NOTE ON METHOD

Society has for some time accepted a hypocrisy according to which writers of fiction avow that there is no similarity to actual persons or events in their work; while at the same time the modern novel is largely judged by the accuracy with which it simulates and interprets reality. This type of writing becomes a game in which the writer attempts to disguise matters to the extent that his source-experiences may not be recognized, at the very time that he tries to give his story validity through the use of familiar patterns of events.

This novel does not pretend to be a complete fiction, for the events described here as of Independence Day, 1937, were derived from the events of Memorial Day, 1937, in the same locality.

The reader may wonder, then, why I did not write a precise history, using the actual names of places and persons. I did not do so because the form of the novel appeared to permit me the most effective interpretation of those events and of the conditions which gave rise to them. Furthermore, the historical pattern had gaps in a few essential contours, where facts had not yet come to light; and I felt that by transferring to fiction I could suggest some content for such gaps. For instance, though it was established that there were industrial spies operating in the actual source-case for this story, the identity of those spies was never disclosed. In other steel plants, however, the identities and methods of operation of industrial spies were revealed. I have transferred some of these methods and some of the circumstances of detection to the Chicago scene.

I have not used the actual names of persons because I have not depicted actual persons. I do not know, personally, the people who took part in or shaped the events of Memorial Day, 1937, in Chicago. I could never have known many of them, wholly. There is greater truth in an author's whole knowledge of his invented characters than in any piecemeal knowledge he might acquire of living persons, or dead.

It will be observed that some individuals in this story are presented reportorially. The head of the steel company, for instance, appears before a Senate committee and repeats verbatim things that the head of a steel company said at the La Follette committee's hearings on the 1937 steel strike. Similarly, officials of the Chicago police department are presented reportorially, saying things that were actually said; I have not, as a novelist, attempted to enlarge upon the personalities of these recorded participants, but have confined myself to paralleling what is in the record. In the case of Captain Wiley, I have indicated a typical youth-background in Chicago, and I believe it is obvious that this is intended only as a technical device, to knit the character of Donovan more firmly to the general pattern of my story, and is not offered as the record of the youth of any living person.

Though the heads of the steel company, the heads of the city government, the heads of the union, being in official positions, are presented reportorially, a different method is used as the action reaches the levels of involved human participation. In these actions, fictional characters predominate. Strikers, organizers, policemen, newspapermen, attorneys, citizens, scabs, are types and combinations of types, rather than parallels of persons. They touch actuality at the points where they do things that were done, and in a few cases even say things that were said before the La Follette committee. In some instances, such recorded statements were so pure that I felt the novelist's art, at least this novelist's art, could arrive at nothing more revealing, and therefore I gave those statements to fictional characters. It was not my intention to attribute to the real persons who testified before the La Follette committee any of the aspects of my characters. The characters are fictional. To make this clear, I shall presently detail such instances.

The differences between these fictional characters and actual people are chiefly in two forms: First, in that some characters are composites. Thus, I present a character called Corcoran, an assistant state's attorney. Corcoran performs duties that must in fact have been the work of three or more persons, all attached to the office of the state's attorney. An assistant state's attorney did appear at a hospital where wounded strike demonstrators were given first aid. An entirely different assistant state's attorney presented the legal aspects of the case before the La Follette committee—which obviously corresponds to my Gottschalk committee. And still a third state's attorney's assistant examined witnesses at the coroner's inquest, my rendering of which, by the way, does not pretend to be exact, since several purely fictional characters are introduced—such as Dr. Whalen, whose statements are not taken from the record of the inquest. (However, I believe the essential characteristics of this inquest are in no way violated by my interpolations; the points of dispute before the actual inquest and before my fictional inquest were similar; I have only detailed them differently, to the extent of liberal paraphrase.) Again, I present a restaurant scene in which the basis for a "deal" between the union and the state's attorney's office is laid, anent the further prosecution of arrested strikers. This scene is fictional; it is inserted for the sake of concretizing events whose outcome, merely as a matter of novelistic logic, seemed to me to involve such an agreement. In short, my character Corcoran is a composite figure representing an office, and neither as a whole nor in his various separate actions is he intended to portray any of the several individuals who may in fact have held such an office or performed similar actions.

Likewise, the police officer Braden is a personalization necessary to the novelist, in order to suggest something of the emotional and moral attitudes of the police; but Braden represents

[646]

no individual in the Chicago police force. It appeared to me a condition of the task I had set myself, in this novel-form, to refrain as much as possible from the introduction of testimony that was not actually uttered before the Senate committee; and therefore, when my fictional characters appear before the Senate committee, they may be found quoting or paraphrasing recorded statements. Braden, for instance, at one point remarks that he considers the police force to be on trial before the nation; a similar remark was made before the La Follette committee by a Chicago police officer, but there his identity with Braden ends. I know nothing of the life of that officer and have not attempted to suggest or depict it. There is also the record of another officer, who was embarrassed before the Senate committee when he was led to identify himself on a photograph showing police brutality; this officer stated before the committee that he was ashamed of such behavior. I have introduced a similar dramatic episode, as part of Braden's experience, and in this case, too, the identity ends with the single incident. I think it will become apparent that, as Corcoran is a composite representing the state's attorney's office, Braden is a composite representing the police force. The tavern scenes in which Braden appears are wholly invented, but I believe they are not exaggerated, as inventions.

The second form of difference to be noted between the actual record and this fictional rendering arises from the need to offer a more completed pattern than was developed by the investigation of actual events. As I have already pointed out, certain details of the Memorial Day massacre never were revealed; I have therefore invented characters whose actions, it seemed to me, could plausibly fill such gaps.

One of these is the police officer Gorcey who, in my story, takes a wounded man out of a first-aid car and arrests him. There was an actual incident at the Memorial Day massacre in which a man with a severed artery was taken from a first-aid car, and that man died. I do not know who ordered him from that first-aid car. I invented Gorcey, and Gorcey's testimony before the Senate committee, like everything else he says and does, is invented material.

Perhaps the most complicated relationship between invention and actuality is represented by my treatment of the Lindstrom family. In the Memorial Day massacre, there was a union man who lost an eye as a consequence of police violence. He made a statement before the La Follette committee, much of which I have placed, verbatim, in the mouth of Oscar Lindstrom. Included in the actual statement was mention of a brother who continued to work in the plant, while a second brother went out on strike.

That statement was extraordinarily moving and poetic; as generative material, it led me to the construction of the Lindstrom family. But, as may be noted, I used the same opportunity to invent and place in my story a family whose history would supply some of the history of unionization in the steel industry; the generations of the Lindstroms are entirely different from those of the actual family spoken of before the Senate committee. I kept this much: a member of the Lindstrom family—in my story it is the father rather than a brother—loses an eye. Another member of the family, a son, is killed in the massacre—a departure from the Memorial Day actuality. A second son continues to work in the mill. This second son—again a departure from actuality—is purely fictionally depicted as a clerk in the personnel department. The entire background and personality of the Lindstrom family are my own invention; I know nothing of the actual family involved in the Memorial Day massacre beyond the external facts given above. It will be apparent that I have in this case availed myself of the common literary device of dramatic juxtaposition, placing in the family of Oscar Lindstrom two sons who take part on opposite sides of a war. And I used the invented Will Lindstrom to fill one of the gaps in the story offered by actuality: the investigations never revealed the precise link between the company management and some outside information and propaganda agents. It may be seen that the

Lindstrom family background is perforce fictional, since that background is constructed in such a way as to make it plausible for Will Lindstrom to perform this function.

Aside from the quoted speech, then, which really served the writer as a point of departure, the account of the Lindstrom family is, like the accounts of all the other slain and their families, total fiction.

There may be some question as to why I changed the names of certain individuals and institutions. The change is not for the sake of disguise but as a constant reminder that this, in the final analysis, is not a report; it is not history, it is a novel. It is not written as an exposure but as an interpretation. The Senate committee is called the Gottschalk, rather than the La Follette, committee to remind the reader that Gottschalk makes remarks which Senator La Follette never made, and that certain incidents are shown to take place in Washington which did not actually take place. The members of the staff of the Gottschalk committee are in no way intended to resemble the persons on the staff of the La Follette committee. Similarly, the steel company is not called by the name of an actual company—for this does not pretend to be a historical report of any company's activities. A Chicago newspaper is called the *Clarion*, and not by the name of any actual newspaper, because it could not be said that the items attributed to the *Clarion* were accurate quotations from any paper, no matter how similar in editorial effect.

And, as a further instance of this type: while Victor Fuchs, the labor board attorney, is shown to be the author of a thesis on labor disputes in Chicago, and while I adapted material from just such a thesis for use in this story, I have no knowledge whatever of the career of the author of the work I used. Wherever he may be, he is certainly not a labor board attorney connected with the case of the 1937 steel strike in Chicago, for Victor Fuchs is a wholly invented being in so far as personality and background are concerned. In case the author of that thesis happens to encounter this book, I should like to take this opportunity to thank him for some very illuminating material.

It may be asked: why was it necessary for the writer to go so close to actuality for his material, without stepping into the realm of history? I believe modern writers are impelled to this method by a sense that the inner human truths of motive and compulsion can be found by examining experiences of reality. By using only actual, attested events as materials, the writer reduces the possibility of arriving at false conclusions. It is not pretended that this method can universally serve, or that it is even a preferred literary approach. For the present work, to the present writer, it seemed the best method.

This story in itself, I trust, is evidence that I bear no malice toward any being, real or fictional.